BELOW THE SALT

BELOW
THE SALT

A Novel by

Thomas B. Costain

Doubleday & Company, Inc.

Garden City, New York

1957

All characters portrayed in this novel are
fictitious. It is a coincidence if the name of
any real person, living or dead, is mentioned.

BOOK ONE

Chapter I

1

J OHN FORADAY had always been quiet and imaginative, and this was the only fault his grandmother had found in him.

"Come, John," she would say in her gentle voice. "This won't do, you know. You should get out and play with other boys more. And you should read the newspaper and—well, take an interest in things. You won't get to be a successful businessman this way."

She had been right about it, of course. He had to make a good businessman of himself. It was the goal he must attain, even though at times he had grave misgivings about it. He must not disappoint his grandmother.

One morning he was sitting at the bare table where he read proof at the printing plant of McMurray and Erbank. The phone rang and Bill Sands, who shared his labors, took the call. He handed the instrument over the table. "Yours," he said.

"Hello," said John, rather puzzled that anyone should be calling him at such an hour; or at any hour, for that matter.

"Is this Mr. Foraday?" asked a feminine voice.

"Yes."

"Mr. Foraday, will you come to the office of Mr. Ross, of Ross, Cullom and Calvin, at two o'clock this afternoon?"

John stammered in surprise. Why should Mr. Christopher Carver Ross, the oldest and most esteemed lawyer in the city, want to see him? His life was not complicated enough to involve him in any legal difficulties. After spending the day at the printing plant he would go directly home to the plain dinner Mrs. Groupy would have ready for him and the whole evening would be devoted to the manuscript of his novel. He had little enough time for reading, none for recreations, and because of the austerity of this daily routine, no friends. The call from the old lawyer's office, he said to himself, must have to do with his grandmother's affairs.

"I can be there," he said, "if Mr. Erbank gives me permission. We're very busy here right now."

"Please tell Mr. Erbank," said the voice at the other end of the line, "that Mr. Ross says it is important. Believe me, Mr. Foraday, it is *very* important."

"Then I expect it can be arranged. I'll be at your offices at two. Thank you, ma'am."

"What's all this about?" demanded Bill Sands, looking at him suspiciously. "Damned if I ever remember you getting a phone call before. Why this sudden mad rush of popularity? Some dame trying to date you up?"

"I'm to go to the office of Mr. Christopher Ross at two o'clock. I can't understand why."

"Must be a mistake. Meant for some other John Foraday. Except there isn't another!"

John had never discussed with his co-laborer the fact that his grandmother had been Lucy Congdon, who had inherited the once great Congdon hat business from her father. It would have seemed pure swank on his part; and anyway it had all been so long ago, his being brought back from Chicago to Crosswich as a boy when his father and mother had died within a week of each other, and after his grandfather, Irvin Byron Beal, had somehow succeeded in involving the Congdon factories and the Congdon retail stores in bankruptcy. His grandfather had died soon after and he had been raised by his gentle and proud grandmother, in the most straitened circumstances and in complete seclusion. The relationship between them had been such a happy one that he could not bring himself to speak of this phase of his life to anyone, particularly since her death two years before. He did not speculate any further, therefore, on the possible explanation of his appointment, for the benefit of Mr. Sands.

He went at once to the office of the general manager of the plant and made his request for as long an absence that afternoon as might be needed.

"You're to go to the office of C. C. Ross?" Mr. Erbank frowned in surprise. "Now what in hell for? To the best of my knowledge, Mr. Ross never has anything to do with clients except his old ones, or perhaps people he's known all his life. If I was to ask him to handle our legal affairs, he'd be insulted. What can he want with you?"

"I've no idea, Mr. Erbank. The call was from his secretary, I suppose."

"Old Liz Candee. She's been with him for thirty years. You'll find, Foraday, that a call at the offices of C. C. Ross is kind of social as well as business. He'll offer you the choice of a drink or a cup of tea. Take the tea. Old Liz Candee spends more time lugging in drinks and dishing up tea than she does typing letters." The head of the printing plant gave a nod as though light had suddenly come to him. "I know what it is. It'll be about your grandmother. Old C.C. knew her. I wouldn't be surprised if he knew her quite well."

"I can't say," said John. "My grandmother seldom mentioned any of her old friends."

"Be there on time," admonished Erbank. "C.C. is a stickler for punctuality."

He was on time for the appointment. At one minute before the hour he presented himself at the small reception grating at the offices of Ross, Cullom and Calvin. Miss Elizabeth Candee admitted him with a friendly smile.

"I saw your grandmother often, Mr. Foraday," she said. "Years ago, of course. You take after her a lot. Of course your hair is real honest-to-goodness red and hers was more golden—when she was young, I mean. But you do look like her. Mr. Ross is ready for you."

The dean of the legal profession in Crosswich was sitting in a creaky swivel chair behind a desk heaped high with papers. The room might be untidy but he himself was quite impeccable in a neatly pressed suit of navy-blue raw silk. He swung around and looked sharply at his visitor.

"I see you're a Congdon," he said. "Nothing of the Beals or the Foradays in you. How does it happen you are working in that plant? I would have expected you to be at college."

"I was in my sophomore year at Harvard when my grandmother died, sir," said John, rather resentful of the need to mention the circumstances in which he had been left. "I couldn't finish because it was necessary for me to earn my living."

"You must forgive me, my boy, for bringing the matter up." The old lawyer looked quite disturbed. "I assure you I had no idea how things stood. I knew your grandmother very well when we were both young but I saw her infrequently after her marriage to your grandfather. After his death she retired into seclusion so determinedly that I never saw her again. To my great regret, young sir." He sighed, as old men often do when their thoughts turn to the past. "But now, since you have been so kind as to come here today, I think we should get to business. Mr. Jacob Samuel Lynch, sitting over there in the corner, is the one who wants to talk with you. He comes from far out in the West. Move your chair up, Jake, and start to work."

John had noticed the presence of a third person in the room when he first entered, a man with a thin mustache curled up at the ends and a pleasant gray eye, who was sitting near the window. The latter maneuvered himself out of the chair and into a standing position and came over to shake hands.

"Young man, this is a pleasure," said Mr. Lynch in a drawling voice. "I've come to ask you some questions. Many questions. On behalf of a client. I hope you won't mind."

John looked at the lawyer before replying, as though seeking guidance. Mr. Ross gave him a reassuring nod.

"I won't mind," said John. "But—may I ask one question first? I would like to know who your client is."

The Westerner looked at Mr. Ross in turn. They both seemed to ponder the request and then gave each other an acquiescent nod.

"Why not?" said the Westerner. "There's nothing hush-hush about this, although Dick did want to stay strictly in the background. Well, young man, my principal in this matter is Richard Jeffrey O'Rawn."

John's eyes opened wide with surprise. "Do you mean Senator O'Rawn?"

"Yes, Senator O'Rawn himself. The great political leader from the wide-open spaces of the West. Who came so close, by the way, to being nominated for the presidency last time."

"But—but why does he want to know about me? What kind of questions are you going to ask?"

"Suppose we begin to ask 'em? You'll find out best that way."

John knew little about the famous senator except that he was still noted for the fire and humor of his speeches, although now an old man, and that he had made a great fortune in Western lands and cattle.

"I'll try to answer whatever you ask me," he said.

"Do you wish me to withdraw, Jake?" asked the lawyer.

"Of course not. On the contrary, I'll appreciate it if you'll draw a hand and sit in. You may be able to help the boy with some of his answers."

Christopher Carver Ross gave John another reassuring smile. "Nothing to be disturbed about, you know," he said. "Mr. Lynch isn't an officer of the law. I rather suspect, although he hasn't confided in me, that his purpose in coming here is a friendly one. Even that it may result in some benefit to you."

"Could, sure enough," said the Westerner.

Mr. Lynch began then to question John about his grandparents, the circumstances which had brought him back to live with his grandmother, his own likes and dislikes, his habits, and finally about his ideas for the future.

"Would you say that you are ambitious?" he asked.

John did not answer at once. "Yes, I suppose I am," he said finally. "There's some doubt as to what I'll try to do with myself. My grandmother wanted me to become a businessman and put the Congdon hat back on the market. I think it was the one regret she had at dying that she wouldn't see me succeed in doing it. She—she took the failure very hard. As though it had been her fault. But I must be honest and say that I myself have a quite different ambition."

"I think I must have been badly informed at the time of the failure," declared Mr. Ross. "I was of the opinion then that the loss of the business didn't seriously affect the private fortune her father had left her."

John hesitated. "It did, sir. She was left with very little indeed. My grandfather had been looking after her investments as well as the business and it seemed he had made—well, rather a hash of them."

"I got word of that later," said the lawyer. "But I still didn't suspect the full truth. The Congdon fortune had always seemed such a gigantic thing. Like the Rock of Gibraltar. I'm sure all of Lucy's old friends thought she could get along on what was left."

"That was what she wanted them to think, sir. I believe she kind of— of fostered the idea."

"Do you care to express an opinion of your grandfather?" asked the lawyer.

John shook his head at once. "No, sir. I never heard my grandmother say anything about him. Anything—well, derogatory. It wouldn't be right for me to express an opinion, sir."

"Well," said the Westerner, "you seem to have been left with a rather tall order. How do you propose to go about it?"

John gave his head a doubtful shake. "I really don't know, sir. Since I've been in the printing business at McMurray and Erbank's, I've been keeping my eyes open to see how things are done. I'm afraid it's something I'll never understand. I've just about reached the conclusion that I'm not cut out for a businessman."

"In that respect," said old Mr. Ross to himself, "you're the exact opposite of your grandfather, Mr. Irvin Byron Beal. That pretentious ass knew no more about business than an unborn babe but he was sure he could run Congdon Hat better than the man who founded it."

"I don't see where I could make a start. I'm sure I'll never be able to save enough out of a salary to get things going again, although I'm trying. I suppose what I need is the capacity to go to men with money and sell them on putting up the capital for a new beginning. Well, that's beyond me. I wouldn't be able to sell the reception girl on letting me past the switchboard."

"You said you have another idea in your mind as to your future," prompted the Westerner.

John hesitated. This was difficult ground. He shrank from admitting to anyone that he hoped someday to be a novelist and that he was using every spare moment to fit himself for that work. He had even gone to considerable pains to keep Mrs. Groupy in the dark, avoiding any heading on the first page of his manuscript or even the mention of the word "chapter." He had dropped devious hints to her about setting down information on the Congdon business and the making of hats.

"It's true that I have another ambition," he acknowledged finally. His cheeks had flushed as red as his hair. "I—I hesitate to say what it is. You will think I'm very presumptuous. You see, I'm writing a novel."

"Well, I'm sure that's a laudable ambition," said the Westerner, although there was a suggestion of doubt in his voice. "It's a rather crowded field, isn't it? And I've heard you can't expect to make much money at it. I seldom read books myself."

"Your grandmother wrote verse when she was young," contributed Mr. Ross, with an encouraging bob of his white-thatched head. "She never let any of her friends see what she wrote but it was rumored around once that a bit of it had been published in a magazine."

"She had a poem published," declared John proudly. "But not in a magazine. In a newspaper. A small country newspaper. I thought it was very good."

"Do you ride?" asked Mr. Lynch.

John shook his head. "No, sir, I don't. I've never had the chance."

"A drawback. But you're young enough to learn. Can you use a gun?"

"No, sir."

"Are you interested in national politics?"

"I read a great deal about what goes on in Washington. But I'm afraid my knowledge is superficial."

"A good word, young man. Do you know anything about the history of the West?"

"A great deal, sir. It's been almost a hobby with me."

The questioning took a new turn. "What was your father's name and where did he come from?"

"My father was the Reverend John Webster Foraday. He was born in Worcester."

"Yes, of course. Foraday Ale."

John shook his head. "He was connected with the ale people. But it was a distant connection. He was a Methodist minister."

"Tell me about your mother."

"My mother was lovely and good. She was small and dark. And always kind of gay. She laughed a lot."

"Did your father laugh a lot too?"

"Not as much. Once I heard my mother tell him he had no sense of humor but, of course, she didn't mean it."

"Where did he get his education?"

"At Harvard. He was quite an athlete. The students called him 'King,' so I think he must have been popular."

"You smiled when you mentioned his nickname. Why?"

"Well, King Foraday, you see."

It was clear that Mr. Lynch did not see, for he went right on with the questioning. "Were you an athlete too?"

"Yes, but not in my father's class. I was a sprinter. I won the hundred-yard dash at high school."

"Which do you take after in temperament, your father or your mother?"

"My father, I think. Whenever I saw him in the pulpit, he looked very tall and sober. I think I'm the quiet type. I don't laugh very much but when I do I laugh out very loud."

"When do you feel so amused that you laugh out loud?"

"Well, I don't know. I do it often when I'm reading. I laughed out loud many times when I was reading *Huckleberry Finn*."

"I hear it's very funny. Haven't read it myself. Are you interested in girls?"

"Yes."

"With one in particular?"

"No, sir. I don't know any of them well enough for that."

"Then you are still fancy-free?"

"Oh yes, sir. Quite."

Miss Candee appeared in the doorway. She glanced inquiringly at her employer.

"It's time to refresh ourselves, gentlemen," said the old lawyer, taking his cue. "Jake, will you have a drink? Or would you prefer a cup of tea or coffee?"

The man from the West drew out a biscuit-thin watch and consulted the time. He shook his head. "I must catch the plane back this afternoon," he said. "There are a few things to attend to in town and I still have some questions to ask this young man. Every minute's going to count with me so I'm afraid I must say no to all three suggestions. Most regretfully, I assure you."

Mr. Ross looked at John. "Will you join me?"

"A cup of tea, if you please, sir," said John.

"Weak or strong?" asked the secretary.

"It really doesn't matter, thank you. We get it kind of hit and miss at home. I'm used to both ways."

The additional questions were asked while the tea was steeping. Mr. Lynch then got to his feet, shook hands with the old lawyer and with John, and made his departure, after retrieving a huge briefcase from behind the first chair he had occupied.

2

Nothing was said for a moment after the Westerner had left. Then Mr. Ross smiled at his young visitor and asked, "Consumed with curiosity?"

"Well—yes, sir, I am. It's been most unusual."

"I wish I could enlighten you. But I'm in the dark myself. Lynch dropped in out of the blue and asked me to make the appointment with you. He didn't volunteer much about his purpose and I didn't feel I could question him. He did tell me he was acting for Senator O'Rawn and that gave me a pretty broad ground for assumptions. Want to know what my guess is?"

"Yes, sir, I do. I haven't been able to make any guess myself."

"Well, young man, I'll have to go back a bit into the past. Lucy Congdon, your grandmother, was an unusually pretty and sweet girl, in addition to being an heiress. She had droves of suitors. I was one. Did you know that?"

John shook his head. "No, sir, I didn't."

"I was never one of the front runners. Lucy liked me but I think she never regarded me as anything more than a faithful friend. But with Dick O'Rawn it was different. He met her at a dance in Boston and he started right in to sweep her off her feet. They were engaged in no time at all and I could see that Lucy was very happy. All the local swains were a pretty sad lot when it was announced. Irv Beal was one of the hardest hit because he had been sure he was first in line. I was a junior partner here at the time—quite junior, in fact—and it happened I had to go up to see Mr. Congdon with some papers for him to sign the morning that the announcement came out in the newspaper. The old man looked at me and said: 'You make me sick, the whole caboodle of you. Letting this outsider step in and cut you all out. I have nothing against young Mr. O'Rawn except that he'll take my Lucy away to the West. It would have suited me if she had picked one of you because then she would have lived here. I didn't want any young Lochinvar carrying her off to the other side of the world. For a time, Chris, I was pinning my hopes on you.' I was feeling so unhappy about it that I suppose I showed how I felt. 'I never had a chance, sir,' I said. 'Lucy couldn't see me with a telescope.' 'Well,' he said, 'I have one consolation. She didn't take that Beal squirt.'"

Miss Candee brought in the tea with a plate of spongecakes thickly covered with white icing. The first swallow seemed to have a reviving effect on the old lawyer. He sighed deeply and resumed his narrative.

"Well, the wedding day was set. About a month before the date, Dick O'Rawn blew in from the West. It had taken him four days by train to reach Crosswich and those who saw him at the station said he looked pale and unhappy. They thought this was the result of the trip. But it wasn't the trip. He saw Lucy and took the first train back. The news gradually seeped out that the engagement had been broken. I didn't see Lucy myself but I heard she was holding her head high and saying nothing about what had happened. Her father was reported to have said at the Crosswich Club that if he had not been out of town the day Dick O'Rawn arrived that young Irishman would have gone to the hospital instead of to the station to catch his train back."

The old lawyer finished his cup of tea and his spongecake. He drew an even deeper sigh.

"Inside of a year Lucy married Irv Beal. I was thunderstruck when I heard she had picked him." He swung around in his chair so he could face his visitor squarely. "Now, young John Foraday, I don't want to hurt your feelings. I don't want to destroy any illusions you may be holding about the man who became your grandfather. Were you fond of him?"

It was clear that John was reluctant to answer. He studied the willow pattern in the cup with a frown. "I don't want to say anything," he began, "that Grandmother wouldn't have wanted me to say. But I think I should be honest about it. I—I didn't like him much. He lived a short time only after I came to live with them. It wasn't long enough for me to get to know him very well. But I never liked the way he acted to Grandmother. He was supposed to have suffered a great blow —about the failure of the business—and his feelings had to be considered all the time. We had to be careful about everything we said. Grandmother cautioned me never to speak of business in his hearing and never to use the word 'hat' under any circumstances. I was just a boy at the time but I was very sure that the blow had fallen hardest on Grandmother and that it was *her* feelings we ought to be considering."

The lawyer nodded his head with great satisfaction. "Then I can say what I meant to. The trouble started with a stag dinner Irv Beal gave a month or so after Lucy's father died. She had gone to visit an aunt, one of her father's sisters, because she was feeling his death so deeply. It seemed odd to all of us that Beal was giving a party so soon and still odder when he served champagne. When we had our first glass, he looked around the table and said: 'This is a celebration, gentlemen. I'm going to take over control of the Congdon interests. I was elected president before Lucy went away.' None of us spoke, we were so astonished. 'I rather think, gentlemen,' he went on, 'that I'm going to show the business world something.' His eye lighted on me and he smirked. 'Well, Chris Ross,' he said sharply, 'what about our bet?' 'Bet?' I said. 'What bet?' 'Don't tell me you're going to pretend you've forgotten. You bet me I would never get control. Didn't you now, didn't you?' Well, I remembered then that we had made some kind of a wager in the heat of an argument. I owned up to it but I said my mind was a blank as to the terms. 'We'll attend to that,' he said, grinning. He produced a dunce's hat, made out of a newspaper, and I had to stick it on my head while I made a little speech of amends. What's more, it turned out I was expected to pay for the champagne. I didn't believe I had been fool enough to make such a bet as that but I paid up without a word." He paused and put his teacup down on the saucer with such vigor that both might have been damaged. He opened his mouth several times as though prepared to give vent to his opinion of Irvin

Byron Beal without restraint, then he shook his head and contented himself with what obviously was an understatement. "I didn't like him, boy, I didn't like him at all."

John had finished off a cup of scalding-hot tea without realizing what he was doing, so deep was the interest he was taking in what the elderly lawyer was saying. He accepted another cup blindly and in a purely mechanical way took a bite from the cake on his plate.

"If you please, Mr. Ross," he said when it became evident that the stream of reminiscence had come to an end, "I don't know much about why the company failed. I've heard some talk, of course, but it has always seemed guesses. My grandmother never spoke of it. I suppose she found it too painful."

"I can tell you what happened in a general way. Irv Beal brought in some fellow to look the business over with a view to bringing it up to date. I don't know what they are called these days but then they were known as efficiency engineers. This particular one decided that Congdon Hat was old-fashioned in its methods and he suggested a policy which suited the new president perfectly. They must reduce costs by cheapening the output while they continued to maintain the high prices for the hat. Then he convinced Beal that the managers of the stores should be changed. They were veterans who knew the hat trade from top to bottom and who had a personal acquaintance with all the regular customers. The men put in their places were young. Go-getters was the word for them, I believe."

The old man gestured with a heat which the passage of so many years had done nothing to abate. "The whole town watched what was going on with fear and amazement. Our prosperity then depended to a great extent on the success of the Congdon enterprises. Will you believe it that one of the retail stores lost so much business that it had to be closed in less than two years? Very soon after they had all been closed and the Congdon hat, the old-time leader and established patrician among hats, was being sold only through regular trade channels. The volume fell off every year, because the new article wasn't worth what they were asking for it. In eight years the business went bankrupt. All of the employees were out of jobs. I tell you, it was a sad time for Crosswich. It took us years to recover from the blow."

John sat in complete silence for some time. "It wouldn't be an easy matter to get things started again, would it?"

The lawyer shook his head. "I'm afraid the public has forgotten the Congdon hat. The name has very little value left, except for the few

old customers who still remember how good it was. It would be almost
a case of starting over again. Of course there are some patented
machines which are good, and there are still a few old employees who
understood the process of manufacture. That's all you would have to
start with, that and the old plant.

"But let's go back to Senator O'Rawn," he went on, after another
pause. "I said I could make a guess as to his purpose in having you
looked up in this way. I never saw him afterward but you may be sure
I followed his career with the closest interest. Now here's what I think:
he has just learned of your grandmother's death and the full extent of
the financial calamity visited on her. I think he has learned more about
it than her thick-skulled friends right here at home. And he has sent
Jake Lynch east to make inquiries. Jake, I know, talked to quite a few
people in town. You may never hear anything more of this, my boy, so
don't go letting your hopes grow. On the other hand, it seems to me
possible that the senator has some definite plan in his head. Perhaps
his conscience is bothering him and he may want to make amends in
some way. That's a kind of wild guess, men don't do generous things
these days. Or so it seems to an old man who has seen the whole world
change—and not for the better."

John responded with more emphasis and feeling than he had yet
shown. "After the way he treated her, I have no intention of letting
him do anything for me. What was his explanation for the way he
acted? I suppose he had fallen in love with someone else."

"No, no. It wasn't that. He never married. There was some good
reason but no one knows what it was. Now, young man, don't go
hardening your mind. Don't jump to conclusions. Wait until you hear
from him again. If you do hear from him, he'll have something in mind
that you must consider fairly. For your own sake. I'm sure, I'm quite
positive, that your grandmother would want it that way."

3

On the fourth morning after the meeting in the office of the veteran
lawyer of Crosswich, John was sitting at the proofreading table as usual.
The hopes roused in him seemed likely now to come to nothing. Bill
Sands, facing him, was inclined to be facetious, and perhaps a little
triumphant about the matter. He grinned across the table at his silent
co-worker.

"John, old stuff," he said, "I'm going to do some sounding off. You've got yourself in quite a bit of a fix by being so damned stubborn. Heck, you're wrong about everything! You go home every night and plug away at your secret ambition, which is no secret to me, instead of seeing life. You've never been drunk. You've never been out with a girl. You don't know what living is, brother. I'll bet when you talked to this fellow from the West you let him see what an old-fashioned square you are. So he goes back and you don't hear anything more from him. Naturally. Say, I'll give you a little bet, three bucks to one, that you never hear from him."

"Perhaps I won't," said John. "Perhaps I don't want to hear from him again."

"There you go, you chowderhead! Willing to let a big chance get away from you."

The telephone rang. Bill answered, said "Uh-huh," and pushed the receiver over to his companion. "I might have lost that bet, *if* we'd made it," he commented.

It was Mr. Ross on the telephone. "John," he said, "I've heard from our friends in the West. The senator wants you to go out and see him."

"But I can't do that, Mr. Ross. I can't spare the time and I haven't the money. And, you know, I'm not very keen about the idea to begin with."

"My boy, everything will be taken care of. Senator O'Rawn seems to be a very thorough man. He's thought of everything. Now, about finding the time for the trip. He wants you to cut loose from that position you have. I suggest you go right down and resign as of this very minute."

"But, sir, I can't do that. I'm expected to give two weeks' notice so I can be replaced."

The voice of the lawyer at the other end of the wire took on a more emphatic tone. "John, I am authorized to arrange things with your employers if necessary. If they make demands, we'll settle with them. Enough to cover any inconvenience they may suffer. Does that satisfy you?"

"Of course, sir. But I'll be out of a job when I come back from the visit, won't I?"

"No, my boy, get it into your head that Senator O'Rawn is planning to take care of things. His instructions to me, which he sent by wire— the longest telegram I've ever seen—are most thorough. They cover all possibilities."

"But, sir, I haven't the clothes for such a trip and I haven't any money."

"You are to go out with me, as soon as you've talked to your employer, to buy what you need. This morning, understand? I'm to go along to see that you don't spare the horses—the senator's own way of expressing it. And I have five hundred dollars waiting for you. To serve as spending money, I assume."

"Five hundred dollars!" John was beginning to realize that this was something which transcended any ideas he had been entertaining with reference to the senator's intentions. This was doing things in the grand manner. "That's a lot of money. Mr. Ross, I don't see—— Well, it really is a full-grown gift horse, isn't it? Now I can leave enough cash with Mrs. Groupy so she won't have money troubles while I'm away."

"I am authorized," said the lawyer, "to arrange for Mrs. Groupy's keep. In fact, her comfort. The senator remembers her in a dim kind of way."

"Say, he *is* thorough, isn't he?" The young man's ideas had changed around completely. This began to sound like an adventure, something he could go into with a clear conscience. "When do you think I should start, sir?"

"You are leaving, John, on the five thirty-two plane today. I have your tickets here."

Chapter II

1

For a half hour the private plane, which had met John at the airport, had flown over wide plains with ridges of clay-red hills cutting them into segments and small streams twisting and turning through them like purple snakes on the dull brown of the land. Then the plane took a sharp dip and began to make a turn, finally coming down on a concrete landing strip with a small hangar at the end. The roof of a wide and gracious house could be seen back of the hangar. From the position of the sun, it was probably five in the afternoon.

A servant escorted John to the house. They crossed a stone-flagged patio where three men were stretched out in long roller chairs, each with a drink in his hand. All three looked at him intently, then nodded and said, "Good afternoon," as he passed them. A woman with auburn hair and a complexion that was almost a youthful pink met him inside the house.

"You Mr. Foraday?" she asked.

"Yes, ma'am."

She shook his hand in a forthright way. "You're just in time to have a bath and get over to the senator's special hide-out. A sandwich now would hold you until you get there and share his late dinner. I think he would like you to do that. But if you need a rest, you can have dinner here and go over in the morning."

"I'll go now," decided John. "And I think I would like the sandwich."

"And a drink, I suppose."

"No, ma'am. I don't drink."

She turned and looked at him with wide-open eyes. "Godalmighty!" she said. "I've watched the dear younger generation at their play and I find this hard to believe. Are you doing this on a bet or something?

Well, of course, you're young. You'll soon learn. And it's just as well you're not going to stay here and have dinner with those three ex-grand masters of the Bone Pickers Union out there on the patio. Give them that much time and they would get everything out of you. Your life story and why you are here and what it's all about anyway."

John gave an involuntary look back over his shoulder and could see two of the recumbent figures. They were men of middle age, well groomed, intelligent and square of jaw, even rather pleasant as to expression.

"Yes, they're good fellows, all of them. I'll introduce you to them before you leave. One is Captain Jastrow, who has charge of all the senator's land and herds. One is Seth Silliman, his political secretary. The third is a lawyer named Al Curwood, who does the legal work. They're loyal and reasonably honest but the senator hasn't a relative in the world and they don't like the idea of strangers trespassing on their preserves. Any fingers that came dipping into the pie would get cut off if these Excluders of Other Heirs caught 'em at it."

"But," protested John, "I'm not an heir. I don't know why I've been brought out here."

"You seem to be a nice modest boy," said the woman, giving him an approving pat on the cheek. "I'm going to like you. In fact I'm kind of fond of you already. By the way, I'm Amy Shirley and I'm the senator's common or working secretary. I'm a career woman, young Mr. Foraday, and I enjoy my work. You'll have to ride to get to the place in the hills. The report on you, which I cast an eye on with a great deal of interest, says you've never been in a saddle. Think you can manage it?"

John smiled doubtfully. "I guess there's no way out of it, is there?"

"None," said Miss Shirley. "A few weeks here and you'll be riding like another Roy Rogers. With your air of innocence and that hair, Red Cloud, you may go and get yourself drafted into the movies."

John stared at her. "Say, that's odd. I mean you calling me Red Cloud. When I was at high school, I belonged to a little group of fellows, and they started calling me Red Cloud."

"It'll get shortened to Red out here. All right now, Red, you'll want a bath first, I reckon."

"Yes, I would."

"Just time for a quick splash. A beef sandwich and a pot of iced tea will be waiting for you here. And I'll be here too. I don't intend to give those three killer hawks a chance at you yet."

2

The guide raised a forefinger and pointed ahead of them. John saw the crenelated top of a round tower protruding above the wooded line of the hills. "That's it, mister. That's where the big boss likes to go so he can give them all the slip. Ye've made it, mister. Ain't ye proud?"

John was both proud and relieved. He was helped down from the saddle and found the muscles of his legs so stiff that he could barely walk. He hobbled across a gravel drive and, obeying a flicker of his guide's thumb, entered the tower through an open door. There was plenty more to the house than the granite-like tower but he was too concerned with the difficulty of controlling his legs to take much in. He got a general impression that the place had a medieval look about it.

Inside, however, this impression faded. The walls were high and of stone, the floors were also of stone and they looked so old that he half expected to find his feet in rushes. The ceilings were massively beamed. At the same time, the interior had a modern note. The fireplaces were not planned for the twelve-foot yule logs which required a whole parcel of varlets to drag them in; they were comfortably small. The furniture was mostly new and well upholstered. The stone walls carried a few fine paintings of early days in the West.

A manservant in a white jacket bowed to John and smiled approvingly. "The senator will be glad you decided to make it tonight," he said in a voice as modern as Times Square. "Dinner has been held up on the chance you would arrive. He's outside, watching the sunset. Come this way, sir."

John found himself on a flagged terrace facing straight into the west. An old man with silver hair was filling a massive chair, his legs stretched out in front of him and his carpet slippers failing to conceal the fact that his feet were bare.

"Is it the young fellow, Peterkin?" asked the old man in a magnificently deep voice. "Ah, it *is* you, John. Come over here, if you don't mind. I'll have to get up for dinner soon, so I'll stay put for the moment. I'm an old man, John, and getting up out of these deep chairs has become an ordeal."

John felt his hand engulfed in a powerful grip and saw a pair of bright blue eyes studying him from under unruly white brows.

"I hope I haven't kept you waiting too long, sir," he said. "We were slow getting over. It was my first experience on horseback."

"And how did you make out?"

"Well, sir, the best I can say for myself is that I didn't fall out of the saddle."

The old man continued to stare at him. "I need no proofs of your identity, John," he said finally. "You take after your grandmother. In many ways. Draw up a chair and we'll talk until the chuck wagon is ready."

By this time John had absorbed a closer picture of his host. Richard Jeffrey O'Rawn had once been a handsome Goliath of a man and he could still sit for a picture of the twilight of a modern god. His shoulders were the broadest John had ever seen and a strong column of well-tanned neck rose from an open collar. His age was unmistakable and yet there remained something almost youthful about his face. This was contributed perhaps by a twinkle in the blue eyes and the unruliness of his ample thatch of hair. There was a great sense of relief for the visitor in his immediate realization that he was going to like his host.

The old man had a long glass in which ice tinkled. "Peterkin says he's sure you don't drink, my boy. How right is he?"

"Entirely right, sir."

"Is there anything you would like while I finish this off?"

"No, sir."

There was a long pause. "I wouldn't be at all surprised," said the senator, "if you've come here carrying a good, solid grudge against me. Because of what happened. Back there so long ago."

John hesitated. "No, sir," he said finally. "All I know is that you were going to marry my grandmother and that it was broken off. If she felt any sense of wrong, she never let me see it. I—I've thought about it a great deal, sir. But I can understand how reluctant you may be to reopen the past."

"My engagement to your grandmother, my boy, was broken for a very strange reason." The senator's eyes were seeing something from the past quite different from the brilliant sunset on which they were fixed. "You would think me mad if I told you what it was. My sweet and lovely Lucy had the courage to believe it. Ah, how brave and wonderful she was! I thought of her continuously afterward. Even now, my boy, after all these years, she is often in my mind."

The old man turned slowly and with obvious bodily reluctance so that he could look straight at his youthful visitor.

"I have never told anyone the reason," he said. His voice was cast in a lower tone but it still carried the suggestion of a lion-like rumble. "But I am going to tell *you*. That's what I brought you out for. I want to explain everything—for reasons you'll understand when you've heard. But not yet. This is the queerest and blastedest story that any human being has ever told; and every word of it as true as though it came right out of the pages of Holy Writ. It—well, it must be led up to. You need to be put into the mood for it. I'll have to give you a bit here and an inkling there. There are some places and things I want to show you first. And then, finally, I'll let you have the whole thing, like a salvo of sixteen-inch guns. Even at that, it will rock you to your foundations, my boy."

"Everything you say, sir, makes me prouder than ever of my grandmother. I think she had to face this broadside without the benefit of these preparations at all."

"That is true, John. Ah, that sweetly staunch, that loyal little soul. When I had belated word of her death—not more than a month ago—I broke down and wept. I assure you that I did, and yet I have been what they call in the West a tough hombre. I hadn't had a glint of moisture in my eyes for half a century."

Peterkin appeared in the door. "Dinner," he said.

Senator O'Rawn may have reached the stage where certain kinds of physical effort were avoided but there were many things he still insisted on doing. He liked to carve the roast at dinner. As he wielded the knife with ease and skill and piled up a substantial mound of slices, ranging from the crisp outside to the pink of the rare center, he talked to his guest.

"Old age has many disadvantages," he said. "In my case I am irked most by the lethargy which follows a good meal. Always before I found the hour when I smoked a cigar after dinner the pleasantest time of the day. I can no longer enjoy it. I fall asleep. And so, John, I must take advantage of the opportunity for talk which dinner affords, even though I once had a prejudice against people who chattered through meals. How do you like your beef?"

"Medium, sir."

"Good. I prefer the two extremes." The old man divided the slices and the manservant placed a well-filled plate in front of John.

"Now in the first place there's the matter of money. Being confident that you and I would get along pretty well, in spite of the past, I took the liberty a few days ago of making you a loan."

"Yes, sir. It was very generous of you. I wouldn't have been able to get out here if Mr. Ross hadn't had that money from you."

"Oh, *that*. It wasn't a loan. It was for expenses. Now here's what I mean. Every so often a new stock comes on the market or some well-established firm decides on a new issue. These kinds of issues are generally oversubscribed and that makes the public hungry for them. The stock goes up immediately. It's a well-established practice for insiders to buy in early for a quick turn. As soon as the expected advance is achieved, they sell and so pocket a neat little profit with practically no risk."

They were deep into their dinner now and the senator was demonstrating that the advance of the years had done little to curb his appetite. Peterkin was refilling his glass with a deep ruby wine.

"Have another wedge of the Yorkshire pudding? Good, you don't often get it as crisp as our cook makes it. Well now, there's been an issue on the market for two days. One of these state-built tollgate jobs. Tax-exempt. A good buy for the long pull as well as for a quick turn. I took quite a slice of it and I put you in for a thousand shares. That's what I meant when I said I had taken the liberty of loaning you some money. If it goes up, and I'm sure it will, you'll make a nice profit on the deal."

"And if it goes down?" John asked himself with a feeling of consternation. He would never be able to pay the losses.

The senator was studying him intently. "John," he said, "I read all those answers you gave Jake Lynch. There was something said about you writing a novel."

John nodded with some reluctance. "Yes, sir. I'm—I'm cutting my teeth on one. My ambition is to be a writer. I don't want to become very rich. I suppose it's too bad that I feel that way because my grandmother hoped I would get hold of what's left of the Congdon business and put it back where it was in her father's time. But I've known all along that I'm not capable of it."

The old man sat back for a few moments and pondered this piece of information. "You know, John, that's an idea. The Congdon hat was terrifically in the vogue. When I was a young buck, no one thought of wearing anything else, if they could afford it. Many's the ten-dollar bill I invested in a Congdon when I could have had a pretty fair hat for three or four. The profits must have been enormous. But you're right about it, my boy; you're not the one to undertake that kind of business resuscitation. Still, I'll think it over. I might be able to start something." He paused and then added reflectively, "For old time's sake, John, for old time's sake."

They were at their salad now. John's taste was somewhat undeveloped in that department and he found the endive much too bitter. The old man downed great quantities of it with every evidence of enjoyment.

"Did you bring the manuscript with you?" asked the senator unexpectedly.

"Why, yes, I did. Just to be safe. I didn't want to leave it where it might be thrown out. Mrs. Groupy is a great thrower-outer. Even though it may not deserve any better treatment."

"Good. I would like to read it."

"No, no!" John's alarm over this suggestion was completely genuine. "It's not in shape yet to be seen. I suspect it's very bad, sir. I—I'm pretty sensitive about it."

"I have a special reason for wanting to read it, my boy. I'll appreciate it if you can get your courage up to the point of letting me have it. What I may think of it will be a secret between the two of us."

"Well." John gulped unhappily. "Just as you say, sir. But it may be pretty terrible. It may make you lose any faith you might otherwise have had in me."

"I studied the answers you gave Lynch with great care, my boy," said the old man, lifting his dessertspoon for a first attack on a mound of ice cream. "One thing pleased me very much: the interest you take in history. He asked you only about American history. Has your reading gone beyond that? What of English, for instance?"

"I've read Green and some of Macaulay. And a new man named Bryant."

"Did you find the story of Magna Charta interesting?"

John nodded. "I found it one of the most exciting stories I've ever read. I suppose it was because my sympathies were so strongly aroused on the side of the barons, representing the people."

"Well, those gallant gentlemen were representing themselves really. But their side of it was the right side. You'll probably be surprised when I tell you that I've made quite a study of that period. For a reason which I won't go into just now. . . . Yes, I feel that I know King John quite intimately, and Stephen Langton and William the Marshal. Those last two, what men they were!"

"Do you think their equal is to be found nowadays, sir?"

The senator had finished his ice cream and was examining the cigars in a round mahogany humidor. "My boy," he said, "there's one truth you ought to get out of reading history. Never undersell the present.

The world *has* advanced. Oh, I know that pessimists sit back and complain that things are getting worse. They don't know what they are talking about because they see only one side. What an eye opener it would be for them if they were compelled to live in the pigsty they called Merrie England in the days of Magna Charta! I wonder how they would like to live under laws which gave a king the power of life and death over them?"

"You seem to have studied that period very carefully, sir."

"Yes," said the old man, who was now beginning to show the first signs of the postprandial lethargy he deplored. "I have had—quite special opportunities to study the period."

3

John wakened with a start the next morning to a realization that he had overslept. The clock on the wall of his bedroom said eight forty-five. A quarter to seven was his regular rising hour and so he sprang out of bed with a sense of guilt. He bathed, shaved and dressed in such a frantic hurry that he arrived downstairs in time after all to share some of his host's breakfast.

The veteran senator, noted for his eloquent and ready tongue, had little to say as he dealt with his steak and corn bread.

"You slept well, John?"

"Yes, sir. But too long, I'm afraid."

There was silence then, which Peterkin finally broke by appearing at the guest's elbow and asking his wishes. Steak, chops, a cutlet, bacon and eggs? John would have enjoyed a steak but he asked for bacon and eggs instead. The coffee, which arrived immediately, was excellent and it was accompanied by a melon, the like of which he had never tasted before.

The silent meal was drawing to a close when there was a sound of hoofbeats on the drive and a pleasant but exacting feminine voice demanding one Abimelech; the groom, no doubt.

The senator said, "That will be Amy with the mail," and became his regular self again with the prospect of normal activities beginning for the day. They could see through the metal blinds that the secretary was accompanied by a man with a large bag, filled no doubt with correspondence. The contents of the bag had been spread out on a table in the living room when they appeared there—cables, telegrams, letters, books, pamphlets, folders, enough mail seemingly for the State Department. John cast an anxious eye on the telegrams and said to himself: "The answer is there! Am I rich or am I going to spend my life grubbing away to save two dollars a week and make good my losses?" His hands were trembling with the suspense.

"Good morning," said Amy, who was looking cool and efficient, and almost pretty, in a pair of tight-fitting riding breeches and a yellow blouse with a dutch collar. "I hope you two strong, silent men succeeded in getting acquainted last night."

"We got along well," answered the senator.

"And you talked about Magna Charta, no doubt."

The old man gave her a suspicious and somewhat soured glance. "We did. John is well versed on the subject. I suspect this is going to be one of your tart days, Amy."

"Plenty of reason. The Three Musketeers were all snoring soundly when I left. How well they sleep when once they can persuade themselves to leave the bourbon and get off to bed. I had words with Porthos last night."

"Let's see now. Porthos—that's Seth, isn't it? What has Seth been doing?"

"He's been giving you bad advice. He's convinced you shouldn't run for another term."

"If he's saying that, Amy, he's merely repeating what I've been saying to him."

The woman began to speak in the most earnest and urgent of tones. "Boss, that's wrong thinking. You couldn't possibly be defeated. Why, you *can't* quit. You're the greatest figure in the Senate. You're the recognized voice of all this great country west of the Mississippi. You're Mr. American West. The country needs you. Washington wouldn't be the same place without you. There wouldn't be anyone to draw crowds to the Senate chamber the way you do. What a scramble there is to get in when the word gets around that Senator O'Rawn is going to speak! The President depends on you. He believes whatever you tell him about the feeling in the West. He takes your advice. Oh, boss, it's unthinkable that you won't be in the Senate any more!"

The old man gave her an affectionate smile. "Well, Amy, I'll say this. You have the issue very much at heart. You feel deeply about it, don't you?"

"I certainly do. I—I do have your best interests at heart, you know."

"But, my dear child, it's not just a case of deciding whether I want to stay in the Senate or not. I would like to be a senator as long as I live. I feel certain I can be re-elected if I stand. But there's something else to be considered and I've told you this before. There is something I must attend to before I die and I can't do it while I remain in politics. Get this into your head, Amy, I can't be off on this other matter if I decide to stand for another term. The other matter would undermine my value as a member of the Senate."

The secretary's face had become quite heated with the intensity of her feelings. "This mysterious other errand *can't* be as important as staying in the government. It just *can't!*"

She began to riffle through the mail. Watching her, John said to himself: "Please get to the one about our deal. *Please!*" His feelings were growing more intense with every second that passed.

"Well, I don't seem to be able to talk you out of your lunacy, boss," said Amy, still unreconciled to what seemed to be the inevitable. She bent her head over the mail and her voice showed hesitation as she went on. "There was one thing I said just now which—which was a great understatement. If you care to think back, you may discover what it was."

It was the senator himself who brought relief to the sorely tried young investor. He looked at John and smiled. "I wouldn't be surprised if our young friend here is anxious to find out what has happened to Western Tollgate on the Exchange. I'm interested myself. What did happen?"

Amy Shirley found the telegram among fifty or so others. She glanced at it without allowing her expression to give away the secret of the news it contained. She handed it to the senator. "There it is," she said. "You tell him."

"It's bad news!" thought John. "I'm done for, that's clear."

The senator read the wire. "Well," he said. He looked up at John. "Satisfactory on the whole," he declared, handing back the yellow slip. "We've made a profit. We got out yesterday afternoon, at practically the top. Well, that's fair enough. The profit on your block, John, will be a little in excess of two thousand four hundred dollars."

"Twenty-four hundred dollars!" cried the visitor.

"Not as good news from Hudson and Sadler, boss," declared the secretary. "We've taken a loss there. And old Jack Hartigan is proving stubborn about those concessions."

"Old Jack Hartigan is always stubborn," declared the senator. "He refused his first rattle in the cradle and dashed his first bottle into flinders. Well, the lean with the fat. I rather think John here is pleased on the whole. Perhaps he would like another go at it. Next week the Boncolenco Power people are putting out a new issue. A gilt-edged proposition if there ever was one. What do you say, my boy? Like to plow your profits back in?"

To his own surprise, John heard his voice replying, "Yes, of course, sir." His voice, moreover, had an eager note to it.

"Good. We'll see that you get in on the ground floor."

"I'll feel much better about this one, sir," John went on without any hint of doubt or hesitation. "Now I have some capital to risk and I could pay it back if we had losses on this new venture, sir."

"That's quite true, my boy. I'm glad to see you are going into this with a commendable sense of responsibility. Well, let's go whole hog this time. We'll cut you in for two thousand shares of the Boncolenco issue."

John caught his breath. He had not planned to take as rash a plunge as this. It had been in his mind, in fact, to say he would go in for five hundred shares. He looked at Amy Shirley and found her watching him. Did she understand what his feelings were? He believed he read sympathy for him in the expression of her eyes.

"All right," he said, after several moments of intense and painful thought. "Let's go whole hog, sir. I'll buy two thousand shares."

"Amy has gone in for two thousand," commented the senator. "That shows how good the stuff is. She can seldom be persuaded to risk more than chicken feed. Well, now you can share your anxieties between you."

John realized that both the senator and the secretary were anxious to plunge into the mail. Hours of intense work undoubtedly lay ahead of them. He rose and excused himself, glad of the chance to get away and give thought to the situation in which he had become involved. The magnitude of this new gamble was causing him to quiver inside as though he had suffered a severe emotional shock. Within the space of a very few minutes he had received what seemed to him a very large fortune and then had found himself putting this wonderful bonanza into peril by pledging himself to an even greater risk! He sat down in his room and thought it over for some time, finally reaching the con- clusion that the West was doing something to him, that the bracing air, or perhaps the bracing viewpoint of his new friends, had made him a different man. Certainly the John Foraday who sat for eight hours every day at the proofreading table in the printing shop would never have allowed himself to plunge so casually into breath-taking risks.

After a time he allowed himself to get away from his thoughts and anxieties. He walked about the house on a tour of inspection and found it peculiarly interesting. On the outside it was, he believed, a remarkably accurate replica of a small castle, a very old variety, Norman in all probability. The walls were of solid stone and they were three feet thick, so that the interior remained comfortably cool, even though the world outside seemed as hot as a frying pan. The inside had been ingeniously converted from the ancient plan, however, and offered every modern convenience. John's own bedroom was as modern as the jet plane or rock and roll, and his bathroom was all chromium and tile.

He spent some time also at the stables, learning how to saddle a horse and receiving more useful information about the business of riding than his experience of the previous evening had taught him. He found himself completely at home in these surroundings. The long rows of stalls with inquisitive eyes at each grating, the smell of fresh hay and liniment, the cheerful whistling of the grooms as they went leisurely about their tasks, the soft twang of their voices—nothing he had ever encountered before had pleased him as much as this. He sat on an upturned bucket and listened to the overseer.

It was apparent at lunch that the morning had been a busy one for the other members of the household. The senator sighed as he took his place at the table and said: "I went through that pile of mail like a buzz saw. But I'm afraid you are in for a day of it, Amy, getting all those letters off."

Amy Shirley was preoccupied, so much so that she did no more than toy with her food. "Just as well," she answered. "This press of work will keep my mind off the *fatal mistake* you are making."

The senator smiled and turned to John. "My boy, this morning I burnt my bridges behind me. I wired the committee that I wouldn't be a candidate for re-election as senator from this sovereign state. That, in other words, I was stepping out of politics for good and all."

The secretary commented furiously. "It broke my heart to type out that message. Such a beautifully worded explanation of your reasons for such an unforgivable step!"

"You die hard, Amy. Well, I've crossed the Rubicon—going backward. And I must say that I feel very free, and lighthearted, and pleased with myself. I'm my own man from this day forward. I won't have great bushels of mail to answer. I won't have to go to stupid public dinners. I won't have to make speeches. And I can now go about this other plan of mine, which has been drawing me toward it as though a great magnet, a great spiritual magnet, had been turned on."

"If you would only tell me what it is!"

"You'll know in time, my dear. No one is going to hear yet. I don't want any dropping of monkey wrenches into the machinery."

"I suspect you are going to commit some incredible folly, boss."

"It may prove to be a folly. But it will not be one of my making or choosing. And now let's get on with these chops. I'm sure, Amy, you'll want only one of the lamb. John, which do you want, lamb or pork?"

"Both," said John.

4

The ride to the house in the hills had seemed to John an interminably long one. Amy Shirley made it twice a day but she was an expert rider and it took her no more than a half hour each way. On the fifth morning he rode out to meet her, looking a little self-conscious but with a sure enough saddle and a good hand. She drew in by the side of the road and waited for him.

"Well!" she said. "You've been coming on!"

"I've been working at it," he explained. "Hard. Every day. And enjoying every minute of it."

"I suspect you had a natural turn for it. Have you breakfasted yet?"

"Yep. Had a bite in the kitchen this morning because I wanted to surprise you. The senator's sitting down to his now."

"That stubborn mule! Have you read the news stories and the editorials about his retirement? The whole country regrets it. Look at that additional bag of mail we've brought today. It's filled with letters, begging him to reconsider. But he won't! I know that stiff-necked old-timer. He's made up his mind and nothing will change him." They were riding slowly along together now and the mail carrier had dropped to the rear. "John, have you any inkling of his reason? I mean, what it is he's planning to do?"

John shook his head. "He hasn't said another word about it. But I have a hunch he thinks something should be done to convince people that radical changes in our way of life and government would throw us back into a stage from which we emerged with the greatest difficulty. He says it took us centuries to escape from slavery and that what these wild-eyed communists are trying to do is to clap the handcuffs back on our wrists again. That sounds pretty old stuff but I think he has some way in mind to drive the truth home."

"And how does he plan to go about it?"

"I haven't the foggiest idea."

There was a moment's silence. "The way he can do the most good is to stay right on his job. Have you ever heard him speak? Well, you've certainly missed something. *That* is when he's really convincing. And you ought to see him in a committee meeting! I have, many times. He's a wonder when he gets his feet under a table and starts to talk common sense. He has the air cleared and a straight, clean path mapped out in no time at all. It's a damned shame that we're going to lose him."

"Well," said John, "whatever it is he plans to do, he's very happy about it. He whistles and hums and once, when he didn't know I was watching, he did a kind of shuffling dance step."

"The old galoot! I feel sometimes that I'd like to take a broomstick to him." They were now on the last upward grade. "Well, the usual is happening. All that a stock ever needs to go down right into the cellar is for me to buy a share or two. We bought into Boncolenco yesterday. And what do you suppose happened?"

"Did the stock go down?" John's face had taken on an expression of the most intense worry.

"Yes. The stock went down, the very instant after the transaction was completed. But only a quarter of a point. Just give it time, and it'll do a lot better than that! At this stage I feel as though I have a profit, I've been so consistently unlucky."

"Don't you think that it's going up?"

"If I thought that," she declared, "it would be a case, as someone said, of optimism triumphing over the lessons of bitter experience."

There was a long pause. "Then," said John with a deep sigh, "I guess it's good-by to the profit I made on the tollgate deal."

But the next morning Boncolenco Power was up a full point. "If it keeps on this way," said Amy Shirley, when he rode out again to meet her, "I won't be out on the deal more than the brokerage charges."

Two days later she waved a hand to him as she came riding along at a faster gait than usual.

"Good morning, partner!" she called to him. "How does it feel to be a rich man?"

"Do you mean," cried John, "do you really mean that the stock is showing a profit?"

"A profit?" The secretary reined in her horse and indulged in a laugh.

"That's an understatement for you! What a young gloom hound you are! John, Boncolenco really started to climb yesterday. Before the market closed, that stock had gone up, up, up—— Of course we got out before the finish."

"How much did we make?" eagerly.

"Take a good hold on the reins now. I don't want you tumbling out of the saddle or anything like that. We each made a profit of something over twelve thousand dollars!"

John galloped the rest of the way up the hill and then turned and came back, waving his hat above his head and cheering wildly. "Yip-ee! Did you say twelve thousand? That means I have more than fourteen thousand profit altogether. Isn't that wonderful! I can hardly believe it. Why, I've got enough now to make a start on that Congdon business."

"Huh! You'll have enough for that after, say, fifty more deals as profitable as this one."

John slowed down at that and looked rather abashed. "Honestly, I thought I could make a kind of a start on it with what I have."

"You'll need a half million," she declared. "Not a dollar less. And anyway you aren't going to have any time for that kind of thing. I rather think the senator has entirely different plans for you."

That evening, after the senator had selected his cigar and was puffing happily, he began to speak again of the days when Magna Charta was signed.

"I don't want you to think I'm hipped on the subject," he said. "But I was wondering. In your reading, did you ever come across the story of a beautiful princess who lived at that time? One so very lovely that they called her the Pearl of Brittany?"

John thought this over and then shook his head. "Don't think so. She couldn't have been mentioned or I would most certainly have remembered her."

"Well," puffing slowly, "I'll tell you about her. In the first place, this was the family setup. First there was old King Henry II and there have been few better than he was. He had married Eleanor of Aquitaine, who was the greatest heiress in the world. She owned half of France, including all the land on the Bay of Biscay. She was beautiful when she was young and a real high-stepper. Now she had settled down and become a pretty wise woman. They had a large family. First there was Prince Henry, the oldest son, who died before his father. The second son was Richard the Lionhearted. The third son was named

Geoffrey, and finally came John. There were a few daughters, all lovely girls. They are known in history as the Plantagenets, you'll remember, because of a flower they wore as a crest. The Plantagenet sons were terrific young fellows, proud, violent, quarrelsome, and fighting fools, all of them. And they were handsome; they looked the way kings and princes are supposed to look, but so seldom do. They were tall and strong and as blond as ripe corn and they had blazing blue eyes; all except John, who was as dark as Satan. The third son, Geoffrey, was the handsomest of them all. He had been married to Constance of Brittany and they had two children, a daughter Eleanor and a boy Arthur. Geoffrey himself was dead by this time and so was the old king, and when King Richard, who was always fighting, got himself killed at the siege of a castle in France, the succession should have come to young Prince Arthur. But John settled *that* by murdering Arthur and grabbing the throne himself.

"Now the princess I started to tell you about was this little Eleanor, Arthur's sister. She looked exactly like her father and so she was probably the loveliest girl in all Europe. Something had to be done about her, so John got her into his hands and locked her up in a castle, the strongest in the country. No one knew where she was and the people of Brittany, who considered her their rightful ruler after Arthur's death, were afraid she had been killed by her wicked uncle. Even after John died, and his nine-year-old son had been chosen to succeed him, the barons of England kept this unfortunate girl under lock and key. They didn't want another claimant to the throne at large. They'd had enough of that kind of thing. They wanted peace, even if it meant keeping her as close as the Man in the Iron Mask. Later the princess was removed to another castle and in a few years it was given out she had died. Perhaps she had. On the other hand, perhaps she went right on living. How do we know?"

The old man settled back into his chair. He began to puff again on his cigar. "John, I want to talk to you about my will. I'm sure you're interested in what I've got to say. Now don't protest. It's only natural for you to feel an interest. I've got a great deal to leave and I could leave it in any number of ways, couldn't I?

"Well, I have very definite ideas about the leaving of property," he went on. "I don't think there's any justification for leaving all you've got to other people, young ones mostly, who don't have to work any more. With what I've got I could make drones or parasites out of a great many people; and there are plenty quite willing to be made into 'em if

I decide to leave them as much as they would like to have. It is my solid and unchangeable conviction, John, that money should be left for the general welfare, and I've devoted a great deal of time and thought to the problem of what I should do with mine. My will, which was made in its present and final form some years ago, is based on that line of thought. But I haven't taken the easy way, which is to leave the money in great big blocks to a few institutions or to certain causes. I've broken it up into many smaller donations—a million here, a hundred thousand there, fifty thousand somewhere else. I've studied the need to which each donation is to be applied and in every case I can see that the benefit will be felt in a personal and real way by a great many people.

"You'll understand now, John," he continued, "that too much of the money is earmarked for this and that to allow for any great fortunes being willed to individuals. I'm leaving legacies, of course, to quite a few people; but in no case will the beneficiary be able to sit down on his or her roundabout and have racing stables and villas in Italy or devote a lifetime to cutting coupons and collecting first editions. I've made only one change in my will in the last few years. I made it yesterday. I signed a codicil, leaving a legacy to you, my boy. One of the kind I've been talking about. A nice, sizable chunk of change but not a fortune."

"Whatever you've done, sir, is more than generous, I'm sure," declared John, finding it hard to speak. "I'm not entitled to anything. I know that. I—I don't see any way of letting you know how grateful I am."

"There may be a way. Pretty soon, in fact. But we won't talk of that now. All I want to add to what I've already said is that I'm putting you into my will because I've taken a fancy to you. And also—well, it's for your grandmother's sake. I've something to make up for, you know. I can't do it this way. I know that. But Lucy will know what I've done and it will make her happy, I think."

Before John could say anything further the old man changed the subject; or, at least, he took up the question of finances from another angle. In a hearty voice he said: "In the meantime, you and I can go on making some money for ourselves. Which will, in your case, sort of back up the bit I'm leaving you. What do you say to another little speculation? A sort of dead certain speculation, if there is such a thing. And how about really going it this time, really going whole hog?"

"Yes, sir!" cried John eagerly. "I've got some capital now. Thanks to you, sir, of course. I've got fourteen thousand dollars. I guess I can afford to go really whole hog."

"I'll put you into a new issue of an industrial concern called El Dorado Light and Power. It's a sound concern. In fact, if the securities of old El ever got shaky we could expect the end of the world—the financial world, of course. So this time it shall be—five thousand shares for you, young Mr. Plunger Foraday. For several days only, I mean."

"Right you are, sir! Shoot the works. Five thousand shares it is, sir."

5

Senator O'Rawn's combination butler and valet was a very tall, very thin, and very pessimistic man whose real name was Peter Cloyne. His employer had started early to call him Peterkin (being fond of quoting from an old English poem about one Peterkin and a famous victory) and the name had stuck. Even the bellboys in Washington had taken to using it.

A week after the last recorded conversation Peterkin came to John about the time of day when he served the senator his single before-dinner cocktail. The suggestion of grimness and worry he always carried about him seemed much intensified.

"Say, young Mr. John," he began. It was perhaps in keeping with his other characteristics that he spoke in a hoarse voice. "There's something going on here that something's got to be done about. I'm speaking to you because the old man's taken a shine to you and I guess you're the one to do it. It's about all this picking at him. Do you know he took a bad turn this afternoon?"

John dropped the magazine he was thumbing through and jumped to his feet. "I didn't know. I started out for a long ride after lunch and just got back. Is it serious, Peterkin? Judas priest, I hope not!"

"It all depends. The doctor's just left. The boss isn't going to have his cocktail tonight. He's in bed and all the dinner he's going to have is one soft-boiled egg. He's mad enough to hang a whole string of hides out on a line."

John was looking very sober and worried. "What was it, Peterkin? Not—not a stroke, I hope."

"Not quite. But I guess he came close to something pretty serious. He toppled over and he was trying to get back on his feet when I found him."

"What is it you want me to do? I'm ready for anything."

"He's got to be left alone, young Mr. John. You can stop all this picking at him. They're at it all the time. 'Don't quit politics,' they say. 'Write another letter,' they say, 'and tell the public you didn't mean the first one. You just got to run for another term,' they say. The worst one of the lot is that Shirley woman. I guess she thinks she's doing the right thing but she just keeps it up. Picking, picking, picking. And she's working him too hard, answering all these letters he gets. They don't need to bother him about these bags of mail coming in every day. Burn 'em, I say, or send out a form letter."

"Peterkin," said John, "he hasn't told me anything about this plan he's got in his head. Does he really want to drop out of the Senate? Or is he doing it because he thinks it's the wisest thing to do at his age?"

The body servant walked closer and leaned a hand on the table beside John's chair.

"Young fellow," he said, his voice hoarser than ever because he was feeling so disturbed, "the doctor told me something. His heart's bad. He isn't going to die in a week or a month or anything as bad as that. But he's not going to have so very much longer. The doc opened up to me because I'll have to look after him, and see he takes his medicines and don't eat or drink too much. No one else knows it but the old man himself. He said to me just a few minutes ago, 'I ain't blaming you about the cocktail. I know you'd get it for me if I wanted it very much.' 'Not a chance,' I said. 'I wouldn't get you one for nothing under the sun.' 'Well, anyways,' he said, 'I don't bear any grudges because I haven't got much time left to get on my horse and be along about my business. I guess I've left it to the very last minute.' There wasn't a trace of fear or regret in him. I would say, young Mr. John, that he's champing at the bit to be off. He said to me, 'Peterkin, I've got the queerest knowledge stored up in this old head of mine and I've got to get it out. This will be the damnedest, oddest journey any man ever took.'"

"Do you think they'll listen to me when I tell them to lay off him?"

"Give it to 'em straight from the shoulder, young Mr. John. Say to them, 'Do you want to kill him with all this stuff?' You can't tell them what the doctor said because I'm not supposed to tell you or no one else. But perhaps you could drop a hint. They've got to get it into their heads that he's done with politics and ain't going to have any more of it."

This very disturbing news kept the young guest awake much of the night and he did not waken from a belated nap as early as usual. In fact he had not finished shaving when he heard the voice of Amy Shirley coming from the direction of the patio. Brushing the lather from his face, he hurried down to have a hand in what was being said.

The old man was stretched out in an extension chair and it was apparent at a glance that he was not himself. His secretary had dumped the contents of three well-filled mailbags on a table beside him. She had lost some of her usual assurance and was regarding her employer with a questioning and rather unhappy air.

"John, we're making plans," said the senator. His voice had not lost all of its bass note but it sounded to John like that of an old lion who had been challenged for the leadership of the pack and had lost. He was, nevertheless, in good spirits. "I'm arranging with Amy to get reservations and to jolt the State Department into getting passports and visas ready in record time. I've made up my mind. I'm going to Europe. Will you believe that I've never been there? I've traveled all over Canada and Alaska and I've flown around the South American countries. But I've never crossed the Atlantic."

Amy spoke up in a voice equally compounded of regrets and determination. "I'm trying to tell him, John, that he's not well enough to go right away."

Some of the boom came back into the senatorial tones. "And I'm telling her that it's now or never. I'm telling her to take these letters back to my office and turn them over to Seth Silliman. They'll have to run things between them while I'm away. As for you, my boy, you're going with me. That is, of course, if you want to go."

The burden of regret John had been feeling about the arrangement rolled away. "I certainly do want to go. Yes, sir, there's nothing I want to do so much as go along with you on this trip."

"I'm going to work you hard."

"That's good, sir. I want to be useful."

"You haven't any idea how hard I'm going to work you. It won't be all sight-seeing and having a good time. Your nose will be at the grindstone."

"You'll need me too," protested Amy Shirley at this point. "What will you do about the letters you'll receive, and the invitations you'll get, and the tickets you'll have to buy?"

"My dear child, I'm going to disregard letters. I'm not going to answer any of them. If I get any invitations, I'll turn them down cold. No, young lady, this is going to be strictly stag. John and Peterkin and I. No one else is going."

Amy turned and walked back into the house with the slightest hint of a flounce. "I don't think you are being very kind," she said. "If you don't need me any more, there's nothing left but to resign and get myself a new job."

The senator looked properly disturbed at this. "Now see here," he called, "you mustn't go and do anything silly, my girl. I'll always need you, even if I must limit my party for this little jaunt." But he was speaking to a closed door.

It was three days before the doctor would permit the patient to get into a saddle. To avoid the heat of the day they started in late afternoon and it was dark when the horses turned into the corral at the O'Rawn ranch. Seth Silliman, looking as solemn as a pallbearer, met them on the wide patio.

"Sorry to hear you've been a bit done up, boss," he said, staring hard at the signs of fatigue on his employer's face. "I'm not sure Amy isn't right about this and that you ought to recuperate before starting. However, we've got everything ready for you. The passports will be handed over at the airport in New York. All the reservations have been made. You go to Ireland first as you stipulated and I judge from the nature of the telegram I received from the management of the Shelbourne that there will be plenty of excitement over the arrival of the great Irish-American senator."

"Clamp down on that kind of thing, Seth," protested the old man. "I'm leaving my political career behind me. It will be a tired old man on a wild-goose chase who'll be arriving. I don't want to make any explanations. What's our schedule?"

"You fly tomorrow in time to make connections with the transatlantic in New York. All you do there is to change over to a transatlantic plane. They'll wait for you if you're late. That much they insist on doing for the finest senator the country has ever had."

Senator O'Rawn turned to speak to John in the dark. "My boy, I'm as excited and chirkey about this as a ten-year-old. It's like the day I went on my first picnic excursion. All my life I've wanted to do this—to get over there and start at this business we have ahead of us. I'm leaving everything else behind me without a single pang."

Two men were at the foot of the steps when the plane landed at New York. One was a messenger from a Manhattan trust who turned over to the senator a package of telegrams and letters, which the latter shoved into a capacious pocket with an almost indifferent air. The second was a brisk young man in a far from quiet tweed suit.

"Senator," said the second man in a guarded tone, "I'm Victor Alfredi. Of the secret service. I'm assigned to see that you get off safely and with the least trouble to yourself."

"It's kind of you, Mr. Alfredi," said the old man. He seemed very tired. "But I'm a private citizen now, you know; or very nearly that. I won't need any official coddling from now on."

The officer smiled. "That's what you think, sir. You've got to transfer to Idlewild and, when you get there, you'll find a big crowd waiting for you. Newspapermen, politicians, some of them top brass too, people wanting favors done for them, cranks, curiosity seekers. Several hundred of them."

"I'm very tired, young man," declared the senator after a moment's reflection. "You see, I haven't been well and I started on this trip before allowing myself enough time to recuperate. Is there any way of avoiding this crowd?"

"That's what I'm here for. We can get into the airport by one of the private entrances and go direct to the plane. Will you mind getting on while they're refueling and loading her?"

"Not a bit. The prospects of getting into one of those reclining chairs and having a quick nap appeals to me more than anything else at the moment."

"It's as good as done, sir."

The senator looked very tired and pale when they were hoisted up into the plane. He confirmed what he had said by falling asleep almost immediately. John settled down beside him. Although he was deeply worried over the condition of his benefactor, he could not help feeling at the same time a sense of exhilaration. He had no idea what lay ahead of them but it was certain they were starting out on an adventure. Something was afoot, something strange and unusual. It would have been less than natural if he had not felt a tingle of excitement as his mind dwelt on what might happen to them after they landed in Ireland.

The plane had been under way for more than an hour before the old senator roused himself. He turned in his chair, grunted once, and then opened his eyes. The steady drone of the motors warned him that they were making progress on the long Atlantic jump.

"Just started?" he asked.

"You've been asleep an hour, sir. We're well out. They'll be bringing our dinners any minute now."

"Lot of good that will do me," commented the senator bitterly. "Peterkin back there will watch every mouthful I eat. I could have sworn I dozed off for no more than a few minutes." His mind went back to the events following their arrival from the West and he reached a hand into a pocket for the mail he had received. "I need a smoke so badly that every last one of the billions of molecules in my body is setting up a holler."

He sorted out the mail with a careless air and handed one of the telegrams to John. "A report on El Dorado Light and Power," he said. Then, without giving his companion time to digest or at any rate to make any comment on the communication, he began to talk of something else. "It's the first time in my life I ever did that. I mean, giving all those people the slip at the airport. I was always careful to treat the public well. Ordinarily I would have shaken hands with every man jack of them, called as many of them as I could by name, listened to what they had to say, made notes of what they wanted. They must have been a surprised lot when they found I had given them the go-by. I expect the reporters will hand me a panning." He seemed worried over the probable results of his maneuver but after a moment he smiled. "What's it matter if they are angry? I'll probably never see one of them again. And I'll never be asking for votes. When we get through with this business of ours, John, and come back to America, there won't be any crowds to greet us. I'll be out of the public eye by that time. I'll regret it a little. I like people. I admit that I've always liked publicity. I've never shrunk from seeing my picture in the papers."

He became aware then that his companion was not paying any attention to him. John had opened the letter from the brokerage house and was staring at it with unbelieving eyes.

"What's wrong? Did old El drop down a little?"

"No, sir," answered John in a small and unnatural voice. "On the contrary. It went up. They sold our holdings before the market closed today."

The senator did not seem much interested. "Well, that's what we expected. The market has been pretty bullish."

"Sir," said John, "I don't believe I'm reading the figures right. I'm quite sure I'm wrong. I wonder if you would look at them."

The old man fitted his glasses on his nose. He studied the figures for a few moments and then turned around to smile at his companion.

"Pretty good, eh? What total did you get?"

"I—I figured it several times and the total was the same each time. I know I must be wrong because what—what I make out of it is a profit for me of $39,655.80."

"That's right. That's what you made on your five thousand shares,

John. After taking off commissions and the interest for the use of the money. You wanted it that way—on a straight business basis."

"Yes, sir." John's power of speech was still refusing to function properly. He finally managed to say: "I don't think I should take this money. I haven't earned it. You are being so generous to me that I don't know what to say or do."

The senator had been watching him out of the corner of one eye. "Don't take it so hard, son. You'll get used to this sort of thing after a while; and to other things which won't be nearly as pleasant. But if it will make you feel a little better, this is the last transaction of the kind we'll be in together. I gave them instructions to sit tight and do nothing until I got back. I don't want to be bothered with cablegrams. It seemed wisest to close up shop for the time being."

He was still watching his young companion with an amused realization of the truth that gratitude is the hardest emotion for the young to express. To save John from further floundering, he began to talk about the unfinished manuscript of the novel.

"I read it some days ago," he said, "but the way the roof suddenly caved in on me, I didn't have a chance to talk about it. John, I have two quite definite reactions to that story of yours. I'm not a critic and I don't know what constitutes good writing but it seemed to me you wrote extremely well."

The youth's face lighted up. He felt more excited over this favorable report than over the great profit he had made on the market.

"The writing was so sound that I read the story all the way through. But I've got to say that I think you picked a trite theme to expend your talents on."

John looked considerably surprised at this. "Why, sir, I thought it would be the other way around. I expected you would approve of what I was trying to do but find my writing immature and—and amateurish. I was dealing with a theme which interested me more than anything else in the world and I've always believed this to be the first test of literary sincerity."

Senator O'Rawn nodded his head. "I see your point, son, and I'm sure you are right. But it seems to me unfortunate that you have to be interested most in an idea that every other budding author elects to write. I'm sure there have been fifty novels published in the last few years about adolescence and the efforts of sensitive youth to get adjusted to the thorny business of living."

"I know that, sir. But I still feel that I had something to say."

"My final reaction is favorable, John. I'm sure you can undertake a job of writing for me. That's what I meant when I said I was going to keep your nose to the grindstone. I want you to go with me and see certain places and listen to something I'm going to tell you. I want it put down in a story that people will read. I feel pretty sure you can do it. Do you want to try?"

"Of course, sir. I feel very grateful that—that you think I can write a little. I was afraid you would be more disposed to laugh at my feeble efforts."

"Son," said the senator abruptly, "I have a question to ask you. Do you think an angel could make a mistake?"

John was puzzled at the sudden change of subject and even more at the nature of the question.

"Why, no. Angels are the instruments of God and so they couldn't be anything but—infallible and omnipotent." Then he began to give the idea more thought and reached a point where he wanted to qualify his answer. "Well now, coming to think of it, it seems just barely possible that there could be an occasional slip. If we accept as truth that there is a God—one God, the head of the whole universe——"

The old man nodded his head with the deepest earnestness and belief. "There is, my boy, there is. Never allow yourself any doubts on that score. Believe me when I say that I know there is a God. *I know.*"

"Well, then, sir, can we believe further that He isn't the kind of God to create a world like ours and then leave it alone, not caring what happens to the creatures existing on it? If He is the kind of God who watches and directs and has a purpose in everything——"

"He is the kind of God who watches and directs and has a purpose in everything. I know He is."

"In that case He must have a tremendous number of angels. Thousands of them to attend to the whole universe."

"Thousands of them, John. Hundreds of thousands."

"Then it's just possible that one of them, a new angel, say, might be responsible for a slip."

The senator laughed and slapped his young companion on the knee. "I've asked a great many that question, my boy, and I've always had the same answer; that an angel could *not* make a mistake. Well, I agree with what you have said. Of course, it may all have been intended in the first place but I'm inclined to think it was a mistake. That a door was allowed to swing open, as someone said in a story I read. Kipling, I believe. And because this mistake occurred, we are going on a journey and you are going to write me a long report of what you see and hear."

Chapter III

1

SENATOR O'RAWN had done himself well at breakfast. Peterkin had grumbled but had finally agreed to the consumption of a crisp rasher of gammon and he had not objected to a long glass of Irish coffee. Now Peterkin should have known that Irish coffee is of a very special kind. It consists of three parts: first, two fingers of Irish whiskey in the bottom of the glass, sweetened with two small spoonfuls of sugar, then the coffee, black, black, black, as black even as the sin of Dermod MacMurrough, and then the thickest of cream floated over the top. As a result of this unusual indulgence, the elderly visitor from America was in the best of spirits when he emerged through the wide-open doors of the hotel at Kilkenny and looked out on the world.

It was a wonderful world, he found, a world of bright sunshine and grass as green as shamrocks, where even the yellow of mountain fern could be seen on the streets of the town. He took a deep breath.

"This is Ireland at last, John," he said. "Just listen to their voices. None of your stage brogue here, John, my boy. Just the naturally sweet tones of a race blessed with gentle nature and the best of speaking cords in their throats."

John was watching the people who passed. No hurry, no noise, no whistling for taxis (and no taxis to whistle for), no extravagance in dress, no hats straight from Fifth Avenue, no high heels.

"Very pretty girls, sir," he said.

"There's no prettier in the world," exclaimed the senator. "Except, of course, the girls of the United States, most of whom have Irish blood anyway. And will you look over there at that shop which has a sign saying, 'Turf Accountant'? Would you know what a turf accountant is?"

"It wouldn't mean a bookmaker, would it?"

"It would indeed. Isn't that just like the Irish? To dignify properly a calling as necessary as undertaking or paperhanging but which is spoken of in disrepute in all other countries of the world?"

There was a small car standing at the curb. A small man got out from behind the wheel and started up the steps toward them.

"Might you be the sinator from Amerika?"

"Yes. And I expect you're the Jamesey Boy Callaghan the landlord told us about."

The little man wore a long and dilapidated coat bound in at the waist by a frayed rope. "It's no secret in any part of County Kilkenny, sor, that I'm James Callaghan, no matter what other names they have for me, the dirty backbiters and faultfinders."

"I was informed you had a car, Mr. Callaghan."

The little man waved a hand grandly in the direction of the contraption at the curb. "And what might that be, sor?"

"I'm afraid, Mr. Callaghan, that automobiles are not like old wine. They don't improve with age. Just how old is that car, so called?"

The Irishman's pride went immediately to the defense of the antiquity of his property. "No man, dead or alive, knows the true lineage of this car, sor. It goes far back into histhry. It's said that Brian Boru himself rode in it."

"It's most clearly a museum piece. When did you buy it, if I may make so bold as to ask?"

"I didn't buy it, sor. It were re-link-wished to me by a dump heap, and my brother-in-law Daniel Oge worked miracles on it."

"Do you guarantee it will get us to Castle O'Rawn?"

The Irishman gave his head a satisfied nod. "Then the information I had, sor, is true. You *are* the great man from Amerika who has come all the way across the seas to visit Patrick O'Rawn. And a fine gentleman he is, even if he is a wee bit hasty at times. It's a matter of regret that I must report him, sor, to be one that will hold a grudge. I have been told not to set so much as a foot on his property and so I can do no more than take you to his gate and depart at once. You'll have the thirty shillings ready for me, so I can get away without any delay, sor?"

"I'll have the ten shillings ready for you and not a penny more."

"It's hard of hearing I am, sor. Did I hear you say twenty shillings and the price of a thrippence mug of heavy for all in the bar up to, say, six?"

"You hear me say fifteen shillings. And it's the last word you're going to hear on the subject."

"Fifteen it was all the time. But it's not blaming me you'll be for trying."

"I'll not blame you if you get us to Castle O'Rawn. I have my doubts whether this car will hold out that far."

The jehu waved his hand airily. "Git right in, sors. It's a broth of a car and in any case it's downhill most of the way."

They rode in uneasy state across the square and looked up with awe at the great frowning castle which Strongbow had built above it and which William the Marshal had enlarged and strengthened. It looked enormous and grim, a very Moloch of a castle. They climbed a grade which led out of town, with much puffing and snorting and bucking, and just managed to make the crest with a final convulsive shudder. They rolled on then through country as sweet to the eye as the hills of Samaria to desert travelers, where they could look down over the greenest of fields to the winding course of the river Nore. As they progressed, Jamesey Boy Callaghan told them a great deal about the owner of Castle O'Rawn. It seemed that he was a man of much pride and a blistering tongue, the rough edge of which had been employed often in pointing out weaknesses in the character of James Callaghan. He was a man who knew horses and might have made a fortune out of them if he had ever been able to afford more than a pair of "plugs" for the use of the family. He was a writer, a writer "of sorts," amended the driver with the air of one who deems it necessary to draw a distinction.

"What sort of things does he write?" asked the senator, who sat in the front seat with him, while John and Peterkin sat in the rear and held onto the sides for dear life.

"Oh, all sorts. The theayter, and books, and wine, and the histhry of Kilkenny. Anything that's uninteresting like and don't matter at all. It's not much that gets published, sor. But it's rolling in wealth he'll soon be, because his niece is the most beautiful girl in all Ireland, including the black country of the north, and she'll be marrying a wealthy American one of these days." At this point he turned to look at the back seat. "Is the young fella a wealthy American, sor?"

Richard O'Rawn kept a straight face. "He is that, Jamesey Boy Callaghan. He has just made a great fortune on the market."

"Has he, now! It's always been the way I wanted to make me living, to drop a shilling in a slot and see the great beautiful gold pieces tumbling out at the other end." Then he gave his head a doubtful shake. "But it's not winning the lovely little Eleanor he'll be doing unless he can talk the birds out of the trees."

The old man turned to look back at John. "Can you?" he asked.

"I've never tried, sir. I don't believe I would have much success at it."

"Unless a young spark can talk the birds out of the trees, how can he expect to talk the little lady off the high perch she's climbed herself up to? But," with another shake, "would it be of any use if he did? It's a title she wants. Are titles to be had in Ameriky, sor?"

"No, I'm happy to say. We don't believe in that kind of folly."

"But *she* believes in them. It's a Lady This or a Duchess That she's got to be. But all this is idle talk, sor, and a waste of time. She says she's never going to marry and all the brisk lads hereabouts are beginning to believe she means it."

Castle O'Rawn, as they perceived when it was pointed out to them from the summit of a steep hill, was not large or impressive and only part of it was old enough to justify any claim to the term of castle. But it had a great deal of charm, standing in the bend of a small stream with a clump of gentle old trees on one side of it and the greenest fields in the whole of Ireland around it.

"It's just as I thought it would be," said the old man in a musing tone. "I've been corresponding with Patrick O'Rawn for a great many years and he's made the home of my ancestors very real to me."

"Will you be jumping out when we reach the gate so I can throw you the bags and get along about my business without any attempt to stop whatever? These brakes are like an old 'ooman's stays which has lost the whalebone."

The owner of the castle had seen them as they came over the hill and he was standing at the gate when the ancient car gave one jerk and almost came to a stop. Peterkin was down first with outstretched arms to help his employer. The senator proved so heavy, however, that the pair of them came close to tumbling on the sod and only John's hand on the old man's arm prevented a catastrophe.

"So you fell into the clutches of that scoundrel!" said the owner of the castle, scowling at the back of the rapidly departing jehu. "I hope you've come to no injury. If you have, I will personally attend to the horsewhipping of Jamesey Boy Callaghan all the way to Dublin and back."

"I'm quite all right," gasped the senator. "How useless the muscles are when you reach my age! Have we all the bags, Peterkin?"

"They're here, sir."

Patrick O'Rawn was very tall and bone-thin, with an undisciplined thatch of thinning red hair. There was an unmistakable air of distinction about him.

"I'm most happy," he said, "to welcome the greatest of the O'Rawns to the home of his forefathers. It is an honor as well as a pleasure. Will you be running for President next term?"

"This is John Foraday, Patrick O'Rawn. And this is Peterkin. I will *not* be running for President. I've dropped out of politics entirely. A matter of old age combined with bad health; and a pressure of time on me for the doing of other things."

They were crossing the lawn and saw ahead of them a beautiful old door with copper hinges sunk into the walls of the ancient part of the house.

"I have no wireless," the owner was saying. "But I've seen you sometimes here and there on what you call newsreels, I believe. You are a most impressive speaker, Richard." He paused at the stone steps. "I hoped my niece Eleanor would be out to do the honors with me. No doubt she has planned some more impressive way of letting you see her first. Sometimes I think that girl should be with the Abbey Players and sometimes it seems to me that she belongs on a tapestry of Norman times and nowhere else."

They were standing in a circular hall of quite considerable height and with open steps winding upward around the wall. The stone of the wall and the darkness caused by the narrowness of the slits which passed for windows spoke convincingly of a great age.

"Your first visit home, Richard," said the host, giving his head a regretful shake. "And right away I see speculation in your eyes. Are you thinking that you stand for the first time in all that's left of the ancestral home?"

The visitor from America nodded. "My mind was filled with it, Patrick. I was indeed speculating on the age of these walls. They are old. But not as old perhaps as you think. And you are equally to blame for this lifelong delay in getting together. You were stubborn also, Patrick. You wouldn't come to America and I couldn't go to Ireland."

"The New World called to me but there was never a time when I could afford the passage. But you were saying something that I propose to dispute most emphatically. About the age of these walls."

"In my humble opinion, sir, this entrance tower was built at least two centuries later than the arrival of the first O'Rawn in Ireland."

The owner's face showed a slight tendency to redness. "Come, Richard, a snap verdict. I'll show you all the evidence there is on the subject. Scanty enough but to me quite convincing. Our brave young ancestor was the architect of these walls, Cousin, although I am free to concede that the rest of the house is comparatively modern. One wing is even Elizabethan." He was now scowling at his guest. "Hell and Biddy Malone, why do you think different?"

"Patrick, the Normans always considered protection against attack the purpose to be achieved in building a castle. Why would Richard of Rawen, who seems to have been a wise young cockerel, select this site? Archers posted on the top of that hill could have riddled you here. I'll take you to the exact spot where the first Rawen Castle stood, Patrick, on the brow of that hill. If we can get a few strong-backed fellows with spades, we'll get down to the original foundations in no time at all. Don't look at me so bitterly. Isn't the truth in such a matter more important than personal pride in a long-accepted theory?"

"The truth is more important than what you call my personal pride, Cousin. But come outside again and point out this site to me." He added over his shoulder: "The stubbornness of the Norman still persists in the O'Rawns, doesn't it? We both have our full share."

John did not follow his elders out for the continuation of the discussion. He had heard a sound from the interior of the house which interested him much more. Someone was playing a harp. What he heard was not the sonorous throbbing of a full-sized instrument but the poignant note of a small Irish harp. The air was an old and strange one, as old perhaps as the tower in which he stood, and the voice which sang the words was a pure and sweet treble. It was like a minor Patti singing a lullaby in a nursery.

"It's the niece," he said to himself. "Should I stand here while they argue outside or should I go in and introduce myself?"

He compromised by going as far as the entrance to a small drawing room, an apartment in which elegance had slowly turned to shabbiness. There were fine portraits on the walls and a long Georgian couch which seemed priceless at a casual glance, but the rugs were worn and not too skillfully patched. A girl sat at the far end, dressed in flowing green and gold, and she was picking at the strings of the harp. Her head, a mass of pure gold, was bent over it.

Peterkin was breathing hard at his shoulder. "Will you look at that!"

he whispered. "She must be an angel. And d'ye see, she's playing a harp!"

John, who had caught his breath in sheer wonder, had no comment to make. He was thinking in a panic: "How can I face this divine creature? How will I be able to talk to her? Peterkin is right. She is an angel."

Then the girl turned and it was apparent to John at once that Peterkin was only partly right. She was angelic in her beauty but at the same time she seemed as imperious as any princess out of history. Her golden hair had been wound around her head with the most artful carelessness; her eyes were of a blue which defied any definition; her features were flawlessly classic but with the delicacy of a cameo. Searching in his mind for similes, John said to himself, "She's like a Plantagenet princess"; and stopped there, for he knew he had found the perfect one.

The girl had risen and stretched out a hand in greeting. The green and gold sleeve had fallen back to reveal a slender white arm.

"You must be Mr. Foraday," said the divinity. Did her voice have a slight hint of royal condescension about it?

"Yes," he answered, his throat so dry that speech was difficult.

"We live a most secluded life here and you are the first American I have seen. You puzzle me rather. You don't look like an American. At least not what I expected."

"Don't I? How should I look?" He was beginning to get hold of himself.

"I suppose I expected you to speak in a high voice and to be wearing one of those felt hats with a very broad brim. All Americans wear them, don't they?"

"Well, no," said John. "Only when they're in the movies or when they live in the hot parts of the country where they need protection from the sun. The first time I saw a cowboy hat worn in real life was a few weeks ago when I went to Mr. O'Rawn's ranch."

"It's strange that such wrong ideas can get about, isn't it?"

"It's the same all over the world, I guess. The people of one country laugh at all others. Why, at one time in America the favorite comedian in a play was generally an Irishman."

He realized at once that this was not the right thing to say. She had drawn herself up and was regarding him with an air that was positively chilly.

"Really! What could you possibly find to laugh about in us?"

John hesitated. "Oh, nothing much. You know, the old things. 'Begorra!' and 'Bejabers!' and red noses and plug hats and shillelaghs."

Her manner had become glacial. "How amazing!" she said. "I didn't believe it possible that even in America there could be such ideas. And as for what I said about you, I was told positively by Dr. O'Markey that he was more impressed by the number of cowboy hats in America than by the skyscrapers."

"Perhaps your Dr. O'Markey isn't a reliable observer," suggested John, who was beginning to get his back up in spite of the spell she had cast over him.

"That is possible," said the girl. "He did say that the Western university where he lectured had several times over the number of students as our Trinity. And *that*, of course, is absurd."

And then, with a suddenness which left him speechless, she changed completely. Her whole face lighted up and she smiled at him. "Oh, Mr. Foraday, how very rude I have been! Getting you into an argument as soon as you step inside the door. I've been trying to tell you that we Irish are the one perfect race and at the same time proving how very tactless we can be. Will you forgive me? And now I think you might like a cup of tea."

To John's amazement she did not reach out to pull the bell cord on the wall behind her but left the room and returned in a very few minutes with a small tray and a pot of tea. The china was almost transparent and obviously very old and valuable and the act of handing him his cup brought her so close to him that he could feel his hand trembling. He hardly dared accept it.

They were sitting together, however, and talking in a friendly way when the two elders returned, still pursuing their argument. They had the room to themselves, moreover, for Peterkin had been taken in hand by the household servant, a gloomy and untidy Irishman named Lacey, and they had vanished together. Patrick O'Rawn came to a stop when he saw his niece.

"So! It was the role of the beautiful harpist at a Court of Love you selected. I hope the young man was properly impressed. Richard, this is my niece Eleanor. She was my youngest brother's youngest child. Now, God be kind to all of them, there are none left but the three of us, Richard, the last of the O'Rawns. I must warn you about this niece of mine. She has gentle and beguiling ways when she likes, she rides like an angel on a white horse in the clouds, she has a mind and a tongue of her own. I love her dearly. I would do anything in the world for her. But there are times when I wish she were still a little girl so I could take her across my knee!"

"Uncle Paddy!" cried the girl in indignant tones. "What an outrageous thing to say!"

"I am putting our guests on their guard."

Richard O'Rawn had nothing to say. He was looking at the girl in a silence which suggested he had experienced both a surprise and a shock. He was thinking: "This passes belief! How strange, and yet how right! How the proofs are piling up!"

2

Eleanor O'Rawn had made John feel like a tongue-tied courtier, a juvenile Raleigh speechless and dazzled in the presence of Elizabeth, a mere private in the Russian Guards on whom the eye of Catherine had rested unfavorably for a moment. His consciousness of the imperious side of her and of his own complete unworthiness had not proven any defense. He had fallen in love. When she retired to change her costume, he sat in a corner of the drawing room, facing a beautifully bonneted mahogany cabinet filled with rare bits of things. The contents of the cabinet made no impression on him. His mind was filled with what he knew was the rarest and loveliest thing ever created. "I'm a goner," he said to himself. "She'll never think of me as anything but a stupid lunk from a country which lacks her royal approval. But she's so wonderful that I'll go on loving her just the same. As long as I live." Recalling a phrase from a classic poem, he added, "I'll love her till I die."

The effect she had on him was quite different when she came down for lunch. He found himself pitying her. The blue and white-trimmed dress into which she had changed showed signs of having been carefully repaired. Even to his far from expert eye the length of the skirt was at least a year behind the style procession. Her mood, moreover, was different.

"Would you like to ride this afternoon?" she asked him in a friendly tone. "I'll lend you my hunter."

John said hastily: "I'm a beginner. I had never been in the saddle until I went out to the ranch a few weeks ago. Any kind of old crowbait is good enough for me."

"He's the best beginner I ever saw," declared the senator, who had been keeping an eye on them. "John, why don't you buy a hunter for yourself? You could get good use out of him while you're here and I'm sure our good friends would provide stabling until we come back. Have I told you, Patrick, that we plan to drop in again after our jaunt through England and Brittany?"

"That's a promise I'm going to hold you to, Richard. And I know where we could pick up a splendid fellow for John. The one I have in mind would be a bit on the expensive side, I'm afraid."

John's mind had been fired by visions of long rides in the company of this golden-haired divinity, during which he might conceivably be able to get on a better footing with her, to win her liking even.

"Let's go and buy him right away!" he exclaimed.

The girl sighed, and thought, "Oh, to be able to like a thing and say, 'Let's go and buy it!'"

John was indulging in an inner prayer. "Oh, Lord, make it possible for me to turn my fifty thousand into fifty million dollars. I want to lay it all at her feet!"

"I am interested in your neighbors, the Tostigans," said Richard O'Rawn when they sat down to lunch.

The Irishman looked startled. "Why, Richard, the Tostigans ceased to be neighbors a great many years ago," he said. "The place has been empty since the First World War when the last of them died. It's been falling into rack and ruin."

It was clear that the American found this information disturbing. "It never occurred to me to ask you about them. I assumed that they were going along as usual. Weren't they a vital kind of family?"

"Indeed they were. The countryside still talks about them—the black, fighting Tostigan boys."

"Bad cess to them!" declared Marty Lacey, the one servant of the household, who had prepared lunch and was now serving it. "Such stories my da told about them. He knew them and to his sorrow it was. Eight was the least there ever was of the brothers and they went in a pack. Been there was a fair or a picnic or a dacent little get-together, sooner or later—said my da—the word got passed around. 'Here come the Tostigans.' And there they would be, the fightin' davils, looking for trouble. They would stand together and they would start to yell fit to curdle the blood, 'Foight! Foight! Foight!' Sometimes the other men would sort of join up and accommodate them, and then what a smashing of tables there would be, and a spilling of good vittles and a breaking of bottles, and a blacking of eyes!" Lacey placed on the table a platter of fish fresh caught in the river. "It was good riddance to bad rubbish!" he finished.

The senator was rubbing the bridge of his nose and frowning with an expression which might be called unhappy. "They were good stock to begin with," he said, as though to himself. Then he straightened up. "As a family they go far back. It is my impression that they came to Ireland at the same time as Richard of Rawen."

"The Tostigans always made that their claim," answered the Irishman. "There's no reason to believe they didn't. Except there are no proofs."

The senator did not speak immediately. He was saying to himself: "No, there are no proofs. That is always the sad thing about the happenings of the past. There are so seldom any proofs." He took a morsel of fish on the tip of his fork, and found it fresh and sweet and quite delectable. He waited until the stout-bellied, long-nosed Marty Lacey had left the room. "Do you know, Patrick, that there is Tostigan blood in all of us?"

The head of the O'Rawns stared at his guest with a questioning light in his eyes. "Now how do you happen to know that? Oh yes, it's true. There's a reference in the family records to a Leueen Tostigan who married Richard O'Rawn in the year 1531. It was my own father who found it. We were—well, we were rather quiet about the whole thing. We didn't want what was left of the black Tostigans descending on us in a body and calling us cousins. You may think we were snobbish about it. But, Richard, you never knew the Tostigans and the clamor they made out of everything!"

"The black, rarin' davils!" said Marty Lacey, coming in with a fresh supply of boiled potatoes.

Patrick O'Rawn placed his arms on the table and turned to lean closer to his guest. "But, Richard, how does it happen that you know? You've never seen the document. You've never been in Ireland before. I thought myself the sole custodian of that secret."

"It was just a surmise, a guess," declared the American visitor. To himself he added, "It was the only possible explanation. It could be nothing else."

"To give the devils their due, they were always fine fighting men," went on Patrick O'Rawn. "The two brothers who were the last, Sigurd and Terence—Sigurd was a family name and there seems to have been one in every generation—were killed in the First World War. They died bravely and well, as Irishmen always do. That, I think, is the one thing we should remember about these very distant cousins of ours. They were born to fight and the quiet existence here was too dull for them."

Richard O'Rawn made no response. His head was lowered and he seemed to be absorbed in his food. But through his mind a series of figures were marching, dark young men who had answered to the names he had never forgotten—Sigurd, the first-born, Harold, William-with-the-Long-Arm, little Patrick.

After a long pause the visitor raised his head. "I'm glad to know about Sigurd and Terence and that they died so bravely."

The host was perplexed by the oddness of all this. Richard O'Rawn knew nothing about the Tostigans. How could he? This was his first visit to Ireland. There had never been any mention of them in the letters they had exchanged. Why, then, this strange interest he was manifesting in the troublemaking clan who had been such a problem in the neighborhood when he, Patrick, was a boy?

"Perhaps I am wrong in saying that none of them are left," he said after several long moments of silence. "It's generally believed that one of them still persists in the ruins of the small tower where the family always lived; and which, by the way, is authentically Norman and goes back, perhaps, to the time of Henry II. I refer, Cousin, to the Tostigan ghost."

That brought about a quick uplifting of the leonine head of the visitor from America. "A ghost?" he said. "This is very interesting, Patrick, very interesting indeed. Tell me about it."

"Understand this first of all. I'm Irish and I think I respond to every chord which stirs in the Irish heart. But I don't believe in the Tostigan ghost. It doesn't rattle a battle-ax on the top of the old tower or tramp with mailed feet up and down what is left of the stone steps. It sits on a stone outside the tower, a stone which is shaped like a high-armed chair."

The American was startled into a comment. "The Marshal's Seat? Was that what it is called? And isn't it very old?"

"It has always been there and I believe I've heard it referred to by that name." The head of the household asked no more questions of his guest. All this was getting beyond him. He contented himself with telling the story of the last phase of the Tostigan family. "I was in the First World War but I was too young to get to France. The Armistice came before I saw the last of the training camp. When I came home the two Tostigans were dead and there was no one to claim the old place where they had lived. It was thought there were uncles and cousins here and there about the world, in Australia, Canada, South Africa, and the United States. Heirs were advertised for and there was plenty of correspondence with people in different parts of the world, although nothing much came of it. No one succeeded in establishing a relationship. The courts are now threatening to close the case and take over the land. It's not especially good land."

There was a long pause. "I think, Patrick, I shall pay a visit to the tower one of these nights," said the old man from America. "It's a most interesting story. When you get to my years, you have a great concern over things which pertain to the past. I can think of nothing I would rather do than exchange a few words with this visitor who sits and contemplates all that is left of what, no doubt, was once a great dream."

"The broken walls of an old stone rookery?"

"There might have been great dreams when those walls were first raised, Patrick."

"Will you let me go with you?" asked the host.

"Of course, Patrick. The same blood runs in our veins. We have the same interest in this story."

"I'd like to go too," spoke up John.

"And I," said Eleanor eagerly, from the foot of the table.

Marty Lacey brought in a dish containing toasted Irish raisin bread. "My da lost four teeth in a go with the Tostigans," he volunteered. "The murtherin' davils!"

3

Both of the cousins were on the impatient order. At three o'clock that afternoon Patrick O'Rawn said to his American relation, "The men with the strong backs will be here in half an hour." The American's eyes lighted up with pleasure. "You're one after my own heart, Patrick," he said. "You've got a bit of a go-devil inside you. Instead of sitting around and talking about doing a thing, you pitch right in and do it."

Three men arrived, each with his own shovel and pick. They were led at once to the summit of the hill and here Richard stood for several minutes studying the lay of the land. His eyes were full of a strange introspection as they studied directions, particularly when they rested on a stand of trees, behind which lay the domain of the now extinct Tostigans. Finally he nodded his head.

"Here," he said, touching a spot on the ground with the tip of his cane. "Start at this point and dig your line due west. I don't believe you'll have to go down far."

Whatever the reasons he had for saying that the remains of the foundations of the first Castle O'Rawn would be found where he indicated, it was soon apparent that he was right. In ten minutes the pick of one of the husky trio encountered a block of solid stone.

"Here we be, sor," said the one who had made the find. "Man McCluskey, it's as solid as the hills at Knocktopher, sor!"

"Go easy, Tim Murphy." The American was on friendly terms already with the working crew. "Clear the ground on each side."

Patrick O'Rawn's eyes, as he watched, changed from skepticism to a reluctant conviction. "That's early masonry," he commented. A few minutes later he was certain that it was Norman work. When the earth had been cleared away for a considerable distance on each side of the ancient masonry, he capitulated completely. Here, he said, was where Richard of Rawen had first built. What other explanation could there be?

The elderly American stepped off distances and drew lines on the surface for the digging crew to follow. At the northwesterly angle he inscribed a circle which corresponded accurately (as a later measurement demonstrated) with the line of the newer tower. When the picks of the workmen reached this point, they encountered the wide circular foundation of the original tower. At this juncture Patrick O'Rawn drew his cousin to one side.

"Richard, what is all this?" he demanded. "You've picked like a magician with a wand the exact spot where the tower was raised. Are you a modern Merlin? Is the first Richard standing at your shoulder and whispering in your ear?"

"Castle O'Rawn," said the American, "was included in a book of ancient Irish homes. I studied it most carefully. There was a plan drawn to scale. I happen to remember all the details."

The deep Irish blue of Patrick O'Rawn's eye still held a measure of doubt. "You're holding something back," he charged. "That article did *not* say that the first castle was built on this hill. It assumed that it had always stood on the present site."

"It seems," was the reply, "that the writer of the article was not fully informed. Or he didn't use common sense."

By five o'clock the squad with the sturdy backs had cleared all of one side and the angle where the tower had stood.

"Enough for today," said the owner of the property. "Be back to-

morrow morning at eight sharp. And stop at the kitchen for a drop of
tay on your way home."

"Perhaps, Patrick," suggested Richard, "you'll allow me to anticipate
the pay settlement with a bit on account now. I haven't heard any
jingling in their pockets."

"By all the saints in hivin, that manner of talk is music to the ears!"
cried one of the trio.

"Is American money any good here?" asked the visitor, drawing out
a handful of loose bills.

"As good," was the reply, "as sweet little bits of gold chipped off
the Blessed Gates. And, I'm thinkin', a little bit more on the handy side.
They'll recognize it at the pub where I fear my weary feet will come
to an unwillin' halt through sheer fatigue, sor."

"Your weary feet had better take you straight home," said the owner
of the castle sharply, "because you and your friends must be here at
eight tomorrow without fail, Johnny O'Keefe."

When the money had been distributed and the three had departed
with unanimous briskness and no hint of fatigue, the two elderly men
turned in the direction of the present home of the O'Rawns. Any sense
of pique which the owner had felt over the revelations brought about by
his guest had vanished. He was filled with enthusiasm over the results
of the digging.

"Richard," he said, "I'm going to write a report of all this. It will
make a capital article and I'm sure it will sell to a better publication
and get me a larger price than the piece I've been laboring away at so
long. I've been doing something on the character of Richard III and
taking a few bits of skin off that lady who tried to whitewash him. I
was getting doubtful of it. But *this* will be of interest to everyone. We
must have plans drawn to scale and take some photographs."

"A capital idea, Patrick."

"But," declared the host with an accusing frown, "I'm going to find
it hard to make your role in this sound believable. I won't be able to fob
the readers off with anything as flimsy as this explanation you're giving
me. They'll believe you've found some secret documents. Or that you
were transplanted back to the days when the castle was built; like that
fellow in the Mark Twain book."

"The story of the Connecticut Yankee and King Arthur's Court? Be
easy in your mind, Patrick. All this will put a bit of mystery into your
article. There will be letters sent in about it. That's what editors like,

I understand. Articles which bring in plenty of letters." He was silent for a moment. "Patrick, your niece is like a very lovely princess."

"I sometimes call her that," with a smile. "Whenever she gets hoity-toity or begins ordering everyone around. Which is an almost daily occurrence."

"Who was her mother?"

"My brother Connie took up land in New Zealand and he married a girl out there. I never saw her but Connie sent me a picture. She was small and dark. The child was sent home to me when her parents died, five years ago. Richard, you could have knocked me over with one puff when I set eyes on the child. I said to myself, 'Holy Mother and all the blessed saints, is this a fairy queen in human guise?'"

"We can be sure of one thing. She's a throwback to some lovely lady of Castle O'Rawn of many centuries ago."

The Irishman agreed. "Nearly a thousand years, I think, Richard. She may have been the mistress of the castle when it stood back there on the crest of the hill."

"I keep wondering what will happen to her, this very unusual child. What does life hold for her?"

"She'll marry soon, I'm afraid. In course of time she'll become matronly and the gold in her hair will become brown. I don't want to be here to see that day."

"This princess of ours," said the visitor, "has no more of common clay in her than a sculptor could hold on the point of a trowel. She'll be lovely to the day of her death."

4

The senator continued to speak of his desire to visit the dismantled tower which had been the home of the Tostigans but somehow they never did get around to doing it. Every evening after dinner, with a long black cigar in his lips and a look of utter content on his face, he would say something to this effect: "Shouldn't we go over and see the Tostigan ghost, Paddy? A fine night for it." His host would rouse himself from the slight torpor into which he had fallen after the removal of the coffee cups and mutter: "What—what did you say, Cousin Rick? Oh yes, the ghost. Yes, we ought to do it tonight. No time like the present, eh? But, hell and Biddy Malone, I'm so sleepy I can hardly keep my eyes open. This very instant I'm thinking with longing of the comfort of my bed and how fine it will be to get my head down on a soft pillow."

There would be a pause. "I might as well confess, Paddy, that I feel exactly the same way. I don't think I can stay awake long enough to-night to catch that ghost at his tricks. Well, let's leave it that we'll go tomorrow night without fail."

But tomorrow never came, as far as the quest of the Tostigan ghost was concerned. Each evening, after the two elderly men had gone upstairs to their beds, a change would come over the princess (they had fallen into the habit of calling her that, all except John, who did not dare) and her eyes would begin to dance with excitement. She would say to John: "Let's go for a ride! The moon's out and it will be gorgeous to cross the ford and ride up into the Calverstock."

John never failed to spring up with alacrity. "A grand idea! Let's go!"

For he had his hunter. It had been inspected and purchased on the second day of the visit, for a good round price, a handsome bay with a long reach and strong quarters. The princess had taken one look at him and had said to herself bitterly: "My poor little Bridie will be hard put to keep up with this fellow. And think of the dozen or more decent Irish boys, without a shilling in any of their pockets, who would sell their immortal souls to own him."

She had been willing enough, however, to coach the fortunate out-sider in the finer points of riding. She had been very severe about his posture and his hand on the reins. "Sit up but give him his head!" she would cry. "He knows more about fences, this fine bay honey, than any dozen of you could name." Or, "Easy, you idiot, easy! Do you want to saw the poor fellow's mouth in two?"

Under such exacting tutelage, John had improved rapidly. So rapidly, in fact, that one day she gave him a searching look and said, "Don't tell me you haven't any Irish blood in you. No mere Yankee could pick things up as quickly as this."

"There's not a drop of Irish blood in my veins," answered John cheer-fully. "I'm New England for ten full generations. And proud of it."

"If I believed that," she declared grimly, "I wouldn't be devoting all this time to you, John of the Fine Hats."

The reference to hats stemmed back to an early stage of the visit when John thought to establish himself higher in her esteem by men-tioning that his great-grandfather had been the maker of the best head-gear in America. The Congdon hats, he had explained.

"Congdon hats?" The princess, it seemed, had never heard of them; which was not strange. "Do you mean riding hats?"

"No. Hats for everyday use. Fedoras, mostly. And bowlers and straws."

"But," she had demurred in a puzzled tone, "the best hats in America would be riding hats. That stands to reason."

"Not one person in twenty thousand has ever been on a horse in America. So riding hats are of small importance."

"It must be a dreadful country. Everything you tell me makes it seem worse, John of the Fine Hats."

Her own life seemed bound up with riding. Sometimes she would be out before breakfast and she would come in just in time for the meal, looking flushed and beautiful. She would put her crop on the table in front of her and look scornfully about her. "Sluggards!" she would say. "Wasting the mornings in soul-clogging sleep. Coffee, I beseech you!" John generally shared her afternoon rides and always went out with her when she decided to serenade the moon with a fast gallop. Unfortunately this did nothing to advance his suit. The princess rode like the wind and conversation was out of the question.

Her changes in mood were rapid and unpredictable. They might part on the worst of terms because of some disagreement over nothing and then she would come down to dinner in a green frock which made her look wonderful; and she would take a chair beside his with a gay "Hello, Sir John." She would smile at him between voluptuous sips of her cocktail. Her hair would be piled up high on her head and the light from the lamps would cause it to glow softly. Her eyes would be bright while her cheeks had a rosy tint; and her haughty mood would be dissolved completely in tenderness. John would think of Eleanor of Aquitaine (because she had been the mother of the Plantagenets and was said to have been beautiful and fascinating) and Helen of Troy and Cleopatra, and he would decide they were all old hat. She would chatter throughout the meal and John's fork would remain unused and his fingers would toy aimlessly with the stem of his glass. Even when he unintentionally lifted something to his mouth it would be done with no realization that the mutton was supreme or that the raisin pudding, sloshed with custard and thick cream, was a heavenly dish for lovers as well as dolts and gluttons.

5

It was only by accident that he was enabled to see beneath the surface of this contradictory creature. Rising early one morning, he heard sounds from the floor below and went down to investigate. The youthful chatelaine was in the drawing room and busily at work with a broom. Her hair was neatly tied up in a handkerchief and she was almost engulfed in a huge apron. The broom moved with a precision which spoke of long practice.

"I knew it," he said accusingly. "I knew it wasn't Marty Lacey who kept this house as neat as a pin. You've been slaving for our comfort."

She stopped work and looked at him over the handle of the broom. "Why all this sudden indignation? The housework has to be done. And who else would do it, if I didn't? Uncle Paddy? He attends to the outside work when Marty Lacey's too busy to do it. Which is all the time."

"But there's too much for one pair of hands. There must be some way of getting around this. Can't we all help?"

The corners of her mouth twitched briefly. "What could you do, for instance?"

"Who does the heavy work? Scrubbing, for instance."

"Do you think you could?"

"Certainly. There's no knack to scrubbing."

The girl placed the broom against the wall and left the room. When she returned, she was carrying a bucket of hot water, a bar of soap, and a scrubbing brush.

"Here you are," she said. "Never make an offer like that if you don't want to be taken up. You are now the official scrubber for the household."

John shook his head. "I've been doing some thinking and I've got a much better idea. I know your uncle Patrick would refuse any financial assistance. But I also know that the senator will be leaving you a legacy in his will. Why shouldn't he settle an allowance on you now?"

She gave him a cold look. "Is this any business of yours?"

"None at all," he conceded. "But if no one else will think about such things, I'm going to make it my business. After all, I'm not suggesting anything new or out of the way. I believe it's the practice over here. And I don't need to tell you that he's very wealthy and the most generous man in the world."

The princess left the room with the scrubbing equipment. When she returned, empty-handed, it was clear that she had been doing some thinking also.

"It's true that it's often done," she said. "Here in Ireland the head of the family—the one who inherits the estates—gives allowances to the younger brothers and the girls of the family. That is, when there's any money to do it with."

She had changed completely. Gone was the usual hint of condescension in her manner, the assurance she had always shown. He detected instead a hint almost of entreaty.

"An allowance for me? Do you really think it could be arranged? Has Uncle Rick ever spoken about it?"

"I'm sure that all I have to do is mention it and things will begin to happen so fast your head will spin."

"But—but we must think about it first."

She did not think long. Her eyes opened suddenly until they were large and round and shining. "John, it would be *wonderful!* Do you think—do you really think, he would be willing?"

"I'm sure of it."

"But—but will you do the speaking to him?"

"Of course. I'll speak to him this morning."

"John!" she said, her voice falling to a whisper. "You have no idea how poor we are! Sometimes there's no money in the house at all. When we knew you were coming, I begged Uncle Paddy to let me sell my hunter, so we would have enough to see us through. He refused, the dear lamb, and said we would manage somehow." She looked up at him with sudden penitence. "I shouldn't have told you that. Please, never repeat what I've said. Not to anyone, certainly not to Uncle Rick. I shouldn't have said a word about it."

He spoke to the senator that morning. During the afternoon the heads of the two elderly cousins were close together in a long conference. The next day they drove into Kilkenny and did not return for several hours.

John and the girl met on the landing above the main stairway as they were starting down for dinner. She was clutching a handsome bag in one hand.

"Do you know what I have in this?" she asked excitedly. "A purse, John, a purse. And the marvel of it is that there's money in it. Twenty pounds! Three fivers and five ones! John, what you suggested has been arranged. My wonderful uncle from that wonderful America has settled an allowance on me. For life. There had to be cables and drawing up of papers. It will be some time before I can have the allowance but the bank agreed to advance me the twenty pounds. Oh, glory be to St. Patrick and all the blessed saints, and to my dear uncle Rick!" Her eyes were filled with tears. "I'll be grateful to you, John of the Fine Hats—and I'm sure they were very fine—all the rest of my life!"

"I hope," said John, swallowing hard, "that your uncle Patrick was in full sympathy with the idea."

"Oh yes. Uncle Paddy is very happy about it. After I was told the news he patted me on the cheek. Then he whispered, 'It's the generous Irish strain in him, God rest him and keep him!' My only anxiety is that Uncle Paddy may not let me do all the things I have in mind. We are going to have a man to look after the horses—we'll get a small string now—and a maid in the house. That's all understood. But, oh, if he would only give in about these other things: a telephone, central heating, proper plumbing and drains, even—even a car!"

"You'll bring him around," said John. "Be slow about it, and tactful. Play your cards carefully."

"We should live now as befits our station. It was all very well to do without things when we had no money. We could hold up our heads and say, 'It doesn't matter, we are the O'Rawns and what if we are poor?' But now it would be—well, eccentric, don't you think? Uncle Paddy must *not* be pigheaded."

"Don't put it to him in just that way."

"Oh no, I'll be cautious. I'll think it over very carefully before I say a word to him."

They walked slowly together down the steps and found Richard O'Rawn waiting for them at the foot. He was regarding them with a grave intentness.

"Uncle Rick, Uncle Rick!" said the princess when they reached the bottom. "I'm so happy I don't see how I'll ever be able to sit through dinner. What I want to do is to go out for a ride. I want to ride like mad."

"I suppose you've been making plans."

"My head is full of them. Just trivial things so far. Like going to Dublin for a full day's shopping and then staying overnight at the Shelbourne. I need gloves and stockings in particular. I've always needed them."

"When you get around to more important matters," cautioned the visitor, "keep it in mind that your uncle has an honest and deep-seated aversion to having gas or electricity in Castle O'Rawn. He likes things as they are."

"I know. Uncle Paddy is as stubborn as a mule."

"I hope you won't be as stubborn on the other side."

There was a pause. "I'll try not to be. I suppose it will come down to trading. I'll give in about the lighting——"

"He says your hair is much more lovely by candlelight."

The girl raised her eyebrows slightly. "Really? I hadn't thought of that. Well, I'm ready to let him have his way about the lights and I'll be content with wood fires, if he'll give in about a motorcar. Don't you agree, Uncle Rick, that we *must* have a car?"

The senator nodded. "Yes, I'm with you there. Using horses only is a luxury you can't afford when you live this far out from town. Yes, my dear, we'll have to gang up on this uncle of yours. In fact I would like to see you with two cars around the place, one a station wagon— I mean a shooting brake, in your language—and a sports car, for you."

When they entered the drawing room, where a few friends were due to assemble for dinner, the senator drew John to one side.

"A word of advice, my boy," he said in a low tone. "Don't let yourself get in too deep. Emotionally, I mean. She's different from the rest of us, you know. I understand her. In fact I feel that I know her very well. She—well, this may seem farfetched, but I'm sure she's marked by destiny for something unusual. God alone knows what. But whatever it is, she'll follow the course marked out for her. Even if it means leaving everyone far behind her. You and me and all the rest of us."

"I know, sir. I've been aware of that. I've known that falling in love with her is like playing a long shot. As much as a thousand to one in my case."

"Well, my boy, I've decided we had better be on our way before you are hopelessly sunk. I'm going to tell Patrick that we must leave by the end of this week."

Chapter IV

O F A L L the unusual places that Senator O'Rawn chose to visit in England, two remained most firmly fixed in John Foraday's memory.

The first was a stretch of flat green ground along the south side of the Thames in close proximity to Windsor. This meadow was bounded on the south by a wooded hill or ridge, with a ravine running along the base of the high land. John looked out of the car window and felt something take possession not only of his mind but of his heart as well.

"Runnymede," he said.

"Why do you think that?" asked the old man, leaning out of the window on his side of the car. "I'm sure there was no mention of our coming here today."

"There's a sense of history about the place. I felt something stir deep down inside me. And besides, this is just about where it should be."

"You're right, my boy. This is Runnymede. I wanted you to see it. I wanted very much to see it myself."

The car came to a stop at a point where two cottages faced each other across the paved road. The senator got out and stood with uncovered head, gazing intently about him.

It was a glorious day. The sky was blue and clear, the sun was pleasantly warm. A breeze stirred the tops of the trees along the ridge and soon had the white locks of the eloquent senator standing up on end. A swarm of crows had settled down on the raised land and were keeping up a continuous cawing. "History says there were crows at Runnymede on the day when King John signed the Charter," stated the old man. "Did they caw in derision of that very bad man who had been forced so reluctantly to his knees? I've always liked to think that they did. But why are they keeping it up? Mankind still enjoys the benefit of what was done that day, so what we should hear is a chorus of praise. I guess the truth of the matter is that crows have a poor opinion of men in general and raise their raucous voices whenever they are near us."

An official had come out of one of the cottages and seemed disposed to give them whatever information they might desire. The old man asked, "What is that raised land called?"

"Cooper's Hill, sir."

"A recent name, no doubt."

"Oh yes, sir. Perhaps not more than a century old."

"Isn't it true that the ravine running along the base of Cooper's Hill was once the bed of the Thames?"

"I believe so, sir. But that was a long time ago."

"Then it's quite probable that the land we are standing on *was* an island when the Charter was signed?"

The official nodded.

"The historians don't seem at all clear on the point. But it's certain in my mind that the channel over there was once filled with water."

"But," declared the official, "that channel has been dry for—for centuries, sir."

2

Rawen Priory, lying close to one of the tributaries of the Thames, was not sought out greatly by tourists. Even the belief that Dunstan had been concerned in the building of it (although it was *not* at Rawen that he had caught the Devil's nose in red-hot pincers), and that William the Conqueror had been responsible for closing it, did little to bring visitors. The Earl of Baudene had been charging a shilling for years but had barely cleared expenses.

The owner, in a flannel suit which actually had a tinge of pink to it, was standing at the entrance to the refectory when a party in cars came slowly down the dirt road.

"Odd," he commented, being a man of few words.

"Why?" asked his sister, the Lady Birdie, who stood beside him.

"The name. O'Rawn and Rawen Priory."

"Coincidence."

The eyes of the earl clouded when he saw that there were three cars. "Swank," he muttered.

"Nonsense." Lady Birdie then indulged in a streak of loquacity by adding another word. "Workmen."

She proved to be right. The first car contained Senator O'Rawn, John Foraday, Peterkin, and a rather famous antiquarian named Robert Underpeck. The other two disgorged workmen with picks and shovels, a photographer with a great deal of equipment, and a stenographer prepared to make notes.

When the necessary introductions had been made and they entered the refectory, the senator paused and looked about him with an air of astonishment and gratification. This ancient hall, where the monks had satisfied their appetites on the sparest fare, still boasted a roof in good condition. The stone floor was intact and it was clear that the walls had not suffered at the hands of restorers. Little remained of the steps leading up to the reader's niche, despite the fact that the stand itself was in excellent condition.

"My lord," said the senator to the peer, "these walls, which it is your great privilege to own, have more truth about the past concealed in them than a shelf of histories."

With meticulous care he proceeded to pace off distances and then tapped with his foot on a large square stone.

"With your permission, my lord," he said, "I'll have them raise this one. But first, Mr. Photographer, I would like a picture of the stone before it was disturbed."

The cement of time had settled the stone into place more securely than all the labor of monkish trowels could have achieved; and it took almost an hour of hard labor to raise it. When this had been accomplished, a yawning space leading down into a dark vault was revealed.

There was a slight quiver of excitement at the end of the nose of aristocracy. "Odd," commented the peer.

The senator was staring intently into the darkness of the small space below. "I am very happy to observe," he said, "that the steps have not crumbled away. I begin, in fact, to be quite optimistic about our quest." He glanced over his shoulder at the antiquarian. "How long do you suppose it has been since this stone was raised last?"

Robert Underpeck gave the point some thought. "Several centuries, I expect," he said finally.

"I agree with you, sir. In fact I shall be rather more explicit. Seven centuries." The senator turned then to the earl. "There's little room down there. I'll be needed to decide where to attack the wall and that will leave just enough room for one of the men to swing a pick. Will you object to watching from here with the others?"

The earl had no objection, so the senator provided himself with a large lantern and went down the steps. John stood at the head with another torch while the antiquarian knelt on the stone floor and watched with the utmost interest.

The senator studied the walls and then pointed to one where the surface of a stone had been raised in the form of a cross. "The one above," he said to the workman. "It's not mortared in and I don't believe you'll have much difficulty in getting it out."

"Just a moment," said the antiquarian. "I desire to ask you a question, sir. What do you expect to find behind this stone?"

There was a long pause. When the senator finally spoke, there seemed to be a difference in his voice as well as in his choice of words and phrases. It could easily have been believed that someone else was speaking.

"Divers wonderful things," he answered, almost in a whisper. "It will be found, good sirs, that behind the stone there is space enough to hold a small wooden chest. In the chest there was once a document; a paper, sirs, of such great use to men that its value was above that of gold and rubies and pearls. It is no longer there. A need arose for it and it was removed. A long time, a very long time ago.

"There was in the space also," he went on, "a hoard. Of pennies. Not a great hoard, not the wealth of a landholding Norman thief, who could save by the thousands and still leave enough for chantry priests to pray in supplication for him for centuries. This was the hoard of a Saxon thane, and so a small one. There was also a ring, a plain gold band which was of small value save that it had been worn on a very special finger. There were other articles of less interest. But as to what is still there, I cannot say. Perhaps we will find nought but empty space."

They had it open in short order. The senator plunged an arm into the cavity and then nodded up at John. "There's something in there still," he said, smiling and winking with excitement. "Let's have that square of canvas."

The canvas was held under the opening and all of the contents swept into it. The corners were then tied and the bundle handed up to those above. The senator followed it with eager steps.

The canvas was spread on the floor and Mr. Underpeck took charge of things. He first gathered the coins into one pile.

"Henry I," he said, holding up a penny. "See the quatrefoil design on the reverse? Made by one Humphrey of Bristol. This one is Stephen's. See the name, Stefi. Most of them are of Henry II's coinage.

They carry the Rex Ang. Ah, here's one of the Conqueror, with the side-face portrait and the single cross fleury."

"Not many," commented the earl in a disappointed tone of voice.

"I warned you of that." There was a moment's silence and then the senator added: "Count them. I think you'll find there are eleven hundred and fifty-six."

The peer's eyes seemed to pounce at him, as though saying, "Now we'll have you." He seated himself beside Mr. Underpeck and began to build the coins up in piles of ten. When this task had been completed, the antiquarian took a pencil from one of his pockets and made some calculations on the back of an envelope. He stared hard at the paper when a total was reached and then made a recount. He said, "Huh!" and looked up at the circle of faces above him.

"Eleven hundred and fifty-six," he announced solemnly.

During the silence which followed this announcement the Earl of Baudene got to his feet. He confronted Richard O'Rawn.

"Magic?" he asked. "Like sawing the lady in half?"

"I'm not a magician."

"You won't deny," said the antiquarian, looking up with the same puzzled expression on his face, "that you have some special source of information?"

"No, I don't deny that. I have special sources of information."

"Do you intend to tell us about it?"

Richard O'Rawn shook his head. "Not yet. A little later."

The peer whispered in Underpeck's ear. The latter then asked: "Would you object to giving the story out to the press? His lordship is anxious to have it printed."

"Two shillings' worth," said the peer.

The senator smiled. "I think, sir, you will be justified if you double the entrance fee now." He went down suddenly on one knee and reached into the dust and debris left on the canvas. He held up a band of tarnished gold and mused over it with reverence for a long time. "Yes, this is the ring I spoke of." His voice fell to a whisper. "See how plain it is. *And how thin!*"

The earl reached out a hand for the ring, looked at it a moment, and then slipped it into a pocket of the pinkish flannel coat.

"Treasure it, my lord!" said the senator. "It is worth more than all the pennies minted by all the Norman kings. It belonged to a lady. A gracious and great lady."

3

Back in London, they did not get rid of Robert Underpeck and his insistent questioning until it was time to dress for dinner. Richard O'Rawn was off then to the American Embassy. He did not return to their suite at the Watling until nearly midnight, so it may be assumed that he had found the company stimulating. John had not gone to bed but was sound asleep on a couch in the sitting room. He got to his feet slowly and stretched his arms.

"You look tired, Uncle Richard," he said. He had fallen into the habit of addressing the senator in this way since the trip began. "I was going to ask you some questions but I can see we'll have to postpone our talk until tomorrow."

The senator fumbled with his white tie and then unbuttoned his collar. Seating himself in a chair and kicking off his patent leather shoes, he sighed with relief.

"I'm wide awake," he said. "We might as well have it out now. I know what you are going to ask, of course. It's about the coins. John, I believe I heard them counted—*seven centuries ago.*"

John had been expecting some such answer but now that he had it he found himself filled with doubts and fears. Was his benefactor beginning to lose his mind? Had he fallen into the grip of a strange obsession?

"My boy, it seems that I may have been here in England in King John's day. Either that, or I saw it all in dreams."

"You asked me once if I believed an angel could make a mistake," prompted John.

The old man smiled and nodded his head. "This is what I was driving at. There's something hidden away at the back of our minds, and I expect it's not intended for us to know what it is. But the shutter which closes off that part of the brain sometimes begins to rattle and slip and yaw, which gives the possessor of the head an occasional glimpse of what's behind it, a brief flash of memory. Perhaps the angel, who is supposed to see that all these shutters are tight and shipshape, has been careless. Perhaps this new and raw assistant was so careless once —in my case—that he let the shutter swing wide open—and it never was closed. Does that sound very farfetched to you?"

"I'm afraid it does, sir." Recovering from his first shock, John asked a question. "When did this return of memory occur, sir?"

"This will make it still harder for you to believe. Fifty years ago!"

"But—but why have you waited so long to tell about it?"

The senator, knowing that they were now embarked on what would be a long talk, opened a humidor and carefully selected a cigar. He lighted it and gave a satisfied pull.

"John," he said slowly, "you must consider the position I was in. I had a promising political career ahead of me. What would have happened if I had told my story then? How many votes would I have received? Not one, my boy. No one would cast a vote to send a crackpot to Congress, a man who believed he had seen the signing of Magna Charta. You see that, don't you?"

John managed a grin. "Yes, I can understand that."

"What's more, I would have been laughed out of business. No one would have trusted me. There might even have been talk of clapping me into an insane asylum. So—I have kept a still tongue in my head."

"But things haven't changed. Of course, you're getting out of politics but you'll be laughed at just the same. People will say you are out of your mind."

"I've been preparing for that. What happened today, for instance. The Earl of Baudene will give the story to the newspapers because he wants to get two-shilling entry fees to the priory. And he'll have plenty of witnesses. I took Patrick O'Rawn to the site of the first castle and then uncovered the stones of the foundation. There were four witnesses to that. I had never been in Ireland and yet I knew about the Marshal's Seat." He looked at his youthful companion with a hint of a smile on his rubicund face. "What about you, my boy? Do you believe me?"

John hesitated. "I—I can't think of any other possible explanation. I confess that what happened today—well, it has shaken me up."

"I have a reason for telling the story now. You know what people are saying in all parts of the world, that the present system of government deserves to die. Because some people have easier lives than others and a larger share of worldly goods, they want everything changed. To achieve complete equality—or what they hope will prove equality—they are willing to forgo the personal freedom we have won so slowly and painfully over the ages, the right to think and say and do what we please. They are willing to bring back the tyranny of absolute government. Ah, if they only knew! If they could look back into the past and see for themselves what mankind has emerged from!" The senator's eyes had lighted up with determination and zeal. "John! I can pull the curtain aside. I must do it!"

"But can you make people believe? Won't they say it's just a story, a piece of fiction?"

"Perhaps. But we must try. We must make the effort, you and I. I have been taking you over the ground and showing you many places which come into the story. Now I will turn my memory inside out for your benefit. I will describe everything in minute detail. And I want you to get it all down on paper."

After a long silence the old man resumed. "Well, my boy, I've told you," he said in a more normal tone. "I can see you would like to believe me but that incredulity still has the upper hand. You think that all of this may have been a dream. Perhaps that *is* the explanation. But did ever man have such a dream before? Can a whole life and a strange world be created for the sole benefit of one mortal?

"There will be other proofs beside the coins. In time, I think, you will come around," he went on. "But there can be no delay. I'm an old man and memories fade quickly when your feet begin to approach the last step. The dream, if it is a dream, may fade suddenly. The shutter in my mind, which opened and let me remember the past, might close again. We must seize the chance before that can happen. Tomorrow, then, we get to work. I shall start at the beginning and tell you everything. Every detail, no matter how small and unimportant it may seem. And you will take down what I say and then put it into such form that it will not be hard for people to read. Will you humor an old man to that extent?"

"Of course, sir. I am eager to start."

BOOK TWO

*The narrative set down
by John Foraday from
the story told by
Richard O'Rawn*

Chapter I

I T W A S a day in June in the year of Our Lord 1175. There was peace in Merrie England but in the north and west of France the old English king, who was called by his subjects Harry Secund, was waging a fierce and bloody war against a great golden ingrate of a son named Richard. The division between Saxon and Norman was still wide in the island kingdom. It was easiest to believe that more than a century had passed since the Conquest when the eye noted such things as the decay of the empty walls of Rawen Priory, from which the monks had been expelled for disobedience to the Norman king.

Here, in the ruins of Rawen, lived a handsome and strong but very unhappy man who was called Edward the Saxon. On this particular day, which fairly sang with sunshine and the green of the fields and hills, Edward started out to ride to the market town. He had no particular business to transact there and nothing in his pocket for the purpose. Being of a touchy pride and a sharp temper, he had few friends and, indeed, wanted none; but he had a great desire, nevertheless, to cut a good figure in the eyes of the world. His supertunic was neat and showed touches of bright embroidery at neck and wrists, and the feather in his hat was new and without a hint of tarnish.

He sighed deeply as he eyed the rich rolling land through which he rode and the sturdy trees against the sky line. He said to Sigurd, his servant, who cantered beside him: "My great-great-grandfather was robbed of the sweetest land in England. Think you that God is punishing Duke William for the suffering he brought to England?"

When they reached the point where the narrow, rutted road from the priory joined the highway running north to Baudene Castle, a long mounted train came into view. Through the dust raised by the hoofs of many horses the two Saxons could see a glint of steel and a show of cowled heads as well as burnished helmets.

"Master," said Sigurd, his square and well-tanned face alight with interest, "the man of Baudene is returning. With his Norman bride."

"We'll wait here for them to pass," instructed Edward the Saxon. "And there must be no hint of greeting. No raising of hands and no touching of forelocks."

The two men sat their mounts in motionless disregard as the train passed. There were a number of women in the party, including one who rode beside the earl and who had loosened the ends of her wimple so that her black locks had fallen down to her shoulders.

"It has been said, master," declared Sigurd, watching the slender figure beside the earl, "that the new wife of the man of Baudene is fair to look upon."

There was no need to call her attractiveness to the notice of the young thane. He had eyes for no one else. The bride had the blackness of hair and the whiteness of skin so often found in Norman women but her eyes set her apart. They were a dazzling blue. As he watched her ride by, without so much as a glance in his direction, the thane felt his heart doing somersaults like a painted clown at a fair.

When the long train had passed the junction of the two roads and the horseman in the rear had sounded a derisive note on his horn, Edward touched heel to his horse's flank and they resumed their journey in the opposite direction.

"Am I to spend the rest of my days coveting my neighbor's wife?" he asked himself. "The priests call it a sin. But truly Hugh de Baudene has been a bad neighbor, as cruel and arrogant as that hawk on his wrist. And I recall that in the Bible it is always a rich man who covets the wife of a poor shepherd or a humble grower of vines on a hillside. I think perhaps it often happens that a poor neighbor falls in love with the fair wife of a rich man and that he isn't judged wicked because of the hunger he conceals in his heart."

At the same moment that these thoughts were running through his head, the bride in the rich burgundy cloak, with a hand touching carelessly the gold chain about her neck, was asking her lord a question. "Who," she wanted to know, "was the tall young man with the golden hair who sat so still back there? He didn't raise a hand in greeting as we passed."

"A scurvy knave," answered her spouse. "A stubborn Saxon who skulks in some ruins and dares to think himself my equal."

The grim castle that the Normans had built at Baudene, on taking over the land, had been decked out gaily for the arrival of the bride. The drawbridge was ankle-deep in roses, the cables of the portcullis were wrapped with summer flowers, a company of gleemen sang romantic songs from the battlements, and a goliard, disguised as a fawn, skipped fantastically before the party as they crossed the moat. The bride tried to enter into the spirit of the occasion but, when she urged her lord and master to join her in a measure in the courtyard, where the servants had assembled to greet them, he shook off her hand and grumbled, "I was never one to trip a light foot, wife."

There was much excitement and confusion in the bride's dorter when her clothes were produced from the saddlebags, with many exclamations of delight on the part of the maidservants. She joined in the talk and asked many questions, declaring that she could not wait to become acquainted with this beautiful land of green fields and thick brush where she was to live. There was much comment, therefore, about this and that and it required no more than a single discreet word to bring forth a flood of information about the neighbors and particularly the lonely Saxon who dwelt in the ruins of Rawen Priory. He was, the bride learned, about twenty-eight years of age and unmarried, refusing to bring a wife to such a sorry home and such dim prospects. He lived an austere life, although women threw themselves shamelessly at him. At early dawn his horn could be heard as he rode out to hunt, wakening the echoes like the piping of Pan, and at night the last faint blast as he returned tired from the chase.

"By'r Lady, it is well I am married and settled down," thought the Lady Maude, "or perchance I would pursue him shamelessly also."

Her almoner, Father Alonzo, who had been born in Anjou, contributed one disturbing piece of information about the unfriendly neighbor. "His family owned all the land hereabouts before the Conquest," he said. "This man still holds to a sense of grievance. Our wardens are under orders never to set foot on his meager acres for fear of having their ribs tickled by a Saxon arrow." He added as an afterthought: "He went with the marshal to the Crusades."

"It seems to me," thought the bride, "that this poor man has reason for feeling as he does."

A few months later the Lady Maude's confessor fell ill and she rode on a Sunday morning to hear mass at the little church of St. Willibald's in a nearby village. It was a measure of her devotion that rain was falling heavily and that she had to be so completely bundled up in a cloak that only her bright eyes could be seen. She did not at first perceive the tall and lonely neighbor dismounting at the same instant. He also was wrapped up and in the very shabbiest of cloaks.

They came face to face on the stone steps of the church and the lady was so startled that her lips parted as though she intended to speak. Then her cheeks flushed and she stood perfectly still on the rain-washed stone. But she looked steadily into his eyes. Lowering her head after a moment, she began the ascent of the steps ahead of him. Her heart was beating furiously and her hands clasped the missal as though it offered her the protection she needed.

She heard him say behind her, in a whisper which could not have reached other ears, "May God bless this most wonderful and memorable of days when I have seen my lovely lady face to face."

It had become clear to both of them that neither would forget the other, even though they might never meet again.

A year later Hugh de Baudene was killed in a tournament held rather secretly in a hamlet off the New Forest to avoid the restrictions that the old king had laid on this costly sport. As his wife had borne him no children, the question of what would happen to the huge Baudene holdings became a bone of contention at court. The king, jealous of all the rights and privileges of the crown, and needing the money more-over, was determined to sell the hand of the bereaved Lady Maude to a second husband of his own choosing. The royal anterooms—for the king was back briefly from the civil wars in the south—were filled with candidates for the fair widow, all of whom were prepared to pay Henry handsomely. The bids kept mounting up in a steep spiral.

One morning in August, Edward of Rawen donned his best raiment and rode off from the priory. Male attire was rather plain in these days but the materials used were of the best. Even this poverty-stricken thane wore soft green shoes which fitted his calves tightly and his super-tunic was of silk from the East, held at the neck by a large garnet which had been in his family since the days of great King Egbert.

The first hay had been cut and the field hands were taking it in ox-drawn carts across the lowered drawbridge when he arrived at Baudene Castle. The hoofs of the Saxon's horse had reached a point directly under the portcullis before a guard emerged from the entrance to the outer bailey and barred further advance with a steel-tipped pike.

"How now, Sir Stranger?" cried the man, not recognizing him and rather awed by the fineness of his attire. "What errand brings you so boldly to our gates?"

"I am Edward of Rawen and I desire speech with the Countess of Baudene."

The guard threw back his round head and roared with laughter. "Geoffrey-with-the-Whiskers will have you fed to the dogs!" he exclaimed. A man perched on top of the nearest load of hay joined in the merriment. He lifted an arm and a forkful of hay descended over the head and shoulders of the bold visitor. The guard was still making threatening gestures with his pike and muttering maledictions on all Saxon swine when a plump individual in a gray tunic came stumping out from the gloom of the courtyard.

"Our gracious lady will see you," said the newcomer with an unwilling nod. "You are to follow me. But tread not too closely on my heels, for there is already a heavy odor on the air which offends my nostrils."

The Lady Maude came to greet him in a small niche off the Great Hall. Her blue gown was so long that it frothed with every step she took. Edward the Saxon caught his breath. She was without a wimple on her head and so for the first time he was seeing her in all her beauty and charm.

They stood some distance apart and looked into each other's eyes as intently as on the day when they met at St. Willibald's.

"Do you share the opinion of your servants that I am presumptuous in coming thus to see you?" he asked finally.

She advanced a step nearer and put out a hand hesitantly to remove a wisp of hay from his sleeve. "I hope you will forgive the rudeness of your reception," she said. Then she raised her head and smiled. "No. I have been expecting you. At least, Sir Knight, I have been hoping you would come, and—and thinking you were tardy."

He leaned down to touch the top of his handsome green shoes. "I could not come unshod, my lady," he said. "I am a poor man, as you doubtless know. It has taken me a full year—ever since that day when we met in the rain—to acquire a suitable wardrobe. I have had to clothe myself piece by piece, and the shoes did not arrive until yesterday. I have lost no time in paying my respects."

"I feel much honored, gallant neighbor."

"What a sweet voice she has," he said to himself; "rather throaty but soft and full." She did not slur her words, as most Saxons were inclined to do.

"I had to see you today or put my hopes away forever. A friend at the king's court sent me some word last night. It seems that the bidding for your hand has reached as high as two thousand marks. King Henry will soon be reaching a decision. That is why I am here." There was a long pause during which he kept his head lowered. "Yes, I am presumptuous. I am presumptuous beyond all measure. How daring it is of me to believe that it was your heart which spoke when you said you had been hoping I would come."

Dark lashes closed over her eyes for a moment. Then she opened them wide again and smiled. "It was my heart which spoke," she said.

For several moments the scene in the rain on what Edward had called that memorable day was re-enacted. Nothing was said. Eye looked into eye, questingly, trustingly, passionately.

"Words are so often of small use," he said finally, in a tone little above a whisper. "There was once when they were not needed between us. And now I think we have reached an understanding without them. But there is one question I must ask. Have you any fear of consequences?"

"None!" she cried. "I will tell our liege lord the king to his face that I married once on the command of my parents and that now I marry for love. I am prepared to face any consequences." Then she paused and it was in a lower and less assured voice that she finished. "Save, my dear knight, as they may concern you."

"Then there must be no delay. We must wed at once. Before your powerful suitors can put obstacles in the way. And have no fears for me, dearest one. If the king should exact my life, I would count it well lost for a few moments of happiness with you."

It was their good fortune that the king found it necessary to go to France again. He was at Le Mans when he received word of the marriage of the widow of Baudene to Edward the Saxon, who seemed to him most surely the least eligible candidate in the whole of his kingdom. His face turned an angry purple when he read the report.

"By God's splendor!" he cried. "She must be taught a lesson, this pretty wanton. She must learn that the flouting of my wishes is a dangerous pastime!"

The choleric king thought of insisting that the marriage be set aside but was finally convinced that this could not be done. Then he turned his mind to punishments and he decided, first, that a large fine would be the most satisfactory kind of retribution because it would put money into his pockets, which were almost bare at the moment. Accordingly he sent a message to the chancellor at Westminster that the fair widow must be amerced to the extent of three thousand marks, which was higher than any of the bids he had received for her hand.

As it happened, however, the royal messenger fell into the hands of a patrol of Prince Richard's men. The contents of the bag he was carrying seemed of little consequence to that prince of sultry moods.

"Burn all this," he ordered. "It will be the better if some of my gracious father's plans go astray."

The newly wed couple lived at Baudene Castle in a state of bliss which could not be shaken by the shadow of retribution hanging over them. The only event which had threatened their happiness directly was the arrival in London of one Gilles de Baudene, a distant connection of the Lady Maude's late husband. This cunning Norman was the owner of a few sour acres of land in the Cotentin and he saw a chance for profit in the situation which had developed. His first move was to give notice of suit for possession of all the Baudene lands, as the closest surviving relative of the late earl.

At the offices of the chancellery, the claimant from across the Channel was treated with scant respect. The officials were certain that King Henry had his own ideas with respect to the Baudene estates and that a distant kinsman would not be allowed any part in them. This did not seem to disturb Messire Gilles too seriously. He spent his days in the chancellery anterooms, biting his nails and watching everything that went on with his cold gray eyes. His nights were spent in the cheapest tavern he had been able to find.

The officials of the department fell into the habit of saying to him each morning, "You are still here then?" To which the claimant never varied in his reply: "Marry, yes. I am here until justice is done me by God and the king."

2

It must now be told how the hand of misfortune and grief finally touched the devoted lovers. The Lady Maude gave birth to a son whom the parents named Richard after the old king's son. The father stood out against this selection but his wife for once insisted on having her way. Letting her head rest against his solicitous shoulder, she whispered: "It may win some favor for our little son. I am afraid he will need much of it in the life ahead of him."

She had no illusions as to her own fate. The travail of motherhood had taken heavy toll of her strength. "Sweet husband," she said, "I will not be here much longer. They will try to take away all the land. Fight hard to keep my dower rights at least for him, our poor little son. And take good care of him. He must grow up as tall and strong and straight of leg as his sire."

"You will share these responsibilities with me when your strength comes back, my loved one."

Her strength did not come back. The boy Richard was no more than a week old when her long lashes closed for all time over the unusual blue of her eyes. The stricken husband sat beside the bed until they came to prepare the body. He rose then without a word and walked to the cradle of the child.

"You and I, my son," he said, "have long hard years ahead of us, I fear. I must fulfill my promise to your lady mother, and see that you are raised to be strong and honorable and brave."

He turned to the nurse who hovered over the cradle. "You have lost no time in binding him up in swaddling clothes, despite what I told you."

"My lord, it is the custom!" protested the woman.

"You needn't tell me that. I know it is always done. I know that four infants out of five die before they are released from the swaddling board. Poor little slaves of a hideous custom! How long do you plan to keep him thus, unable to move hand or foot?"

"A year," she stammered. "It is the rule."

"Free him at once!" exclaimed the father. "I won't have my son die because silly mothers and ignorant midwives have invented something as cruel as chaining prisoners to the wall in damp cells. He must be allowed to kick his legs and use his arms as God intended children to do."

"It is sacrilege!" cried the nurse.

"You will obey my orders." To himself the father added: "He must be as free as though he had been born under a hedge and his parents trod the open road. When he is a year old his legs will be strong and, moreover, he will be using them. This much, at least, I can do for him."

3

Edward the Saxon was in the bathhouse, a dark and ill-smelling cavern under the keep.

It had been a sore point with the servants at Baudene that he was such a believer in cleanliness. They commented in wonder and umbrage on his demand for a bath once a week. It meant that they had to fill a large metal tank with water and build a fire under it, stoking the blaze until the bathhouse was filled with steam.

"He will kill himself with all this womanish scrubbing and he'll break our backs a-doing it," they would mutter among themselves. "If the men of God in the monasteries are allowed a bath only four times a year, why should this penniless Saxon pamper himself?"

Edward had envied his lady wife the luxury she enjoyed of bathing in her own rooms. Each day while she was alive there was a procession of maids with small leather buckets filled with steaming water, hurrying between the bathhouse and the sleeping chambers of the chatelaine. He would have made similar arrangements for himself if he had not realized that scorn would have been heaped upon him if he had.

He did not know how the rite was carried out in his lady's chamber. Once he had entered unannounced and had caught a glimpse of his beautiful Maude standing beside a porcelain vessel from which steam rose in a scented cloud, while her maid, Gilsey, labored over her with busy hands. It was a very slender and white body which he thus saw for the first time. However, he caught no more than a fleeting glimpse, for Gilsey had rushed in his direction with a look of horror on her broad face, indignantly waving her hands.

"No, no, master! You must not come in. It is wrong."

The woman had pummeled him on the shoulders until he hastily turned and withdrew.

That night as Edward and his wife lay in each other's arms in the grand high Norman bed, after the last maid's suppressed giggle had been heard in the corridor and the hooting of the owls had begun on the battlements, Maude had laughed delightedly over the incident.

"Sweet my love," she whispered, "you could have stayed for all of me. I—I hoped you would. How nice if you had come and kissed me, although you would have got very wet if you took me in your arms. But, ah, dear Mother of God, it could not be! What a scandal it would have caused!"

The fact that the lady of the castle bathed regularly was almost a scandal in itself. Most ladies considered the use of water superfluous when such fine perfumes were being brought from the East.

As for the servants, they had a reluctance to cleanliness which caused Edward some concern. There was, for instance, a pretty little flaxen-haired thing who fluttered about the castle on duties which he had not been able to identify. Passing her at close range one day, he had become aware of such an unpleasant odor that he stopped and asked her when she had last taken a bath. The maid looked at him with surprise in her round eyes, as blue as cornflowers.

"Good my lord!" she tittered. "It is like my mother washed me when I was brought into the world. But never since has a drop of water touched me. Of course, my lord," she added with a conscious air of pride, "I wash my face and hands every morning without fail."

"You'll never catch yourself a husband, my girl, if you aren't more careful."

The girl giggled at that. "My lord, it's little you know," she protested. "I can have my pick of husbands. I've been asked and asked. And once with promise of a proper churching."

As for Sigurd, the brawny servant, his opinion on the matter was the voice of the kitchens, the psalteries, the forges, and the hayfields where men labored. "Do I want my belly crying shame at me," he asked once, "if I treat it like a lady's with soap and warm water?"

Edward's mind, as he stood in the steamy atmosphere and sloshed water over his head and shoulders, had gone back to the gentle reticences of his deeply mourned wife. Although her eyes had always filled with unshed tears of happiness when he spoke of the depth of his love for her, she had found it very hard to tell how much she reciprocated his passion. She had carried her child for months before he, her husband, knew that the experience of parenthood was to be his. If she had divulged the secret sooner, it was possible that things could have been done with drugs and charms so that she would have been saved when the day of her ordeal came. He fell into a deeply melancholy mood and did not speak at first when Sigurd's huge frame materialized before him like Blunderbore weaving through a mist.

"Master!" said the man.

"What is it, Sigurd?"

"Come with me, my lord. It is better you get this over quickly for once. There is something afoot."

"What has happened?" asked Edward, drying himself with a sudden alacrity.

"I know not, master. But whatever it is, our little Bulchin is very pleased and so I know it is bad. He shouted at me to ask where you were."

Bulchin was a nickname they used for the seneschal of the household, a Norman named Gillikin who had been kept in charge after the death of Hugh de Baudene. He had always been antagonistic and had dared to show his feeling openly.

The seneschal stood under the arch leading into the towers where the family lived when Edward and his man emerged from the cavernous temple of cleanliness. Several of the castle guards stood behind him, all with pikes in their hands and a certain apprehension in their manner. Gillikin was wearing a smirk in which it was easy to read both malice and triumph.

"I have received—this!" he said, flourishing a letter with a seal attached to it. "The castle and landholdings of Baudene are being taken over and will be administered by the king's servants until such time as the courts decide on the rights of succession. A royal steward is on the way and is expected to arrive tomorrow. It will be necessary for you, Sir Saxon, to rid the domain of Baudene of your presence."

"On *your* word, Master Gillikin?" Edward the Saxon laughed briefly and angrily. "You will give me that letter in your hand. It was intended for me undoubtedly."

When Gillikin hesitated, Edward took it forcibly into his own hands. The perusal he gave it was, on the surface, a thorough one. Actually his small knowledge of writing made it impossible for him to decipher more than a few words. After a suitable pause, he handed it back with a gesture of indifference.

"It is a matter to which," he said, "I must give some thought."

"As stated in this order," asserted the seneschal, "my lady's son will become a ward of the king although the writ has not yet been received."

"These are matters to be discussed with the royal steward when he arrives." Edward's manner gave no hint of the fear which had gripped him. It was the custom, he knew, for wards of the king to be placed in the hands of guardians appointed by the Crown. He might never see his little son again.

The seneschal threw out his chest importantly. "I give you a piece of advice, sirrah. Be off before the king's officer arrives."

Sigurd had been standing behind the seneschal while these few words were exchanged. His face turned an angry red at the impudence of the man. "Very well, my Bulchin!" he exclaimed. Reaching out with both hands, while the castle guards stood by and gaped, he seized Master Gillikin by the neck and the small of the back. His grip was so powerful that the servant was unable to move as he was hoisted high in the air. Carrying the stiffened figure to a large cistern which collected rain water from the roof through a lead pipe, Sigurd dropped the seneschal in. Gillikin opened his mouth to cry for help but the only result was that he swallowed enough rain water to make him splutter in impotence and rage.

"Norman swine, that will teach you how to address your betters!" said Sigurd, forcing the seneschal farther under the water with a stout rap on the head. "Come, master, let us go where we can fill our lungs with air that carries no Norman taint."

An hour later Edward the Saxon rode out on the horse which had brought him to Baudene Castle. His sleeping son, now two months old, was carried in one arm. Sigurd cantered behind him on a stout roan which had been a gift from the Lady Maude. Edward was smiling for the first time since his wife died.

"I am glad," he said, "to leave these walls which throw an alien shadow on the land of my forefathers. The rights of my little son will be passed over. We must be reconciled to that. But all men with English blood in their veins are accustomed to such injustice. We must wait for better days."

When they came in sight of the gaunt walls of Rawen Priory and could see the stone and wattle house which had been Edward's home before he married his Norman lady, the owner nodded with satisfaction.

"Sigurd," he said, "it is the Lord's will and I begin to think it may be all for the best. My son will grow up a Saxon. He will have your little son Tostig for a companion, and he will wax healthy and strong on the plain foods and the solid drink his forefathers knew. But," he added, his mood losing abruptly all of its satisfaction, "am I to sit by in silence and see him robbed twice of the broad acres they now call the domain of Baudene? Someday there will be a reckoning and we, my son and I, will take back the rich lands which rightly belong to us."

Sigurd shook his head at this. "Do not count upon it, master. You know what old Godgifu says, that the lands will never be ours again. And it's true she can see things that none of us see and hear voices that are silent to all else. She has the gift, my lord."

Chapter II

1

THE BOY was called Richard of Rawen from the beginning. To give an idea of the kind of life he lived, it becomes necessary now to tell how it came about that this once powerful family subsisted under the roofless walls of the old priory, and of the way in which their living was contrived. After the Conquest, William had divided up the lands among his own followers, and the extensive holdings of one Cymric the Saxon were given to Odo de Baudene, who had been in the first charge at Hastings. The rightful owner, who was a close connection of the once great Earl Godwine, was allowed to retain no more than a small parcel of rather sour land which included the priory from which the Saxon monks had been ejected. Finding himself in a desperate pass, Cymric had built himself a wattled structure against a part of the east wall, and his successors had continued there ever since.

The boy did not realize that the house in which he lived was small and mean. Compared with the thatched tofts in which the peasants lived, it seemed grand and pretentious. What if there was only one room on the ground floor? It had three windows with hinged shutters, a large hearth on which five-foot logs could be burned, and an oak cupboard which actually contained bits of silver and pewter. That the peaked solar apartment above, reached by an outside tier of wooden steps, was the only other room and that all members of the family slept there together, except Dirk the villein, did not detract from his conviction, nor did the fact that most of the pointed stakes in the defensive wall around the house had rotted away like the teeth in a miser's head.

Young Richard lived in the company of Tostig, the son of Sigurd. Tostig was three years older and a fine sturdy lad with a square face

and gray eyes filled with courage and intelligence. It was the stout
Tostig's duty to see his master's son through all the crises of boyhood
and to initiate him into the ways of life. The days began at dawn and
ended with the coming of darkness at night. When cocks began to crow
somewhere within the priory walls, Tostig would stir on his pallet of
straw and raise his head from the billet of wood which served him as a
pillow.

"Master Richard," he would whisper, "the day begins."

Richard would whimper a little. "It would be nice, Tostig, to sleep a
little longer. Just for once. I'm very tired."

But Tostig was a hard taskmaster. "Up!" he would command. "Don't
you want to grow up to be a fine, strong man like your father?"

"But, Tostig, couldn't I sleep just a little longer and grow up to be
half like my father?"

"Master Rick," said Tostig in a voice loud enough almost to disturb
the boy's father, who slept in the one bed the household boasted at
the other side of the solar, "if you don't foot the boards at once, you
will grow up to be a man like Dirk."

This was a dire prospect which could not be disregarded. Dirk was
as old and dirty as the sin-eaters who were always to be found at
funerals, ready to assume the sins of the deceased for a hot dinner. He
sat down with the family at meals, but always at the far end, so the
odors of the fields and the manure pits would not be too noticeable,
and he slept in what was left of the abbot's house at the far end of the
enclosure.

Richard rose at once. He was *not* going to grow up like Dirk. But, as
he drew on his hose and trussed up his points, he said to Tostig: "All
right, you old Tostig. I'm up and no one can stop me now from growing
up like my father. But you'll have to play *Stip, Step, Stirk* this morning
to make up for it."

Tostig was about ten years old at this point and, to the amazement
of everyone who watched him, he was already a skillful archer. He
could send an arrow from one end of the monks' enclosure to the other
and hit the mark every time. He was, naturally enough, so proud of
his skill that he was always glad to display it. So, as soon as they were
dressed, he took up his station at the farthest point from the abbot's
house and both boys began to chant in loud voices:

"*Stip, Step, Stirk! Dirty old Dirk!*"

As their shrill voices sounded joyously on the morning air, Tostig shot arrow after arrow at the door of the black little hole which the abbot had once used as a detention cell and which Dirk had picked as a bedroom because it was the only part which still had a ceiling over it. Tostig did not miss once, and the bolts landed with a fine *zing* and remained quivering in the wood. Needless to state, old Dirk did not dare open the door until they tired of the sport and went somewhere else, by which time his breakfast was cold.

Tostig taught his charge everything that he knew himself about the woods: how to set traps and how to skin rabbits and squirrels. He ran races with him (and sometimes managed to lose), he taught him to ride, he taught him the tricks of wrestling and how to swing a quarterstaff. When Richard was very young he would take him to the one arm of the now dismantled cloisters and hold him on the edge of the stone trench which had once served the convenience of the monks. They bathed together in the little burn which twisted its way through the grounds. They went fishing in the spring and in the autumn tramped great distances to gather nuts in canvas bags which would be carried up to the solar to dry out. They kept watch on the small herds of cattle and sheep which Edward the Saxon owned. In the winter when the cold blew down from the north and west they would see to it that the poor animals were sheltered in the cloisters and the slype, a passage leading to what was left of the chapter house. They wove branches into covers for the gaping holes in the masonry which had once been windows, to keep out wind and snow.

Tostig saw to it also that Richard adopted the right attitude toward the people they encountered. For the men who worked in the fields with plow and shovel he himself would have a wave of the hand and a friendly word, but if his charge did the same, he would growl under his breath. "No, no! They're beneath you. You can't be familiar with any of them. Raise a hand as you pass. But not too high! Just high enough to show you've seen them."

When they met members of the great families thereabouts, he counseled the same restraint but for a different reason. "You're as good as they are, Master Rick. Better, even. Let them speak first. If they don't, ride by and don't turn an eye their way. No eagerness, mind you. Always remember this, Master Rick. Your fathers were kin to great Earl Godwine and to brave King Harold. These people are robbers. They came over and stole our land, the lying, sneaking Long-Noses! Look any Norman straight in the eye and he'll turn his head away."

Richard followed these instructions but sometimes it was hard. There was one occasion when they encountered a knight and his lady and a girl of about his own age who rode on the saddle in front of her father. She was a pretty girl with long curls and she was dressed as sumptuously as her mother, who was also pretty. The girl looked curiously at Richard as she rode by but her parents paid no more attention to the two boys than they would give a villein with a hoe in his hands.

"Who was that?" asked Richard when the Norman family and their long train had passed down the road.

"The Lord of Doreham and his lady."

Richard had heard much talk about the Lord of Doreham and his lady. They were very rich, very influential, and very stiff-necked. "There was a girl with them," he said.

"Their only child," commented Tostig, who seemed to know everything. "Her name is Adela."

"I didn't know girls could be as pretty as that," said Richard. After a pause he added, with as much enthusiasm as he might have shown over a fine pelt, "She has red hair!"

2

On one of the few occasions when Richard rode out alone, he found himself at a rather considerable distance from the priory and in unfamiliar surroundings. He was on a narrow dirt road which followed the course of a swift stream. The may flies were rising and he was so interested in this that he was not watching the road and came almost head on with a party riding from the other direction. It was a group of three, two of them keepers of the game, the third, who rode in the lead, a youth of his own age.

The latter reined in and regarded Richard with a lively dark eye. "By St. Hubert!" he said, aping the speech of his elders. "This is lucky. I know who you are. You're Richard of Rawen."

"Yes," answered Richard. There was something very genial and friendly about this strange youth. Remembering Tostig's instructions, however, he strove not to let his appreciation of this show too plainly.

"Do you know who I am?"

"I have never seen you before but I think you are Alain of Casserlie. I have heard much about you."

"Yes, I am Alain of Casserlie," said the other. His bright eye continued its survey of Richard and it was clear that he liked what he saw.

"We could be friends, you and I, Richard of Rawen. I'm Norman and you're Saxon. But what of that? In any event, you are half one and half the other."

The latter reined in and regarded Richard with a lively dark eye. He liked this smiling Norman youth and agreed enthusiastically that they could get along together. "I would like to be friends," he said.

"Do you know that my father is sheriff of the county?"

Richard nodded his head. Everyone knew the Lord of Casserlie and the great black castle he had built. It was on an island and the walls were thicker and higher than any others. Richard had seen them in the distance and had been Saxon enough to feel his heart contract, thinking of all the prisoners who had died in the cells of Casserlie and the unfortunates who had swung on the gallows there. Roger de Casserlie was a stern administrator of the law.

The sheriff's son dismounted. "See, Friend Richard," he said, "we will go over there by the stream and sit down. We can talk. There's nothing like talk to get to know each other."

If talking led to close acquaintance, then the friendship of the two boys was cemented that day for all time. They sat together on the bank of the stream and their tongues clacked incessantly. At least, Alain's did. Richard had much less to say because he felt inevitably the inferiority of his position; but he was in agreement with everything that his companion expressed.

Alain was most handsomely attired in a fine garment which was called, in court circles and in all company where men of rank gathered, a cyclaton: a particolored tunic in black and yellow, which was quite long and had sleeves which tapered most correctly to the wrists. He wore a brimmed felt hat, turned up in the back and encircled by a curled plume, and yellow shoes as pointed as a field hound's nose. Richard looked very plain in comparison, wearing a tunic of the abbreviated length of the quilted doublet called the *pourpoint* (which came into general use a little later), and everything about him was a solid unrelieved green. His shoes were made for utility and without so much as the hint of a point. Was it any wonder that he assumed the role of the listener, and reveled in and believed everything he heard?

Alain's talk wandered far afield but always came back to a subject of which Richard had heard only the faintest echoes: chivalry. Nothing else in life, it seemed, counted at all. A man must live to do brave and honorable deeds, to rescue maidens in distress, to fight battles with dragons and men of false heart, to die if necessary and with great cheerfulness for his liege lord and his king. The perfect exponent of chivalry, according to the glib recital of Alain, was the prince who would be the next king of England, Richard of the mighty sword and the irresistible lance, Richard with the heart of a lion and the golden hair and flashing eye.

All this was so new to young Richard that he listened with wide-open eyes and mind, and he rose at the finish of the talk a fully confirmed believer in this new and exciting code.

Alain's final dictum, delivered in a rather scornful tone and with a lofty gesture, proved equally acceptable to the new devotee. "A man must raise a family," he said. "There must be sons. To carry on the name and assume the overlordship of the land. But if you want my honest opinion, Friend Richard, it's all a very trifling matter. Women are—well, let's put it this way: women are a nuisance. They take a man's liberty away from him. Oh, we must come to it in the end. Even you and I, Friend Richard. But my wish is that we both have a long period of glorious freedom before we become entangled in this web called marriage."

Chapter III

1

THE YEARS of Richard's early boyhood had been uneventful and even humdrum. Nothing had happened to take him more than a few miles at any time from the narrow confines of his father's few acres. Then, without any warning, the pattern of his life was upset by a rapid succession of events.

Over in France the wars between King Harry and his rebellious sons had been going on almost without interruption. Inevitably the old man's spirit was broken and, beaten to his knees, he died in great mortification of spirit. Richard succeeded him and came to London, full of plans for the great army he was going to lead to the Crusades. A wave of religious exultation swept over England. Men were seen everywhere displaying the cross as a sign that they had enlisted with the new king. Fiery priests preached in every town and village, exhorting men to go. Great bells were heard tolling in the skies and miracles were reported from shrines where the bones of martyrs lay. The common people of England marched and sang and prayed with an enthusiasm which nothing could check.

But among the leaders of the nation the enthusiasm began to wear a little thin. Richard, it developed, was going to extraordinary lengths in raising money for his army. He was selling everything he owned. The royal castles were being disposed of right and left for very large sums (and later they were taken back by the king without indemnity to the unlucky buyers), the offices of Church and State were being auctioned off to the highest bidders, the decisions of the courts were being awarded to the litigants who paid the most substantial bribes.

"By God's feet!" this fine king was reported to have said. "I would sell London itself could I but find a purchaser rich enough to pay me the price!"

One day the new king had a discussion with his chancellor, one William de Longchamp. The latter, a small man with a crooked back, had seemed a curious choice to everyone in England for so high and honorable a post, although the wonder ceased when it became known that he had paid the king three thousand pounds for the office he held. He was proving himself an adept instrument in the raising of money by dishonest means.

King Richard was sitting cross-legged in his chair, a list of names in his hand. He was a true Plantagenet, golden of hair, blue and handsome of eye, the possessor of a gladiator's shoulders and chest, and of hands made to grasp all the fair wide provinces and the immense power his father had left him.

"Gilles de Baudene," said the young monarch, reading from the list. "I know a little of him. A contemptible fellow. A cur, a coward, and a skimp cheese. If he doesn't take the cross, we must find reason for putting a fine on him."

The chancellor looked slyly at the king. "I think, sire," he said, "we can make better use of this man than putting a sword into his hand. He is not a soldier but he *is* a claimant for the Baudene landholdings."

"Hah!" said Richard. "That is different."

"He is a haggler over pennies but he won't hesitate to pay a large sum for a decision in his favor. I have discussed the point with him. How he wriggled, like a fox caught in a trap! But he agreed to go to the moneylenders."

"Drive a hard bargain with him, Sir Chancellor."

When word came to the priory that the long-deferred decision about the Baudene land had at last been handed down, Edward the Saxon led his son out to sit on the tumbled stones of the gatehouse where no one could hear what was said. They presented a singular contrast now. The boy was growing into a tall youth, with straight back and limbs and a fine spread of shoulder. Edward the Saxon, once so strong himself, had been aging rapidly. He had developed a condition which slowed his step and hollowed his cheeks. He seldom went out these days. His bow hung beside the chimney and the arrows rusted in the quiver.

"My son," he said, "we have lost!"

"Do you mean," asked the boy, his face becoming very still and pale, "that the suit has been settled? That it has gone against us?"

Edward the Saxon nodded. "The Norman gets everything. The information which comes to me is that he paid so large a bribe that it will take him many years to clear his debt to the moneylenders. Still, he has won. The land is his. And all the honors." Here his face flamed with sudden passion. "What else could we expect? A Norman king, a Norman court, a Norman suitor! There is no longer any justice in England."

The boy's reactions to this bad news were curiously divided. Through his undivulged friendship with Alain of Casserlie, he had been gaining a sense of pride in the blood he had inherited from his beautiful Norman mother. The Normans, as Alain put it, were the rulers of the country, they were brave and chivalrous, and they went to the wars and won themselves much fame and glory. Why shouldn't he be proud that his mother had been Norman? Why should he not look forward to the day when he himself might wear the gold spurs of knighthood? Why should he not regard King Richard as the greatest of all warriors, a king for whom he should be glad to lay down his life?

But the fact of the decision was not easy to swallow. He got slowly to his feet and his eyes turned to the west where the sun was sinking under the tops of the trees which marked the boundary of the land still belonging to them. "Then," he said with a sweep of his hand, "this is all I shall ever have?"

His father rose also and placed a hand on his shoulder. "This," he said, "and a heritage of pride which has always seemed to me more important than any possessions. There is, moreover, a trust. When the time comes, my son, I shall have something to tell you. Something that was told me by my father when he knew he was going to die. It may not be long now before I feel that the trust should be placed in your hands."

They walked slowly together across the untended sward. The last narrow rim of the sun vanished behind the cover of the trees and the air seemed of a sudden to become cold. The thin shoulders of Edward the Saxon drew together in a shudder.

"You have a new friend, my son," he said.

Richard paused and gave a startled look at his father. "It is true," he answered. "I have a friend. I have such a liking for him that, if he were to appear now, I would feel as though the sun had changed its course and come up again over those trees."

"He is the son of the Butcher of Casserlie."

"How did you know?"

"Bits of information come to my ears. I have known of this for some time."

"Alain is brave and fine, and a true friend!" cried the boy. "I sometimes think we must be like David and Jonathan."

"My boy, it is good for you to have a friend of your own age and station. But it was not good that you didn't tell me." They had reached the door and Edward opened it with a hand which trembled. "I suspect that I have little time left to enjoy your company and your confidence. I have no fault to find with you, my fine son, but perhaps a word of advice would not be amiss. Do not accept everything your friend Alain says without question. He has nothing but Norman blood in his veins and his father holds land today which was stolen from your forefathers. Does the Butcher know of the friendship between you?"

"I think not, Father."

"Then this infamous decision may make no difference. Had Roger de Casserlie known, he would have judged you an unfit companion for his son."

There was a small fire burning on the hearth. Edward turned toward it eagerly. He sat down and hunched himself over the blaze. He had been losing his teeth and this had brought the tip of his nose close to what had once been the strong line of his jaw.

"Now that our last hope has gone," he said in a low tone, "there is little to live for. I think, Richard, that the time is close when I must transfer that trust to you."

2

Edward the Saxon slept little that night. He tossed and turned while his mind wrestled with the problems of the future; not his own future, for he expected to have little of that, but the poor prospects stretching ahead for his son. At dawn he heard old Godgifu, from behind the curtain which screened her from the rest, groaning and mumbling her prayers. He was aware of the heavy step of Sigurd on the uneven planking and the urgent tones of Tostig addressed to the reluctant Richard. Then he finally fell asleep and did not waken until the sun was high in the heavens and pouring through the narrow window beside his bed.

Edward felt for once that he did not want to get up. What was there for him to do? His heart was too weak for work in the fields. He was on the point of turning over to avoid the sunlight when he heard the thud and clatter of horses' hoofs on the road. Alert again immediately, he sat up in bed and so could see that a party of perhaps half a dozen horsemen had arrived. A sleeve crossed his line of vision. It was black with bars of green. The livery of Pembroke!

The owner of Rawen Priory was out of bed in a trice. "William the Marshal is paying me a visit!" he said to himself. "It must be that he has had my letter. Perhaps he has come to say he can take the boy into his household as I requested. If that is it, I shall be able to die with an easy mind."

William the Marshal was so long of back and leg that he needed a tall steed and in consequence the lady beside him, on a black palfrey with silver gear and bright plumes in its mane, looked very small indeed. William had a fondness for feeling the wind on his face and through his hair, and so he was riding bareheaded. He was in his fifties but his bold features showed no signs of age; a handsome man with fine gray eyes in which no trace of guile or malice could be found. The lady with him was his new-made wife, Isabella, the daughter of Strongbow (who had led the conquering Normans into Ireland) and the greatest heiress in the land. She was dainty and dark blue of eye, and very much in love with her husband, to judge by the many occasions she found to touch his gauntleted hand or lean her head against his arm.

"Edward!" cried the marshal when the Saxon appeared at the gate. "It is many years since I have seen you. Not indeed since we returned together from the Crusades. But, old friend, I have thought many times of the well-directed lance you brought to my aid on a certain occasion when the paynims were pressing me hard." He came to a sudden stop, having had a chance by this time to notice the change in his friend's appearance. "Edward, are you ill? You are no longer the bold blade who set out for the Holy Land with me."

"That was a very long time ago, Sir Marshal," declared Edward, "and in the meanwhile the years have been taking toll of me. But not of you, my lord! You seem as young as ever."

"And lucky for me it is," said the old warrior. "When a man waits to my age before taking a wife and is rewarded then with the hand of the loveliest lady in Christendom—well, he does not relish looking as old as I—as I really am."

"My sweet lord," said the bride, "I am happy you waited so long. Otherwise I would not have you now and some hussy would."

The marshal looked down at her, and quite a distance it was he had to look, and smiled with so much warmth and affection that Edward, watching, lost for a moment his recollections of William as a great fighting man, as a steel-clad scourge in the lists, as the knight who had never been worsted.

"But, my small bride," said the marshal, "there is no denying that I am an old man and you are a mere girl. You are so very young! You should have been given a chance to choose for yourself."

The bride tossed back her head and laughed. As she did so Edward noticed that along the bridge of her very shapely nose (perhaps because of the outdoor life she had lived on her huge Irish estates) there ran a barely discernible line of small freckles.

"My sweet, my very sweet lord and master," said the bride, "you give me too small credit. Do you think I had no say in selecting you from the others? From all those others who were willing to have me—and my lands and honors? I went to some pains to see you and then I demanded a word with my liege lord the king—the old king, it was—and I said to him, 'I shall wed the marshal and none other.' He looked at me like a thundercloud because he had other ideas. He didn't want to give me to you because you had not offered to pay him anything at all, so little did you desire me——"

"Come, sweet chuck," declared the marshal, still smiling down at her, "I would have given him everything I possessed—and that would still have been next to nothing."

"Well," continued the small and sprightly wife, "I made it very clear to Harry Secund—and later to King Richard as well—that it was you or no one. Even though some of the others had offered *huge* sums, I was going to be the wife of the marshal of England or I would remain unwed to the end of my days. And now you know the whole story."

The marshal turned to Edward, who had been trying to convince himself that he could offer them wine, the best in the house being of very poor quality. "We are riding through to Pembroke, where we hope to have a brief rest. And I thought we must not pass so close without halting a brief moment to see an old comrade in arms." He paused and gave Edward a solicitous glance. "I heard of the decision. A foul injustice, my friend! I had received your letter. This son of yours seems to be in much the same position that I was once. I had no prospects whatever and so I went to Normandy to serve an uncle. 'It would be a sound idea, indeed,' I said to myself, 'for my stout old friend's son to come into my household—as a page, then a squire, and finally a belted knight to ride in my train.' He would have the same chance then that

I had, to feather his nest with tournament prizes and perchance to pick up a little bit of land here and there."

"Sir Marshal, I can think of no better future for my poor, dispossessed son!" cried Edward, his spirits rising so high that a touch of the old fire showed in his eyes.

The lady asked a question at this point. "Sir Edward, could I see the young man? It is necessary first, I believe, that I should like him and that he should like both my lord William and me. He would be living with us and having much to do with the many children we expect to have; and so we must all be sure."

Edward turned back to the threshold where a trumpet, made from a ram's horn, was hanging. He placed this to his lips and sounded a loud blast. Almost immediately a boy's voice answered from the thin cover of woods in the west. The master of Rawen then blew three times in rapid succession.

"That is a signal to come at once," he explained to the visitors. "As my lands are small, it will take him no more than a few minutes to get here."

When Richard arrived in a breathless state a very few moments later, with Tostig running at his heels, the marshal took no more than one look at him before saying: "My boy, you have a fine long leg and a good back. I am disposed to think you will grow up to be as tall as I am. That long back is perfect for the saddle. You won't be an easy one to jolt from your seat. Let me test your muscles. Ah, splendid! They are long and will never gather up into tight little knots on your arms and legs." He nodded to Edward. "I like your son, my old friend. He has a good eye. Gentle he will be unless aroused and then he will be like a roaring lion in his wrath. At least, that is what I read in him at this one quick glance."

The Countess of Pembroke then commanded the boy's attention. She leaned over to take both his hands in hers. "Richard," she asked, "would you like to come with us and serve us, first, as a page? Later, of course, my lord would assert himself and take you away to learn the arts and tricks of war."

Richard's eyes lighted up as though he had been shown all the kingdoms of the earth. "Oh yes, my lady, yes!" he cried. "To be a true knight is my only wish. I will serve you faithfully and well, my lady."

The countess continued to study his face. "Yes, it is true, you have a good eye. And I like the way your hair grows down on your fore-head. It is my opinion that you will grow into a handsome knight." She glanced then at Edward the Saxon with a hint of sympathy for him in her eyes. "Sir Edward," she said, "I am very much afraid that we are going to rob you of your son."

After it had been arranged that Richard should join the marshal's household on their return from Pembroke Castle to Cavenham, the home which was their favorite among the scores of places they owned, and that Tostig was to go too (for the discerning eye of the young wife had seen how close the friendship was between the pair), the marshal turned his horse to leave and his lady gave them a warm inclusive smile before gathering up the red leather reins into her gloved hands and following after him.

Edward said to the boys, "Come with me," and led the way back into the cluster of ruined walls behind them. In the stype there remained a stone bench large enough to seat three. "You must not think, Richard, that being a page—or filling whatever post they find for you, Tostig—is going to be easy," he began.

They seemed somewhat surprised at this and he went on to explain. "A page is a household servant, in everything but name. At first he's supposed to pay special attention to the lady of the house. He stands behind her chair at meals and he must not only serve her but anticipate her needs. Before she can say, 'Bring the hot-water ewer,' her page should be at her shoulder, tilting the handle so she can dip her hands in.

"You will discover a custom when you get out into the world which sets all men into the mold of caste. There will be a tall salt cellar about halfway of the board. Above it sit the family, the high officers of the household, and prominent guests. Below the salt are the squires, the house servants, the field churls, the dusty travelers of low degree; and you, Tostig, will be among them. As for you, Richard, you will not have a seat at meals. You will remain in attendance at the head of the board until everyone has been served, even the least-considered varlet at the foot of the table. You will get for yourself then whatever is left, and it may be no more than a crust of bread or a well-gnawed bone.

"You won't go to bed until your master and mistress are couched for the night and then you will probably curl up on a skin outside their door so you will be wakened at dawn by the first servant to appear.

"When a page becomes old enough to be a squire," he went on, "he is allowed to carry a streamer or pencel of his own on the end of a lance. Now things are different but even harder. He polishes armor and burnishes swords and he is always very busy with the horses. In battle he fights behind his master, going to his assistance when necessary and procuring a new horse if his master's is killed. After the fighting, while the knights feast and drink and then snore the night away, the patient squire is still repairing the ravages to armor and garments and getting ready for another day of rampage and fury. If he survives all this, he becomes in time a knight himself and carries a banneret on his lance and has squires of his own."

Richard gave his head an ecstatic shake. "A wondrous life!" he said. "What more could a man ask than to serve? For it is clear that, while the squire serves the knight, the knight serves the earl, the earl serves the king and the king serves his God. I shall be happy to begin a humble life of service."

His father nodded wryly. "You will be lucky indeed, my son, that it is William the Marshal you are to serve. He was a landless wight, just as you are, and so he had to make a place for himself with his strength and his skill with weapons. Have I ever told you that he fought in five hundred tournaments and won them all? No knight has there ever been to compare with William, and yet he is always kind, with a smile for the beggar by the wayside as well as for the courtiers about the king. He has been a slave to duty. When he sees his way clearly before him, nothing can change or swerve him. He was always the most loyal to the old king when the princes began to rebel against their father. Once, very near the end, old Harry Secund was forced to retire because the French king and Prince Richard were out in great force against him. He was retreating from Le Mans and young Prince Richard rode hard after him in pursuit. But it was William the Marshal the prince encountered. He was holding the rear guard in hand with great skill and courage. 'God's feet, Marshal!' cried the prince. 'Do not slay me!' 'The Devil slay you, for I will not!' answered the marshal, unhorsing the prince by killing his mount." Edward paused before adding: "I know of nothing more to the credit of Richard than this, that on becoming king he held no grudge against the marshal but continued him in his post and put no obstacles in the way of his marriage to the heiress of Pembroke."

"What will I need to take with me?" asked the boy in an anxious voice.

"You will be expected to go to him suitably clothed," was the answer. "It is customary to have a woolen tunic, two pairs of hose, without a patch on them, a dagged cloak of scarlet wool with enameled buttons, a leather belt, and two pairs of good shoes. You will ride your own horse and it must not be an ancient crow but a young animal of good spirit."

There was a moment of silence. "It will cost you much to send me to the great earl's castle."

"Yes, my son. It will be a difficult matter. But somehow," with an involuntary sigh, "it will be accomplished. A ring that your lady mother gave me will have to be sacrificed, I fear."

"It has always been this way," added Edward after a pause. "When there has been need of something for you, my son, we have fallen back on what your lady mother provided. You get your looks from her. Your sense of high lineage. Your high pride; although perhaps I share in that, never having been of a humble turn. The few objects of value which adorn this poor habitation came from her. And now, with a gift from the past, she gives you the chance to go suitably clothed into the years of preparation for knighthood. It is no wonder, Richard, that you take such pride in the Norman blood in your veins, knowing that it comes from that gracious and lovely lady. It is to be expected that you—that you take more pride in it than in the Saxon share."

The boy said nothing for a moment. He had listened to his father's low voice with a sudden sense of shame. He was realizing for the first time that, without desiring to do so, he had shown little regard but rather contempt for the Saxon tradition, for that half of himself. Suddenly his shoulders began to shake and tears streamed down his cheeks.

"My father, I have been blind," he said. "I have been unfair. It isn't true that I think only of my mother and never of you. But—but I never saw her and she is in my mind so much of the time."

"Richard, Richard, I am not blaming you! It is natural for you to feel as you do, although I hope you will come in time to perceive the glories of the Saxon line from which you spring."

Chapter IV

1

W H E N all the preparations for the departure had been made, and the new tunic and the dagged cloak of scarlet wool (this term applied to the material, which was quite special and would wear for generations, and did not mean that the color was scarlet; it was more often brown or green) and the horse of spirit had been obtained, Richard rode out to meet his friend Alain of Casserlie and say farewell.

Alain arrived at the meeting place a little late but his eyes were shining. "I have news," he called.

"And I also," answered Richard. "Great, glorious news!"

"I'll tell mine first," said Alain, which was typical of him. "What do you think of this, Rick-with-the-Frown? I am to be wed. Oh, not at once. The articles have been agreed to but it will be a few years before we have the churching. My fair bride must have a chance to grow up."

Richard looked soberly at his friend. "When that happens, it will be an end to everything between us, Alain," he declared. "You will forget me when you leave the chapel with a wife on your arm."

"You groutnoll! Romance means nothing in my life. I grant you that the small Adela is a sweet chick——"

"So it's *that* one."

"You have seen her? Then I don't need to tell you that her hair's a wonderful red and that she's as pretty as a kitten. But when she rode away with her parents, I was glad to see the last of her. Oh, when it comes to wedding, I suppose I'll get as soft and moon-struck as anyone but that's years and years away. In the meanwhile I have my spurs to win."

"Well," said Richard after a pause, "now for mine. I'm going away. To be a page in the household of William the Marshal."

Alain's voice had been changing. Once a fine and high tenor, it had now taken to breaking up and down the scale in the most unpredictable ways. It was almost with a screech that he responded to this piece of information. "Richard!" he cried. "My good old Rick, my Dick, my Dickon, my very best friend! What everlasting luck!"

"My father went to the Crusades with the marshal," explained Richard, his eyes shining with the enthusiasm which filled them. "Yes, it's a wonderful chance. It makes up for everything bad that's happened to me, even the loss of Baudene."

Alain leaned over in his saddle and placed his hands on Richard's shoulders. "Best of friends, I wish you joy of your great good fortune but I can't help being jealous. Rick-with-the-Frown, I would change places with you this very minute. I would sell you my birthright for the chance, and throw in everything I'll ever inherit from my father, and all the honors and lands which will come to me with my Adela. Nay, I would throw in the little redheaded Adela herself and still count myself the winner in the deal!"

2

The night before Richard and his companion were to leave, Edward the Saxon leaned over and touched his son's forearm during the evening meal. "Tonight," he confided in a whisper, "I shall place in your hands the trust that has been mine since the death of my father. You see, my son, I have no illusions. I do not expect to see you again."

Richard looked at the thin, lined face of the prematurely aged man and a sense of fear gripped his heart. "I will be allowed to return," he protested. "There will be times when I am not needed and then I shall ride back to see you. If this were not so, I would change all the plans and not go with the marshal at all."

Edward shook his head. "It may be so. But I know it will be better for you to put this life far back in your memory and think only of the future. Nothing must stand between you and the winning of your spurs. It may be that the Lord and His blessed Son will be kind and grant me a longer time to live, in which case I might hope to see you come riding down the old road on a tall black horse under a curling banner and the gold glittering at your heels. But I am not asking such a boon. There is a hand which beckons me to the life beyond. I speak the full truth, Richard, when I say that I will welcome the chance to—to wear the cross a second time." There was a long moment of silence between them. "And so tonight you must hear the story and see—what there is to see."

When that harsh but just man, Henry, the youngest son of William the Conqueror, came to the throne of England (said Edward the Saxon) there was much rejoicing among the Saxon people. It was not only because Henry had made vows at his coronation to rule well and to have regard for the rights of all men, even the lowliest, but because this also was known of him: he had seen the fair Saxon princess Matilda, the great-granddaughter of Edmund Ironside, and wanted her for his wife. There was some doubt about the rightness of this, because the princess had been living in a convent under the stern rule of an aunt. Had she taken the vows of heaven? The princess said no, she had made no pledges, and in this she was upheld by the court that the good Archbishop Anselm held at Lambeth. And so, in due course, she rode beside the new king to Westminster, her eyes filled with happiness, her flaxen hair glistening like gold under its rich woven net, and was crowned queen of England.

She was a good woman and a good queen and, had she lived longer, things might have been much different in England. But after no more than a brief span of years as queen she felt the hand of death reaching for her shoulder, and she performed a brave and farseeing act before her death which made it possible to preserve for all time the benefits of the king's earlier intentions. And this (continued Edward the Saxon) leads us to a story of some strangeness.

On a stormy spring night in the year 1118, Cuthbert of Rawen was sitting longer than usual over his wine. Cuthbert was a man of strong character and it irked him more than it had his father and grandfather before him that the great domain of the family had been taken from him. The small house which stood against the walls of Rawen was like a prison cell to this bold and ambitious man. He had faith in his destiny and he believed he would march in the van when a certain long-awaited signal came.

As he sat and glowered unhappily at the dying fire on the hearth there came a knock on the gate in the barricade of stakes which then stood high and strong. He sat up at once. The hour was late. No ordinary visitor would come knocking at his door when the night was as far advanced as this. Cuthbert knew a moment almost of fear. The Devil was said to come to men's gates in the dead of night and knock loudly.

He heard the cautious voice of his servant raised in a note of interrogation. In a matter of seconds the door in the oaken screen swung open and an old man came in.

Old age does either one of two things to men: it shrinks them into useless, wrinkled husks or it intensifies the qualities which have been in them from the beginning. The visitor was very old but he stood in the door and looked at Cuthbert with eyes which had lost none of their fire. His almost fleshless hands were clasped over the end of a staff and in the bend of his back there was no hint whatever of surrender to time.

"My son," he said, "I come at a late hour. It was necessary."

Cuthbert of Rawen went down on one knee in front of the holy man to receive his blessing and to ask a question which tingled on his tongue and sent waves of excitement racing through his body.

"Father Aelred!" he whispered tensely. "Has it happened? Does this mean that the bell is rungen?"

The old priest answered in an equally low tone, although they had the room completely to themselves. "No, my son. The time is not yet. The bell will not ring until we are ready."

"I am ready. Are not all other men equally so?"

"It is not a question of what is in men's hearts, my son. Our oppressors are still too strong. We must have more men, more weapons, more money."

Cuthbert got to his feet and for several moments the blazing black eyes of the old priest stared hard into those of the Saxon thane, which were bold and of a steely blue. They had ceased to be priest and layman. They were members of a captured race which lived on for one thing only.

"I won't hear the bell, my son," said Father Aelred, after several moments had passed. "My days are numbered. The leader will not come in my time. But you should live to hear it, and to follow the leader, whoever he may be."

"God grant it, Father Aelred!" The voice of the thane was deep and fervent. "God grant me this boon, to live long enough to draw my sword and stain it deep with Norman blood on that day of days!"

The venerable priest made his way to a bench before the fire and sat down. He brushed away Cuthbert's offer of wine.

"My son, I am the bearer of bad news," he said. "The queen has not long to live."

When Cuthbert joined him at the fire, seating himself on a log of wood, the old priest amplified his statement. "She has been ill for a long

time. The king neglects her and runs after foreign women. She is unhappy because of this but her greatest regret is that she sees in him a
tendency to forget the promises he made." Father Aelred studied the
pattern of the slow flames. "I have been with her now for many years
and she has often sought my advice. Often she has followed it." (Often,
indeed! It was known everywhere that it had been his wise counsels
which guided her.) "You know, of course, that after his coronation
vows the king prepared one hundred copies of the promises he made
and sent them out to all parts of the kingdom. He was a zealous young
king then, and his bride was at his side to whisper sound advice in his
ear; and so he wanted it known to all men that he intended to be a just
ruler. He regrets this now, having no further wish to be bound by the
generous impulses of his youth. It is in the queen's mind that, as soon
as she is gone, he will take steps to regain all copies of the written
Charter and to destroy them. She has asked me to act to this end, that
one copy at least will be placed beyond his reach. This, my son, is the
errand which brings me here, like a thief in the night."

The priest fumbled in a leather bag under his girdle and produced a
gold ring which he handed to the thane.

"The pledge of our good queen. So you may know that I come at her
command and that you may put full trust in me."

It was a plain gold band, with the royal initials and insignia stamped
on the inside. The master of Rawen studied it with a reverent eye while
the priest went on to explain his mission.

"I have brought a copy of the Charter with me. Unbeknown to the
king, she has always kept this one in her own possession. It is her wish
now that it be placed in other hands. I mentioned you to her and she
agreed that a better custodian could not be selected. I shall leave it with
you and it must be so well hidden away that no one, except you and I,
may know where it is."

Father Aelred drew then from a capacious pocket on the inside of
his robe a plain wooden container which he placed in the hands of the
thane.

"It is short," he said. "But it contains the wisest precepts ever laid
down for the guidance of a king. It may well serve as a covenant to be
exacted of all future kings. You must guard it with your life, if necessary,
Cuthbert of Rawen. You are to surrender it only if someone comes to
demand it who bears a replica of this ring. Give me your promise to be
true to this trust which has been placed in you."

"I swear," said Cuthbert solemnly, "to guard the Charter with my life and to reveal the secret of its existence to no one, as long as there is breath in my body; save if it should be necessary when I come to the end of my days to hand the secret on to my eldest son."

"Your willingness to become the custodian of this paper has lifted a weight from my heart. I know that it is in the best of hands." The priest studied the travel-stained condition of his sandals with a weary eye but rose nevertheless to his feet. "So that no word may be noised abroad of my having been here tonight, I think it wise to ride on to St. Wulstan's." He allowed his voice to fall to a whisper. "Do not despair, Cuthbert of Rawen, the bell will be rungen in God's own good time. Our fathers thought it would be Hereward when he sent out the war arrow and resisted the Conqueror so long on the Isle of Ely but the people of England were too badly beaten down to respond. There will be another Hereward or a brave Harold to rise up and lead you. It must be seen to that the English king who rules after the ringing of the bell has agreed to all the terms in this paper I leave with you."

Such was the story that Edward the Saxon told his son on the eve of the boy's departure. When he came to the end, noting with satisfaction the rapt interest with which the boy had listened, he added: "No messenger has come since with the other ring and, of course, the bell has not been rung. The masters of Rawen have continued to save whatever they could for the day when the bell will ring and money will be needed. The contributions have been smaller as the years passed. I have been able to add no more than a few pennies."

"And the Charter is still here?" asked the boy. "In this house?"

"It is still here."

"Your father told this story to you?"

"On his deathbed, Richard. I am the fourth to be told the story and to learn of the place where the Charter is hidden. You, my son, the fifth, must adhere to the same oath that Cuthbert swore."

"I swear," said the boy eagerly.

The small household had scattered while father and son talked at the head of the table. Sigurd had already made his way up to his straw pallet above and no doubt was sound asleep. Dirk had disappeared. Old Godgifu was in the kitchen and they could hear her muttering to herself over her tasks. Only Tostig remained and he had betaken himself to the far end of the table. The torches placed at the head and foot of the table had burned down low and the drafts threatened momentarily to extinguish them.

Edward the Saxon rose to his feet. "And now," he said, "it remains to show you the place where the Charter has been kept. I think," he added after a moment's hesitation, "that we must make some use of Tostig. He will accompany us, for part of the way, at least."

3

Father and son walked out through the broken palisade, Tostig following with a mattock over his shoulder. Edward looked up at the sky in which a brightly burnished moon was yielding so much light that they could see all the way through the broken-backed arches of the cloisters to the clumps of stone marking the line of the western wall.

"It was on just such a night that my father led me out for this same purpose," he said as though to himself. "It seemed to me that every bird flying on wings had come to attend us. They rustled in the ivy and twittered among themselves and the owls were hooting. I thought they were saying, 'These poor mortals, stealing out at dead of night on their silly little errands.' My father was so weak that he clung to my arm and he could barely whisper. He died before morning."

A sudden and angry fluttering of wings greeted them at the entrance to the refectory. A single owl hooted from above the abbot's house where, no doubt, Dirk was already fast asleep.

"Nothing seems to have changed," muttered Edward.

"The vines should be rooted out, master," said the practical Tostig. "Give them time and they'll have all the walls down."

The refectory, being so securely roofed, was very dark inside. Tostig laid down his mattock and lighted a torch.

"It is well that the roof holds," said Edward. "Once it comes down, these stones underfoot will yawn and give up what is beneath."

He began, still making use of the boy's arm, to pace off distances from two of the walls. When convinced of his correctness, he tapped on one of the large square stones with his foot.

"This one, Tostig," he said. "It is to come up. Put your back into it, my lad."

The sturdy youth had the stone up quickly and, for a moment, the three of them stood together and looked into a dark vault below. The light of the torch made it possible to see the outline of a brief flight of stone steps leading downward. Edward took the torch into his own hands.

There was a stone in the vault below which had a cross chiseled on its surface. Edward pointed to the one above. This yielded easily to Richard's pick and it was found to be of a few inches in thickness only. There was a dark space behind it, from which the questing hand of the father drew out the wooden case containing the Charter.

He stood and looked at it in silence, his fingers trembling with excitement.

"As you know, my son," he said, "I cannot read. And yet I am certain of this, that there is no document in the world today, saving those of divine origin, which is of importance equal to this. It contains the hint of something new. An idea, a belief! That all men—even those who work in the fields and follow their overlords into battle—have the right to think as they please, to speak their own minds, to live as they desire, to be punished for misdoings only by due process of the laws of the land." He replaced the paper in its container, as though afraid to let the light touch it. "Your head is full of dreams, my son, and it may be that this idea does not stir your heart yet as it does mine. But someday, I am sure, your eyes will open to the light."

The next article removed from the open space was a bag of coins. Edward's inability to read did not detract from his capacity to figure. He proceeded to count the coins on the damp floor of the vault.

"Eleven hundred and fifty-six," he said. "You must never forget, my son, the purpose for which these coins were accumulated and hidden away. The total has grown little since Cuthbert of Rawen died, the difficulties of mere existence having become so great. It was started soon after the calamity of conquest befell us, at a time when every man of Saxon blood was certain we would soon be able to rally and drive the invaders out. They did not estimate the Normans at their full strength, having no idea how tenacious and greedy were the fingers of the invaders in their mailed gloves. They saw the strong, high castles being built at all strategic points but did not sense how difficult this would make any effort at liberation. The truth of the matter was that our people needed a great leader. The leader will come, never fear; and so we must keep this humble contribution of our ancestor's storing. Every penny, as well as every man, will be needed, Richard, when the bell finally rings. I charge you not to take a single piece from this small hoard for any other purpose."

"You have my promise," declared the boy.

When they had climbed the steps and replaced the stone which concealed them, Edward the Saxon produced another document. "This," he said, handing it to Tostig, "makes you a free man. It has been legally drawn and properly attested and from this moment you are no longer bound to the land. Your life is your own. You may marry as you wish and the children you bring into the world will be as free as you are."

Tostig's strong hand trembled as he accepted the document. "Is it mine?" he asked. "Am I to keep it?"

"It is yours. And you have earned it fairly and well." The weary eyes of the head of the household took on a degree of warmth as he studied the sturdy figure in the plain gray tunic, and the close-cropped head. "My hope, Tostig, is that you will continue to serve my son."

"I ask nothing better, master."

"You have a sound head on your shoulders. And a sense of caution which, I fear, my son lacks. He will need you, Tostig, in the years ahead." Edward paused and then held out a hand to the newly freed man. "And remember this. From now on you call no one 'master.'"

The next morning, as the first rays of the sun lighted up the sky, the two adventurers took to their horses. The saddle cloths were of the plainest gray material, the snaffle bits were of unadorned iron, the stirrups lacked any hint of inlay, the saddlebags were of woolen cloth without any armorial embroidery. The travelers looked exactly what they were—a poor young lad and his servant, starting out on a journey.

When they reached the point where the road forked and one arm went to Baudene, they took for the first time the other arm which would lead them to London town.

Chapter V

1

RICHARD OF RAWEN sat his favorite horse Messire on the edge of the tilting grounds at Savran-Dupré, one of the residences in Normandy of the marshal and his highborn wife. It was a busy scene, for all the squires were out, nearly a score of them, and as many of the pages as could escape from domestic duties. The boys were practicing at the quintain, a fixed target with a knight's shield, at which they could ride and sharpen their aim. The squires were pounding away at each other with sword and battle-ax and quarterstaff.

Richard was master of all he surveyed. Having won his spurs on the march to the relief of Arras, and having, moreover, entered many tournaments and won them all, he was second only to the old marshal himself in the eyes of the younger men of the household. They had fallen into the habit of seeking his advice, and they marveled at the length and strength of his limbs as well as the extent of his worldly wisdom.

Guy de Coutrand came over to join him, riding a gray horse with a fine mane. "Shall we splinter a lance, Sir Richard?" he asked.

The new knight looked first at his friend's mount and then quietly smoothed the black mane of Messire. "Gladly would I measure skill with you, my good friend Guy," he said, "but my old fellow here would refuse."

"The horse?" cried the young Norman.

"The horse. You see, that is a good steady war horse you are riding—Amadis, isn't it?—but he isn't a proper charger, trained in the ways of the tilting grounds. Messire knows this as well as we do. He would not move from his station."

"God's chin!" cried the Norman. "I've heard it said that horses sometimes get such notions. But I've never believed it."

"You were not here the last time it happened," said Richard. "I was against Bertrand of Belsize. He was riding a fast, skittish roan. The trumpet sounded, the roan got into full stride, the spectators roared. Messire did not stir an inch. I cried to him, 'At them, Messire! Our honor is at stake!' He did not move, except to toss his head scornfully. Bertrand reined in his mount and glared at me. 'What is this?' he demanded. 'You seem to be amused.' 'Yes, I am amused,' I said. 'At this foolish fellow of mine.'"

"But I am not amused now!" cried Guy de Coutrand.

"Let me explain. Let me tell you what is going through his mind. He is saying to himself, 'Why should I ride against this great looby of a horse who might swing out of line or tumble in a heap and throw his rider off balance? I might get his lance in my eye instead of it striking the shield of my master. Besides,' he is thinking, 'there is the matter of my rights and my dignity to be considered. I should not be asked to ride against colts or green loobies, I am Messire and I am a champion.'"

The other horse, the gray, seemed to understand the situation. He was standing quietly by, with his head down. He knew his own shortcomings and that he was unfit to ride against the lordly black.

"*Ma foi!*" cried the Norman. "Never have I given ear to such folly!"

"Demand of the grooms a trained charger, Guy de Coutrand, and Messire and I will gladly run a course with you."

A servant with the Pembroke lion on the green of his sleeve came at a brisk run from the direction of the castle. He bobbed his head at Richard and delivered a message. He, Sir Richard, was wanted. By his lordship, the marshal. At once, as it was a matter of importance.

The mood of the black charger had changed. He rubbed his long nose along his master's sleeve.

"My good fellow, my find old rampager!" said the young knight. He turned to Tostig, that stern disciplinarian. "I detect a gleam in your eye as though you think something should be done about this. If you please, Tostig, we will not be hard on Messire this time. Instead I would suggest"—he gave the squire the benefit of a broad grin—"a measure of oats."

"No disciplining then," assented Tostig. "But," in high dudgeon, "no oats!"

The marshal of England was seated in a corner of what was called the Great Hall, although it was in fact rather small and dingy. The bench he had chosen was lacking in the necessary strength for his great weight and was creaking a little. A back door had been left open and several dogs and a huge hog had come in and were rooting about among the rushes on the floor on a quest for food.

"I would not have asked you to see me here but there is no privacy anywhere in this place," said the marshal. He looked at the animal intruders with distaste. "It was a mistake to come here, Rick. It's one of my few personal properties and I'm not at all proud of it. But that lovely little wife of mine has an insatiable curiosity. She's determined to visit all the places we own if it kills both of us. I don't think we'll stay here long. Last night she was looking at everything in a very thoughtful way, it seemed to me. We'll be off for somewhere else in the winking of an eye."

Richard was sorry to see in the revealing light of day that the marshal was beginning to show his years. There were fine lines and wrinkles about his eyes and mouth and a general air of weariness.

The marshal sighed and proceeded to explain his reason for summoning the young knight. "My boy, I am sending you on an errand of great delicacy, nay, of secrecy. You must leave at once. For Brittany."

"Yes, my lord," assented Richard eagerly. He would be glad also to get away from Savran-Dupré. The night before he had slept under the table with a round dozen other bachelors and he still ached from the roughness of his couch.

The marshal frowned as though uncertain how to explain the mission. These were parlous days, with John not yet firmly established on the throne of England and fiercely suspicious of everyone. The new king was well aware that young Prince Arthur of Brittany had a better claim to the throne and that most of his subjects thought so.

"I want you to see Prince Arthur," said the old soldier finally. "A whisper has reached my ears that our bold and not too well-advised prince is contemplating a step which"—there was a pause—"which will have *dire consequences*. For him. My message must be no more than whispered in his ear, after exacting a promise that it will go no further. You are to inform him that—well, that the step he contemplates, which is neither right nor politic in the first place, has ceased to be a secret. It may seem strange to you that I am willing to make him aware that I have this knowledge. I cannot see that unfortunate prince walk blithely into a trap. In any case I feel it is better for the peace to be kept."

Richard could not help wondering how much consideration the young prince would be likely to give to advice coming from William the Marshal. Had not the old soldier been chiefly responsible for pro-

claiming John the king of England on the night when word had been
received of Richard's death at Chaluz?

2

It had perhaps been a whim that induced William to take his young
squire with him when he rode to Rouen on that fateful night. It had
been just as well that he did, for the Countess Isabella had whispered
in Richard's ear that she would depend on him to see that her husband
and lord wore a surcoat over his armor and a covering of some kind on
his head, and that he should break the long ride for a rest. He was the
only one in the train she could trust with these instructions. Actually,
she had added, it was not Richard himself she trusted so much, it was
his squire Tostig, who had made a reputation for himself in the household as a man of much good sense. Between them, Richard and Tostig,
they had seen to it that the marshal did not overly tire himself on the
ride over the rain-swept roads to Rouen.

They arrived in that ancient city a full hour after sundown and made
their way to the Abbey of Saint-Ouen, which was generally used as
the residence of the Norman kings. Despite the warmth of his fur-
lined surcoat and the woolen bascinet under his helmet, the marshal
had begun to show signs of fatigue. Richard advised him to go at once
to bed and take up his duties in the morning.

"Not so," said the marshal, looking down at his young knight with a
critical frown (he stood two full inches above the tall Richard). "There
are matters of state to be settled before there can be any thought of
slumber. We must go at once to the archbishop's palace."

"My lord," protested Richard, "you have ridden all day. And you
are the custodian of Rouen. Why shouldn't the archbishop come to
you?"

The marshal did not seem to hear. He was rubbing his unshaved
chin and frowning thoughtfully. "The streets were crowded when we
rode through. I know the reason. The place is filled with mercenaries, it
is stuffed with them to the very eaves. I don't understand but this is always happening. Let there be the merest taint of blood on the air and
these beasts of prey collect. They seem to come out of nowhere—from
the Low Countries, from Burgundy, from Italy, from every corner of
the Teuton countries. Great hulking brutes, all of them, wild boars in
human guise." He turned to Richard. "Death lurks in the streets tonight.
We must go in full force to the palace."

The rain had stopped when they ventured out but this, they realized at once, was not to be considered a turn for the better: the birds of prey might have stayed within and steamed in their damp clothing before inn fires if the moisture had continued to descend but as it was they were in the streets, looking for throats to cut and purses to filch. Tostig strode in the lead, holding a lantern with horn slides above his head, a furtive porter at his shoulder to point out the way. A dozen knights followed, then the old marshal with head sunk forward in deep absorption, and after him a score or so of stout yeomen. They traversed the Rue de la Grosse Horloge, the main artery of the old town, and found it advisable to walk in the center and to huddle closely together. Heads peered at them from doorways and voices muttered in alleys but no one ventured to dispute the passage of so strong a body; and in due course, with a bitter wind whipping their surcoats about them and the clouds above in wild confusion, they came to the gloomy stone building in the open square of the cathedral, where Walter de Coutances had his abode.

The archbishop's palace was a damp and sour old rookery. There must have been leaks in the roof, for streams of water were running down the walls and all the furnishings were mildewed and malodorous. The old churchman fitted into this picture perfectly. He had been in his bed and his scant gray hair formed a comic fringe to the tonsured baldness of his pate. A bed covering of some kind was wrapped about his shoulders and his feet were so affected by the chilblains that he hobbled rather than walked.

The room was drafty and the candles guttered and went out and had to be relighted continually by shivering attendants.

"Ha, Marshal!" said the archbishop. "A sad matter, this. The archer who loosed the bolt has been skinned alive but that won't bring our great King Richard back."

The marshal nodded grimly. Perhaps because he wanted an intelligent witness he had brought Richard with him into the long cold room with its gaping black hearth, leaving the rest of his train in the regions below where warm fires blazed. "My lord bishop, I have an order with the king's own hand to it, that I am to take charge here. There is some recruiting to be done—which will be an easy matter—and the peace to be kept, and the royal findal to be guarded."

"Little enough of *that*, my good friend." The bishop snuffled scornfully. "He kept drawing on it and I question if you'll find much left.

He, the great Richard, had only one use for gold, to make it fly in all directions."

There was a moment of silence and then the marshal sighed heavily. "All such things are as nothing. It is for us, you and me, my lord bishop —yea, you and me and none else—to decide who will be proclaimed here in Rouen. John or Arthur? Have you a stout stomach for the making of such a decision as that?"

The archbishop squinted up at the tall soldier. "The King's Son of Heaven settled it for us, Sir Marshal," he said. "Forty years or so ago when a son was born to King Henry II and given the name of Geoffrey. A few years later the king and his good queen were blessed with another son and they named him John. Geoffrey is dead but his son Arthur stands in his place today."

"My lord bishop," declared the marshal, "I have been much in England in the last years and I know what men are saying there. They are saying, better that we take John, whose faults are known to us, than a French princeling of thirteen years who has never set foot on English soil. The Lady Constance of Brittany, his mother, has trained him to hate us, to hold all French ways right and all English ways the ways of swine. With the barons of England, I do assure you, it is ten to one for John. And remember also it was the declared wish of our dead king that his brother succeed him. Ah, I know what you are thinking, my lord bishop," he went on, before the voice of the prelate could be raised in protest. "I know as well as you that John has been false to his vows, and a bad son and brother. But it comes to this. We can have John and peace or Arthur and civil war. This is no time to have a minor as king."

They disputed the question back and forth, the bishop vehement in his belief, the marshal sadly resigned to the choice of the barons. The latter stood out so determinedly for the lesser of the two evils that finally the churchman gave in. Sinking his numbed hands into the folds of his voluminous gown, he faced the English paladin with a resigned air.

"So be it, Sir Marshal," said the bishop. "Sound the *Rouvel* as a signal that the townspeople are to assemble. Let your heralds proclaim it to every housetop where the leopards flap in the breeze. Command the trumpets to sound. Richard is dead, long live King John! It will be given out from every pulpit tomorrow at dawn." The narrow Norman eyes of the churchman became no more than slits in his sallow face. He intoned in a solemn voice, raising a forefinger in the air: "Nothing of which you have done, Marshal, will you have such cause to repine as this!"

Richard had listened to this discussion with emotions which churned inside him and made him want to cry out: "The barons and the bishops who stand out for John the Traitor are old men! Does it not seem to you that the youth of England would prefer our brave young Prince Arthur?" He succeeded in biting back his dissent, however.

There was a sudden tumult in the streets below: men's voices raised in wonder and anger, a clash of arms and the thump of drums. The archbishop walked to a window and looked down into the square where in less turbulent times the merchants had been allowed to set up booths. The whole space was now black with people.

"The word is out," he said, turning back to address the marshal. "I tried to keep it a secret until such time as a successor could be named. But now they know out there that Richard is dead and they are waiting for a proclamation. We can't delay it any longer, Sir Marshal."

The two high officials of the Crown left the room and for a quarter of an hour Richard stood alone at the window and looked down over the crowded and noisy cathedral square. Rain had started to fall again, a moody kind of storm which seemed to drizzle in despondency but at intervals would goad itself into a fury and lash angrily at the rooftops and the turrets of the massive church. Nothing, however, could discourage the crowds which had gathered on the square. It was clear now that the word had spread everywhere of the death of Richard of the Lion-Heart. Wild rumors as to the cause and manner of his death were being circulated. It was a plot of the treacherous French king, it was the work of the landless Prince John who wanted the throne for himself, it had been carried out by fanatical heathen from the East who had been sent by the Old Man of the Mountain, one of Richard's deadliest enemies. "Kill! Kill!" was shouted in many tongues, together with more direct demands for the heads of the French king and John Lackland.

"The common people are not for John," said young Richard to himself, standing close to the window so he could see everything that was happening.

Then he heard the sound of trumpets and a silence settled quickly over the square. A loud voice proclaimed, first in French and then in English, that King Richard was dead and that his brother Prince John was to succeed him. As the words "Long live King John" rang out, there was a wild outburst from the crowds which might have been the result of pent-up feeling but which could be construed also as evidence that the succession was not a popular one. "The Black One" was a name by which John was known in taverns and market places and in shops where the tongues of apprentices clacked, partly because he was black of hair and eye in contrast with the blond Plantagenets, partly because of his record for treachery. The term was heard repeatedly now as the excited voices below commented on the proclamation. "It's some of his work, the Black One," men were saying. And, "Jack Lackland has done for our great Richard at last!"

An hour passed. The townspeople reluctantly dispersed and left the square to darkness and the persistent rainfall. Richard was summoned to attend the marshal and found him sitting in a small room off the chapter house where a decent fire blazed on the hearth. He had cold meat and a flagon of wine on a table beside him but did not seem to be much interested in them.

"The die is cast," said the marshal, motioning to the young knight to seat himself. "I have done the right thing; but will I be justified by the results? Whatever the outcome, we have sent word to John, proposing that he come here to be crowned first as Duke of Normandy. He will have his hands full for a time keeping the French provinces in line and his coronation in England will have to be delayed." He paused and looked at Richard with a hint of weariness in his wide-spaced eyes. "John will not be a palatable dish to many. Here in Normandy they have not been able to forgive him his landless condition, believing it a fault in anyone not to show a proper degree of acquisitiveness. They have a nickname for him. Jack Lack. Do you suppose they will be pleased with King Jack Lack?"

"No," answered Richard bluntly. "I find it hard to believe that anyone will be pleased."

The marshal sighed and passed a hand over his brow. "I am at home when there is man's work to be done but I am out of my depth when it comes to haggling about policy." His voice fell away to a low mutter. "Priestly concerns," he said. "Juggling of words and weighing of this and that. It's not for me. Richard was my liege lord and my duty was to obey him. He gave it out as his will that John should succeed him. Richard is dead and so I am now John's man. There is no other course for me but to stand by him; even though I may feel doubts as to his fitness for the responsibilities of kingship. It is most difficult."

"Have you any doubts about Prince Arthur, my lord?" asked Richard.

"Prince Arthur is a gallant boy. As handsome as his father, who was the best in looks of all the Plantagenets. He's brave, high of spirit, chivalrous. I am very fond of him."

"Then surely he would make a good king."

"As to that, one can only guess. There are reasons for doubt. His father was hot of temper and both sly and treacherous. His mother was capricious and filled with a bitter pride. If the prince is like his parents, he would not make a good king. But how can we be sure?" He sighed a second time. "This responsibility, which I did not seek, is proving a heavy burden. I wish the decision had not rested on my shoulders. I will bear the blame if things turn out badly."

3

And now Richard himself was to take a hand in the tangled relationships of the English royal family. He was beginning to entertain some doubts about the mission with which he was being entrusted.

"This is a weighty matter for one so inexperienced, my lord marshal," he said.

"You may be the very best envoy," was the answer. "Let me see. You are twenty. Prince Arthur has just turned sixteen. Youth will speak to youth. You will understand each other. And no one will suspect so young a man of being the bearer of important advices.

"You will need a strong party," the marshal went on. "Half a dozen men-at-arms, a groom, a body servant, a priest to act as interpreter. And, of course, the worthy Tostig. You will need a suitable pretext for traveling at this particular moment and I suggest you declare yourself as seeking a chance to splinter lances with the knights of the western provinces. You can hold your own with the best of them. It wouldn't surprise me, in fact, if you emptied them all out of their saddles." He frowned unhappily. "I am against deception of any kind but I'm afraid we must be somewhat devious in this case. To the extent, certainly, of carrying letters to prominent men in Bordeaux and Gascony. It may not be necessary to deliver them or to go to either city, for that matter; but they will be in your possession and they will justify your presence on the road."

Richard had another question to ask. He hesitated over it, fearing that he had no right to inquire too closely into the matter in hand. Still, it would be better if he knew. After a moment or two of doubt he finally spoke. "Would it not be advisable, my lord, for me to know what this action is that the prince proposes to take and which you regard as dangerous?"

The marshal was now the one to show hesitation. He frowned at first and shook his head. "I am playing with fire," he said. "The fewer who

know, the more secure I will feel. Still—you will be in a position to
speak with more authority." He paused and then continued in a low
tone. "King John is in England but his advisers here are in possession
of the information. The king would not agree with the course I am
taking but I know that I am right and that I must follow the dictates of
my conscience. In the interests of justice and peace, the boy should be
warned to give it up. The King of France has finally roused himself to
positive action and is going to take the field by leading an army into
Touraine. Of course we have always known that he won't be content
until all of France is in his hands and the English have been driven
out. But now Arthur is going to take sides with the French."

"Can he be blamed for that?" asked Richard.

"No, perhaps not. It's still firmly fixed in his mind that he was robbed
of his birthright, although he no longer blames me as bitterly as he
did at first. I've seen him twice and we got along well. He's bright and
courageous and I don't want anything to happen to him. But he'll make
a grave mistake if he follows his present plan. He proposes to cross the
Loire with the strongest force he can raise and attack Mirebeau."

The marshal looked surprised when the young knight made no comment, and after a moment of silence he said: "It must be, Richard, that
you don't know who is living in the castle at Mirebeau. The old queen.
Queen Eleanor, the widow of my first liege lord, King Henry. She is
Arthur's grandmother, of course, but he is prepared to take the castle by
storm and make her his prisoner."

Richard now saw the folly of such a course. "He would be condemned
by every man with any regard for the code of chivalry!" he exclaimed.
"He would never be forgiven."

"It's his father coming out in him," declared the marshal. "Prince
Geoffrey would stop at nothing. Blood ties were of no concern to him.
You are right that the prince would put a stain on his name and I am
determined to persuade him against it. You must not discuss the military
side of it with him because we can't give *our* plans away by the same
kind of loose talk he has been indulging. But I must tell you this much:
if he strikes at Mirebeau, he will draw all our strength against him. As
I said before, there will be dire consequences. I am hoping you can
dissuade him from a course which would be fatal to him and most
unpleasantly expensive to us in every way. Before you leave, I will go
over with you the various arguments I think you should use.

"A final word. The young prince is in the hands of bad advisers. He
seems to be listening at this time to a wily and dangerous churchman.

A man of Breton stock who won the nod of Rome and has been made a cardinal, no less. His name is Pourtran and he is called the Red Cardinal. Steer clear of him, whatever you do. He's double-tongued, treacherous, and without a human scruple. The nature of your talks must be kept from the knowledge of this red-bearded priest if you hope to have any success.

"And now," continued the old man, "there's another matter which concerns you personally. My boy, I am going to kick you out of the nest."

When Richard displayed his surprise by making no comment, the marshal proceeded to explain himself. "It's time you ventured out into the world to make your fortune. As I did—so many, so very many, years ago. You are well trained now in the use of arms and I believe you have no superior in the lists. The world is full of opportunities for a young man with your qualifications—and your good appearance. And I don't mind stating my opinion that you will be well advised to stay out of the civil warring in which we will be constantly involved. It's always a sad and unprofitable thing when brother fights brother—or uncle fights nephew. You should go to Rome. There is a Pope there today who is going to shake up the world. It was a good thing that, when the camerlingo tapped with his silver mallet on the forehead of Celestine and called him by his name, the old Pope could not respond. He was dead, as dead as a brown leaf tossed by winter winds. And so the cardinals sat down and selected Innocent III.

"Innocent sits in the Lateran now and his head is full of wonderful plans. Go to him, my bold Richard. He will have work for you. But before you go, ride about France for a time and enter tournaments. As I did when I was your age. I'm certain you have it in you to pick up a tidy fortune that way. When your eye has been sharpened and your backbone has become strong, leave the fields of make-believe and see what real work Innocent will offer you."

4

Richard's opinion of the estates of Savran-Dupré did not improve as a result of the visit he paid to the solar above the Great Hall. In the first place, it could be reached only by an outside staircase, on the steps of which a large flock of chickens had congregated. The knight stamped his way through them, sending them flying off with much indignant squawking. The solar itself was low-roofed and cramped and it contained one bed only. It was filled, moreover, with such a clatter of feminine activity that at first Richard hesitated to enter. Half a dozen handmaidens were busily repacking the clothing and supplies which had been brought the day before.

"Such a dismal hole it is," said the countess, giving the knight a nod and smile of welcome. "We'll be on our way—somewhere—by this time tomorrow."

She was as comely as in her earlier years but showing a tendency to the matronly in figure, having brought a child into the world each year with great regularity. With the passing of time she had become more unconventional, even to the extent of discarding the wimple and going without a head covering of any kind when indoors. The long train of her tunic of blue baudequin (from Baghdad, no less) had been annoying her to such an extent that she had ordered it cut off; and the remnants lay in a heap beside her chair with the golden scissors which had been used in the operation. A small handmaiden was down on her knees, removing the jagged effect with a busy needle.

"My very dear Richard," said the countess, "I am quite desolate. You have been with us so many years, and always you have seemed like another son."

"But my liege lord is right. It is high time I began to make a place for myself in the world. I have had the best of training and I have won my spurs. My lord has been giving me much good advice which I will surely follow." He looked down at her with a hint of unhappiness in his eyes. "But for a time I shall feel quite lost."

"But you will not . . ." The countess hesitated. "You will not go over to the other side? I know your sympathies have always been with Prince Arthur."

"My lord's advice is to take no part in it. So I am going first to try my luck against the knights of the west and then I am off for Rome. I hope to find a place in the train of some bishop palatine."

The countess sighed and lowered her voice. "How fortunate that you will escape all this strife! No one is more strict in adhering to the dictates of honor than my dear lord and he finds it necessary so often to stand against the wishes of the king. Sometimes he comes to me very pale and very tired of it. But he does not give in, even though the king charges him openly with disloyalty. The charges are always quickly retracted, of course, for the king knows he cannot get along without him."

A childish voice said from somewhere close at hand: "You are very rude to me today, Richard. You haven't even noticed that I am here."

Richard turned and saw that one of the smallest members of the family was seated on the bed, kicking her heels against the sides and holding onto one of the posts. She looked very small indeed, seated up there, for the bed was large enough to accommodate both her father and mother and herself at night. She was very pretty, with the fine blue eyes of her mother. No one had yet thought of contriving clothes for boys and girls and so they were dressed like little men and women. The slender child on the bed wore a replica of the Lady Isabella's blue gown, even to a train, and she had also a gold chain around her waist from which depended three loops of gold cord.

"I apologize most humbly, my little Lady Isabella," said Richard, bowing very low to her. "I didn't see you, seated away up there."

"But you *should* have seen me, Richard."

"Leave Richard alone, child," said the countess sharply. "He has much on his mind today."

"I know he has much on his mind, dear Mother. And it's because of what he has on his mind that I think he should have noticed me. He is going to leave me."

"The children will all be disconsolate," declared the countess. "You have always been a great favorite with them, Richard. I sometimes believe that all my little girls harbor a secret attachment for you."

"I do," declared the Lady Isabella.

The servants had been keeping their ears open and at this point all of them burst into involuntary laughter. It subsided quickly, for in spite of her usual kindliness and tolerance the countess could be very stern. She glanced about her now with an accusing eye and every head dropped and every pair of fingers went back feverishly to work.

The child stepped down off the bed and walked toward the stairway.

"Isabella, my child!" called her mother anxiously. "Where are you going?"

"I am not sure," was the reply, in a voice which showed the child was close to the point of tears. "I am going where I will not be treated this way. I hope to find my father. It is nice in his company because he never scolds or allows anyone"—her eyes swept stormily around the room—"to laugh at me."

"With your permission," said Richard to the countess, "I will escort my lady Isabella to her father."

"Yes, Richard, do. While I have something to say to these lazy and impertinent people of mine."

They went down the outside steps together, the small hand of the child raised high to rest on Richard's arm, quite properly and primly, however. "I was very glad, my dear Lady Isabella," he said, "to hear that you have a good regard for me. I hope it means that you won't forget me entirely now that I am going away for a very long time. Did you know that I leave today?"

The girl nodded her head slowly. "Yes, Richard. And I think it is very wrong of my father and my mother to let you go away. You will soon forget all about me."

"No, no, my lady," said Richard. "The shoe is on the other foot. You are a very pretty child as, of course, you know. When you grow up, you will be as beautiful as your lady mother."

"Everyone tells me I will be more beautiful than my mother. And more beautiful than all of my sisters."

"You will be beautiful enough to break the hearts of many men, that is certain. And you will be a great heiress. You will have so many suitors that it will be hard to make a choice and it's certain you will marry an earl, at the least. Perhaps your husband will be a prince of the royal line. By that time you will have forgotten all about a poor, landless knight like me."

"No," said the child firmly.

Chapter VI

1

I T R A I N E D at intervals during the long ride across the north of France and it was not until they had crossed the borders of Brittany that the weather made amends and became as gracious and warm as a lovely woman's smile. There were other changes at the same time which interested the party more. Gone were the chalky hillsides, the broad and leisurely rivers, the prosperous farms with their sleek herds. Gone the thrift and orderliness of the Normans. Richard shook his head in wonder at the round stone fences which they now encountered, and the hedged-in fields, and the haystacks built so high around the trunks of trees that only the top branches showed. The roads were beginning to climb and the wildness of the hills closed them in. Sometimes they saw heath lands dotted with marshes and glowing with the golden tangle of broom and gorse but mostly it was a different world, dark and unfriendly with its gnarled trees and narrow valleys where the sun did not penetrate and the trillium grew thin and reedy.

As the roads led farther up into the fantastic hills, the wonder of the wayfarers grew and they felt a tensity of mood, even a prickling of the spine, for a sound was always in their ears: the song of water pouring out of tangled brush. The brooks of Brittany seemed to have gone stark mad. They boiled in a frenzy to be away (unaware that this gorgeous freedom would end so soon in the eternal sameness of the sea), they leaped with the delight of escape from the bondage of the immovable earth.

"We are a people of contradictions," said Father Pasquitien, the interpreter, who was a Breton. "We are as jealous of our liberty as these violent little streams of ours and yet we will not struggle against fate nor clamor for new rights like the English. We maintain these old graves of the long dead which we call dolmens because we have such respect

for the past, and we have a saying, 'You will be wiser dead than living.'
Perhaps that is why we do not strive to bend this life to our will like
the grasping Norman."

"What I would like to know is this," said Richard. "Whether your
people will struggle and clamor for the rights of Prince Arthur."

"He bears the name of the great king who slew the giant of Mont
St. Michel," was the answer. "But I don't believe, Sir Knight, that the
Breton people felt any deep disappointment when he was not made the
King of England. We are as ready as any people to cry out against injustice but at the same time we do not want our good young prince to
be exiled from us in London. We think it right that he should stay
here and rule Brittany." There was a pause. "Still, you have asked
a question and I shall answer you. Yes, my lord, we are ready to fight
if he gives the word. What is more, Anjou and Maine and Touraine
will stand behind Arthur against John."

"If that be true," said Richard to himself, "my mission is doomed to
failure."

Tostig was riding in the van as usual, watching every foot of the
land and unerringly finding the right road. He turned at this. "You
want Arthur to be the Duke of Brittany but not the King of England?"
he asked. "Can he be the one without being the other? Since the
Plantagenets came to England nothing is simple any more. An ordi-
nance in London must be acceptable to the winegrowers of Bordeaux.
And a king in England must rule also in Normandy and Brittany and
Gascony."

They were climbing a road which twisted along the banks of a
particularly turbulent stream and the noise of the water made speech
difficult. It was not until they came out suddenly on a level stretch of
land filled with sunshine from which could be seen the heights looming
over the Forest of Rennes that the priest had more to say.

"I am not an oracle to tell you what my people will do. But it seems
to me rather more than probable that, should Arthur go to London,
we will demand that his sister, the Princess Eleanor, be made Duchess
of Brittany."

Richard looked at the gray-clad priest in surprise. He had not been
aware of the existence of a Breton princess.

"While the prince stays at the court of France and lays plans with
the French king—who will, of course, break any promises he may make
—his sister acts here in his stead," went on the priest. "We have become
strongly attached to her. She knows the laws and she is prompt and

just. It is the general opinion that we could have none better. And she is so beautiful that people call her the Fair Maid and sometimes the Pearl of Brittany. Our young men would gladly die for her. And yet she is the most unlucky woman in all Christendom."

Richard turned in his saddle. "If she is as beautiful as you say, and if she rules the country so well, how then can she be counted unlucky?" he said.

"She has been the pawn of fate, young Sir Knight. She is a year older than Arthur and should before this have been married. Three times her hand has been sought in marriage by the most eligible of princes. First it was the brother of Saladin and they were to rule as King and Queen of Jerusalem. But he refused to change his religion. She was betrothed to the son of Leopold of Austria when the negotiations for the release of King Richard were under way. Some quirk of statecraft led to the breaking of the match. Then she was to marry Prince Louis, the heir to the throne of France, but when Richard made up his mind that John should succeed him, the French king decided it would not do for his son to marry a mere Breton princess. And so the Pearl of Brittany, the loveliest of them all, remains unwed and is like to share the fate of the Unwanted Alice of France."

"All this makes me think I have lived too narrow a life," commented Richard. "In the household of the great marshal we thought of nothing but the proper use of the lance and the care of our chargers. If any whisper reached us of the existence of this unfortunate lady, it passed in one ear and out the other." He looked with some suspicion at his cowled companion. "Can it be, Father Pasquitien, that you are exaggerating the charms of the lady?"

"You will soon be able to judge for yourself," was the answer. "In my opinion it will need no more than a glance. You will see our golden-crested princess with her eyes as blue as the heavens above us, and you will fall as completely and desperately in love with her as a full thousand men of knightly degree have done before you."

Tostig turned at this point and winked broadly at Richard. "Good priest," he said, "Sir Richard of Rawen has unhorsed at least a score of French knights in the lists. Do you think him so weak that he will go down with one glance from a French maid who has already been jilted three times?"

"The rules are far different in the lists of love, Sir Squire," declared Father Pasquitien. "A strong arm and a firm seat in the saddle avail the candidate nothing."

2

The turn in the weather had caused the ducal household to desert the tall granite castle within the walls of Rennes; which had been a place of some greatness, it should be said, long before the Romans invaded Gaul. Ten miles to the north, within sound of the brawling Vilaine, there was another castle to which the court had repaired. It lacked the high towers and the dizzy tourelles which were a feature of the strongholds of the day, and being in the form of a U, it was wide open to the warm breezes of spring.

When the party came within sight of this somewhat unorthodox abode, the plains west of the castle walls were covered with tents, over which floated the flags of Brittany and France. There were joint banners also above the barbican tower. The leopards of England were nowhere to be seen.

"I have no liking for this," said Tostig, shaking his head. "They are arming for war. Can't you feel it in the air? And hate and anger as well? We will be in luck if we come out of this alive."

A paunchy man with a thatch of black hair and intense eyes under heavy brows crossed the drawbridge and elbowed his way through the guards who were standing there. He stationed himself inside the barbican and glared belligerently at the newcomers.

"That is Robardi," said Father Pasquitien. "It means trouble, my young friends."

"Who is Robardi?"

The priest motioned in a southerly direction. "He came from the wine country. In the days of the imposition."

Richard frowned in lack of comprehension. "The imposition?"

"That was the name we had for it. When the father of our Prince Arthur and of the Princess Eleanor was killed, the old English king compelled our Duchess Constance to take a second husband. He made the choice: a Norman earl from England. It is to be doubted if they were ever man and wife because there was nothing but dislike between them from the first but nevertheless the earl took over the control of everything. It was a very bad time for the people of Brittany because he imposed Norman laws on us and he brought in many Normans and imposed *them* on us. One of them was this carrion knave Robardi. He was humble enough then, a barber and drawer of teeth. He carried all the teeth he had ever extracted on a string around his neck. The other officers are gone now—but Robardi remains. He is a man of some importance, young sirs, the seneschal of the ducal household."

The black-a-vised man made a gesture in their direction and called out something in a tongue unknown to the Englishmen.

"It is for me," said the priest.

He joined the seneschal and for several moments the pair talked in their native tongue. Robardi spoke in loud tones and gestured emphatically, keeping his eyes for the most part on the silent travelers. Father Pasquitien returned then and gave them a worried nod.

"Word of our coming has preceded us," he reported. "Robardi says you are spies and must be treated accordingly. At any rate, you are to be questioned. Young men, I beseech you to be careful in what you say. Weigh your words well and—and tell them as little as possible."

"Is this black spider to do the questioning, Sir Priest?" asked Tostig.

Father Pasquitien shook his head. "No, my sons. You are to go before the cardinal himself. I am to conduct you there."

As they passed through the guards massed at the end of the drawbridge, the two Englishmen were more conscious than ever of the antagonism of the people of Brittany. The soldiers glared at them and exchanged sullen remarks in undertones. They were like chained dogs, ready to spring if the leash were slipped.

"We are walking into a trap," declared Tostig. "I would enjoy getting the throat of this barber into my two hands. He would spit out all of his own teeth before I was through with him."

It was in the late afternoon and the sun was still in its friendliest mood. By way of contrast, the churchman who received them in a small room opening on the inner court was not friendly at all. This was the Cardinal Pourtran of whom the marshal had spoken in words of warning. He was as bald as a cube of ivory and so the name by which he was known, the Red Cardinal, could be ascribed to the glowing and well-tended beard which covered much of his chest and, perhaps, to the smoldering brown of his continuously active eyes.

"What brings you to Brittany, Sir Knight?" he asked in a grating voice.

"I am English——" began Richard.

"That," declared the cardinal, "is a point which need not be explained. There is something unmistakable about the faces of you insatiable islanders. Also, I think I know something of you, young Sir Richard. You ride in the train of the Earl of Pembroke, marshal of England. Is it not so?"

"Yes, Your Eminence. I have been fortunate in the lists and I am venturing out in the hope of finding opportunities to splinter lances with some of your knights here in the West."

"You choose a strange time for this jaunt," declared the churchman, who sat in an oversized chair, with his bare feet stretched out over a stool to get the benefit of the breeze. He turned his head abruptly and stared at Richard over his shoulder. "Is it possible that your splendid old marshal, who can be admired for his prowess at the same time that his slowness of wit is to be deplored, has assumed the role of Joshua, son of Nun?"

"I do not understand, Your Eminence."

The cardinal indulged in some incoherent grumbling as he dropped his splayed feet to the stone floor. He took a sip of wine from a flagon at his side and rubbed the moisture from his lips with the end of his stole.

"Do the young men of this degraded age have no knowledge of the Scriptures?" he demanded. "Good St. Cyril and all the martyrs, deliver me from these barbarians who are concerned only with violence and bloodshed! I see, Sir Knight, that I must inform you of my meaning. Joshua, the great leader who took the children of Israel across the Jordan, sent men in advance to spy out the land. Is my meaning clear now?"

Richard responded in heated tones. "I have taken the vows of knighthood, Sir Cardinal. Do you think I would descend to such baseness as spying?"

The churchman shrugged his shoulders. "It is well known," he said, "that the men of England have no scruples." He indulged in more grumbling and then suddenly pointed a finger at Richard. "The Devil is loose in France! Get yourself back over the border before we hang you and your whole party! I give you this advice in all honesty and in the hope you will have the good sense to act upon it."

There was a light knock on the door and a young girl was admitted whose very great attractiveness caused Richard to think she might be the Princess Eleanor. A second glance, however, convinced him that this could not be the case. Her hair, under a wimple of coarse white linen, was of the brownness of honey instead of the vivid gold which Father Pasquitien had described. He noticed also that her tunic was of homespun and that her bare feet were in sandals bound with woolen straps. She spoke to the cardinal in the native tongue and he answered her sharply.

It was clear during the conversation which followed that the cardinal did not approve of the message she brought, for he shook his head emphatically and addressed her in brusque tones. Finally he gestured resignedly and turned to Richard.

"Sir Knight," he said, "it seems that our princess, who generally displays more good sense, has a desire to speak with you. She will receive you, briefly, before you start on your way back."

"It will be a great honor," declared Richard. "But I beg to point out, Your Eminence, that I have not stated my intention of accepting your advice."

"But you will," was the prompt response. "You have your choice. An immediate departure or the dance of the chats for you and your whole party. And," he added with sudden vehemence, "see to it that your men do not stick their stinking Norman snouts into matters which do not concern them! Tell them to ask no questions and to keep their eyes on the ground. A single false step on the part of any one of them and you will all pay the penalty for it."

3

The girl dropped each of them a curtsy and then indicated that they were to follow her. Her footsteps, even in the wooden sandals, made scarcely a sound on the stone floor as she led the way from the room.

Expecting to find Tostig deeply concerned over the difficulties of their position, Richard was surprised to see the eyes of his squire studying the trim lines of their guide. "She is graceful," whispered Tostig. "This girl's eyes are not only lovely but they are filled with a great sweetness. It's clear she is a servant but there is a fineness about her which I do not understand."

"She is probably the confidential servant of the Princess Eleanor. They always have one."

Tostig sighed. "How lightly she walks! Her hands are not the hands of a servant."

They crossed a U-shaped courtyard from which the crowded tents of the encamped forces could be seen. Beyond this was a dirt road which curved away in the general direction of Dol. A heavy cloud of dust obscured this road at the point of the horizon.

"More troops coming," said Richard in a low tone, realizing the danger of such comments. "Horsemen. A goodly company by the looks of things."

Tostig sighed again. "There is not a trace of the servant in her voice."

The room where the princess received the knight was long and airy, opening on a garden where spring flowers blossomed in great profusion. Over the stone wall, which enclosed the garden, the colors of France and Brittany waved with what seemed an air of arrogance. In this respect they matched the mood of the royal lady who had summoned him to appear.

She was seated in the midst of a group of her ladies, all of them young and of apparent vivacity. They served no purpose so well, however, as to enhance her beauty by contrast. Father Pasquitien had given a valid report of her; the Pearl of Brittany was of exceeding fairness.

She gave Richard the benefit of a long and thorough look, but did not extend her hand to be kissed. Then she turned to the lady who sat on her right. "He comes from the island of England, Marguerite," she said. "Does it seem to you that he bears a fair imprint of the races from which he springs?"

The girl had not expected to be questioned. She flushed self-consciously and stammered in answering. "I know not, my lady. I have given no thought to it."

"It is a cold and foggy land," declared the princess, transferring her gaze back to Richard. "It is perhaps because they have to struggle for a mere existence that the people are so cold and treacherous." She selected another of her attendants. "You, Guillaumette. Does it seem to you that he is of a knightly appearance?"

The girl Guillaumette was more self-possessed than the first one had been. She answered promptly. "He is indeed, my lady."

The response surprised the princess. "Do you really think so, Guillaumette? I am surprised. Now tell me this: does it not seem to you that the hint of baseness in him, which is very easy to detect, tends to destroy whatever pretentions he may have to comeliness?"

"No, my lady." Guillaumette gave Richard a quick glance before lowering her eyes. It was as though she had said, "I have my own opinions, Sir Knight, and I will insist on liking you no matter what she may say."

Richard had not moved his position while this brief discussion was carried on. The resentment he felt caused him to stand even straighter and to hold his head high. His cheeks were flushed. He took his eyes away from the angry princess and studied instead the peaked tents and the massed pennons showing above the top of the wall.

In spite of the feelings she had aroused in him, he realized that her attitude was a natural one. She could not be expected to forgive the country which had passed over the rightful claims of her brother or the people who acquiesced in the injustice.

"If your curiosity is satisfied, my lady," he said after a moment of silence, "I beg your permission to withdraw."

"I have other things to say." She gestured imperiously. "The men of that distant island must be very tall, Sir Knight, if you are a fair sample of them."

"I am above the usual height, my lady."

There was another moment of silence which gave Richard a chance to study her more carefully. How haughty and regal she was, but how wonderful the beauty with which she had been blessed! The priest had called her golden-crested but this seemed now a dull measure of praise for one whose fairness seemed to rival the sun. She had the Plantagenet eye, that blazing blue which could flash with temperament as readily as melt into disarming tenderness. It had now, alas, no hint of the latter quality.

If there had been time he would have been impressed, without a doubt, by the contrast between her rich apparel and the drabness of the room. The furniture consisted of a few benches, very stiff and hard, and some chairs equally uninviting. The stone floors were bare, the walls were cracked and damp. The chimney seemingly had no capacity to carry away smoke and the ceiling was black with the fires of a generation. In such surroundings the Princess Eleanor seemed like a gorgeously plumed bird in a dismal cage. Her gown was of velvet, a scintillating green, most elaborately embroidered with thread of gold. A collar of miniver was turned down in a deep V to display the pure white delicacy of her neck. A girdle sparkling with jewels encircled her waist. Her shoes were sharply pointed and of a rich yellow velvet.

"Your reputation has preceded you, Sir Knight," she said. "You perform well in the lists. But it must be that your success has gone to your head because we are told you have come to match your skill against the best knights of our country. Is this not a case of overweening pride in one so young?"

"I am prompted by a desire to learn, my lady. Such skill as I have was acquired under the training of the marshal of England. My purpose in venturing out now is to add to it by pitting myself against better men than myself."

"You have a quick tongue. This surprises me because I have been told that the men of that gloomy island are slow of wit and clumsy of words."

"Your Highness seems to think very poorly of us indeed."

Her temper, which had been held on a loose rein, flared at this. "Can you and your countrymen be held in respect when you refuse to acknowledge the just claim of the Prince Arthur to the throne of England? It has always been said that your marshal is a man of the highest honor. Why then did he take the side of the traitor John?"

"The decision was made for him, my lady. By the late king, who had declared his desire to be followed by his brother."

"It was done in a moment of resentment because King Richard and my gracious mother did not agree about the training of my brother. Can a kingly whim override the acknowledged law of succession?"

Throughout this brief passage of words, the Pearl of Brittany had remained in a taut posture and there were patches of color in each cheek. At this point, however, she seemed to feel that she had gone far enough in making a visitor the butt of her resentment. She dismissed the question of the succession and began to ask personal questions.

"From what line do you stem, Sir Knight?"

"I come in direct descent," he answered proudly, "from the line of Sigurd of Rawen. Until the division of land after the Norman invasion, we were holders of extensive estates west of Windsor. My mother was of Norman birth. Her husband, before she married my father, was the Earl of Baudene."

"Oh! I have heard about *that*. You are the disinherited son. You are indeed a champion in the lists. Have you also a voice for song?"

"I have nothing of the minstrel in me, my lady. Such voice as I have is suited only to battle songs."

The delicate arch of her very lovely nose seemed to twitch with distaste. "It sounds most barbarous." She studied him with what seemed a degree of increasing disfavor, noting the plainness of his tunic and the lack of adornment on his hose (even though his long legs filled them with elegance) and his low shoes of fretted felt. "Our good cardinal, who is usually a man of the quickest decision, cannot decide about you. He does not know whether you should be sent out of the country, with a strong enough guard to make sure that you recross the border, or whether it would be better to hang you as a spy at once."

"He mentioned both possibilities, my lady."

"I confess I find it hard to believe that one who has taken the vows of knighthood could descend so low as to act as a spy."

"I appreciate your lack of conviction on that point. Allow me to assure you that I had no such purpose in coming to Brittany. I no longer belong to the household of the marshal of England. I am going out into the world, to make my fortune or to die in knightly adventurings. When I leave here I hope to go to Rome."

"This is most enlightening, Sir Knight. I may now make a suggestion which occurred to me as soon as I heard of your rash desire to face some of our knights in the lists. That wish can be gratified if you defy the worthy cardinal and stay for another day. You have heard, no doubt, of the Captal de Cham?"

Richard had heard a great deal about the Captal de Cham. He was a knight of Poitevin stock who had won such a resounding reputation in the lists that he had become a popular idol with the people. Because of his enormous size and the deadliness of his tactics in competition he was called the Sire Tohu-Bohu, which could be construed rather freely to mean pandemonium, terror, death and destruction and fire from the clouds, severed limbs and broken equipment and bloodstained hauberks on the turf. The Captal rode an enormous black stallion, the largest no doubt since the ancient Eohippus had been transformed into a horse.

"Yes, my lady. I have heard much of the Sire Tohu-Bohu."

"He happens to be in attendance here. If you still have any appetite for a test, it could be arranged for you to run a course with him tomorrow."

It had never occurred to Richard that he might be called upon to face the Captal de Cham. Because of his great size, the latter was not included when men spoke of the relative merits of the knights of the day. He was considered a cast-back to the time of the paladins of Charlemagne when men fought like gods.

Despite the dismay he could not help feeling, Richard bowed and answered, "It shall be as my lady wishes."

The Pearl of Brittany studied him for a moment with raised eyebrows. Had she expected him to decline? Richard had been keeping his gaze elsewhere but, when she made no immediate response, he looked directly at her. Their eyes met, and held. It was as though she were seeing him for the first time. He could tell that she was experiencing a change of sentiment toward him. The antagonism was gone and in its place he was sure he detected respect and approbation. There was, even, a hint of something deeper, a personal liking; and the possibility that this was true caused him to feel sudden exultation.

"Are you quite sure, Sir Knight," she asked finally, "that you want to meet the Captal de Cham in the lists?"

"I am quite sure, my lady."

There was a pause. She seemed reluctant to have the matter settled. "Then," she said, "the arrangements will be made at once. You have our permission to withdraw."

Richard left the room in a state of conflicting emotion. Uppermost was a feeling of resignation which might be compared to the sensation a prisoner of noble blood experienced when he had been convicted and was led from court with the edge of the ax turned toward him. Tostig was standing in the hall in the company of the maid of the princess.

"We are staying for another day."

The maid gave Richard a startled bow. "Then I shall show you to your room, my lord," she said.

"Is it wise?" asked Tostig in a whisper, as they followed her down the hall. "Have you forgotten what the cardinal said?"

"I am quite sure it is not wise," answered Richard. "But we remain nevertheless. I am to fight in the lists tomorrow. With the Captal de Cham."

"Master Rick!" Tostig's voice was an indication of the consternation he felt at this prospect. "The Captal! He's not a man, he's a monster, a creature from the Pit! No one can face him. This—this is utter folly!"

"A folly from which there is no retreat."

Tostig stopped still and regarded Richard with unhappy intentness. "There must be a way. Has not the cardinal ordered us to leave the country at once on pain of death? Could we have a better excuse for leaving?"

"His decision has been overruled. We have the permission of the Princess Eleanor to remain another day. If I drew back on any such pretext, I should never again dare show my face in knightly company."

"By St. Willibrod!" exclaimed the squire. "This is a serious pass to which you have brought yourself. I tell you, Master Rick, the man has the strength of a fiend. He has never been unhorsed——"

"He never faced the marshal of England."

"That is true. But the marshal had a strength granted to few men. It would have been a meeting of giants had they ever met in the lists. It may be that in time you will be of the same caliber but you haven't reached your full strength yet. Are you aware that many of the knights who have faced the Captal have not lived to tell the tale?"

"It is a risk I must take."

It developed that one concession was being made to Richard's rank and reputation: it would not be necessary for him to sleep on the rushes in the Great Hall with all the other visitors. There may have been another reason: that he must be kept from seeing or hearing too much of the preparations for war which seemed to fill all of Brittany. At any rate, he and his squire were escorted to a room they would share together, a tiny cubicle below the level of the ground. It lacked a single stick of furnishing, and a narrow slit near the ceiling, through which the water from the moat washed at every disturbance of the surface, provided the only relief from darkness. The floor was covered with rushes of such age and moldiness that the room stank of disintegration. Tostig proceeded to take the rushes together into two piles which would serve them later for couches, and in doing so disturbed a whole family of toads. These he tossed out into the moat through the slit in the wall.

"Giselle heard some of what was being said," declared the squire as he performed this task. "She said the princess was in an angry mood."

"Her name is Giselle? Do you realize that she bears a resemblance to her mistress? I was aware of it as soon as I entered the room. In the face of the reproaches heaped upon me, it slipped from my mind."

"It is natural that there should be a resemblance," declared the squire. "They are sisters."

"Sisters! Are you sure?"

Tostig nodded. "I caught a glimpse of the princess when you were shown through the door. I saw then how much alike they were. I asked Giselle about it. At first she shook her head and said nothing. But I persisted and finally she gave in. Prince Geoffrey was a handsome man and he seems to have had a way with women."

"A failing that most princes have."

"Her mother was a domestic in the household of a goldsmith in Rennes. She died when Giselle was young but the girl was kept on as a sort of drudge. The two sisters saw each other for the first time when Eleanor was riding through Rennes with a large party and Giselle ran out to the street to watch her pass. The poor child was dirty and almost in rags but the princess reined in her horse at once and said to her attendants: 'There can be no doubt about it this time. Here is another of them.' She seems to have taken a fancy to the child and, when her mother the duchess died, she had her brought to the palace."

"Are they still fond of one another?"

"Giselle worships the ground on which the princess walks. She enjoys many privileges. From the few hints she gave me, I concluded that she has the confidence of her sister."

Richard smiled at his squire. "Never have I known you to take such an interest in a woman. Can it be that the stern and practical Tostig is no different from other men after all?"

The gravity of Tostig's face did not lessen. He nodded soberly. "This is the woman for me," he said. "None other would ever suit me."

"You don't often come to a decision as quickly as this. It's barely an hour since you first set eyes on her."

The squire answered in an almost rapt tone. "I did not need as much as an hour, Master Rick. She is so sweet, so wholesome, so pleasing to the eye. She won me at the first glance. While you talked with the mistress, I made good use of the time. I pressed her with questions. She was reluctant to answer many of them, being of a becoming modesty. But I had a thirst to know everything about her and I would not be denied."

"It is unfortunate," said Richard, "that Englishmen are in such bad odor here. I'm much afraid the fair Giselle will not look with favor on your suit. If it's your intention to go to such an extreme length as offering to marry her."

The squire's face took on an even greater suggestion of gravity. "Such is indeed my intention," he declared.

4

Sounds of revelry reached the ears of the English visitors that evening from the direction of the Great Hall but they were not permitted to participate. Instead, servants brought in dishes of the roughest earthenware and flagons of wine, which they placed on the damp and sour stones between the two mounds of rushes.

"They are taking every precaution," said Richard. "In case we *are* spies."

He was disappointed, for he had hoped to see the beautiful princess again when the company sat down to dine. The food brought them, however, was both ample and satisfying. Richard recognized all of the dishes, for they had sometimes appeared on the bountiful table set for William the Marshal. There was a dish of *bouilli*, steaming hot in spite of the distance it had been carried from the kitchens. There was also

La Bardette, a cabbage stuffed with larded hare, quail, and mashed chestnuts. This was a famous Breton dish. It would generally be carried in to the sound of pipes and with cooks and jesters capering and prancing in front of it. There was also a fish from Lower Brittany and, finally, a monstrously sweet concoction of wine and honey and saunders, cooked with figs in a batter of flour and cut into crisp leechings.

The two men had small appetite for such satisfying fare. They sat on either side of the dishes and picked lightly at the food.

"Father Pasquitien was right," said Richard, who had fallen into a thoughtful mood. "The rules are indeed different. To look into eyes as lovely and proud as those of the Pearl of Brittany is more dangerous than the thrust of a lance. Every word she said to me expressed scorn and yet—and yet——"

"Like master, like man," said Tostig.

"Did your fair Giselle tell you much about herself?"

"She was very guarded at first but before we were through she was chattering like a magpie. Such a lovely magpie! Her great fear is that she will be forced into a marriage. There was an old man in Rennes, a notary with very considerable property. He had won the ear of the Baronne Verduse, who is the head of the household—where the girls have coined a name for her, Madame Attifeuse—by the offer of a handsome present. But the princess saw that Giselle was against the idea and she said no, a much better match must be arranged. There is now another suitor. He is even more persistent than the elderly notary. It is this carrion knave, the seneschal."

"The man Robardi?"

Tostig nodded grimly. "The fellow pretends to be much in love with her. He stares at her with his evil eyes and follows her about. The poor child is helpless to do anything about it, particularly as the princess has not yet declared herself." An angry flush mounted on the squire's cheeks. "What I think of Master Robardi is this: I think he is a spy of King John of England."

Richard considered this possibility. "I believe you may be right. It's said the king pays well for information and that he has his spies everywhere. This ex-barber might be one of them." He nibbled at a crisp stick of the batter pudding. "You seem like to suffer a great disappointment, Tostig, for I can see no way in which you may advance your suit."

"And what of yours, Master Rick?"

"Mine?" Richard indulged in a laugh which was intended to show lack of concern, even scorn. "I grant you that the princess is hard to resist. Every glance she gave me was like a sword thrust, and yet my admiration continued to mount. But it will never go beyond that."

The squire was not easily taken in. "God grant, Master Rick, that you have the sense to resist her charms. There will be trouble and unhappiness for you if you don't." He paused. "I had no more than a brief glimpse at her through the door. Is the resemblance between the sisters so marked?"

Richard nodded thoughtfully. "The princess has golden hair, which makes a great difference. In point of features they are much alike. They have the same nose and the same line of brow. There is, more particularly, a matter of expression, a tendency to widen the eyes in smiling; which, no doubt, they got from their Plantagenet father. Dress your Giselle up in silks and furs and put a golden wig on her head. Then it would be hard to tell them apart."

The conversation dwindled at that point and finally ceased. The shadow of the Sire Tohu-Bohu settled over them and they thought of the dire things which might happen the next day. Finally Tostig bestirred himself and rose.

"I must have a look at this great bogeyman," he said. "How can you hope to hold your own unless you have an accurate measure of him? You must know how to direct the aim of your lance. I must see what bits of information may be picked up. There will be much talk about the match among the servants."

Richard protested. "It's against the cardinal's orders. If you are caught asking questions, we shall all hang. I would rather not come to my end in any such sorry mess."

"The risk must be taken. It's my duty as your squire to bring you such information as I can. Who knows, this great Goliath may have certain weaknesses. If he has, it will be talked about where the squires sit down to meat. Yes, Master Rick, it must be chanced."

5

The first flush of dawn was in the sky when Richard wakened. He had the room to himself save for a rustling in the rushes.

Richard stirred uneasily, fearing that the absence of his squire meant trouble. Something slithered by on the slimy floor and he hastily drew his feet up under him and crouched against the wall, having no liking for this kind of visitor. Further reflection brought some reassurance. If

Tostig's activities had been detected, he himself would have been involved in the consequences by this time.

His mind resumed the train of reflection which had filled it during his last waking moments. He repeated every scornful word spoken by the Princess Eleanor. He carried a perfect picture of her in his mind, the proud tilt of her golden head, the coldness of the eye she had fixed upon him (in which, nonetheless, there was a hint of tenderness, although not for him, alas), the delicate modeling of her nose which no goldsmith could ever hope to equal, the ivory perfection of her hands.

The instinct of the poet, which was latent in all men of Saxon blood, wakened in him. "My great and lovely lady," he said aloud, "you are the most contradictory of all human beings but the more desirable for that. You are like the red gold of dawn and the burning sunshine of midday but also you are the quiet blue of dusk and the silver path that the moon makes in the silence of the woods. You can be like the storm which comes out of an angry sky but to those you deign to favor you are the rainbow which marks its end. Your loveliness is beyond description or comparison or even comprehension." He paused at that and grinned guiltily in the darkness. "Truly my head is full of flummery. I know I shall never see this beautiful lady again, this angry demoiselle who has such contempt for me."

There was a cautious step in the stone hall and Tostig entered the room. He carried a lighted torch which he fixed in an iron ring on the wall. Then he turned and regarded Richard with a somber eye.

"Time to be up," he said.

It was like the old days when he had been such a severe taskmaster. Richard stretched his long legs and ran a hand through his tousled hair. "Have you been out all night?" he asked.

"I drank with the last of them in the guardroom. Then I came back and had a few hours' sleep. It was just as well I came, for a black water snake was curled up at your feet. An hour ago, I went out again."

"Have you anything to tell me?"

A grim intentness settled over the squire's face. "I saw your opponent last night. He sat beside the cardinal and he made the churchman look like a sly little red squirrel. The fellow is a full half foot taller than you and he has a face like an angry, grinning owl. They tell me his horse is an enormous black."

"What were they saying in the guardroom?"

"You should have heard how they laughed last night, thinking what their man would do to you. Such cackling and blowing off and slapping of thighs! I took one of them outside, a hulking codshead, and I rolled him in a muck heap!"

"They are all certain he'll win?"

"Huh! The slutching fools are sure you'll be spitted like a gamecock and carried off the field in pieces." He came to a halt beside the pile of rushes and stared at his master; for although a free man he still thought no other term proper. "There's one chance, Master Richard. If you try for his shield, you'll think you have come dead on against an iron mountain on hoofs. You must aim for the visor. I sat for hours, listening to the jabber of these country fools, and I found out one thing. No one has ever tried for the visor because he sits so high above them. He'll be taken by surprise. You must contrive to hit him high and hard."

"One chance only in ten that I could do it," declared Richard, getting to his feet and buckling on his sword belt. "It would be like aiming at the moon."

"I tell you it's the only way," said the squire earnestly. "He's as slow-witted as a bull. If you seem to be aiming for his shield and don't swing your lance upward until the last moment, he'll be taken so much by surprise that you may scoop him right out of his saddle."

"I must win! I must!" declared Richard passionately. "She must keep that much memory of me at least!"

"Yes, you must win. And a little practice before anyone rubs the sleep out of his eyes will be useful. There's a quintain behind the seats. I'll raise it to allow for the extra height in the saddle. The spot to strike is where the visor is attached to the helm. If you get him there, he'll take the impact of it on his forehead. It will unsettle his wits if it does nothing else—and he'll go into the second running with his head in a whirl."

Tostig was talking in this vein to strengthen the young knight's confidence. Both of them knew that the giant would come down the course like a black wind trussed in steel, like the high waves of an angry sea. Only by the greatest skill could such sheer brute strength be met and sustained.

"Fetch Messire out," said Richard, "and I'll practice at the quintain. I'm sure you are right. This is my only chance."

Tostig returned Messire to his stall and then joined Richard in the room under the moat. The latter was still sweating from his efforts in the practice field and his spirits had lifted perceptibly. They stood still for a moment and smiled at each other.

"Ten drives at the quintain," said Tostig. "Nine times you hit the spot I had marked, fairly and squarely. The other time you were two inches high. Beware those two inches, Master Rick. They might cause your lance point to slip off the rounded surface of the helm."

There was a knock on the door and Richard's "Come!" brought the maid Giselle into the room. She hesitated on the threshold and looked at them cautiously, first at one and then the other.

"Good Sir Knight," she said, addressing Richard in a tone little above a whisper, "there is something you should know."

"You have risen early to tell me."

"No, my lord. We rise with the dawn. My mistress stirred as soon as I did and her ladies came in to sit on her bed and drink their morning posset together. It is always the pleasantest time of day for them. They are not yet trussed up so tightly and their feet are free. They sit about and gossip and it is very nice. I am permitted to sit in the room and listen. So I heard everything that was said."

"I am sure," declared Tostig, "that they were saying the same things that I heard in the guardroom last night. That Sir Richard of Rawen will have no chance against their great Captal."

The girl looked at him with deep concern in her eyes. "You should not have been there!" she exclaimed. "Oh, messire, I trust you asked no questions. It is said the cardinal will have you all hanged if you are inquisitive."

Tostig's face flushed with gratification at this proof of her concern for him. "I learned first that none of the guards have any reason for loving the cardinal. There will be no tale-telling for his benefit."

"Messire, I trust not! It would be a very sad thing if any of you came to harm."

"But," interrupted Richard, "have you been wise in coming to see us here? What would the Red Cardinal think about it?"

Giselle stole one glance at him and then lowered her eyes. "It does not matter. All that matters is for you to know what was said. Guillaumette, who always spits out whatever comes into her head, was the first to speak of it. She said what a pity it would be if such a fair and graceful knight came to grievous hurt because of being matched against one so heavy and strong. All the others agreed with her and there was much shaking of heads. My mistress said it was a matter of no consequence. 'He is only an Englishman,' she said. 'But such a handsome one!' cried Guillaumette. 'It will be one less to stand in the way of their rightful lord and king,' declared my mistress. But, my lord, I knew she did not mean it. I always know what she is thinking. I said to her, 'Dear lady, your head is beginning to ache. You are going to have one of your spells.' 'I am afraid so, my child.' 'I must darken the room,' I said. 'You must not say another word. I will get the hot bandages at once.' So all her ladies left and I came right here to tell you."

"But how does this concern me?" asked Richard, frowning.

"My lord, my sweet mistress has no headache. That she was willing to pretend was because she wants to give you a chance to escape this dreadful jousting. You see, my lord, the tilting would have to be postponed if the Princess Eleanor could not be there. Word would then be sent to the cardinal that she thought it unwise for you to remain longer in the country and he would send you on your way. Not a word was said between us but my mistress knows I am here and she is hoping that you will be sensible and go."

"My honor is at stake," declared Richard.

"Oh, good Sir Knight, there would be no dishonor!"

"What will your mistress do if I am not sensible?"

"She will fall into a rage. She will say to me: 'Take these bandages away and open the curtains! Bring all those chattering trollops back so I can speak to them.' When her ladies come, her eyes will be full of fire and she will say to them: 'My head no longer aches, which is good because now I shall be able to watch our splendid Captal split this presumptuous Englishman like a larded cock!' "

"You make a good advocate, my girl, but I have no intention of forcing the princess to remain a prisoner for as much as an hour to save me from a compact into which I entered of my own accord. Convey my thanks to your mistress for her kind intent but assure her that nothing can prevent me from breaking a lance with the mighty Captal as arranged."

"But, Sir Knight!" The girl's eyes had opened wide with compassion and fear. "He is a giant, an ogre! He can break a lance in his two hands. And they do say he has made a bargain with the Devil! No man can stand before him. He will kill you!"

Since tilting at the quintain, Richard was feeling somewhat easier in his mind. "When in his prime, my liege lord, the marshal of England, could have broken your mighty Captal in two as easily as *he* can break a lance."

"Your champion is large and strong," added Tostig. "But there is still, by Our Lady, the matter of skill to be considered."

When the girl had left, reluctantly because she had failed in her purpose, Richard said to his squire, "Your little Giselle will make you a fine wife."

"Neither one of us," declared the somber squire, "will live to see another day!"

Chapter VII

1

T HE NINE shrewd blows he had directed at the quintain, the skill he had learned from the great English marshal, the suppleness of youth—these were points in his favor, as Richard knew well. But he knew also, even before he saw the great Captal de Cham appear in front of the red silk pavilion which had been pitched for him at the other end of the lists, that all the advantages he could claim might not be enough. Weight and strength count mightily in the sport of chivalry, and there was a legend of invincibility behind the dread Sire Tohu-Bohu which would add assurance to his lance and security to his saddle. The Princess Eleanor had been right on one count: he, Richard of Rawen, had shown presumption in declaring his desire to splinter lances with the champion of the west. He needed the additional strength of arm and weight of bone which a few more years would bring him.

Tostig was adjusting the metal chausses on his thighs. It was not necessary to wear poleyns over the kneecap in tournament play but after a moment's pause the cautious squire laced them on. "Why take unnecessary risks?" he asked. "This great codshead of a Poitevin is as clumsy as a bear; he might miss the shield and strike the knee, and it would be a sad thing to be lamed for life because of a moment's lack of care.

"Master Rick," said Tostig, transferring his attention to the shoulders and attaching ailettes carved with the Pembroke lion. "The people out there are in an ugly mood. They will be calling for blood. To them you represent the traitor John and the barons of England who have robbed their prince of his rights. They won't be satisfied to see you unhorsed. Nothing will suit them so well as to see this great Blunderbore kill you or injure you so you'll never ride again."

Richard walked to the entrance of his pavilion, which was smaller and not nearly as richly decorated as that of the giant, although it carried a red lion standing on one paw. He raised the flap over the entrance. The sun by this time was so directly overhead that it seemed to be watching what went on in this small space of ground enclosed by wooden palisades to the exclusion of the rest of the world. There was not a cloud in the sky and the air was so still that the pennons flying above the pavilions and at intervals along the barricades were as limp as the tails of sick hounds. Rooks had congregated in colonies in the nearby trees and were keeping up a monotonous cawing, in curiosity or protest according to the mental attitude of the individual spectators. Jugglers and tumblers, vying for attention on the outskirts of the crowd, were having small success.

Richard's eyes took in the noisy mobs pressing against the palisades and he shook his head. "I had no idea there would be so many of them," he said.

"The roads from Rennes and from Dol in the north have been black with them since dawn. Noblemen with long trains of retainers and great ladies in their curtained litters, and the common rabble trudging on shanks' mare. They're all out there now—gentlemen and priests and men-at-arms, thieves and cutpurses and peddlers with their wares. Not half of them will be able to see what goes on. But if there's a riot afterward, they'll be having a hand in it." Tostig had joined the young knight at the entrance and was staring out from the other side of the flap. "If you tumble him out of his saddle and the crowds break through the palisades—as they may—get your sword out quickly. Keep it in your left hand and the lance in your right, and use them both right briskly. If we must sell our lives, let's exact a high price in sluggish Breton blood!"

Richard's gaze was now turned to the raised seats reserved for the spectators of high degree. They were already well filled. The ladies in their gorgeous tunics, and with jeweled barbettes in their hair, and the men in cloaks with heraldic devices on breast and arm and brimmed hats with long dyed plumes, made a brilliant combination. Only a space in the exact center was still unoccupied.

"The princess is late in arriving," he said to himself. "We will know when she comes by the stir it will make. How they will wave their hats in the air and cheer for her!"

"The little Giselle will not be here," said Tostig. "She hadn't the heart for it, fearing the outcome as she does."

"How do you know that?"

"I saw her," explained the squire, with a not too successful attempt at casualness. "As I led Messire out from his stall, she was passing with a bundle in her arms. A most fortunate chance, I thought it. I had a few words with her."

There was a sound from all parts of the field and hats were waving everywhere. The empty space had been filled. The princess, Richard saw, was gowned in blue with ermine at her throat and wrists.

"We shall conquer or die," he said, "with the loveliest eyes in the world watching us."

He parted the silken curtains and stepped out into the open. Tostig followed, carrying his lance.

Richard walked to Messire, who was pawing nervously at the sod, and laid an affectionate hand on his mane. "My brave Messire," he said. "This will be a test for both of us, my old friend. We may not come through it alive, either of us, but of this I am sure: you will have no fear of the black stallion we must ride against. There will be no standing on ceremony this time, no refusing to run against an ill-trained charger."

Messire raised his head and shook it as though in answer. He pawed at the ground still more vigorously and snorted in defiance.

"That is the spirit!" said Richard. "If we lose, it will not be your fault."

The voice of the herald could be heard, proclaiming the nature of the event.

"To horse!" said Tostig in a restrained voice.

"The time has come, Messire!" said Richard, giving the glossy mane a final affectionate tug.

When he had helped Richard into the saddle, the squire busied himself with adjusting the gear of the restless horse. "Remember what I said, Master Rick," he whispered. "Those two inches. Be not too high. Smite him squarely on the forehead."

"Yes," the knight whispered back. "May God and all the saints direct my eye!"

In accordance with usual custom, Richard as the challenger rode directly down the field and struck the shield of the Captal de Cham, which was hanging over the front of his pavilion. It was unusually large and kite-shaped, as black as night, and bore the moline cross because the Captal had been an eighth son and was therefore devoid of inherited land. Richard smote it vigorously with the steel point of his lance and it rang out as loudly as a church bell and seemed likely to slip its attachments and fall to the ground.

"A outrance! A outrance!" cried the crowd, delighted that it was to be a duel with naked lances and not one with blunted tips.

Richard then began the customary progress around the field with his lance held high in the air. With his other hand he touched the neck of his proud charger. "Head up, my old rampager!" he said. "Tail high, and give it a good swish. Remember this, that the eyes of a proud, scornful, beautiful lady are on us."

Messire responded by tossing his head and beginning to caracole as he followed the oval line of the enclosure. When they passed the raised seats, Richard lifted his lance still higher in the air as a salute to the princess and her ladies. He was rewarded by a barely polite spatter of applause from those around her which was drowned out by the massed crowds behind the palisades, who hooted and hissed and bellowed their unfriendliness.

2

As soon as Richard had reached his station, he saw that his opponent was already in position at the opposite end of the lists. He caught his breath in surprise. All that he had heard of the size and might of the great Sire Tohu-Bohu had not prepared him for the actual stature of the man. The Captal's black charger was enormous enough to seem like a creature straight from the least probable pages of mythology but it appeared barely capable of sustaining the weight of its rider. On what anvil in Valhalla, asked Richard of himself, had such a breastplate been fashioned, such a gorget and vambrace been hammered out, such taces and greaves and sollerets? The knight with whom he was to compete in the grimmest of all the grim games that a rough age had been capable of conceiving seemed as little human as the ogres he had believed in as a boy. He took his eyes away from the motionless partner of Death at the far end of the courses and gave a glance up at the sky.

"God and the King's Son of Heaven and Our Merciful Lady can't mean me to die," he thought. "Not on such a perfect day!"

Standing beside him, the grim-lipped Tostig repeated his word of warning. "Remember that narrow margin of space. Be wrong by as much as two inches and you will fail. Clip this bogeyman under the helm, Master Rick."

There was a flourish of trumpets and the Princess Eleanor raised a baton of gold above her head. The chargers at each end of the lists sprang into action. No holding back this time on the part of the eager Messire. He knew this was war and he plunged forward with a burst of

speed which carried him beyond the halfway line. The Captal on his
black steed came on at a less precipitous gait but this did not detract
from the aura of menace which rode with him.

It was a matter of seconds only until they met but Richard had time
to think of many things. It had been an easy enough matter to clip
the quintain time after time on the exact spot marked by Tostig but
now he was not charging a dented shield hanging loosely on a wooden
post. His mark was the most dreaded knight in all France and behind
the visor, which he must strike, was a face as fiercely hostile as a
hunting owl's. He could see little but the distended and fiery eyes of
the black stallion and the point of a lance stretched out to bear him
to the ground.

Richard kept his lance low and it was not until the tossing manes of
the horses seemed to mingle that he guided the point upward and struck
the visor of his antagonist.

He knew at once that he had found the exact spot. The point did
not slip away from its mark and the impact could be felt all through
his body, while the lance splintered in his hand. At the same instant
he experienced a sensation as though the earth and the mountains
thereof and the sun and the stars had all fallen upon him. The lance
of the Poitevin struck his shield with such force that he was crushed
back against the rear of his saddle. Even in this moment of chaos, when
earth and sky split wide open, his hand did not loosen on the reins.
Messire, checked in his top stride, reared up on his hind legs, pawing
frantically at the air and screaming in the excitement of conflict. Could
any human or equine sustain such a shock without collapsing backward
on the green turf? Could even so skilled a hand as Tostig's have tight-
ened a girth to hold under such a strain?

In the fraction of a second Richard's mind cleared and he found
himself clutching the side of a precipice formed by the upright back of
his splendid steed. He realized that he had not been hurled from his saddle by the hammer blow on his shield. It was equally to be marveled at
that Messire had kept his balance.

His opponent had not been as fortunate. The unexpectedness of the
blow on his visor had bent the Captal so far back that no saddle
devised by the shrewdest armorer could have kept him in his seat. He
was floundering on the turf, his feet higher than his head, his splintered
lance still grasped in his gauntleted hand. His charger, floundering beside him, had not yet found its feet.

For a moment no sound came from the stunned spectators. Then throats regained the power of loud utterance and the air resounded with cries pitched in bitter rage and menace. The fondest legend of the Western world had been shattered, the invincible Sire Tohu-Bohu had gone down before a mere stripling and would no longer be a name to dangle in pride before the rest of the world!

Richard, sitting erect in his saddle without motion and with his sword drawn, saw the wave of angry humanity break over the flimsy barricades and come rolling out into the enclosure. He thought, "Have I survived one danger to encounter an even greater?" Then he saw that Tostig had managed somehow to reach him and was standing at his stirrup with a pike in his hand, and a sense almost of relief took possession of him; the companion of his whole life was here and might find a way out for them as he had always done. At the worst, they would go down together.

But the resolution and mettle of the angry mob was not to be put to the test. A sound of trumpets was heard outside the lists. The onsurging wave paused, then came to a stop. The wooden gates at the challenger's end of the field were thrown open and a party of horsemen rode through.

At the head of the newcomers was a very young man in light armor, with a sleeveless surcoat of gold and purple samite over it. His head (which was as gold-crested as that of the fair Princess Eleanor) was covered by a felt hat instead of the usual metal cap. A squire rode behind him, carrying his shield. There was not a moments' doubt in the mind of anyone as to his identity. Prince Arthur had returned, somewhat sooner than he had been expected.

They heard him cry in a high boyish voice, "Maledictions, we are too late!"

"It seems so, Your Highness," said one of the knights riding behind him.

"And yet we came on at a rare good pace, messires and good companions, once the word reached us of what was afoot." Then the prince observed the recumbent figure of the champion of the West still stretched out on the turf. He stiffened with amazement. "God's ribs!" he cried, in imitation of his Plantagenet uncles, each of whom had chosen some part of the celestial body for purposes of emphatic speech. "The Captal is down! What has happened? Was he thrown from his horse on entering the lists?"

The explanation was given him and he sat his horse for several moments in puzzlement and a sense of loss. "By all the saints, it is hard to

believe!" he declared finally. "I would have wagered a half of my possessions—*all* of which my fair uncle is claiming—that our great champion
would have brushed this English youth aside like a bothersome gnat.
Perhaps it is as well, messires, that we were spared such a bitter sight."

Then he grasped the significance of the crowded course. His share of
the violent Plantagenet temper drove all semblance of beauty from his
boyish face.

"*Mordieu,* what is the meaning of this?" he demanded. "Who has
allowed this greasy rabble to invade the field of honor? Clear them out.
Rid the lists of them at once. If they resist, hang every man jack of
them!"

Fortunately the noisy crowd was driven back behind the barriers by
less drastic means.

3

Through all the years that Richard had been a member of the household of the marshal, he had never known comfort. Never once had he
eaten, slept, dressed, undressed, or washed alone. They had been like a
movable beehive. They swarmed down on a castle, filling it to the
battlements and eating all the supplies of food and making great inroads on the wine casks before moving on. The Norman castles in
England consisted of the Great Hall, the kitchens, and the guardroom
for the most part. The lord and his lady slept in tiny niches sunk into
the thick walls, which offered little privacy and no comfort. A pallet of
straw was the closest he himself had ever come to the softness of a bed.

It was a surprise, therefore, to find that the castle on the Vilaine
was large enough to absorb the train of the Breton rulers and still allow
some privacy. When Richard received a summons to wait on Prince
Arthur, he was led through the Great Hall and into a passage from
which opened many doors. They came to a corner apartment, at which
point the attendant announced, "The English knight, my lord duke,"
and vanished, leaving Richard alone on the threshold. It must not be
assumed, however, that the room represented any high degree of luxury.
There were tapestries on the walls but under them the masonry was
damp and there was an unmistakable mustiness on the air.

The prince had a bright, shining face and a liking for color on his
back. His jacket was red, his diamond-checkered hose blue and gold, his
shoes (turned up at the toes in a fantastic exaggeration of the style)

green. He was thin but handsomely proportioned and he seemed to walk on springs, making no sound when he moved.

He looked at Richard and nodded his golden head. "How did you do it?" he demanded abruptly.

Richard knew, of course, to what he referred. "I went for the visor," he answered. "High. I struck just under the helm. It threw him completely off balance."

"God's ribs, supposing you had missed!" cried the prince.

"I would have been disgraced. I took the chance of that, my lord duke."

The prince repeated his "God's ribs" and declared he would regret his absence to the end of his days. "You know, Sir Knight," he confided, "I was not entirely sorry that you won. He's a sour old dog, this Poitevin. I don't believe I've ever heard him speak. He grunts. He eats enough for three men. His wife is as big as a Flemish foot soldier but all his mistresses are tiny creatures. There's nothing human about him."

He drew his sword and made a high pass at the wall as though repeating the lance stroke which had destroyed the legend of the invincible Tohu-Bohu but his mind had gone on to something else. "Foxy says you're a spy. Are you?"

"I am not a spy, my lord prince. I don't return to Normandy when I leave here. I go to Rome."

A pleased look took possession of the prince's face. "I knew he was wrong. It's a good thing to catch him this way; he's always so right about everything that I grow tired of his perfection."

It was evident that he spoke of the Red Cardinal. After a moment he gave his head a knowing nod. "But you *are* here for a purpose, young Englishman. I am sure of that. Confess now that I'm right."

"You are right, my lord prince. I came to see you. To deliver a message. A warning."

"I knew it!" The prince was so pleased with himself that he indulged in something resembling a caper. "I can hardly wait to tell Foxy that he was wrong and I was right."

"Unless I have your promise, my lord prince, that you won't discuss it with His Eminence, I am under orders not to deliver the message. It is for your ears only."

"That means it's from William the Marshal. Dismal Will. I suppose he wants me to sit down quietly and wait to be gobbeted like a trout. Oh, his intentions are good, I'm sure. He thinks I'll have no chance if I show fight." He straightened up suddenly and gave his head a shake.

"I give you the promise you demand. Now what does the marshal want you to tell me?"

Richard proceeded to enumerate the arguments which he had been given to show the danger of any resort to arms. He bore down particularly on the folly of putting reliance in the promises of the French king.

The prince heard him out with a serious mien, and then proceeded to argue the matter point by point. In doing so he showed an almost mature perception of the military aspects of the case and a surprisingly sound judgment of the main figures involved. He spoke, however, in jocular terms, as though the situation appeared to him in the nature of a game. He had facetious names for everyone concerned. His uncle was never referred to by the dignified name he bore nor even as the king; he was always Jack Lack. The marshal was, as already shown, Dismal Will and sometimes Old I-Do-My-Duty. The King of France was the Big Promiser and the Red Cardinal was never anything but Foxy. His sister was, affectionately, Puss-in-Silks.

The prince paced up and down the small apartment as he talked, with the springy step of perfectly co-ordinated muscles and a tendency to gesture with some flamboyance. It was clear from the beginning that he took an optimistic view of things. He was not, he said, aiming to take the throne of England from the perfidious uncle who had robbed him of it. The sole purpose of the present moves was to assure him the possession of Brittany and its allied provinces. Could there be any legitimate objection to his taking some at least of the lands which were rightly his? He laughed easily when Richard repeated the words of the marshal, that he must beware the consequences of failure. There was no thought of failure in the minds of his associates and friends. He would be deemed a poor creature if he sat down and did nothing. He must stand up for his rights, he declared with flashing eyes, or forever after be counted a poltroon and a fainthearted cullion.

"Enough of this," he declared finally. "You have said your say. I have listened and weighed everything. No word you have uttered will go outside this room; you have my word on that. And, of course, I expect you to be equally reticent. All I can tell you now is that I will give thought to the marshal's message."

A wave of the hand brought the discussion to a close. The prince called, "Pierre!" and, when a man-at-arms answered, he gave an order: "Tell them to send up wine." Then he swung around to face Richard with a smile of the utmost friendliness.

"You'll have to leave at once. Old Foxy is insisting on it. If you don't go, there's no telling what he will do. He has a very bad habit of acting first and then explaining himself when it's all over. I don't want him hanging you and your man and then coming to me with trumped-up proofs that you were spying on us."

The wine arrived and the prince had a goblet poured for Richard. "When it's all over and I've shown Jack Lack that I can't be treated like a child," he said, "you must come back. Ah, what good times we'll have! We'll hunt old Oncle Verrat [the wild boar], and we'll splinter lances every day. I will be expecting you to teach me a great deal about *that*. And we'll play Tables. Are you a good hand with the dice? I am. I'm the best in all Brittany. Everyone says so." His eyes, as brilliantly blue as his sister's, were shining. "I like you, Englishman. We are going to be great friends."

4

Richard and his party left at an early hour next morning. There was a hint of triumph back of the gray eyes of Tostig as they rode out to the southern highway.

"She has agreed," he said.

"You refer, of course, to the little Giselle. But to what has she agreed?"

"Master Rick, she has a fondness for me and she has promised to wait for me to come back. How soon do you think that will be?"

"You are a lucky man, Tostig," said Richard as they clattered noisily over the drawbridge. "But it will be several years before we can expect to come back."

"God grant that she will be alive and here to greet me," said Tostig soberly. "The princess rides with her brother to Mirebeau and it is arranged that Giselle is the one to go with her."

Richard was startled beyond measure. "What folly is this?" he cried. "Do they think it is a pleasant little processional they are starting? Don't they know that the King of France is so occupied in the Vexin that he won't be there to help them and that they'll have to meet John and his army alone? The princess may be killed or taken prisoner. This is sheer madness!"

"Giselle told me the real reason," said Tostig. "The Princess Eleanor has no love for the old queen. She was to have been married to the Dauphin of France but the widow rode all the way to the court of Spain and brought back another grandchild, Blanche of Castile, to become the dauphine instead. Eleanor would have been a much better Queen of France than the plain Blanche. She wants a chance to charge the old lady with her unfairness and duplicity."

"Nothing but ill will come of it!" cried Richard.

They were climbing the road to Rennes and Tostig turned back for a last look. An expression of rare felicity crossed his face and he raised an arm above his head and waved. Richard swung around in his saddle and saw a figure standing on the low battlements, violently agitating a red kerchief. It was clear even at the distance that it was Giselle.

"Lucky Tostig," he thought.

But Tostig was not to have all the luck. For a brief space they had been aware that a small party was riding ahead of them, skirting the edge of the woods and stopping at intervals to study the sky.

"Hawking," commented Tostig.

Richard nodded and threw back his head to look upward. At the moment there was nothing on wings within sight.

"Three ladies with them," said the squire, gazing ahead under a cupped hand. "Two of them seem to be attendants. The third one, in the pink cloak, is—I believe it's the Princess Eleanor."

After a pause Richard said, "Yes, it's the princess." The lady in question was wearing a mantle over her head but her hair was not covered completely and there was no mistaking the Plantagenet yellow. She had been so much in his mind that he had other means of identifying her; the way she carried her head, a characteristic manner of raising her arms.

"Is it a peregrine on her wrist?" asked Tostig.

"It must be. No woman, not even a princess, is allowed to have a gerfalcon."

"They're not having any luck. The bird is mantling."

The line of trees drew in closer to the road and the royal party came slowly within speaking distance.

"Sir Knight," said the clear, high voice of the princess, "you ride early."

Richard did not respond at once. She had addressed him in English! There had been some talk in the Breton tongue during the two days of their stay at the court but everyone with whom Richard had come in contact had spoken French.

"My lady, I am much surprised," he said. "I did not know you could speak our language."

"My mother was most ambitious," said the princess, choosing her words with deliberate care. "She never doubted my brother would someday be King of England. And so she said we must both speak English, even though our father had not a word of it. The English is —much difficult. I speak it, Sir Knight, most badly."

Richard could not restrain himself from smiling. "You speak it very well, Your Highness. There is a trace of an accent but I find it delightful."

"That is greatly kind. I speak it so little now. I knew you were leaving. My brother told me he had given advices to you to go without delay. He liked you, Sir Knight."

Richard bowed. "I am happy to know that His Highness approved of me."

Her manner had been somewhat aloof but at this point she seemed to relent. "Was it clear," she asked, smiling, "that when you came I did not approve you very much?"

"Yes, Your Highness, it was very clear."

She glanced about her to be sure no one was within hearing distance. "But when you won from that—that great beast, that giant with face of bird of prey, I began to regret with my princely brother that you would not stay. Where do you go?"

"First to Tours. I may ride then to Bordeaux but sooner or later, my lady, I shall go to Rome."

There was a moment of silence. "We hoped," she said, "that you might—how is it said?—cast your lot with us. Perhaps not now but later."

She had reined her mount in so closely that they could now speak without any risk of being overheard. Her party had drawn off on some concern of the sport and Richard's men were keeping a discreet distance. He felt his heart pounding because of her nearness. On the other occasions when he had seen her, she had been in green or blue but the pink cloak she now wore with black headdress and gloves seemed even more becoming; it was less regal most certainly and more feminine, even, he thought, coquettish.

The peregrine preened itself again, spreading out one wing and stretching a leg, as though in protest at this long interruption. The princess spoke to the bird in affectionate undertones.

"Will you be returning to England soon?" she asked then.

"Not for years, my lady. I have my fortune to make, and small chance there is of that in England."

She made some adjustment of the chain which held the peregrine on her wrist and this kept her occupied for some moments. Then she looked up again.

"Do not, I beg you, Sir Knight, put wrong construction on what I now say. There is no plotting to invade England. No such thought is in my brother's head. But is it wrong to think that a kind and wise God may provide a chance someday for a great injustice to be—to be set right? If this should happen, I have a hope you will be there."

"My sympathies," declared Richard, lowering his voice, "have always been with Prince Arthur."

"It is possible then you might someday ride in his train. No, say nothing more. Words are dangerous things. What we have said must be locked as a secret between us."

The attendants of the princess drew closer as though they thought the conversation had been unduly long. Eleanor smiled and bowed, and then raised one hand in a gesture of farewell. The party returned to their sport.

"I am lucky also," said Richard to himself. "I have a memory which I shall cherish all my life."

Chapter VIII

1

RICHARD OF RAWEN rode all over France and put in an appearance wherever a tournament was being held, once journeying down into Navarre and once venturing over into Genoa. His strength had increased and his skill had reached its high mark since he stretched the mighty Sire Tohu-Bohu on the turf. He emptied saddles wherever he went; and every time he knocked an opponent off his horse he filled his pockets with gold, it being the rule that the gear of the loser was forfeited to the winner: his charger, his saddle, his armor, his supply of weapons, everything but his shield, which carried his armorial bearings. Sometimes the loser would buy back his equipment but generally the winner found it necessary to visit some soft-spoken Lombard banker in an inconspicuous shop and sell his winnings for the best price he could negotiate. Richard emptied so many saddles and filled so many pockets with gold that in the course of a short time the money belt around his waist was stuffed with pieces of the precious yellow metal. He was being heralded as second only to the once great William the Marshal.

Wherever they went they heard talk of the wickedness of the King of England. John was loudly cursed as a usurper, a perjurer, and a foul murderer. The frightening train of events which had followed close on the heels of Richard's departure from Brittany was seldom out of the young knight's mind. He and Tostig talked about it continuously as they rode from town to town, and their faces would darken and their fists would clench and a desire for revenge would show in every word they said. Soon after their departure from the ducal palace near Rennes, Prince Arthur had collected his forces and marched against Mirebeau as planned. Although the garrison was taken by surprise, the castle had been defended stoutly under the fierce urging of the old queen, Eleanor of Aquitaine, whose dark eyes still burned in her wrinkled face with the same fire as in days gone by when she had been the most beautiful and most willful woman in Europe. They could not have held out indefinitely, of course, and the final stage was in sight when King John, rousing himself from his customary lethargy, had acted for once with proper dispatch. He arrived on the scene with a considerable force and shattered the Bretons under their brave but inexperienced young prince. Many prisoners were taken, including the prince himself, the Princess Eleanor, and all of the knights in arms.

All Christendom had shuddered over the sequel. Prince Arthur had not been heard of again and it was believed that the enraged monarch had murdered him. Twenty-four of the captured knights had been sent to England, bound together in pairs in open carts. Incarcerated in Corfe Castle, a gaunt stronghold in the Isle of Purbeck which John used as a political prison, they had been starved to death; a method to which the amiable king seemed addicted. As to the fate of the princess, nothing was known. Was she still alive? Had John placed her in one of his black prisons, not daring to outrage world opinion with an assassination even more unthinkable than that of the unfortunate Arthur?

The fate of the lovely Eleanor had seldom been out of Richard's mind since. Tostig would always remember him at this stage as a silent figure with knuckles tense on the hilt of his dagger. Sometimes the knight would burst out into loud self-reproach. "What am I doing here?" he would ask. "Playing at war and fattening my purse while this wild beast holds our lovely lady in captivity! I should be back in England where it may be possible to do something for her. I should at least be willing to aid her cause by clamoring against her infamous jailer!"

Tostig would answer with the sound common sense which never deserted him. "We can't go back to England. The king knows what you have been doing, that you favored Arthur from the beginning. Do you want to give him the satisfaction of putting you in some foul prison to starve to death? Would it serve the cause of the princess for you to die and for me to be hanged on the nearest gibbet?"

"It might set men to thinking."

"They are thinking, Master Rick. And if they think long enough, they may reach the point of acting. *That* is the time when we should be there."

Tostig felt as deeply apprehensive as Richard but he restrained himself from speaking openly on the subject. He knew the young knight was still convinced that his first duty was to serve his king and, if needs

be, die for him. But if it had been possible for the squire to see into
Richard's mind, he would have found there the beginnings of doubt.
Richard Coeur de Lion had shaken his namesake's faith in some degree.
Despite the splendor of the warrior king's exploits in the Holy Land,
it had been hard to swallow his callous disregard of the interests of
England, his eagerness to grasp by corrupt means the gold for his in-
cessant fighting in France. And now the malevolence and the coward-
ice of John had convinced the unhappily puzzled knight that allegiance
to this particular incumbent of a throne was impossible.

Richard in his bewilderment had even reached the stage of asking
himself: "If one king can be so bad that tavern knaves spit at the
mention of his name, is there something wrong with the system which
puts all power in one pair of hands?"

He dismissed the suggestion quickly whenever it obtruded itself on
his mind; but it kept coming back.

What was destined to be the last tournament in which Richard of
Rawen played a part was held in a small town about twenty miles
south of Paris. It drew a large number of competitors and attracted
spectators by the thousands. Six challengers, the cream of the Gallic
stock, set up their gaudy pavilions at one end of the lists and a large
canvas tent was raised at the other end for those who would come to
face them. In spite of the reputation he had gained, Richard was among
the latter.

At a late hour of the morning, while the babble of thousands of
tongues rose from the galleries outside and the brassy piping of the
heralds could be heard every few minutes, Richard was putting on his
armor in a corner of the common pavilion. He was in a confident mood
because he had prevailed over four of the challengers in previous meetings and did not anticipate any difficulty with the other two.

A mendicant friar in a black robe (which indicated a certain lack
of orthodoxy) came into the pavilion on bare feet. As a man of peace,
he found himself ill at ease in this atmosphere and he held his head
down, raising his eyes at intervals only and then dropping them hastily
as though he shrank from what he saw. Finally his gaze became fixed
on Tostig and, with considerable hesitation, he crossed the crowded
space to address him.

"Eenglish?" he asked.

Tostig straightened up and looked at him questioningly. "English?
Yes, I am English, Father."

The friar hesitated still more noticeably over his next question. "Name, Tosty?"

"My name is Tostig."

The friar gave his head a satisfied nod. "The same. Tosty. From Eengland. I have message for Tosty."

Tostig drew the black-robed figure into the corner where their talk could not be overheard. "You have a message for me?"

"Oui, messire. Message. 'One who serves great lady bids Tosty know both she and mistress alive and well. Well as—as can be.'"

Tostig grasped the friar by the arm. "What else? There must be more. Where is she?"

"Not know."

"But the one who sent this message and her mistress are in England." The black robe nodded. "I think, yes. In Eengland."

"How," demanded Tostig eagerly, "did you get this message?"

"It pass from one to one. I am eleven to have it. Now *you* have message. That is good." The man in the black robe turned to leave the pavilion. "My son, give up violent ways. Turn feet to heavenly path."

"Thank you, Father," said Tostig gratefully. He realized that the mendicant friar had taken a great risk in drawing attention to himself in this way. He and his like lived precariously under the stern disapproval of the Church. Finding a coin in a pocket under his belt, Tostig held it out. "For the common purse."

The friar accepted the coin with a furtive caution and glided out from the pavilion.

"Master Rick!" exclaimed Tostig, returning to complete his task of adjusting buckles. "Did you hear what that friar told me? The blessing of all the saints descend on his humble head! They are alive and well. The princess and Giselle. The word was sent to us by Giselle, and has been passed along from one to another."

Richard had been on the point of settling his steel headpiece into place. He paused and regarded his squire over the rounded top of it. A light was beginning to kindle in his eye. "Did you question him? Are you sure he speaks the truth?"

"I have no doubts on that score. The message has been passed on by word of mouth. That is all I know. But we can be certain now that they are alive, both the princess and Giselle. And they are as well as might be expected. What better news could we have?"

"None! I haven't felt so happy since we learned they had fallen into the evil hands of John. Father in heaven, I thank Thee! Thou hast watched over them and preserved them from harm."

Richard was so delighted with the news that he went out to play his part in the lists in a highly exalted state of mind. Having small concern for anything else, he performed his tasks with nonchalant skill and sent three of the challengers sprawling on the pitted sod. This was all he was called upon to do and after that he needed only to acquit himself well in the mêlée, which would bring the contest to a close, in order to be acclaimed the champion of the day. A mêlée was a pleasant exhibition in which the knights took sides, thirty against thirty, and fought it out with lance, battle-ax, and sword until the judges decided there had been enough bloodshed.

But when, late in the afternoon, Richard issued forth for his last appearance and swung himself up into the saddle, it became apparent that the final exhibition of mayhem was not likely to take place. A priest had stationed himself on the elevated ground back of the common pavilion and had drawn most of the spectators from their seats in the wooden galleries. A dense circle had already been formed about him. His voice could be heard clearly all over the field and a dedicated fire had taken possession of his angular countenance.

"Who is that?" asked Richard.

Tostig was holding Messire by the bridle. "I suspect it's a priest preaching the new crusade."

Richard listened to the persuasive voice of the priest and then slipped down from his saddle. "Tostig," he said, "I think we should listen to what this man has to tell us."

The tournament came to a complete stop, for everyone, even the highborn ladies from the gallery, which was called the Bower of Beauty, had left their seats and ranged themselves around the impassioned priest. His face was as full of light as a beacon fire, his voice as resonant as the trumpet of a herald. He depicted the evil days which had fallen on the Holy City, which the Saracens again held, in the most vivid terms. The Holy Sepulchre was befouled, the Temple of Solomon resounded with the shrill voices of infidels, Moslem inciters to violence had taken the place of the gentle and lowly Christ. Why did the Christian world sit slothfully by? It was time to draw the sword again!

"It's said he's a servant of the young Pope," whispered Tostig.

Richard did not hear him. He was listening with such close attention that he was unconscious of everything save the voice of the eloquent priest. His thoughts were following the preacher a long distance into the East, to the ground where the Temple of Solomon had once stood, high above the Valley of the Cheesemakers, to the humble home in the Wall of David, to the Mount of Olives where the treetops stirred gently when a breeze was wafted down from the scarred face of Jebel Kuruntul and where, it was still believed, a devout eye might find the imprint of a sacred foot.

It was when the speaker turned to the defaming of the holy places that his eloquence reached its peak. He made them see the narrow streets, close and dark and dangerous, doubly dangerous now that infidels lurked in every twist and turn. The Wailing Wall no longer rang with supplications, it was reserved for the chaffering and bickering of desert traders who called on the name of Allah. Men knelt on the Dome of the Rock and prayed to a God who was not the God of Israel. More disturbing still, because it could be more easily shared, was the picture drawn of the plight of the pilgrims who took their sins to Jerusalem: cheated, scoffed at, pelted with dung, seized with sudden furious hate (if any strayed away from their fellows) and sold into slavery to infidel masters, maltreated for all the days of their lives, no more than one in six getting home to tell their story and wear in their hats thereafter the silver sprig of the palmer. What, O men of good faith and stout heart, was to be done about this?

At the finish Richard was one of the many who stepped forward and professed a willingness to serve. When the ceremony was over, he looked at the cross he wore on the breast of his tunic and said to Tostig, "We won't go to England for a long time now."

"No," was the answer. "Perhaps our pleas will reach the ears of the Lord more surely this way."

Richard turned and looked at his companion. His eyes displayed a sudden surprise and he pointed at Tostig with an accusing finger.

"You are not wearing the cross! I was too absorbed to notice. But I thought—I was sure—you had taken the oath also."

"No," said Tostig, "I didn't take the oath. I tried to reason you out of it but I don't think you heard anything I said. You seemed in a trance. Don't look at me so accusingly! I haven't committed any offense against God and Holy Church. I have made use of such common sense as I happen to have."

Richard was frowning in a perplexed way. "Common sense has nothing to do with it."

"I'm afraid it has. I don't mean that you shouldn't have taken the cross; but, as you have, it is doubly necessary for me to be free. I think I understand the situation in the world today better than you do."

Richard's perplexity was growing by the minute. Never had Tostig spoken to him like this before.

"We've been hearing a great deal about the young Pope," declared Tostig. "How strong he proved himself in Italy when he chased the Germans out. How much he has the interests of suffering humanity at heart when he builds these great hospitals of the Holy Ghost. How wise and strong he was in sending an army to capture Constantinople and so unite Eastern Christians with the West under one Pope. Everyone has told us he has a greatness in him which the others lacked, those venerable ones who've been sitting in the Lateran. But there's something I know which you may not, Master Rick: that the young Pope was deceived and cheated. He didn't want the crusading army to go against Constantinople. He knew the first step toward setting the Holy Land free was to capture Egypt. But the men of Venice, who think of nothing but money and trade, were expected to supply the ships and those sharp foxes held back until they were allowed control; and *they* chose to tear down the power of the Eastern emperors instead. It looks at the moment as though they won a victory but all they succeeded in doing was to defeat the plans of the young Pope for a successful crusade."

"How does it happen," demanded Richard, "that you know so much more than anyone else about such matters?"

"Master Rick," said Tostig earnestly, "you've laughed at me because I like to talk to all kinds of people. Well, I enjoy sitting down with them and listening to what they have to say. You'll laugh at me again when I tell you the common man keeps his ears open and hears many things which escape his betters. A keeper of an inn very often has a shrewder view of affairs than the lord of the castle or the abbot in his snug nest. The news that comes out of Constantinople isn't good. That great monster of a city has a habit of swallowing those who try to conquer it. Do you know that London town could be dropped in one corner of it and never be noticed again? Well, it won't be long before the Eastern Empire will be back where it was before—free of the West, free of Rome, and free of the Pope. And all the crusading zeal of the young Pope will have been expended in vain. He knows it, never fear; and that is why he is striving so hard to get another crusade under way. He wants another army and another chance to carry out the original plan. That's why he has sent out these priests to rouse the world."

"Is that why you stood aside?" asked Richard. "So you could go back at once to England?"

"Though I won't be wearing the cross," declared Tostig, "I will go with you wherever your conscience takes you. Surely you know that."

A sense of contrition took possession of Richard. "Forgive me, Tostig, for what I said. I didn't mean it. I know how loyal you have always been."

"Well," declared the squire, "this is the position we are in. We can't stand around waiting for marching orders from the Pope. It may be years before he's in a position to give them. Our best plan will be to ride at once to Marseilles and take a pilgrimage ship to Rome."

"To see the Pope?" Richard clearly was elated at the prospect of this.

"Perhaps," was the answer. "But to see another man first. An Englishman. A very great man, the greatest Englishman alive today. He stands so high in the esteem of men that I heard much talk of him here last night when I had my glass of wine in the common room at the inn. His name is Stephen Langton."

Richard frowned. "I have never heard of him."

"Where you sit the talk is all of war and fighting and doing brave deeds. But even the beggars of Paris know of Stephen Langton. They say he will be the next Pope, if he outlives Innocent. The young Pope knew him when they were studying in Paris. One of the first things Innocent did when he was elected was to summon Stephen Langton to Rome. He made him a cardinal and he asks advice of him more than of any other man. My idea is this, Master Rick: that we go to see Stephen Langton and ask his counsel. Whatever he tells us to do will be wise and right."

"When do you propose to start?"

"Now. I think we should be on our way before the sun goes down. It's a long ride to Marseilles."

Richard indulged in a somewhat rueful laugh. "Am I not to have time to collect my winnings? The gear of those three knights I upset today will bring us a handsome sum. Although I haven't much stomach for bargaining at the moment."

"Let me talk to them," suggested Tostig. "I won't let them off easily. You may be sure of that."

2

Tostig looked with a grimace of distaste at the slattern ship tied up in Marseilles Harbor. "They build them for the pilgrimage trade," he said. "They're good only for hugging the shores. Sometimes they buy old ships of war and then remove the cabins to make more space for passengers on the decks."

The master of the ship in question was a huge fellow named Cornelius. He had a tangled mop of hair, scowling features, and no more than a part mouthful of teeth. His naked belly could not be spanned by an ordinary pair of arms. He came from somewhere in the Baltic area but he addressed them in a vulgar mangling of the French tongue.

"You will pay double for the horses," he said. "They will be stabled on the orlop deck. Supply the forage and feed them yourselves."

"Your terms are hard," said Tostig.

"Then don't take 'em!" cried the master in an angry voice. "I can sell every inch of space I have. I have no stomach for gentrice, if you want the truth, my masters. They demand too much. They want hot food. They want cabins and they light candles and they set the curtains afire. Many a ship has been lost because of them. I want none of these high-nosed lords. Give me a deckful of humble fellows who don't squirm at maggots in the bread and take a kick in the backsides in good part." He interrupted this harangue to roar at an assistant. "What's this you're bringing out, you miserable, sniveling codshead?"

"It's the wine," mumbled the man. "T' cure the seasickness."

"My fine malvoisie!" bellowed the master. "Look at the sea, you blind ox! As smooth as a stinking pond. There will be no seasickness today. Take the wine back." Then he turned again to the Englishmen. "There won't be another ship for two weeks. But don't let that change your minds. I will be glad to see the last of you."

"We have no choice," said Richard.

He shuddered when he followed the horses to the orlop deck. Bilge water churned through the foul sand at every movement of the ship. The offal from many voyages had not been removed and the stench was indescribable.

"When they have a corpse to be buried ashore, they give it temporary burial in the sand here," said Tostig, who knew a great deal about everything. "Sometimes, they say, you can see arms and hands, and even heads, sticking up before the end of a voyage."

They tethered Messire at one end and supplied him abundantly with hay. Richard ran a sympathetic hand down the charger's muzzle. "My poor fellow!" he said. "It's not right for a fine horse like you, a horse of high degree, to be penned up in a pesthole like this.

"Let's pray for a short run," he remarked as they came up on deck.

They found that conditions there were almost as bad. The deck was already filled with men of all sizes, shapes, and nationalities. They wore the gray cowl, scrip, and scarf, and the slouch hats turned up in front, which marked them as pilgrims. Most of them had breviaries at their belts and all carried staffs. Cattle and sheep were penned at each end and chickens were roosting everywhere.

"Where will we sleep?" asked Richard.

"We'll sleep on the deck and we won't have more than an inch of space from our neighbors. Cheek by jowl. St. Christopher, watch us with a kindly eye!" Tostig studied the horizon and gave his head a shake. "We're going to have weather by nightfall. This tub will pitch and toss like a cork."

His prediction proved accurate. By the time the prayer to St. Julien brought the evening services to an end, and the pilgrims were stretched out on the six feet by two of space to which they were entitled, the deck was pitching drunkenly and most of the passengers were already sick.

It took twelve full days to circle the Tyrrhenian Sea on the way to Rome and by that time the unfortunate pilgrims were sadly emaciated. Master Cornelius, who seemed impervious to the weather, stamped about and cursed his luck at having to feed them so much longer than he had expected. He was, in point of fact, lucky; for the pilgrims were too ill to eat the nauseous food and they learned early it was no use begging for wine. There were deaths every day and the bodies were piled together under canvas and buried in the sea after night had fallen.

Richard slept between Tostig on one side and a burly Swede on the other. A hen insisted on roosting on his shoulder. He would shoo it away a dozen times but waken in the morning to find it back. Sometimes, as though by way of payment, he would find an egg on the deck beside him and would scramble bitterly with the Swede for it. On the last occasion that this happened he conceded the egg to his neighbor without a struggle because it was evident that the once strong Scandinavian was a very sick man.

On the last night, when they had spied the rooftops of Ostia by the final feeble rays of the sun (to the dazed men everything seemed gray and sickly), the Swede, who had not moved for hours, finally succumbed and his body was hauled away. A greasy Levantine took his place with an eagerness which should have aroused some apprehension; but both Richard and Tostig were too enfeebled to give the newcomer a thought. They settled down heavily to get as much sleep as possible before the disembarkation in the morning.

Richard wakened to a bright and warm sky overhead, a steady deck, and a view of the shore which was unbelievably inviting. The Levantine was gone, which allowed him enough space to stretch luxuriously in the expectation of comforts ashore. His satisfaction, however, was short-lived. A lack of constriction about his waist caused him to drop a questing hand to that area.

"Tostig!" he cried. "I've been robbed! My belt is gone!"

Tostig's response was fraught with at least an equal degree of dismay and anger. He found that his belt had also been removed during the night.

One of the other pilgrims sat up and said that the Levantine was a thief and had been suspected of other robberies during the course of the voyage. "If you had money in those belts, you should have slept with your hands under them," he volunteered.

They ran up and down the deck, looking for the missing passenger, but saw no trace of him. Master Cornelius, when they invaded the quarterdeck with their frantic complaints, supplied the explanation to the disappearance of the nimble-fingered Levantine.

"He's gone," he said. "Did a neat cat in a pan. A half dozen of them took a shore boat around dawn. They've landed by this time." The master seemed not at all disturbed over their loss. In fact there was a hint in his eye of secret pleasure. "I knew him for a nip as soon as he come aboard. You'll have this much satisfaction: he'll be becked and hanged one of these days."

Richard was white of face and sick inside over the loss of all his winnings of nearly three years but the effect on Tostig was even more noticeable. He was white with consternation and anger.

"If you knew him for a cutpurse, why didn't you warn us?" he demanded of the master.

Cornelius exploded into one of his familiar rages. "Why didn't I warn you?" he thundered. "Didn't he wear his cloak and his hat and his staff? Didn't he even have the bell at his belt, and how many of them do? Didn't he pay in his money, with an extra shilling or two? Am I to judge what's inside those slungy shirts they wear? Let me tell you this, Master Squire: we have them on every run, these users of the cant. This fellow now, the one who's got your money and is burning his soles to get away, he's riding on pilgrim ships all the time. Is it concern of mine? There are plenty of them, playing low and crafty. On my last turn I carried three ladies. In disguise as pilgrims, mind you. Two were running away from their husbands, the sluts. The third—well, *she*, the slyboots, wasn't up to anything good." He allowed his voice to recede several degrees to a more normal pitch. "There, Master Squire, that's what we have to face, and who am I to do anything about it?"

This contradictory tirade left Tostig in an angrier mood than before. "What you mean is that the forces of evil congregate to rob and pillage the pilgrims. That the owners and masters of the ships know this but won't do anything about it."

"That, my loud-crowing cockerel," said Master Cornelius, turning and walking away from them, "is what I mean."

That was how it came about that, when they went ashore, their waists were still free of the satisfying encirclement of their money belts, and in their pockets they had no more than a few small pieces of silver.

3

It was in the church of St. Chrysogonus, which stood in the sparsely settled part of Rome on the far bank of the river Tiber, that the two weary travelers first saw Stephen Langton. He was preaching, and the church was filled to overflowing; a well-dressed congregation for the most part, and eagerly attentive. The voice of the English cardinal filled the edifice without difficulty.

The pen of a narrator, which may plunge blithely into descriptions of lesser men, pauses when it becomes necessary to depict a Stephen Langton. He was not tall nor were his features conspicuous in any marked way. Not even his eyes could be considered an easy index to his character, for at most times they were thoughtful and reserved; and it was only when his tongue took fire that their cool gray turned a deeper shade and they held the watcher in complete subjection. It was when he spoke that the measure of the man could best be had; his voice was deep and unhurried and compelling, and what he had to say, no matter how difficult or how simple the theme, seemed lucid and convincing.

Richard's eyes wandered a little as the sermon progressed, taking in the handsome velvets and looped gold chains of the sallow-faced men and the dark beauty of the women but Tostig never took his gaze from the speaker. At the conclusion he whispered to his companion, "This is the man needed in England, Master Rick."

Stephen Langton received them later in an austere stone room off the atrium. He looked tired, as though the delivery of the sermon had drawn on his strength.

"I am happy to welcome fellow countrymen," he said. His eyes looked Richard over carefully, noting the lithe lines of his tall frame and the hint of great strength. "So you are Richard of Rawen. I am a man of peace but I confess that pride caused a tingling in my veins when I heard you had overthrown the Goliath of the West, and at word of your many victories since. You are wearing the cross! I am happy to see it, and I am sure His Holiness will count it an example which will bring us many recruits." He studied them both for a brief moment. "There is a reason, no doubt, for your visit to Rome at this point."

Richard looked rather shamefaced as he replied. "Our purpose in coming was for inspiration and guidance. There is an immediate need, however; for a bed tonight and, perhaps, a meal."

The broad brow of the churchman drew into a puzzled frown. "I am sure there is a story behind this."

He listened to the tale of their misfortune with eyes which had become dark and somber. "It will not be new to you, then," he said at the conclusion, "that there is a conspiracy to rob the men who take the staff of the pilgrim and set out to see the Holy Land with their own eyes. It is not confined to low criminals of the stripe of this man who robbed you. It extends as high as governors of provinces and even to—to leaders of the Church. The pilgrimage ships pay huge profits. But the worst thing of all is the way these poor brave fellows suffer when they reach the Holy Land. They are robbed and mistreated, they are sold spurious relics, they are even sold into slavery. The money filched from them every year runs to fabulous amounts." After several moments of unhappy thought the cardinal seemed to brush the evil picture aside. "It is well you came here, my sons. His Holiness has need of men such as you. I shall make it my concern to take you before him at the earliest moment. In the meantime you must consider yourselves members of my household. It is a humble one. Peter's pence does not suffice to maintain the offices needed about the papacy and we are always pressed for funds. But I can give you beds and seats at my table until such time as His Holiness decides the use he may make of you."

"You are most kind, my lord cardinal."

The churchman sighed as he sat behind the plain desk where he did his daily work. "Have you been in England since John became king?"

"No, my lord. I have made no secret of my feeling about his choice over the unfortunate Prince Arthur; and of what has happened since. It would not be safe for us to return."

The churchman paused briefly. "These are bad days in England, my sons."

They were summoned to an audience with the Pope the following morning at an hour which would have been surprising to anyone who did not know the habits of the young occupant of the Holy See. The early sun was striking warmly on the roofs of the Lateran Palace as they crossed the river but there were few signs of life in the streets. Most of Rome still slept.

They passed through a succession of long high halls into which little light penetrated and through which sounds carried reluctantly, although the smallest of them created slow and mysterious echoes. Two of the Ostiarii stood with pikes at each door and there was a continuous rustle of alb and stole and chasuble as the clerical staff moved with studious calm about their duties.

An anteroom was reached finally where a young officer of the Ostiarii was on hand to receive them. He wore his silken cloak and carried his baton and he was so very young that it was doubtful whether his chin had yet known the touch of a razor. His manner was jaunty and he did not seem to have relished the need of rising so early. At any rate he was yawning openly.

"I am Ralph of Mincamo," he stated. "Welcome, my good fellow Norman. You are from England and I from Sicily. We are each of us half Norman, as a point of fact. Which is good. The Norman character, as I see it, benefits always from some form of blood mitigation. Eh, my friend?"

"My father was English," said Richard. "I am proud of it."

The officer continued to talk with an easy garrulity but in a low tone of voice. "You are going to be with us. You may not know it yet but I assure you it is all settled. We will serve together, I trust, but there will be this difference between us: you will owe your appointment to merit and accomplishments in the field, I owe mine to family influence pure and simple. I have done nothing to earn a post of any kind. I am like the lilies of the field; at least, I toil not. And why should I? An uncle of mine is an archbishop and there are three counts in the family, and *much* wealth."

Richard was thinking anxiously. "Is His Holiness waiting while this chatterbag talks to me?"

The young man from Sicily must have sensed what was passing through his mind, for he said: "He's not ready for you yet. There have been matters to disturb him already and I suspect he's reaching for the thunderbolts in there. Still, he won't be hard on you because you come from the Silent One. Anyone who comes from the Silent One is greeted with attention and even respect."

Richard asked in a puzzled tone, "Do you refer to Cardinal Langton?"

"Yes, the new cardinal," answered Ralph of Mincamo easily. "He's English too, Langton. When the tension gets to a point here, we sigh with relief when we hear the Silent One has arrived. He has a way with him. A way of seeing the best thing to be done under any and all circumstances." The young officer raised a hand which boasted a handsome oriental ring, with a stone gleaming like the eye of a cat, and an opal bracelet. "Please, my good fellow Norman, do not misunderstand me. I mean no lack of respect. I have the greatest admiration for the one who sits inside. He is going to be a great Pope."

"I heard that said of him on my travels," stated Richard.

Ralph of Mincamo nodded. "If he lives long enough, he's going to be the greatest Pope of all time. He will rule Christendom from in there if he gets his way. And it's my opinion, Sir Giant-Killer, that he *will* get his way."

There was still no word from the inner room. The officer took advantage of the delay to speak further about the young Pope. "He's admired by everyone here; and that is unusual because some of the staff have served under a half dozen or more Popes and can compare them. There's one man, in the Archives, who can remember back as far as Adrian IV, nearly fifty years. And he says that Innocent is going to be stronger even than Adrian, who was a very strong Pope. The Lion of the North, they called *him*."

"I seem to have heard something about him."

"You should, Sir Englishman. He came from England. Nicholas Breakspear was his name. The only Englishman to reach the exalted post; putting aside all that silly nonsense about a Pope Joan. And he'll be the last, in my opinion. Unless the chance comes to the Silent One, which is highly unlikely."

Everything that the loquacious officer had said served to make Richard increasingly doubtful of the result of his audience. How could he hope to make a good impression on a man as great and difficult as this? He said something to this effect but Ralph of Mincamo brushed it aside airily.

"You won't need to talk. He won't even ask you any questions. It's a rule of his to know in advance everything he needs to know about a man. I promise you he has your pedigree at his fingertips already."

A priest emerged from an inner room and said, "Richard of Rawen!" Richard stepped forward and bowed.

"Come with me. His Holiness is ready to receive you. Your squire is expected also."

"Good luck, my new friend," whispered Ralph of Mincamo. "Stand up straight and have little to say. And don't get in the way of any thunderbolts."

The room where the Pope sat was in sharp contrast to the loftiness and grandeur of the halls and reception apartments. It was plain with sober walls and a large outer door which opened directly to the east, through which he could gaze and ponder on the problem which sat so heavily on all pontifical shoulders: the freeing of the Holy City; not that Innocent ever took much time to gaze or ponder, his waking moments being given over to endless work. It was a busy place, with two secretaries at corner desks, scratching away with pens, and the walls covered with plans and maps. The plans, it is perhaps unnecessary to explain, were of the East, and it was to be seen at first glance that they were far different from the usual kind. The map makers of the day were indifferent performers, with no exact knowledge of topography and a tendency to let imagination fill in where detail was lacking. It may have been that the plans which Innocent kept about him were the work of oriental hands, the men of the East being far superior to their Western brothers; they were excellent, at any rate, with precision taking the place of allegorical flourish.

Nothing they had heard of this extraordinary man had prepared them for what they found. The face of the pontiff did not suggest his relatively few years. It was lined and seamed already, and the sunken cheeks and intensely alive eyes suggested that his soaring spirit made too heavy demands on a frail body. The eyes were deep-set and magnetic. The two Englishmen, on comparing notes later, realized that they had been captured by the first glance he turned upon them.

"Richard of Rawen," said the Pope, his glance passing from one to the other, "and you also, my son. I have good reports on both of you. I have a fondness for Englishmen. Once, when I was very young, I paid your country a visit, to pray at the shrine of St. Thomas the Martyr. I can still feel the intense emotion which took possession of me when I gazed at the spot which had been washed with his blood." After a moment's reflection devoted to that early experience, he went on: "Your country impressed me as a land of milk and honey and my desire was to return often. That privilege will now be withheld from me."

The pontiff concluded a close study of both visitors and then straightened up in his chair. "It is gratifying," he said, "to see the cross worn by so doughty a champion. It is my hope that you will remain here, my son, until such time as we are ready to strike a blow. There is much you can do."

"I am at your command, Holy Father."

"I cannot promise you any substantial reward, my son. A living has become vacant in one of your northern shires and I shall so arrange matters that a portion of the income will be set aside for you. It will be a circuitous arrangement, and one extremely vexatious to me. The appointment will go to a clerical member of my household, who will retain a purely nominal share. Part will then have to be paid to a native-born vicar who will perform the functions of the office. The balance, such as it is, will be yours." His voice carried a slight note of apology. "It will be small. No more than enough to meet your most pressing needs. That is all."

"I ask for nothing better, Holy Father."

The passionate eyes of the young pontiff began to burn under the penthouse of his brows. "This will be the three hundred and twenty-fourth appointment of this kind in England alone. No defense need be entered because they can afford to contribute thus to our ever increasing costs. But I repeat for your benefit what I have said many times, that it is humiliating to depend on such devices and to be under the continual necessity of breaking down the opposition of the national churches." He brushed away the papers in front of him with an impatient hand. "It is to be hoped that soon we shall agree on a better method. In the meantime it continues necessary to implement our funds in this way.

"As for you, my son," went on the pontiff, turning to Tostig, "I have the best advices as to your capacity and your character. I trust it will be agreeable to both of you if I make use of your time for work which will take you to other countries. The nature of this work will be explained later. There is a need for secrecy about it. Do you have any knowledge of Latin?"

"No, Your Holiness."

"Are you able to speak the language now used by the Latin people?"

"No, Your Holiness."

"My advices are that you are quick in acquiring the use of other

tongues." This was quite true. Tostig spoke French more easily and
fluently than Richard, who learned slowly. "It may be necessary to gain
a slight grounding in one other tongue before you venture on your
chief mission." He reached out with a sudden briskness of manner for
the papers on the desk. "That is all, my sons."

Rooms were allotted to Richard in one of the smaller buildings in
the vicinity of the great state banqueting hall, which was called
Triclinium Major. A short hall led off one of the main corridors, ending
in an ascending flight of six stone steps. The door at the top was of
massive oak and gave admission to his small suite. The rooms, three in
number, had some advantages, however, the chief being the chance
they offered him to see back over the walls and study at his ease the
great city where so much history had been made. He had two men-
servants, a valet and a cook.

On the whole he was more comfortable than he had ever been before
in his life. As the ceilings were high and the walls were of thick stone,
he did not suffer too much from the summer heat (but, ah, how cold
they were to prove in winter!) and he had a large and stately bed
which he did not need to share with anyone. The valet was a devoted
little pod of a man and worked long hours for small pay. The cook
was an accomplished rascal who spoke Latin fluently but who robbed
him over the food bills.

His work was not exacting. He stood in the anteroom of the Pope
whenever prominent visitors were expected, and sometimes he would
be called in to take part in any discussion which dealt with the possibility of another crusade. The men he came into contact with in this
way were familiar with his exploits in the lists; and so he was greeted
with respect and his opinions, when sought, were received with attention.

Most of the talking on these occasions was done by the Pope. He
was still heart and soul in favor of a new and vigorous blow in the
East. His eyes would glow with passion, his tongue would become
eloquent as he depicted the need for immediate action. The visitors
would go away convinced, and many of them would make promises
of personal participation.

Chapter IX

1

ON A MORNING in late summer, when the air was soft and warm and the orchards were full of color, Richard, having nothing better to do at the moment, set out on a tour of the gardens. "I wonder," he thought, "if my lady is allowed to enjoy such beauty as this?" He sighed when he reached the neighborhood of the gate, for here the monastery raised its gloomy roof high above the walls, with such a hint of seclusion about it that he was reminded of the rumor that the Princess Eleanor was being held behind the dark walls of a political prison.

He found that three of the Ostiarii had placed themselves in line across the roadway to prevent the entrance of a party of perhaps half a dozen dusty travelers. He gave an interested glance at the invaders, for there was something about them which seemed faintly familiar; perhaps it was the shape and color of their faces, perhaps the sound of their voices.

In the forefront was a priest who waddled and shook, partly with indignation, partly because of his excessive avoirdupois. He had a round face and a nose which resembled a button on the red biretta of a cardinal, and he moved with an air of comic self-importance. With angry gestures of his pudgy hands he was demanding in a high-pitched voice that he and his party be admitted at once.

Losing interest in the visitors, Richard turned onto one of the paths leading back into the gardens. He stopped, however, when he heard a member of the party address the leader in English. A second spoke up. English again.

"Sir Priest," said Richard, approaching close to the group and addressing the leader, "I am an Englishman. Could I be of assistance to you?"

The leader turned at once in his direction. "Well may you ask, my son," he stated, drawing himself up to his full height, which, it must be said, was far indeed from impressive. "I am Reginald of Canterbury. I seek audience of His Holiness, having just reached the city and daring not to delay by as much as an hour to get the papers and permissions demanded by these minions."

Reginald of Canterbury! Richard turned the phrase over in his mind with a growing sense of perplexity. The Archbishop of Canterbury was Hubert Walter, who at one time had been King Richard's justiciar. By what right did this shrill little clown assume such a designation?

Feeling unable to cope with the situation, he stated that by a happy chance Cardinal Langton was a visitor in the Basilica. With their permission he would inform the cardinal of their arrival, and, no doubt the permission necessary for their entrance would be forthcoming at once. Reginald of Canterbury, whoever he might be, frowned majestically and seemed prepared to lodge an objection on the point of delay. But Richard was already on his way.

He found the English cardinal and informed him of what had happened. Stephen Langton seemed very much disturbed.

"He has been expected," he said. "A sorry tangle, this! What a web to be woven by a parcel of stupid monks! My son," addressing Richard, "Hubert of Canterbury died some weeks ago. A group of the monks of Christ Church took it on themselves to elect their subprior to the vacant post. None other than Master Reginald who now demands admission at the gate. Word of his coming reached us two days ago."

Duty summoned Richard elsewhere and it was not until late in the afternoon that he again had a free moment. He sought out Tostig, who had just returned from one of his long journeys to Constantinople, where he had gathered information. The latter did not disappoint him; he seemed to know the whole story of what had happened.

"Everyone is talking about it," he said. "His Holiness saw Master Reginald. It seems that at first the little man strutted and puffed out his chest. But at the finish he was on his knees, blubbering and mumbling explanations, his little nose as red as a ripe cherry."

"Who is this Master Reginald?"

"One of the stupidest men in all England," declared Tostig. "A rancid little puffin, filled to the ears with conceit of himself. It has long been a matter of tradition that the right to elect archbishops has rested with the monks of Christ Church but old Harry Secund put an end to that. He told the monks they could elect anyone they saw fit, provided it was the candidate he wanted.

"Well," went on Tostig, "the younger monks at Canterbury got it into their heads that this was all wrong. They were going to assert their ancient right at the first opportunity. When Hubert Walter died, they rose secretly at midnight—not all of the chapter, just a select group of the younger spirits—and they hied themselves to the chapter house and proceeded to an election. This fat little donkey of a Reginald was their immediate superior. He was a notorious gabbler, a true jolthead, but these young dictators of destiny lacked the vision to see beyond him. So they chose Reginald. They recruited a party to accompany him, they raised the necessary funds and packed him off to Rome to secure confirmation at the hands of the Pope. One measure of caution occurred to them. The utmost secrecy must˙be maintained. The good Reginald was already beginning to puff and wheeze with importance but he agreed not to give anything out until he knelt in the presence of the vicar of Christ. Reginald's pride was not equal to this severe test. He began to announce himself as soon as he set foot on Norman soil. The result was that the word got back quickly to England.

"King John fell into a rage. He had his own candidate in mind, one John de Grey, Bishop of Norwich. He summoned the whole chapter before him, dictated to them the selection of the bishop, and then sent a deputation off for Rome for confirmation. A party of twelve, all of them thoroughly well bullied into doing what the king wanted. They left under strict orders to ride night and day and so reach Rome before Reginald, who was reported to be dawdling along like an old woman carrying eggs to the market."

Two mornings later, at an early hour, Richard lay in his wide and handsome bed and gazed out across the roofs of the great city. He was thinking of the days of Rome's glory, when the legions marched out to conquer the world with the golden eagles flying proudly above them, of Caesar and Pompey and Scipio Africanus and the gallant Gracchi. As he pondered such matters he heard a footfall on the stone steps which led to his apartments. A firm stride, unmistakably that of Tostig.

"They've arrived," announced the visitor, coming in with a broad grin. "A sorry-looking lot they were, all mud and dust. They tumbled out of their saddles like so many bags of meal. Word of their arrival, and of the condition they were in, was taken to His Holiness, who ordered them to bed immediately with permission to sleep the clock around before seeing him." Tostig gave his head a brisk nod. "I was up and about and I saw them come ambling through the gate on their weary horses. A saddle-galled lot and yet in spite of the ache in their bones there was a certain smugness about them. They have come to select the new archbishop under the watching eyes of the Pope of Rome. No wonder they wore grins like cats stuffed with cream. But," he added, "I fell into talk with one of the servants accompanying the party. He was a windy fellow and he told me that, although the monks will pretend they can make the selection of their own free will, the king made each of them swear before they left not to vote for anyone but his choice."

"Do you still think the Pope can circumvent them?" asked Richard.

"I think he will. Innocent will find some way. He'll have his plans made before the weary crew wake up. Make no mistake, the new archbishop will be of his choosing."

2

Pope Innocent differed from most of the pontiffs who had preceded him in more ways than the question of his years. He was unconventional and did not resort as much to the traditional ceremonies; particularly the slow and stately processionals about the Lateran in his chair. He was not only stirring up the whole of Christendom with his mighty plans, every detail of which he worked out himself, but he was striving to make Rome the final court of appeal in legal disputes. He presided tirelessly in the pontifical courts. There was little time in such an active life for the endless ceremonies which had made up so much of the lives of many of his predecessors. Often he traversed the halls of the palace on his own determined feet and the officers closest to him were always being surprised by his sudden appearances.

Innocent wasted no time in settling the dispute over the English archbishopric. He summoned all the parties concerned to appear before him. They were brought into one of the halls of justice where the pontiff sat on a high raised chair and the resident cardinals occupied seats below.

The Pope did not pause to meditate for any length of time on the evidence. He straightened up and declared in firm tones that the election of Reginald had been illegal from every standpoint and was therefore void.

The hearing on the second election, that of John de Grey, by the whole chapter under the lowering gaze of the king, took a longer time. The discussion was opened by the Pope calling upon Stephen Langton for an opinion.

The English cardinal had taken no part in the proceedings up to this point but the delegates from England had been fully aware of him as he sat quietly among his fellow cardinals. Although none of them had ever seen him, he had been a legendary figure in England for more than a decade. Every eye was on him when he rose slowly to his feet.

"Your Holiness," he said, "I have not been advised of all the circumstances of the case. Moreover, I am conscious that it has been many years since I set foot on English soil. There is not so much as a drop of alien blood in my veins, yet I do not believe that today I can appreciate fully what is happening in that green isle of my memory. Murmurs reach us from across the water. The people are stirring under the heavy hand of tyranny. The sound rises high, then ebbs, like the beat of storm waves on a fretted shore. It is clear, Your Highness, that there has been a change in the thinking of Englishmen.

"This is a matter of the utmost importance; for the man who is sent to the great See of Canterbury at this juncture must be a leader. He must be clear-sighted and he must be capable of sifting out on the granary floor of opinion that which is good and rejecting that which is no more than the froth of mob passions.

"I have no acquaintance with the man John de Grey. I have heard nothing of praise for him, nor anything harsh or derogatory. That the king favors him is clear enough, and so it may be assumed that he would be an able administrator. The quarrel of parish against parish, the dissensions always found in high places—with these he would have a sure hand. I am confident he would fill a niche comfortably at the king's court, with the apt words always to bless a kingly endeavor and the unction to smooth ruffled royal feathers.

"But, Your Holiness, I cannot judge if the man John de Grey has eyes to see what must be seen. How can we judge of him as a leader? The head of the Church must be zealous in the fight which is beginning for the rights of the individual. Would he be strong enough to resist tyranny? Would he be prepared to receive on an unbowed head the full fury of monarchial wrath?"

Richard and Tostig were among the few spectators permitted to attend the session of the court. From their station well back toward the high mosaic wall, they had watched the proceedings with an almost breathless interest. While Stephen Langton spoke, they sat motionless, letting his words fill their hearts as well as their minds.

"Surely," whispered Richard, "they must all see that this is the man who should be chosen archbishop! Do you suppose, Tostig, that the Pope has thought of him?"

Tostig laughed confidently. "The young Pope thinks of everything. Of course he has considered Langton for the post. Why else would he call upon him first? He wants the delegates to see the light for themselves. Look at them! They are drinking in every word."

Tostig was right. The Pope had thought of Stephen Langton for the post. He had not, as it soon developed, thought of anyone else. Much as he valued the work that Langton was doing in Rome, he realized how much more he was needed in England.

It is possible that he did not take sufficient care to assess in his mind what Langton was saying or, at any rate, to follow his reasoning through. Had he done so, he might have had a prophetic vision of what would come from this inspired type of leadership. He might have caught a fleeting vision of a broad green field on a bright summer day, where armed men bestrode their chargers and a pavilion stood in the midst of them and a king sat in futile efforts to avert the storm he had sown. Innocent III was too deeply committed to the elevation of the temporal power of the Church to feel too much concern for the needs of the common man. And so, years later, when Langton had achieved the first step in what he preached, they would cease to see eye to eye and the balance of their lives would be lived out in constant friction and suspicion.

But that was all in the future. On this particular and momentous day, the young Pope saw in Stephen Langton the inspired instrument of his will. He watched with a sense of satisfaction the faces of the delegates as the English cardinal spoke. When the end was reached and a silence fell over the hall, the Pope proceeded to strengthen the fabric of reasoning thus set up with the nails of legal ingenuity.

"It becomes necessary now," he declared, "to consider that the election of the Bishop of Norwich occurred before the previous election, that of Reginald, had been set aside. It is on that account as uncanonical as the first choice and must be declared void as well. With the ground thus cleared, we may now proceed to a legal and binding settlement."

This ingenious statement had not been expected. Blank looks were exchanged among the king's delegates, who had been confident up to this point of an easy victory.

The pontiff did not pause for any discussion of the principle thus laid down. He followed his first blow with one of an even more sweeping nature.

"It has come to our ears," he declared, "that the delegates before us are not as free as we have been led to believe. It is true that they have already, in sessions at Canterbury, voted for John de Grey. It is known also that the King of England has promised his assent to whatever decision they may reach here. But, to prevent any shifting of opinion, he secretly exacted from each and every one of them a promise, given under oath, to vote for none other than his choice."

After pausing to allow the confusion among the delegates to become apparent to everyone in the assemblage, the Pope raised a forefinger solemnly in the air. "You are hereby absolved from the oath thus demanded of you. You may consider yourselves free to debate the issue and to arrive at your decision without regard to any earlier commitment."

The pontiff next proceeded to make his purpose abundantly clear. "There is one among us today," he said, "of great gifts and of such dedication that no one excels him in understanding and in the expounding of the Word of God. A fit man indeed to fill this vacancy, and an Englishman as well."

A stillness fell over the hall. Stephen Langton's face could not be seen, for his head was lowered. His hands gripped the rail in front of him and it was clear that he was saying a silent prayer. Later he let it be known that it had come as a surprise, that nothing had been said to let him know of the Pope's purpose.

Innocent addressed himself again to the delegates from England. "The issue is in your hands."

The Canterbury monks filed out through a side door, their faces reflecting the varying emotions they felt. The pontiff was too busy to spend any length of time in waiting on a decision of this nature. In a few minutes he retired but word reached the chamber later that his attendance had been requested by the delegates to decide some point of canonical law. He spent a quarter hour with them and undoubtedly took advantage of the opportunity to make a more direct and forceful presentation of his wishes. At any rate, the delegates filed back into the hall soon thereafter.

They had chosen Stephen Langton with only one dissenting vote.

3

It was dark when Richard passed through the gates beyond which the will of the Pope was the law. Rain clouds filled the sky and the first damp gusts of an approaching storm moistened his face and caused him to hasten his steps. His cloak was damp by the time he reached his own doorway and he paused to give it a thorough shaking.

Inside he found Tostig, busily engaged in superintending the stripping of everything from the chests and the walls, and having them packed in saddlebags. The latter looked around with a triumphant air.

"We are going!" he cried. "At dawn tomorrow. God grant the storm has passed by that time."

"To England?" asked Richard. He could feel his heart beating with excitement.

"To England. In spite of everything, Cardinal Langton is going to cross the Channel. His Holiness, knowing the temper of our good king, fears he will meet with a violent reception. That is why he is sending us."

Richard seated himself in the nearest chair as he was finding it hard to breathe. "Tostig, Tostig!" he said. "This is the best word we have had for many years. How I have longed to go back!"

Tostig crossed the room and leaned down to whisper in his ear. "Perhaps now we shall be able to do something about the two fair ladies the king holds in captivity."

"You may soon be a married man, Tostig. Your Giselle is not a prisoner."

Tostig shook his head. "Giselle will never consent to leave her sister. I know her well enough to be sure of that." He brushed such speculations aside. "We have a long day's ride ahead of us. You must get as much sleep as possible."

"Sleep!" cried Richard. "Waste these golden moments in sleep? No, Tostig. There won't be a wink for me tonight. There's too much to think about."

Chapter X

THE PARTY which accompanied Stephen Langton did not reach England. On learning what had happened in the matter of the election, John's violence knew no bounds. He proclaimed that anyone acknowledging Langton as archbishop was a traitor. He had the Canterbury monks, who stood their ground, expelled in a body. Even the father of the new archbishop, an old and feeble man, had to fly for his life.

On instructions from the Pope, the party halted at the Cistercian monastery of Pontigny in Burgundy. Once before this institution had offered sanctuary to an incumbent of the Canterbury see who had been exiled: when Thomas à Becket had been forced by Henry II to flee the country.

No one in England, least of all the king, had believed that Innocent would carry out his threat of placing the country under an interdict. But when John showed no signs of amending his conduct, the Pope acted.

One night three of the bishops of England, on instructions from Rome, entered their episcopal churches. Each wore the violet robes of mourning and they were followed by priests carrying torches and chanting the *Miserere*. The shrines and the crucifixes on the walls were shrouded under cloth, the relics removed, the Wafer of the Host burned. A proclamation was then read that all the land of England had been laid under an interdict.

Instantly the lights were extinguished. They would not be lighted again, nor would services be held for burials, for weddings, or for christenings, until the ban had been lifted. The darkness of pagan days fell over England.

The two years that Richard spent in Pontigny seemed interminable. The monastery could not accommodate all of Langton's train and so the knight lived in the house of a miller who was called Old Huitre. All day he stood in the archbishop's anteroom to guard against any aggression from across the Channel. At night he shared a meal with the miller and slept in a dusty room above the wheels. To sleep was never easy. He would toss about and let his thoughts go back over the years since the two short days he had spent in the royal castle of Brittany. A thousand times he thought of the morning when he had ridden away. How long it seemed; longer than time, an infringement even on eternity!

One evening Richard was sitting at supper with Old Huitre (which means Old Dunce) and finding it hard to enjoy the cold mutton, cheese, and black bread which decorated the table between them. He had fallen into the habit of eating the last meal of the day with the miller because the enforced silence in the refectory at the monastery sat ill upon him at the close of his long and tedious days. It had become obnoxious to him to follow the sign language which was used to indicate wants, such as holding the tip of a first finger to the first joint of a thumb to convey the request, Pass the beans, or both hands joined obliquely to mean, More cheese.

"My ancient friend," he said, having noticed that the old man had never once during the meal looked him in the eye, "something tells me that your sight gets no better."

"No," answered the miller, fumbling for the pewter platter which held the cheese. "It will not get better, young sir." There was a long silence between them. The old man mumbled his cheese. "You are more observant than the others," he said finally. "Yes, I am blind. The light went out of these poor eyes a full two years ago."

"Old man, it cannot be! I have watched you going about your work. You have served those who brought their grain to you. You find your way to church and the market place. And no one has suspected."

"Nonetheless," declared the miller, reaching in three directions before locating his knife, "I am blind. As the means of calculation are withheld from me, I have no way of measuring the time. Except that my old bones have felt the cold of two long winters since I lost the use of my eyes."

"But why? Why have you gone to such pains to conceal it from everyone?"

"Why? I will tell you, my kind young friend. I have kept up this pretense because of fear. Fear! Nothing else."

"But surely there is no need. You have five sons who would lend you their aid. You are well liked, you have friends."

"Sir Knight," said Old Huitre in a tone of voice which reflected both grief and desperation, "my five sons are married and have their own homes but they watch me all the time, fearful of losing their share in what I have to leave. If they knew my sight had left me, they would be here day and night, watching, prying, waiting for the moment when I would betray the hiding place of my savings. If my sons did not do this, their wives would give them no peace about it. They would come themselves, those tight-lipped women. They would slip in when I could not see them, to search and turn everything upside down. Those who bring me grain to grind would give me short weight and take more than their due of flour. Pity me, young man, I don't dare to be blind! I would be robbed of my money and my mill would be taken from me. Life would hand me a cane and say to me, 'Go out on the streets and beg, Bartimeus.'

"So, you see, I haven't dared let them find out. I have had to make myself so certain of every bit of space about me that I can move with assurance. I keep my eyes lowered so no one will detect the lack of response in my useless eyes. You, and you only, have guessed the truth. You must not betray me."

"I will never give you away, my ancient friend. I will do everything in my power to help you. Think of me as a staff on which you can always lean."

The blind have compensations in the sharpening of their other senses. The miller proceeded to demonstrate this by declaring that someone was coming to the mill. Richard turned to listen but heard nothing.

"He who approaches is from that house of safe stone walls where most of my flour goes to fill fat bellies," declared Old Huitre. "One of the monks, surely, for I can hear the slish-swish of his sandals. By Gis, he is in a great hurry. I can hear him panting. Something has happened."

In a few moments Richard himself heard the scraping sound of sandals and almost immediately thereafter a monk appeared in the door of the mill. As the miller had declared, he was panting furiously and he had hitched his robe above his knees to facilitate a free use of his limbs. The newcomer addressed the Englishman.

"You, m'sieur, are wanted. It is a matter of consequence. You will come at once, if it please you."

2

It was indeed a matter of consequence. Tostig had killed a man and, in doing so, had saved the life of Stephen Langton.

When Richard arrived, they were still in the abbot's garden with its high stone wall thick with vines. Stephen Langton was standing quietly under the wall and Richard saw that his heavy woolen gown had been ripped down one side and that blood was running from a wound in his shoulder. The body of a man was lying on the grass and Tostig was beside it, still holding by one leg the wooden chair which he had used in disposing of the archbishop's assailant. The portly figure of the abbot could be seen approaching in waddling haste from the direction of the cloisters with several monks at his heels.

It has been said that Stephen Langton was not unduly impressive in appearance but on this occasion he held all eyes. His face had gone white but it was the pallor neither of fear nor of relief at his escape. He was regarding the body at his feet with a look which held only compassion. He seemed completely unaware of the injury he had received.

"You were right, my son, and I was wrong," he said to Richard in a composed voice. "There was danger, after all. I stood in the eye of our Father in heaven and so I could not die; but truly the Lord was all-wise in His choice of an instrument to carry out His will. How quickly our good Tostig moved to defend me!"

It seemed that, soon after his frugal supper, Stephen Langton had expressed a desire to walk in the abbot's garden, the evening being warm and pleasant. Tostig, of course, had gone with him. Richard had made these arrangements. He himself was in attendance on the cardinal throughout the day and the squire was on hand for the rest of the twenty-four hours, even remaining outside the door while the great man slept.

It was so very pleasant out, the evening air being heavy with the scent of the ripening apples and pears, that the archbishop had lingered longer than he intended and finally dusk had fallen about him. He was pacing up and down with his arms locked behind his back and his head bent forward in meditation; and so was an easy target. A figure had sprung out suddenly from the shadow of an apple tree, a knife raised in the air. Because of the churchman's desire for solitude, Tostig had been following at some distance but he moved with such instant decision that he was in time to stay the blow of the murderous unknown with a chair he had picked up as he ran. One blow of the chair had broken the man's skull. That he was dead was not to be deplored except that he was beyond the reach of questioning; and that was unfortunate, for now they could only speculate as to his motive.

"Who is it?" asked Richard, looking down at the body, which was lying in a most unnatural position with one leg doubled under the other.

"I think it's Tuddual," answered Tostig. "I caught a glimpse of his face as he fell."

"You mean the gardener who was ejected on the order of the abbot a month ago?"

Tostig nodded. "A thoroughly bad one. He was drunk much of the time and he had been convicted of theft, blasphemy, and the Sin."

"He was an attacker of women?"

"Three times."

Stephen Langton continued to look down at the inert body. "Poor fellow! He had no chance to repent of his sins. He is beyond redemption."

The abbot arrived at this point. "My lord cardinal!" he cried. "How can this have happened? Within our very walls! I am at a loss to account for it."

One of the monks who had followed him recognized the body and his explanation drew a sharply incredulous cry from the abbot. "Tuddual! I thought we were through with that wicked man. I cast him out a month ago and the order was given that he was never to be allowed inside again." His voice was reedy with exasperation. "My lord, I beg your leniency. There has been some grievous error."

"My kind and indulgent host," said the archbishop, "you must spare yourself any blame. It would be an easy matter for one as familiar with the establishment as this man to find his way back in. The Lord was watching and supplied a strong arm to fend off the blow. I have come to no harm."

"I am not sure of that, my lord cardinal," exclaimed the abbot. "You have suffered a wound which should have attention at once. I shall have Father Sosthene attend you to dress it. You are more badly hurt than you realize."

"It is probably no more than a deep scratch."

One of the monks had been examining the body. He rose to his feet at this point, holding a well-filled purse in one hand.

"My lord abbot, I found this under his belt."

"May I be permitted to examine it?" asked Richard. He took some coins from the purse and bent over to study them. "It's just as I thought. These are English coins."

"Ha! The motive is now clear," said the abbot, happy to place the blame elsewhere. "Someone crossed the Channel with the intention of attacking you, my lord cardinal, and found a ready instrument in this man who has been a thorn in my flesh for so long. But I blame myself for not being severe enough with the rogue. He should have been kept in prison where he could do no harm. But come, my lord cardinal, you suffer while we talk. Do you feel capable of walking?"

"Quite," answered the archbishop, smiling. He turned and took Richard's arm. "But it may be wise for the surgeon to see to this shoulder at once."

The injured man and his escort left the garden through a gate which creaked on rusty hinges. They crossed the cloister garth and mounted a short flight of stone steps to the suite of two rooms which served the visiting prelate. In the inner one he kept a plain pine table for his correspondence and a narrow cot on which he slept. The outer served as both oratory and anteroom and it was here that Richard remained in attendance during the day and Tostig through the night. It had one high and narrow window so it was often hot and breathless in summer. There was no hearth and it had to be heated in winter with a small brazier; so in all seasons it was an abode of unremitting discomfort.

"Come inside with me, my zealous young men," said the archbishop, leading the way into the inner room. There was a single candle burning low on the table. Stephen Langton looked at this as though considering the substitution of a fresh one; but, possessing in a full degree the churchman's sense of frugality, he decided that this was not necessary.

"Sit down, young men," he said, falling into the chair behind the desk with a deep sigh of relief. The wound had begun to bleed freely and he was suddenly conscious of weakness. "Before I explain what I have in mind, I desire to thank you, my stout Tostig, that I am alive this minute. With what miraculous speed you came to my assistance! The Lord must have lent you wings. One second more and I believe the knife would have found a vital spot. I owe it to our kind Father in heaven, and to you, that I am alive and sitting here this minute."

Not being blessed with prophetic vision, none of the three men in the ill-lighted room could know that Tostig's celerity had done much more than save the life of the Archbishop of Canterbury. If it had been allowed them to see ahead and know the shape of things to be, it would have been clear that the whole world had benefited. Had Stephen Langton died, there would have been no historic document signed on a meadow beside the Thames in a matter of a few turbulent years. Perhaps mankind would have waited a long time for the impetus to personal freedom which began with the Great Charter. A century certainly, two centuries, three perhaps. It would have come about in due course without a doubt, for the tyranny of absolute rule could not have been endured forever. Sooner or later the will to be free would have broken the bonds.

Some dim sense of this may have been in Stephen Langton's mind. At any rate he said in a reverent voice, addressing Tostig, "If a miracle brought you so swiftly to my aid, it was not to save my poor life but for a greater reason. . . .

"This has convinced me of one thing," he said when the surgeon had withdrawn. "You have been right, my good young men, in anticipating trouble. I am sure now that the situation in England is reaching a final stage. The king would not have gone to such lengths—for this attempt must have had his sanction—if he had not felt that things were reaching a desperate pass.

"What other conclusion is possible?" he went on. "The man had no grievance of his own against me. The English money in his purse was conclusive evidence. Yes, he had been paid to put me out of the way. No doubt the agent who hired him was skulking outside the walls, with horses to make good their escape." There was a pause. The archbishop frowned down at the papers on the worn surface of his plain pine table. "I receive reports from England, as you know. The latest makes it clear that the interdict weighs heavily on the people of England, that they are paying an unbearable price for the obduracy of the king. I would like to have a more thorough report on what is happening.

"The benefit of another viewpoint from that of my correspondents, who are mostly living under cover, is what I must have. There should be a test of the temper of the common people. Someone must go from one end of the country to the other, talking to men in the shops, in the fields, even in the taverns. I must know if I may count on support if I cross the water and issue a challenge to the king." He turned and looked steadily at Richard. "Are you ready to undertake this?"

Richard's face shone with a sudden exultation. During the tedious months and years that he had been serving the archbishop, he had entertained one great hope. To get back to England, to solve if possible the uncertainty, the mystery, which weighed heavily upon him.

The fate of the lovely Eleanor had seldom been out of his mind. The uncertainty had haunted him as he idled the time away in the dark anteroom of the archbishop. There had been a feeling of certainty in his mind that he could get at the truth if he were in England. And now he was to have the chance.

"Yes, my lord!" he exclaimed, his eyes shining with eagerness. "I am ready to go. At once, if such is your will."

The dream which had filled his mind as a youth had been dispelled. He was returning to England to work against the king.

Like the scouts who were sent into the land of Canaan by Joshua to spy out the land, the two emissaries lost no time on the road. They traveled mostly by night and slept during the hours of daylight. So vigorously did they push along that they came within sight of Calais well ahead of the usual time. Before venturing into that gray old town, which had become a veritable hotbed of treachery and where every third man was a spy or a professional soldier since the ban of the Church had closed over England, they donned the garb of goliards, the wandering minstrels who were so heartily welcomed in every corner of England. Their new clothes were particolored: one leg blue, the other gray, their tunics checkered and greasy with use, their hats boasting stiff feathers rising a full eighteen inches above the head. Richard carried a gittern over his shoulder, having gained some skill in the handling of it. A clever piece of facial disguise had been performed by Tostig which made the young knight look like a student who had been expelled from his university for good cause and had taken up the easy way of a life on the road. Tostig himself, with tunic bursting at the seams in an effort to encompass such broad shoulders, could easily be mistaken for a tumbler.

They went aboard on foot. A groom would follow with the horses on a later boat.

Chapter XI

T H E Y were most successful as a pair of goliards, drawing crowds about them and afterward sitting down in the taverns to chat about this and that and the state of the nation. It was frank talk to which they had listened. The country seethed with discontent and the interdict weighed heavily on the public conscience. True, priests could perform marriages outside the Church and there were services for the dead though none could be buried in consecrated ground. But the people of England could not accustom themselves to the locked and empty churches (for the bells had been removed and laid away in straw and all the holy vessels had been taken down from the walls and the lighted candles had been blown out), nor to the feeling of insecurity which weighed on their minds at being thus abandoned to the wiles of the prince of evil.

Everyone, it seemed, despised and hated John. It was not only because he had taken the consolations of religion away from them by his feud with the Pope. They hated him because he had murdered Prince Arthur, because every man's life was in danger from his vile rages and his disregard for the law, and because no woman was safe from his lustful ways. They despised him because he was losing the war with France and letting the Angevin Empire (of which all Englishmen were secretly proud although they ranted at the cost of it) break up as a result of his lack of energy; calling him John Softsword and sneering because he preferred to sleep late in bed with his beautiful young wife (who had been stolen from another man) instead of being early up and busy with affairs of state.

Ways had been devised of sending back word to Stephen Langton of what they were finding, and so it had been certain that their mission was a success.

But it had become too successful, largely because of Tostig. That astute young man had not been content to contribute his feats of strength and balance to an evening's entertainment. He had fallen into the habit of running comment on things in general as he went about his exhibition of skill. Having developed a dry sense of humor, he threw his audiences into gales of laughter. No one was spared the barb of his homespun wit but it was King John who bore the brunt of it. The squire had coined a phrase, "What lack ye, Jack?" which he interjected into his talks at suitable moments. Why, he would ask, had Normandy been lost to the French king? Why had the impregnable Château Gaillard, which Richard of the Lion-Heart had built, been surrendered to the French? *What lack ye, Jack?* Why were all fences in the forest being destroyed? Why did the king hold two little Scottish princesses as his prisoners? Was he more successful in making war on women? *What lack ye, Jack?*

The men in the taverns who listened to him and the crowds who gathered at village crossroads or in forest glades found this recurrent question much to their taste. They would take it up after him and shout the words with loud guffaws.

Finally Tostig wrote some verses for a more telling use of the phrase. He was discovering new powers inside himself and one was a way with words. The verses had an immediate effect whenever he used them, bringing audiences to their feet to shout and cheer.

> *Why are the steeples empty and still?*
> *What of this king who rules us so ill?*
> *What lack ye, Jack?*

It did not take long for word of the activities of the wandering pair to reach the ear of authority. One day they ventured into London and it so happened that King John had chosen this time also to pay the city a visit. They watched him ride down Cheapside, a stout dark man in a cloak stiff with gold thread and a huge ruby dangling at his neck. His errand, it was known, was to induce the merchants to make him a loan, and so he was surrounded by calculating nobles and sour churchmen. There were no ladies riding with him, not even his very beautiful queen (who had been worth stealing if beauty counts that much), nor was there any conspicuous rattling of armor nor a sign of the motley. On occasions the king could summon enough amiability to greet his subjects with a good humor verging on levity but it was clear that he had no thoughts this day beyond his great need for pounds, shillings, and pence; certainly he paid no attention to the noisy crowds assembled to greet him.

Richard was studying the much-hated king with close attention when he felt a hand pluck at his elbow.

"Follow me," said a cautious voice from behind.

He turned quickly and saw that the speaker was a man whose neatness of attire bespoke high rank and whose dark, thin features were intelligent and alert. Brushing his lips with a forefinger to enjoin caution, the stranger turned about and began to make his way through the crowd. After a moment's hesitation Richard motioned to Tostig and they followed after him.

The eyes of the population were fixed so intently on the puffy face of the monarch that no attention was paid to their departure. The stranger led the way inside the porch of one of the small churches which were so numerous in London. It was dark inside. The windows were covered with strips of canvas and not a single socket had its guttering candle. As a result of the interdict the walls were vacant and the shrines were stripped bare. In this gloom the paintings on the walls, which depicted the tortures of the damned, filled the interior with a sense of realistic horror.

"Thanks to the king's stubborn will, there is no place so private in all the world as an English church," declared the stranger with a wry smile. Then he sank his voice lower. "You must leave London at once. It's known you are here and our worthy king has declared in no uncertain tones that he wants you laid by the heels. As it happened, I heard what he said. 'I will show this mangy pair that I lack all compassion in dealing with base traitors,' was the way he put it. It is clear, young sir, that you have been a burr in his saddle and a gripe in his stomach for many a long day."

"Friend," began Richard, "for friend you must be to take such risks on our behalf. What advice have you for us, if we are to get away safely?"

The stranger spoke in low and hurried tones, for it was apparent that he desired to be free of them as quickly as possible. "Follow this street until you reach the river. There you will see a tavern with a sign, the Two Crones in Bice. Go in and ask for the landlord, Humphrey the Toss. Humphrey will set your feet in the safest path." He raised a hand in warning. "Lose no time about it. Our good king will have no manner of luck with the guild masters today and he will be in a savage mood."

Several decisions were reached that night in a dark room at the rear of the Two Crones. First, they were to separate. Tostig was to adopt the loose shirt and the tight leggings of a sailor and take his place on a wool barge which would unload farther down the river. From there he would ship to Flanders and make his way overland to Pontigny. Richard was to assume the garb of an itinerant merchant and take an empty barge on its return trip up the Thames. This was because he had declared his intention of continuing his journeyings about England alone. Having fulfilled the purpose for which he had come, he was free now to devote himself to the quest which lay so close to his heart.

At every stage of their journey they had heard speculations as to the fate of the Princess Eleanor. A few believed she had shared the fate of Arthur but most people were convinced she was being held a prisoner. The Lost Princess, they called her. In Norwich the two minstrels had been told that she was in Bristol. In Bristol it was said she was in a northern castle, right on the coast, in fact, so that the waters of the North Sea swirled about the foundations. The citizens of London were firmly convinced that she was in the Tower. "Ay," said a stout individual who had come down the Thames on a wool barge and was holding forth in a tavern, "I saw her taken there. I was no more than a hop and a jump from her—if you leave out the hop. Ay, she was a beautiful lass, with hair as black as mine."

A small landholder in the Oxford district was convinced he knew the whole story. "They're keeping her in a cell." He waved a hand vaguely in a westerly direction. "It's a dark little hole with no more than a slit for a window. Every day they hand in a loaf of bread and a jug of water. That's where the Lost Princess is—in case she's still alive, that is." He gave his head a rueful shake. "It stands to reason that she's dead and gone and tucked away with a spade by this time."

Richard's hopes rose and fell, according to the nature of the guesses and conjectures they heard. Once, in an East Anglian village, Tostig found him sitting in silent dejection on the low stone enclosure of a cemetery. A dozen plain wooden coffins were piled up along the outside of the wall, awaiting the time when the interdict would be lifted and the dead could again be confided to consecrated ground. Storm clouds were blowing down from the north and a wind was shaking the trees in the grove behind the graveyard. It did not require a vivid imagination to believe that the sound came from the neglected souls being denied their proper rest.

"What is it, Master Rick?"

Richard shook his head despondently. "It is quite possible, Tostig, that she's dead and waiting for burial like this. She might even be in one of these coffins. Who knows where she is?"

"You may be sure of this: if the king has had her killed, the body will be so well disposed of that it will never come to light." The squire studied the sad face of the young knight. "She's alive, Master Rick. I am certain of it. Giselle is with her and would have died at the same time; and I know that *she* is alive. I have seen her in my dreams and she always looks at me with a cheerful smile."

2

One night Richard was sitting at the long and hospitable board of his old friend, Alain de Casserlie. He was seated near the end of the table. Alain, sitting at the head with his beautiful young wife beside him, had no idea that he was being honored in this way; for Richard was dressed in the plainest of cloth tunics and was being most careful to keep out of the earl's range of vision. Alain had developed into a handsome man, rather heavy, it must be said, and florid of face but most pleasant and complaisant in manner. He and his auburn-haired bride were so devoted to each other that they paid little attention to any of the guests. They whispered together and laughed often, and once the slender wife allowed her head to rest fleetingly against his shoulder.

"Alain is a lucky man, and a happy one," thought Richard, with an inward sigh.

It was his hope to have a few words later with his old friend but he realized that Alain must not show any recognition of him in full sight of the household. Accordingly, he kept himself as much out of sight as possible behind the lubberly shoulders of his neighbors and took no active part in the talk which filled the oak-beamed hall.

Sleeping accommodation for the casual visitor was always limited, even in castles as large as Casserlie, and Richard found himself put to the necessity of choosing a place for himself on the rush-covered floor of the Great Hall. A half dozen others were already snoring in a huddled group near the hearth. He found himself a spot at some distance from the others, for the good reason that he was wearing his sword under his long woolen tunic and did not want anyone to discover it. With a rounded length of firewood to serve as a pillow, he stretched himself out and fell promptly to sleep.

He was wakened by someone tugging at his shoulder. The Hall was in complete darkness.

"Richard! It *is* you, isn't it?"

He realized then that it was his old friend who had roused him and he sat up with great pains to make no noise.

"Alain?"

"Yes, Rick, old friend. But don't make a sound. We must not waken any of the flea-bitten rabble."

They walked on tiptoe, making their way out through the oaken screens. Here the head of the household retrieved a candle he had left in an alcove before venturing into the Hall. By the light thus afforded he studied Richard for a moment.

"I recognized you at once, my old rogue!" he whispered. "But I gave no sign. It would have been very difficult for both of us if I had, because you have succeeded in rousing our gentle and puissant king to a state of most unusual ferocity."

"I should have left the country with Tostig but there—there was something I had to attend to first."

"May I ask what it was?"

"I must know what has happened to the Princess Eleanor."

There was a pause while the owner of the castle studied his visitor quizzically by the flickering light of the candle.

"Then there *was* some truth in the rumors which reached us."

Richard looked his surprise. Brittany had seemed a long way from England and, in any event, it had all happened years before. "What was it you heard?" he asked.

"Well, there was a story whispered about, here and there. The princess, so the story ran, had been very brusque with you when you arrived in Brittany and goaded you into the fight with the Captal de Cham. When you unhorsed him—ah, my old friend, what a thrill I had when the news of *that* reached my ears—then she began to look at you with different eyes. It was even said she was sorry you had to leave so soon and was inclined to mope for some time thereafter. Such, at least, was the way the rumor went."

"The princess won my entire allegiance!" declared Richard. "I would risk my life at John's hands if I could do anything to clear up this mystery. I would die gladly in her behalf!"

Alain remained silent for several moments, turning the candle downward and holding a hand above the flame so it would cast no light on them. "I can see it would have been wiser if I had kept my tongue between my teeth," he said finally.

"Alain!" said Richard, clutching his friend by the arm. "You know something! What is it? You must tell me. Are you sure she is still alive? Do you know where she is being kept?"

Alain indulged in a long hesitation. "If I did know something and was rash enough to tell you, I'm certain you would rush in and get all of us into serious trouble. There's a mad look in your eye." A further period of hesitation followed. Then the owner of the castle gave his head a sudden nod. "Yes," he said. "Yes, to both questions. The princess is alive. I know where she is being kept."

Only concern for the welfare of his host kept Richard from shouting aloud in sheer exultation. Eleanor was alive and the secret of her whereabouts was known to his friend! The weight rolled from his heart.

"Alain, you will tell me? I must know. I must."

"Having involved myself to this extent, I suppose I might as well go on. Yes, I will tell you. But not here, old friend. We might be overheard. Come, we will go up to the chamber I share with my wife. She will be asleep and dreaming sweetly by this time, my rare little beauty, and so we won't disturb her. It's the only place where we will be able to speak safely."

Alain lighted a long candle when they reached the solar and then bolted the door behind them. The guest looked about him with some hesitation, feeling very much of an intruder. He perceived that the room, which was large, contained a high French bed. Unlike the English type of tester bed, this one had curtains which rose above the top of the frame in a spiral and reached almost to the distant ceiling. The curtains were tightly drawn.

The room was surprisingly bare: a crucifix on one wall, a table, two chairs. A half-opened door revealed a closet in which clothing hung. A vessel in one corner, shaped on the order of a tulip, might have been a bath. All the windows were closed tightly, which made the room quite warm. Richard understood the reason for this. On arriving that afternoon, he had realized that the volume of water in the moat had shrunk through evaporation and was failing to carry away the scum which ran down the outside of the walls from the privies above. The late summer odors which always hung about great castles were, as a result, more prevalent than usual.

"Let us sit here in a corner," said Alain in a whisper. "We must not disturb my little red-crested bird."

"She is wondrously lovely and appealing, your lady," said Richard. "I found it hard to keep my eyes from her face this evening. I am sure you are a completely devoted couple."

"She means everything to me," declared the lord of the castle. "I love her so much that sometimes it is like a great pain in my heart. And to think there was a time—although you may have forgotten it—when I told you I would give all my lands and my prospects, and even my chance to marry her, if I could go with you into the service of the lord marshal!"

"So!"

A voice had spoken behind them. Turning with a feeling of guilt, the two friends saw that the curtains of the bed had been parted sufficiently to allow a face to peer through them. A delightful face, but an indignant one. A face from which all traces of sleep had been banished. A face with crisply curling hair, which had seemed auburn in the light of the candles at the table below but now looked more nearly red.

"So!" the owner of the face repeated. "That is how much you care for your unhappy, despised, uncared-for, unwanted wife! You were willing to trade her for a chance to go into service where you would wait on other ladies, and perhaps make love to them when their husbands weren't about, and spend all the rest of your time wrestling and fighting and tilting! How fortunate it was that I wakened and so discovered the truth about you!"

"My sweet wife whom I adore above everything else on earth!" cried Alain, running to the bedside and casting himself down on his knees. "It was when the match was made by our parents that I said those idle, meaningless words! We didn't know anything about each other. You were twelve years old and I was sixteen."

"I loved you," said the indignant beauty in a voice of increased hauteur, "from the very first moment I saw you. I went home in a glow of happiness! Why do I demean myself by telling you now? Because you—well, the truth is out. You didn't care for me at all."

"My angel from heaven!" cried Alain. "I wouldn't give you up for all of Christendom, with a slice of the moon thrown in, and all the light from the sun and enough stars to make a necklace for you! And I would include all of Prester John's country and the Land of Cockayne itself with its piecrust turrets and gingerbread walls, and its miles of blazing kitchens with chines of beef and haunches of venison hung up on pegs!"

There was a pause after this sweeping profession of devotion. The light of battle began to recede from the blue eyes peering through the curtains. After a moment a smile replaced the stern line of the mouth.

"Your apology is well and truly spoken, my Alain," said the young chatelaine, "and you covered a great deal of ground, didn't you? On the whole, I am inclined to accept it and say that we will forget the whole matter. But I am treating you much more leniently than any other wife would."

"You are the only perfect wife that ever sat by a man's side, and teased him with her sweet moods, and slept so prettily in his bed!" cried the now happy husband. Remembering then that this little conjugal scene was being conducted in the presence of a third party, "My dearest Adela," he said, "this is the friend of whom I have spoken so often, the companion of my youth, Richard of Rawen."

"We meet under somewhat unusual circumstances, Sir Knight," said the young wife, extending an arm between the curtains. This was quite a feat because, of course, it was customary to sleep in a state of nature and she had to leave herself one hand for the manipulation of the curtains. The extended arm was white and shapely and also, it must be confessed, a slight degree on the plump side.

Richard dropped on one knee and printed a kiss on the small hand. "I am your devoted servant, my lady," he said. "To intrude on you in this way is, I know, unpardonable——"

"It is all my fault, my heart," declared Alain. "We had to find a place where we could talk and it seemed to me that only here would we be free of possible eavesdroppers." He gave his head a nod. "I've promised to tell him, my love. What the tailor and his wife told us."

The head between the curtains looked startled. "But, Alain, my own, have we the right?"

"Of course, sweet chuck. . . . It was this way, Rick. A month or so ago a party came by late and begged beds for the night. We welcomed them, of course; it is our rule to turn no one away, except for just cause. They were curious people."

"Alain, if it is to be told, let me tell it. There was a man and his wife and two maids, who turned out to be seamstresses, and a bodyguard. They came from London where they made the costumes for the court."

"The man," said the lord of the castle, "was Rene of Tours and he was a tailor, of course."

"Yes, he designed all the robes, and the wife and the seamstresses did the fitting and the sewing. The wife's name was Suzette."

"They had a sumpter horse loaded with all manner of rich stuff."

"Alain, this is the part I can tell best. Ah, Sir Knight, it was a sight to gladden the heart! Such rich materials! Silks and satins and samite of heavenly colors. Light blue, lined with orange. Scarlets to be edged with ermine. Velours so stiffly embroidered that it was almost like chain mail. Such girdles and tassels and buttons! Such velvet for little caps and pearls strung on thread of gold!" She had become so carried away that she extended an arm through the curtains and then, with a startled cry, withdrew it in a great hurry and wrapped herself up to the neck again. A look of alarm settled on her face. "Alain, I don't think we should tell any more."

"Yes, my heart. Rick has a right to know."

"You think so?"

"Of course."

The delicate face, framed in the plum-colored hangings, looked quite sober at this. "Well, if you think so. You see, Sir Knight, this Rene of Tours was a boastful man. He said, 'Ah, what beauties we will make of these three little ladies at Corfe.' 'But, Master Tailor,' I said, 'there are only two of the Scottish princesses at Corfe.' He shook his head, 'True, my lady, but there is the other one'—he winked at me, the great, fat, soft creature—'the one who has been there all these years. And, 'swounds, my lady, she is the most lovely of the three and as slender as ever.' 'Pay no attention to what he says!' cried his wife. 'There are only two princesses!' 'Three!' persisted the tailor. 'Then,' I said, 'the third one must be the Lost Princess.' The wife got out a long, sharp needle. 'Thou very Tim of simpletons!' she said. 'I ought to run this clear through your gizzern! There may be three of them but there will only be two of us to be hanged if the king hears you have been blabbering, you soft-mouthed fool.' The poor wife begged us to treat the matter as a deep secret and we gave them our promise."

Richard's joy knew no bounds. "Then all the stories I have heard have been false! She hasn't been a prisoner in the Tower. She is not being kept in a dark cell without a window. She is safe and well."

Different moods had been chasing themselves across the pretty face of the wife; a genuine delight in the finery and the pleasure of telling a very great secret, as well as the doubts she felt over the fitness of telling anything. Now she was, clearly, filled with uneasiness. "But, Alain, I feel very guilty. We promised them so faithfully not to whisper a word to anyone about there being *three*."

Alain brushed this aside. "Come, come, my heart, my precious little worrier. What nonsense! A promise to a tailor? It means nothing when the interests of a knight are at stake."

"But we promised——"

"Rick will make us a promise that he will tell no one; and that, being a pact made by one knight to another, will be a secret matter. So no harm has been done at all by telling him."

There was a frown still on the brow of the young wife. "But he could tell another knight and *that* would be a sacred vow, would it not? Where might it end? If the king knew the tailor had told us, it would go hard with that stupid man. I fear I am very dull but what is the difference in promises?"

"My sweet child, the same as the differences in birth and rank. A promise to a cook, a servant, a barber, a tailor? *Pouf!* It is nothing. Surely you must see that."

"And would a promise from a knight hold good against a demand from someone higher in rank? From an earl, from a prince? From the king himself?"

Alain pursed up his lips as he considered these questions. "An order from the king must be obeyed." Then he paused. "But not all orders; no, no, not all. We are finding there are times when we must refuse the royal will. Rick, do you agree with that?"

Richard, who had once been so convinced that unquestioned obedience to the king was the first law, slowly nodded his head. "I have seen coffins piled high against churchyard walls, I have been everywhere in a country where the priests of God hide in cellars and caves. Yes, I agree with what you have said, Alain."

"As there is still a frown on that sweet brow, I think we must demand that not a word of this, not a whisper, will ever be spoken."

"You have my most solemn promise. I shall be away by dawn and so no one will ever know, no matter what befalls, that I have been here. No blame can ever fall on the shoulders of this gossiping tailor."

"And where are you going?"

"To the Dorset coast. Where a certain tall and grim castle stands. I am going to—to spy out the land."

Chapter XII

1

T HE autumn rains held off and the market towns were brisk with the activities of harvest as Richard tramped through them. In the New Forest the deer were wary and all other wild animals hostile and sulky. The same feeling could be felt in Winchester, which was already suffering from the loss of Normandy and the encroachments of the eastern counties in the wool trade. It was downhill from that point and Richard took advantage of the favorable grades to hurry his footsteps. His heart sang within him, "She is alive and I know where to find her."

South of Salisbury the downs opened up and the roads ran through country of such plenty that it was impossible to harbor any feeling but thankfulness. The stubble fields were speckled with red and gold and the late roses massed themselves over the stone fences. A homeless dog attached itself to the dusty heels of the passer-by but became lost in the confusion of a cattle market.

After passing Wimborne the freshness of the sea reached him and he knew that his journey was drawing to a close. Alain de Casserlie had spoken of an inn in the village of Corfe Castle and Richard had hoped to spend the night there. He was a little weary by this time, however, and his feet lagged. Dusk began to close in around him, the roads were suddenly flinty, and he had to pick his way carefully. He was on the point of giving up and seeking shelter at the first house which presented itself when he became aware that he was at the outskirts of a town or village. The going was smoother and there were cottages on each side of the road. There was a solid dark mass high on the sky line which must be Corfe Castle. "This is the place," he said to himself cheerfully. "I hope the landlord will have something simmering on the fire."

The village, he found, clustered at the foot of the hill on which King John's great castle stood. The square, in fact, ran straight to the castle gate and the village church faced the barbican tower across the paved surface. There was an inn on the eastern side of the square.

The place was ominously quiet. There was no sound to be heard save the tramp of his own weary feet. Not a light showed anywhere.

"Halloa within!" he cried, knocking vigorously on the inn door. There was no response.

He was considering the advisability of making his way into the dark interior when a welcome sound reached his ears, the clop of heels on the cobbled square. The figure of a man had emerged through the metal door in the tower.

"A traveler, eh?" said the newcomer, who was dressed in shapeless russet and wore a plated sallet on his head. "They didn't expect that."

"Is the whole village deserted," demanded Richard in some dudgeon, "or has an enchantment been laid on the place?"

"The women and children will be abed by this time," said the man. "Sit down and wait. It won't be long now."

"If I knew of any other place to spend the night, I would be on my way. This silence makes my skin creep."

"If you were a minstrel, they'd welcome you in the guardroom tonight. My name's Marcady and I'm one of them. When I left, they were sitting around and growling in sheer dullness of spirit."

"I made my living once as a wandering minstrel," confided Richard, seeing the glimmer of a plan. "A poor living, I must tell you. Now I have this pack on my back filled with goods for sale."

"Peddlers are let in often. To please the women."

The man Marcady was studying the wanderer as closely as he could in the darkness. "It's dead against orders at this hour," he said, as though to himself. "Robardi would be in a rage if he heard about it."

"Robardi!" cried Richard.

"Ay, the tim of tollers. He came from Brittany when the king sent over his prisoners. He's second to the governor but it's said that it's always his word which goes. And that makes it hard for everyone." The man made up his mind to the bold course and nodded to Richard. "You come with me. We can get in through the postern in the other side of the hill and you can get away by dawn."

"Robardi mustn't lay an eye on me," said Richard. "He saw me once. Across the water, it was, when I was not a peddler."

He had made up his mind to take the risk. An inner excitement had gripped him which he found hard to conceal. Here, he said to himself, was a God-sent chance to get inside the castle, to study its gates and walls, and to pick up information from the members of the garrison. A dozen Robardis, with malice in their heads, would not keep him away.

"What brought you here?" asked Richard of the guard.

"An idle mind and nothing better to do," said Marcady, grinning. "As I told you, things were dull so I spoke to Old Skull-Cruncher, who's in charge, and said I was willing to stroll over and get the news of how things went. 'You'll run into Old Scratch if you do,' he said. But everyone was anxious to get the story. So here I am. Know you aught of Nicholas of Acre?"

Richard shook his head. "This is my first visit in this part of the country."

"Two days ago he sat in his garden looking peacefully to the south where the fresh winds come. Dame Gildy left him alone for a short hour and, when she went back, he was off on his last campaign. To-night they are burying him in St. Martin's churchyard. Just back of the church over there."

"But, my friend, no one can be buried in consecrated ground! Not while the interdict lasts."

"Nicholas of Acre was a great soldier. He went to Ireland with Strongbow and a bit of land is there in his name. He marched behind William the Marshal in France, and it was at Acre, where he fought under our grand King Richard, that an arrow struck him in the eye. Ever since he has been sitting in his garden, with one side of his face puckered in a hideous scar but the other eye full of wisdom and kindliness. The people around here loved the old man. Would they let him rot by the roadside because of the stubborn moods of a king who never went to the Crusades?"

"So that is it!"

"He's laid away in his grave by this time," said Marcady. "Each man in the village was to take his turn at the digging so the blame couldn't be fixed on a few of them." He peered into Richard's face. "If ye want to come, we had best be on our way."

"Lead, then," said Richard.

The heavy gray-black of the sky seemed to undergo a disturbance as they began to skirt the high hill. A wind perhaps was responsible for a visible stirring in the leaden quality overhead; at any rate, a menacing black seemed to develop above this little corner of the earth where a group of bold villagers were defying the laws of the land and the dictates of Rome. The two men stopped of one accord and looked up.

"Is it because of what they're doing over there in the churchyard?" asked Richard in an awed tone.

"I think not," answered Marcady. "Father Bernard will be there to say the words over Old Nicholas. They're coming back, you know, the priests who ran away or went into hiding when Jack Lack swore he would skin every one of them alive that he could get his hands on. I saw the stringy old neck of Father Bernard through a window in the village the other day."

"I have heard of other cases. Think you it is going on all over the country?"

Marcady nodded confidently. "There were two churchmen at the castle a fortnit ago and I heard some of their talk. Yes, friend, the priests are coming back. And they are saying services for the dead and performing marriages. A sister of mine was wed up on the edge of the Marcher country a month ago with a procession to the church, and kneeling under the carecloth, and dancing of prinkcam-prankcam afterward."

"What does the king think of it?"

"He smiles his broadest smile and winks at his ministers. Will he worry if the people refuse to obey Rome any longer? He wants them to toss the interdict aside like a worn shoe."

"But," said Richard, "there is a power above both king and Pope. There will be no smiling or winking in heaven over this kind of disobedience."

The mood of the soldier changed. "Ay, and that's a true word you've spoken. When the Church sat down and folded its hands, the Devil came to England; and he's never left. You, friend, have been across the water and you don't know of what has been going on. Old Scratch has had a great trade in English souls. He's seen all the time, searching around the coffins in vaults and by the sides of roads. He always has a bag over his shoulder and *something in it that squirms and cries out*. A brother of mine saw him at it and the look the Horned One gave him from his terrible black eyes left my brother in a dead faint which he didn't recover from until the sun came up. He's no clunch, that one, he's everywhere at once. He's been seen twenty places in the kingdom at the same time—prying and stealing and smiling his terrible smile. Do you know that six times bells have tolled in empty steeples? An urgent, desperate ringing, as though the bells were crying out to the people to awake."

"Do people live, then, in a state of dread?"

The soldier laughed in a scoffing tone. "The people are the real clunches," he said. "At night they lie in bed and tremble, but when the sun comes out they forget all about it. They get out of bed, these brave, bold fellows, and they laugh and say, 'Where is this Old Scratch? Let me see him and I'll show him how poorly I think of all devils.' They never learn. Even though the fierce winds sweep up from hell, and horrible shadows fall across windows at night, while chains rattle and voices moan at keyholes. I'm sure they marched boldly over there to St. Martin's with the old man's body on their shoulders but they'll come back with their tails dropping, because the Devil will be following them in a great rage and he'll buffet them with unseen hands. All this night long he'll roam the streets of the village, his eyes blazing like the wildcat's."

The battlements of Corfe Castle had been high above them as they talked. Richard was glad when their stiff climb up the rear of the hills brought them to the back exit in the mountainous walls. A moment later the gate clanged behind them, shutting out the dread and mystery of the night.

2

From the outside, Corfe Castle had seemed black and forbidding, without a single light shining in its walls to hint at human habitation; a jumble of high towers on the crest of a hill and extending far up into the uneasy sky. Lights greeted them, however, as soon as they entered by the northern sally port. They had come directly into the inner bailey and to their left stood the towers in a formidable clump. Plenty of lights twinkled now in the lower part of the buildings, all below the level of the walls and so not to be seen from the outside. Richard lingered behind his guide long enough to study the largest structure, which, he knew, must be the King's Tower. It stood a full hundred feet above an open paved platform; the favorite residence of the king, perhaps because of the safety it afforded him. It was, he knew, the keeping place of the royal regalia. Beyond were lesser structures, one of which would be the Queen's Tower, where the constable was lodged.

They reached the platform by means of a long stretch of open stone steps and here Richard paused again to look about him. William the

Marshal had often said that Corfe was one of the strongest castles in the known world and Richard could see enough to agree with that opinion.

"You couldn't be taken here by direct assault," he said to Marcady. "Does the king spend much time here?"

"Too much," was the grumbling response. "It was an easy life when he was away but now that the Scottish princesses are here we have heavy duties. The staff that came with them will be in there now, swilling themselves full of the king's wine."

"You seem busy tonight."

They turned through a narrow door into the keep where the guardrooms were located. "Yes, we are busy but it's always this way since the two plump bratlings from up over the border were sent to us," explained Marcady. "Lords and ladies and tutors, and this and that. We can't tuck 'em away comfortably in cells with a platter and a jug shoved in twice a day and water for washing twice a week. They've set up a household of their own, like a core in an apple. They ride out every day, they have their own little ceremonies with six tall fellows galping away on their bagpipes. At home these tomfools fill their stomachs with sour oats like horses but here nothing suits 'em but roast mutton and fresh fish and puddings rich with suet."

Richard's first impression of the inside of the castle changed quickly to one of apprehension. Something about the place spoke—nay, cried aloud—of cruelty and terror. The walls seemed higher and darker and colder than any he had seen. Footfalls were heavier on the stone floors, and echoes came back when a voice was raised. Men seemed to slink, not walk, and to have a fearful eye always over the shoulder. Richard began to think he could hear faint whispers on the air, from desperate men and women confined in small, dark cells, dying of hunger and unable to make their plight known.

"A friend with a tongue to talk and a voice for singing, if rote or harp can be found for him," was the introduction Richard received when they made their way into the low-ceilinged guardroom where the last stages of a dismal meal had been reached.

His singing proved a success, such a success that Marcady had to caution his fellows repeatedly against joining in the choruses. As it was, Richard found it necessary on one occasion to conceal himself behind a stack of bills and pikes when Robardi came down to ascertain the reason for so much noise. Fortunately the prying eyes of the seneschal did not discover anything amiss.

When the company broke up for the night, Richard drew his sponsor to one side.

"My good friend Marcady," he said, "I have a request to make of you. Could you arrange for me to have a word with the maidservant Giselle?"

Marcady's mouth fell wide open at this suggestion. He looked both frightened and horrified.

"St. Wilfrid deliver me from this madman!" he exclaimed. "Does he want to get us both hanged? Does he think it a safe matter to trifle with the furious tempers of Robardi?"

"All I ask is a few seconds. Just long enough to whisper one sentence in her ear."

"All he asks is a few seconds with her! He might as well ask to see the queen in her bath or the soul of Morgan le Fay in torment."

Richard laid a solicitous hand on the man's arm. "It is a matter of life and death, good friend."

"It's only a matter of death so far as I'm concerned. No, no, Sir Merchant, who are no more a merchant than I am. It can't be done." The guard was frowning as he found new grounds for puzzlement in the request. "How comes it you know anything about this girl?"

"Is it not enough that I do?"

"Get this through your head, Sir Merchant. We have a mystery on our hands. Why is this girl Giselle here? It would be worth a stretch on the rack to ask. Does she serve the strange lady who is never seen and about whom no one dares speak? What reason is there for them to occupy the top floor of the new tower, which can be reached only through a narrow tunnel in the stone wall? Why is it ordered that no one is to be within eyesight when the lady comes out for a walk on the battlements? I want naught to do with such dangerous mysteries, Sir Merchant."

Richard indulged in no further urging. Marcady frowned and ran a hand speculatively over his jaw. He seemed to be giving the matter more thought. Finally he said, in a grumbling tone: "After all, we're friends. There would be no great harm done if I showed you the Short Gallery, would there? Cropper is on guard tonight and he never knows what's going on. Come along, my fine singer of ballads."

The Short Gallery was a stone corridor which ran off the Long Cham-

ber. It was dark and damp and unwholesome. Cropper was leaning
against a pillar with heavy-lidded eyes.

"It's this way, Cropper of the Stout Heart," said Marcady. "My
friend here wants to see one thing. And nothing more, mind you. Just
the entrance to the shaft. Master Ballad Singer, tickle the paw of this
brave warrior and see if he gives us a nod."

Richard dropped a small coin in the outstretched palm and Cropper
of the Stout Heart nodded and grinned. Marcady led the way to the
end of the gallery where the beginning of a passage in the wall could
be seen. Richard looked up the shaft and gave a shudder. It was round
and black and it went up at least forty feet, so that the opening at the
top seemed no wider than a man's hand. Only by shifting and squeezing
could a man of size make his way through it. The steps were mere
stone projections from the wall and not more than two inches wide.

"It's a cat climb and naught else," said Marcady, at his shoulder.
The guard gave an appraising rub of his stomach which was a well-
rounded specimen. "It's not for me, although you might get up. Father
Ambrose, the lady's confessor, tried it once and his fat belly got stuck.
He lost a lot of skin scrambling back, and he hasn't tried it since. So
the lady has to come down to him."

Richard continued to gaze up into the shaft with a mounting sense
of horror. To anyone who feared heights or close confinement it would
be a terrifying nightmare.

"No saint in a dark cell or hermit in a cave is so well hid as this
mysterious lady of ours," contributed Marcady.

"Does she make the climb often?"

"Most days. They say she's deathly afraid of it and is ready to faint
every time. But there's Father Ambrose to be seen and it's the only
chance to get a breath of fresh air out on the battlements. So what
else can she do?"

"My poor forlorn princess!" thought Richard. "What a cruel punishment for being born with a claim to a throne!"

"I don't need to tell you that no two people can pass in it. They
have two bells, one at the foot and one at the top. The one at the foot
is called the Ascent Bell and it's supposed to be rung before anyone
starts to climb. The one at the top is the Descent Bell and it's used the
same way. When the unknown lady is coming down it rings twice, and
that's a signal to clear off. No one's supposed to lay an eye on her."
The guard winked at his questioner. "Robardi pays no attention to sig-
nals. If he hears the Descent Bell, he's as likely as not to go up anyway.

You see, when a man going up meets a girl coming down, he can take all manner of liberties with her before she gets free of him. He tried it on the mistress once and she kicked him so hard he carries a scar on his temple to this day."

Richard's mind was filled with maddening conjectures. How could they be rescued from an eagle's eyrie reached only by this shaft? The king couldn't have thought of a more diabolical scheme to keep her safe! And yet she couldn't be left here any longer. It would drive her mad.

"Do you know who she is?" he asked his companion.

Marcady indulged in a snort. "Of course I know who she is. But her name has never been on my tongue. I don't want to find myself strapped on the rack or my foot in the boot. If you know her name, my friend—and I suspect you do—keep *your* tongue away from it."

None of this agreed with what Alain de Casserlie had told Richard. "I thought they were supplying her with beautiful clothes and caps with pearls on them, and warm furs," he said.

Marcady nodded. "That gives them an excuse to say she's being treated well. Where could she use fine clothes? Up there at the top of the shaft? Watch, my friend." He took ten steps down the gallery. "Three rooms," he said, "and they don't take up more space than that. There's a chamber for the lady, with a shrine and a bed, and under the bed a mattress for the maid Giselle to sleep on. Then there's a day room with a hearth and a window near the ceiling. And there's a kitchen where the manservant sleeps. He does the heavy work and he's called Sunric the Gill because he looks like a fish. My lady can trail her finery up and down these rooms and nowhere else."

As they left the gallery, Marcady contributed some further information about the conditions in the cells above the shaft. "One basket of wood every three days, winter and summer, so most of the time they eat cold food. There's only the one window and they can't see out of it and the sun gets in at dawn only. The place is like midnight by noon."

Richard was searching in a pocket under his belt. What he produced was a piece of money of such size that Marcady's eyes opened wide. "I will amend my suggestion. Get a message to the girl Giselle and this coin is yours. Get word to her that . . ." He paused, thoughtfully. "Just let her know that Richard is here and will be leaving at dawn. That is all."

Marcady plunged both hands down deep into his tunic pockets. His brow became furrowed with the intensity of his thinking. It was apparent that cupidity and fear were fighting a battle in his mind. When he finally emerged from the struggle, cupidity had won. "Dame Fritch has been up several times," he said. "She'll do anything for me. Flip me the coin, Sir Merchant. Your message will be delivered."

Richard was escorted to the outer bailey and to a dry nook in a hay tallat, where he was to spend the night. Here he stretched himself out and waited in such a fever of impatience that he could not keep still but threshed around from side to side and in doing so buried himself still deeper in the fragrant hay.

It was the better part of an hour before Marcady returned. He stood beside the rick and seemed to be engaged exclusively in moving the horn slides of the lantern he carried.

"She says," he whispered, "to be here just before dawn. No one is like to be around that early and the sentries have orders to keep their heads turned outward. But it will be wise to stand under the overhanging roof of the salterie, which will hide you from the sentries in case they get inquisitive. No matter what happens you must keep your mouth closed. Is that clear?"

"Perfectly clear, Master Marcady."

"I won't see you again. In fact I've never seen you. Except in the guardroom, and I had no part in getting you there. Is that clear? Very well, you must be away from here before the sun reaches the walls. Leave by the rear exit gate. Old Ned will let you out and he won't ask any questions. Drop a penny in his dirty paw and he'll call you Gabriel and Michael. Pick your feet up and place them down fast; and never look back."

He gave the lantern a swing and Richard could hear his cautious footsteps crossing the bridge over the dry moat which cut off the inner courts.

3

Richard did not sleep at all, his mind being filled with the problem of rescuing the Lost Princess from her stone prison up in the Dorset sky. No plan which offered any reasonable prospect of success occurred to him and he was disposed to give up in despair when the sound of discreet footsteps in the darkness reached his ears.

"Good Sir Knight! Can you hear me? It is Giselle."

"Where are you?" he asked in a whisper.

A hand groped for his in the still unrelieved darkness. With fingers interlocked, he followed her to what he recognized as the low arch which led back into the inner courts. Here they came to a stop.

"The light will soon reach us," whispered the girl.

In a matter of a very few minutes the first break came. The eastern sky had turned to gray.

"I am not to walk with my mistress this morning," explained Giselle. "There are things I must tell you. Sir Knight, if anything is to be done for her, it must be at once!"

"I have no purpose in life save to see her free again!" he exclaimed fervently. "But I am still in the dark as to how it can be done. Your one window is so narrow that no one can get through. In any event, it is a sheer drop of one hundred feet to the ground and so escape is impossible on that side. That leaves the shaft in the wall and it ends on a corridor where there are armed guards day and night. What method of rescue is left, then, unless an army can be assembled to take the castle by storm?"

"All of that I know. I have gone over it a thousand times!" There was a hint of hysteria in the girl's voice. "If it is impossible to save her by any earthly means, we must leave it to God and His Son and all the angels; for my poor mistress must be free of this soon. She grows desperate and I fear she will throw herself down the shaft. Or even hang herself with the rope."

"What rope do you mean?"

"There is a winch at the top of the shaft. But a prisoner cut off most of the rope and tried to escape through the window. It was a miracle that he got himself through but it was of no avail, for the rope was not long enough. The sentries saw him hanging there and they filled him full of arrows. The body was left to dangle for several days as an object lesson."

"How much of the rope is left?"

The girl spanned her slender throat with her two hands. "Enough," she whispered, "to enable my poor mistress to escape from this earth."

"It is possible that Tostig will find some way of getting you out," said Richard in a tone which suggested that he did not entertain much hope, even from his resourceful squire.

"May I ask a question?" Her voice carried a hesitant note. "Is he— is Tostig here?"

"No, he left me some time ago to carry reports to the archbishop at Pontigny. I sent a messenger to summon him back as soon as I learned that the princess was in Corfe. He may arrive within the week. And, of course, there is always the chance that our longheaded Tostig will see some way that everyone else has missed."

"Yes!" The girl's face showed a hint of eagerness. "We must not give up hope yet."

A shaft of pale light had touched the crenelated line of the battlements. Richard could now make out that they were standing at the upper part of the outer bailey and that the grounds fell away sharply beneath them. There was a pronounced dip also in the high wall surrounding the lower court. He was examining the defenses with an eye eager to detect any weaknesses when a light step was heard on the stone rampart above them.

"My mistress is coming," whispered Giselle. "She begins here at the Plakement tower and walks to the Gloriet and back three times."

It had become light enough for him to see the pale face of his companion for the first time. She was showing some of the effects of the long years of confinement. Under the kerchief wound around her head, he could see a streak of white in the brown of her hair. Her eyes had lost some of their freshness. Her cheeks seemed to carry a flush, however, and he concluded that this was due to the brief mention of Tostig.

He stepped out from the overhanging eaves of the salterie and found himself directly under the wall. Glancing up, he saw a figure emerge from the stone arch of the Plakement tower. He knew it must be the princess, although she was muffled up against the morning chill and her face was covered with a veil.

She became conscious of his presence at the same moment. Her steps slowed and she raised her veil.

She was fragile and pale but it seemed to him nevertheless that she was as beautiful as ever. The tips of hair showing under her wimple were still golden and she carried herself proudly. Then he saw for the briefest moment the tragic entreaty in her eyes. His love, which had become a compound of pity and habit over the years, returned again as a tumultuous force, urging him to bold action. He wanted to fight for her singlehanded against all the dark forces of John, to ride away with her on his saddle over the Dorset hills.

She began to speak in such a low tone that he found it hard to tell what she was saying.

"Richard of Rawen! Is it indeed you, my good friend?"

"You must not answer," Giselle admonished him in an anxious whisper.

"I thought I had been forgotten," went on the princess, her slow pace carrying her beyond the spot where they stood. "Kind and brave Sir Richard, let my friends know. I beseech you, let them know what has befallen poor Eleanor of Brittany!"

The heavy tread of a sentry could be heard behind her. Giselle's arm guided Richard back under the overhang of the roof. The princess, adjusting her veil, continued her slow descent of the wall.

Chapter XIII

1

RICHARD took the road that skirted the base of the hill, stumbling often in the dark, and finally reached the inn, which faced on the village square. Despite the earliness of the hour there were signs of activity within and he tapped lightly on the door.

The landlord came out to greet him, wiping his hands on a huge towel. He was huge himself, having the broadest of shoulders and great, powerful arms. Widely spaced gray eyes gave him a look of courage and reliability, both of which qualities he was to display amply in the course of their acquaintance. Richard would learn, moreover, that it was the master of the inn who had talked the villagers into the audacious frame of mind to lay away old Nicholas of Acre in the church graveyard.

"You'll be wanting the room above," said the landlord, whose name was Silverdown. "They all do."

"A bed to myself," stipulated the guest.

"And you'll be staying a matter of a fortnit or so."

"Perhaps." Richard swung the peddler's pack from his shoulders and deposited it at his feet.

"They all say 'perhaps' but they stay nonetheless." The landlord nodded his broad head. "I've come to know the signs. They're all on the same errand. Someone has been taken and put in the stone cage up there. A father, a friend, a son, or even a wife. They come here to my inn and they put in the time sitting where they can see the walls of that great black pile. Ay, and there's a look in their eyes which tells how unhappy they are. They ask all manner of questions and it's clear they are thinking and wondering—wondering if there's any way of getting them out. But after a time it grows clear to them that nothing is going to happen and that there's nothing they can do. Then they pack up and go away, very slowly and sadly. Ay, I've seen it happen a round score of times, my good young man."

"Are there many prisoners?"

Silverdown nodded slowly. "There's always a great many. They come under heavy guard, the brave young men and the wise old ones, mostly priests. Once there was a lady. A handsome lady, with her young son beside her. They never appeared again and the word was whispered that they had starved to death in the one cell. You know who *she* was?"

"The Lady Braose, whose husband had been such a favorite once with King John."

"Ay, that unfortunate lady it was. She was looking very close at everything as she rode through—the sky, the hills, the houses and the hedges, and the people who came out to watch. *She* knew she was looking her last at the world." The landlord stood with his feet far apart, his hands on his hips. "It's not an easy death, being starved in a cell."

"What of the twenty-four knights from Brittany?"

Silverdown's brow clouded. "I saw them!" he said. "And the cruelest sight I've ever seen in my life it was! They were brought here just as they had been started off on their journey across the water. Chained together, two by two, in open carts. They were thin and white, the poor young men, and their clothes were damp and covered with sea salt and their wrists were raw and bleeding from the chains. There was a hopeless look on all their faces. As long as I live I'll remember the creak of the death carts as they came slowly down this road. One of the knights pointed with his free hand to the castle up there and said something in an outlandish language. The rest tried to cheer but it was a dismal effort. They had no strength for it."

Richard had been listening with a look of horror in his eyes. "Rumors of all this got back to the Continent where I was at the time. We did not believe it could be true."

"Not a bite of food did they have after that, and not a drop of water." Silverdown's voice was as deep as the indignation which stirred within him. "They were so weak when they arrived that they didn't last very long."

Richard was given the upper room with a bed to himself, a very large bed in which no fewer than four tin merchants had been known to sleep at one time. The meals were good, the ale brown and satisfying, and so he was quite comfortable. But he was in no state of mind to enjoy such privileges. He sat outside, as Master Silverdown had predicted he would, and seldom took his eyes from the forbidding walls of the castle above him. He was always there at dawn, hoping to see a slender figure emerge from the tower to begin a sad progress of the battlements; but for some reason he failed to catch a glimpse of Eleanor at any time. He speculated grimly on the details of her life up there in the bare rooms allowed her. Did she have books to occupy her mind? Was she given paper and ink? Did she have harp or dulcimer to raise her spirits with music? Was there a carpet on the cold stone floors?

His mind was filled with speculation and plans. How could an escape be carried out from such a stronghold? All the methods he thought of were built on hope and none had much relation to reality. The truth of the matter, as well he knew, was that the castle would have to be taken by force; and that entailed a large army and several months of time, not to mention mangonels and battering rams and catapults capable of hurling large stones against the walls. Certainly it was no task for a lone knight and his very capable squire; providing that Tostig had received his note and was already on his way to join him. He thought of many ways also of getting in touch again with Giselle but each entailed the help of some members of the garrison staff, as well as the co-operation of the villagers; and he was not yet sure enough of any of them, even of honest Master Silverdown, to risk revealing his identity and purpose. The best he could hope for was that she would get in touch with him. She was in a position to select those about her who could be trusted.

Perhaps the devoted Giselle did not feel justified in placing so much faith in anyone. Perhaps it had not occurred to her that he would remain in the hope of getting word from her. At any rate no message was received. The days went by. The weather remained open and mild. Nothing happened and the sun went down at the close of each day with a finality which sent him in despair to another sleepless night on his ample couch. He began to long for the arrival of Tostig, knowing how much more resourceful the squire was. He dared not leave until Tostig arrived; otherwise they might never get together again but would rattle about hopelessly like two dried beans in a bushel bag.

He had been ten days at the inn when one morning the landlord came out to join him, carrying two tankards of ale, one for each of them.

"Sir Knight," said Silverdown, for it had been long before understood between them that Richard was neither a peddler nor a wandering minstrel, "you ask me no questions. That is unusual. In all other cases I have been questioned to death. Can it be that you put no trust in me?"

"My good host," said Richard, "I have no doubts of your honesty or your courage. If it were my own safety only that was at stake, I would be persistent. But any question I might ask would involve others."

"Of course. On the other hand I may be able to supply at best part of the answer to any question you might ask."

Richard thought this over, and the more he studied the honest face of his companion, the more convinced he became that his host could be trusted. A start had to be made somewhere. Could he hope for a better chance to begin?

"Master Silverdown," he said, "you told me of seeing prisoners brought through the village. Did you see them bring the Lost Princess?"

The landlord took a deep pull at his tankard, keeping his eyes fixed the while on the high ramparts of Corfe Castle. "Ay," he said after a long pause. "At least I saw a lady brought down this road at night. It so happened that I was in a state of mind about this and that. I couldn't sleep and so I lighted a candle and went downstairs to prowl about. I heard horses approaching with muffled hoofs. I put out my candle and went to a front window. It was a large party, twenty men at least and armed to the teeth. There was a lady in the midst of them, wearing a black mask and bundled up to the chin. I guessed at once who it was, for it was a few weeks only after the word had reached us of the capture of the poor little prince and his sister. Later we found that my surmise had been right. It was the Princess Eleanor." He put down his tankard and looked full at his guest. "Is it because of the princess that you have come, to sit and watch and ponder?"

Richard nodded. "Yes. It is her fate which concerns me."

"But you are English, Sir Knight."

"I happen to be one of the few Englishmen who believed that Arthur had a just claim to the throne."

The landlord seemed quite suddenly to have put two and two together and arrived at four as his answer. A light took possession of his eyes.

"Can it be that you are the knight who fought against the great black foreign devil and knocked him clear out of the saddle?"

Richard hesitated and then decided that an evasive answer would serve no purpose. "Yes," he acknowledged. "I am Richard of Rawen.

By telling you this I have placed myself in your power, as you must realize. The king would like nothing better than to get his hands on me."

Master Silverdown got to his feet and began to pace ponderously about the paved space in front of the inn. He planted his large feet down loudly, he cracked the joints of his fingers, he made odd faces and, in general, gave evidence of an intense inner excitement.

"Richard of Rawen?" he said in an awed tone. "Kind Father in the sky, guide me now to a right and proper decision! How best may I serve this gallant knight who has put his very life in my hands? Should I tell him to go back at once to sanctuary across the water? Or should I—should I put him in the way of aid in the purpose which brought him here?"

Finally he reached a decision. He gave up his slow pacing and placed himself in front of Richard. "For right or for wrong, Sir Knight, I have some word for you. First, there is a rumor that the king intends to pay Corfe a visit very soon. A word to the wise: you must be far away from here before he comes. Second, the harvest dance will be held in a matter of ten days. On the square outside. It has always been the custom for some of the people from the castle to come out and join us. Women as well as men."

Richard pricked up his ears at this piece of information. He said to himself exultantly, "Perhaps this is the idea I have been trying to find!"

"The wives of the officials of the castle come sometimes and this year we expect many of them."

"Truly, this is the miracle I have sought!" cried the knight.

Silverdown nodded his head. "There is a chance, a slim one, I fear; but it is worth the trying. And now for the third. There is a man hereabouts who thinks much as you do. His heart is right and he hasn't a drop of Norman blood in his veins. It is a cool and resourceful head that he carries on his shoulders. Most important of all, he is in a position to lend aid to any worthy enterprise such as we have in our heads this moment. Say the word, Sir Knight, and I will send a messenger to ask that you be allowed to wait on him."

2

The directions which Silverdown gave him took Richard farther down into the Isle of Purbeck and then over a road to the west. This he followed for the better part of a day. The hills dipped down to the water's edge in places and so the roads were circuitous and the grades were steep. He was thoroughly weary when he came in sight of the domain of Adelbert of Halterlo, which stood well above on the high lands. The sun, sinking in the west, cast a warm glow over the long thatched houses and on fields ripe and ready for the sickle of the harvester.

The house had seemed squatty and almost mean on the outside but the interior was much more impressive. The walls were of stone and tightly lined with racks for the tools of war. Above the racks there were many rich articles on display: tapestries, prayer rugs, and rare articles of gold and silver and copper from the East. At the end of this room, behind a section of carved wood which did not extend to the ceiling, was the Great Hall. A circular stairway of stone led off to the right.

A servant led the way up the stair and Richard found himself in a small apartment with a hearth, a table of magnificent wood, and two high-backed chairs, in one of which sat a man with a white beard and a hoary mane of hair above a wide brow.

"Welcome, stranger," said the owner of Halterlo, rising courteously to his feet. When the diminishing clatter of heels on the stairs gave proof that the servant was out of earshot, Adelbert added in a cautious tone, "You are Richard of Rawen, are you not?"

"Yes, my lord Adelbert."

"Then you are doubly welcome. You have the key to open every Saxon heart and door, the pride we take in your great exploit in Brittany."

He was, as could be seen at first glance, a study in contrasts: of an advanced age, with the brow of a thinker and the well-thewed legs and broad shoulders of the fighting man, inspiring confidence by the frankness of his eye and respect, but also fear by the inflexible line of his mouth and jaw. Over his shoulders he wore a tippet of blue velvet handsomely lined with white fur, which suggested that the chill of age had settled in his bones; and yet there was vigor in every movement.

"To you, who come of a line which suffered bitterly in the confiscation," said the older man, "it may seem strange that I dwell in such comfort. I should like to explain how it comes about." He paused as though giving careful consideration to his words. "My great-grandfather, five times back, for whom I am named, was both a builder and a sailor of ships. It must be confessed that he was not above an occasional venture into the lucrative field of piracy. He had the gift of making all his ventures pay him well. After Hastings, where he had wielded a stout battle-ax, his lands were confiscated. He went to Duke William and offered him a substantial sum to be left in possession. 'Sir Duke,' he

said, 'give part of what I am offering you to the man who would otherwise be allotted my lands and keep the rest for yourself. If you do, we
will all three be better off.' The Norman leader looked at him sourly
and asked, 'What is there to prevent me from taking the lands and
picking your mangy hide of every coin you possess as well?' 'Just this,
Sir Duke,' declared my ancestor. 'I would die under torture before I
would reveal the place where my money is kept. You would get the
land and nothing more.' So the duke thought it over and said: 'Very
well, Sir Saxon. Bring me the gold and you shall keep your lands.' Needless to state, perhaps, my ancestor became a very rich man in time.

"My father took after him closely," continued Adelbert of Halterlo.
"He wore the cross and came back with a ship's hold full of loot from
the East. This house is filled with what he picked up in the course of
his crusading. I shall be happy to show you what there is a little later."
He paused and looked reflectively down the length of his handsome
nose. "I am not telling you this with any sense of pride. I want you
to understand my position. I am among the very few men of Saxon
blood who have wealth and so they come to me when help is needed.
I am indispensable in any effort to improve the lot of our people."

The tall master of Halterlo seated himself on a corner of the table and
crossed one knee over the other. It was then apparent that there was a
great neatness and gentility about him. His hose fitted him like his own
skin and his shoes had thin cork soles while the tops were of elegant
velvet laced tightly about his ankles with silk cords.

"There is one thing you must recall," he said abruptly. "Your father
waited long and patiently for the bell to be rung."

Richard nodded his head. "I heard him speak of it. He hoped for it
until the end."

"My young friend, I am going to open my mind to you freely. The
bell will remain silent and the Normans will never be swept back into
the sea. They have been here too long for that. There has been much
intermarrying and much property changing hands. The two races are
slowly merging. It is a hard thing to stomach but it must be accepted
now as true and beyond change. You will never get back the lands of
Baudene." He made a deprecating gesture. "There, you see? I spoke of
your family estates by the Norman name. That is an indication of what
habit does to us. But"—and the deep-set eyes under heavily thatched
brows came to life and shone with conviction and purpose—"but there
will be other ways. The present king, this cruel and base man, is a gift
from the God who weaves the web of destiny with such sureness. Men

are stirring under the foulness of his despotism. When the interdict
comes to an end, we believe there will be at the same time an end to
Master Jack Lack."

Richard was listening to this daring talk with an interest that verged
almost on fascination. He had never before heard the thoughts which
filled the secret places in most men's minds expressed with such boldness.

"And after John, who? We won't put his infant son on the throne.
The chaos of the interdict can't be followed by the evils of a regency."

"I can give the answer to that!" cried Richard, springing to his feet.
"Who? The Princess Eleanor, of course!"

The elderly man regarded him with studious care. "Then you are one
of those who believe her descent can be traced back in a straight line
to that greatest of kings, Arthur of glorious memory?"

"Yes, my lord. I have seen the charts prepared by the College of
Heralds of the Pendragon line. Now that her brother has been killed,
she has first claim to the throne of England."

"I am told you have seen the princess recently. You have even
spoken to her."

"A few words only. Spoken as she passed me on her morning walk
along the battlements."

"And do you think she would make a good queen?"

"She is beautiful and gracious. It is my belief also that she is wise
and brave."

"The Plantagenet kings have all been handsome and, when they
cared, gracious. They have been brave to a fault and some of them
have been wise. But other qualities are needed. Discretion. A sense of
fairness and of the responsibilities of kingship. Honesty. Godliness. Has
she all of these?"

Richard gave an honest answer. "I don't know. But I believe so. To
me she is everything that is right and good."

"I fear you are a partial witness, young Sir Knight," said the master
of Halterlo with a smile. "But I welcome such testimony, for I believe
her to have many of these qualities. Certainly she has the gift of winning
devotion. And, like you, I am convinced of the soundness of her claim
to the throne.

"I am speaking without reserve," he went on, dropping his feet to
the floor. "We must rescue the princess from the power of the king
as soon as possible. I am told you have a plan."

"A vague one. I have hopes it will succeed but I can make no promises."

"I am not certain the time is ripe to put her forward as claimant of the crown. The barons are ready enough to put curbs on the power of John, even to the extent of supporting a successor, but they are not organized into a party yet. If you succeed in your plan, I would have certain of them meet the princess as a first step. That, I am convinced, would start a movement in her favor. But while the sentiment for her was growing and taking hold, we would have to provide sanctuary for her. There is only one answer to that. Wales."

Richard agreed at once. It was in Wales that the memory of the great King Arthur was kept alive and green. As a descendant of the Pendragon, she would be guarded well.

"The Prince of Gwyneth won't welcome the idea. He has extended his hold over all the Welsh provinces and is taking on royal airs. Besides, he's married to a love child of John's and thinks himself high in the esteem of his amiable father-in-law. No, we can't count on the prince. It will have to be Owen ap John."

Richard looked puzzled at the introduction of this name. He had lived so long abroad that he knew little of what had been happening at home.

"Owen ap John," said Adelbert in explanation, "is a strange and dangerous man. He doesn't bend the knee to Gwyneth and can afford to refuse because of his wealth. He has a castle on the great bay, not far from the Teifi, and they say he lives in state like a very king. It's true, of course," giving Richard a sober glance, "that he's the head and shoulders, not to mention the brains, of the slave trade with Ireland. Many's the thousands of fine young serfs from England and Wales that he's sold to the plantation owners and the neat little Welsh girls he has placed in prostitution."

Richard was frowning in serious doubt. "Is he a safe man to take the affairs of the princess in hand?"

Adelbert seemed completely confident on that score. "He keeps up a court as elaborate as Arthur's at Camelot. Gentlemen of this and that, and ladies in waiting. He's such a climber that he would swathe our lady in cloth of gold and set her up on a throne. A fine and honorable man would not serve our purpose as well as this uncouth striver after greatness. He would be willing to wage war on Gwyneth on her behalf and spit in John's beard. Yes, my young friend, Owen ap John was born into the world to fight the cause of Eleanor of Brittany." He paused and pondered over the situation. "Can you tell me yet what you will need in the way of help?"

"Horses. Six, at least. Two reliable men. And money. Plenty of money because it will be necessary to buy the help of people inside the castle. They will be demanding."

Adelbert nodded slowly. "I can promise you what you need, then. The horses will be spirited and fast, the men able to cut a way through opposition and not squeamish about killing on sight. I promise you the money out of my own purse."

3

Richard was roused at daybreak the next morning by the sound of many voices coming from the direction of the main gate. Going to a window, he saw that a large number of men in rough garb had gathered there and that one of them, a tall fellow with a face the color of his russet tunic and a bristling black beard, was addressing himself to Adelbert. The master of the land, in a surcoat of handsome tan and a hat with a gay feather, was listening politely to what the spokesman had to say.

As far as Richard could make out, the dispute between them had to do with the labor the men were expected to supply. Adelbert was concise and firm in his statements and several times the workers flared into noisy dissent. The listener left his window before any conclusion could be reached and, while he dressed himself, he could hear the meeting break up. The villeins apparently returned to their work.

Adelbert was having his breakfast when Richard reached the Great Hall but he was not alone. A pretty little woman with dark hair and eyes sat beside him. The guest looked at her curiously because she had not been in evidence the night before, and he had been told that the head of the household had been a widower for many years. An inkling of her position came to him when he saw the broadness of her hands and the cheap materials in her dress. Adelbert, who liked apparently to stick to the proprieties, had moved over to a corner of the table. This brought him close to her without the necessity of seating her above the salt. The other servants, acting perhaps on orders, did not speak to her.

Richard asked no questions concerning her but he liked her at once, noting the sweetness in her dark eyes and a wistful quality in her quite infrequent smiles. He did not even learn her name. His host seemed to rely on the word "Come" in addressing her. He would say, "Come, will you have more to eat?" or "Come, tell me what you think." Her voice in answering bespoke her peasant origin but there was always good sense in what she said. Once, during the meal, she allowed her hand to touch the master's lightly and briefly and once also she smiled up at him.

After devoting himself to his food with good appetite, Richard ventured to ask his host about the dispute he had overheard. The head of the household seemed disposed to brush it aside. "It was nothing," he said. "It's always this way when the autumn days run short. A dispute over corvée.

"They were contending," he went on in a completely matter-of-fact tone, "that it's late in the season for them to be giving me all their time. They're afraid the autumn rains will be on us before they can get their own crops in. All of them are tenant farmers, you see."

Richard knew enough about the land laws to realize that, as lord of the manor, Adelbert could insist on the tenants coming at any time he issued a call, in addition to the regular days they gave him each week. Only when he did not need them could they attend to their own crops.

"What was the outcome?" he asked.

"I refused, of course," answered the landowner, going on calmly with his meal.

"But, my very kind lord," began his female companion in hesitating tones, "the weather is getting unsettled. There will be rains soon. Perhaps tomorrow."

Adelbert was eating a mixture of eggs and fish with evident relish. He continued with his meal. "I think it quite certain that we'll have rain. That is why I want my crops in tonight."

"But, O my kind lord, what will happen to *their* crops?"

"There will be nothing left of them." His tone was quite casual. "I am not responsible for the rains."

"It is God who sends the rains."

The master laid down his knife and looked at her with surprise. This, quite clearly, was the most he had ever heard her say. "That is the point," he declared after a moment. "The Lord sends the rain, and if it ruins their crops, it is a sign that He is angry with them. They have been guilty of some sin and He is punishing them. Perhaps they have taken His name in vain. Perhaps they have been speaking ill of me. Why haven't they been like the provident ants who labor all the time and are never in need of food?"

"Because," in gentle tones, "you have demanded all their time for the past two weeks, my lord."

The woman hesitated to continue the discussion and it was several moments before she regained her courage to speak again. "Oh, dear master, oh, my kind and sweet lord, have you any idea what it is like to live through a winter in one of their houses, their cold and drafty little tofts? It is hard at any time but how bitter it is when they haven't enough food and must get along on roots and the scrapings of the salted fish barrel which have turned rancid, and flour made of husks and acorns! Many of the children will die of hunger this winter if you do not allow their fathers to work today on their own crops— their pitiful little crops! I beg of you, give them today free, at least."

The lord of the manor had shoved his meal aside and was regarding her with a look of deep surprise. "Come," he said, "this is most unusual. You are quite an advocate, child! And it comes to me that, in all the time you have been with me, you have never asked for anything. You have never bedeviled me with demands for silks and dresses, for ribbands and gauds, for land of your own, or an earthen pot in which to hoard your pennies—and the pennies to fill it. Because you have never been demanding of me, it is hard to refuse you now. So be it! I will release them for today and tomorrow. But mark you, it is you who must carry the message to them. You must make it clear that I give in solely to please you. They must not expect me to do it again."

The woman sprang up from the table and fairly ran to the door at the end of the Hall. Here she turned and smiled at him with misty eyes, even making a gesture as though to throw him a kiss but thinking better of it. "For this I shall love you all my life and pray for you with my dying breath!" she cried.

"It is surprising," declared the lord of the manor, "how pleasing she can be and how nice her habits, considering what she is." He turned to his guest. "I'll have reason, God wot, to regret what I've done. The rain will start before they return and part of my crops will be lost. I shall have to buy flour before spring comes and haul fodder for the horses. It will cost me much. Was I weak, Sir Knight? Or do you agree with what I did?"

"My mind has ceased to be clear on such points," answered Richard. "It was all so natural and easy when I was a boy. The king could do no wrong and one should be glad of a chance to die for him. The only things in life which counted were faith in your God and in the lady you wed, and obedience to the vows of knighthood. The only great pleasure was to measure your strength in honorable combat with one of equal birth. No sunset was so lovely as the sharp cutting edge of a well-wrought sword." He shook his head. "But now it is different. I have seen so much to unsettle me in these last days, I am all confused in my mind." He paused before answering his host's question. "I am sure, my lord, that you did right. The lady pleaded so well for them that you couldn't stand firmly on your rights." He added in a solemn voice, after some thought, "I'm not sure I will ever be able to believe completely again in any of the things I accepted as a boy."

"But never lose your faith in the wisdom of the land laws!" declared the master of the estate. "Without them there would be chaos, with shoddy in the saddle, and sow's ears instead of lady's colors on the tips of lances!"

Richard saw the lady of the breakfast table a little later, when he was preparing to leave. She was crossing from the stairs leading to Adelbert's apartment above and she was holding her head so low that it was clear she did not desire to be recognized. He stepped toward her nevertheless, saying, "I am on my way, my lady, and will not have the pleasure of seeing you again." This seemed to disturb her. Stopping in what was almost a panic, she gave him one upward glance with her warm brown eyes and whispered, "Thank you, good master," before disappearing behind the oak screens. "Odd little creature," thought Richard, staring after her.

Chapter XIV

1

IT WAS late that evening before Richard reached the inn near Corfe Castle. The landlord met him at the door with a mysterious wink. "My good merchant," he said, "I have another guest who will share your room and bed. He is upstairs now."

"I had your promise——" began Richard, in high dudgeon.

Silverdown winked again and said in a whisper, "It's your squire, Sir Knight, after a hard ride down from Dover way."

Tostig was sitting on the floor, for the room contained no chairs, and was busily overhauling his riding gear. He got to his feet with a wide smile.

"Master Rick!" he exclaimed. "I had your message as we were leaving Pontigny. I couldn't come at once after landing because my lord the archbishop instructed me to proceed to Canterbury. I came as soon as my task was completed." His eyes were shining in his bronzed face. "You did not set things down in so many words but I gathered that—that you know where they are. I rode in a frantic haste to get here."

Richard motioned toward the shadowed walls on the hilltop which could be seen through the window. "She is there. And, of course, Giselle is with her."

As he told the story of his visit inside the castle and what he had seen and heard there, the smile left Tostig's face and his expression grew grim and unhappy. It lightened somewhat when Richard spoke of his plan and of the results of his visit to Adelbert of Halterlo.

"Now that we are assured of help," declared Tostig at the conclusion of the narrative, "it should be possible to get them free of the tyrant's claws. Escapes have been made from castles as strong as this foul den."

"Is the interdict being lifted?" asked Richard.

"Well, peace is being patched up between the king and the archbishop. The raising of the ban waits on the good will of the Pope in Rome."

A step was heard on the stairs and Silverdown put his head through the door. "May I come in, young sirs? I have a hint for you. Nay, it may be more; it may prove the key to what sits so heavily on your minds. I believe I can get you into the castle." His eyes darted from one to the other. "Have you read in God's Word?"

Tostig nodded, having taught himself to read since entering the service of the archbishop. He had dipped zealously into the Bible. Richard shook his head. He had some knowledge of reading and writing, as much as he would ever acquire, but was hardly equal to a venture into Holy Writ.

"Then, Sir Squire," said the landlord, "it may be you have read the story of Rahab."

Tostig answered eagerly. "One of the greatest of all the Bible stories. What a wondrous thing that the walls of Jericho came tumbling down when the trumpets of Israel sounded! Rahab was the harlot who lived atop the walls of Jericho. Ay, Sir Landlord, I know the tale from beginning to end."

"You will recall, then, that she helped the Israelite spies to escape from the city and she attached a red cord to her window on the wall so that Joshua's men would know where she was and spare her from the sword. Young men, there is a Rahab in the village. She doesn't live on a wall, which is our good fortune, for if she did I would not take you to see her. She lives in a neat cottage on the other side of the village. There is Spanish blood in her and she goes by the name of Sanchia."

"How does it happen that a Spanish woman lives in this country?"

"It's said her mother came over with the old queen, Eleanor of Aquitaine. As for Sanchia, she says never a word about herself. This is how she put it to me once when I was being inquisitive: her present is something not to be talked about, her future belongs to God, but her past is her own." He gave a rather self-conscious nod. "The woman is comely and clean in her ways and I—well, young sirs, I have been long a widower and I sometimes go to see her. Many men of the garrison, even some of the officials, visit her little stone house. One thing I have learned is that she is anxious to redeem herself in the eyes of God. I have spoken to her and I believe she may be persuaded to bespeak you a chance to get inside."

"Can we trust her?" asked Richard.

"Ay, Sir Knight. I will swear to her honesty. And she's not a gossip. Her trade has made her closemouthed."

"When is the harvest festival to be held on the square?" asked Tostig eagerly.

"On Tuesday next. Five days in which to act. If your thoughts lie in that direction."

The house of Sanchia was vastly different from the tiny domain of Rahab on the sun-baked walls of Jericho. It stood apart, in an acre perhaps of garden and behind a stone wall, and there was an air of seclusion about it. Not a light was showing when they came to the gate. The landlord gave his head a satisfied nod.

"When she's not alone," he whispered, "she puts a candle in the window to show that she has company and mustn't be disturbed. We are free to go in."

The woman who opened the door to them was quite different from most of the sisterhood of Rahab. Although no longer young, she was still slender and there was a suggestion of neatness about her. She wore a large gold ring on one finger. There was wariness in her eyes, however, and she looked doubtfully at the two tall men standing behind the landlord.

"They are those of whom I spoke," said Silverdown. "Must we kick our heels here on your doorstep or will you let us in?"

"Come in," said the woman.

The house was in darkness but she lighted a candle and held it up toward the faces of her visitors. She studied them long and questioningly.

"This one," she said, nodding her head at Richard, "is of gentle house. The other," looking at Tostig, "is neither gentrice nor of the land."

"I am a free man," declared Tostig briefly.

"Yes, I can read that much in your face." The woman turned almost fiercely on the landlord. "Old Silver, you ask too much! Why should I risk my skin for men I have never seen before and a woman who would have nothing but scorn for me?"

"I am putting my own head in the noose," declared Silverdown. "I think God will smile on such an effort and that the angels will write it down fair of us in their book."

The woman began to speak in a tense whisper. "There is only one I would dare broach such treasonable matter to. He is hard and selfish but he keeps a close mouth about everything. He would take any risk, for money. But his price would be high."

Richard touched a hand to the purse under his belt. "I can pay well."

She was a woman of quick moods. Her eyes flared darkly. "For me, I would take nothing! I sell only the pleasure I can give men. If I risk my life, it will be to win favor in the eyes of the God who seems to have deserted this cruel and lawless land." Her attitude became less heated. "Only one could go. Two would mean overmuch risk." She considered them both and then tapped a forefinger on Tostig's broad chest. "This one."

"Then you have made up your mind to it, my brave Sanchia!" cried Silverdown.

"May that same God help me! I have decided to try, Old Silver. And I think I shall be burned as a foreign witch because of it."

2

Tostig left the house of Sanchia the next night, stalking at a discreet distance behind a man who led him with great caution around Corfe Hill; the same path that Richard had taken on Marcady's invitation. No word was spoken when the rear postern was opened to them but they were admitted unquestioningly. Inside, the guide moved with new caution, glancing continually about him and pausing often to listen to sounds in the dark halls. When they reached the entrance to the shaft in the short gallery, he gave the Ascent Bell a most cautious tug. Two rings sounded immediately from above.

"Up with you!" said the guide in an almost savage undertone. "Be back in half an hour or I will leave you to your fate."

It was not an easy climb for one of such rugged frame but Tostig managed to haul himself through the narrowest parts of the shaft. He reached the top with a sigh of relief. An eager pair of hands took possession of his as he emerged.

"Oh, it is you! I hoped it would be!" whispered Giselle. "Tostig, it has been so long! I have thought of you—overmuch."

There was a single candle in a sconce behind her but it afforded them little light. All he could see was that the girl's eyes were shining with excitement and delight.

"I have come in the hope of getting you and your mistress out of this foul hole," said Tostig. "We have a plan. A sound one, I believe. If it proves successful"—he paused as he returned the pressure of her hands

—"I shall claim a reward. A very great reward. The right to protect you and keep you free of trouble for the rest of your days."

Her answer was so low that he found it hard to hear what she said. "I could ask, dear Tostig, for no greater happiness."

"We received your message," he said.

"Oh, how glad I am! We didn't expect you would get it, because we knew only that you were somewhere on the Continent. An old friar was found at the rear postern. He was sick and close to starving and they brought him into the kitchens. I saw him there; and when he had finished a bowl of soup and seemed to be getting back his strength, I asked him to do what he could. The brave old man smiled at me and said he would try. The best he could promise was to pass the message on."

"That was how we got it. It was in a town south of Paris. A tournament was being held and an old friar came into the pavilion. He whispered the message in my ear."

"It was a miracle, surely!"

"He was the eleventh in the chain to carry it. I can't tell you how happy we were to learn that you were both alive." He lowered his head to study her face more closely in the dim light. "Have you withstood the close confinement well?"

"My health is good."

"And your mistress?"

The princess had come to the stone arch leading into the small room which served her as bedchamber and oratory.

"Is it Tostig?" she asked.

"Yes, Your Highness," he said. "I am alone. It was thought wise for one only to come tonight."

"We are allowed one candle each week so we have to be very careful of them," explained Giselle, in apology for the darkness of the rooms.

It was impossible to see at any distance from the feeble light in the wall sconce and so Tostig got no more than a dim impression of the Princess Eleanor. She seemed well dressed for a prisoner, even one of royal degree. Her tunic was of rich material with fur at the neck and wrists and her pointed shoes had bows of gold ribbon. Immediately thereafter, however, she moved within the narrow radius of illumination and he saw that the gown, although it had once been fine, was old and worn. It even showed signs of careful darning. The bows on the shoes were tawdry and badly tarnished, and there were holes in each toe.

"There will be scant time for all we have to say," declared Eleanor, leading the way under another stone arch which opened, he found, into the day chamber. Giselle retrieved the stub of candle and followed them in, finding another sconce for it beside the stone chimney.

The princess seated herself on a wooden bench before the hearth. Giselle and Tostig remained standing for a few moments and then, on Eleanor's suggestion, they seated themselves side by side on the uneven stone floor.

"We can speak freely," said Eleanor. "I sent Sunric downstairs on an errand and he won't be back within the hour."

Tostig plunged at once into the plans which had been worked out in the long talks held with Richard and the landlord of the inn. Giselle was to express a desire to take part in the dancing on the village square, if necessary making her request of Robardi himself and being as friendly about it as her feelings for the man would allow. "Suggest a dance with him," urged Tostig, seeing the reluctance she felt. "Freedom is worth a step and a twirl." When his consent had been obtained, the princess was to request an audience with the constable of the castle, Peter de Mauley, at which she would plead for the brief pleasure of going down and watching the frivolities from the shelter of the barbican gate.

Eleanor nodded her head at this point. "I will say that I am sure the Scottish princesses will want to watch and that I can be placed in the care of their guards. Surely he will not refuse such a modest request. He is a hard man but a knight of good repute. Although he has to follow the king's orders, he has been kind enough to me on several occasions. I shall play on his feelings and flatter him. He's vain and so I think he can be won over."

"The permissions are in your hands," said Tostig. "Our plans have progressed to this point. There will be a disturbance on the square when we see that you have arrived outside the gates. It has been arranged for a party of sailors off a boat at Swanage to appear on the scene. They will be well fortified with ale and will be looking for trouble with the villagers. In the midst of this the iron basket at the side of the square, which provides the light, will be knocked over. In the confusion and darkness, you should be able to slip away among the dancers. Richard will be close enough to you, Your Highness, to act as your guide and I will do the same for Giselle. If it is a very dark night, there may be uncertainty and we may not be able to reach you at once. In that case wait for someone who says, 'Beyond the king's writ.' Follow where he leads.

"We will meet first at a house a short distance beyond the village.

Here each of you will change at once into a shirt of mail and a steel hood. We must expect a furious hue and cry, with the whole countryside watching for us. Even though we ride by night and stay under cover by day, we are certain to be sighted. If the word is passed that two ladies have been seen riding northward with a company of men, we would have the hounds on our trail at once. You must dress in male attire until we cross the Wye."

The princess nodded her head. "It is a wise precaution, Sir Squire."

It had been apparent as they talked that Giselle had something she wanted to tell. "My mistress——" she began at this point.

The princess interrupted her. "No, Giselle, we are sisters," she declared. She addressed herself then to Tostig. "We have been confined here together for so long that all other ties have become unreal. No one has ever been so blessed as I have been in the devotion and care of my dear Giselle. Seven years! In these three little rooms! With little light and scarcely any heat, even in winter. No letter have I received in that time. I have had nothing to read. No sound of music has reached my ears. I am sure I would have been driven mad long ago but for the loving watchfulness of my sister."

Giselle had begun to sob. "But he must be told what I did. The awful thing I did without consulting you! I feel so guilty, now that a chance for freedom is opening for us."

"Your intention was good," said the princess. "Come, dear Giselle, we can't allow our feelings to use up the little time we have."

"But it must be explained." Giselle turned to the visitor seated beside her on the floor. "Not being committed as a prisoner, I am sometimes allowed a little freedom. I have been permitted to go for walks outside the walls. In the company of guards, of course, to prevent me from speaking to anyone. It occurred to me that the resemblance between us would make it possible for her to go out in my place, and so her escape might be brought about. She refused when I suggested it because she feared for me. I did not care! Her freedom would mean more to me than anything, even my own life." She nodded her head emphatically. "I had my plans all made. You see, we can be told apart because of my sister's golden hair. I thought that if I—if I had the golden hair, instead of her, then it would not be hard to get her free. No, don't shake your head. I tell you, I had a plan! If she would cut off her hair, it could be made into a wig which I would wear. You must not laugh! I am in earnest about it."

"I am not laughing," said Tostig. "It is not a laughing matter. It is a

plan for which I have nothing good to say. Do you realize this: that if
the escape of Her Highness could be accomplished in this way, it would
mean you would have to remain behind in her place? The disguise of
the wig might not be enough. What would happen to you if you were
found out?"

"That is what I said to her," declared the princess. "I was against
the idea. I refused to discuss it."

"I also am against it," said Tostig with every evidence of deep feeling.
"Now may I proceed with the rest of our arrangements?"

"But—but I haven't told you all," declared Giselle in hesitating tones.
"When I found my sister was against it, I became desperate. This was
after Sir Richard had been here and had gone away again. When no
further word reached us, it seemed that our one chance had been lost,
that our only contact with the rest of the world had been broken. We
were both in the deepest despair and that is why I thought I must force
her to agree. One night, when she was sleeping very soundly, I took my
scissors and cut off her hair. I clipped each lock with such great and
loving care that she was not disturbed."

"Even in this dim light," said the princess with a rueful attempt at a
laugh, "I prefer not to let anyone see how I look. I am sure I must
resemble a small dog my brother had when we were children. We called
it Louis after the Dauphin of France because its head was covered with
funny short curls." Her mood changed as a recollection of her wrongs
swept over her. Her eyes burned angrily. "It is the unkindest thing of
all that my jailers refuse me a mirror. For seven years I have not seen
my own face! I have no idea how I look. I may have become a yellow
and wrinkled old woman!"

In the dim light provided by what was left of the weekly candle, it
was clear that time had been infinitely more lenient than she suspected.
She was still slender and graceful in her movements, her neck (most
vulnerable part of all) was firm and round, her eyes had gained character from the few wrinkles collected about them. In repose she looked
sad but the imprint of the years vanished when her moods and passions
returned.

Giselle began to weep. "I don't deserve to be forgiven. How could I
have yielded to the desperate mood which came over me?"

"Now that it has happened," said Tostig, "I think we must make the
most of it. Permit me to have a wig made. When Your Highness is free,
there will be times when it could be used for special appearances. If it

can be made quickly enough, I can find means of smuggling it in to you."

As time was passing rapidly, he proceeded then to go over the course of action ahead of them in very considerable detail, telling them what they must do and what they must not do, what they must say and what they must leave unsaid. He coached the princess in the reasons she must give the governor and instructed Giselle in what she should say to Robardi. They went over everything several times and he did not hesitate to correct them when they did not seem to have caught the spirit of his instructions.

"You must realize this," he said finally, "that it is easy to make plans but hard to carry them out. Things go wrong. A mistake is made at a critical moment. An outsider intrudes himself. Something unexpected turns up. It may be that the light in the basket will continue to burn after it is knocked over. The sailors may get too drunk and make their appearance too soon. They may turn ugly at the last moment and refuse to obey our orders." He gave his head a somber shake. "And so we must be prepared for failure. But remember this: if we fail this time, we will come back and try again. You mustn't be discouraged. You will not be forgotten. That much we solemnly promise you." He glanced up at the Princess Eleanor. "There are people all over England who regard you as their rightful queen. Thousands of prayers are said every day for the Lost Princess. Never give up hope, no matter what happens.

"One thing remains to be settled between us," he went on. "We must keep in communication. On the last morning, if you have been successful in getting permission to attend the festival, you must signal us. I suggest that you do as Rahab did from her house on the walls of Jericho. Attach a red string to the bars of your window so that we can see it from below."

The time allotted them had slipped by. Tostig rose slowly to his feet.

"God grant that nothing happens to upset our plans," he said.

The princess fell to her knees on the floor and her lips moved in a silent prayer. Giselle walked beside him to the head of the shaft, her hand in his. "No matter what befalls!" she whispered. "No matter what befalls!"

Tostig rang the Descent Bell twice and heard a single response from below which meant that it would be safe for him to go down.

3

The days that followed were filled with feverish activity. A barber was found in the neighboring village of Wareham who used the beautiful long tresses of the Pearl of Brittany in making a wig. Through the efforts of the Spanish woman the wig was smuggled into the castle and up the shaft to the two anxious women above. Two shirts of chain mail of suitable size were found. Adelbert of Halterlo was persuaded to supply six men instead of two, with horses for all. A rendezvous was established in the woods a few hundred yards from the stone house and here the horses would be held during the evening. Richard and Tostig and the zealous Silverdown sat in solemn conclave and went over the preparations time and time again, looking for weaknesses in the plan and probing for the unexpected things which might arise to upset them, and where possible arranging countermeasures. On the night before the festival they went to their couches convinced they would succeed in spiriting away from Corfe Castle the most romantic and important prisoner it had ever held.

Even the weather indications were favorable. The old men in the village had been questioned and had been a unit in predicting clear weather. "The young 'uns will be at ta dancing," one of them declared. "The sun winked once afore going down and that is a sign. And ta face was red as harvester's."

The day came in clear and warm. Tostig studied the dawn from the window in the bedchamber with mixed feelings. "No rain," he said over his shoulder. "But tonight the moon may be out. Put in a prayer, Master Rick, for some late clouds." He paused and then said in a tone of satisfaction: "Old Silver is bringing out his horse for the ride to Swanage. St. Hubert smile on his efforts with that cross-grained bosun who must keep his squad in line for us."

At an early hour Tostig paid a visit to the small stone house outside the village and handed the chain-mail shirts to Sanchia.

"Two?" said the woman. "Then you are taking the baseborn sister as well as the princess."

"Of course. Would we leave her behind to bear the brunt of the king's savage humors?"

He was thinking how different the woman was from others of her class, as well as housewives in general. Instead of appearing in the loose garment customary in the mornings, she was neatly and carefully clad.

The hearth was clean, the kitchen utensils hanging on the walls shone with the fineness of copper. The floor was freshly sanded.

"There is trouble," she said. "With our friend in the castle. He came last night and demanded more money. When I told him it was unlikely you could pay him more, he grinned most evilly and said in that case he would have to tip the beck. Do you know what that means? He'll tell his story to Robardi."

Silverdown, knowing the man, had warned them to expect this. "How much is he asking?"

"Ten marks."

"Ten marks? The man is a brigand. You could buy the soul of a Norman abbot for less."

Sanchia nodded in agreement with this estimate. "But what can you do?" she asked. "I am afraid of him. He comes at noon to know what you have decided. My advice is to leave five marks with me. I will give him two and let him see the color of the rest, which he will not get until everything is over. I am afraid of him because he is a very bad man and will die on the gallows. But," looking up quickly, "not because of his part in this. He will not die for several years."

"How do you know such things?"

Her expressive dark eyes smiled for the first time. "I think Old Silver has spoken of me as the Spanish woman?"

"Yes. But that is all he knows about you."

"And that, young sir, is a guess. You are not of the village and I think you will keep a still tongue if I tell you the truth. My mother did not come from Spain but from the East. We belonged to a much older race. We can trace our descent back to Hagar, the Egyptian servant of Abraham who was driven into the wilderness of Shur. We call ourselves by a name which has never been on other lips, the Rom. My mother married a tall white soldier who came on the Crusades and she was cast out by her people. I too had a Christian husband and I was married before a priest. The people of the Rom would not take me back when my man died; and so here I am. My people can read both the past and the future from the lines of the hand and I had looked at his—this greedy knave who demands so much. Never before have I seen the mark of the gallows so clear on a life line. But even though we are sure he will die the death of a thief, we must meet his terms."

Tostig counted out with reluctance the five marks from the funds supplied by Adelbert of Halterlo. "Can you read what is on your own palm?" he asked.

There was silence for a moment. "Yes, young sir. I have lived out my share of happiness."

4

The single window which admitted light in limited quantities to the three tiny rooms was so high that Giselle had to use both of the chairs they possessed, one on top of the other, in order to reach the bars. She attached the red cloth, torn from a tunic which had fallen into rags and tatters, to the outside of the bars with a sense of jubilation. She had spoken to Robardi and had secured his consent. The princess had been equally successful with the constable of the castle.

"It is clear and warm outside," she said to the Princess Eleanor, who was holding the top chair steady. "The sun is strong. It looks so wonderful out. Oh, God and the Holy Mother look down on us tonight, and help us to our freedom!"

"I have almost forgotten what a midday sun is like, and the feel of it on my face," said the princess.

When she got down, the half sister's mood had changed. She seemed despondent. Instead of going about such small duties as their stone habitation provided, she seated herself on a stool beside the hearth and rested her head in one hand.

Despair was so much their prevailing mood that at first Eleanor paid no attention. Finally she could not ignore it longer. She called to Giselle: "Why are you moping like this, my poor child? Have you lost faith?"

"Almost," was the response. "I am afraid I won't be equal to playing my part."

"Your part? It is nothing. You dance once, or perhaps twice, with Robardi and then you wait for what will happen."

"But, my sister, I am not good at acting a part. When I went with my request to Robardi yesterday, I did not dare look him in the eye. I stammered. I hesitated over my words. I am sure his suspicions were aroused. Although he said, 'Very well, I shall be generous this once,' I think he was wondering what was behind it. And now I must see him again tonight. I must try to be pleasant when I dance with him. I am sure I shall be so awkward that he will know there is something wrong."

The princess walked to the hard wooden bench and seated herself there. "Do you really fear him as much as that?"

Giselle shuddered. "My flesh creeps whenever I see him. He is like a black beast of prey. I expect him to pounce and sink his terrible claws in me."

Eleanor gave this difficulty some thought. A solution came to her finally which caused a brief smile to cross her face. "There is one thing we could do to spare you. You could wear the veil and watch the festival from the gate. I could put on your dress and wind your blue scarf around my head, and meet the charming Robardi on the village square." She even indulged in a light laugh. "It might be amusing. He would think the music of the country fiddlers had gone to my head—to *your* head, rather."

"Wouldn't that make him more suspicious than ever?"

"I would allow him no time to think," declared Eleanor. "It will be too dark on the square for him to get a close look at me so we needn't be afraid he would find us out. Yes, my little sister, that may be the solution. Oh, I would be careful. I wouldn't be too different. I would keep my eyes down and only allow myself an occasional upward fluttering glance. I would smile, of course, and perhaps even laugh; but my gaiety would seem like a slow growth under the influence of his unexpected charms."

Giselle still entertained doubts. "What will our good friends think? Will it upset their plans in any way?"

"I can't believe so. Well, we have all day to think about it. Perhaps we'll find some better way."

The time passed slowly. Sunric had been summoned below to help in the kitchens for the day, so the preparation of the meals fell to Giselle's lot. She climbed down the shaft at noon and went to the head cook, who gave her a small smoked fish, half a loaf of fresh bread, and a beaker of rather sour wine.

"I hear you are going out to the square with us tonight," said the cook.

Giselle did her best to seem happy and excited over the prospect. "Yes, Dame Grout. I have not danced in a very long time."

"Better watch out, my lass. Robardi is not one to give favors without his full return." The woman lowered her voice. "The king comes at the end of this week."

Alarm showed in the face of Giselle. "Oh, Dame Grout!" she exclaimed. "Think you it will mean ill for my mistress?"

"Nothing good. You can be sure of *that*."

The mood of the princess had changed when Giselle returned with her meager supply of food. Eleanor was a Plantagenet and her temper was never far from the surface. Her eyes flashed and a spot of stormy color showed in each cheek when she saw what they were to eat.

"They feed us like lepers!" she cried.

She took one mouthful of the fish and then carried the rest of it to the hearth where she tossed it into the ashes. Returning to the table, she proceeded to content herself with the bread and the wine, making wry faces over the latter.

The hours passed slowly. Every so often Giselle would climb again on the two chairs and gaze up at the sky in an effort to guess at the time of day. Finally she announced that the afternoon was over and that the sky showed the first signs of dusk. Eleanor cried out with pleasure in the prospect of action at last. "And now for the test!" she said. "Do not worry, little sister. I shall carry things off with a high hand. Give me your dress to wear and then wrap the blue scarf around my head. I have decided to assume the task of deceiving that most considerate of jailers and most persistent of suitors, Messire Robardi."

The changing of garments gave further proof of the close resemblance between the two sisters. They were equally slender and shapely, in spite of the years they had spent in prison confinement. Their arms had the same roundness and grace, and this could also be said of the limbs which came into view on the discarding of the plain tunics each had been wearing. There were facial differences: a slight divergence in the arch of the nose and in the width between the cheekbones. But it would have taken an observant eye to detect them. The one important matter was the hair. Eleanor's was still the gold of the Plantagenets, Giselle's a light brown shot through with gray.

"You will wear my veil," said Eleanor when the change of costumes had been completed.

Giselle went into the bedchamber where the few articles of clothing they possessed were hanging in a corner. She drew out the wig first from its hiding place under the bed. It fitted her quite well and she carefully patted it into place, wishing there was a mirror so she could see what change it made in her appearance. Would it look real? Would it be possible for her to pass as the princess, if the need should arise? It was maddening that she had no way of knowing.

"Who can tell?" she said to herself as she placed the silk veil over her head and tied it securely under her chin. "It may prove very useful tonight."

"I think the time has come!" whispered Eleanor, becoming very tense.

They stationed themselves at the head of the shaft. Sounds reached them from below of many footsteps and of voices raised in excited anticipation. Giselle reached for her sister's hand and began to recite from the Psalms.

"'Be merciful with me, Oh God,'" she said, her eyes filling with tears. "'Be merciful unto me: for my soul trusteth in Thee: yea, in the shadow of Thy wings will I make my refuge, until these calamities be overpassed.'" Eleanor took up the thread of the words, saying with her: "'I will cry unto God most high; unto God that performeth all things for me.'"

The bell below sounded once. This was the signal for them to begin what they hoped would be their last journey down the dreaded shaft.

Chapter XV

1

THE harvest festival of Corfe Castle village was an event which attracted visitors from all parts of the Isle of Purbeck and even from the farthest confines of Dorset. In the afternoon an archery contest was held in a field outside the village in which bowmen from far away competed, although the champions almost invariably were local men. Many had been acclaimed over the course of the years and eight of them now lay very quietly on the other side of the churchyard wall; although it was a generally held belief that, when the contests were close, the graves of these silent archers would stir ever so slightly, as proof that the occupants could not entirely restrain themselves.

When the gate of the castle swung open that night and a group of the younger people poured out across the drawbridge, the square was already crowded. The dancing had begun and the fiddlers were sawing away like good fellows and the pipers were blowing until their distended cheeks threatened to burst. Robardi, always careful and always observant, felt a twinge of apprehension. He looked about him with an anxious eye, thinking how easy it might be for anyone to melt away into the crowds.

His mind was easier after he approached Giselle and claimed the dance she had promised him. She was not thinking of escape. On the contrary, she acceded readily and then danced with a grace which surprised him. She even had enough good will to look him in the eye and talk as they tripped through the measures.

"This is a new mood," thought the ex-barber. "And a most pleasant one. Is she beginning to relent? Ah, what a lightsome little dabchick she is!"

But Robardi had not watched the quiet Giselle all these years with-

out getting a very clear picture of her in his mind. This nymph, who
danced with such ease and who even laughed, seemed a different being. He caught a close glimpse of her face in profile and his appre-
hensions increased a thousandfold. Could it be imagination on his part
or was there something unfamiliar about the patrician arch of the nose?
She was dancing with someone else now and he watched her closely.

"There is trouble afoot!" thought Robardi. "I must take a look at the
other."

He was not the only one who felt surprise at the gaiety of the usually
quiet Giselle. It was Tostig's role to take her in charge when the light
was extinguished and he was hovering about and watching with the
same doubts.

"I don't understand this," he said to himself. "It must be Giselle and
yet . . ." His mind was quicker than that of the stolid Robardi and it
jumped unerringly to the explanation. "This is the princess," he thought.
"Now what are these foolish creatures trying to do? I must see about
this."

He first went to one of the men who had been sent by Adelbert to
assist them, an upstanding young yeoman named Alfred. "My friend,"
he said, "keep a close eye on the pretty woman with the blue scarf. If
I am not beside her when the hurly starts, go to her at once and say,
'Beyond the king's writ.' Then take her out of here. Take her to the
stone house. Remain there until the rest of us come."

The yeoman nodded his head. "A fair task, Sir Squire," he said. "I've
kept ta eye on her. A comely lass, that 'un."

In the meantime several things which had not been anticipated happened. Richard was standing close to the small group of people from
the castle who had crossed the drawbridge but were limiting their
share in the festivities to watching. There was a slender woman among
them who wore a veil and he kept his eyes fixed on her while he
waited for the action to begin. It must have been that someone in the
group had known him, for he heard most unexpectedly a challenging
and peremptory male voice cry, "Richard of Rawen!" Realizing the
danger, for himself and for the successful execution of the plan, he
promptly edged away and concealed himself among the dancers. "What
an unhappy chance!" he said to himself. "Now I must be doubly careful."

At almost this exact moment Robardi approached the princess and
spoke to her. "My lady," he said, for the fiction maintained about her
did not permit the use of other titles, "may I bring you wine?"

Giselle shook her veiled head. "I have no thirst," she said.

There was a difference in their voices, a slight one but sufficient to impress itself on the sharp hearing of the onetime barber. He was so certain there had been a substitution that he took a great liberty. He reached out and raised the veil.

The result was so opposed to what he had expected that he gasped with dismay. It was the princess after all! There could be no doubt about it, for the face under the veil was framed in the unmistakable golden hair.

"Your Highness!" he exclaimed. "I crave your pardon. I am filled with mortification."

Giselle was saved the necessity of replying, for at this moment the disturbances began. A loud altercation broke out in the corner of the square where the iron basket was supplying the light. The sailors from Swanage had arrived and were starting with great enjoyment to play the part for which they were being paid. They were quarreling with the villagers and fists were beginning to fly. Women screamed, the music stopped, and then over went the basket, causing a flurry among the dancers who were close to it. The sparks, which had been sent flying above the rooftops, died down. The late clouds, which Tostig had solicited so anxiously, had been contributed by some watchful agency, and so the square was plunged into almost complete darkness.

Richard had remained as close to the veiled figure as he dared and he now plunged eagerly forward, striving to reach the princess before the light could be started again. He was aware, as he elbowed his way through the people at the foot of the drawbridge, that Robardi was shouting in a frantic voice, demanding that the guards at the gate come to him. The head jailer's agile mind had read danger in this disturbance, so suspiciously timed, and knew it was his first duty to get the princess back safely into the castle.

Struggling through the agitated group, Richard realized that they were moving across the drawbridge and he redoubled his efforts to reach the princess in time. Perhaps the response to Tostig's wish had been too thorough. Certainly it would have been easier for Richard to carry out his part if the darkness had not been so dense. He could not tell one figure from another. The sound of a man's voice, raised in terror and anguish, gave an impetus to the retreat of the watchers. He crossed the bridge and stood under the arch in a state of desperate frustration, peering at every face which passed him, repeating, "The king's writ," hopefully.

By the time the light was replenished the square was almost completely deserted. The villagers had hastily betaken themselves home, knowing only too well the brutal methods of the castle guards. Visitors from outside had withdrawn silently to the sides of the square, having no appetite for this kind of disturbance. The sailors could be heard singing some distance up the road.

As Richard crossed the bridge to the paved square, his mind filled with the dismal realization that the plan had failed, he was startled to find that there had been one casualty. The body of a man was stretched out on the cobblestones, face down, with the hilt of a dagger sticking up from between his shoulder blades. The victim lay so still that it was clear he was dead.

Richard felt a hand pluck at his elbow. The voice of Tostig whispered in his ear. "Hurry, in God's name! The guards will be back in a trice and they mustn't find us here."

It was barely light enough on the square for him to observe his squire's face clearly but from what he did see he was aware that Tostig's passions had been aroused to a degree verging on frenzy. The disruption of their plans had wakened in him both rage and fear. His eyes seemed to have drawn closer together, his lips were clenched tightly.

"We've failed!" he said in a tense whisper. "Oh, God in heaven and the Holy Son, save her from her fate!"

Impatiently he took Richard by the shoulder and directed him to an open space on the west side of the square. Here there was a narrow opening between two of the small houses. This had been remarked earlier and selected as the best route for their departure. They ran down a flagged walk in complete darkness, scaled a stone fence, and found themselves on a back road.

"It was my fault!" gasped Richard as they began to run at top speed. "Someone recognized me in the group where the princess stood and called out my name. It was clear the whole plan would fall through if they got their hands on me at that stage. I did not dare venture closer until the lights went out."

The clouds were dispersing and a cluster of stars showed through an opening above them. Tostig raised a fist in that direction. "Why did this happen when everything was going so well? Did You not think these unfortunate women worthy of Thy pity and Thy aid?" Then he achieved a better control of his feelings. "Forgive me, O Lord, for laying our mistakes at Thy door. We have failed somehow. But it is now in

Thy hands, O Lord. Do your best for our brave and generous Giselle."

"Giselle?" cried Richard.

Tostig's angry impatience brought both arms into play. He waved them above his head in a gesture of impotence. "It's not the princess we are leaving behind. It's Giselle. For some reason, which cannot be explained in the light of reason or sanity, they had changed places."

"Then," cried Richard, "the princess has escaped!"

This mention of the successful issue of part at least of their planning did nothing to ameliorate Tostig's mood. "I think so. I did not realize what they had done soon enough. But, when I did, I left Her Grace in charge of Alfred. If no womanish whim has prevented him from following the instructions I gave him, she is safe by this time."

They had turned onto the road which ran direct to the cottage of the gypsy woman. Richard was feeling a guilty sense of relief. If one of the sisters had to suffer because of this tragic mistake, it was better for it to be Giselle. She was not a prisoner and so, he tried to convince himself, she could not in reason be blamed for what had happened. Second thoughts robbed him of any sense of satisfaction. They could neither expect nor hope that Giselle would escape blame when the enraged king began an investigation.

"Do you think she can play the part?"

"Do you mean, can she act as the princess? No, Master Rick, no! I cannot believe she will deceive them all. Not even wearing the wig of her sister's hair—if she has it. All we have accomplished is to deliver her over to the fury of this bloodthirsty king!"

"She may have escaped in the darkness," said Richard. "She knew that was her only chance. If she did, she may have taken refuge in one of the houses. Or she may have found her way to the gypsy woman's."

"She may this or she may that! All false hopes, Master Rick. But we'll have the truth now, for here we are."

The gypsy woman had not been losing time. She had stripped off the clothing of the one sister to reach her house and, when the two men entered, she slipped the shirt of chain mail over the slender shoulders of the princess. It was, in point of fact, a man's hauberk, the smallest they had been able to find. This defensive garment of closely fitted iron scales reached to her knees and the sleeves were long enough to cover her hands. A change for the better was effected when the belt was buckled about her waist. It was good that the gray cloak Sanchia fitted over her shoulders was also too long, for it hid the fact that the leather shoes on her feet were much too large. When the gypsy woman had covered her closely cropped yellow hair with a metal hood, the princess was ready for departure.

Tostig had stationed himself at the window, to watch and listen for signs of pursuit. He turned at this point. "Better be off, Master Rick," he whispered. "Alfred will go with you. He knows the roads. Get to horse at once. Our first duty now is to see that her ladyship gets safely away."

"Where is my sister?" asked the princess. Her eyes had been on the door, hoping to see Giselle join them.

"We are not sure yet," said Richard. "She has probably found refuge in the village."

Tostig waved impatiently to them both. "No time for that! Make your explanations when you are in the saddle. Be off now, in God's name! Leave the man Egbert and three horses. I'll wait here."

2

They got to horse as soon as they reached the trysting place but the princess refused to follow when Alfred led the way down a narrow wooded path.

"I know something has gone wrong," she said in a tense whisper. "You must tell me. Where is Giselle?"

"My lady," Richard answered, "I fear she did not succeed in getting away from the watchers at the gate. But we can't be sure. The dark was so intense at that time."

Her voice rose to an almost hysterical pitch. "But we can't ride away and leave her!" she cried. "We must wait. Take me back to the village. We must find her. She may be hiding."

"That is possible. We thought of it, of course, and Tostig is remaining behind. If she got away from them, he will find her. And now, my lady, we must not wait here. They may be down on us at any moment."

"I can't go! Do you think me such a coward as that? No, no! I would rather be caught than leave my poor Giselle."

Richard placed a hand on the reins of her horse. "It would be of no service to her if they got you back. What good could we do by returning to the village now? There will be armed men all over the place and horsemen patrolling the roads. We can't rescue her if she is in their hands. If she is free, Tostig will find her, and they will follow us."

"My poor sister! My sweet Giselle!" she said, beginning to weep. "Oh, Holy Mother in heaven, why should this happen to her?"

Richard touched the flank of her horse with his foot and started it into motion. "Keep your head down, my lady," he cautioned. "We will be riding through woods for some time."

"I shall never forgive myself if evil befalls her!"

They took off at a gallop then, the man Alfred in the lead, Richard riding beside the princess, and three guards behind. The horses' hoofs were muffled in heavy canvas and so they made little sound. In a matter of minutes, although it seemed an eternity to the anxious Richard, they turned into a second passage through the trees which was so narrow and low that it was necessary to ride in single file and to keep their heads lowered. In a short space of time they splashed through a stream swollen to unusual width by the autumnal rains. Then they crossed an open glade and became engulfed again in an obscurity of trees.

Three times they crossed streams and once they doubled back on their tracks for more than a hundred yards before taking to the woodland paths again. Alfred seemed to know every foot of the way. He never paused to consider or investigate. After an hour of this Richard said to him, "I think we must have thrown them off the scent by this time."

"That we have, praise to God and good St. Christopher. They'll need tomorrow's sun to trace our course, and not much of that will there be." The guard paused to listen for any hint of pursuit on the air. He nodded confidently. "They've lost us, so it's straight ahead now."

Eleanor had fallen into a deep and unhappy silence. She rode automatically and kept her eyes fixed ahead.

"Was there anything that could have been done?" she asked once.

"Not after Robardi became suspicious of the substitution. I saw him leave you and start to make his way back with frantic haste in the direction of the gate. This was almost immediately after I had been recognized by someone from the castle. I knew I couldn't venture closer."

"My poor Giselle!" cried the princess. "All the years we have been together it has been the same. She has always sacrificed herself for me, for my comfort, for my peace of mind. 'You are Eleanor of Brittany,' she would say. 'It is my duty to serve you.' Never has there been one more gentle or loyal." She choked back a sob. "And, of course, this is all my fault. I suggested we change places. I was too free with that terrible man and so planted the seeds of suspicion in his mind. It is even possible, Sir Knight, that my sister did not attempt to get away in the darkness because she knew her presence would delay the pursuit."

They had been at the gallop for something in excess of an hour before the princess laid aside her vain regrets to ask a question. "Where are you taking me, Sir Richard?"

The road had become wide and firm and so Richard had no hesitation in edging his mount a little closer to hers.

"We've had the aid of a splendid man whose name would mean nothing to you," he said. "He supplied the horses and the men, and the money. Tonight we must ride as far as a hunting lodge in the hills which belongs to him. We'll remain in hiding there all of tomorrow. The hue and cry will be on, so we won't dare do any traveling by day. There is better than a hundred miles of riding ahead of us. Our object is to reach the Wye and cross over into the country beyond the river where the king's writ does not run. To be on the safe side, we must steer clear of Bristol and ford the Wye above Chepstow. Once there, you are to remain in close seclusion in a small castle belonging to our great friend and benefactor.

"He has been in touch," he went on, "with many men of power and property who are sorely dissatisfied with the state of affairs in England and it's his hope to unite them in your support. Now that we've succeeded in getting you out of the king's hands, he will write these others to come and see you. And, perhaps, to discuss plans for the future."

"All this will take much time," she said after a moment's reflection.

"Yes, my lady. I believe his plan is to keep you at his castle for a brief while only and then take you to a more secure sanctuary in Wales. The Welsh people are still loyal to the memory of their great King Arthur and will receive you with open arms. That, Your Highness, is as much as I know of the plans. My own part, I am sure, will be a small one from now on."

Her voice suddenly became warm with gratitude. "I owe everything to you, my best of friends. Ah, how lucky that you came to Brittany! You have been generous to overlook my taunts and the harm I might have caused you when I arranged the tilting with the Captal de Cham. Why, why are you so forgiving?"

Two hours before dawn they reached a high place in the downs. Here the valleys were lush but the sheepwalks on the hillsides had been cropped to a dark monotony. The first sound of a tentative bleating reached them from far off in the hills.

The man Alfred showed the way up a road which seemed no more than a ledge on the rocky slope. It led into a wilder district where nature had taken control, where the road became no more than a path through the thickets. This was hunting country, abounding in game. Alfred said with a satisfied nod: "Trocking is just ahead. No one will follow us here."

Trocking turned out to be a small lodge, buried away in thick green trees. It had been built obviously for the use of rough men who came to kill game; a low, flat-topped building, surrounded by a palisade of untrimmed trunks. It consisted of a single long room with a chimney at one end and a narrow window to admit light. A rope had been strung around one corner on which new hides had been hung. Behind the curtain thus provided was a pile of newly cut boughs. This, quite apparently, would serve the regal visitor as a couch. There was a rough table at the other end, laid out with a cold joint, a loaf of bread, and a flagon of wine.

The princess looked about her. She was content to accept the limitations of a lodge dedicated exclusively to St. Hubert but she could not prevent the tip of her sensitive nose from quivering slightly.

"There is food, Your Highness," said Richard. "Would you care for some venison?"

She shook her head. "I am too excited and also too tired. But I am thirsty and would like a cup of wine."

Richard studied with a critical eye the liquid which he poured from the flagon. "I am afraid, my lady," he said, "that you will find it thin and sour."

She accepted the wine without demur. "I have been taught to expect no better," she said. But she drank very little of it before returning the cup to him. "Where am I to sleep?"

"Behind the curtain of skins, my lady." He added in an apologetic tone: "Things are very rough here. But we shall spend only the day and be off again by nightfall."

"I have no complaints to make. Have you forgotten that I have lived for seven years in dark stone cells?"

"I shall sleep outside the door, within call if you should need me."

She hesitated. "Please, will you sleep inside? At least one of my ladies has always been in my room at night. I think I would be afraid of the dark if I were alone."

"Very well, my lady."

She vanished behind the barricade of hides. Richard stretched himself out on some straw near the door but with no thought of sleep. The fear of the hunted still kept its grip on him. At any moment the pursuing party from the castle might come upon them and surround the lodge. Even though one of the men had been posted as a sentry near the road, he must remain vigilant himself.

Eleanor had pleaded weariness but it was soon evident that she was not finding the relief of sleep. He could hear her toss and turn and once, for a few moments, she indulged in a spell of weeping. Finally she spoke in a very low voice.

"Sir Knight!"

He sat up at once. "Yes, my lady."

"I can't sleep in this coat of mail. But I find myself in a difficulty."

Richard got to his feet and lighted a torch in a wall sconce near the door.

"Never in my life," she said in a whisper, "have I lacked the aid of other hands. I have always had my ladies to dress and undress me. I am at a loss about getting free of this armored coat. Besides, it seems to have caught on something at the back. Would you deign to be of assistance in this dilemma?"

"Of course, my lady," he responded in a voice which suggested a breathless awe.

He extended an arm over the bearskin wall and his hand encountered the back of the chain mail which had been turned to him. Investigating with the nervous care of a neophyte moving a sacred relic on a shrine, he discovered where the links had become entangled on the garment beneath. He separated them with fingers which had become clumsy, keeping his eyes turned up to the ceiling. But even in the darkness back of the barricade, and in spite of his resolution to see nothing, he caught one guilty glimpse of the slender outline of her garnet-colored hose.

"And now," she asked, "how do I get it off?"

"It is customary, my lady, to slip it up over the head." She did not say anything and he sensed some hesitation on her part. "If you will raise your arms, I will be able to take it off for you."

When the task had been successfully accomplished, she said with a sigh, "And now, I shall sleep. If I can get my mind off my poor Giselle."

The afternoon was well advanced when Richard wakened from a sleep of a few hours. Sunlight was reaching the open door of the lodge through the cover of trees and laying a narrow bar of brightness across the moldy earthen floor. At first he thought he had the place to himself but then he became aware of rhythmic breathing behind the barricade. It sounded, he said to himself, hardly more noticeable than the purring of a kitten. He rose to his feet and, at the first sound he made, the breathing stopped. For several moments complete silence reigned in this shrine sacred to the patron saint of hunters. Then a whisper reached his ear.

"Is it you, Sir Knight?"

"Yes, my lady," he responded.

"Has there been any word?"

"None. We seem to have shaken off the pursuit. A sentry has been kept to watch the road but nothing has been seen or heard."

"There has been no—no word from Tostig? No news of my poor sister?"

"None yet. But we must hope for the best."

There was a pause. "You could be of service to me again," she said in a hesitating voice. "I must have water, hot water. And, if you please, soap. Giselle made up a bag of certain very great necessities but, of course, she carried it herself. And as there is no Giselle with us, there is no bag. I would be very happy if you could obtain for me also a brush and a comb. Do you think it at all possible you could get me some perfume?"

"Not perfume, Your Highness. Not even if I stood beneath Merlin's Tower and could command his aid. As for the rest, we shall see."

He left the lodge and returned in about ten minutes, carrying his inverted helmet in both hands. Steam was rising from it and he handed it over the curtain with great care. She reached little more than the tips of her fingers to take it, from which he drew certain conclusions.

"Thank you," she said. "And now the soap, if you please."

"I could get nothing but the water. I even had a time heating it, there being nothing in the way of a pan or a kitchen pot in this charming abode. The members of our escort are most devoted to you. I am sure they would die for you. But they can't obtain any soap. In fact they seemed quite hazy on the whole subject of soap."

"Then I must do the best I can. I think it will be necessary now for you to leave me. But please remain somewhere within call. Other needs may arise. Am I asking too much?"

"Gracious lady!" cried Richard. "I live only to serve you. I am prepared to fight with any weapons, even to do battle with my naked hands, to fulfill your slightest fancy." He permitted his long-suppressed devotion the fullest rein. "I am your slave! I would crawl to your feet and lie there forever in the hope that you might condescend to use my head for a footstool."

There was a perceptible pause. "Your devotion I have taken for granted," she said. "But this seems to go somewhat beyond the bounds of mere loyalty."

"Yes, Your Highness. I shouldn't have allowed such freedom to my tongue. But as I have said what is in my heart, I wouldn't recall my words, even if I could."

She seemed to become involved in difficulties at once and Richard, who had stationed himself just outside the door, heard her call, "My good friend!"

"Yes, Your Highness."

"I need your help again. Sanchia trussed me up in this manly costume and I am finding it most hard to—to get the same results."

"What is wrong?"

"These—these *points*, I believe they are called. The leather thongs which attach the top of the hose to the belt."

"That is quite a simple matter, Your Highness. You tie the points first to the hose and then through the eyelets along the bottom of the belt. You should use a score of the points."

"I have done that. I have tied them all. Sanchia had me trussed up so I could hardly move but, at any rate, my hose fitted perfectly. I must have done something wrong because now everything seems to—to sag."

"I think," said Richard, "that you need some instruction in the tying of knots. There's a knack to it. Perhaps you are not using the right kind of knot."

"I am certain it isn't the right kind. Would you be good enough to show me how to do it?"

Richard removed one of his own points and held it high enough for her to watch. "This is the way it's done. See. After you pass it through the eyelet, you twist it twice like this. Using your thumb and first finger."

The princess was watching closely but was finding it necessary to grip her lips together to prevent herself from smiling.

"Let me try." She took the leather thong and began to twist it in

the manner prescribed. It seemed quite firmly knotted when she was
through. She said in a triumphant tone, "I think I have the knack!"

3

They had scarcely finished their one meal of the day, a stew of
venison with no hint of flavoring and thick slices of stale bread, when
the sound of a voice reached them from the direction of the nearest
road.

"The sentry, I think," said Richard, getting hurriedly to his feet.

The princess rose also and came around the table. Her face had
turned pale.

"Have they found us?" she asked.

"I don't know." He loosened his sword and felt hurriedly for the
poniard in his belt. "You must leave here. Take the path which turns off
to the right. Alfred tells me it leads to a cave. Two hundred yards
back in the woods. The entrance is not easy to find. Look for a stunted
oak. It will be wise to stay out of sight there."

Another voice could be heard now and, after a moment of tense
listening, Richard sighed with relief.

"It's Tostig. But to be perfectly safe, my lady, I think you had better
stay out of sight in the woods until we can be sure."

Richard walked down the road to meet his squire. Tostig was accompanied by the man Egbert and a plump woman of middle years, for
whom Egbert was carrying a large bundle. Tostig was tired and gray of
face but his eyes lacked the tortured look they had worn when the two
men parted.

"Then the word is not bad?" asked Richard.

"It might be worse."

"You must have ridden all day," said the knight. "Was it wise to
follow us in broad daylight?"

"My lord Adelbert thought it safe. There has been no hue and cry.
They think at the castle it was Giselle who made off during the disturbance."

Richard frowned in doubt. "But what of Robardi? He knew what was
afoot. Has he some reason for keeping his evil mouth shut?"

Tostig smiled as he answered in a tone of almost complete indifference, "That he has. The best of reasons. It happens that Robardi is
dead."

"Then," cried Richard, "it was his body I saw lying near the draw-bridge!"

"That was Robardi. I killed him."

"You!" The calmness of the announcement had given an edge of incredulity to Richard's voice.

"He was holding hard to Giselle in the confusion. I knew he thought it was the princess. So I tried to get her free of him and he fought back fiercely in the dark, cursing me in his barbarous tongue. I had to be rid of him quickly, so I gave him the benefit of my poniard. There was relish in the one blow I dealt him and he crumpled up under it. It took no more than a minute but that was enough to defeat our plan. In the meantime my poor Giselle had been swept back inside the walls.

"The talk in the village is all of the death of Robardi," went on Tostig. "They seem to think"—he hesitated and indulged in one of his formidable frowns—"that it can be explained by the disappearance of Giselle. Knowing how infatuated he was and how he had pursued the poor child, they think he came to his death in trying to prevent her escape."

Richard questioned him with a sudden access of fear. "Will they charge her with it if they discover she is still in the castle?"

"There would be an inquiry. But there are two points in our favor. No one has the smallest suspicion of the real state of affairs. They are convinced, inside and out, that the sister still in the castle is the Princess Eleanor. And it's true that everyone from the constable down had nothing but contempt and dislike for the ex-barber."

"But I very much fear that things will take a different turn when the king arrives. Robardi was a special creature of his. John will want to avenge his death."

"The king's arrival has been delayed. He is progressing by slow stages in order to visit some of the barons.

"If the king discovers the truth," went on Tostig, "and he may do so, for he has a sharp eye, I don't believe he will take any immediate action. We can be sure he's well aware of the discontent among the nobility. He may even know of the interest some of them take in the princess." There was a shrewd gleam in his eyes. "I think he will reason this way. It will be to his advantage to keep Giselle under his thumb. If the barons rise against him he will be in a position to say that the real Princess Eleanor is still in Corfe Castle and that it was the base-born sister who got away."

Richard nodded his head. "That is true. It didn't occur to me but I can see how likely it is he will act in just that way."

"Not until he has put the real Eleanor out of his way," said Tostig, "will he think it wise to acknowledge the truth about the substitution. He will express then his deepest regret over the mistake which led to her death and he will proceed to lay the blame on the designing sister who aimed to take her place. Oh yes, it all fits in. That is how the king's mind will work."

The princess, unable to control her desire to learn the news which had been brought, had come back by the path through the close encircling woods.

"Tell me what has happened to my poor Giselle!" she cried.

"Nothing, my lady," declared Tostig. "Nothing as yet. She is acting in your stead and no one yet has seemed to suspect the truth."

Eleanor's face showed a quick relief but then clouded over again. "How long can she keep up the pretense?" she asked. "I am afraid not for any great time."

"My lord Adelbert——" began Tostig.

"The man who has helped us so much," said Richard in explanation.

"My lord Adelbert is not convinced of the need for apprehension, my lady. With Robardi dead——"

"Robardi dead!" A look of intense surprise took possession of Eleanor's face.

Tostig nodded. "He was killed during those few moments of darkness on the square. With his prying eyes closed forever, it may be that the change in identities will not be discovered."

It was not possible for the princess to believe that things would be as easy as that. "There must be no delay in doing whatever we can to help her," she said. "I am certain she cannot maintain the pretense long. And then what will happen to the poor child?"

Nevertheless the news that Tostig had brought was better than she had thought possible and her face lost some of the evidences of strain. The plump woman had carried the bundle inside the lodge and she now came back to the door, bowing and smiling.

"I am ready for you, my lady," she said.

Eleanor disappeared with her behind the barricade and Richard turned at once to Tostig with questions. Who was the woman? Where had he found her? And why had it been considered safe to bring her over the same route they had followed with the princess? Would this not leave a dangerously easy trail to follow?

"It was my lord Adelbert's plan," explained Tostig. "He did not see any danger in providing the kind of help we couldn't get in any other way. The woman is French, the widow of a mercenary who was killed in the king's service. She is known as Dame Jehane. It's intended to have her take Giselle's place until—until we can save our brave little Giselle."

"When did you see Adelbert?"

"As you may have suspected, he was close at hand all the time. After you left the house of the gypsy woman, I returned to the inn, and there he was. He was sitting in the dark in your room and watching everything that went on below. He had already received word of the general opinion in the castle and, on that account, he was convinced we could set out to overtake you. First, of course, we had to get Dame Jehane and collect the clothes for the princess. It was nearly dawn when we started."

"Did he know of Robardi's death?"

Tostig nodded. "But he didn't know how it came about; nor did I tell him the truth of it. He asked me to warn you of the need for speed in everything we do. We must get the lady to his Castle Furmain in the Marcher country as soon as possible. Any of the barons who come to see her must do it before winter sets in. Because of this, he suggests you ride over at once to see Alain de Casserlie and persuade him to throw in his lot with us. He stands first in his county. We need him."

"When does he think I should go?"

"Tonight. He's a man of decision, my lord Adelbert. The rest of us will continue on the north road to Furmain while you turn to the east. If you are not delayed in seeing the lord of Casserlie, you may reach Furmain as soon as we do. I brought your piepowder cloak and your wide hat, as well as your case of goods. It will be wise to ride to Casserlie in disguise."

Richard observed the grayness of his companion's face and the shadows about his eyes. "Have you slept since I saw you last?"

Tostig shook his head. "There has been no chance for that. But I doubt if I could have slept if the chance had offered." He moved his position slowly and painfully. "There is another reason for quick action. A feeling is growing up among the barons that it would serve no lasting purpose to dethrone John and put someone in his place. His Grace the archbishop is saying that what England needs is a law to bind the king, to put restrictions on his power—not only on John but on all the kings who will follow him. He speaks much of a charter." The tired eyes turned to Richard with an arresting intentness. "I say he is right, and yet there is this about it: if we are to open the prisons and release all who are unfairly held, we must get rid of the king. To curb his powers will not get our poor Giselle free."

Richard was frowning uneasily. "I am all confused with this kind of talk. I think I would rather see a bad king deposed than the holy order of kingship changed by man-made laws. It goes against everything I have believed."

"There will be a charter," declared Tostig. "The archbishop works for it continuously and those to whom he talks listen intently and seem to be convinced. But if we move at once, we may have our own way about it. We can dethrone John and put him out of the way——"

"Do you mean kill him?" There was both horror and incredulity in Richard's voice.

"There is no danger so great as the existence of a deposed king. A country can know peace only when he has been sent where he can make no more trouble. It is always done."

"I agree that the king as a man deserves any punishment we can visit on him," said Richard. "But to kill a king, save in the heat of battle, would be an abomination in the sight of the God who put kings to rule over us in the beginning."

"It is a worse abomination in the sight of the Lord to hold innocent people in dark cells," declared Tostig.

Richard gave the matter more silent consideration. Finally he said, with a sigh of half conviction, "This much I give you, that I'll ride to Casserlie tonight and try my persuasive powers on my friend."

While they talked there were sounds of activity behind the barricade of skins. They could hear the deep tones of the Frenchwoman and the excited treble of the princess. Finally Eleanor raised her voice. "I am coming out!" she cried. The tone she used took Richard back to the time when he had first seen her at the court of Brittany. It even had a hint of gaiety in it.

She stepped out through a space provided by the muscular arm of Dame Jehane, walking slowly and rather sedately. Her appearance was proof of the liberality of the wealthy Saxon who had supplied her new wardrobe. The robe she wore was of white with an embroidered gold collar and a belt of intricate links, the end of which reached almost to her knees, where it terminated in a large emerald. Over the robe was a loose cloak of blue brocade, extending to the floor and held in place by a single band of gold across her neck. Only the tips of her shoes showed as she walked but it was apparent that they were elaborately embroidered in garnet and gold.

"How do I look?" she asked, giving her skirts a slight swish and pivoting about. "I am properly tired for the first time since I fell into the gentle hands of my royal uncle. Ah, how wonderful it is to be bathed and powdered and scented and pomandered after all these years!"

"May I present to my lady a gift from the provider of all this?" asked Tostig, stepping forward.

Eleanor turned her eyes in his direction. "More gifts?" she said. "How very generous he is!"

Tostig drew from under his belt a shining round object with a short handle. This he placed in her hands. "It is a mirror of glass," he explained. "He—the one who sends it to you—says that it came from the Far East and that there are very few of them in existence. It is so fragile that the slightest blow might shatter it into pieces."

The princess turned it over in her hands as carefully as though it possessed magic qualities. "A mirror of glass! Truly it must have come from Merlin's Tower. This is so very light. I have never seen mirrors save those of heavy steel or silver. Is it possible to see oneself in it, my brave Tostig?"

"Yes, Your Highness. It reveals the face more clearly than the most highly polished metal."

The princess looked about her as though in search of a chair. The lodge contained nothing of the kind, so she remained standing in the middle of the floor. She held the mirror tightly in both hands but did not raise it in the direction of her face.

"Try it, Your Highness," urged Tostig. "It will give you a surprise such as you have never had before perhaps."

"I am afraid of it." Eleanor looked at Richard for sympathy in her plight. "My good friends, you must bear with me. I have not seen myself for seven years! What will I find now? That I am old and wrinkled? That I carry the stamp of the prison on my face? I think I should not put it to the test. You, my friends, will be kind enough to flatter me always and tell me that I still look young. But this—this magic glass will tell me nothing but the truth. I think I should be content with what you tell me, even if I suspect it has more flattery than truth in it."

"You need have no fears, my lady," urged Richard. "Look in the mirror! It will prove to you that nothing we might say could be flattery. I think it will enable you to see yourself as you are for the first time in your life."

"I am still afraid." She turned the mirror over several times. The back and sides were carved out of ivory. An impudent monkey peered over the top. "My kind friend Richard, what will I see if I make the venture?"

Richard smiled warmly. "You will see—the Pearl of Brittany!"

"I can't believe it. But——" She made up her mind suddenly and raised the mirror in front of her face. "How strange!" she cried. "It's so clear that I can see myself peering out from this magic glass." She turned it over and examined the back. After a moment she raised it again and stared intently into it, her face reflecting the conflicting emotions which filled her. "It *is* magic! What else could it be? But I find it a sweet magic, for the long years have not treated me as badly as I feared. True, there are wrinkles around my eyes. And my hair is so absurd that I must not let anyone see it again. My good Jehane, bring me a wimple at once, if you please. I must always wear one until nature repairs this terrible loss."

It was not until the commotion over the mirror had ended that she noticed the costume Richard was wearing. He had assumed the cloak of the itinerant merchant and was holding in his hands a large felt hat with a dusty feather. The pack was strapped over his back.

The Princess Eleanor studied him with surprise and also a faint hint of resentment. "Why this strange garb?" she asked.

"I must leave at once," said Richard. "The leader of our group thinks I should see a friend of my boyhood who has now become one of the leading barons of the west. He hopes I will succeed in persuading him to join us."

"But, my good friend!" protested Eleanor. "You are in command of my train. You must escort me safely to Furmain. I—I would have no sense of security if you left me."

"You will be well guarded, Your Highness. I believe it possible that I can accomplish my mission and still reach Furmain as soon as you do."

Her face showed a slight flush and her lovely brows were puckered up into the semblance of a frown. "But how can I get along without you? My brave Richard, I have come to depend upon you so very much."

"But we have so little time," he urged earnestly. "If my friend is to join us, he must come to Furmain with the rest. That leaves me with no other time to see him save the present." He lowered his voice. "My lady, I have no thought but to serve you. We need him, we need him badly. It is in your best interests for me to see him at once."

"That is probably true." Her color was still high. "But I think you might have consulted me before making this decision."

There was a pause. "Yes, Your Highness. I was at fault in not explaining the need to you first."

"Well, it seems you must go. I am sorry, because I had counted on your company." Then she smiled and seemed to cast her resentment behind her. "I shall try to forgive you by the time you rejoin me at Furmain."

Chapter XVI

1

I T P R O V E D to be a long and slow ride to Casserlie, for rain fell all night and the roads became almost as dangerous as quicksand. Not until noon of the next day did his tired eyes espy the round towers of the island stronghold of his friend. The sullen mood of the guard at the outer gate was intensified by the sight of his muddy cloak and the condition of his boots.

"Ye expect me to let ye in, ye filthy dog?" he said. "Look up there, Cheat of the Roads. What do ye see?"

"The royal standard," said Richard in dismay.

"The royal standard it is. Is it not enough to have the king come riding here himself last even with a hundret in his train, without so much as a by-yer-leave? Must we take in as well a dusty-heeled jack peddler?"

Richard's first thought had been to ride away as fast as his tired horse could carry him but on second consideration he decided it would be better to remain.

"A word in the ear of my lord," he said, "will win me admission, my brave fellow."

"My lord rides in the north and late tonight it will be when he returns. Be on your way!"

This information was of an alarming character. No woman, no matter how high her rank, was safe if left alone and at the mercy of the lascivious king. Richard did not hesitate, therefore, to produce a coin from under his belt and flip it into the palm of the warder. The latter motioned over his shoulder. "In ye go," he said. "The same inducement will get ye a bone and a crust of bread at the kitchen. Ye'll be wise, my friend, to seek no better bed than six feet of hay in a tallat."

There was a sly humor prevalent among the buff-jerkined men-at-

arms, with golden leopards on their sleeves, when Richard joined them
at the midday meal; a tendency to wink and slap each other on the back,
to indulge in coarse hints, as they sat in a circle on the paving stones
and dipped their spoons in rotation in the pot. Had the king been having
ill dreams that he must go to sleep in one bed and waken in another?
Should husbands with red-haired young wives be so careless as to leave
them at home alone when the king was on his travels?

All desire for food deserted the new arrival when these hints reached
his ears. He wandered in growing distress of mind about the service
quarters, not daring to venture inside where he might be singled out for
questioning. His mind was a prey to the most disturbing fancies. Was it
nothing but guardroom gossip or had the king, who gave no consideration to the rights of other men, been so disdainful of the laws of hospitality as to force himself on his host's wife? This was hard to believe,
even of one so universally hated as this king, but he obtained some confirmation when he encountered a housemaid carrying a punnet filled
with soiled clothing to the steam house. The girl's eyes were red, as
though she had been weeping.

"When will my lord be returning?" he asked her.

"Better nor my good lord ever come back. No wife'll he find when he
does."

"Do you mean that my lady has gone away also?"

Tears filled the red-rimmed eyes again. "It's the truth," she whispered. "God and the Holy Mother watch over my lady, who set out for
the convent of Sisters in Holy Will soon after dawn this morning. There
will be no coming back for her, I'm feared. It bodes ill, it bodes no good
at all."

Richard spent the rest of the day in search of information, hoping
that he could chance upon something that would be of help to his friend.
He learned that the king had spent most of the morning in bed, rising
just before noon and strutting down to a midday meal; smiling to himself and winking at his confidants, and finding many sharp things to say.
Most of the regal afternoon was passed in talk with advisers, including
a moneylender who had ridden up from Winchester to see him. It was
whispered that he was uneasy about his gold and jewels, which were
distributed for safekeeping among no fewer than sixteen monasteries.
Messengers rode in with letters and rode away again with the answers
supplied by the royal scrivener. Once the door of the cabinet where the
king sat swung open and the royal voice could be heard in the worst of
tempers, reviling the bishops and the barons and the Pope and all his

cardinals. Nothing further was heard of the unhappy chatelaine nor was there any word of the husband who would find a pair of cuckold's horns waiting for him on his arrival.

Richard wandered aimlessly about the courtyards, keeping his hat drawn far down over his eyes. He spent some time at the swinecotes, marveling at the size and the number of animals kept there to supply the demand for the noted bacon of Casserlie, which had enabled Alain's father to amass a considerable fortune. There were many hundreds of them and the stench was almost enough to overpower the stale odor from the scum-coated moat.

"Dangerous beast!" thought Richard, looking at a huge boar with red eyes and slavering jaws.

It was a combination of curiosity and foolhardiness which led him that evening to find a seat in the Great Hall. He had a desire to see this much-hated monarch at close range.

He looked closely and with an almost fascinated interest at this king who was charged with so much cruelty and oppression. John was in a bodily sense the black sheep of the Plantagenets, because in a family noted for its dazzling fairness he had black hair and eyes. His face was full and it might have been said that his brow had something of nobility about it if the eyes beneath it had not been set too close together. There was nothing about him otherwise to hint at the furious tempers into which he fell; he might have been a merchant of good standing, a high official in a chancellery, a goldsmith, but never a fighting leader of armies. Despite this touch of the humdrum about him, he was oddly ostentatious in dress, wearing a long robe of black velvet with elaborate patterns traced in pearls and gold thread, a chain of heavy gold links wrapped many times about his neck, and a smother of rings with precious stones on his fingers.

The king was enjoying his meal. Talking almost continuously, he kept those about him in loud laughter, sometimes forced, sometimes genuine.

It was not until one of his men strode up on the dais to stand behind his chair and whisper in his ear that the king relaxed his attention to the food. He laid down his knife and looked with sudden curiosity along the line of faces at the far end of the table. Richard felt a sudden stirring of apprehension. Had his presence been detected?

He was not left long in doubt. John placed both hands on the board and spoke in a voice which carried a note of excitement.

"You all look alike down there," he declared. "As much alike as pigs at a trough. And so I have no way of detecting the black traitor who sits among you. You harbor—unbeknownst to all, I hope—a most vicious character; an English knight with no sense of loyalty to his liege lord and king, a recreant who prefers service with a sourbellied tool of the Pope, who, moreover, has wandered in disguise about my dominions, spreading treason. He has even dared to raise his voice in mockery of his king." There was an ominous stillness about him as he concluded, "Richard of Rawen, stand up and show yourself, traitor and spy!"

Richard had known when the first furious words fell from the royal lips that this was the end. His heart had seemed to stand still and he realized that he was facing death. His lips moved slightly as he said a prayer, an almost frenzied appeal for divine aid in his desperate pass.

"Stand up!" cried John. "Are you afraid to face the king you have so affronted?"

Richard had been wearing his wide-brimmed hat but at this repeated command he took it off and rose to his feet. He turned to face the king.

"And where," demanded the angry John, "is the companion of your travels? The bold squire who amused the rabble with his treasonable discourses and his snatches of doggerel!"

Richard found it hard to speak. "We parted company some time ago, my lord king," he managed to say finally.

"How lucky for him! But his luck will be of short duration. Now that I have you, I shall soon lay that braggart dog by the heels, never fear."

The king's manner changed suddenly. The anger stirred in him by his first sight of Richard seemed to subside. He became like a cat which enjoys toying with the mouse within reach of its paws. He even indulged in a smile, a fleeting movement of his mouth which gave Richard no sense of comfort whatever.

"I think, Sir Knight," said the ruler of the land, "that I must give some thought to the manner of your death. It must be a fitting end for one who has offended so greatly. Remain on your feet, Richard of Rawen, until I have made up my mind. I think I shall finish my meal before dealing with you, which will serve a double purpose. It will give you a chance to pray for the remission of your sins, and it will enable all my people to benefit by the sight of an arrant rascal who is going to die. There are so many excellent and ingenious ways in which I can have you killed! I must not hurry my decision." He paused and then spoke more slowly, as though savoring the words. "One thing only have I made up my mind to; you, base traitor, must die within the hour."

Richard had been leaning his weight on his hands pressed down on the table. He became aware that his arms were trembling and he began another prayer. "Oh, God, grant me the resolution to die well! I must strive to meet my fate as a good knight should but my flesh may shrink from the ordeal. Give me, O God, a stout heart for what lies ahead of me!"

He had heard a whisper from someone near him, "What think ye now of Jack Lack?" but the snicker which accompanied the question was not echoed by others. The condemned man sensed that the humble folk who had been dining around him felt a sympathy which they dared not express. This was not a new thing for any of them; the temper of the vicious king often exploded in this manner, and death always rode with them when they were numbered in the royal train.

To those who took the vows of knighthood the thought of death was never fully out of mind. They swore to die gladly in the service of their liege lord, to take any risks, to perform any brave but hazardous deed which chance presented to them. Death could not be something, then, from which to shrink. And yet Richard found himself dreading the fate he faced. It was one thing to die in battle or on the field of honor and another to go to a tortured end like a common malefactor. For a moment his mind turned to the one source of relief he could find. "My dear lady will weep when she hears," he thought. "Perhaps it is well for me to die before long absence dims her memories of me." There was some consolation in this but not sufficient to blunt the fierce rejection of death in one who had youth and strength and the prospect of a long life ahead.

He felt a pair of hands grip his shoulders like the steely claws of an eagle. One of the guards, who had been directed by the king to take charge of him, removed the sword he wore under his loose robe and the dagger from his belt.

"Stand as you are," he warned. "Not a move, not a word out of you."

The king had gone back to his meal but he paused long enough at this point to say: "Give no thought to escape or resistance, Richard of Rawen. Unless you prefer to be hacked to pieces."

But it did not require the implacable hand on his shoulder to convince Richard that escape was impossible. Death had overtaken him. To struggle against his fate would be futile as well as unworthy of one who had taken the vows of knighthood.

He became so immersed in his contemplation of the life he had lived, which would soon be opened to divine appraisal, that he had no idea how fast the time was passing. The meal was nearly over before he was roused to a consciousness of what went on about him. There was a sound then of horses' hoofs on the drawbridge.

"Our good host has returned," said John, looking about him with a sly glance.

There was considerable delay before the lord of the castle made his appearance. Richard forgot his own desperate trouble when he saw that his friend's face was as white as fresh alabaster. Alain stationed himself beside the king's chair.

"My liege lord and king," he said in a voice devoid of all emotion, "I did not know I was to be so honored."

"We have missed you, Alain de Casserlie," answered the king, "but your lady wife has been most attentive to us. We have been well entertained."

"My beloved lady left this morning, leaving a letter for me," declared Alain. "I have just read it. You know, I think, what it is she tells me."

John answered in a casual tone, "It is a matter between you and your lady, Sir Earl."

"Nay," said Alain. "You also, Sir King, are concerned in her message. I know, of course, that under the law there is no redress for a man who is dishonored by his king."

John did not seem in any degree embarrassed. It might almost have been thought that he was enjoying the situation.

"The law forbids a subject to challenge the monarch who has done him this harm," went on Alain. "He may not strike his liege lord with any weapon, not even with his hand. He must keep a close tongue and say none of the things which fill his mind."

"You are making too much of it, Sir Earl," said John. "Take your seat and pledge me in a cup of your excellent wine."

Alain made no move to obey but maintained his position beside the king's chair, his face still white, his eyes lowered so no one could read what was in them.

"Is it your purpose to remain overnight, my lord?" he asked.

"Most decidedly, Sir Earl. The hour is too late to venture farther on the journeyings which lie ahead of us."

Alain took a step backward. "It becomes necessary, then, to adopt other means," he said. Without bowing, he turned and left the Great Hall.

"My poor Alain!" thought Richard. "Even if he knew the death I face, I think he would gladly change places with me."

King John looked about him with a heavy frown. "I am deeply displeased," he said, "at the attitude taken by this young man. He lacked my permission to withdraw. What ill-considered folly has he in mind?"

Almost immediately there was a sound of furious activity on the floor above, of heavy blows struck by some weapon and the splintering of wood.

"By God's teeth, the man has gone mad!" exclaimed the king. He motioned to an officer who sat some distance down the board. "You, Godfrey-with-the-Squint, hie yourself up and see in what absurd way he is venting his spleen."

The uproar from above continued for some minutes, augmented by voices raised in dispute. Then Godfrey-with-the-Squint returned to report to the king.

"Well, my man, what folly is this?" demanded John.

"My lord king," answered Godfrey, "I think the Horned One has taken possession of him. He has smashed with his battle-ax the bed in which Your King's Grace slept. When I found him, he was at work on another bed, the one in which the lady of the house slept. He acts, my lord king, like a madman."

John's voice rose to a high screech. "Go back and tell this insane fool that I have had too much of his crackbrained folly. Let him know that I demand his presence at once and that he must present to me a face of penitence for his mad behavior!"

"He swears, my king, that he will not come down."

John's face, which was over-ruddy in hue at most times, had turned white. This was particularly noticeable at the nostrils, which twitched and flared.

"How can I give thought to the manner of death I shall want for this black traitor standing down there, while all this noise and confusion surrounds me?" he cried. "And what, moreover, am I to do for a proper bed tonight?"

He had scarcely finished speaking when a louder and stranger sound assailed the ears of the company in the Great Hall. The uproar began with the barking of dogs and the sound of men's voices urging them on with much cracking of whips. Gradually another sound could be detected, the grunting and squealing of frightened animals from the rancid pens. The latter noise soon tended to drown out all others, until it became clear that the pens had been emptied and that all the occupants thereof, the rampageous boars, the fattened hogs, and the young and vociferous grice, were being herded in the direction of the castle.

"Another outrage!" cried the king, looking about him as though not able to accept the evidence of his ears. "Has the fool taken leave completely of his senses? Godfrey, Tancrid, Willikin, out, all of you! See that this display of madness is ended at once!"

The order came too late. The words had barely left his lips when it became evident that the pigs were in possession of the courts of the castle. Pandemonium seemed loose in a topsy-turvy world when the invaders reached the sculleries and the larders and the salterie, and then flowed into the kitchens. In a matter of seconds, it seemed, the scratching hoofs and the angry squealing of the animals filled the corridors. The oak door burst open and the maddened creatures, still goaded by the baying of the pursuing hounds, poured like the Gadarene swine into the Great Hall.

Nothing could stand in the way of such a living tidal wave as this. A great boar, with rage and hate in his small red eyes, butted against the king's chair and toppled it over, sending John himself in a heap under the table. Here he was trampled upon and rolled about until he found himself far down the Hall, his velvet robe hanging in tatters from his bruised shoulders, one leg bleeding from the glancing blow of a reddened tusk. Still they came, leaping upon the tables to seize remnants of roast and fish and fowl and to snuff up fragments of bread and vegetables and lap up the wine which flowed from broken flagons, kicking over chairs and benches, and driving the panic-stricken company before them. The king, who was not known for courage in emergencies, joined in the rush, his thick legs carrying him out through the screens and under the portcullis, and down the drawbridge until he stood outside the walls of the castle. A breathless rage had taken possession of him.

"He shall hang for this like a common criminal!" he cried. "The scaffold I'll raise for him will be higher than the gallows of Haman! Here, some of you, form a guard about me. I have no stomach left for further contact with these horrible creatures. The rest of you, drive them away! Drive them into the moat." He looked about him and raised both arms above his head. "Bring Alain, Earl of Casserlie, before me. Do you hear me? Bring him here at once, so I may pronounce sentence upon him!"

But Alain, Earl of Casserlie, was not to be found. His determination to rid his domain of this king who had betrayed him was not yet exhausted. One of the circle gathered about the king raised a hand and pointed.

"My lord king!" he cried. "The castle is on fire!"

This was the final stage of the purification that Alain deemed necessary, the destruction of the huge castle his grandfather had raised and in which he had been born. The wooden buildings in the baileys were already a sheet of flame, and the trumpeting of the frightened horses and the domestic stock drowned out the squealing of the swine. Before applying the torch, Alain and his men had been humane enough to free the animals. They began to pour out over the drawbridge, horses, dogs, cattle, sheep, the bellowing of the poor creatures raising the volume of sound to an indescribable pitch. Some of the king's men tried to capture the horses but succeeded with no more than a dozen of those which had resorted to swimming the moat in their haste.

Alain appeared for a moment on the drawbridge after the exodus of the stock had come to an end. He raised an arm for attention and then called out in a defiant voice:

"I bid ye welcome for the night, Sir King! But your couch will be one of smoldering coals, I fear. A foretaste, perhaps, of the bed which will be yours for eternity!"

He disappeared then into the smoke which poured out under the portcullis.

"Carrion dogs that ye are!" stormed King John at the men who stood about him, all in soiled tunics and cloaks tattered by porcine tusks. "Drag that man out for me, even if you have to go straight into the fire to lay hands on him. Kill every man, woman, and child you find in the place. Bring as many as possible alive, for I want to watch their heels kicking on thin air!"

But all the domestics in the castle, male and female, knowing the fate they would suffer if captured, had already decamped through the rear postern and taken refuge in the thick woods which grew close to the castle on the east. John's eyes, smarting still from the smoke, darted about him for other victims when this information was conveyed to him. It was then he bethought himself of Richard of Rawen.

"Where is the traitor?" he demanded. "Diccon, bring me that black scoundrel I confided into your hands. I have thought of a death which will make him bear on his one pair of shoulders the punishment for everything that has been going on here. Not, I may tell you, that I have given up my intention to make them all suffer in time."

But Richard was nowhere to be found. Diccon and the other guard were brought before their terrible master, trembling and white-lipped, to explain that they had been caught in the stampede with the rest of the royal party. They had lost all trace of the prisoner in the confusion and had been trying in vain since to lay hands on him again.

John looked at them with smoldering eyes. "Was ever king so badly served?" he cried. "I plant the royal standard for an invasion of France and my barons do not join me! I refuse to accept the mandate of a foreign despot who calls himself Pope, and my subjects conspire to weaken my resistance. I capture a spy and place him in the care of two able-bodied men, and what happens? He slips through their clumsy fingers like a will-o'-the-wisp!" He continued to glower at the two unfortunate guards. "I shall not be cheated entirely of my vengeance. You, Diccon, and you, Bernard, shall pay for your carelessness."

So the two guards were taken by their reluctant fellows and strung up from the stout limbs of a nearby tree. This act of summary justice completed, a select number mounted the few horses which had been caught and rode away for the nearest castle. The rest were left behind to round up the stray horses and to watch for stragglers from the burning castle. The instructions given them were to procure prisoners, for the king's thirst for vengeance must be slaked later.

2

The stampede from the swinecotes had caught Richard as much unprepared as it had the king and his men. His feet were swept from under him and he was trampled over by the porcine horde. One of the pursuing hounds had given him a glancing blow from its teeth as it leaped by him.

The attack of the scrambling animals had brought him a sudden hope. Here was a heaven-sent opportunity to make his escape. He struggled to his feet and looked about him. The two guards had been swept away with the rest. He leaped over the hairy back of a huge boar, which had paused to consume a round of beef, and found himself outside the screens. Remembering his way from his first visit, he plunged in desperate haste down a dark passage and came in a matter of seconds to an arched entry into the inner bailey. From there he made his way to the stables, saddled his own horse, and rode down through the outer court to the rear postern. It was swinging open after the passage of the stampede.

He kicked a heel exultantly into the flank of his stout roan and crossed the rear bridge over the moat with a thunder of hoofs. Heaven had opened a way to liberty; he must make the most of it. A path from the outer wall led straight up into the woods and he cleared the open space with head turned to catch any signs of pursuit. It seemed clear enough that his escape had not yet been observed.

Richard would have ridden away at once, having made up his mind that the best plan would be to return to the country from which he had come, the wooded lands beyond the Wye where the king's writ did not run. Before getting too deep into the woods, however, he perceived that the castle was on fire and this caused him to rein in. He realized that the royal party would be faced with two necessities before they could think of sending out parties to round up fugitives; they must recover their horses and give thought to the question of lodgings for the night. His mind turned then to the case of his friend who had subjected the king to this series of indignities. He and Alain were now in the same plight. They must share the perils of their position.

Accordingly he drew up after reaching an open spot in a corner of the woods from which he could observe what was going on below. The fire was spreading throughout the castle and already flames were licking at doorways and archery slits and shooting up above the battlements. From his observation point, Richard saw the king and his small mounted guard ride away while those left behind engaged themselves in efforts to capture the rest of the horses. The castle staff in the meantime had disappeared into the same woods which were serving Richard himself as a screen. Knowing that Alain would now be concerning himself with the task of seeing his people to some kind of sanctuary, he turned his horse and followed into the forest depths from which sounds reached him of the hurried exodus.

Chapter XVII

1

I T W A S nearly a fortnight later that Richard saw the whitish walls
of Furmain Castle rising up from the tops of a thick tangle of
trees. He had been riding hard and fast since dawn, thinking
perhaps to ease his conscience by a great burst of speed at the finish.
Not that the delay was in any sense his fault; he could not have left
Alain sooner.

As he prodded a spurless heel into the flank of his fine roan, he asked
himself the same questions that had been plaguing him all the time.
What had been happening in his absence? Was the Lady Eleanor safe?
At the same time he gave some anxious thought as to what his reception would be. There had been more than a hint of coldness on her
part when he left. It seemed to him quite possible that, after this long
stretch of time, she might not have a welcome for him.

The road to Furmain ran down into a crowded and dark valley and
then up a gradual rise on the other side. He had reached a spot where
he could see straight ahead to the raised drawbridge of the little castle
(although capable of a stout defense, Furmain was not one of the
great strongholds of England) when he passed a dirt path which came
in to join the main road at an oblique angle. A sound of horses coming
at a gallop down this path reached his ears at the same moment. A
cloud of dust rose up above the topmost branches of the stately trees. He
reined in by the side of the road and waited.

There were three in the party and one of them, on catching sight of
him, left the others well behind and rode up beside him. It was the
Princess Eleanor and her eyes were shining with pleasure.

"Richard! Richard of Rawen!" she cried. "It's you at last. I have been
so frightened. I was certain something terrible had happened to you."

With a skillful pull on the reins, she brought her mount to a stop beside him. "Richard!" she said in a low tone. "I am so relieved! I am happy you are back."

"I was afraid," he answered, "that you would not be glad at all. That my long absence would not be forgiven."

"Oh, there were times," she said, "there were times when I was impatient and angry. When I thought you had given me up. But always I knew quite well that you had a good reason. I was certain you would come as soon as you could, my best of friends."

"It will be a long story in the telling, my lady. And a very sad one."

They began to ride slowly up the final stretch of the narrow road. The two horsemen who had accompanied her fell back to a discreet distance. A bell began to ring in the chapel of Furmain, which stood a short distance away from the castle. The morning mists were rising in haste and a bright and warm day stretched ahead.

"I had almost given you up," declared Eleanor. "It is two weeks that you have been gone. There were so many dangers besetting your path and I feared the worst. Tostig was no comfort to me at all. Since poor Giselle was left behind, he is indeed a Job's comforter. He did not hesitate to tell me that he feared you had fallen into the hands of John's men. I became tired of his frowns and his headshakings and his dire predictions and I haven't spoken to him for three days." She looked up at him and her eyes were warm with the pleasure she was feeling. "But here you are!"

They finished their ride together and crossed the drawbridge in the best of spirits, the princess telling Richard of some amusing episodes during their journey north. It had been uneventful otherwise.

Furmain Castle seemed to be in the process of making. In the first place, it was small and it had few of the usual features of the Norman stronghold. Richard noticed at once that nothing seemed to have been finished. They rode under the portcullis and dismounted in a court which was only partly paved. Piles of cobblestones attested to the intention once of making a thorough thing of it. Passing in through a door so low that Richard had to stoop, they found themselves in a great black cavern, with a well in the center and an elaborate winch for the raising of water. There were stalls along one side and mountains of hay at one end. The neighing of horses and the lowing of cattle mingled with the grunting of pigs and the cackle of hens. They went to the floor above by means of a flight of wooden steps which lacked a rail, although the materials for one leaned against the wall.

The space on the next floor lacked the proportions of the customary

Great Hall but it was serving the same purpose. There was a long trestle table and wooden benches, and a hearth of some size at one end. Behind a low barricade of oak at the other end could be seen the kitchen. It had been intended, clearly, to close the kitchen off and a scaffold had been set up for the purpose. This had been a long time before; but the scaffold still stood and would probably never be removed.

A second unrailed stairway led to another floor which was divided into half a dozen small rooms. One possessed both a window and a bed but the rest had no furniture save pallets of straw. Holes in the partitions had to suffice for light and ventilation.

Tostig escorted Richard to this floor and selected one of the rooms for his use. "Her Highness has the corner one, with the bed," he explained. "Dame Jehane is next to her."

"What is above?" asked Richard.

"The quarters of the garrison. The archers have their stations up there. The servants share the hay in the basement with the chickens."

Richard frowned uneasily. "How long do you think we could hold out if a strong force came against us?"

"The defenses are better than you suppose," declared the squire. "The walls are of stone and the moat is deep and wide. The well has a continuous flow of water and we could live for a long time on the livestock below."

Later in the morning the princess joined them in front of the hearth in the Great Hall and Richard proceeded to tell of the destruction of Casserlie Castle. "I found Alain some distance back in the woods," he continued. "He had gathered his people together and was leading them to a manor house on the extreme tip of his landholdings. My poor friend was so distraught that I could not get his mind off his troubles at first."

"I hope he had the delicacy not to intrude himself on his wife at once," said the princess thoughtfully.

Richard looked puzzled. "But," he said, "it seemed to me he should lose no time in getting to her. She needed him. I advised him strongly to go."

"Then I trust he didn't take your advice. At such a time a woman wants to hide herself. From her husband most of all. She must have a chance to recover from the shock. The proper course was to send a letter, saying he would fly to her as soon as she was ready."

"As it fell out," said Richard, "that was what he did. I thought he was making a great mistake."

"No, no. He may get his wife back because of it. Is she fair to see?"

"She wouldn't look well wearing a crown," answered Richard tactfully. "You see, my lady, she is rather small. She has bright red hair, and eyes as blue and trusting as a child's."

"Exactly the kind, I expect, to appeal to the fine instincts of my royal uncle. Does your friend, the husband, feel disposed to join us?"

"He looks forward to the day when John will be thrown from the throne. His head is filled with it. As soon as his own problems are brought into some kind of order, he will be with us."

2

To understand how an escaped prisoner of great political importance could thus vanish from official sight, it should be explained that the land lying between England and Wales, which was known as the Marcher country, was in a continual state of war and confusion, belonging neither to Wales nor wholly to England. It was controlled by the Marcher barons, who were English and who held their land for their services in restraining the wild Welsh tribesmen. They were all old battling war horses, these barons, chosen because of their toughness and their lack of scruples. When there was no fighting to be done with the Welsh, they fought among themselves. It was a grievously unhappy strip of land, taking in all the western sections of Monmouth, Hereford, and Shropshire, and only in cases of extreme need would anyone seek sanctuary there. The barons made their own laws and had their own bloodthirsty ideas of justice. Even in the severe and orderly days of old Harry Secund the itinerant justices, sent out to hold assizes throughout the country, had never penetrated into this seething no man's land.

It is perhaps needless to state that at Furmain Castle every precaution was taken. Whenever the drawbridge was down, two men stood in the narrow gateway, ready to lower the portcullis in case of trouble. Two sentries stood on the ramparts night and day. An armed attendant was stationed at the head of the stairs on the floor where the princess slept. Horsemen scouted the neighborhood at all hours. The princess was attended by an armed escort whenever she ventured out for rides.

Adelbert arrived the day following. It was clear from the first moment he set eyes on the Princess Eleanor that he had conceived an admiration for her. She had been riding and was wearing a cloak of the color known as Lincoln green, and on her closely cropped hair she had a cap of the same color with a jaunty feather. The Saxon went down on one knee and declared his fealty to her in fervid tones.

With so many matters pressing on them, they went into a conference at once. Eleanor seated herself before the hearth while Richard and the new arrival faced her on a wooden bench. Tostig remained standing behind them. His mouth had become drawn in a taut line by the strain under which he labored.

"All was quiet when I left," said Adelbert. "The village still seethed with talk of the death of Robardi and, I assume, the people in the castle showed at least an equal interest in that mysterious incident. Another maidservant has been selected to serve the—the one who was left behind; but the man Sunric is no longer with her. The prisoner has been seen walking on two occasions on the battlements."

Tostig hesitated and then interjected a question. "May I ask how she looked? Was she—was she well?"

"There is proof that she is well," answered the Saxon. "A message was smuggled out of the castle. By word of mouth. It reached the woman Sanchia first and then came to Silverdown, who repeated it to me. Just two sentences. 'I am well' and 'No matter what befalls.'"

The princess showed some signs of puzzlement over the words but to Tostig the meaning was quite clear. If the others had been watching him they would have seen a slight hint of color in his cheeks. The message had been meant for him and, for a brief moment, nothing else counted.

"The king was in Corfe briefly and it is not known whether he saw the prisoner."

There was a moment of silence. Then Eleanor shook her head. "If he saw her," she said, "he could not have been deceived. He would know almost from the first word that he was not addressing me. Things passed between us soon after he took me prisoner which no one else knows about. This was after I was certain he had killed my brother. I did not know how it had been done but there was no doubt in my mind that he had removed my poor little Arthur from his path. But I *did* know that he was stunned by the feelings aroused by his foul deed. I am going to tell you now of something I have kept closely to myself. The king invented a story to account for Arthur's death. It would have cleared him of all blame but—it would not be accepted unless I supported it. He offered me my freedom and many castles in England if I would swear to the truth of it. I refused. He then offered to make me Princess of Wales. I still refused. When he became convinced that I could not be bribed to help him, he sent me to Corfe Castle where I was lodged in those tiny stone cells at the top of the shaft. He hoped to break my will that way. Each time he came to Corfe, I would be summoned to his presence and asked if I had changed my mind. My answer was always the same. . . .

"My poor Giselle knew nothing of this," continued Eleanor after a long pause. "He would realize at once that she was completely at sea. And he would soon trip her up, that cunning fox. If he saw my sister, why has he done nothing? What evil scheme fills that cunning brain?"

"It may be," suggested Adelbert, "that he still hopes to clear his record of the stain. He may have suggested to the poor woman that she continue to play the part of the princess and that she begin by acknowledging the truth of his story."

"Giselle would never agree!" cried Eleanor. "She would never play me false."

Tostig had been on the point of speaking when the princess came so vehemently to the support of her sister. He smiled at her gratefully.

"We must not forget that the king is in a position to bring pressure to bear," said Adelbert. "In the case of Your Highness, he feared public opinion. He had killed the Prince Arthur; and he did not dare fly in the face of world opinion by disposing of you also. But with your sister it is different. He may not hesitate to use the rack or the leaden cope. If she succumbs under it, he can always say, 'It was not the Princess Eleanor, it was a shameless impostor who deserved her fate.' He could justify anything he did by his need to find where the real princess is. On the other hand, if Giselle lacks the strength to hold out, he can then say that you are the impostor."

A silence settled over the group. They looked at each other and the same dread could be detected in each of them.

"What will he do next?" asked Eleanor finally.

"I think he will wait," answered Adelbert, whose shrewd mind had been at work. "He will give himself time to break down your sister's resolution. If she gives in, he will commit himself to an acceptance of her as his real niece."

"And what of me?"

"Let us hope," said the Saxon, "that we will succeed in asserting your rights and so provide the answer to that." After a moment he proceeded to speak of another phase of the situation. "The death of Robardi remains a mystery. The king is said to have taken slight interest in the matter, and it is being whispered about that he considers himself

well rid of that wicked man. Perhaps Robardi knew too much. Whatever the reason, nothing is being done."

Richard looked at Tostig out of the corner of one eye. The squire's
face had not changed expression, although he continued to stare at the
pattern of the stonework under his feet.

Suddenly the princess sat up straight in her chair, her eyes flashing
and her color high. "All this makes it clear," she exclaimed, "that we
must lose no time! The king is cunning. If we allow him time, he will
find ways of winning back the support of the barons. He will be full of
promises and they may be weak enough to listen to him."

"Her Highness is right," declared Adelbert. "It is indeed a case of
now or never. I trust the visitors we are expecting will see matters in
that light."

In the hills above Furmain there was a small lake around which
wound a straggling path. This had become a favorite place for recrea-
tion, and on the day after Adelbert put in an appearance, Richard
took him there for a walk and a private talk.

Adelbert did most of the talking. "She has dignity and decision," he
said. "And I was pleased to see she has kept much of her beauty. I am
sure my lords and gentlemen will be well impressed with her." He
paused and turned back to Richard, who was walking behind him on
the narrow path. "She is a true Plantagenet. She likes her own way. It
will grow on her when she has power in her hands. You have noticed
this?"

Richard nodded. "Is it not natural? As you say, she's a Plantagenet
and they are all of a high temper. We must remember also that she
has been badly treated. Seven years in that ugly cold pile with nothing
to do but brood on her wrongs. Would you expect her to come out
gentle and forgiving? I would think ill of her if her temper did not
flash at times."

"Even at the expense of her friends and benefactors?"

"My lord Adelbert, these little fits of temper are like the—the in-
stinctive arching of a kitten's back. They never last. One moment she
is in a fury, the next she is smiling."

"We must warn her about the highborn barons who will come to
see her. They also have great tempers, and with them it's more like
the surliness of a she-bear than the spitting of a kitten." He fell into a
reflective mood. "A few of them are men of honest purpose and high
ideals. They want a better ruler on the throne. They have been

scandalized by the bestiality of John and humiliated at the ease with which Philip of France has taken away our overseas provinces. Then there are some with personal grievances; and they are ready for action. But most of them are concerned only with their own selfish ends. They see a chance to better themselves by having a hand in the ousting of a king. It's the prospect of favors to come which attracts them. Men of this stamp can't be depended upon. If anything goes wrong, they vanish quickly.

"I expect the first of them in a day or so," he went on. "A very great man, particularly in his own esteem. He will come under an assumed name, having a great tenderness for his personal safety, but you will probably know who he is when I tell you he is the greatest land-holder in the western counties. He has twenty-six castles and manor houses in all, and he can bring an army into the field; but as he insists on commanding it, the results are likely to be disastrous. He is, in my esteem, a man of boundless conceit and a witless fool into the bargain. I am telling you this so you will know how to accept him. I think I should tell you also that he's a newly made widower and that he will probably consider himself the perfect and inevitable choice as husband for the Princess Eleanor."

Richard's mind filled with resentment. The princess would have to marry, of course; that much he had always understood and accepted. But he felt a bitterness against this presumptuous baron who considered himself worthy of her.

"They are a prickly lot," cautioned Adelbert. "Once it is seen that he holds these ambitious designs, the others will turn against him. It's my belief he will be shrewd enough to lose no time in coming, hoping to impress our lady with his worthiness and his manly charms before the rest arrive; and so have her committed to a preference in advance. I am so convinced of this that I expect to see the gallant fellow come riding up that road at any minute, with pride breaking out on him like a rash."

Adelbert proved correct in his surmise about the wealthy and ambitious baron. He arrived the next morning. Richard was in the courtyard looking up at the sky, which was heavily overcast, when a loud and confident voice was heard from the drawbridge.

Two horsemen had reached the outer approach. The one who rode in the front had something vainglorious in his manner which left no doubts as to his identity, even before the arrogance in his eye could be noted.

"Here he is," said Richard to himself, "this swaggering, loud-prating fellow who aspires to the hand of my dear lady. He comes in all his finery like a bridegroom."

The newcomer rode across the drawbridge at a gallop and drew up with a clatter of hoofs in the courtyard. He gave Richard the benefit of a haughty stare.

"Who are you?" he demanded to know.

"I feel free to tell you this much only," answered Richard. "I came here from the south."

"Ha! Then you are the doughty rescuer of damsels in distress. The wielder of so sly a lance, moreover, that you unhorsed a certain monster of great reputation some years ago. Am I correct?"

Richard gave no more than a nod in response. The newcomer dismounted slowly. He looked up and studied the meager proportions of the castle with a critical eye. "A mangy cage to hold so gorgeous a bird," he commented.

"It is not large."

"I feel under compunction, Sir Knight, to offer my congratulations. You did more than I expected. There was magic in this rescue. God's chin, you must have sought aid at Merlin's Tower!"

"There was no magic about it," Richard said shortly.

He had taken a greater dislike to the newcomer than he had expected. The peer was a handsome fellow, thickset and slow in his movements, carrying the tip of his nose almost as high as his heavy brows; his hair the yellow of autumn leaves and his eyes blue and overbold. The surcoat he wore over his chain mail was of the finest material and elaborately fashioned, but careless use had reduced it to shabbiness. If self-esteem was evident in the indifference of his manners, it could be read also in the rents in his tunic. At close range the plumes in his hat were seen to be tarnished. "Neatness is for lesser men," his slovenliness seemed to proclaim.

"I'm curious about how you unhorsed that fellow and will have some questions to ask you when you unbuckle your belt of caution. I might even consider giving you a chance to splinter a lance with me."

Richard had observed the clumsiness of his descent from the saddle. "It would be a simple matter," he said to himself, "to beat this juffler, who is so very sure of himself."

Richard was not on hand when the new arrival met the princess. The meeting consumed the better part of an hour and, when Richard encountered Eleanor on the stairs, there was a hint of fire in her eyes and a patch of color on each cheek.

"He is a simpleton!" she said in bitter undertones. "Must I bear much more of his inane talk? His first words to me were, 'Our meeting under these circumstances, dear lady, will be recorded in history.' When he finally condescended to leave me, it was with the air of a conqueror."

"Has Adelbert talked to you about him?"

The princess gave her head an angry nod. "He told me the man has a pride like so much tinder and that I must strive not to displease him. I am of the opinion that *my* temper is more to be considered."

At the evening meal the princess sat in the center at the head of the table. She was in purple and white, in which she looked regal as well as lovely, and there was a plain gold circlet on her head. Her glances at Richard, who was sitting on the other side of the board with the priest of Furmain, showing she had little liking for the seating arrangements. The new guest was at her right, wearing a handsome sky-blue tunic with a stain which hinted at a lack of care with soup. Adelbert, on her left, had a wary look in his eyes, as though he did not expect things to go well.

The visitor took matters rather completely into his own hands. He made a huge meal, requiring the constant services of the staff, snapping his fingers for attention and growling over a moment's delay. He used no fewer than four pieces of bread as tranchoirs, his method being to place the bread on the table in front of him and to lay a slice of meat on top of that. By the time the meat was finished, the bread would be well soaked with the gravy and he would scoop it up with his knife and consume it with every evidence of relish. Refusing wine, he kept the yeoman of the ewery, who was waiting on table, very busy filling his mug with ale; and after each swallow he wiped his mouth with the back of his hand.

He talked incessantly and never deviated from his favorite topic, himself. When interrupted by any remarks dealing with general matters, he would wait impatiently and at the first hint of a pause resume his personal recital. He spoke freely of his first marriage and confessed that he had only ten children, which he considered unworthy of him when it was taken into consideration that eight of them were illegitimate. With an arch look in his large round eyes, he let it be understood that he expected to do much better with his next venture.

Eleanor watched and listened with a helpless dismay but the two watchers were disturbed in turn when they noticed a telltale flush taking possession of her cheeks. "How long can she stand this fellow?" was the silent question that Richard flashed across the table to Adelbert and the shrewd Saxon shook his head apprehensively as though he feared the worst.

Eleanor took advantage of the first opportunity, as they left the Hall, to whisper in Richard's ear. "When I was a very small child, I was quite undisciplined," she confided. "I sometimes bit the maidservants and once, when I was only four, I kicked my royal father in the stomach. There were times tonight when I longed for the privileges of childhood!"

3

The next morning, at an early hour, the princess went for a ride with the visitor, taking the road which led to the lake. Richard watched them go with misgivings but he dismissed such thoughts from his mind when Father Exiguus came to him with alarming news.

"I must tell you of a strange rumor which has reached us from over there," said the priest, motioning toward the lowering backdrop of the Welsh foothills. "It concerns that Godless man, Owen ap John. It seems that he has gathered into the cells of his castle at Cromlath a very large number of hapless youths and maids who are to be transported to Ireland and sold there as slaves. The Toegs are a patient lot and they have accepted much bitter treatment at his hands, God wot. But this time he is going too far. The rumor is that the men in the mountains back of his castle and in the valleys which run down to the sea are stirring and arming themselves. When the slave ship comes in to Cromlath, there will be resistance and a most determined effort to win the poor young people free." The deep-set eyes in the thin face of the priest were glittering with excitement. "I am a man of peace, my lord, but if the chance came to me to have a hand in whatever may befall, Our Heavenly Father would have to look with leniency on my backsliding."

This was disturbing news, for it meant that the chance had almost certainly been lost to find sanctuary for the princess in Wales. But the morning was to bring forth an even more upsetting development. Richard heard of it from Adelbert.

"Well, we have lost the support of our self-confident baron and I conceive it is my fault," said the owner of Halterlo. "I should not have allowed him to come here in the first place and most decidedly I should not have permitted our lady to go for this ride with him. It seems he took advantage of the opportunity to propose marriage. According to the version she has just confided to me, she tried to be very pleasant and conciliatory, telling him nonetheless that she was not free to decide such matters for herself. He was not to be put off, this great blustering noddypeak. He insisted it was the best possible match and that the opinions of others need not be considered. Finally she was driven to refuse him in most unmistakable terms."

"Good!" cried Richard. "I am more than happy to hear it."

"Our gallant fellow became white with anger. He said she had been refused by the German prince and by the Dauphin of France and even by a third man of black skin, meaning the brother of Saladin. Then he said he was one of the greatest noblemen in England and that she, having been spurned three times, should be only too glad to have the offer of his hand. 'What happened to the soiled Alice of France,' he demanded to know, 'when your Richard Coeur de Lion refused to wed her? They married her off to a tuppenny French count. You should be thankful I am willing to save you from the same fate, my high and mighty Eleanor from Brittany.' That was more than our lady could stand. She seized his mace and dealt him a blow with it. It couldn't have been a very heavy blow, but it was sufficient to make him lose his seat in the saddle. He, this boasting fool who talked of breaking a lance with you, fell over into the water with the loudest splash. It happened to be a shallow bit of water and so the gallant baron was in no danger of drowning."

Adelbert was silent for a moment and then he burst into laughter. "It may prove a great blunder but, Sir Knight, I love her for it. She has convinced me that she has the right spirit to be the Queen of England." His mirth subsided quickly. "I fear it is a sweet muddle in which we find ourselves. I met the great man as he came tramping back on foot. He was fissling like a she-bear. He waved a clenched fist at me and said he was leaving at once. What will be his next step? Will he run to the king with his story in sheer malice and spite?"

He had barely finished speaking when the hostile baron emerged from the castle and called sharply to his squire, who had been hovering about the stables. "A wondrously fine idea, Sir Saxon, to put a vain and capricious woman on a throne!" he said. "How fortunate that I decided to come and look into this festering treason for myself. I have no intent to join myself in your scheme. I may add, you conniving swine, that I never had any intention of joining."

"So that is to be his story!" said Adelbert under his breath.

The departing baron spat contemptuously into the moat as he galloped off across the drawbridge. Then he turned and called back an epithet applied to Eleanor which caused Richard to reach furiously for his sword. His companion laid a restraining hand on his arm.

"Let him go!" he said in a low tone. "We can keep a watch on him this way and see what he does. Would your man Tostig undertake to follow them at a discreet distance?"

Richard nodded at once. "We couldn't leave it in better hands," he said.

"His nearest castle lies in the northeast, a number of miles above Worcester. If he takes that road, we will know he is running to save his own skin. The king is in Winchester at the moment."

When Tostig was apprised of what had happened, his mind leaped at once to what he knew would be the inevitable result. If the hint of a conspiracy got about, the king would not continue to play with the situation. He would strike furiously and the first victim would be the prisoner in Corfe Castle. On this account, he professed himself as not only willing but eager to undertake the task of following the departing horsemen.

4

It had seemed strange that one so rich in possessions as Adelbert could countenance any habitation as bleak and bare as Furmain Castle. There was nothing gracious or fine about this little block of stone in the Welsh foothills. Even the corner room where the princess slept was sparely furnished with not a hint of color or a feminine touch. A table and three wooden benches, with a high oaken bink which had been converted into a sideboard of sorts, was all the Great Hall could boast. There was good reason for this. At any time of day or night a rapacious baron might descend on the place and carry off everything it contained or set it to blazing with a neighborly torch. Adelbert maintained the castle for reasons of his own but he had no intention of putting any of his prized property at the mercy of men who resembled the wild boar in everything but the possession of tusks.

He maintained a room for his own use, however, the exact location of which was known to no more than a few members of his household. A dank passage led there, opening behind the hay piled up on the ground floor, and so low that a tall man would have to bend over in traversing it. To this sequestered nook Adelbert led his three guests immediately after the return of Tostig, because it was certain they would not be overheard.

"We were afraid something had befallen you," he said to the squire, placing the princess in the one chair and motioning the others to sit on the straw-covered floor. "For three days we have been watching the bend of the road down there and wondering what ill turn of fortune was detaining you."

"I had to be certain," declared Tostig. "And I had to be cautious. If one of them had caught a glimpse of my face, they would have been down on me at once." He looked soberly at the others. "He will cause no further trouble, Your Highness, and my lords, being as thoroughly dead as a frozen fox in a trap."

"Dead!" cried Adelbert.

"He seems to have had many enemies and one of them took advantage of a chance to send an arrow in his direction as he rode by. I saw him lying in a ditch, with the arrow in his chest. I turned my horse and came back with the word of his ending as fast as my horse could run."

Adelbert crossed himself. "Peace to his soul. But I am compelled to say that his departure from this life removes a most uncomfortable threat."

Richard did not discuss the matter any further until the time came to retire that night. He and Tostig climbed the stair together.

"The death of our late guest," he said in a lowered tone, "removes the immediate danger hanging over Giselle."

"When he turned onto the Winchester road, I felt as though he had her death warrant in his pocket," responded Tostig.

"Was there any clue as to who did it?"

"None that I heard."

"Then you think it is like to remain a mystery?"

"As to that, I can't say."

They had reached the top of the stair. Richard lingered for a moment in the open door of his room. "I trust, Tostig," he whispered, "that you took every precaution."

For a moment nothing more was said. It was dark where they stood and Richard could not read the expression on his squire's face.

"I took the greatest care," answered Tostig in a tone so low it was hard to follow him. "And I may tell you, Master Rick, that never before in my life had I taken aim with such precision."

Chapter XVIII

1

VISITORS to Furmain Castle seemed to bring trouble, but an arrival on the day after Tostig's return was perhaps the worst of all: a snowstorm, which began as the sun dipped behind the horizon and continued through the night and the next day, until the trees lost all natural semblance and began to look like oversized and outlandish goblins. The roads disappeared and even some of the hedges, and through it all the bitter cursing of the guards could be heard from the battlements, from which the beautiful and damned stuff had to be cleared regularly. The large soggy flakes had been dropping straight down from the leaden sky but, when the storm was resumed on the fourth day, it brought with it a wind with teeth of steel, which lashed the countryside and cut the drifts into fantastic shapes.

Albie Oakyard, the head huntsman, predicted dire things. The larder would soon be empty if this plaguy state of affairs lasted much longer. He growled his troubles into the ear of Tostig. "Nothing as runs on four legs or flies on two wings will venture out on these devil-sent days. It's all very well to say, 'Albie, go out and find us game.' I might as well hang up my bow and toast my shins by the fireside. We've had to open up the first cask of salt fish laid by for the winter."

Adelbert did his best to keep the princess amused. He shook dice with her for pennies and played at Tables, and generally managed to lose. She was always a little distrait and he guessed she would have found the company of Richard more to her liking; but being a shrewd man, he saw to it that his younger confederate was kept busy elsewhere. One topic of conversation never failed to win her full attention: the question of when they might expect the friendly barons to arrive. She was beginning to entertain doubts on that score.

"The English treat queens badly," she said on one occasion. "There was my great-grandmother, Queen Matilda. They soon took the throne away from her."

"She was arrogant and proud and cruel," declared the old Saxon.

"She was the only surviving child of King Henry I. And so she was their rightful queen."

"We must be patient," urged the old man. "They can't get here with the snow three feet deep on the roads."

On the morning of the fifth day, while the wind howled about the battlements, the princess was standing in a window of the Great Hall and staring out at the slanting attack of the snow. When Richard came up the steps from below, shaking his hat free of it, she called him to join her.

"How much longer will it last?" she asked.

"Father Exiguus, who knows more about weather than anyone else, says there will be two more days."

"Two more days!" she cried. "Will anyone be left alive in England? Will I live to see the flowers again, and the sun?"

"Yes, sweet lady, it can't be long before the sun comes out and drives the Devil away. It is the Devil who brings the storms."

The princess shuddered. "I am afraid of your English Devil. He is black and blustering. Now in the fair lands of the south he is suave and well mannered and one does not mind him so much. He goes about a great deal and he sings a good song; and he has a quick eye in his head for a pretty lady."

"We never think well of him here in England, my lady."

The princess leaned her arms on the stone sill. "How it comes down!" she exclaimed. "Will you believe it that last night I dreamed of snow? I dreamed I was in a land where it always stormed like this. All the men of this cold country had wings on the sides of their helmets and they were very tall and strong. I lived in a great palace which I thought at first was made of shining marble. This was wrong, I found: it was built of ice and it glistened in the sun. These huge men with the wings on their helmets kept saying to me, 'You are our queen and we would gladly die for you,' and I kept answering them, 'No, no, I am not your queen. I am going to be the queen of England.' They would laugh at that in their great rumbling voices and they would drink toasts to me. I had to sit at the head of their table all through the night so they could go on drinking and lifting their flagons to me.

"I was very unhappy because they told me I would never be able to leave. The snow was so deep that the rest of the world was cut off and they said it would always be that way. Then one day they came to me in great excitement and told me that the prince of the other half of their kingdom had come to demand my hand in marriage. When he was brought in, I saw that he was very tall and handsome. He was wearing a robe made from the skins of white bears and the crown on his head seemed to be of precious stones. But his crown was not made of precious stones, because he got excited when he began to tell me that he had loved me all his life and the crown started to melt. It was made of ice and that was why it shone so brilliantly. The water streamed down his face but I did not laugh. I was sorry it was only a crown of ice because I had made up my mind to accept him and I would have liked to have one made of precious stones for myself.

"And," she concluded, changing to English and watching him with a warm smile, "who do you think the prince was?"

Richard had no idea who the claimant for her hand might have been.

"You were the prince."

Adelbert entered the Hall, followed by Tostig. When he saw the pair in the embrasure, standing so close together that their shoulders touched and there was almost no distance between their heads at all, he stopped short and turned to look at the squire. There was an expression of consternation on his face.

"I hadn't thought of the possibility of *this!*" he said. "I see a mission must be found for our brave knight which will take him away for a long time."

2

The snow continued to fall for two more days, as Father Exiguus had predicted, and then it turned to rain. For three days and three nights it rained steadily and heavily and at the end the snow had shrunk to dismal hummocks. At odd moments the sun peered through the clouds, wanly and uncertainly, but did little to alleviate the chill in the air.

Of the people of the castle only Albie Oakyard ventured out, to replenish the larder, and of visitors there were none. Adelbert fell into an uneasy mood and his steady pacing in the narrow confines of the Hall was an indication to the others that he did not like the turn of events.

The princess became very quiet and it was clear that she was un-

nerved. She berated Dame Jehane loudly and found fault with everything that was done for her. She did no more than nibble at her food.
The corner chamber, where she slept, commanded a view of the road
and she spent most of her time sitting there, watching out with somber
eyes.

When the rain finally stopped, Adelbert sought out Richard in the
courtyard, where he had gone to stretch his legs. "Rick," he said, "if no
one comes today, we may as well consider that we can't count on aid
from any of them."

"They are a pack of cowards!" charged Richard furiously.

"Let us say rather that they have come to respect the firmness with
which their heads sit on their shoulders. Take my own case. I see nothing now for me to do but to stay here where the king's hand can't reach
me. John will be fully advised of the part I have played." He frowned
unhappily. "Our brave little lady is taking it hard. It is not easy to have
a crown dangled before you and then see it snatched away."

"Do you think it has come to that?"

"If no one puts in an appearance today, I shall reckon our cause a
lost one," declared the owner of Halterlo.

They climbed the stairs to the second floor and found Eleanor there,
staring out morosely at the empty road. She greeted them without a
smile.

"My good friends," she said, "I have heard this country spoken of as
Merrie England. We believed in Brittany that it was a land of milk and
honey. So far I have seen nothing to justify either description."

"Your opportunities for observation have been unfavorable, Your
Highness," said Adelbert.

"During my endless walks on the battlements of Corfe, I could see
nothing but the line of the hills. At first they seemed friendly and green
but gradually they became a part of my prison. I could not break
through the walls and I could not see through the hills. And so much of
the time they were wet with rain or wrapped in fog.

"A few nights ago," she went on, "I had a dream of being cut off from
the world by mountains of snow. Now I am imprisoned in reality by
rain and fog. No, this is not a land of milk and honey, it is a land of bitter
ale and salted herring. The people are never 'merrie.' Their faces are
long and they have voices like crows. How stolidly they danced that
night when we ran away from Corfe Castle!"

"Princess Eleanor," said Adelbert in earnest tones, "you should not
speak ill of the people you may someday rule."

She turned to him quickly. "Do you still have hopes of that?" she asked.

He spread out the palms of his well-tended hands. "I have not yet given up all hope," he answered. Then honesty compelled him to add, "But the chance grows slighter with every hour."

Despite his years, Adelbert had all the daring of youth in the matter of his attire. On this occasion he was wearing the knee-length tunic which younger men were adapting from Europe, thus displaying his well-turned calves in ruby-colored hose. The tunic, moreover, was of great thickness. Six depths of silk thread had gone into the weaving, so that the material (it was called samite) was stiff and very costly. His shoes were of the softest leather, with the tops turned back to reveal the yellow lining. Richard looked plain beside him.

"As I said, gracious lady," went on the Saxon, "you have had no opportunity of judging the merriness of England, nor the fine qualities of the people. I think your eyes would be opened if you could see, for instance, an archery contest. There you find the yeoman at his best, his eyes alight, his arm strong, his aim sure; and such chaffing from the onlookers and so much raillery among the contestants, and such a healthy love in all of them for good brown ale. If you want to learn of their temper, you do not think of English soldiers in victory, when they are like all others, gloating and plundering and ravishing, but in retreat when a greatness comes out in them. Times I have had to fall back with my men when the odds were great against us, and never have I known them to falter or show a tip of the white feather. Rather they have been ready to turn again and again on their pursuers, to strike and fall back, and finally to die with their backs to the wall.

"Then there is the carver with his chisel and mallet, who can make faces come out of the gray stone; he is to be found in every hamlet but he gets no more of earth in the end than the clod with a hoe. And above all else, there are the nights when the moon is hidden and the word is passed that a friar or a hedge priest is to speak in the woods. Times I have gone to such meetings, with my hood down low over my eyes, and always it has been good for my soul. We who own the land have long since abandoned hope that the bell will be rungen but the man who carries a bill and yokes himself to a plow still believes the leader will arise to drive the Normans into the sea. It is in these dim glades, by St. Clement, that the true spirit of England persists, and you see the real Englishman; a fellow with a strong back and a touch of the poet in him, and whose eyes still light up when he thinks of the day when the war arrow will pass secretly from hand to hand."

The day passed without incident. At the evening meal Richard sat on Adelbert's left and could watch the face of his beloved Eleanor over the handsomely embroidered sleeves of his host. Ordinarily he would have enjoyed to the full the haunch of venison which the skilled bow of Albie Oakyard had provided but he could tell by the expression on the face of the princess that she was deeply disturbed, and so his appetite failed him.

Adelbert also sensed drama in the air and, when the last bone had been tossed by greasy fingers to the dogs snuffling hopefully in the rushes, he raised his hand in a signal. The lower table emptied at once, leaving the trio, together with Father Exiguus, in sole possession of the Hall.

Eleanor began to speak at once. "My good friends," she said in a repressed voice, "you are going to think me the most ungrateful of mortals. But I must say what is in my mind." She turned her head and looked steadily at Adelbert. "Can anyone deny that the English are a treacherous race? Is there no honor in this country? Have the men of England no regard for what is just and right, or for the Lord's will?"

"I believe, Your Grace, that you have every reason to feel bitter," said Adelbert. "And yet all the questions you propound may be answered with a no. There is treachery to be found among the English, it is true, but no race is free of it. Truly there are men everywhere who put personal interests first and are prepared to go to any lengths. As for the rest, I know of no land where there is a higher sense of honor than among men of this country. Even," he added, "if evidence to the contrary may be put forward."

"Why," demanded the princess, her color high and her eyes stormy with passion, "did they select John as king instead of the rightful heir, my brother Arthur?"

The old Saxon was clearly unhappy under her questioning. He paused for some time before making any reply.

"There were many of us who thought the crown should go to Prince Arthur," he said finally. "We had no chance to assert ourselves. There were reasons of state for the decision. The unfortunate prince, your brother, was young and he had never set foot on English soil. It was the expressed will of Richard that John should succeed him."

"Why," she demanded with mounting tension, "did you permit this

evil man to remain as king when it became known that he had murdered my brother?"

"There are times, sweet lady, when the hands of right-thinking men
are tied. After Arthur's death I felt a tension everywhere and a growing dislike and distrust of John; but there was no leader to rouse the
forces of dissent. I, for one, would gladly have risked my life then in an
effort to remove John from the throne. Even as I do now."

"This vile king has been a failure!" she cried. "The French have
taken Normandy and Anjou away from him. The leopards of England
have been trampled in the mud. But still the men of England bow
meekly to the will of your John Softsword!"

"Not meekly, Your Grace. A storm is gathering which will sweep
him from the throne. It is gaining strength every day."

The princess rose to her feet to deliver her final charge. "These brave
gentlemen who were to rally to my support, where are they? Are they
slinking in their kennels like whipped curs? They no longer have the
excuse that the roads are impassable; and yet not one of them has
come."

"Your Grace," said Adelbert, bowing his head before the storm,
"there are forces at work in England today which are hard to understand. Men are thinking of remedies for the evils under which they live
which may prove more important than whether John is to be left on
the throne or who is to succeed him. They are asking themselves what
restrictions may be placed on kingly powers which will free them for
all time from despotism."

"What treason is this?" cried the princess. "Do the people of England
think to set limits to the power of the kings who are ordained by God to
rule over them? Is this what the friars and hedge priests preach at those
midnight meetings of which you spoke?"

"Even so. There is a temper in England today which is new and
strong, though it may take time to assert itself."

Richard, watching and listening in silence, was thinking that he had
never seen Eleanor more beautiful. Never had skies been bluer than
her eyes as she stood and faced them, never had sun shone with a more
penetrating light. The passion which possessed her made her seem truly
regal in every line of her slender figure. "She is like Boadicea, standing
so bravely and proudly in her war chariot before charging the ranks of
Suetonius," he said to himself.

"If I become Queen of England will I be subject to these restrictions
of which you speak?" she demanded to know.

Adelbert nodded his head slowly but firmly. "Yes, Your Grace. The English people are making up their minds to submit no longer to any form of tyranny."

Eleanor turned to leave the Hall, tossing her head high and saying over her shoulder: "Then it may be well, my lord Adelbert, that none of these honorable gentlemen came to see me. They would have found me unwilling to accept such terms."

When the silken rustle of her skirts as she climbed the stairs could no longer be heard, Father Exiguus shook his head sadly. "The poor child is overwrought," he said. "We must not judge her hastily. And it must be agreed that she has no reason to feel well disposed toward Englishmen after what she has suffered."

Adelbert sat very still for several moments, studying his hands, which he had spread out on the table in front of him. "What are we to do with her?" he asked.

They discussed the problem at some length but without arriving at any conclusion. It was only too clear to all of them that the situation they faced offered no ready solution.

After a quarter hour had passed they heard a footstep on the stair. Turning their heads in unison, they saw that the princess had returned. She had donned her coat of chain mail and had buckled a sword around her waist. Her eyes were blazing with a new resolution.

"Only one course is left to me," she said. "It is my purpose to take horse and ride out openly to claim my rights. Are you willing to go with me?"

Richard sprang to his feet without a moment's hesitation.

"Yes!" he cried.

Adelbert rose also but more slowly. He too answered with one word but it was a clear and unmistakable "No."

The princess drew the sword from the scabbard and held it above her head as she completed the descent of the stairs. "I cannot blame you," she said, addressing herself to Adelbert. "Nor will I blame anyone who fails to come forward in my support. The risk is indeed a great one."

Adelbert did not answer at once. When he did, it was in a deliberate tone and with carefully chosen words. "My lady," he said, "in giving you my answer, I had no thought of my own safety. My life is already forfeit. The part I have played in your cause is no secret. As long as John remains on the throne, I will never dare return to my possessions in the south. I confess that the bold plan you propose has an appeal that stirs my blood. But, my lady, I am thinking of your own fate. Have you any hopes of success?"

"There is always hope," she answered. "Many brave men might come out to ride under my banner once it was known that I was free and making a bid for my rights."

"It is true," he said slowly, "that there is always that hope. But a wise leader does not make his plans on hopes alone. He must have some feeling of assurance that the odds favor him, that he has at worst an even chance. To throw down the gage when the odds are overwhelmingly against you is a very great folly indeed."

"It may be the only course that honor allows!" she cried. "I would rather die than go on living in hiding like this! Not daring to show my face!"

"If it were only a case of dying, I would gladly say, 'Let us ride out tonight. Let us unfurl the banner of the Pendragon and make our bid against the power of the king.' But, my lady, if we failed—and I must say that in my estimation we would have no better than one chance in ten—those who died in the fighting would be the lucky ones. You must have heard of the amiable methods this king uses in dealing with those he considers traitors. Many of the valiant knights and brave boys who had come out to serve you would die in dire torment."

"Isn't any death better than to slink in dark holes and hide our faces from the tyrant?"

"My lady," said Adelbert slowly, "your own fate would be the hardest of all. John would reserve a very special punishment for you. He would put you back in one of his prisons and you would soon realize that the conditions under which you existed at Corfe Castle were luxurious compared to the state in which you would drag out the rest of your life. My flesh creeps when I think of you in a dark cell, never seeing the light of day, never seeing a human face, never hearing a voice, nor any sound save of your own making. A hand stretching in once a day to deposit the morsel of cold food and the pan of water which would keep you alive. A pallet of foul straw to sleep on and nothing to cover you in the cold of winter. You would become disease-ridden and verminous. My lady, my very dear lady, to whom I have pledged my allegiance in full faith, I cannot be a partner to a mad gamble which holds out such an ending as this!"

Eleanor glanced at Richard. "My good friend, do you still abide by your pledge?"

"Yes, Your Grace. I am prepared to face any risk. But I am compelled to say there is wisdom in what my lord Adelbert says. It may be wiser to wait for a more favorable time."

"If King John were here," said Adelbert, "and listening to this discussion, he would rub his hands with glee. Nothing would suit him better than to have us venture everything on one cast of the dice. For the dice, my lady, would be heavily loaded in his favor."

There was a moment of tense silence. Then Eleanor turned and began to retrace her steps, replacing the sword in its scabbard as she did so. "It seems," she said, glancing darkly over her shoulder, "that in addition to their other faults, Englishmen are cowards!"

Nothing was said until the sound of her ascending footsteps ceased. Then Adelbert spoke. "I've heard that when John is beaten or thwarted in a desire he rolls on the floor in rage and chews the corners of the rugs. His father, old Harry Secund, did the same. It is a Plantagenet trait. We must not blame our lady too much because she shares it in some degree."

"She will blame herself bitterly when her mood changes," declared Richard.

Adelbert frowned thoughtfully at his hands resting on the board. "Has it occurred to you, Sir Richard, that she may decide to ride away alone? We must provide against any such wild adventure as that. I will give orders to the groom not to saddle a horse for her and not to lower the drawbridge. As a further precaution, I think we should get our hands on her armor." He looked up at Richard. "I don't think it wise to leave it to one of the servants to do. Your room is close to hers. Will you undertake to get it?"

Richard hesitated and then agreed with a somewhat dubious nod.

3

The sentry at the head of the stairs was sprawled back against the wall and snoring loudly. From the small rooms on each side of the hall came the rhythmic sound of profound slumber. Richard walked on tiptoe to the corner room which the princess occupied and paused there to listen. When he heard no sound from within, he pressed a hand cautiously on the door. It gave under the pressure. The room was not in complete darkness because a candle was burning on a chair but the figure in the bed did not move. He could see the mail shirt lying on the floor and took a cautious step toward it.

"Richard!"

Eleanor had roused and was sitting up in bed. The candle cast enough light for him to see that she had been weeping. Her eyes looked swollen and unhappy.

"What is it you want?" she asked.

"I am ashamed of my errand," he said. He held up the chain mail. "I came for this. We were afraid you would be bold enough to venture out by yourself."

"No," she said in a voice little above a whisper. "I realize now that no good would come of it." She brushed back her hair from her face. "I must be a sorry object. Are my eyes very red? I have been weeping ever since I came up. How unfair I was to you! I know now that I—that I shall never be Queen of England. The chance has slipped by. And I have insulted my best friends."

"There is no reason to give up hope. How can we tell what the future holds?"

"Nothing good, I am sure. Am I to blame for our failure?"

"No, sweet lady! You have acted with great courage and dignity."

She began to weep again. "Richard, Richard," she whispered. "I cannot face the future without you. Must we part now?"

"I desire nothing in life save the chance to remain with you and serve you!"

And then he forgot that she was a princess of the royal line and that he was a plain knight, without land or prospects. He remembered perhaps the whispered conversation between them in the window embrasure. He was aware of her need for comfort and of the great love he had for her. His arm went about her shoulders and he drew her head down against his arm. There was no hint of reluctance on her part, although for several moments she continued to weep.

Many minutes passed without a word being said, how many he could not tell. He came to himself with a sudden sense of guilt when he realized that he had kissed her; not once, not twice, but many times, and that she had accepted his kisses and had even returned them.

"Your Highness!" he whispered. "I have most surely gone mad!"

She reached under her pillow and found a handkerchief which she applied to her eyes. "Richard, I am doubly unfortunate," she said. "I have none of the privileges of royal birth but I must suffer from the restrictions. I know there are things in your mind which you will never dare say. So—so I must say them in your stead." She stirred in his arms and pressed her face more closely against his shoulder. "You came to remove a temptation from me by taking away my armor. But your coming has created a still greater temptation."

Adelbert sat at the head of the table when Tostig went in for breakfast. It was apparent that the owner of Furmain had something on his mind. He frowned as he kept his head lowered over the food and his voice was sharp when he addressed the servants. It has already been made clear that he was against any departure from established custom. Because of this he finished his meal and then left his own place and went to sit with Tostig some distance down the board.

"A final blow has been dealt us," he said in a low tone. "A runner from Cromlath arrived early this morning. Owen ap John, it seems, was on his way here. When I heard this, my hopes rose again. It seemed quite possible we could place the princess in the sanctuary of his castle and then proceed with the making of plans at our leisure. But the messenger informed me also that Owen had turned back. News had reached him that the peasantry, who have been sullen because of his part in the slave trade, took advantage of his absence. Two nights ago they rose in arms and secured possession of Cromlath Castle, with the aid no doubt of some of the guards. They released the prisoners, who were to have been put on a boat for Ireland—some unbelievable number of them, in excess of two hundred—and then proceeded to dismantle the walls and the keep. I think the garrison must have had a hand in it. At any rate, they turned the place into a pretty shambles." Adelbert's face was a study in anger and frustration. "Owen ap John has ridden back to Cromlath. He will be so concerned with rebuilding the castle and settling his accounts with the peasantry that he won't be able to take any part in our plans. And so, my good Tostig, our last chance has been lost."

Having finished his breakfast, which consisted of a salt fish and an apple of the codlin variety, Tostig retraced his steps to the floor above, to tell Richard of the blow which had been dealt them. Richard's door was closed, so he rapped cautiously. When there was no response, he opened the door and looked in. The room was empty. A second glance made it clear that the bed had not been slept in.

Tostig, a prey to the most intense anxiety, stood in the doorway for several minutes, turning over in his mind all possible explanations. He was convinced that Richard had not left the castle. What possible reason could he have had for venturing out during the night? Convinced that the reason must be found elsewhere, he turned and glanced up the narrow hall. The door of the corner room was closed. He had been surprised not to see the princess below for breakfast. She was an early riser and it had been her custom each day to have the morning meal with their host. In contrast to his moroseness of mood, she had always been talkative and even rather gay.

"It can't be," said Tostig to himself.

He retreated into the little dark room, which lacked a window and which served him as a bedchamber, and seated himself on a corner of the straw pallet. It did not take him long to become convinced that there was no other explanation. He was so sure that he said to himself: "This is a complication which never occurred to any of us. It is something with which Father Exiguus will have to deal."

Chapter XIX

1

"I LIKE to spend Christmas here at Pembroke," said Sybilla, the third daughter of the earl and countess, as the family descended from the high chapel where Father Sosthene had conducted the first Yuletide service, "but I *don't* like getting up so soon after midnight. Do you, Isabella?"

"No," said Isabella, the second daughter, who has appeared once already in this narrative and who was now as beautiful as she had promised to be then.

The two girls were wearing warm cloaks and hoods which almost hid their smooth blonde hair. There were mittens on their hands and fur-lined shoes to protect them from chilblains. Even as well protected as this, they shivered a little in the dead, dank cold of the high halls.

"I think," went on Sybilla, "he took a very long time chanting the genny——"

"The genealogy," said Isabella in a superior tone. "Of St. Matthew."

"I nearly dropped off to sleep again while he was at it," declared the younger girl. "*Brrrh!* It's cold, isn't it? I think, Isabella, if you don't mind my saying it, that you would enjoy Christmas here at Pembroke much more if Mother had allowed you to invite some of your suitors to visit us."

"Not at all. When you reach my age, silly goose, you will know how wise it is to disappear at times and leave all the men kicking their heels."

"The nicest suitor you ever had, Isabella," rather wistfully, "was that one years and years ago. Oh, seven or eight years, I think. When I was very young. He had just been knighted and he was very handsome. You were terribly in love with him."

"Who do you mean?" sharply. "I had no suitors seven or eight years ago. And if he was just a plain knight, he couldn't possibly be a suitor."

"I mean Richard. Richard of Rawen."

"St. Agnes assoil us!" exclaimed Isabella. "So you mean that one. Whatever made you think of him, child?"

"You must think of him a great deal, Isabella."

"I had almost forgotten him. Why, he hasn't entered my head in years. And do you know, Sybilla, I have no recollection of what he looked like. None whatever. My interest in him, if I ever had any, ceased long ago."

"You said," protested the younger sister, "that he was going to wait until you grew up."

"What a very stupid little girl I must have been!"

They had reached the ground floor and the flames from the chimney in the Great Hall were rising ten feet in the air and casting out sparks in all directions. William the Marshal took his old bones to a chair in front of the fire. The Yule log had been carried in the preceding evening but the younger members of the family had not seen it. Isabella cried out in a delighted voice, "Oh, it's the largest one we've ever had!" She began to hum a popular carol which was all about English ale and Gascon wine, stopping almost immediately to say to her sister in a low voice, "When they elect the Lord of Misrule, I would like to be made one of the pages."

"I have pretty legs too," said Sybilla primly, "but I don't intend to show them off in public like that. You would have to wear tight hose, Isabella."

"I had no such thought in my head! But I do want to have a part in the ceremonies. It isn't amusing when you have to watch, because they're sure to elect Mum Peter again. His only idea of being funny is to wear a false nose and kick up his heels."

The Countess of Pembroke, whose hair had turned most becomingly white, was sitting on the arm of her husband's chair when her personal maid approached her. "It's very mysterious, m'lady, but there's a man says he must see you," she whispered.

"A man to see me? At four o'clock in the morning! Gertruda, there must be some mistake."

"No'm, m'lady. He says his name be Tostig and he was of the household once. Mum Peter thinks he remembers him."

"Why didn't you tell me all this at once?" demanded the countess in an impatient tone. "Where is he?"

"I ustered him into the small stone room that m'lord uses so much. It seemed the best place, seeing as how secret the man was."

The countess left her dozing spouse and the comfort of the leaping flames to venture again down one of the chilly halls, carrying a candle above her head. "I won't need you, Gertruda," she said when the maid showed an intention of accompanying her.

Tostig was standing in a window embrasure and looking up at the stars, wondering perhaps if their position was favorable for the enterprise he had in mind. He stepped out and bowed. "My lady, it is kind of you to see me."

"Too kind perhaps," said the countess, "in view of the strange hour you have elected to visit us."

"I knew you would be up early for the Christmas chants. I could have waited until morning before coming but it seemed to me wiser and safer to come under cover of darkness."

"Safer?" A dubious frown showed itself on the comely face of the chatelaine. "Does that mean you are in trouble, Tostig? More trouble than usual?"

"Your ladyship, I never seem to be out of trouble."

"So we have heard." She held the candle closer to him in order to study his face. He was travel-stained and weary, with the wool cap of a peasant on his head and huge gloves of red wool. "The last glimpse I had of you was when you set out for Brittany with my young knight, Richard of Rawen. You have both been involved in most curious enterprises since. *Such* bad reports have reached us!"

"Yes, my lady. It is not likely that the king holds any affection for us."

"Where is my nice Richard? And why didn't he come with you to pay his respects? I think ill of him for neglecting me."

"My lady," explained Tostig earnestly, "we felt it would be unwise for him to come, because it might involve you and my lord in difficulties. And I—I rather took things into my own hands. I came, your ladyship, to make a suggestion about which he knows nothing." He paused a moment before adding, "He is in Wales. At Milford Haven."

"Have you come from Milford?"

"Yes, my lady. But I did not dare take boat or use any of the ferries. I had to ride quite far upstream."

A sudden draft almost extinguished the candle held by the countess. Tostig moved a screen which stood against the wall and propped it up around her, so she would have no further trouble.

"What is Richard doing in Wales?"

"He is there with his lady wife."

"His wife!" exclaimed the countess, her voice rising with surprise. "Richard is married? Why did I not know of this? And who is the bride?"

"He is married"—Tostig seemed reluctant to give voice to such dangerous information—"he is married to the Princess Eleanor of Brittany."

"This is utter nonsense! You can't know what you are saying, Tostig. The princess is a state prisoner. She is held in one of the king's castles. I believe it is Corfe, although I have never been able to get any information from my husband. He may not know himself."

"She escaped from Corfe Castle several weeks ago, my lady."

The countess stamped a foot in disbelief and exasperation. "You *can't* mean what you are saying! This is unbelievable. You stand there and tell me with a straight face these extraordinary things." She laughed indignantly. "Go on, my man, go on. You must tell me everything now. If it is true that the princess has escaped, then I know that you and Richard had a hand in it."

Tostig indulged in a smile, the only expression he had displayed since the talk began. "Yes, your ladyship, you might truthfully say that we had a hand in it. Moreover it was our plan, although there were others helping us." He hesitated before going on but realized almost immediately that he must be more explicit. He explained how they had succeeded in effecting Eleanor's escape but was careful to say nothing of the political plans which had failed of success. "They think now of going to Rome to claim the protection of the Pope. They have been three weeks at Milford Haven, waiting for a ship to take them to the Continent. But I am convinced it would be a mistake. Now that she has married a landless knight, the princess would not be an asset in the plans of His Holiness. I am not even sure she would be safe there."

"The princess must have lost her head completely!" exclaimed the countess. "Although she was a state prisoner, she remained high on the list of succession. By running away and marrying a commoner, she has forfeited all chance of high preferment."

"She has lost her liking for heights, my lady. The cell in which she was confined was very high. It was at the top of a forty-foot shaft in the castle wall. She was kept there for seven years! She prefers now to live on a less exalted level, even though it means being the wife of a poor knight. My lady, they are very much in love with each other."

A note of impatience showed itself in the voice of the countess. "That is no excuse for rushing into matrimony. Love comes after marriage and very seldom before. And now that they have been so rash, what are they to do? I am inclined to agree with you that it isn't wise to trust

themselves into the hands of the Pope. Why should they not remain in
Wales? The Welsh people will accept the princess as a descendant of
the great Arthur. Have they been keeping their identities secret?"

"Yes, my lady."

"I am glad they have had that much discretion." A crease showed
on the unwrinkled brow of the countess. "You know, of course, that we
would be in serious trouble if it became known you were here?"

Tostig bowed. "I am so conscious of it, my lady, that I have been
most cautious. Old Micklebury took my horse when I arrived. As you
know, he is not the one to tattle. I think it would be wise if I remained
under cover all day and did not leave until darkness had set in."

"I will have Gertruda bring you something to eat," decided the
countess. "She is loyal and not a gossip. Also she must bring you a
blanket so you may get some sleep. You look very tired. As for the key
to this room, I shall keep it myself."

2

William the Marshal had not been too far gone in slumber to know
that a visitor had arrived. "Who was it?" he asked when his wife seated
herself beside him at the breakfast table which had been set up for
greater warmth in a smaller room off the Hall. A crackling fire behind
them was dispensing comfort and good cheer.

"I will tell you later, dear William." The countess frowned doubtfully.
"A most unusual matter indeed."

There is always something sad for parents in Christmas festivities.
The Marshal brood of ten had all escaped the perils of infancy and
were growing up, handsome, the lot of them, and healthy; but, alas,
they were beginning to scatter. William, the oldest son, who would
someday succeed his father as the marshal of England, was already
deep in the councils of those who opposed the king and was continuously
from home. Richard, the second son, who was to inherit the family
estates in Normandy, was abroad. Matilda, the oldest daughter, was
married and living with her husband in Norfolk. Four of the younger
children were still asleep in their beds but would be down soon, in time
for the convening of the court of the Lord of Misrule, when their noisy
enthusiasm would add much to the gaiety of the occasion.

"I wish William could have been here," sighed the earl. "What has
kept Gilbert away? Is he so steeped in his books that Christmas means
nothing to him? And I miss that dear Matilda so very much!"

"Good my lord," said the countess. "I suggest you take charge of those who are here today. You will have no time for regrets, if you do. You might even be less conscious of the absence of our older children."

The earl turned his attention to the food and did not speak again until his wife, who was eating little, asked him a question. "William, do you ever wonder what it would have been like if Arthur had been selected and not John?"

The earl sighed and pushed away his wine with a gesture which meant he was finished. "Often," he replied. "Always I think of it when the cup of the king's iniquities seems ready to overflow. But I have no feeling of fault or regret for the part I took. It had been settled that John was to succeed. I would do the same again. But many times, sweet chuck, I have felt badly for the poor prisoner who is locked up in Corfe Castle."

"So!" said the countess. "You knew it all the time and you never told me!"

"Didn't you know?" The marshal's manner suggested that he had been honestly unaware of keeping the matter from her. "She must be kept in restraint, of course. We can't have another civil war in England, not with the situation on the Continent so acute. If conditions had been favorable, that rascally French king would have an army of invasion in England today."

"How is the Princess Eleanor lodged at Corfe?"

"I understand she lives in some comfort, even a touch of luxury."

"Have you ever made it a point to find out?"

The earl thought for a moment. "No, dear wife, I don't believe I have."

"William," whispered his spouse, after a moment of silence, "you are so guarded of tongue. I don't believe you have ever confided to me your full and honest opinion of King John."

The marshal leaned his head down close to her ear in replying. "My love, I am the servant of the king; and even though he may be the worst man in Christendom, I must obey his orders as long as I remain in office." There was a pause and then he continued in a low whisper. "Dear heart, he is all of that, the worst man in Christendom! Soon I must make up my mind that I may no longer serve him. It is only my desire to keep the office in the family and my fear of who might be appointed in my place which holds my hand. He is surrounded by thieves and mountebanks and would undoubtedly select one of them for the post if I stepped out."

The countess had contented herself with no more than a mouthful of bread which had been made especially for her and had come to the table hot from the ovens. She sighed even more deeply than her husband.

"William," she whispered, "I hope the times will mend before our children are called on to play their parts."

The marshal glanced at their two daughters, who were sitting together. They had kept on their cloaks but the hoods had been thrown back, freeing their long tresses of golden hair. He himself was still handsome in a long-nosed, square-jawed way of things, but the two girls had the delicate features of their mother. They were chatting in such a lively vein that the head of the family got to his feet. "If you will excuse me, my heart," he said, "I think I will sit for a few minutes between my pretty little flibbergibs over there."

3

When William the Marshal discovered a half hour later, on accompanying his wife to the small stone room, that the nocturnal visitor was none other than Tostig, his face beamed in welcome and he said in hearty tones: "Ha, you young scoundrel, this is a surprise! I am glad to see you because now I shall have the whole story of how our Richard unhorsed that hulking monstrosity of a Poitevin. Did you know that I came close to splintering a lance with him once? It was many years ago and we were having a pleasant little running at Rouen. There were three of us ready to take on all comers. This great black bustard was the first to offer himself and I felt an itching in the palms of my hands because I had long wanted the chance to have at him. But he passed my shield by, the lumbering ox, and struck that on my left. He beat my comrade and was content then to rest on his laurels."

"You would have had little difficulty with him, my lord," said Tostig.

The marshal was fair to a most unusual degree. "Who can say?" was his answer. "I think perhaps I might have bested him, because he carried so much suet above his waist. Still, it was never put to the test."

Having thus disposed of the Sire Tohu-Bohu, William gave the squire a highly critical stare. "We've been having infamous reports of the pair of you. Going about the country in disguise and singing these songs about your liege lord, the king. By the head of St. Peter, I expected you to be well hanged long ago!"

"We were sent to England on a mission," declared Tostig defensively.

The marshal nodded. "I knew you had been with the archbishop at Pontigny. It came to my ears, in fact, that you were much in his confidence."

A sudden ray of light touched one of the windows. The first flush of dawn had appeared in the sky. The old champion turned and walked over to observe it, leaning his noble height on the bars. He tilted his head to look up into the clouds and so his long gray hair fell back from his fine brow. An almost ecstatic look spread over his face.

"How many thousands of times have I watched the sun rise!" he said. "And I still wonder at the glory of it! Each night I pray that I shall be spared to see it many times still."

The countess took advantage of his absorption to say to Tostig in a low tone: "I know you have some plan in that calculating head of yours."

"Yes, my lady. I have thought much of Ireland as a place for the princess and Master Rick to go."

"They would have to go far inland to avoid recognition."

"As far perhaps as Kilkenny."

The countess regarded him with a highly critical eye. "You are always perhaps a little too shrewd, my good Tostig. You are quite aware that my lord has great estates in Ireland."

"Which belonged to your grandfather, my lady, when he was King of Leinster."

"You know, I need hardly mention, that all of Kilkenny is included in our holdings."

"Exactly, my lady. His lordship has such wide holdings that Richard of Rawen could serve him well on the western boundaries of Leinster. He could help to keep order and to repel aggression from the wild tribesmen of the west. And Kilkenny, my lady, is like a foreign country. The people there know no more of England than we know of Thule. Nothing that happens there is ever heard outside."

"There is some truth in what you say."

"My lady, a man who goes to Ireland is accepting exile. He is gone out of sight and mind."

The lady glanced in the direction of her spouse. The marshal had drawn a chair to the window the better to watch the coming of the dawn but it seemed that the early hour of his rising was already claiming its toll of his wakefulness. His head had fallen forward on his chest.

"Tostig, I am going to trust deeply in your sense of honor and your discretion. There has always been in my mind a sense of regret over the killing of Prince Arthur, a feeling almost of complicity in that terrible tragedy. My good Lord William has never said a word to warrant my belief that he shares this with me; but I am certain he does. Understand this first of all, he did his duty that night at Rouen. The people of England did not want Arthur as king but—but they did not want Arthur murdered and his beautiful sister thrown into captivity. This seems to me, Tostig, a chance to rid our consciences of some of this feeling. If we take the risk of helping the princess now, we may ever after rest a little easier over the consequences of the decision my good William reached at Rouen."

"Yes, my lady," said Tostig eagerly.

"Would this poor foolish Eleanor take an oath renouncing for all time her right to the throne? Would she swear never to reveal by word or deed her real identity?"

"I did not discuss this thought of mine before starting out, my lady. But I am certain she would gladly take these oaths."

"They would need a good story to tell to account for themselves."

"Richard would claim to be of Irish birth, although he had lived most of his life in England and on the Continent. His name, Richard Patrick O'Rawn. His wife, a Breton girl he met on his adventurings in France."

The eye of the countess expressed even more of suspicion. "You have it all worked out, haven't you? You came here expecting us to agree with your design."

"Yes, my lady. Knowing the greatness of your hearts and the courage you share."

The countess fell into a mood of abstraction which lasted for several moments. "On the river, some miles beyond the town of Kilkenny," she said finally, "there is a lovely stretch of land. It is called the Little Farm of Green Hedges. But it isn't really small. There are about four hundred acres in all. The house *is* small but it could be added to." She sat in silence for more moments of earnest speculation. "The people of Kilkenny know nothing of England. To them it's as far away as the Land of Cathay, and the less they hear of it, the happier they are. Richard and his princess could settle among those fine simple folk without any fear of being recognized." She turned to face her dozing spouse. "William, William!"

The old marshal stirred and drew the back of a hand across his eyes. "Yes, my love. What is it?"

"William, I have a problem to lay before you."

"My dear Isabella!" He heaved a deep sigh. "I hoped I could live through this Christmas without a single problem to solve. I seem to do nothing these days but make decisions. I am very weary of making decisions."

"Then we will leave this until later. But tell me this, dear William. Where is that ship you built to break up the slave trade between England and Ireland?"

This, apparently, was a subject which interested him very much. He straightened in his chair and the sleepy unconcern left his eyes.

"It's laid up for a few days. The hull needs caulking. Very soon I intend to pay my respects to the pirates on Lundy's Island." The marshal's face took on a determined look which boded ill for the Bristol corsairs. "It's the most unforgivable form of treachery. Preying on the commerce of your own country! They should all be hanged."

"It may be, dear husband, that I'll want you to sail to Ireland instead."

The face of the marshal brightened. He always enjoyed a visit to the green island. "You know my weakness and play on it like the witch you are. There are many things that need doing in Ireland as it happens. I must have some words with that old adder, the Abbot of Ferns. He claims I stole some land from him."

"William!" cried his wife. "Have no more dealings with the Abbot of Ferns. He will lay a curse on you."

The marshal indulged in an unconcerned smile. "No man who has been to the Crusades need fear the curses of a stay-at-home abbot. The Lord would listen and say, 'Who is this windy fellow crying out against My good servant who fought the paynim in My name?'"

"I may want you to send the ship to Ireland at once. With three passengers."

"My lady," corrected Tostig. "Two passengers only."

"Don't you intend to go?" The countess studied the squire's face as well as she could in the still dark room. She saw that he showed a fatigue greater than could be charged to his night's ride. There were shadows under his eyes and he wore an air of deep sadness. His fatigue clearly was not all physical.

"No, my lady. I feel I should return, for a time at least, to the service of my lord of Canterbury. And there is another need to keep me in this country. The half sister of the princess is still a prisoner at Corfe." His voice showed a tendency to break. "I cannot leave. I must remain to do—whatever can be done in her behalf."

Chapter XX

1

THE first glimpse that the homeseekers had of the Little Farm of Green Hedges was a most favorable one. The weather had been raw and cold and their journey across the water rough. Eleanor (for she had forsworn her right to the title of princess) had been unhappy and had clung often to Richard's arm, crying: "Fog, fog, fog! Will we ever be free of it?" But the sun had come out when they cantered down the wide gray stone streets of Kilkenny and saw the river Nore winding along in the valley beneath them. The grass was remarkably green for so early in the year. Eleanor gave a relieved gasp of "How lovely!" and it was not long before she gripped his arm (for, of course, they rode side by side) and cried out ecstatically: "There it is! Over there. That stretch of heavenly green land!"

She was right. It was the Little Farm of Green Hedges. There was no mistaking the hedges, for they were taller and greener than any yet seen, and they did not have the geometrical precision of a chessboard but went in every direction to suit the windings of the river and the lay of the land. Besides, Fergus MacDatho, who was riding in the lead, turned his horse down a narrow dirt path with a wave of the hand to them to follow.

"This is where we cross, my lord and lady," he called, grinning back at them in the most friendly way. "The river can be waded here at this season. It will save us much riding."

The Earl and Countess of Pembroke had been more than generous in their endowment of the newly married pair. The cavalcade consisted of six horses: one for Dame Jehane, who had wanted to continue in the service of her mistress, two pack animals, loaded as heavily as camels, and a frisky roan for Fergus MacDatho, who was very sure in the saddle. This genial young man bore a fine Irish name but his branch of the family was not a prosperous one. He had been attached to the Irish household of William the Marshal since his earliest years and had been selected by the countess to act as interpreter for the new occupants of the farm. A deep attachment for them had already grown in his easy, unselfish mind.

He drew up on the brink of the slowly rolling river and called back, "My lord, it will be best if her ladyship tucks her feet up on the saddle, so she won't get them wet."

Richard rode closer to Eleanor and saw to it that this advice was followed. To make it easier for her to retain her seat in this awkward posture, he wrapped an arm around her shoulders.

"I suppose a bride must be willing to submit to such unnecessary precautions," said Eleanor.

Her eyes were bright and happy as they splashed through the water and then climbed the grassy banks. They rode over springy turf to a long low house of gray stone.

The house surprised them by a certain degree of spaciousness. Even though the ceilings were low, the rooms were quite large and there were enough windows to admit the sun and air. The high wooden barricade of split logs which surrounded it had fallen into such a state of decay through long lack of use that it did not keep out the light. Inside, the furnishings were scanty but the crackle of fire in several chimneys filled the place with a comfortable warmth and spread an odor which caused the new mistress to wrinkle up her nose in curiosity. "How very odd!" she said. "What is it, Fergus?"

"Peat, my lady," answered the interpreter. "It grows in the fields and they cut it in the fall. It burns well."

The domestic staff was drawn up in the main room. It consisted of two small and rather young girls with a lively sparkle in their gray-blue eyes, and a very tall and muscular youth whose eyes lacked any kind of expression at all.

"These," said Fergus MacDatho with an offhand wave, "are your servants, my lady. The girls are of native stock. They are as pert as sparrows and you will have to beat them at times. But if you go light with the stick, they'll bear no grudges. The boy's name is Harboth and he comes from Cornwall. He was illegitimate so his father got a good price for him from an agent of Owen ap John and he was sold over here as a slave. He's strong but not bright."

The interpreter spoke to the trio and the two girls curtsied very low, saying together in piping voices as though reciting a lesson at school:

"Welcome, dear mistress. We are very happy you have come. We will serve you well."

Eleanor responded in the tongue of Brittany, which had some resemblance to theirs. Their pink and white cheeks became wreathed in smiles which had not been rehearsed.

A very tall and very dark man appeared in the doorway and studied the newcomers from there with an air of complete hostility. He was wearing a ragged green tunic, tied about the waist with a branch from a tree, and his dusty feet were bound in wooden sandals. He addressed Fergus MacDatho in deep and what seemed menacing tones. The latter listened attentively and his voice, in answering, suggested that he held the visitor in some awe.

Eleanor whispered to Richard, "He looks like another wrathful Moses, come down from the mountains with the laws under his arm."

"Or another Goliath," answered Richard.

After several sentences had been exchanged between the interpreter and the visitor, the latter turned about abruptly, spat copiously on the ground, and stalked away, muttering to himself and waving his arms.

"That, St. Ultan be kind to us, is Conn Ragen of the Dark Moods," explained Fergus. "The horses are in his care. He is not feeling friendly."

"I was warned," said Richard, "that he wouldn't be friendly. At least, not at first."

"My lord, Conn Ragen never changes," said the interpreter. "He is very thorough in his hates. He hates Danes and Welsh and Saxons but most of all he hates Normans. He says you are Norman."

Richard stood up stoutly for his story. "I am Irish," he declared.

"I told him that. Conn Ragen says you might have been born here but that you are not Irish. He hates everything. Women and children and even old grandmothers. He hates soldiers and priests and minstrels and poets, and gentry riding in armor and silks. He hates cattle and sheep and the hills and the gentle moon in the night sky. He even hates the Little People."

"The Little People?"

"My lord, have you been away long enough to forget them?" cried Fergus MacDatho. "The Little People are not to be found anywhere but in Ireland and only the Irish can see them. I've seen them, my lord, often's the time. They are so small they can sit on an oak leaf and hide under the petal of a flower. Your ears have to be good—and it *is* said we have the best ears in the whole world here in Ireland—to hear the voices of the Little People."

"And you say Conn Ragen hates them?"

"St. Ultan forgive him, he does. He says they bother the horses. There's only one thing he doesn't hate. Would you care to make a guess what it is?"

"Himself?"

"Ach, no, my lord. It's naught but bitter contempt he has for himself. It's the horses. He loves them. Ach, how he loves the horses!"

"This afternoon, Fergus MacDatho," said Richard, "I think we must ask Conn Ragen to show us the horses. I will love them myself."

It was late afternoon when Richard returned from his tour of the farm, in the reluctant company of that greatest and most thorough of haters, Conn Ragen. He found Eleanor seated in front of a fire, with a look of weariness on her face and yet also a certain note of triumph. She had been keeping her staff of three very busy all afternoon. The whole house had been swept and cleaned. There were rushes on the floor, and on the wall the ivory crucifix which Tostig had brought from Constantinople as a gift for Richard.

Richard walked over and drew her face up toward his, with a hand on each ear. He kissed both eyelids, then the bridge of her nose (which he admired excessively), and then her lips.

"You are an insolent dog, Richard Patrick O'Rawn," she said. "But I don't suppose you would be such a good husband if you didn't have this particular vein of insolence in you."

"My sweet wife," whispered Richard, "I still live in the greatest awe of you. And I am still ready at any time you say to prostrate myself at your lovely feet and let you rest them on my devoted head."

Eleanor sighed. "What will we do if the stubborn English change their minds and want me as their queen after all?"

"There would be no difficulty about it," answered Richard in easy tones. "This marriage of ours would be considered no more than an indiscretion; and isn't a beautiful queen entitled to one indiscretion? I would not be allowed to stand in the way. My good lords and gentlemen would contrive to put me out of sight. They would remove me so thoroughly that I would never be heard of again. I wouldn't even be mentioned in the histories the monks write. In time my existence would be doubted. I would be no more than an unconfirmed rumor."

Eleanor looked up into his eyes for several moments in a tense silence. Her own eyes had narrowed, her lips were slightly parted. Dame Jehane had bound her hair in green silk bands but the few strands which

escaped showed that the growing process was well under way and that
the new locks would be richly golden.

"My dearest Rick," she whispered, "I would never accept any condition of life in which you would be no more than—than an unconfirmed
rumor."

They sat down to dinner at a small round table near the fire on which
had been set out a fish caught fresh in the river, a supply of bacon,
and a warm loaf of bread. Richard drew their chairs close together so
they could lock arms. The pieces of crisp and pleasantly salted bacon
that he raised in his free hand were never conveyed to his own mouth,
and Eleanor reversed the process for his benefit. They drank from the
same cup. One of the two maids, whose name had been Normanized
to Bridgidette, was waiting on table and she giggled continuously.

2

The honeymoon, to borrow that term from the relatively civilized
era in which it would be coined, was not always happy. Richard spent
his time in the fields. He was intensely busy, having reached the conclusion that he could make himself prosperous on these lush acres. Once
he said to Eleanor: "Here we have the richest land in Ireland and here
we can raise the best horses. I am going to make it profitable to raise
them. Do you know how?"

Eleanor yawned and looked at him over the hand she had promptly
applied to the task of concealing her indifference. "No," she said.

"I am not going to be content to use all these beautiful fields and
hillsides for grazing. I am going to grow crops."

"Indeed?"

"Mostly oats. So it won't be necessary to buy what we need. In fact
I hope to sell to our less provident neighbors. And wheat, of course.
Also barley."

Eleanor was sufficiently interested to ask a question. "Why is our
land better than these other farms around us?"

"That," was the answer, "is what I must find out. As usual, my sweet
child of clouts," meaning a doll, "you have sent an arrow straight to the
mark. I suspect that Conn Ragen knows the answer."

When the days were clear Eleanor was perfectly happy, for she rode
continually. She would be awake soon after dawn, demanding that her
favorite mount be brought out for her. Conn Ragen would attend to
her wishes himself, scowling blackly and scolding at her as he adjusted

the gear. She would return with her color high, her eyes fairly blazing with the delight of it. Conn Ragen would rush out to examine the horse, to inspect her mouth (Eleanor had selected a small and high-spirited mare), to ascertain if she had suffered any injury on such a harum-scarum race over hill and valley. Eleanor would dismount without any help from him (none was ever offered) and say: "There, you will find nothing amiss. What's more, she likes me, this sweet little hinny." She always addressed him in the Breton tongue, so that he could get the meaning of it. His answer would be in an intense voice. If Eleanor had been able to understand more than a few of the bitter phrases he employed, she would have known that he was saying something like this: "You are a foreign woman, an Egyptian, and your hair is Godlessly short like the days of a heretic. You think my gentle silken Biddy likes you but that is all in your pride. She could have naught but hate for the Norman woman that you are. But you whisper in her ear, you wheedle her like a Jezebel, and it goes to her weak head; as it would go to mine, saving that my head is a good Irish head and not weak. So she gallops her hardest and she takes fences and hedges that are too high for her." He scowled at Eleanor still more darkly. "Someday neither of you will come back."

On days when it rained—and most days, alas, were wet and cold—she would be compelled to stay in the house. She would stamp from room to room and make life very miserable indeed for the three servants and for Fergus MacDatho, if that usually discreet young Irishman had not succeeded in disappearing. Her head was always filled with bitter thoughts. "Why," she would ask herself, "did I swear away my rights? Did I expect to be always happy as the wife of a common knight and living in a wallow like this?" At times she would go many steps further in her rebellious thoughts. "Why shouldn't I go back openly and say: 'Here I am. Return me to my cell, for I am Eleanor of Brittany and I must live according to my destiny. Let my baseborn sister go free. She will marry her squire and I am sure she will be happy in this very kind of life!' "

Richard would encounter the dregs of these moods when he returned from the hills. He would feel at once how very short she was with him and he would say: "So, my sweet wife has flown away and left in her stead a princess who is bitter over the bargain she made. I am compelled to say that I do not blame her." She would relent in time, of course, and the reconciliations would be tearful and sweet.

It was the arrival of a very old wandering minstrel which brought about, in a most indirect way, the solution to Eleanor's uncertainties and misgivings. He crossed the ford on foot and came to the rear of the house in a very wet and famished condition, holding his small harp above his head to protect the strings. Eleanor had seen him from one of the windows and sent word to the kitchens that he was to have food and drink and dry clothing, and then to be sent in to her.

His name, it developed, was Brian; at least, he thought that was it. He had been born in the far north, or was it the south or even the west where the great ocean roared in on the shingle of so many tiny bays? The truth of the matter was that he had outlived most of his memories and his chief reason for keeping on the road, apart from his need of daily food and an occasional bed, was to recover the knowledge of his birthplace. A short, intense man, with long white hair in matted locks and the bold hooked nose of an Old Testament prophet, he sat down in front of the mistress of Green Hedges and proceeded to play and sing. The strings responded to the wizardry of his stiffening fingers and filled the room with strange music. At times he would stop and an eager look would take possession of his face. He would seem on the point of a discovery. Then the memory would elude him and he would heave a deep sigh.

"Faith, my lady, I had it that time on the very tip of my mind. So clearly could I see the tall fine trees around a bend in the road and a wind playing through the branches which said, 'Welcome, Brian, welcome home, old minstrel!' But now it is gone again and I don't know where the bones of my ancestors are buried, whether it be in the north, or the south, or the east, or the west."

In the course of an hour he had several such lapses and in that time also his fancy added to the greatness of the home he could not find. A turret was added to the battlements of the castle and at least three musicians to the company which played and sang in the minstrels' gallery for the edification of the ladies and gentlemen below. "Such greatness and nobility, my lady," he sighed, "the like of which has never been seen." It was, he believed, the very spot where the foot of St. Patrick first touched Irish soil, although many of envious mind were ready to steal away that honor. If he could only recall the name of the village, or stumble across it in his endless travels, so he could settle down there and be at peace for the rest of his days.

Eleanor found his music so diverting, and she conceived moreover such a liking for the addled old wanderer himself, that he was urged to stay with them and forget his wearisome quest. The certainty of regular meals and a place beside a chimney with its warmly smoldering peat was too much for Brian ("Not that I can swear to it, m'lady, that such is my name") and he soon became convinced that this was in reality the goal he had sought, that it was at the Little Farm of Green Hedges he had first seen the light of day. "Then it was under a hedge he was born, the dirty old spald!" declared one of the pert maids.

His talk was all of the past and of the folklore of the Irish people. Once he asked Eleanor, "Is it known to you, my lady, that every well in Ireland is under a spell, good or bad?"

When she replied that this interesting state of affairs had never before been called to her attention, he proceeded to explain at some length. "It is the truth, my lady. Sometimes there is a spirit lives in the well, if it is a deep one, but always a spell is laid, be it good or bad; and more often it is bad, such being the mood of these queer creatures. If it is a good spell, nothing can go against those who draw the water from it. The men become strong and brave and the ladies fair and virtuous. But if it be a bad spell, then those who must drink of its waters are mean of spirit and sour of mind, with aches in all their joints and red noses which always drip, and it's little satisfaction they get out of living at all."

At this Eleanor dropped the fancy seam on which she had been sewing and looked the old man over most thoroughly. "This is very interesting, Brian of the Quest," she said, having already picked up many Irish manners of speech. "I think we must have you inspect all our wells, to see which are evil, if any, and which are good."

It was because of this talk that the old minstrel found himself that very day beside a well under the tallest hedge on the property, which cut off the Cullin Meadow from the rest of the land. It was used for watering the stock and Eleanor had never been close to it before. Richard had inspected it once and had been rather taken aback by the depth of it. He had dropped a pebble and had been shocked by the long interval before a faint splash came back to him. The wall was round and made of stout gray stone. The winch was of ancient wood and quite rickety but, when this was pointed out to Conn Ragen, he had refused to have it replaced or repaired.

Brian stood beside the well for a long time and stared intently into its moist depths. When he looked up, his dark eyes were alive with excitement.

"It is under a good spell," he announced with a flamboyant wave of his arm. "I can feel it all about. A whisper of peace comes to me. I am sure the good spirit who lived at the bottom of this well found it a pleasant home."

"Do you think there is a spirit down there?" asked Eleanor, going over beside him and gazing downward. Her voice had a catch of awe in it.

"No, m'lady, I think the spirit has gone. But there was one here once. Ach, yes, m'lady, you can see all the signs. It was a female spirit. But it is likely the people were too curious about her; and, of course, there was a continual raising of water and the screech of the winch and the bump-bump of the buckets. Would any decent spirit have wanted to stay?"

Eleanor was delighted with all this. "How can we be sure she isn't still there?" she asked breathlessly. "It is too bad if she has been driven away. I am sure it would be very pleasant to know a lady who lived by choice at the bottom of a well. There are so many things I should like to ask her."

"We shall make a test of it, m'lady."

The old man seated himself on the top of the stone wall and proceeded to play on his harp. He kept a steady eye on the water so far below him while his aged fingers picked out eerie notes on the strings. When this produced no results, he began to draw single notes from the harp, sometimes high and strange like a faint echo from heavenly birds, and sometimes low and with an earthy gaiety. He kept his head turned in order to catch any response which might come back from the depths.

"If you are there, sweet spirit, give us a sign," he begged again and again. "A ripple in the water, the merest whisper."

But no ripple or whisper rewarded his efforts and he finally gave his head a shake and slipped down from his seat on the stone wall.

"She has gone," he declared. "She would have roused if she had been there to hear my music."

Conn Ragen had been standing off from them a short distance, watching every move made and, no doubt, hearing every word spoken. His visage had attained to a new high level of unfriendliness. When they turned to leave, he came forward and began to hoist water from the well with furious energy.

That evening Fergus MacDatho had interesting news for them. "The old one is right, my lady," he said. "There *was* a spirit lived in the well once, and a lady it was too. They used to hear her splashing in her bath and sometimes, when they spoke to her, a reply came back. A very low trilling sound like the singing of the Little People when the

moon is high. But the poor little damp lady got tired of all the questions they kept asking her and of trilling back to them. Boys began to
chuck rocks down into the well. Boys had no more reverence or respect
then than they have now. This was too much. The gentle spirit spread
her wings one evening and rose right up out of the well, and she was
never heard of afterward. But being a kind spirit, she did not change
the good spell she had placed on the well when she first took up her
lodgings there."

"When was it that she left, this gentle water sprite?" asked Eleanor.

"A short time ago," answered MacDatho. "Not more than two hundred years, my lady."

Not having been at the well when the old minstrel made his tests,
Richard listened to the talk with great interest. "It's clear we must make
a change here," he said. "The household must be supplied from this
well. We should be taking advantage of the good spell laid on it."

This resulted at once in conflict with Conn Ragen. He came storming
up to the house, his eyes fired with anger, his tongue pouring out a
torrent of abuse. Just so many buckets of water could be taken from the
well each day and there was barely enough for the horses as it was.
He refused to consider using any of the other wells. Did they not know,
he demanded, that it was because of the water from this one that the
horses of Green Hedges were finer than the stock anywhere else in
Ireland? Had they not realized it was the charmed water which gave
them good bones and fine strong frames, as well as glossy coats and
proud tossing manes?

When one of the maids went down the next morning for a pail of
water, she found Conn Ragen standing at the side of the well like a
guardian angel. A two-handed sword stood against the stone wall as
evidence that he would resort to violence if necessary. He sent the girl
back to the house with an empty pail but a well-warmed behind from
a whack or two with a sound Irish stick.

This brought Richard into the conflict. By this time he had picked
up enough of the native tongue to be able to communicate with the
iron-willed Conn Ragen and they had a long and bitter clash of opinion
on the subject of the use to which the well was to be put. The best
Richard could gain was a compromise. They might draw water each
day for the sole use of the lady of the house, enough for a daily bath
and for a full ewer to stand always at her elbow on the table. Conn
Ragen gave in this far with the utmost reluctance.

"Is it not better," he demanded, "that our sweet little fillies have glossy coats than one selfish woman should keep her skin unnecessarily white?"

"We will dispute no further!" said Richard firmly. "The matter is settled."

"Why can't she be content with a bath each week instead of each day? By St. Sechnall, it is a trick, a subterfuge. No lady needs a bath every day. It is a dirty Norman habit!"

3

The agreement made with the cross-grained yeoman of the horses was adhered to, and so only Eleanor used the water drawn from the well in the Cullin Meadow. Two months later Richard came in from the fields in late afternoon of a cold and blustery day. He made his way at once to the floor above.

The bedchamber was in no sense an imposing room. The roof sloped down abruptly on one side and the only window was surely as poor an excuse for a window as ever builder had contrived. But there was a fire burning on an open hearth, there were candles in extravagant number, and there was Eleanor herself, seated in a comfortable chair and wearing a gown of the very reddest tuly silk, and behind her Dame Jehane brushing skillfully at the fast-growing golden hair. Richard would have been perfectly happy with this much if he had not observed that his wife's cheeks were pale and that her manner had a strange lassitude.

"Are you ill?" he asked, bending over her.

"It has been a wearisome day," she conceded. "You may leave me now, my good Jehane. A few words with my lord and husband will restore me."

When they were alone, she went on in the same rather dispirited tone. "I was thinking before you came in, my Richard, that if I were queen of England tonight, or just a princess in Brittany, there would be much shaking of heads and frantic summoning of doctors and telling of beads. The old wives would be saying what should be done for me and thumbing over their herbs and simples. The heralds would be ready to issue forth with white pennons on their trumpets. Ah, yes, my Richard, there would be a great concern over my well-being."

"Not more than I feel!" cried Richard. "My sweet Eleanor, I left you in good spirits not more than a few hours ago. What has happened to bring about this sad change?"

Eleanor's answer left him even more mystified at first. "The charm laid on the well was most potent, it seems." She smiled then and drew his head down close to hers. "Why are you so slow tonight? Can you not guess? This is what I am telling you, dear Richard: I am going to bring a little Irishman into the world."

All the next morning Eleanor could see Richard tramping about on the top of the rather steep knoll which occupied all of the northeastern corner of the land. Fergus MacDatho had accompanied him and there was continuous communication between them by the waving of hands and sometimes she could even hear their voices as they called back and forth. She had no idea of the purpose of all this and so there was a hint of impatience in her greeting when he finally came down for the midday meal.

Richard's eyes were shining with the light of accomplishment. "You do not love the Normans," he said, "but I am sure you will concede, my wise and lovely wife, that they know how to build castles. It was their uncanny eye for strategic points and their thoroughness in raising thick and impregnable walls which held the English in bondage after the Conquest." He sat down beside her and went on speaking in low tones. "Well, I am going to build a castle. Up there on Brehon Knoll. It is the best site in all Kilkenny. I am going to build the walls high and thick and strong."

Eleanor looked much puzzled at this declaration of intent. "Do you know what the cost would be? Great fortunes have been spent on the raising of these Norman castles. Your King Richard emptied his treasury to build Château Gaillard."

"I shall have to sell many horses!" exclaimed Richard. "Somehow it will be done. It must be done." He walked to the door and looked down the steep steps leading to the floor below. Then he returned, leaving the door open so they could hear if anyone came up. "Eleanor," he said, "you have sworn an oath to resign all claims to the throne of England and to keep your real identity a secret. But this oath will not be binding on your children. If it became known that you are here and that you have a son, they"—he paused and then proceeded to define those to whom he referred—"the king, his ministers, his bishops, and his barons would fall into a panic. They would know that he, the boy, was the rightful King of England. What would they do about it? Oh, sweet wife, you know they would stop at nothing to put him out of the way. Assassins would be sent over to kill him. You also, for they would not want you to bring more sons into the world. If they drew the line at assassination, they would try to get their hands on him, so that he would spend all his life in some grim Norman castle. That is why I am going to build my own castle which will be a home and a sanctuary for you— and for this fine little Irishman of ours!"

Chapter XXI

1

ARCHBISHOP LANGTON, finally established at Canterbury, had little love for his palace at Lambeth, which stood on the south bank of the Thames River, almost directly opposite Westminster Abbey. It irked him that he never succeeded in traveling the distance between Canterbury and Lambeth in less than a week. His difficulty was that he had to take an immense train of officials and clerks; and as the see owned no fewer than thirteen manor houses in Kent alone, he found it impossible to goad his followers into progressing farther in one day than the distance from one to another. Living as he did under a sense of divine urgency, straining like a hunting dog on a leash to be up and about the Lord's business, and having lost so many years through the obduracy of John, he had a furious distaste for delay. Nibbling at his bread and cheese and sipping a cup of milk, he did not find the spectacle of his plump officeholders sitting down so happily to rich stews and pastries an edifying one. Many times he said to himself, "How unfortunate that Our Lord and the King's Son of Heaven have to depend so largely on the aid of gluttons and simpletons!"

The noisiness of Lambeth, when he arrived there, was highly unpleasant. His appearance brought every disgruntled clerk, every applicant for preferment, swarming about his door. It was true also that the Thames cut Lambeth off from London. At this particular bend of the busy river the traffic thickened perceptibly. It was filled day and night with the wool barges and the conveyers of tin, racing for the estuary, where the crews would be paid according to the time it had taken them to get down the river and shift their cargoes to the outgoing ships. If there were men on this earth more quarrelsome and blasphemous than the wool-barge men, the saintly archbishop had never encountered them. "God's chilblains!" he would hear them cry; and, if they found no harsher term to apply to a competitor than "this fresh-gutted cods-head," they were paying him a compliment. Worse still, they did not hesitate to ram and sink apologetic craft which ventured to cross the river with loads of visitors for Lambeth. If a few shaven-polls went down for the third time, so much the better, they had been sent a little sooner than they had expected to share in the delights of paradise.

Furthermore the archbishop's palace was much too large and grand to suit the tastes of so dedicated a man as Stephen Langton. From the wharves stretched the archbishop's garden, which certainly was an effort to create on this earth a picture of the aforementioned delights of the next world. The Great Hall, or the Magna Camera Domini, as the monks called it, was an imposing structure, nearly two hundred feet long and with a ceiling which soared up to a height of forty feet. Behind this demonstration of worldly glory was the Presence Chamber where preceding archbishops had received their visitors; and this again was something to marvel at. Between these two awesome apartments there was a tiny anteroom. A dark little hutch, hot in summer, cold in winter, and of a truly monastic order in its furnishings. Here Stephen Langton sat all day long and sometimes far into the night.

One day in August 1214, Stephen Langton had three visitors in this dark anteroom. It was evident that they had been working together for some time, for the talk between them had the casual note of give-and-take which comes only from mutual interests and engagement in a common cause. One was Tostig, who had returned to the service of the archbishop. The second was a small monk with a simian type of face, who was called Father Trist. The third was Alain de Casserlie.

"There is word from the king in France," said Langton, reading from a letter which had just arrived. "The campaign goes badly. As badly as everyone, saving the king himself, knew it would. He is in a furious mood because so few of the barons responded to his command to go with him. Such as you, my dear Alain."

"I received the summons," declared Alain in a grave voice. "But I am sure the king had no idea that I would go to fight his battles with him. I have made no secret of the hatred I bear him."

And then the archbishop said something that caused all three of his listeners to sit up very straight and stare at him in amazement. "What a fortunate thing for England," he declared, "that this wicked man has been such a bad king! I mean it, young men. It is part of the Lord's plan—if I may make so bold as to express understanding of it." He stopped for a moment to study the faces of his three companions. A change had come over his own. His eyes, generally so calm and judicious, had taken fire. He looked inspired. "Hear me!" he said. "We have had weak and bad kings before; and men have bowed their heads before them and accepted their haughty will and their wrongdoings. It needs a supremely bad king to rouse the people to action—and the wise King of Heaven has sent him to us. Yes, it is God's plan. I can see it in everything, even in the long years when England lay under the interdict and the Devil's darkness covered the land."

Stephen Langton laid his tightly clenched hands on the table before him. "The hour will soon strike! These dispatches say the king is planning revenge. He is placing the blame for his humiliating defeats on the barons who refused the call to arms. He will lay fines on all of them. He will impose new taxes. He will maltreat the Jews and grind the faces of the poor. Young men, the great day dawns! The issue between this bad king and his subjects will now come to a head."

Alain de Casserlie, who had lost his florid plumpness and was looking gaunt and unhappy, was the first to comment.

"The day cannot come too soon, my lord bishop," he said.

The archbishop gave a moment to a frowning consideration of the situation. "But will we be ready? There is so much to be done. There are so many men whose courage needs rallying." He leaned forward on his elbows and studied his three aides. "In a few days I shall preach in St. Paul's on the moral issues before the men of England today. I won't speak one word of what I have said to you but the service will serve its purpose. It will bring them all together. Afterward a meeting will be held in the town house of one of the great northern families which has been loaned me for the purpose. Only those of whose discretion we are completely sure will be there." He lowered his voice. "At this meeting we will make definite plans to organize the barons of England into a body to oppose the king and compel him to grant our demands. By force of arms, if necessary.

"Young men," he went on, "at this meeting we must not have one coward, one traitor, most particularly not one of loose mouth to spread abroad the whisper of what is afoot. We must weed them out. As you know, we have been making tests. The written reports I have had drawn on each man who might be expected to support us in a clash with the king have been in your hands. I have now divided the names into two lists. On the first list are the men of whom I entertain no doubts.

These will be invited to attend the meeting. The second list is made up of those of whom there may be some question."

He glanced at each of the three earnest faces about him. "I have invited those on the second list to visit me here. They will be arriving at different hours for the next few days. I want you to look them over very carefully. First you must read the reports on them again and then I want them weighed according to the special knowledge that each of you has. You, Alain, will know the men of noble rank who present themselves. You will know the antecedents of each one, his reputation, the opinion of those who have lived with him or near him. You, Father Trist, have worked with the men of lesser degree, the merchants, the guildsmen, the goldsmiths, the bankers. You can, I am sure, judge their courage and honesty. You, Tostig, will know none of them; but you are a shrewd judge of human nature as I have observed on many occasions. I trust you to look at them all impartially."

Stephen Langton proceeded then to explain matters in detail. "Each man on arrival will be asked to wait in the outer lobby. Behind the lobby there is a small closed chamber with narrow slits in the walls. You see, my friends, an archbishop represents God and the Pope but he is only human and so there are times when he needs every bit of help he can find. This chamber has been used for a long time by those who preceded me in office. It enabled them to appraise visitors before they were allowed to go in for an audience. All the men who are coming over to see me will be held in the outer lobby while you, my shrewd jury, will watch and listen. There must be no talk between you, no exchange of views, because the slightest sound would put them on their guard. I want each of you to write one word, Yes or No, on a slip of paper. These slips will be brought in to me before I see the man in question. If your feeling is against him, I shall talk to him pleasantly about some other matter and send him away. If you are favorable to him, I shall accept your judgment and invite him to the meeting."

At the end of the discussion, Stephen Langton rose to his feet and accompanied them to the door. He had become thinner since returning to England and the ruddiness seemed to have deserted his cheeks. His high-bridged nose gave him a look of hawklike sharpness. He dropped a hand on Alain de Casserlie's arm.

"One last word, my young men," he said. "There is always danger in what we are doing, and always responsibility. I know that the danger does not concern any of you but at this moment all of us have responsibility weighing heavily on our shoulders. One error of judgment on the part of any one of us, an error by which one wrong man gets into this meeting, a man loose of mouth or weak of heart, and the opportunity which our Master in heaven is making for us will be lost."

On their way out from the anteroom, Alain de Casserlie fell into step with Tostig. "Tell me, my good fellow, what word is there of my friend?" he whispered.

"I have had no word from him," answered Tostig in equally cautious tones. "There is too much danger in the sending of letters or messages of any kind. I hope soon to be allowed the time to go and see him."

"When you do," said the nobleman, "take him a message from me. Whisper in his ear that—that my difficulties are not yet resolved. Put it that way and he will understand. Tell him also that I do not despair. That I have hopes of being happy once again." His face hardened in expression. "But, of course, that cannot be until this matter in which you are engaged as well as I, my good Tostig, has been brought to a final issue!"

2

When the last of the visitors had been observed and judged (receiving an emphatic No from Tostig) and had duly returned across the river, Tostig went back to his regular task, which was to stand on guard in one of the outer rooms. It may be remarked in passing that much history has been made by individuals who did nothing seemingly but stand in anterooms. Here he saw the men of the first list paying their calls on the archbishop and he applauded the judgment of the latter. They were quite different from most of those on the second list, keener of eye and more straightforward of manner, many of them having the sloping brow of the soldier.

Sometimes he heard what was said in the cabinet of the head of the Church and, as he had grown to know every intonation of Stephen Langton's voice, he realized that one point invariably came up. These large landowners and titleholders were prepared to do battle with the royal forces in order to remove John from the throne and put someone else in his place. They seemed to favor the very young son of John, a boy of three or four named Henry, for then they could have a regent of their own choosing and the days of oppression would be over. What of the future? Marry, my lord archbishop, let the future take care of itself!

They seemed convinced to a man that no king would ever consent in writing to a document which limited his powers. When this point came up, Stephen Langton's answer was always the same.

"Sir Earl," he would say, or Sir Knight, as the case might be, "one king did put his name to a document of the kind. Of his own free will, when he was young and idealistic and wanted to be a good king. The charter he signed might very well serve as a model for the much more substantial one which we should now demand."

He would then proceed to tell of the Charter of Henry I, of the hundred copies made and distributed, of the change of heart on the part of the king and his demand years later for the return of the copies; and finally of the receipt of ninety-nine copies only. Sometimes his visitors had heard of this rather vaguely. A few of them asked if the archbishop had the hundredth copy to show them.

Stephen Langton's answer to this was the same in all cases. "The whereabouts of the hundredth copy remains a mystery but I have not abandoned hope that my Master in heaven, Who knows all and amends all, will see that it reaches my hands."

Tostig heard this said several times and on each occasion something seemed to rap insistently at the back of his mind as though demanding to be heard. There was a familiar ring about this talk of a missing copy of a very old paper. When had he heard it before? Finally the answer came to him. The last night he had spent with his onetime master, the talk had been of such a paper. From his place at the other end of the table, and without any conscious effort at eavesdropping, he had caught scraps of the talk. The opening of the vault under the floor of the refectory had followed. What documents had Edward of Rawen and Richard climbed down into the vault to inspect?

When the fourth visitor had received the same response from the archbishop and departed, Tostig took his courage in hand and tapped on the prelate's door.

"Your Grace," he said, when permission had been called for him to enter, "I have heard you speak of a missing document. I pray you, do not think I have been listening of deliberate purpose. But the tones of your voice, my lord, have become most familiar to me and I cannot escape knowing something of what is said."

"Could anyone else have heard me?" asked the prelate, with an anxious frown.

"No, my lord bishop." Tostig hesitated. "This missing paper, Your Grace. It is possible I know where it is."

Stephen Langton's head had been bent over his papers. At this he looked up and stared at Tostig with an air of amazement.

"My son, do I hear you aright?" he asked.

"Yes, Your Grace. But there are two reasons why I have hesitated to speak about it. The first is that I cannot be certain it is the same document. The second is a more serious one. I am not supposed to know of the existence of this paper and to speak of it, even to you, my lord, is like breaking faith."

"My son, your doubts do you credit. Let me be the judge of whether you do ill in telling what you know. Let me hear your story first."

So Tostig told of the night when he had been ordered to bring a mattock and assist Edward of Rawen and his son in raising a stone in the refectory floor. The archbishop listened intently. His eyes seemed to gain in luminosity with each detail recited. He was thinking, no doubt, of what he had said to his callers: "I have not abandoned hope that my Master in heaven, Who knows all and amends all, will see that it reaches my hands."

At the conclusion of Tostig's story he began to ask questions.

"When was it that this strange priest visited Cuthbert of Rawen and left the paper with him?"

"More than a hundred years agone, my lord archbishop."

"What was the name of the queen who sent him on this errand?"

"I heard no more than a name that the people of that day used for her. She was called Good Queen Mold."

The deep-set eyes of Stephen Langton seemed to burst into flame as when the sparks from tinder find the dry leaves waiting for them.

"Good Queen Mold!" he repeated in awed tones.

"Yes, my lord."

"Was the name of the strange priest Father Aelred?"

"Your Grace, I did not hear his name."

"Did they bring the document up from the vault with them?"

"No, Your Grace. I was under the impression that they examined it in the vault and left it there."

"Do you think it is still there?"

"Yes, my lord bishop. No one could have disturbed it in the meantime."

"Did I understand you to say that it is to be produced only when a certain message is received?"

"I heard something said of a ring, a duplicate of which was to be shown."

"Can Richard of Rawen be reached immediately?"

"No, my lord. It would be a matter of some weeks to get an answer back from him."

The prelate joined his hands together and bowed over them in silent prayer. When he looked up, it was as though his face had been transformed. An expression of solemn joy had taken possession of him.

"Father forgive me!" he said aloud. "I have allowed my weak and doubting heart to entertain no more than a half belief in Thy willingness to help Thy servant."

Then in a brisk voice he said to the waiting Tostig: "My son, you must leave at once. I shall provide a companion for you and fast horses. Ride, my son, to where the document is hidden and bring it back to me. If there is any question later of your right to act in this matter, I will deal with those who raise the point. Go with a clear conscience."

3

Tostig returned from Rawen Priory after thirty-six hours in the saddle, dusty of gear and gray of face. He made his way at once to the room where the archbishop sat.

"My lord bishop, I will make a bargain with you!" he cried. "The Charter of Henry I for the release of the prisoner in Corfe Castle."

Stephen Langton looked up eagerly from the papers in front of him. "Do you have it?" he asked. "Are you sure it is the missing copy of the Charter?"

"Yes, Your Grace. I have it and, as you will see, it carries the signature of Henry." Tostig paused and a musing look took possession of his face. "I read it, my lord, and it is full of wondrous promises. Not only for the lords of the land but for all people, even the lowliest. In one place it says, 'And I enjoin on my barons to act in the same way toward the sons and daughters and wives of their dependents.' My lord bishop, has such a care for the good of common people ever been shown before?"

"You speak of a bargain," said Stephen Langton sternly. "Do you not realize, my son, that there can be no question of bargaining where the business of Our Heavenly Father is concerned? That it may not even be spoken of?"

Tostig, in a properly humbled mood, laid a scroll beside the papers on the table. "There it is, my lord," he said. "If there can be no talk of a return, then I beg of you a promise that you will do everything possible to get the release of the poor prisoner. Could it not be a part of the terms you propose to demand of the king?"

Stephen Langton read through the document, which was not long, consisting of no more than a score of clauses. He sat in silence for a long time, his head bowed over the yellowed script.

"Truly, it is what I need," he said then, as though speaking to himself. "With this I can convince the barons that the king can be brought to the point of giving a written promise to govern only by the consent of the governed and according to the laws of the land—a promise which will be binding on every king who follows him, on all the thrones of the world perhaps. This," touching the script with a reverent finger, "is only the beginning. We will enlarge on the promises made here and we will force the king to make such concessions that never again will there be any form of tyranny. After the charter which we will present to him, there will come many more measures of such a sweeping nature that we cannot conceive of them now; save that they will bind the rulers of the future to rule as the Lord intended, with fairness to all, so that all men may indeed be free."

His eyes were moist with emotion when he turned to address the bringer of this historic document. "Tostig, you have done us a great service," he said. "How can we reward you suitably?"

"I have told you, my lord bishop. I ask nothing else."

The archbishop considered the point for some time in silence. "The king resents any form of interference on my part," he said. "The last time I protested to him about some violation of the law, he turned on me furiously, crying out at me, 'Rule you the Church, Sir Bishop, and leave me to govern the State.' I do not wish to make you any promises which I might find later are impossible. He is as unpredictable as a wild animal."

"This much at least!" cried Tostig. "Get from him a promise that she will be moved at once from the dark high cells at the top of the shaft in the wall. Demand for her quarters which are comfortable and safe. Don't allow her to be treated any longer as a common criminal."

"That much I promise you," declared the archbishop firmly. "I will see to it that in future she is treated well." He paused for several moments. "I will get from the king a pledge that no harm will come to her. To get the pledge, I will play on his greatest weakness. Even though it does not influence him to better conduct in this life, the king has a great fear of what will happen to him after death. He turns white and mumbles for forgiveness of his sins, when he thinks of the life hereafter. He is convinced that unless he can trick the Devil his soul will be taken by that cruel prince of darkness. Once, with a face ashen from fear, he begged of me to see to it that when he comes to die he will be buried, not in robes of state, but in the robe of a pilgrim and with a pilgrim's hat drawn down low over his brow so the Devil will not recognize him. That much I shall assure him if he will promise me in turn to treat the prisoner well. Nay, I will go a step further. I will give him my word to see that he is buried between the bones of two saints."

The narrative of John Foraday was interrupted at this point by a need for additional information. This will be explained in an interlude which follows.

The Interlude

1

JOHN FORADAY walked out on the open porch from which it was possible to see, over a wall of jagged rock, the waters of the Mediterranean. It was late afternoon but the air was still bright and warm, and the sea below was dotted with the sails of small yachts and the black stacks of large ones. The winding road below was filled with long, reptilian cars in the brightest of colors, and there was scarce a moment free from the arrogant honking of their horns. The resorts along the Riviera were having a banner season.

Senator O'Rawn was dozing in a reclining chair, a magazine on the flagged floor at one side of him, a newspaper on the other. A glass of fruit juice (practically untouched) was on a table beside him.

"Uncle Richard," said John, halting to thumb over a small book of notes.

The old man stirred and looked up. "What's your trouble, Johnny?" he asked.

"There's something you forgot to tell me," declared John. "Either that or there's something wrong with my notes for the rest of the story."

"Fire away!" said the senator.

"Well, you said to that caretaker on the day we visited Runnymede that you remembered the place when the river ran directly under that line of bluffs. The only other time when you could have seen the field was when you were Richard of Rawen. But on checking over my notes I find that Richard was not present when the Charter was signed."

The senator slowly elevated himself to a sitting position. He had aged a great deal in the year which had passed since they flew from New York to Ireland. He had lost weight and his clothes seemed to hang on his great bony frame. After grimacing at the glass beside him, he bellowed for Peterkin. "Can't I have something decent to quench this terrible thirst on me?"

Having lost the argument, he turned to John and proceeded to drop a depth charge. "My boy, did I ever tell you that I was Richard of Rawen?"

A startled look stole over young Mr. Foraday's countenance. "Well," he said, "perhaps you didn't tell me in so many words. But, of course, I've always known you were Richard."

"What made you so sure?"

"Well—the names for one thing. And the story is all about Richard, isn't it? You certainly told me this was *your* story we are writing."

"It is my story, sonny. My personal, honest-to-God, unchanged, undiluted story. I saw or heard the things I have been telling you, or I was able to put two and two together and so arrive at the truth. But—well, I was not Richard of Rawen. Don't look so flabbergasted, boy. Make a guess as to who I was."

John tried to pull himself together from the stunning effect of this announcement. He hastily assembled the cast of characters in his mind, seeking for the one whose part in the drama and whose character resembled most closely that of the great Western senator. He came up triumphantly with what seemed to him the right answer.

"I know!" he exclaimed. "William the Marshal!"

There was a pause and then the senator motioned to John to draw up a chair beside him. "I haven't told you much about William the Marshal," he said. "In my opinion he is one of the greatest men England ever produced and he's certainly one of the most underestimated. Why, I've read histories in which he isn't even mentioned. No other knight ever withstood him in the lists. He was gentle and loyal and honorable —but a lion in action. This story of his life, written in verse by his squire, which turned up in a French monastery a century ago, gives a remarkable picture of the man and of the times. I knew the fellow who wrote it. Have I already told you that?"

"No, sir."

"That you think I might have been William the Marshal," went on the old man, "is the greatest compliment ever paid me. But, no, I was not that doughty old champion. Try again."

A still more brilliant thought occurred to John Foraday. "I have it!" he cried. "Why didn't I think of it at once? You were Stephen Langton."

"My boy, my boy, you overestimate the part I played. Stephen Langton was one of the greatest men who ever lived. All the world owes him a debt. And he isn't entirely appreciated in England yet. Otherwise they wouldn't have left his bones all these centuries in that coffin which sticks out through the wall of Canterbury Cathedral. We didn't get to see it, did we? It was just as well. It would have riled me." After a pause, he added, "No, John, I was not Stephen Langton."

The young man frowned in concentrated thought so long after this that the senator became impatient. "Use your head!" he cried. "Look below the salt, man, look below the salt!"

And then the light came to John. He smiled with the pleasure of discovery and exclaimed: "Of course! Why didn't I guess it at once? You were Tostig."

"Yes," said the old man. "I was Tostig."

After a moment the senator continued. "There you have it. What is more, I am not ashamed that my father was bound to the land and that I was more than half a serf until I was given my freedom. I glory in it."

"How stupid can a person be? I never saw any connection between you and the Tostigan family—the black, fighting Tostigans. But I'm still rather mixed up about things. How is it that you are descended direct from Richard of Rawen and have his name?"

The senator looked with aversion at the glass of fizzy water which Peterkin had placed within reach of his hand. "All this talking is hot work," he complained, "but that unfeeling man of mine has no sympathy for my sufferings at all." He settled his large frame as comfortably as he could in the chair. "Have you forgotten Leueen Tostigan?"

"Of course! That explains it. You are a descendant of both of them, Richard of Rawen and Tostig. That makes everything clear except—except why you are here at all."

"As to that," said the old man, shaking his head solemnly, "your guess is as good as mine. Perhaps I presented problems. You see, I was a product of the times. They were rough, cruel times and I was as rough and cruel as anyone. I put that knife into Robardi and I shot the arrow which killed the baron in the Marcher country without any compunction because I knew it was necessary in both cases. Perhaps it was felt that there was something to be done in this world which required a knowledge of earlier days. It may have been that the shutter was allowed to swing back in my mind as part of the plan." He gave his head a reflective shake. "It is possible also that what I know of the past was conveyed to me in a dream. The longest and most detailed dream that any human being ever had."

There was a long pause and then the old man smiled at John. "Whatever the explanation, you may take it for granted that what I said about the river was true."

2

John returned an hour later. The sun had just slipped down behind the line of hills. The old man was in the same chair but Peterkin had wrapped him up in an opera cloak.

"I have won an argument," he said jubilantly.

There was a cocktail in his hand. A martini, no less. He raised it and took a sip, the smallest imaginable sip. "Have to make it last out," he said. "I won't get another out of that fellow Peterkin. Especially as he's dropping the bars and letting us have a steak for dinner, a thick, juicy one. This is going to be a wonderful evening, John. Of course," he added after a moment, "I'll feel terrible in the morning."

John drew up a chair. "I have some questions to ask you."

"I expected it." The senator smiled knowingly. "About our little Eleanor back in Ireland. You are very much interested in her, aren't you?"

"Yes," said John. "I'm terribly in love with her."

"I expected to hear you say so. What do you want to know?"

"Supposing that you actually were Tostig, could she have been Eleanor of Brittany?"

The senator shook his head emphatically. "No, no. I wondered about it at first, the resemblance between them being so great. I put her through all sorts of tests, asking questions, dropping hints, probing into her memories. They don't go back beyond her girlhood in New Zealand. We can take it for granted that she happens to be a cast-back."

"The princess could not have been as beautiful as our Eleanor."

"John," said the old man, "I am going to be perfectly honest with you. I love our little Eleanor back there in Ireland very much indeed and, in any comparison between them, I would prefer to give her the nod. But it's the other way. Her hair is as golden as that of the princess, her eyes as blue, her features as beautifully chiseled. But there was something in the assembling of them. The princess was a Plantagenet of Plantagenets! When I first saw her at the court of Brittany, she was as dazzling as the sun. Poor Richard took one look at her and was lost. Even after the years in prison, she was truly lovely."

"Were they as much alike in character?"

"Our Eleanor is a cast-back in point of character also. She can be pretty hoity-toity when she doesn't get her own way, as you must have seen. She has a temper, and a flash in the eyes, and a foot to stamp. But again it's a matter of degree. The princess was a true Plantagenet. She didn't chew carpets when she became angry, although I expect she often felt like it. Our Eleanor, that sweet child, is no more than an imitation of Eleanor of Brittany when it comes to temperament."

A silence fell between them for a few moments. The senator sipped his cocktail with great content. "When Peterkin condescends to make one for me," he said, "he does it right. I'll say that much for him. This one is really dry. John, you say you are in love. Let me give you a piece of advice. When we go back there on our way home, play a bold game. None of this weak, namby-pamby, John Alden stuff. Whenever you hear the bell, come out of your corner fighting! That's the only way to get anywhere with this girl. Now don't forget what I've told you."

"I won't."

The drink was making the old man unusually talkative. "I gained the deepest respect for Eleanor of Brittany," he went on. "If she had been made Queen of England, she would have been a great queen. She had courage and imagination and judgment. And I think she had a sense of fairness. For all her faults, she was cast in the mold of greatness. Yes, if she had become queen, there would have been another name to put in the top bracket of history: Isabella of Spain, Elizabeth of England, and Catherine of Russia have it to themselves now. I think Eleanor of England might have headed the list."

Chapter XXII

1

OF THE historic field of Runnymede, where Magna Charta was signed, Tostig saw very little. Of the great pageant enacted thereon he caught a few glimpses only.

Early on the first day he stood far off to the eastern side of the field among squires and archers and body servants, stout fellows who knew their place in the scheme of things and found little fault with it as yet. Between the thick tanned necks in front of him he could glimpse the splendid pavilion the barons had erected but he did not see the approach of the royal party until there was an excited rustling in the ranks and a cry was repeated from one end of the field to the other:

"Here they come! Here they come!"

By standing on the tips of his toes he saw King John and his company riding in from the Windsor road. It was a dark and heavy morning and so it could be said that the weather partook of the royal temper. There was no more than a handful of men in the train of the king: Archbishop Langton and William the Marshal, whose official duties compelled their attendance, the papal envoy, the Grand Master of the Templars, a bastard brother of the king riding under the lioncels of Salisbury, a bishop or two, and a few knights. By way of contrast, the field of Runnymede was filled with the embattled barons and their followers, thousands upon thousands of eager men, armed to the teeth and furiously ready to put the issue to the test of arms if necessary.

The king himself rode with a contemptuously casual air and did not seem concerned at the silence which settled over the open field where the barons and knights sat their splendidly caparisoned horses. The royal herald cried, "The King of England!" The pennons rustled in a sudden breeze, a horse neighed, but no other sound was heard.

The king, who always yielded to a liking for low comedy at solemn moments, raised his left arm in the air and twiddled his mailed fingers.

"Had ever king such a comedown afore?" asked a stout yeoman beside Tostig.

"There wur impriss as fled at dead of night from Uxford all dressed in white like a ghost," contributed a man from the west country. "She wur grandmother to they king, and men had took a fair bellyful o' her bad tempers."

Tostig paid no attention to what was being said. A glow of exultation had taken possession of him. Here was the beginning of a new hope, a new faith, perhaps of a new world. Never again would the hand of tyranny weigh heavily on men of England. The turn of the page would bring liberty to the prisoner at Corfe and, if she still loved him, they would have many sons and daughters, and after that grandchildren. Never again would English feet be bound to the land. Never again would the consent of the lord of the manor be needed when youth sought maid in marriage. Never again would it be necessary for harried tenants to leave their own fields and go to reap the landlord's harvest first.

"She does love me!" said Tostig to himself. "She has only affection and nought of deceit in the sweetness of her eyes."

The time was close at hand when the release of Giselle could be demanded. Of this he had no doubts. Keeping his eyes fixed on the pavilion, above which the leopards of England coiled lazily, he was convinced that a cowed monarch would emerge, and that immediately the hinges would creak as the doors of prisons opened all over England.

His mood of satisfaction, however, did not blind him to some puzzling aspects of the situation. The baronial ranks were magnificent without a doubt. The mounted knights were a perfect picture of the finest side of chivalry. But he saw no signs of the prosaic activities which should have been keeping all men of low degree busy. Where were the horse lines? Where the field kitchens? There was no welcome scent on the air of meat roasting in the pits to feed this great body of men.

Around noon, with the discussions still continuing behind the closed flaps of the pavilion, the men on foot began to grumble and hunt through the bags over their shoulders for scraps of food. The knights began at the same time to open their saddlebags. A man in clerical garb came slowly through the jerkined ranks, his sharp eyes darting in every direction. Tostig stepped out to meet him when he recognized the newcomer as Father Trist.

"Sir Squire," said the priest, "I have been looking for you everywhere. My lord the archbishop desires your presence."

As they neared the blue and yellow pavilion, it became apparent that the first session had come to an end. The baronial leaders had emerged into the open and were standing about in groups, their heads together. They were talking and nodding and expostulating over the progress made or, perhaps, the lack of it. Father Trist led the way to a clump of trees some distance in the rear, and here they found Stephen Langton sitting rather wearily on the stump of what had once been a noble oak. A number of his people stood in front of him, one displaying the episcopal cross. They made way silently for the newcomers.

"My son," said the archbishop, "we face a difficulty, because of the optimism of our brave barons. It seems they expected the Charter to be drawn up, approved, and signed in a matter of hours. No arrangements were made for the feeding of their followers. It is now quite clear that we shall be here for several days; and so something must be done to correct the error in their calculations. As usual, in the case of such emergencies, I turn to you."

"I am at your service, my lord."

"It will be necessary to purchase food in quantity without delay. If this isn't done, the men will begin to forage for themselves; and that must be prevented at all costs. It is my wish, my good Tostig, that you undertake this for us."

Tostig gave the matter some thought. "I will need many helpers. I can't be running back and forth to deliver the livestock I manage to find."

"Choose as many helpers as you need."

"Field kitchens will have to be set up and trenches dug. All that will have to be attended to separately."

The archbishop nodded in agreement.

"It will be necessary, Your Grace, to pay money for what we buy. The peasants put no trust in the promises of lords and knights. They've had too many of them made and broken."

"That need, my son, has been foreseen. Father Trist will go with you and make such payment as you find necessary."

"For how many days must we provide, Your Grace?"

"Three, my son."

Tostig gave a whistle of dismay. "That will be hard, I fear. This part of the country is heavily wooded and not much livestock is raised. We shall have to range far afield to feed so many mouths." Then he lowered his voice. "My lord, may I make bold to ask a question? Do things go ill?"

The archbishop shook his head. "So far we have encountered a strange degree of compliance. You may recall how ill he took our first demands at Northampton."

Tostig grinned at the recollection. "His storming could be heard all over the castle, Your Grace."

"Today he has hardly spoken. He nods his head over the very points to which he objected so vigorously before. The additional time we shall need will be for the phrasing and not for the rights involved."

Tostig raised his eyes until they encountered those of the archbishop. "Your Grace, that is not good," he said.

"No, my son. It is not at all good."

"If I may be so bold as to give an opinion, my lord, it is against his nature to yield so easily."

"He sits there and smiles," said the archbishop in a low voice. "But I can see a sneer back of his eyes. He is giving in to us now because there is no other course open to him. He will sign the Charter when we finish it. But—he does not intend to rule by it. He will bide his time. When the chance comes, he will strike."

"May I ask, my lord, how they"—nodding his head in the direction of the barons who still stood about in argumentative clumps—"how they are taking it?"

"I think they all sense the same thing in the king's attitude. That group nearest us, the large one, is made up of the younger men. It is to Alain de Casserlie that they listen. He is urging them to take immediate action. He wants the king deposed and the young Prince Henry put in his place. He would even disregard the promises of safe-conduct we gave the king. What, he asks, would King John do if our positions were reversed?"

"That smaller group," went on Stephen Langton, indicating a rather silent knot of perhaps a half dozen, "is in favor of deposing the king and putting Eleanor of Brittany in his place. They have not said much thus far."

"Are they like to win much support, my lord?"

"Very little. Our good barons have been told too many stories of the tantrums of the Empress Maude to favor another woman on the throne. I am convinced the large majority favor leaving John to rule, after shackling him with legal restrictions. They consider the Princess Eleanor a foreigner."

"Then, my lord bishop, you gain nothing by this?"

Stephen Langton had begun to walk slowly in the direction of the pavilion but at this question he turned back. "We gain as much as we could ever expect from John of England. No matter what steps he may take to have it annulled, the Charter can never be erased or forgotten. There it will stand on the records of history, with the promises of a king set down in plain words and his signature at the bottom of it. Even if he destroyed all the copies in existence, as Henry tried to do, the memory of the Charter would still stay in the minds of men." He indulged in a bleak smile. "It comes to this. If we can maintain a united front, we shall compel him to rule fairly and decently. If we let him get the upper hand—then there will be noble heels kicking on thin air beneath hundreds of high trees."

2

For the balance of the day, and for two days thereafter, Tostig was kept extremely busy. He found and purchased cattle, sheep, and hogs, and great quantities of poultry. He and his helpers gathered up all the eggs in the countryside, they set the housewives to baking bread, and they left nothing but empty vats in the breweries. In spite of the assiduity with which he pursued his duties, he could not achieve any kind of a surplus. He circled farther and farther afield, going finally well west of Windsor into the rich green fields of the Vale. Sometimes the stock owners showed a reluctance to sell at the relatively low prices he offered; and if browbeating had no effect, he did not hesitate to take them by the neck and shake some sense into them.

"It isn't money we are giving you in return for your stock," he said many times. "It's freedom—the freedom that's being won for you on the field of Runnymede."

He did not take the word of anyone but went himself into the fields and up along the sheep runs in the hills. He even foraged into what was left of the winter hay and in the underbrush, coming out with his pockets filled with eggs. Men reviled him and women spat at him; but he kept a continuous supply of food moving toward the once fair field on the banks of the Thames.

For his runners, when they returned to him, he had one question. "How does it go?"

The answer never varied. The baronial leaders continued to argue over the wording of the clauses in the Charter. The knights who had no part in the discussions sat on the ground and grumbled over the delay. The squires and the archers, on the extreme edges of the field, squatted on their haunches and rolled dice. "What of *him?*" Tostig would ask.

"The king still sits quietly. Sometimes he scowls and sometimes he laughs. But he has little to say."

This made Tostig more certain than ever that John was merely going through the motions of compliance.

"Does he send out messengers?" he asked once.

The answer was in the negative.

"Has his following increased?"

On the contrary, was the answer, one of the bishops had left and two of the knights. This had not seemed to disturb the king at all.

"Which may mean," he thought, "that they left to carry out his orders. But it seems more likely he will wait for the barons to disperse before he makes any move. Then the mercenaries will pour into the country to fight his battles. Whatever he lacks, it is not cunning. He has already laid his plans. It may even be that the Pope will support him."

John having gone through the ceremony of declaring himself a vassal of Rome two years before, that most ambitious of pontiffs Innocent III had been showing a tendency to support him against his subjects. Tostig had heard Stephen Langton say that he expected the Pope to declare the Charter null and void. This, quite clearly, was one of the reasons for the lack of fight the king was showing. The more drastic the terms exacted from him, the surer he could be of pontifical support.

"This is just the beginning," thought Tostig. "We'll have to fight this king every step of the way." He sighed deeply at the prospect. "He will refuse to release any of his political prisoners."

On the evening of the third day a dusty messenger reached him as he drank a flagon of ale before an inn which stood in full sight of the figure of the White Horse. The Charter would be signed next morning and the barons would disperse after a triumphant final meal. Could he produce something suited to such a great occasion?

When he turned in to a farm on a bend of the tiny Usk River and saw a spotted calf of the proper age for butchering, he thought at once of the fatted calf of Holy Writ. He made a deal with the owner at once. But the surly farmer was not the only one who wanted a say in the matter. A door hanging loosely on a single hinge swung back and a girl of perhaps ten issued from the squalid interior of the one-room house. She wore nothing but a ragged shift and she was not exactly clean but under better circumstances she might have been pretty.

"Nay, my father," she protested. "You gave me your word. The little Gibby was to be mine. He was not to go to the butcher."

The money was already safely laid away in a purse the farmer carried under his belt. "Go away!" he said to the girl. "Another word out of you and you'll feel the back of my hand."

Tostig decided to leave at once. He threw a rope around the calf's neck and confided it to the far from gentle care of one of his men.

"Please, good sir, do not take my little Gibby away from me!" wailed the girl.

"Be still, Bessa," said the father, "or it's the handle of this pick ye'll be feeling and not my hand."

The girl, weeping hysterically, seized the calf by the tail and held on when Tostig's man tried to lead it away.

"What are tender young calves for but to feed fine lords and fat bishops?" asked Tostig. "Let go, child, as your father bids."

But the girl held on, weeping bitterly the while. Tostig found it necessary to drag her away and toss her into the arms of her irate father. Her despairing cries followed them as they rode off.

This had no effect on Tostig until his thoughts turned to the only subject which brought him any peace of mind, the happy time ahead when Giselle would be released from Castle Corfe and would become his wife. It was at the back of his mind that he would then take up land in Ireland, a few acres perhaps beside those of Richard of Rawen. It would be the best place to raise the strong sons and pretty daughters he was sure would bless his union with the half sister of the princess. It was fortunate, he thought, that his daughters would have a better chance for a decent life than the unhappy child he had just left. Perhaps there would be some resemblance between them and this towheaded girl who bewailed the loss of her pet. He did not at once ask himself the question, however, as to what his attitude would have been if this had happened to a daughter of his own.

She was a pretty enough child. Supposing she had been one of his own get, his and Giselle's? Would he have allowed her to be treated as the girl Bessa had been? This was a distinctly new line of thought for Tostig. At first he was no more than mildly disturbed about it, even though he could not get it out of his head. "Am I going soft?" he asked himself, when he realized that he could not think of anything else.

"That filthy brat! It's no concern of mine. She would have to give the animal up sooner or later."

They had gone the better part of a mile before he realized that he would have to do something about it. He reined in his horse.

"Will the state tremble and fall if my lords do not have fine browned veal to break their fast tomorrow?" he asked aloud, with an edge of bitterness to his voice. "Let them grease their chops with bacon instead. I am more concerned over the grief of this child."

He called to the man who had the calf in his care. "Turn about, my bold Humphrey," he said. "We are taking the beast back."

The girl Bessa threw her arms around the calf's neck when she realized it was being restored to her. But her father looked black with apprehension.

"Ye'll be whipped within an inch of yer life, my girl," he said, laying a protective hand on the purse at his waist. To Tostig he protested, "The bargain wur made, Sir Squire."

"I don't want the calf."

"I'll not be handing the price back to ye. Ye needn't expect it."

"Keep the money," said Tostig gruffly.

He felt at peace with himself for the first time in a long while. He had done something which was wrong and foolish but which also was generous and considerate. He felt completely free to cast his thoughts on what the morrow would bring, the glory which would come into the world with the dawn when the Great Charter would be signed.

3

Tostig slept that night some distance from the field of Runnymede in a moldy hay tallat which had been left over from the previous autumn. For three days he had lacked the time to shave himself and it was a roughly bearded face he turned up for a look at the sky of early dawn.

It was going to be a gorgeous day. There was not a cloud in sight. The sun turned quickly from a beautiful red to a burning glare as he watched. Nothing less would have done for this day of days. A light from heaven must fill the skies as well as the hearts of men.

When Tostig reached the field, he found it seething with excitement and filled with the greatest of expectations. Eyes beamed at him out of faces as heavily bearded as his own. The knights had already donned their armor and were watching the pavilion, over which, surprisingly enough, the royal standard floated. John, a chronic laggard, had arrived early to put his hand to the measure of his submissions.

Tostig found foot space on an overturned farm cart from which he could see what happened. He was there when the flap of the pavilion was swung back and one of the baronial leaders appeared, carrying a manuscript in one hand. The knight raised it solemnly above his head.

A great shout went up from all parts of the field. The knights lifted their lances in the air and shook them, so that the many-colored pennons looked like a fairy-tale forest in a flutter of wind. The common men threw their hats in the air, jumping up and down in their excitement, their faces glowing, their eyes afire. Tostig leaped about until the planks of the cart threatened to crack under the strain.

"The blardy king has put his name to it!" shouted an archer, dancing on the cart beside Tostig. "Jack Lack, the blardiest of them all."

A laughing voice in the crowd took it up. "What lack ye now, Jack?"

A yeoman on the edge of the shouting, milling crowd put an arrow in the notch and sent it soaring up into the sky. It described a low arc and then fell into the waters of the Thames. Immediately every possessor of a bow followed his example until the air was black. The twang of the strings and the humming of the shafts as they climbed filled the air with a drone as though all the great birds of mythology were flying across the field in formation.

The barons who had been sharing in the discussions emerged from the pavilion in a body and were surrounded immediately by those who had only watched and waited. Much loud talk ensued, with nodding of heads and gesturing of hands, all with a jubilant note. No one caught a glimpse of the humiliated king. Apparently he had left through the rear and had galloped from the field with his abbreviated train.

The sun was mounting high in the heavens, warm and benign and (or so it seemed to Tostig and, no doubt, to many others) with a suggestion of triumph. It was easy for these jubilant men to believe that nature shared in their satisfaction.

Preparations for departure began at once. Trumpets sounded, the voices of heralds were raised in strident instruction, the colors of the nobles were hoisted high to serve as rallying points. Men were shouldering their bags and slinging their bows on their backs, calling farewells to the new friends they had made during the long wait. Unfortunately they did not share the respect that wild things have for the woods and the greens and the running water that nature has provided for them; so that they are born, mate, make war, and die without leaving as much as a scrap of hide for the questing eye. The barons of England and their followers had stayed idly on the broad acres of Runnymede for three days, and they were leaving a shambles behind them. The ashes of their fires were scattered everywhere, the empty spits drooped above the trenches, the ground was covered with scraps of food and discarded shreds of clothing. The droppings of horse and man made care in walking a necessity. The air was filled with the stench of fish heads and offal.

Tostig, who loved the quiet and the beauty of the woods, looked about him with an eye suddenly aroused to the indecencies of the human race. He said to himself: "Could we not have remained a day longer to leave these fields as we found them?"

He heard a voice calling, "Tostig! Tostig!" and saw Alain de Casserlie coming in his direction through the turbulent crowds. The young earl had donned his shining breastplate and his steel helmet, so that he moved clumsily and with a loud clanking sound.

Apparently he found it hard to recognize Tostig when they came face to face. "Is it you?" he asked. "Good St. Hubert, you look like a brown bear."

"I lacked the time to shave since we came here," said Tostig.

"I find it hard to tell you fellows apart, clean-shaven or not," said Alain carelessly. "You all look alike in those green caps and jerkins. It's easier for me to recognize my horses and dogs." He paused and rubbed his own jaw, which had not made the acquaintance of a razor in some time. "I've heard it said you've been making yourself useful. Finding food for the lot of us. And there's been words bandied about of something else. I didn't get the gist of it. But you seem to have been helpful to His Grace of Canterbury."

Tostig nodded his head but made no response. The fine edge of his content had been most effectually blunted. He was still just an unrecognizable face under a green cap, without worth or dignity. Would the signing of the Charter make no difference at all?

"I want a letter writ for me," Alain de Casserlie was saying. "I can't make a fist of pen and ink myself. A letter to my lady, to tell her we have won our case and that I am following after the letter in a furious haste to carry her back home with me. Can you write it for me?"

"I lack the tools," said Tostig.

The earl produced a pen and an ink case from under his belt. "I have them. Borrowed from one of the scriveners over there. He was ready to write it for me but—well, as even you must see, the matter is one of some delicacy. I prefer to keep my affairs from a clerk with a sly look about him and a vulgar beak for a nose who would whisper and snigger about it all over London town."

"I will write you the note, my lord," said Tostig quietly.

He began work with great care, using the boards of the upturned cart as a base.

"Make it strong," instructed the earl. "But at the same time make it gentle. I want my love and devotion to show in every word."

Tostig nodded as he slowly indited the note. Alain de Casserlie followed the careful stroking of the pen with an impatient eye. "Make haste!" he cried. "I am afire to send it on and to follow fast after it."

"I have little skill," declared Tostig. "And I must take pains so that your lady will have no trouble in reading what I have set down."

The earl accepted the completed note without a word of thanks nor so much as a nod of farewell. Tostig watched him as he made his way through the throngs to where the colors of Casserlie, a red hart on a black background, fluttered in the breeze. "Is the Charter to make so little difference then?" he asked himself again.

When Tostig edged into the pavilion, to stand in a corner with other attendants, he saw that Stephen Langton was still briskly at work. The archbishop sat at a table and dictated notes to three clerkly assistants, turning in rotation from one to another. The table was piled high with papers and hastily scratched notes. Langton looked up once only and, when his gaze encountered Tostig's, he relaxed long enough to give him a smile which seemed to convey some such message as this: "We have scored a complete success! And you had a busy hand in it." There was so much warmth in the prelate's eye, in fact, that anyone more egotistical than the squire could have deduced from it that he was being given a share of the credit.

For half an hour the steady dictation continued and the fingers of the busy trio were given no rest. Finally the archbishop leaned back against the central pole of the pavilion and gave vent to a sigh of relief.

"There, my good helpers," he said. "I think we may now prepare to leave with nothing pressing on our consciences. We must return direct to London."

One of the baronial leaders, who was seated beside the archbishop, asked a question. "Where has the king gone?"

"The king," said Stephen Langton, "left without addressing a word to any of us. Did you observe, Sir Earl, the difference in his manner this morning? He was not in a gracious mood. Certainly his eyes burned like live coals whenever they encountered mine."

The baron frowned uneasily. "I wish we knew what he has in mind."

"Sir Earl, I think we may take it for granted that the king will go into seclusion for a time."

"Like a bear, to lick its wounds," suggested one of the onlookers.

Stephen Langton did not seem to favor such open disrespect as this. He looked sharply at the speaker but did not make any comment. Instead he informed those about him that he believed the royal party would ride direct "to the Isle of Wight where the king would enjoy a rest of which he no doubt feels a great need. As do all of us." There followed a few moments devoted to last instructions. The voice of the prelate was cool and incisive as he set his train to the tasks before them. Then, disregarding the few members of the baronial party who stood about and seemed desirous of words with him, he rose and walked to the corner where Tostig was standing.

"I cannot let this moment pass without telling you of my appreciation," he said. He spoke in a low tone of voice which suggested that he had kept to himself the story of the recovery of the hundredth copy. "I have been so embroiled in affairs of state, my son, that there has been no chance to speak with you. You have understood, I trust, that my silence has been entirely due to this pressure of events."

Tostig bowed his thanks and then began to speak in an equally low tone. "I know it is too much to expect that this agreement will make all men equal, my lord bishop. But may common men expect an easing of their burdens? Is it now our right to raise our heads and look other men in the eye?"

"Tostig," said Stephen Langton, laying a hand on his shoulder, "I do not believe the time will come on this earth when all men will be equal. Is there equality in heaven? The King's Son sits on the right hand of His Father while the souls of myriad good and true men stand off at a far distance. Are Moses and Elijah and all the blessed company of the saints no more noteworthy in heaven than the good little priests who served in humble corners? The time will come when all men will have the same chances and the same rights before the law. This Charter we have won today for all mankind is no more than a step in that direction but you will find it contains the basis for real justice. It says, 'A freeman shall not be amerced for a small offence . . . and none of the said amercements shall be affeered, but by oath of good and lawful men of the vicinage.' And again, 'No freeman shall be taken, nor imprisoned

. . . but by the lawful judgment of his peers, or by the law of the land.' This will lead to many great changes in the course of time. I see no reason, my brave squire, why you should hesitate today to look a king squarely in the eye or to speak your mind to a bishop of the Church. But you must not base false hopes on this foundation we have laid. The Charter will not bring about any social change.

"There is one change which I sincerely pray will come about ultimately as a result of what we have done here in four momentous days. A custom, little understood and viewed with horror, called the right to vote. I have witnessed a conclave in Rome when a new Pope was chosen. The cardinals were closeted together, lacking all contact with the outside. Their votes were recorded on slips of parchment. If not enough votes were given one candidate, the slips were burned; and when the smoke rose from the chimney, the world knew that a decision had not yet been reached. They kept on voting until an agreement was reached. When a certain period of time passed, and no smoke arose from the chimney, the anxious watchers knew that a choice had been made finally.

"My son, I am sure of this: that the right to vote will someday be given every man and woman in the world, and that the voice of majorities will decide who are to be the rulers and by what laws and practices they are to rule. I may be the only man today on the green footstool of the Everlasting God who believes this. In this conference, with no appreciation of the meaning of what we do, we have taken the first firm and resolute step in that direction."

Chapter XXIII

1

AYEAR had passed. It was mid-October and the North Sea rolled sullenly beneath heavy skies while a raw breeze invaded the land with a slight edge of rain. The Fossdyke Wash seemed to resent the presence of living things and sent tentacles of foam and water up over the path which Tostig's sure-footed mare was following. Above him he could see the peaked top of a barricade and over that again the thatched roof of an insignificant manor, the green of a thick clump of woods closing off the sky back of it. There was something about it that reminded him of the Rawen domicile, which leaned so dependently against the gray walls of the Priory. He was convinced this was his destination.

"I seek one Saire de Fontie," he said, when a man in steel and leather met him at the gate in the timbered outer defense.

"I am Saire de Fontie," was the answer he received. The speaker was a Norman of Normans; a man of long bones and long nose, with a calculating eye and a jaw which seemed to clamp rather than close.

"I have a letter for you, messire. It comes from one whose name needs no mention between us." Tostig had been entrusted with the missive by one of the baronial leaders who remained neutral in the tragically strange situation which had developed in England since the signing of the Great Charter.

Saire de Fontie grunted as he took the note. He was in no sense a scholar, for he read it with the utmost difficulty and deliberation, nodding his head and mumbling the words under his breath. "Tell him," he said, "if you see him again soon, that we'll have regard for what he suggests."

A number of men, who had some points of similarity with the owner of the manor house, came out to join them. They seemed to know

about Tostig and his activities, and when they learned he had recently
returned from Rome, they began to bombard him with questions. Their
curiosity focused on one point: how was Stephen Langton faring in his
efforts to convince the Pope that the Charter should not be rescinded
by papal bull?

Tostig shook his head somberly. "His lordship the archbishop has had
no success. The Pope granted him one audience but allowed him no
chance to state his case. There is no measuring the aspirations for
power that His Holiness feels, nor the anger he has for the people of
England. He, and he alone, he believes, should have control over John.
Since that first day the archbishop has been kept waiting in anterooms where no one speaks to him. The other cardinals pass him by
without a glance. He writes petitions which are never answered. I was
present, my lords and gentlemen, at the Lateran Council when the question of the Charter was introduced. Stephen Langton sat among the
spectators, not being allowed to take his seat, and was given no chance
to raise his voice. The Charter was unanimously condemned. The Pope
will no longer permit the name of Stephen Langton to be spoken in
his presence."

"Why does he stay?" asked Saire de Fontie.

"He's still under suspension and may not leave Rome without the
Pope's consent; and Innocent has no intention of letting him come."

"God's bones!" cried the baronial leader. "It was a bitter day for
England when our great bishop decided to go to the Vatican to fight
the case. If he had remained here, he could have snapped his fingers
at this Pope who wants the world to knuckle under to him. Our fine
Army of God and Holy Church fell to pieces as soon as he left. John
couldn't have worsted us so easily with his mercenaries if we had kept
a united front."

"Yes," said Tostig to himself. "It did not take long after the king came
out of seclusion and the soldiers from the Continent arrived. A bleak
day for England!"

"And it was a very sorry day for England when some of our mis-
guided leaders invited Prince Louis of France to come over and help
us," said another member of the group.

"Word of the French invasion reached us in Rome," declared Tostig,
"and no one could believe it at first. The Pope was livid with rage and
seemed to blame it all on Stephen Langton. It was because of this that
my lord of Canterbury sent me back. He knew his letters were being
seized and he thought I could find some means of keeping him advised."

Saire de Fontie shook his head with deep concern. "Now that the French are here, we may never get rid of them," he said. "Every time this prince takes a castle, he gives it to one of his own knights. Sometimes, even, when the rightful English owner is fighting in his ranks."

"I have heard even worse about these thieving French," declared a third member of the party. "Prince Louis swears he will drive into exile every man who stood for the Charter at Runnymede. He says we were traitors to our king. How these kings hang together! Step on the corns of one and all of them cry out in pain and anger."

"And yet," said Saire de Fontie, "this stupid Louis—for, God knows, he has no qualities of leadership in him—makes John's misrule his excuse for leading an army into England. Only another king may take steps against a ruler who has been unbearably false to his coronation vows."

"London was full of the Frenchmen when I came through," reported Tostig. "The inns were alive with them and they had taken over the houses of the nobility. Decent citizens didn't dare appear on the streets. They were called English swine when they were foolish enough to take the chance, and were sent back with empty pockets and their shirts cut to ribbons on their backs. I had to travel by night and hide of days in stinking hogsheads and dog kennels."

The wind off the sea was freshening. The unhappy group at the entrance of the manor house stared out at the unfriendly waters and brooded over the bitter pass to which Englishmen had been brought. They had nothing before them but a choice of masters, one as bad as the other.

Their presence here in a group could be explained by the need to keep a watch on the movements of John. Since the landing of the French, the English king had left garrisons in all the fortresses along the Thames, with the intent to contain the invaders in the small corner they now occupied, and had then struck north to deal with the barons who were gathering their forces to join Prince Louis. If he could scatter them, he might then recruit more strength and turn south to deal with the French.

"What is the fool doing so far north?" grumbled Saire de Fontie, who did not agree with this strategic conception. "How can he hope to bring in more men and supplies, if he leaves London and the channel ports in the hands of the French?"

"I saw him pass," said Tostig. "At a discreet distance. He was moving slowly because he has a long wagon train with him."

"I can tell you the reason for that," said a priest who stood on the edge of the group.

No one paid any attention to the quiet churchman; they continued to ask eager questions of Tostig. Were the royal forces large? Were they well armed? What roads were they taking?

"I did not venture close as they passed," explained Tostig. "But I swear there was scarce an English face in the whole train. They were black-whiskered Brabanters and towheaded Germans. They're well armed and most fearsomely well trained. They will be hard to beat, my lords and gentlemen." He paused and then said in a tone of sudden passion: "I passed the manor house where he slept last night. This amiable king took a torch and set it afire with his own hands before getting to horse. I heard it said he has burned every place where he slept on his way up north. A chivalrous return for the hospitality afforded him!"

"He belches hatred of the people of England after every sup of wine!" declared Saire de Fontie.

The priest, who was small and frail, pointed suddenly into the south. "Here they come!" he piped.

All members of the group turned and gazed intently in the direction indicated by the forefinger of the little churchman. A cloud of dust rose from the road which hugged the line of the sea. A glitter of metal could be seen under the cloud and an occasional glimpse of standards.

"If they see us here, they'll send horsemen up to cut us to pieces," said Saire de Fontie. "I think we must be prudent and take shelter in the woods behind us."

Tostig lingered, however, and watched the oncoming horsemen from behind a tall oak. When he finally joined his companions in the shelter of the spinney, he had seen enough to carry a pucker of surprise on his brow.

"It's clear they intend to ford the river where it flows into The Wash," he said. "And yet the tide is beginning to rise."

"It will be a great folly if they do," said the owner of the manor.

"When the tides rise and meet the current of the river," said the priest who, quite apparently, was a native and knew the conditions, "there is such a tossing and churning of the waters that neither man nor beast may exist in it. I have seen the sea come in like a mighty bore and the river fight back. When that happens, the foam of the conflict is thrown fifty feet in the air. A most fearsome sight!"

"From what I saw of the land over there on the other side, it is very marshy and offers no cover," said Tostig. "They won't be able to build fires. I swear it will be a most uncomfortable wait for them—if they decide to wait. Do you suppose the king doesn't know about conditions and may decide to come through?"

"God have pity on them if they try it!" cried the priest.

2

The approaching horsemen grew larger by the minute and at the same time the tidal waters of The Wash became steadily higher. The air was still but in its very stillness there was a hint of sinister intent. It could now be seen that a long row of creaking carts followed immediately after the van where the royal standard was carried.

"Never have I seen so many wagons with so small a force," said Saire de Fontie. "Twenty, twenty-five or more. I believe there may be as many as thirty carts creaking along there."

"He has need of them all," said the priest, who was known as Father Ambrose. "Did you hear me say I knew about the assembling of this train? I even know what is carried in those wagons."

"Tell us then what you know, Sir Priest."

"It fell out a month or more aback that I was sent on a mission to the monastery at Waltham," said Father Ambrose. "I had scarce arrived when a royal messenger came on a badly winded horse with instructions for the abbot. The king wanted the valuables he had left in the care of the treasurer of the abbey. What was more, he wanted them without a day's delay. So there was much confusion getting the treasure off under a heavy guard. The place was filled with whispers about what was going on and I was able to piece it together and get the whole story.

"Our dread liege lord, the king," went on the priest, "is not one to put trust in other men. He did not deposit the crown jewels and the royal treasure with the Templars in London as had been the custom. Not King John, messires! He preferred to place his treasures in the care of the Church. Ah, but not all with one institution. Again his suspicions rose up to instill greater caution. He divided the treasure into sixteen lots and deposited each lot in a separate monastery—Waltham and Bindon and Merton and Rufford among them. The same demand for a return of the gold had been sent to all sixteen. My sons, everything of value that the king possesses is packed in those wagons we see approaching."

"For a sly and suspicious man, he is taking an enormous risk," said Saire de Fontie, staring at the approaching cavalcade. "Do you suppose those human tigers he has hired to make up his army have any idea of the treasures they guard?"

"I doubt it very much," said Tostig. "The precious stuff is probably concealed in the bottoms of the carts under camping supplies and spare arms. It is easy to see why the king desires to reach safe lodgings before night falls."

"What all is there in the treasure, Father Ambrose?" asked one of the party.

The little priest, pleased to have their full attention at last, was quick to respond. "I had a detailed description from the good monks at Waltham. First, there are the crown jewels. There is the crown, which is in the form of four strawberry leaves with countless pearls and precious stones. Then there is the Cross of Alfred, the scepter, the orb, the four swords including *Curtana*, St. Edward's Staff, and the ring of the Confessor. You must all recall how the holy Edward gave the ring to an ancient beggar and how it was returned to two English palmers in the Holy Land by a very old man who called himself Johan Theuangelyst? Besides our national regalia there are the pieces that the Empress Matilda smuggled out of Germany a hundred years back, including the sword of Tristan. There are more than two hundred standing cups and flagons and goblets, all of gold or silver and all richly jeweled. In addition there are smaller pieces of a variety that balks any effort at numeration—rings and crosses, thuribles and belts and pendants. There are whole sacks of uncut gems, rubies and emeralds and sapphires. Above everything else, there is the king's gold. It is reported, young men, that he is a very rich king; but as to that I cannot say. All I can vouch for is that they carried out from the vaults at Waltham many sacks supposed to contain the king's money."

The faces of the listening knights were alive with interest and apprehension. "If those birds of prey he has hired learn about this," said Saire de Fontie, "the greatest theft in all history may be enacted before the end of the campaign."

It was now possible for the concealed watchers to see the bronzed and bearded faces of the men riding in the van of the king's force. Saire de Fontie cried out suddenly that he recognized the king himself. "He's in the third rank," he said. "See! There's no mistaking him, though as usual he's dressed simply to escape attention. Still he always wears a chain of gold around his neck with his favorite emerald. It's his luck piece, and I can see it quite plain. Ay, it is the king. And he's in a villainous bad humor."

"That is not surprising," contributed Tostig. "The king is in bad health. I was told he had to be helped when he set the manor house afire this morning and that he carries his gouty leg in a sling when he rides."

"That is true! There is no armor on one of his legs. I think it's supported in a sling. Certainly the stirrup is dangling empty."

For a moment Saire de Fontie said nothing more. Then he turned to Tostig, who was kneeling beside him in the underbrush. There was a resentful gleam in his eyes which increased momentarily until it resembled a glowing fire. He whispered to Tostig, "He suffers greatly, I trust?"

"Yes, Sir Knight. Our liege lord finds the need to take the field in his present condition a great hardship. I heard it talked of everywhere."

"He did me a great injustice once," said the knight in a deep and bitter tone. "I need not tell you the nature of it, Sir Squire, but it was a dastardly and treacherous blow to my pride. Ever since I have prayed that the day would come soon when he would be thrust into the fires of eternal punishment. Perhaps the time now draws close. God grant it is so."

"Allow me a question," said Tostig. "Should the king die, who will you favor for his place? Prince Louis of France because he has married the Spanish granddaughter of Henry II? Or the sister of Prince Arthur, who has the best claim of all?"

"The Pearl of Brittany? I hear she is kept in close confinement. At Corfe Castle. Nay, Master Tostig, I would not favor putting a woman on the throne. For my part, I would say let it be this young son of John. That would mean a regent, one of our number, to rule the country as it should be ruled. In accord with the rights and the needs of the governing class."

"And who would you favor as the regent?"

Saire de Fontie was very sure on that point. He did not hesitate in answering. "Who but William the Marshal? The old man is able and honest and as strong and true as a great oak. None other, my man. Old Will, of course."

Tostig asked no more questions. He had learned what he wanted to know, and what he hoped to hear. If this line of reasoning were shared by most of the bishops and barons of England, then he could rest easily. If John were dead and William the Marshal served as protector of the realm, it would be an easy matter to obtain the release of Giselle from Corfe Castle. He settled down to a resting position with a feeling of intense satisfaction. Perhaps things would work out for the best after all.

The horsemen in the van were now crossing the ford. The water was not yet high on the shingle between river and sea; just high enough to dampen the bandaged foot of the gouty king in its painful sling. When he had crossed to the firmer land beyond, John reined in and looked carefully about him. He studied the river, the slow-rolling sea, the sky which had turned to the cold gray of approaching night. He looked back at the line of wagons ready to follow his guards across the sandy track. He seemed to be calculating the risk.

Then he straighted up in his saddle and raised an arm in the air. He motioned to the drivers to advance. The order was taken up by the royal heralds, who sounded a brisk fanfare on their trumpets.

Father Ambrose, from his place in the thicket, began to speak in a voice thick with emotion. "Young men, do you recall the story of the Crossing of the Red Sea? How the children of Israel, fleeing from oppression and servitude, came to that wide arm of water, with the chariots of Pharaoh swarming behind them in pursuit? And how the Lord saw their plight and gave heed to their supplications, by causing the waters to divide and draw back and so left a dry path for Moses and his followers to take? And finally how the waters closed in when the Egyptians attempted to pursue them and the chariots were engulfed and the soldiers of Pharaoh drowned in the sea?

"I wonder," he went on, "if the Lord will hold back the waters of The Wash today until the wagons of John with all their treasure have crossed in safety?"

3

The wheels of the treasure wagons turned with painful slowness. The water had been close to the hubs when they began to cross and every successive wave rode in higher. The navigable track was narrow and so the advance was performed in single file. The drivers cracked their whips and shouted to the straining horses. The voice of the king, pitched high in an extremity of sudden fear, shrilled his demands for more haste.

"See how rough the surface is becoming," said Father Ambrose, raising his head higher in the brush. "Is God watching from behind those clouds?"

"Down!" admonished Tostig. "Do you want the foreign devils to see you? We'll all feel their filthy steel in our throats if they do."

Nothing happened for one strange and brief moment. Was nature waiting for the orders which came when the children of Israel crossed the Red Sea? Then, with a dramatic suddenness, the beat of the waves turned to a roaring crescendo as The Wash thrust its augmented flood into the funnel of land. The water swept across the wagons, tearing the drivers from their seats and entangling the screaming horses in the wreckage of shafts and harness. No human voice could be heard above the mad clamor of the battling forces of nature. The king, refusing to accept the impotence of human effort, still cried out orders which could not be obeyed, to men who lacked the power to hear.

"I can see the face of God in the clouds!" cried Father Ambrose.

No one else had eyes for anything but the treasure-laden wagons engulfed in the maelstrom. One by one they vanished from sight. Not a single driver succeeded in reaching dry land. The horses perished in a helpless threshing of imprisoned limbs. The king still cried instructions to his men to bring out the contents of the wagons. A futile demand: no eye ever rested again on any part of the train. The wagons were washed away by the flood and the contents carried far out by the undertow. Gone forever was the strawberry-leaved crown, the sword *Curtana*, the ring of the sainted Confessor, the mighty blade of Tristan. Gone also the gold of the king who would now lack the means to pay the mercenaries he had brought to England from every city on the Continent.

Tostig found to his consternation and amazement that he was standing on the edge of the raised land in full view of the king's men. He had no recollection of leaving the cover of the trees. Apparently he had been drawn unconsciously forward by the horror of what was happening. Then he perceived that he was not alone. The same irresistible impulse had brought his companions out from the safety of the trees. They stood in a silent clump and watched with strained fascination as the maelstrom tossed spume into the air higher than the line of cover behind them.

Tostig's first reaction was to lead the way back into the woods where they had tethered their horses. No such action was necessary, however. The king's men were too numbed by the spectacle to pay them any attention. The king did not look in their direction. He had fallen forward in his saddle, defeat showing in every line of his slumping figure. The king, who had made so many mistakes, had now made his last and most dramatic one.

"Young men," said Father Ambrose in solemn tones, "did you observe the fearful precision with which the vengeance of the Lord was exacted? The waves did not strike until every wagon had come within their reach!"

4

The next day visitors began to arrive at the small manor house of Saire de Fontie. They were barons of the county and large holders of land thereabout. Thrust into the background by these newcomers, Tostig sat in the dreary kitchens with the other squires and the servants of the household. The rain, which had threatened the day before, now fell violently, penetrating the imperfect wooden shutters and forming pools on the floor. The storm beat down the chimney and made it difficult to keep a fire going. The smoke, unable to escape, collected in the room until the eyes of the people gathered there smarted painfully.

Rumors reached the kitchens of the news which the visitors brought. John had ridden ten miles the night before to a Cistercian monastery at Swineshead. Here he had partaken of a heavy meal, ending with a heaping bowl of late peaches. Immediately thereafter he had been taken violently ill and had complained of a great pain in his right side.

"He swore they monks had put poison in food," was the word brought to the kitchen from the front of the ramshackle house. "And it *is* said as they put blood of toad in his wine. The king made one monk drink first of it and the gray-cloak went out to garden and died like the plague had him."

Because of this suspicion, perhaps, the king had taken to horse again and ridden on to Sleaford, rolling in the saddle with pain and cursing the day he was born. One of the grooms heard that he was already on his way to Newark. The pain was so great that he was being carried in a horse litter.

The royal army was trailing in confusion after the king. They were living off the land, stripping every traveler they encountered and robbing the houses as they passed. The troops might have been expected to scatter but the king owed them their wages. An alien soldier in a strange land does not like the feel of an empty purse.

Without taking any part in the deliberations which went on among the assembled barons and knights, Tostig knew how sanguine they had become. If the king died, and it seemed almost certain that he would, the situation would be improved and simplified. The barons could then unite under a new ruler and apply themselves to the task of driving out the French invaders; and they could exact of the new king obedience to the terms of the Charter.

On the second day Tostig was summoned to the front room where he found the company eating a midday meal. The shutters were bolted tight and the candles on the table did little to supply light. His feet crushed fishbones on the floor and two dogs were snarling over a sheep's head in a corner.

One of the noblemen, who seemed to be accepted as the leader, grunted a curt greeting. The rest regarded him with some curiosity. It was clear that they knew the confidence placed in him by the archbishop and that they were both puzzled and affronted by this willingness to make use of him, a mere squire, in such ways.

"We hear," said the leader, "that you went to Rome with the archbishop."

"Yes, my lord."

"It is said he listens to your advice. What a great pity you didn't persuade him to remain in England."

"His Grace felt that duty called him to Rome."

"When will he be coming back?"

"He must remain in Rome at the pleasure of His Holiness the Pope."

The spokesman scowled anxiously. "We have heard that it is impossible to get letters to him. Is that true?"

"Yes, my lord. His movements are watched and no letters are allowed to reach him."

"Have you any means of getting news to him?"

Tostig nodded. "Before I left, we made an arrangement by which letters may be exchanged."

"Then," said the baron, "get word to him at once of what is happening. Say that the Army of God and Holy Church has need of his guidance and leadership. Tell him we earnestly pray he will find means to leave at once, without regard to the Pope's orders."

"I have already sent him a full report, my lords," said Tostig. "I let him know the urgency of his return. The messenger left this morning."

"It seems," said the spokesman, "that you are a very shrewd fellow, Sir Squire."

On the fourth day word reached the anxious company in the rain-drenched manor house that King John had died in the palace of the Bishop of Lincoln. In his last moments he had dictated a note of instructions in lieu of a will. The care of his young son Henry had been left to the one man the king had trusted, William the Marshal. As soon as the breath was out of the royal body, the marshal had taken to horse and ridden off by the road to the west.

"Where is he headed for?" Tostig asked the messenger who had brought the word.

It seemed that the marshal was riding to Gloucester. The queen was known to be at Exeter and word had been sent to her to go at once to Devizes Castle where the young Prince Henry was staying. She was to bring him on to Gloucester where they would meet the marshal.

Tostig hurried out through the rain to get his horse from the gloomy ruin of stone and wood which served for stabling.

"Are you mad?" asked the groom Swithin, emerging from the region of the stalls. "It's no weather to be out in."

"Yes, I am mad," answered Tostig. "Mad with joy. I am riding to Gloucester also. There is much for me to do there."

There was indeed work for him to do in that ancient Roman town. He must get the ear of the earl and win a promise of the release of Giselle from Corfe Castle. He felt an extreme urgency about this. He must get to the marshal first.

The groom came forward with a shovel in his hands and looked at Tostig with, it seemed, a note of entreaty.

"Are you freed man?"

"Yes. I was given my freedom many years ago."

"I would give the sight of both eyes to stand in your boots. I am bound to the land." The voice of the groom was filled with the deepest feeling. "Once I was allowed over Willestrem. Once I was five miles to Abbot's Sotherby. Two villages I have seen in the whole of my life and two churches. I see ships in Wash." His eyes began to gleam with intense feeling. "Take me with you, Friend Tostig. You are shrewd, wise man. I work for you."

Tostig felt pity for the earnest suppliant who sought escape from a condition which came so close to slavery.

"How could you get away?" he asked.

The lumbering figure motioned behind them where the horses of the visitors were tethered. "I take one," he said. "That dappled one. It belongs to thane from near Sotherby. No one will care what happens to *him*. Someday I pay for it."

Tostig shook his head. "There would be a hue and a cry. Your master would want you back, even if they didn't care a straw about the thane's loss. I would have to bear a share of the punishment when they found us."

"Would they follow as far as Gloucester?"

"I think it likely they would. I am sorry, Friend Swithin, but the errand on which I ride will allow no delays. And no brush with the law."

The groom gestured hopelessly. "When I was told about you and how you wur close to archbishop, I said to myself, 'This is chance you've wanted so long.' I thought you could do summat for me."

They began to tighten the saddle on Tostig's horse. The hands of the groom fumbled and it was clear he was bitterly disappointed.

"Are you married?" asked Tostig.

There was a hint of anger in the shake that the groom gave his head. "No, no, Sir Tostig. I'll not father sons to be bound to land as I am. Better let them stay unborn."

The horse was ready. Tostig led him out and climbed into the saddle. He looked up at the sky, which was showing signs of clearing.

"There will be stars out. I'll ride all night." Tostig looked down at the groom, who stood with shoulders bent and hands hanging at his sides, the very picture of despair. "When the archbishop returns from Rome, I shall speak to him. Perhaps he can arrange to buy your freedom."

"I am strong," said the man. "And willing. My feet say to me, 'Go, go!' but my head say, 'Go where? To prison and whipping post?'" He did not seem hopeful that anything would come of Tostig's promises. Perhaps he had heard such things before. Turning slowly, he walked with a hopeless shuffle to the interior of the stables.

In a moment, however, he was back. Gloom had given place to determination on his face. He held up a hand to delay Tostig's departure.

"There is girl," he said. "I always wanted her. She loves me. We talk often of running away. Now I think we go. Why us stay and be bound to land?"

Tostig thought it advisable to point out the hazards of flight. "No priest will marry you," he said. "The girl will be a hedge wife only. Her children will be bastards."

"That we know. We are ready to face it."

"Wherever you go, the magistrates will throw you both in prison. Sometimes they'll send you to the stocks and the whipping post. You'll be branded. That's what happens to those who run away from their masters."

"We know it full well. Better it is to sleep under hedges and make the open road our home than stay and have lord of manor say we can't marry. He has a fancy for this girl himself."

Tostig turned in his saddle and looked down at the aroused groom. "Make me a promise, Friend Swithin. Be in no haste to run away. Wait until I have had time to put my affairs in order. Then we'll see what can be done for you and this girl you fancy."

Chapter XXIV

1

TOSTIG met with several delays. His horse fell lame and it took him some time to replace it. An abbot and his train were held up a few hours before he reached a village in the vicinity of Northampton. The priestly party had been robbed of all their possessions and even stripped down to their shirts before being sent back to the village afoot. When Tostig arrived, he was stopped and informed that all travelers were being held until the guilty parties were found. He spent a full day in a tumble-down tavern with guards at all the doors, before the bandits were traced.

He had his anxious moments during the twenty-four hours of his detention. The archbishop had been liberal in his pay and so Tostig had been able to dress and equip himself well. The tabard he wore was of English cloth but it was well woven and embroidered with silk at the wrists and along the slits under the armpits. His saddle was of the best leather and his spurs were of bronze. The curious officials knew he was neither knight nor simple squire but somewhere between the two orders, and there was much speculation as to who he might be. Tostig was relieved that their curiosity was still unsatisfied when his release could no longer be withheld.

He did not arrive in the solid old Roman city until the second day after the boy king had been crowned in Gloucester Cathedral. The town was in gala mood. Flags fluttered from every rooftop and all the inhabitants, acting on a royal decree, wore chaplets of autumn flowers on their heads. Hogsheads of wine had been broached on the public square, at which every citizen and his wife could stop and drink a toast to the boy king. This had made them all merry and loose of tongue.

Tostig reined in at the edge of the square and addressed himself to a middle-aged citizen wearing his chaplet aslant and looking like an intoxicated and portly edition of the god Pan.

"Why all the rejoicing?" he asked.

The citizen winked drunkenly. "The old 'un is dead," he said. "Young Harry, t'ird of the line, wur crowned day afore yest'day. Crowned and rubbed with holy oil and loaded with jew'ls, and prayed over and sung at and kneeled to and ah'd at and oh'd over, all right and proper and 'cording to custom. Nine years of age, young Harry. But Old Will of Pembroke will rule in his stead and that means good times for one and all."

"Where is William the Marshal?" asked Tostig.

"In meetin'. King's Hall be full of 'em—dukes and earls and knights and bishops. There be Pope's legut and Peter des Roches, Bishop to Winchester, and Rafe Mustard, the castellan. They been at it for hours. It's said Old Will be trying to beg off."

Tostig frowned in sudden apprehension. William the Marshal trying to escape the responsibilities of ruling during the boy king's minority! That would make things difficult again.

"Can he be seen, do you know?"

The citizen gave him a bleary wink. "See Old Will? Not today, Sir Half-and-Half."

Tostig applied half a dozen times to the guard who stood at the door behind which the meeting was being held. The guard was, oddly enough, of a friendly turn and confided to him finally that the main meeting was over and that William the Marshal was now conferring with three of his immediate staff in a smaller room down the hall. The door of the smaller room was open and the sound of voices reached their ears. As Tostig stood beside the guard, he heard a voice, which he recognized as that of the marshal, declaiming in a high tone. "By God's glove!" the old champion was saying. "The advice is good and true. If all should abandon us, I would carry the king on my shoulders, one leg here and one in Ireland. I would carry him from island to island, and from land to land, and I would not fail him ever!"

The guard winked at Tostig. "D'je hear that? It's all settled," he said. "Old Will is a-going to act. He told 'em no at first. Said he wanted to take things easy the rest of his days. But he's give in to 'em and one can tell from his voice he's pleased about it. Now he'll fry that codshead of a Frenchy to a crisp turn and chase him back cross the Sleeve."

Three men emerged from the open door down the hall, one of whom was familiar, the marshal's squire Earley (who would write later a report of all these happenings).

"Now's yer chance," whispered the friendly guard. "Slip in afore he closes door."

William the Marshal was standing before the chimney with his back to the threshold when Tostig acted upon the guard's suggestion. He turned at once and gave an exclamation of surprise.

"You have a knack of turning up at strange times," he said. "What in the devil's name brings you here? And how did you get in?"

"I come on a matter that calls for amending at once, my lord earl."

"The last I heard of you, Master Squire, you were in Rome where our good archbishop has got himself boxed up by a hectoring individual who—who shall be nameless." His voice, when heard down the hall, had seemed confident but it could now be seen that weariness showed in every line of the old man's tall figure. "As for this matter, there is no need to tell me what it is. You have been most damnably persistent about it. It's about that troublesome prisoner."

Tostig had always found it possible to speak his mind in dealing with the marshal. "You are right, my lord. But it would be closer to the truth if you said that 'unfortunate' prisoner."

The old man's mood softened at once. "Of course, of course. It's you and that daredevil of a Richard of Rawen who have been troublesome. It's a wonder, my bold Tostig, that you're not carrying your head underneath your arm this very minute. But in truth the poor young woman is the victim of cruel circumstances."

"I'm sure, my lord, you will see no reason for keeping her in such unjust confinement."

"God's glove, do you think it as easy as that? The truth is that nothing can be done for her."

Despair gripped Tostig and for a moment he could not speak. Then he burst into words. "My lord marshal, I rode all the way from the North Sea to get here before any decision could be reached. Do you mean you have already decided?"

"Yes, the decision has been made, my zealous Tostig." The marshal nodded his head gravely. "The Council discussed it this morning and concluded it was out of the question to release the prisoner. I felt sympathetic to the idea of letting her go free but the others compelled me to agree that considerations of state made it impossible."

"But, my lord earl," interrupted Tostig, "you are now regent. Isn't it your right to settle such matters yourself?"

"The power is mine. But in such things it is wise to listen to the others. They were unanimous. You see, we have the French to beat and it can only be done with a united country. There must be no quarreling now over the succession. The boy Henry is king and no other claim must be allowed to interfere. The only safe course is to keep the claimant in safe custody."

"But after the French have been driven out, what then?" Tostig propounded the question in desperate earnestness. He approached the old man and spread out his arms in appeal. "It will be possible to right this great wrong then."

The marshal frowned. "It is possible," he said. "But I make you no promise. I may find the Council still solidly against letting her go. I can do no more than guess as to how far they may relent."

Tostig decided on a bold gamble. "My lord, have the councilors any idea that the prisoner at Corfe Castle may not be the true princess?" he asked.

William turned to face him squarely, his heavy brows drawn down in a sudden frown. When he spoke it became clear that, even if he had learned the whole truth from the countess, he had no intention of acknowledging it. "You speak in riddles, Sir Squire," he said.

"Permit me, my lord, to amend the question. Are the members of the Council convinced that the prisoner at Corfe is the Princess Eleanor of Brittany?"

"Of course. What else is there to believe?"

The marshal left his position in front of the cheerfully crackling fire and walked to a small table on which a meal had been set out. There was a large slice of crisply brown veal, a chop, a mound of mashed turnip, and a loaf of bread which had just left the oven. Here he seated himself. "Sit down, my good Tostig, and join me in a glass of wine."

Tostig felt a lump rise in his throat. This was the first time in all his life that he had been offered a seat in the presence of his betters. He nodded in refusal but accepted a drink of wine.

The marshal applied himself to the meal, cutting the veal with his knife and using his other hand to convey the pieces to his mouth, with a fastidiousness rare in an old soldier. "You must put away any thought," he said, "that the Council acted hastily or with any feeling of hostility for the prisoner. It comes to this: England can't be torn by civil war any longer, we must take any course that assures us of peace. There are always factions to espouse any cause. If the princess were set at liberty, there would soon be an active party, demanding that she be placed on

the throne. They might even resort to arms. *You* should be a good judge
of the possibility of that. It seems cruel and arbitrary to keep her under
lock and key, to refuse her the right to marry. But," nodding his head
with determination, "when the doing of an act of justice will lead to
fighting and bloodshed, and suffering for millions of people, we must
close our eyes and ears and even refuse to listen to the dictates of
conscience."

A minstrel appeared in the doorway and gave a preliminary sweep
on the strings of a small harp. The marshal lowered the chop bone at
which he had been munching and glared at the intruder.

"Go away!" he said. When the man had withdrawn hastily, Old William turned to Tostig. "They seem to think I can't enjoy my meals unless
a bull-necked gleeman is yowling at me. The truth is, I dislike music. I
fall asleep every time a minstrel starts in on one of those ballads of fifty
verses."

A silence settled on the room. Tostig for once was at a loss for words.
What reason could he advance against a course taken on such grounds?
The only possible loophole he could see was to have it declared openly
that the real princess was at large and her place in prison was being
taken by a half sister. This, he knew, would lead to a nationwide effort
to secure again the person of the true princess. Her whereabouts would
soon be ascertained.

"The Council reached another decision," went on the marshal. "The
prisoner is to be removed from Corfe to Bristol Castle where she will
be lodged in—in better accord with her rank. This is to be done at once.
Does that relieve your mind?"

"That she is still a prisoner is due to a lack of precision in a plan of my
making for her escape," declared Tostig. "My sense of guilt is such
that I find little to ease it in this decision of the Council. I am glad," he
added, "that she will live in more comfort."

"I am getting hard of hearing and I didn't catch what you said about
a plan. But don't repeat it, I beg of you. Not here or anywhere else.
And I suggest you pray that the lords and gentlemen who—er—may
have encouraged you in this plan will have enough discretion to say
nothing about it also. So far they have remained commendably quiet."

"Could it be arranged for me to see the prisoner?" asked Tostig, after
some moments of silence.

"I promise to arrange it for you. But not at once. We have a war on
our hands and I am going to need you. I can think of a score of ways in
which your clear head and good arm can be useful to us. You are

needed here much more than in Rome. Will you volunteer me your services?"

"My lord earl, I am at your command," declared Tostig.

There was a long pause. "Young man," said the earl finally, "I'll fight this war with all my might and with every weapon I can command. But the truth is I wish the need for it did not exist or that other men had taken this responsibility on their shoulders. If I were free to choose, I would much prefer the life that my young friend Richard is living. Can anything be more agreeable than raising horses in Ireland?"

2

William the Marshal might prefer the raising of horses to engaging in another war but he went about the fighting nevertheless with great thoroughness. All through the winter he detached the English barons one by one from their support of the French. He kept striking at the outer bounds of the territory held by Prince Louis, recapturing castle after castle and narrowing the French zone.

While this was going on, Tostig was proceeding with the tasks delegated to him by the old warrior. He went from castle to castle, discussing supplies with the barons and the strength which each could lead into the field. He went to Scotland and bought supplies of arms: pikes and spears and side weapons as well as some of the great swords which the Scots called claymores. He visited Wales and gathered some stock of a new weapon the Welshmen were experimenting with called the longbow, a deadly thing as tall as its users, which sent arrows a great distance with the utmost accuracy; and which, moreover, in the hands of Anglo-Saxon bowmen a hundred years hence would cut the chivalry of France to pieces on many historic battlefields. He talked to shipbuilders about the craft needed to meet the French fleet. And finally he went to Ireland to buy horses for the use of the English cavalry, a mission which brought him in due course to Kilkenny.

A ragged kern directed him along the road from town to ford. He splashed through the water and up to the small house, thinking how pleasant everything was and how thickly the rolling hills were tenanted by browsing horses still in their winter coats. To his right the land rose steeply and on the brow of an abrupt knoll the beginnings of a castle wall could be seen. The head of a busy workman protruded above the masonry, and the sound of tools cutting into stone reached Tostig's ears from the space enclosed. A woman came out from the house and watched him under a cupped hand, her other hand holding that of a small boy. A diffidence, to which he had become a stranger of recent years, came over him again when he realized it was Eleanor of Brittany.

"My lady!" he exclaimed, with a trace of stammer.

"Tostig!" cried the chatelaine of the small house. "It is you! What a splendid surprise. Now we shall have all the news of the world. Ah, Tostig, we have been so cut off. It is so secluded and silent here. I am hungry to hear what you have to tell us."

On her order a servant came out of the house and sounded a loud and peremptory call on a horn trumpet. "That will bring Richard: he is over in the valley today with Conn Ragen," explained Eleanor as she turned to lead the way inside. He saw that her hair was almost as brilliantly golden as ever and she was wearing it in two long braids, one over each shoulder. He thought her quite lovely, although it had to be admitted that she was showing a slight tendency toward the matronly in figure.

The boy was a true Plantagenet. Tostig could guess accurately at his age and was surprised at the size he had already achieved.

"This is my son," said Eleanor, her eyes bright with pride. "He will grow up to resemble a certain great-uncle, the one with the heart of a lion. I think, Tostig, that my son is destined for great things."

Tostig looked at the boy with a complete belief in what his mother had said, and a feeling of so much awe that he was on the point of dropping to one knee.

"I am not reconciled to the part of a spectator," said Eleanor. "To being Goody O'Rawn, a mere housewife in the depths of Ireland. Perhaps I'll still have the chance to—to play a part again in the life of my family. But if not, it will remain for my little Arthur Dermot Henry to take his mother's place."

The room was large and filled with the individuality of its tenants. At the chimney an old man sat with a harp at his knees. At their entry he had raised it in his arms and was beginning to strum some introductory chords.

"Softly, Brian," said Eleanor. "We are going to talk."

They sat down together at a small table and a servant brought Tostig a flagon of ale. The boy wandered to another corner and concerned himself with a toy horse. The harp provided a low obbligato for the words which Tostig poured out at the bidding of the eager Eleanor. By the time the sound of a horseman was heard approaching the house he had told briefly everything that had happened. The princess sprang up and went to the door to greet her husband. Her face was white with the feelings aroused by the telling.

"That rumor we heard is true," she said to Richard. "The king is dead. He died a fitting death. But"—her voice rose to a high pitch —"his young son has been crowned king! Richard, Richard, it has happened again! The branch of the family with the rightful claim has been passed over."

Richard looked at her with deep concern. "My beloved one, how have you heard all this?"

"Tostig is here." Eleanor turned and nodded in the direction of the visitor.

Richard entered the room with outstretched hand. "Tostig!" he cried. "How much I have missed you. A thousand welcomes—even though the news you bring us is bitter to swallow." A life in the open had given him additional girth and his skin was as brown as the shell of a butternut. The arm he dropped on Tostig's shoulder was as brawny as the squire's own. "You are looking well. There is something about you, moreover. I am sure you have been accomplishing things."

"Richard," said Eleanor in a tone almost of censure, "I haven't told you all. The choice of a successor was again the work of the marshal. Twice he has interfered to cheat us. Yes, it was the work of that Dismal Old Will, as my poor brother called him. I know we are indebted to him for the roof over our heads. But he has always been the foe of our family. We must not stay in this house another day."

"But, dear wife," said Richard, his handsome face a study in conflicting emotions, "where can we find a sanctuary to equal it? We are safe here, and comfortable. Nay, we are becoming prosperous. The marshal and his countess have been our best friends."

"Richard," cried Eleanor, "he has robbed me a second time of my birthright!" Then her mood changed and she began to weep. "Oh, Richard, I know what you say is true. I love you, my husband, to distraction. Our fine little Arthur is dearer than life to me. And I love every inch of our land and I am proud of our horses." Then, with another lightning-like change of mood, she drew herself up and her eyes flashed. "But am I to stand by and see my rights, and my son's rights, passed over without fighting for them?"

"If I may interrupt," said Tostig, who had been standing by and listening with an air as disturbed as that worn by Richard, "the succession won't be seriously considered as long as there is a French army in London."

"Under the command of the Dauphin of France, to whom I was once betrothed. Richard, this is hard to believe: Prince Louis is claiming the throne of England because his wife, my cousin, Blanche of Castile, is a granddaughter of Henry II. Such arrant knavery! This plain-faced Blanche, who is a shrew and a scold, is the third daughter of the Princess Eleanor. Eleanor was Henry's second daughter, born four years after Prince Geoffrey, my father. She has a better right than this devil's spawn, the son of John; for John was the king's last child; but her claim beside mine is a sorry pretension."

"I heard something of all this some time ago," said Richard, "but I couldn't be sure of the truth of it and so I—I kept it from you until it could be verified." He turned to Tostig. "What headway have the French made?"

"They hold London and all of the southeastern corner of the kingdom. The French king is making a pretense of repudiating his son's invasion but secretly he's pushing it with all his strength. The marshal is organizing a force to give them battle in the spring."

"So, England is fighting again against a French army of invasion. Tostig, the time has come for me to return. Every lance and every strong arm will be needed."

"No, no!" cried Eleanor. "Would you fight to keep the throne for the son of the man who murdered my brother?"

"But, Eleanor, we can't allow the French to conquer England."

"If the French are driven out, this child will stay on the throne. He will grow into a crafty, treacherous man like his hated father. But if the French win, it will be the end of that family of thieves and murderers. Sooner or later the French will be expelled, and then the English people will turn at last to us, the one branch of the family with a clear and honest claim. I would be made queen. Or, if they saw fit to pass me over, my son would be crowned in my place."

Richard refused to be influenced by this reasoning. "We can't work for the victory of France. Can we watch our people reduced to servitude in the hope you would be acknowledged in the event of a successful fight for liberation later?"

Tostig took it on himself to end this phase of the discussion. He addressed himself to Richard. "It would be the height of folly for you to return to England. You would be seized and thrown into prison. And," turning to Eleanor, "it would be doubly dangerous for you to show yourself. All England will be behind the drive against the French. I am afraid they would give your claims no consideration at all."

"It would have been different," declared Eleanor, "if I had been there when John died. I could have talked those dull-witted barons into preferring me to this silly boy."

Knowing that Richard would have nothing to say, Tostig asked a question. "But could you have made yourself heard, my lady, from a cell in Corfe Castle?"

Eleanor was quick to make amends. "I am not blaming you, my wonderful friends," she said, resting her head for a brief moment against Richard's arm. "You gave me life and you saved my reason. I married you, Richard, of my own free will. Nay, I threw myself at your head. I have never regretted it. It's only that sometimes I fear I have robbed my little son of his birthright."

"The future," said Richard, touching her hair gently, "always brings surprises and swift turns of fortune. Your chance may still come. But if it doesn't, we can be sure your son"—he carefully refrained from saying "our son"—"will have time on his side. The great opportunity will come to him sooner or later."

"If I may be permitted to say what I think," interjected Tostig, "I am sure the barons see nothing but an immediate advantage in the present arrangement. During the boy's minority, they'll have things their own way. I know that the marshal has no illusions about it. He said to me: 'John was the worst king that ever lived. His son is going to be the smuggest. He will grow into a very sly man.'"

"What is he like?" asked Eleanor. "This boy they have chosen?"

"He's rather handsome, my lady. He has light brown hair and his features are good. But he has one flaw. One of his eyelids has a droop."

"The sign of evil!" cried Eleanor. "The Devil has put his mark on him." She turned triumphantly to her own son, who had toddled across the room and wrapped both arms around his father's knee. "*There* is the rightful king. The hand of evil hasn't touched him. *His* eyes don't droop like an owl's. My little son—God watch over him and bless him —is without a blemish."

While the servants laid the table for the midday meal, the two men settled down to discuss the question which had brought Tostig to the Little Farm of Green Hedges. They fell so deep into the question of the equine points needed for war service, and the trend of prices, that they paid no attention when Eleanor left the room, taking the boy with her. She returned alone in a matter of perhaps a half hour to hear Richard say: "Then the price is agreed to. You will have the pick of the stock."

She crossed the room and sat down with them. "I have something to say to you, dear Richard, and to you, my good Tostig. It will serve no purpose to inspect the stock. You will find nothing but the runts and the culls. I gave orders to Conn Ragen to round up all the best horses and take them across the river. He obeyed with such eagerness and good will that he has them on the way already." She added triumphantly: "All you have said may be true. You are English. I am only half English and I have had nothing but cruelty from my father's side. I am not going to have any of our fine horses killed to keep the seed of the murderous John on the throne of England!"

3

William the Marshal conducted the campaign against the French with shrewdness and skill. He did not strike early but gathered his forces about him and waited for Prince Louis to give him a favorable opportunity. It came when the bulk of the Gallic army was sent north under the command of one Comte de Perche. Now the Comte de Perche was brave and chivalrous but as little versed in strategy as the most simple-minded of recruits. This rash young man marched his troops farther north than was prudent and finally reached the city of Lincoln. When Old Will learned that the French army, with all its horses and wagons and camp followers, was cooped up on the hilltop in Lincoln between the castle (which was holding out under the brave widow of the owner) and the cathedral, he knew that the hour had struck.

On a blustery morning in late May, therefore, the English forces came down the Old Roman Way in battle order. The marshal rode in the lead, his head bare and his white locks blowing out behind him (how his countess would have worried about this had she known!), his eyes alight with the joy of conflict. He said to the younger men who rode close about him, "God has delivered them into my hands!"

After a victory has been won, there are always individuals to claim they did this, or thought of that, or in some way performed the particular service which made success possible. Many such claims arose after the fighting at Lincoln and it is not the purpose of the narrator to assert that a squire named Tostig, who rode far back in the ranks, had any considerable part in the victory. This much is true, however: that when Old William ordered the wagons and the camp followers to follow closely on the heels of the mounted men so that from a distance they would seem a part of his fighting force, it was Tostig who found flags and pennons for them to carry in order to strengthen the deception. It was true also that he rode on the flanks of the none too eager blacksmiths and cooks and shovelmen and saw that there was no lagging and no tendency to fall behind.

It is recorded also in the brief existing annals of the battle that the French leaders rode out from Lincoln and that the advancing force seemed to be much larger and more powerful than they had anticipated. The Comte de Perche shook his head gloomily. "They are too much to meet in the open," he declared. "We must keep the walls between us; and God and the saints grant that they are strong enough to resist the English attacks."

This was a faulty decision. William the Marshal had received word that a small postern on the west side of the walls had been left unguarded. Well in advance of the main English forces, a small body of archers (some of them carrying, no doubt, the longbows imported from Wales) made their way into the town through the undefended portal. They had stationed themselves on the ramparts of the castle before the battle began. From this vantage point they looked down on the narrow alleys and the lead roofs of the old town where the French forces were huddled together with their horses in such density that they could hardly move. Men and horses alike died under the deadly stream of bolts rained upon them from above. The French fell into such confusion that they could not present any effective front when the English stormed their way into the upper levels.

It was a sanguinary day for the invaders but the English loss was so small that the battle is always recorded in histories as the Fair of Lincoln. A few score only of the English fell in the achieving of this momentous victory.

Tostig had been in the midst of what fighting there was. He was standing at the entrance to a corpse-strewn lane which led down to the cathedral close, with blood on his pike and the dust of battle on his leather breastplate, when an order reached him. His presence was required by the English leader.

Tostig made his way to the square in front of the castle where William the Marshal was stationed. A handful of English, barons who had remained in the service of Louis and had been captured in the dense warren of the upper town, were standing in an apprehensive group at one side; wondering, no doubt, what their fate would be now that the French cause was lost. A few lieutenants sat their horses (none of them from Kilkenny) around the marshal. The faces of the victors were jubilant, their mood far from forgiving. Tostig hesitated to intrude on such lofty company and stood off to one side until the eye of the old leader found him. William commanded him at once to draw closer.

William's face looked tired and old now that the struggle was over. His voice nevertheless was strong and assured.

"There is always much to be done," he announced, "after the Lord in His good hour and mercy has made a victory such as this possible. This is a time to be generous to those who were trapped in an impossible situation." The English prisoners heard this with relief, seeing that he meant to be magnanimous to them. "It is also a time to show appreciation of those whose services merit a reward. There are many who earned today the gratitude of the country. I see before me a man of humble birth to whom an ample reward is long overdue. He not only fought stoutly today. For several years, working quietly and unnoticed, he has rendered great services of divers kinds. With no recognition. Draw closer, my good friend Tostig."

When the squire had obeyed this injunction and stood immediately in front of the leader, the latter said, "You will kneel, if you please." Tostig went down on one knee, his head bowed and a confusion of emotions filling his mind and heart. What reward did the marshal have in mind? In the few seconds of uncertainty left him, he prayed it would take the form of an order for the release into his custody of any prisoner he might select. He had heard of such boons being granted after a battle for the purpose of dividing the ransom money. "If this is what he means to give me, I shall afford him a shock by asking for the release of my sweet lady in Corfe," he said to himself.

But this was not the purpose of the victorious regent. Tostig felt the marshal's sword touch him on the shoulder three times.

"I dub thee knight," he heard Old William say. "Arise, Sir Tostig."

The son of Sigurd, the man who had been born a villein and bound to the land at Rawen until his freedom was granted by his master, rose slowly to his feet. His brief moment of hope had been dashed but his blood raced in his veins and his mind was filled with such a degree of jubilation as he had never known before. He looked up into the skies where a new sun seemed to burn warmly. He felt that everything about life had changed, that everything was new and strange and wonderful. He was realizing that never again would he have to lower his head in the presence of his betters, that never again need he hesitate to speak his mind freely and openly. He knew that never again would he sit at meals below the salt.

Chapter XXV

1

TOSTIG rode to Bristol with a squire cantering beside him. The squire had been a villein on a Yorkshire estate and a wound puckered one side of his face, the result of a sullen blow from the son of his master. His name was Reginald and he was very talkative.

William the Marshal's sense of obligation had gone beyond the act of making Tostig a knight. Under his belt the latter carried a document which granted him a stretch of land in Ireland beside the rich acres of one Richard O'Rawn in Kilkenny. There was also a purse stuffed to the bursting point, not with pence but with zecchins and gold marks. Because of the old protector's generosity he was able to travel as befitted his new station in life. His lance carried a pennon of his own colors, a wide bar of buff on a background of gold. The tabard he wore over his chain mail was also of buff and gold and of handsome material. His spurs were silver.

Tucked in beside the land grant was a second document, a letter addressed to the governor of the castle in Bristol, instructing him to grant the bearer an interview with the royal prisoner.

As they rode slowly across the old bridge, which was wooden and somewhat shaky, Reginald's loquacity was roused by the sight of the castle between the converging banks of the Avon and the Frome, a formidable tower of dark stone behind walls which were higher and stronger than the defenses of Corfe.

"There it be," said the squire. "Looks like giant buzzard made out of stone."

"Yes, Reginald, it has that appearance."

"It was behind they walls the Empress Matilda kept poor King Stepe" (meaning Stephen) "as prisoner. Chained to the wall, he was. Least it's so said."

"Yes, Reginald."

"I don't believe it. 'Tis said empress loved King Stepe. Stands to reason she wouldn't keep him chained up that way."

"Yes, Reginald."

"But," went on the squire, "Stepe's queen, who had been stay-at-home wife, and more 'customed to sewing than fighting, come up with army and captured castle. And that was end of empress, who turned tail and ran away to France."

When they first reached the bridge, Tostig's thoughts had been edged with pride. He had said to himself: "What would my sweet Giselle think if she saw me like this? Riding a fine horse which was given me in Ireland by her own sister, the rightful Queen of England, and with a squire beside me?" Reginald's talk, however, had turned his thoughts into another, and less pleasing, speculation. "What bitterness she must feel, that unfortunate child! How she must scorn us for leaving her in prison so long! If a delicate woman like Stephen's queen could lead an army to rescue him from this very prison, there should have been some way to get her free of *her* chains."

He slumped unhappily in his saddle as his thoughts continued in the same strain. "How can I convince her," he wondered, "that there has never been a waking hour in all these hard years that I haven't thought of her? That she has been continually in my dreams?"

The letter, carrying the signature of the Protector of England, won them immediate admission. Ahead stretched a straight flagged path through the considerable length of the busy outer bailey. The winter and the spring following it had been long and severe and it was clear that the stock in the granaries had been exhausted, for rude farm carts loaded with moldy hay were being brought in by way of the narrow bridge across the Frome River. Tostig had no doubt as to how these supplies were being obtained. Armed parties had been sent out to requisition hay for the livestock and new stocks of food for the castle. They had, he was sure, laid hands on everything they could find. He knew the custom too well to think that the poverty-stricken tenant farmers had received any pay for what had been taken from them.

The governor met them at the high stone gateway leading into the inner bailey in which stood the tall castle keep. He frowned over the contents of the letter, partly because he found reading difficult and partly because of the nature of the instructions.

"Why are you so favored, Sir Knight?" he asked. "The—er—the prisoner, whose name I find here, has had no visitors since being brought to us from Corfe. There she had been kept in the strictest seclusion." He read the order again, to make sure. "Well, it is so written. Follow me, if you please. She will have to be brought down to the Great Hall. And," suspiciously, "you must observe the rules, Sir Knight. There will be a table between you and a guard at one end. Nothing must be handed her. There will be no whispering, no planning or scheming between you. Do I have your promise on that?"

"Yes, my lord governor."

The Great Hall was an apartment of proud proportions, with high arching ceiling and a huge fireplace at one end. Light came in through a half dozen archery slits but not enough to relieve the gloom, while the fire on the hearth did little to alleviate the chill of the place. "My poor Giselle!" thought Tostig. "Condemned to live in darkness and cold while I have passed my days in the grace of God's sunshine and have had these favors showered on me."

"I'll be near the fire," declared the governor in a warning tone. "And I'll be keeping a close eye on you, Sir Knight."

To the right of the chimney could be seen the lower steps of a circular stone stairway. One of the keepers came down, carrying a large iron ring loaded with keys. He nodded to the governor.

"The lady of Brittany," he announced.

Tostig said later that he must have stared like a country gawk at a town fair when he saw her. It was no wonder. Giselle came down the stone steps with all the grace and assurance of a great lady. She bowed briefly to the governor and then came forward to greet her visitor. A maid followed with a proper degree of deference.

"How well she carries it off!" he thought with great pride.

Giselle had changed in every respect; but one point of difference in her appearance was so great that at first Tostig was aware of nothing else. She no longer wore the golden wig, and her hair, still lustrous and abundant, was as white as snow. This gave her an air of maturity without detracting from her beauty. Her gray-blue eyes matched her hair so seductively that at first glance the tiny wrinkles, which clustered about them, were not noticed. She was dressed in a tunic of nutmeg brown, drawn tightly at the neck and the wrists with green braiding. The train was at least three feet, entailing the most expert manipulation.

Tostig stepped forward to meet her and dropped to one knee. She extended her hand, which was white and well cared for, and he kissed it with respect as well as fervor.

"Giselle!" he whispered.

"Tostig, Tostig!" she whispered back. He realized then that her pride and assurance were part of the masquerade she had found it necessary to play. She herself had not changed.

"I am here through the kindness of the Protector," he said, rising from his kneeling position. "He takes a great interest in your welfare." Turning to the governor, he added: "I have matters of a personal nature to discuss with Her Highness. I have no wish to infringe your rules, Sir Governor, but I must request that the guard you propose to station at the table be moved back perhaps as much as twenty paces. I can be watched as well from that distance."

The governor gave the suggestion some thought. "Granted," he said, with a hint of reluctance in his tone.

Giselle seated herself on one side of the table and Tostig took the other, facing her directly. For a few moments they said nothing but looked intently into each other's eyes, both filled with the immeasurable happiness of meeting after so long a lapse of time.

"There is so much you must tell me," she said finally, in a low tone. "And they will allow us a short time only. Begin, begin! Tell me everything."

"The princess," he said, uneasily lowering his voice almost to a whisper, "is in Ireland. She is married to Richard of Rawen."

Giselle gasped in the extremity of her surprise. "Married! Married to Richard! What strange tale is this you are telling me? How did it come about? St. Agnes lend me aid and guidance, for I am hopelessly lost! This passes belief."

"It came about when it was found that the barons who had promised to support her claim to the throne did not come forward. She and Richard were deeply in love and they decided she might as well seek happiness since power was denied her."

"And is she happy?" tremulously.

"As happy as can be expected in view of what transpired after John's death."

"You mean about the succession?" Giselle nodded her head. "The governor tells me briefly the news of the world but I get more from the gossip that my little Trisselda picks up in the kitchens. I know that John's young son is now on the throne."

"The princess has a son also."

Giselle had been keeping her gaze discreetly lowered but at this she looked up. Her eyes were intensely alive with the interest she felt in this part of his story.

"A son! Tostig, this makes me very happy! Is he a fine boy? Is he healthy? Does my ever dear sister find happiness in him?"

"He is a true Plantagenet. With the Plantagenet eye, the yellow hair, the fine manner. Your sister is sure he will grow up to be another Richard Coeur-de-Lion."

A touch of color suffused Giselle's face. For the first time in his recollection she displayed pride. "I too am a Plantagenet. I too am a granddaughter of the great Henry. And so I have the right to feel pride that my sister's son is true to the great line from which he springs."

"Time will bring changes," declared Tostig. "Your nephew may be King of England someday. If it so transpires, he may make a great king."

They compelled themselves then, because of the quick passage of time, to a disciplined attitude in reviewing the things which had come about since they parted. They passed quickly over his own advancement (although Giselle's cheeks flushed again with excitement and pride on learning of his knighthood), they talked of the life of the runaway couple in Ireland, and finally came to her own story.

It was now Tostig's turn to ask questions. "How have you fared since we left you in this dreadful predicament?"

She replied thoughtfully. "It hasn't been as hard as I feared at first. My great anxiety was whether I could carry on the deception. I was helped by having always watched my sister closely. I knew her habits. I remembered every trait. I could imitate her expressions and gestures."

"Has no one learned the truth?"

She shook her head. "I don't believe so. The real test would have come if I had faced the king. Did you know he came to Corfe Castle soon after? I was told he would see me on the second day. I was so frightened I couldn't sleep at all that night. I was sure he would notice the difference at once and that—well, I was prepared for the worst. It was by a great stroke of luck that I was saved. In the morning messengers arrived with news which upset the king very much. I was told he fell into a great rage and ordered that two prisoners were to be hanged at once. I heard later that they were charged with minor offenses only; but the angry king had to find some vent for his evil temper. It would have gone ill with me if he had remained long enough to see me but the news was so urgent that he took to horse at once." She added after a moment's pause: "It was believed in the castle that I had seen him."

"When did you discard the wig?"

"I wore it for a year. I was even careful to keep my maid from seeing me without it. It was always under a pillow when I slept so I could don it quickly if the girl came in. Then I found my hair was turning white."

"My poor Giselle! It was the peril of your position, for which I feel responsible, which turned it this way."

"No, no! I remember that my own poor mother's hair was white when I was a small girl. It must be a trait in the family. At any rate, it gave me a chance to stop wearing the wig. I gave it out that I had used it solely to save my pride and that, as the transformation was now complete, I could give it up."

"I grieve to see so great a proof of the advance of time," said Tostig. "But truly it is most becoming. I think you are more lovely than ever."

She studied him intently. "I am growing old, Tostig, and I know that I show it. But with you the years seem to deal lightly."

"And yet I have lived in great agony of spirit because of my failure to help you. I haven't known a moment's real peace." He paused before going on with his questioning. "Do they treat you well here?"

Her gaze strayed for a moment to one of the archery slits through which a narrow segment of blue sky could be seen. "Yes, I live in comfort. I have two rooms on the floor above this and I use the stairs by which you saw me come down." She did not go on at once and, when she did, it was clear that her thoughts had gone back to the far different life at Corfe. "They tell me that an old priest who was outspoken enough to anger the king is kept now in the cells above the stone shaft. God and the Holy Mother have pity on him!"

"He was there for a few days only. As soon as his story was learned, the Protector had him released. The cells are now empty."

"I have a walk every day and occasionally I am allowed outside the walls. With a suitable guard, of course. I am teaching myself to read. Each day I am permitted to visit the chapel, where there is a Bible, and I am reading slowly—very, very slowly—the holy words. I have come to the Book of Ruth and how she gathered the sheaves. What a beautiful story!" Her eyes brightened. "I have a small harp and am learning to play. Would you like to hear me?"

"I would rather hear you," declared Tostig fervently, "than all the choirs of Christendom or even the holy angels!"

"Nay, you mustn't speak that way. I fear it will be written down as irreverence." She turned in the direction of her custodian and raised her voice. "My lord governor," she said, "may I send for my harp? I desire to play for my visitor."

During the wait, Giselle began to speak in a low tone. "I am reconciled to staying here, dear Tostig. I know it is impossible to do anything for me."

"But," he protested, "I'm certain your release will be granted soon. The marshal is favorably disposed himself but must convince his Council. I have talked it over with him several times and I know he would like to see you at liberty."

She shook her head. "No, Tostig. The people here talk to me freely and they all say I shouldn't hope. They say it is a political necessity to keep me here. The country can't stand more civil war. It would be different perhaps if those who do the deciding knew I am not the real princess. But we must never let them know the truth. Above all my dear sister must be allowed to live in peace." There was a brief pause and then she looked up and met his eyes squarely. "You must believe me when I say I am well content as things are. What better return can I make for the kindness that Eleanor always showed me? It makes me feel that I am like Ruth in the Bible; I am bringing home the only sheaves my hands can reach. And I am comfortable here. Now that I can read and play on my beautiful harp, I fill in the time quite well. What more could I ask?"

"Freedom!" exclaimed Tostig. Then he checked himself and went on in a lower tone. "A normal life. A home. A husband. Children. Are you content to miss everything?"

She did not reply at once. "I realize what I'm missing. There are times when I am very unhappy. But I have trained myself to conquer all such thoughts; and I get over my moods quickly. I think, dear Tostig, I was brought into the world for this very purpose. Shouldn't I be happy to do the Lord's will? They say here that I am a model prisoner. I even think they have come to like me."

"How could they fail to like you!"

"At any rate they do favors for me. I no longer have that terrifying sense of being alone."

He began to pour out his feelings, telling her of his love, of the constancy with which she remained in his thoughts. He had one object only in life, he declared: to win her freedom. What the people of the castle told her was true in a sense but the fear of more strife would soon subside. He was confident the old marshal would succeed before long in convincing the other members of the Council. He repeated this with a passionate sense of certainty, but at the first pause she shook her head.

"What you say disturbs me very much," she whispered, "because I can see that you suffer more than I do. Please, please, believe that I am well content. That I enjoy peace of mind. That I ask nothing better of life. If you will tell me that you understand this, I will be completely satisfied."

The jailer returned with her harp before anything further could be said. It was a small one and, as it lacked a front pillar, it was probably quite old. Giselle rested it on her knees and began to play a quiet air which Tostig recognized as an ancient lullaby. She played with the care of a beginner but with a sure enough touch and an excellent ear. To Tostig, the music she produced was surpassingly sweet and he watched her intently as her fingers (which were as white and finely shaped as her sister's) strayed over the strings. With the eye of a lover, he studied the beauty and delicacy of her profile, beginning to see that the resemblance she bore the princess was far from complete. There were differences: a greater width of brow which gave Giselle a more thoughtful expression, and more of a tendency to taper down to a gentle chin. It seemed to him that she had a sweetness of mien which was not to be found in equal degree in her royal half sister.

He found himself wishing that he had the strength of Samson and could tear down with his own arms these stone walls which held her in captivity.

Giselle came to a stop in the middle of the lullaby. She leaned her cheek against the curved back of the instrument and gave him a long and loving smile. "How foolish," she said, "to waste the little time we have! When we still have so much more to say. I was selfish. I wanted you to remember me playing my harp for you."

"Enough," said the governor, stepping down from his post by the chimney. "I've allowed you more time, Sir Knight, than was intended."

They rose to their feet. There was so much that Tostig still wanted to tell her that he stammered and succeeded only in repeating the words she had used when he climbed up the stone shaft in Corfe Castle. "No matter what befalls!" She had lowered her eyes, perhaps to conceal the emotions which filled her, but at this she looked up and smiled tremulously. "You remember what I said!" she whispered. "Thank you, dear Tostig, for remembering. It will always be the same with me. As long as I live! And now I am sure that you will not forget me. I am happy. Even though"—she paused—"even though this may be a final good-by."

She followed the jailer across the stone floor of the Great Hall. After ascending the first few steps, she paused a moment as though she lacked the resolution to go any farther. Then she gave him a brief and grave smile of farewell and placed her foot on the next step. She vanished from sight, the long train of her tunic trailing slowly after her.

Tostig left the castle with a sense of deep despair. He was afraid he would never see her again.

2

Tostig spent a month in confronting the members of the royal Council. He went first to the Bishop of Winchester, a Poitevin whose name was Peter des Roches and who was destined to be a prominent figure, and the real villain, of the long reign of Henry III. The bishop was a soldier and a diplomat rather than a churchman. He listened to the earnest arguments that Tostig advanced with a supercilious smile on his handsome face.

"The old marshal has seen fit to admit you to the order of knighthood," he said, "but the commoner still shows in you like shoddy in the warp. I see no merit in what you say. It's safer to keep this woman under lock and key. She's probably lost her looks by this time, so what can she hope to get out of her freedom?"

At Dover that stout soldier, Hubert de Burgh, who had held the castle against the French, shook his head at the suggestion of a release for the prisoner. "I had her brother, Prince Arthur, in my charge after he was captured," he said. "I refused to let them burn his eyes out when John wanted it done. Did you know that? Well, I stood in the way of it, so they took him out of my hands. And *that* was the last ever heard of that unfortunate young man. I don't believe they used the red-hot iron on his eyes. I think they killed him in the most convenient way. Some say he was hit over the head with an oar on the Seine and thrown into the water. It's even supposed that John attended to it himself. As to that, I can't say. But I *can* say this. I must not make myself the champion of the sister or everyone will declare my allegiance is given to the Breton line and not to the young king. No, no, I must not prick my chances with my own bodkin."

It required a trip to the far north of England to see the Earl of Chester. He was equally adamant but he proved himself better advised on the real state of affairs than the others. The years were weighing on his shoulders and, as he had never been anything but a low-pocket in stature, he was beginning to seem very small and withered. It was this scion of the aristocracy of the Conquest who had been chosen as the second husband of Constance of Brittany by Henry II after Prince

Geoffrey got himself killed in a tournament. This had made him the stepfather of Prince Arthur and the Princess Eleanor. Constance had disliked the short-limbed, black-a-vised earl and so the marriage was not a successful one; some even asserted that it was never consummated. It had ended in divorce.

That he had once been the stepfather of the Pearl of Brittany did not incline him to a lenient view. "A taunty creature," he said. "I had my difficulties with her." He had indeed, for he was the father that Eleanor confessed to kicking in the stomach when she was four years old. "I would never favor that spite-cat as queen. In fact, I am against putting women on thrones. Only the strong hand of a man can control a country as full of mixed races as this bedeviled kingdom."

Having delivered himself of this opinion, the Earl of Chester looked at Tostig and winked slyly. "I happen to know, moreover, that the prisoner at Bristol is not the Princess Eleanor. It's the half sister."

Tostig was taken aback. "Why do you think that, my lord? Are you not jumping to a very strange conclusion?"

"Not strange at all and not a guess. I *know*. You see, one of the circle of designing barons who thought for a time she could be pitted against John confessed the truth to me. I warned him to keep a closed mouth and not spit the story out again if he wanted to keep his silly head on his shoulders. What's more, I forced the loon to give me the names of some of the others. I went to all of them and finally got a complete list. I read the law to them, I can tell you. I suspended the threat of a charge of treason over them if the story ever leaked out." He indulged in a self-satisfied laugh. "I succeeded in sealing up their mouths forever and a day."

"Since you know the truth, my lord," said Tostig earnestly, "do you not agree that it serves no purpose to hold the sister a prisoner any longer?"

"I do not agree!" declared the earl flatly. "The situation is nicely adjusted in my opinion. The princess is at large and so there is no reason for any of us to feel a weight on our consciences. Not that I ever felt any on mine. The faintest kind of a whisper reached my ears that she had made a fool of herself by marrying some lowborn knight. A Saxon, to boot. She need not be considered any longer as a claimant for the throne. We can rest at peace on that score."

"But why keep the sister, who is innocent of all wrong, in prison in her place!" exclaimed Tostig.

"Innocent of all wrong? Didn't she connive at the escape of a state

prisoner? Hasn't she been carrying on a masquerade ever since? Besides," added the earl, frowning at his visitor as though he did not fully
understand what Tostig was saying, "isn't this woman baseborn? God's
kneecap, does it matter what happens to her?"

So Tostig gave up the effort to win support among the leaders in
the royal Council and betook himself to London where William the
Marshal had moved his family temporarily into the White Tower. He
found no one there save the Tower officials and their armed attendants.
The marshal had been taken so ill that his life had been despaired of
and at his own request he had been moved up the river to his favorite
manor of Caversham.

Tostig realized the gravity of the situation when he turned through
an avenue of oak trees and came in sight of the manor. Armed men
by the score stood about the grounds and tethered horses lined the
hedges and fences. These visitors, as Tostig saw at once, were the
knights and men-at-arms who had followed the marshal to the wars.
Some had come long distances, for their armor was dusty and they
seemed weary as well as sad. A glum lot, they stood about in groups
but found little to say to each other.

One of them spoke to Tostig as he passed. "Old Will is dying," he
said. "It will be the first time he has gone down in all his life to a
stronger lance than his own."

Inside the house Tostig found the countess sitting with her women.
Her eyes were red with weeping and the handkerchief clasped in her
hands was damp. She rose with a strained attempt at a smile of welcome
and led Tostig to the floor above. They stopped in the door of a room
where he saw the long frame of the old warrior stretched out on a bed.
A priest was speaking in subdued tones to a group of the Pembroke
children in one corner but the sick man was beyond taking heed of
what went on about him. His eyes were closed and his arms were
stretched limply beside him.

"He spoke his last words a half hour gone," whispered the countess.
"He asked about two strangers he saw in the room. They were wondrous
fair, he said, and very tall, and they had wings on their shoulders. No
one else saw them. Oh, Tostig, Tostig, they were the angels sent from
heaven to lead him on his way!"

Tostig joined the knights and squires who filled the grounds of the
small estate. Little was said, save to recite some incident in which the
old man had behaved with special valor. There were hundreds of such
known to all of them and it would have taken many hours to recite

them. Sufficient time for that was not allowed. In half an hour a priest came to the entrance and made the sign of the cross.

Tostig mounted his horse at once and rode away. The passing of William of Pembroke had ended his hopes of securing the release of the prisoner in Bristol. Unless, he said to himself, Stephen Langton became the dominant voice in the Council of the young king. He rode slowly, for his heart was bowed down with so much cause for grief.

In the meantime, of course, there was his grant of land in Ireland from the dead marshal. It would be wise to claim it at once, although it seemed of small moment. He turned his horse's head into the west.

Chapter XXVI

1

Tostig reached the grant which was to be his for the rest of his life, and his descendants' for many centuries thereafter, at a late hour of the night. He was accompanied by his squire Reginald and a native of the town who had come along to aid in finding the way. The house on the property proved to be a low structure of one story and with no furnishings of any kind. It had been closed tight for many moons, so that the air was hot and frowsty and small living things could be heard stirring about in the thatched roof. The three men curled up in their cloaks and slept on the uneven earthen floor.

They rose at dawn and proceeded to trace the limits of the grant. There was a level stretch of perhaps one hundred acres enclosed between a brace of hills which were known, according to the native, as the Culleton Slippers because of their shape. It seemed to be excellent land and even the sides of the Slippers were thickly covered and green. Tostig looked about him with the first stirring of a sense of pride.

"This is my land!" he thought. "It is mine, mine! It can be a pleasant thing to be bound to the land—when it is your own!" He studied the easy slope of the hills. "Cattle or sheep. Sheep, I think. I must not attempt to raise horses."

The task of tracing the exact boundaries of the grant took the whole of the morning. It was, therefore, nearly one o'clock before the new resident turned his horse toward the neighboring land which belonged to his onetime master. Entering the O'Rawn tract through a thick cover of trees, he saw Richard standing over a fire in a glade ahead, accompanied by two men in menial garb and a boy of perhaps six years. They were eating a midday meal from a deep iron pot and there was much cheerful talk going on among them. The boy had a shock of yellow hair and blue eyes which, in spite of his tender years, had an almost mature boldness and assurance in them.

"Good morning, neighbor," said Tostig, advancing into the glade on foot.

Richard straightened up and turned his head. He looked first surprised, then startled, and finally incredulous. He dropped the charred branch with which he had been stirring up the fire.

"Tostig!" he cried. "Is it really you?"

The two men shook hands vigorously, their faces glowing with the pleasure of reunion. Richard looked browner, if possible, than on the occasion of Tostig's earlier visit, and perhaps a little heavier of frame. He studied the new arrival with an observant eye.

"Your spurs are silver," he said.

Tostig nodded. "I was knighted by the marshal after the victory at Lincoln," he announced, not quite able to suppress his feeling of satisfaction.

"A well-deserved honor!" said Richard, clapping him on the arm. "You had to wait a long time for it. Sir Tostig, Sir Tostig! It has a fine, bold ring, I must say. I can see you are proud of it; and most justly so."

"Yes, neighbor."

Richard frowned. "That's twice you've called me that. What other surprise have you up your sleeve?"

"That stretch of land back there is mine. I have a grant of it from the marshal."

"The Culleton lands? Tostig, your news gets better every time you open your mouth. So we are to live here side by side. I can imagine nothing that would please me more." He paused. "How generous that old man has been to us. I trust you left him in the best of health."

It was Tostig's turn to look surprised. "It's hard to believe that the news of the world reaches you so slowly. Richard, the marshal is dead. I went to see him, hoping to convince him in a matter in which both of us are deeply concerned and which need not be mentioned. I arrived just before he breathed his last. All England had gone into mourning as I passed through on my way here. He was loved by everyone and I saw nothing but sorrowful faces."

"He was both a father and a god to me. The saddest news you could bring, Tostig." After a long moment of solemn thought, Richard asked, "Who will take his place?"

"I heard it said that it might be the Bishop of Winchester who has the custody and education of the young king. Or Hubert de Burgh."

"My choice would be Hubert de Burgh. The bishop is a foreigner. He has one interest only in England—to bury his greedy fingers deep in English gold."

Tostig was watching the boy, who had been listening with evident interest. "Your son is growing up," he said. "He takes after—after his mother's people. In a most remarkable way."

"There can never be any doubt of that." Richard motioned his son to come forward. "Arthur, this is a very brave man who won his spurs on the battlefield of Lincoln. An honor you will have to earn for yourself someday."

"Yes, Father," said the boy. "I hope it will be at the Holy Sepulchre. I want to take the cross when I am old enough. I will be old enough very soon now, I think. Do you suppose, Father, it will take more than a year?"

Richard gave Tostig the benefit of a quick wink before answering. "Arthur, you must learn to have patience. It will take many years for you to grow up into a man. You would be an unfortunate fellow if you missed them, for they'll be the easiest and perhaps the most pleasant years of your life."

"Do all boys take so long to grow up?"

"Most boys of your age will need at least ten years before they can start to think of themselves as men."

"But, Father," protested the son of the house, "I shall grow up much faster than other boys. I want to be a knight as soon as possible."

Richard had turned to examine the contents of the iron pot. "We made ourselves an excellent stew of beef and kidneys," he said. "But there is very little left. You must bring your company to Castle O'Rawn where there will be food to offer you."

They emerged from the cover of the trees and Tostig saw that a stout stone wall of some height covered the crest of the eastern knoll.

"It isn't finished," explained Richard. "But the walls are up and we have moved in. We live at present in a frame building which will be used for stabling when the stone keep is finished. That will be a matter of several years." His face clouded over suddenly. "I must prepare you for a shock. You will find my lady wife sadly changed. There is no use evading the issue, Tostig; she is in a weakened condition and nothing seems to bring her any improvement."

Reginald had brought the horses through the trees and Tostig was on the point of mounting. He stopped with one foot in the stirrup.

"This is the saddest of news," he said. "She was in good health on my first visit."

"All our people say it is because our special well went dry. Do you remember it? The one where the lady sprite lived hundreds of years ago? The water from it was used only by my lady—and, of course, the horses. When it went dry we did some digging and found that the springs feeding it had changed their course. We have tapped the water again at a spot about twenty feet away from the old well. But everyone contends that the virtue of the water, which came from the charm the sprite laid on it, has been lost."

"Have the horses suffered?"

Richard shook his head. "Not at all. They are as fine and strong as ever. I put no belief now in the story of the charm. I am sure her condition is due to a fall she had."

"A fall from her horse?"

Richard nodded grimly. "She was overbold in the saddle. Conn Ragen kept saying she must be less daring or she would kill both her horse and herself. Well, they fell short of clearing the Domligh Crest. It's the hardest jump for miles around but nothing could stop my lady from finishing every ride there. This time the little mare broke her neck and my sweet lady had a bad fall. It was a wonder she lived through it." After a moment's silence he went on. "Old Brian was alive then and he wrote a long ballad claiming that it was due to the drying up of the well."

"Is the old minstrel dead?"

"His harp has been still for six months."

Richard took his son up in front of him when they set out to ride across his much-hedged estate. The boy did not seem satisfied with the arrangement and informed Tostig that he had a pony of his own and rode it all by himself.

"Come, come, my boy," admonished his father, as they started off briskly for the castle. "I don't want my old companion to think me so indifferent a father as that. You have your pony, of course, but there is always someone with you when you go a-riding."

"I am a good rider," declared Arthur. "I am a better rider than any other boy. They all say so."

"It's quite true," agreed Richard, with a chuckle. "But I could wish him less confident in making his claims."

The castle proved to be most strategically located. Not only was the ascent steep on all sides but across the face of the knoll there was a deep cut. This was spanned by a temporary bridge of tree trunks lashed together.

"Keep a tight rein," said Richard. "Your horse doesn't know the trick of getting across. Someday soon I'll have a proper drawbridge here and then the cut will make a fine dry moat."

When they had made their way across without mishap, Tostig reined in under the gateway. It was a gate in name only, being in fact no more than a hole in the wall. Tostig dismounted and looked the situation over with a discerning eye.

"As you say, a dry moat is all you will need here for defensive purposes," he remarked. "I've given some study to fortifications since the days when the old marshal used to talk to us on the subject. Do you remember how important he thought it was? I'm sure I could construct a proper portcullis and drawbridge for you. That is, if a good smith can be found to make the castings."

"There's a splendid fellow in Kilkenny," declared Richard enthusiastically. "I've been taking things too easy. The cut here should have been bridged long ago. But I've been busy with the horses and have let everything else go by. My sweet lady wife sometimes despairs over this matter of the bridge. And so, if you can get it done for me—well, I shall be as always your most grateful friend."

Inside the tall blank walls, and somewhat to the right of the space left for an entrance, there was a frame structure of no great size. Richard called to a groom to take the horses. He vanished inside and in a few moments Tostig heard the high-pitched voice of Eleanor through the open door.

"My lady is very happy," said Richard, appearing there. "And very excited. She wants to see you at once."

2

There were no listeners when Tostig had his talk with the princess. Richard had many things to discuss with Conn Ragen as well as the need to produce food for the unexpected guests. This was just as well.

Eleanor was sitting in a high-backed chair in which a soft nest had been created by the use of pillows. She was very thin and fragile. Her features had sharpened and the hand she extended to him was white and limp.

"I am back in prison again," was her greeting. "The arms of this chair are my four stone walls. Oh, Tostig, Tostig, there is no escape for me this time. Richard has to carry me, with the greatest gentleness, to and from my bed. I can't take a step. Sometimes I lack the strength to hold out an arm."

"But," he protested, "you will regain your strength."

"Never!" Eleanor shook her head. "My back is injured and I shall never be better again. I am a prisoner for life this time." She looked up at him and smiled. "You come with your proud silver spurs, Tostig. I am most happy for you."

The room in which she sat was neither very large nor very light. The place had been designed, Tostig concluded, for its ultimate purpose and not to provide comfort for its present occupants. On the other side of one wall he could hear grunting and other animal sounds, which indicated that the building served a double function. Hens were scratching at one end of the room. Although the sun was high outside, it was necessary to keep candles burning to break the gloom. All of the furnishings, including the bed and the chair in which the invalid sat, were of the plainest construction. A ladder at one side gave access to the floor above where, no doubt, the boy slept with the members of the staff. On the ride across the domain, Tostig had been told that the house where they lived at first was now being used for stabling the horses.

"We need you," said Eleanor in earnest tones. "Richard is a sweet and kind husband but he's so concerned with his horses that he sees much more of Conn Ragen than he does of his poor invalid wife. I do not complain. We are becoming prosperous; and we must think first of the future of our little son. But no attention is being paid to the finishing of the walls, and of that I do complain. Did you observe? A gaping hole for an entrance! No bridge, no means of defense whatever. If they ever find I am here, particularly if it becomes known that I have a son, the rightful King of England, they could walk right in. I keep urging Richard to finish the gate and build a drawbridge. He promises me that he will. But he is always so busy." She paused for breath. The effort of speaking was almost more than she could sustain. "Tostig, I am going to depend on you. You will have your own place, I know, but I think— I am sure—you will see to it that Richard does not delay any longer. I feel that every day counts."

"You have my promise, my lady," said Tostig.

"I sit here with nothing to do and my mind fills with the most terrifying visions. It is the fate of my little son which worries me most. Have you seen him?"

"Yes, my lady. He was in the woods with his father when I rode over. A handsome little fellow."

"I think," she said proudly, "that there has never been his equal on this earth. Not even my poor brother. And he was something to gladden the eye."

"Has your son been told?"

Eleanor shook her head with more vigor than she had yet displayed. "No, no! He has no idea that the blood of royalty flows in his veins. But he is a prince in every line, and in every thought and action. What frightens me is what he will do when he learns the truth. I know he will not be content to stay here. He will have no thought after that but to drive the usurper from the throne of England. When that time comes, I will not be here."

"I think, my lady, if you were here you would ride by his side, as you did when your brother led the advance to Mirebeau."

"But, Tostig, I see the need for careful planning. There must be no rashness, no setting up of standards on empty moors, no riding to London with a handful of brave but foolhardy followers. What I dread most of all is that someday he will lead a forlorn effort against the armies of the king. *He must not be told until he has reached the years of discretion.* I have visions of my son being taken to the block or put away in a dark cell to rot alone for the rest of his life! It frightens me so much that I struggle to escape the same walls which seem to be closing in about me and pinning my arms to my sides. My son must not suffer such a dreadful fate!"

"What can I do to help?"

"Richard has promised me that the boy will not be told until the time is favorable or until he's twenty years of age. I will not be here to prompt him of his promise but you will. Tostig, I shall depend on you. I want you to prevent any steps which you judge to be premature."

"I promise you, my lady, to do everything that lies in my power."

The invalid settled back with a weary sigh into the cushion of blankets. "You see, Tostig," she whispered, "I know exactly what my son will feel. I was ready to sally out from that little castle with only my dear Richard and you with me and ride to London, believing the country would rally to my support. What a folly it would have turned out to be! My little Arthur will feel exactly as I did. There will be times when your sage advice will be needed."

"Come, Tostig!" called Richard cheerfully, from the rear. "There's food ready for you. I want to hear about your plans and to tell you everything I am doing myself. Are you going to breed horses too?"

"No, not horses. Sheep."

"Good. We will not be against each other."

Eleanor delayed him for a moment. "Richard tells me you saw Giselle," she said.

Tostig paused before leaving and gave her a rueful glance. "I am afraid it may have been for the last time. She is comfortably lodged and is finding ways of using her time. I will tell you all about that later." He was on the point of leaving but turned to say to her, "Has it occurred to you that the plan we made for your escape——"

"And which you carried out so bravely and so boldly."

"—that it has, nonetheless, been a complete failure? You are both prisoners still. Giselle behind iron bars with no hope of freedom and you, my lady, the victim of an accident met in the exile forced upon you by circumstances."

"Has Giselle any regrets? Is she bitter over her lot?"

"Not in any degree, my lady."

"I must strive," said the princess, "to accept my misfortune in the same spirit."

3

The walls of Castle O'Rawn were finished finally, and the drawbridge was constructed and the portcullis erected above it, with Tostig acting in the capacity of overseer at all stages. It was on his insistence also that Richard completed the stone keep, in time to move Eleanor into the comparative comfort of a room with an alcove serving as an oratory and a tapestry on one wall and even a small cupboard which always contained wine and fresh water from the well. It was on the floor immediately above the Grand Chamber so that she could be carried down without much difficulty to sit before the fire blazing on the broad hearth. It had been a close thing, however, for the once beautiful Pearl of Brittany (who never lost her beauty and charm completely, although she became frail beyond belief in the last stages) was not to enjoy the fruits of high feudality very long. She had the privilege of seeing her son grow into a robust youth. It was a glorious period for him. He developed, in addition to the Plantagenet hair and eye, a nose artistically modeled to express pride, scorn, indifference, and also boldness and courage, a strong mouth and chin, and perhaps the longest and finest legs in all Ireland. He never lost his desire to take the cross, although crusading began to go out of fashion with the continual failure to accomplish anything. To compensate him for his lack of opportunity in that direction, he always had good horses to ride and all the girls of the county to dazzle with his fine looks and bold ways. It was a wonder that no one recognized him for what he was; but Ireland caught no more than the faint echoes of what went on in the rest of the world, and Kilkenny itself was far inland and too remote to know much even of the life in Dublin. Arthur passed, therefore, as the handsome scion of a relatively new family of Norman roots and no one tried to probe behind his immediate paternity.

The charm laid on the well continued to manifest itself in spite of the shifting of the springs, for the horses grown on the O'Rawn acres were still strong and glossy of coat, as a result of which the family enjoyed a comfortable prosperity. It must have been that the land allotted to Tostig lacked some at least of this richness. The sheep that the new owner raised were nothing remarkable, and the slopes of the Culleton Slippers did not provide as much pasturage as he had hoped. However, he did well enough and succeeded in building for himself a small stone house with what might be called the hint of a round tower at one corner. He went to England at intervals, when new members achieved prominence in the Council of the volatile and unreliable young Henry III. Stephen Langton had returned but he was an old man and did not concern himself with the complications of this long reign; and so his word carried no weight. Tostig had not given up hope of arousing a sentiment in favor of the prisoner of Bristol Castle. Few of the new councilors would listen to him, however, and none saw any reason for loosing another claimant on the kingdom. He was denied another visit with her. Even his efforts to send her letters were promptly blocked.

Richard and the slowly weakening Eleanor tried to convince him that he should marry and raise a family of his own but to such advice Tostig returned no answer save to snort bitterly and walk away. He made it clear that he intended to continue faithful to his memories and vows. Had he not repeated Giselle's "No matter what befalls"? He realized, in spite of this determination, that certain ladies of the neighborhood looked on him with interest and favor. It was clear that one in particular, the blue-eyed and slightly buxom daughter of the owner of lands west of the Slippers, where the setting sun turned the green of the slopes to purple and gold, would return an affirmative answer if he were to propound a certain question.

When the spirit of Eleanor finally deserted her shattered body, Richard had become massive and slow in his movements and rather more like the Sire Tohu-Bohu than the dashing young David who had unhorsed that Goliath of the Gallic west. All the dash and romance of the family now centered in the son who would have been a prince if things had been right in a topsy-turvy world. As a disgruntled swain put it, the ladies without exception groveled at his feet. Arthur went into strict mourning for his once beautiful mother. He and his father would sit in long silences in front of the fire and he was generally the one who broke them with passionate outpourings of his regret. For a long time Richard, living in his memories, found little to say.

The last word of Giselle reached them soon after the death of Eleanor. One of the knights who rode under the colors of the Marshal family happened to be passing by and stopped to inspect and admire the horses.

"The king is resting easier these days," he said.

"Why is that, Sir Knight?" asked Richard.

"She's gone," was the answer. "The Lost Princess. She's lost for good now. Died in Bristol Castle some weeks ago."

Richard tried to speak casually so the visitor would not notice the effect of this news on him. "I take it you mean the Breton princess. The one who had first claim to the throne."

"Not just the best way to speak of it if you are at court," said the knight, with a grin. "The king, who is testy about everything, is particularly testy on that score. He preferred not to have anything said about the poor lady. Still, as man to man, it's the truth. The princess had first claim after her brother was done away with. They say she was very beautiful once."

"Yes," said Richard slowly. "She was very beautiful once." After a pause he asked, "Have you learned anything of the manner of her death?"

"They say she just faded away. It's a wonder she survived as long as she did."

Richard rode over with a leaden heart to break the news to Tostig. The latter was standing outside the door of his small stone house and he needed no more than a glance at his visitor's face to know the errand on which he came.

"Is she dead?" he asked. "I have been expecting it. I sensed the shadow hovering over her that day at Bristol."

"Yes, she's dead. Our fair ladies have left us, Tostig."

There was a long pause. "How did you find out?"

Richard recounted the circumstances of the knight's visit to O'Rawn Castle. Tostig listened intently but asked no questions. At the end he went inside the house. Richard, following behind, saw him take up his riding boots, which stood on the floor beside his bed. He detached the silver spurs from the heels, bound them together with a piece of rough cord, and threw them into a corner.

"I shall never wear them again," he said. "I am not fit to have silver spurs."

Richard struggled to find words of comfort. "Come, Tostig," he said finally. "You mustn't take this so hard. I know the efforts you made on her behalf. No one could have done more."

"I shall send Reginald back to take service with some other knight. There will be a place for him in the household of one of the marshal's sons." He paused for a moment and then burst out passionately. "I took a vow, as all knights do, to serve the lady of my choice, to risk everything for her, to do brave deeds in her name. And what did I do? I left her to die in prison. And so I tell you, Richard, I am unfit to wear the spurs again." His face was filled with this conviction of his unworthiness. "Richard, there must have been a way! I don't know what it could have been but I—I should have known. Perhaps I should have stood outside the walls of the prison and cried out to all who passed the story of this great injustice. That would have kept her in people's minds. It might have led to something. Oh, I thought of it! But I hoped against hope that the minds of the Council could be swayed in her favor by other means."

"You blame yourself unfairly, Tostig. You did everything that could be done. It would have served no purpose to stand outside the prison like a leper with a bell. A few days of that and they would have hauled you away to a prison cell of your own."

"There must have been a way, Richard! There must have been; but I was incapable of finding it."

4

It was a year or more after the death of Giselle that Richard rode over to pay his onetime squire another visit. He puffed a little as he swung himself down out of the saddle. Inside the house he looked about him and was impressed by the neatness of everything. The floor was covered with fresh rushes. The table was clear save for a bowl containing flowers. The oaken bink against the wall (a form of wooden bench much in use) was polished until it shone.

"For an unmarried man, Tostig," he said, "you keep things most neat and comfortable. Now my place . . ." He paused and sighed deeply. "Since my sweet lady died it has fallen into rack and ruin. Even in her last days she kept an eye on things and saw to it that the servants did their work well. Now they pay no attention to me. They fawn over my son and see that all his wishes are met. But for me? The points tear loose from my belt and I can't do anything with needle and thread. My bed coverings are musty."

"I know you too well to suggest that you find another wife," said Tostig.

"Another wife!" cried Richard with a passion which brought color into his cheeks. "Tostig, it was my great privilege and honor to have as my wife the loveliest lady in all the world. She was a queen in her own right, although it was never acknowledged. Could I degrade myself, and put shame on her memory, by finding another wife to take her place? Never, Tostig! I would rather live like a hermit in rags and filth.

"But I have a purpose in seeing you, Tostig," he went on, after a moment of saddened reflection. "I have come to ask a favor of you. It seems to me on looking backward—which is the only direction I dare look since the future is so black and dreary—that I have been asking favors of you all my life. It began with the time when I depended on you to help me cover my small feet on top of the monk's rail at Rawen Priory. You, my good friend, never failed to do whatever I begged of you."

"It was my duty and my pleasure," answered Tostig.

"This concerns my son. He has at last made up his mind. From the bevy of daughters and sisters and nieces of our neighbors—all of them ready to jump if he crooks a finger at them—he has chosen to marry the Lady Brigitta of Sillerdown."

Tostig gave this announcement a few moments of thought. Richard, watching him, was surprised to find that his hair had turned an iron gray and that his neck and shoulders had thickened perceptibly.

"A good choice, I think," was Tostig's conclusion. "I've seen her on occasions. A young lady of high spirit. And her dowry should be quite as handsome as her face."

"It's substantial," agreed Richard, nodding his head. "Some land, closer in to Dublin. A house in Kilkenny. Considerable money. What I want to say to you, Tostig, is this. Before my sweet lady left me, I made her a promise. You know what it was. She feared the boy's temper and pride would lead him into trouble if he knew of his descent. She didn't want him to know too early and I promised to keep it a secret until the proper time. I've kept the promise." He stopped for a moment and studied his companion's face as though wondering how far he should go with this explanation. "I might as well tell you the whole thing. I still have doubts. It's hard for a father to say this, but there is a streak of rashness in him, and other traits which I fear."

"If he is ever to know," said Tostig, "this is the time. Before he compromises his chances by marrying this girl."

"It's because I believe the same thing that I've come to you for advice. Should I act now?"

Tostig nodded gravely. "I think you should. Arthur has come to man's estate and should not be kept in the dark any longer. It's his own life and he should be allowed the chance of living it as he sees fit."

"It means that I shall lose him," said Richard, getting to his feet with a sigh.

"I am afraid the little Lady Brigitta may lose him also."

"He will resent my long silence. He lacks the fine brave quality of his lady mother. Ah, if she were only here! I dread the telling, Tostig. I dread the blame he will heap on me. He will blame me not only for keeping him in the dark so long but for being his father in the first place. Naturally he will realize that having a commoner father will prove his greatest handicap."

5

One night during the next week Richard went out into a cold rain to make sure that his prized stock was being properly looked after. The next morning he did not rise from his couch but coughed and tossed about in the grip of a heavy fever. The chirurgeon summoned from town could do little for him. He bled the sick man, of course, and tried to induce him to swallow many nauseous mixtures. Yielding unwillingly to these ministrations, Richard got no good from them. The fever gained on him, his breath turned to an ominous wheeze, his face was highly flushed. On the fourth day he ventured out on a new trail which he hoped, if he were capable of any kind of coherent thought, would bring him where the illustrious lady, who had been his wife, waited for him.

Tostig was away at the time of Richard's death. A certain Irish chieftain, with a band of poorly armed followers from beyond the Slieve Bloom, had raided the country along the Nore with an eye to the fat cattle and fine horses of that favored district. There was nothing unusual about this. Raiders could be expected at any time. A force would be hastily gathered and there would follow a few days of desultory skirmishing before the final clash, a hurly-burly of screeching kerns and shouting men-at-arms. A few throats would be cut, a few souls would wing their way upward or downward as the case might be. Sometimes the raiders would succeed in driving off some valuable livestock, although mostly they went back empty-handed.

On this occasion Tostig had led the defending force and had succeeded in administering a sharp check. He had returned well enough satisfied with the results although an arrow wound in the muscles of his left arm was proving highly painful. He sat very still in the saddle and his face went as white as those of the men who had fallen in the fighting when the news of Richard's death was conveyed to him by an aging Conn Ragen.

"Conn," he said, "this is hard to believe."

"It's God's truth, and unhappy I am in the telling of it."

Silence fell between the two men. Tostig was looking with stony face into the distance and wondering what life would hold for him now. The three people with whom his interests had been twined were gone. Now his days would be filled with the drudgery of work and the direction of the handful of people who worked on his land. Time, stretching ahead, had nothing to offer him.

"It is bad days we will be having," said Conn Ragen. He had never reached a friendly footing with Tostig but the fact of a mutual loss seemed to be lowering the barriers. "Himself loved the horses. But the son . . ." He shook his head slowly. "He brings them in covered with lather and with blood on their flanks. He beats them and he shouts his loud curses at them. And it's no more respect he has for flesh and blood. Sir Neighbor, he talks of getting rid of everyone and going down to the boats to buy slaves instead. One of my best young men ran away because he loved a girl down Wexford way. He," meaning the new owner of Green Hedges, "pursued him for a week and brought him back, and he applied the whip himself when my poor Godbin was tied to the post."

"The man had run away," said Tostig. "It's the law."

"Is it the law or is it not the law," cried Conn Ragen, "that a man may be pursued for four days only? It was six before Godbin was found. Sir Neighbor, it was the master who broke the law." There was a vibrant pause. "I am much feared there will be nothing but breaking of the laws from this day on."

Conn Ragen turned to ride away. "He is to be married within the month," he said over his shoulder.

Tostig was too surprised for a moment to make any response. Then he ran a few steps to overtake the horseman.

"Who is he to wed?"

"The one from Sillerdown. He pays no heed to his father's death."

Tostig said to himself as he walked away: "Then it's clear he hasn't been told. My poor Richard died without speaking to him. That young man would be looking for a different match if he knew the truth. Nothing less than a princess would satisfy him."

When his wife died, Richard had provided a grave for her in a clump of trees on his land and had raised a plain stone at the head which carried nothing but the name "Eleanor" and the date of her departure from this world. Tostig went there at once and looked down with saddened eyes at the new mound raised beside the first.

"Master," he thought, instinctively going back to the form of salutation he had first used, "you have left your old servant alone here and very unhappy. There is little in life for him, nothing but work and a final ending to it with no kind faces beside his last couch.

"And do you realize, master," his thoughts ran on, "that you have left me with a problem? I am the only one alive now who knows that your son is a direct descendant of Henry II." This was true because the Countess of Pembroke, the only other to share the knowledge, was long since dead. "What do you want me to do? Do you want me to tell and leave it to him to shape his future course? If I am to tell him, it must be done at once. To princes of the royal line an early marriage is an obstacle which can be removed. It has often been done. But I think your son would prefer to start without weights attached to his eager feet.

"What am I to do? If there was any way you could direct me, I would wait for your word and obey your wishes. But here, in the silence of the grave, I can do no more than guess. I am sorely perplexed because the answer must be found soon."

Before he found the answer to that question, he had an encounter with the young owner of the domain of Green Hedges which led to a change in the course he would otherwise have taken. He discovered one morning that a score or more of the valuable O'Rawn horses had been turned into a corner of his own pasturage. Riding out to find how this had come about, he encountered the debonair Arthur on his way there also.

"Young neighbor," said Tostig, "your men have made a mistake. This land belongs to me and I have other uses for it."

Arthur smiled with complete unconcern as well as a trace of scorn. "Not so, Sir Herdsman. This particular piece of land is mine. Most certainly mine."

"My grant says otherwise. See, to the left of your horse's hoofs, there is a whitewashed stone. Cast your eye down to that clump of oaks where the stream dips in closely. Do you see that white mark on the edge of the grass? That is the second stone. The line which runs between the markers, straight and true, is the boundary of the two properties. Your horses are right of the line, which means they are on my land. I have an immediate use for it. I am sorry to say that I am always short of proper pasturage."

"A pox on your marking stones and your boundary lines! I am certain it is land of mine. At one time all the land you occupy, right up to the Slippers, belonged to the holdings which are now mine. I am not being unreasonable, Sir Herdsman. I am taking back only a small strip."

Tostig was aware of a greater anger growing inside him than he had ever experienced before in all his life. But by the exercise of all the will power he possessed, he strove to master it, even to keep it from showing. He spoke quietly enough. "I am loath to quarrel with the son of the man I esteemed above all others. The grant I hold was made out under the eye of William the Marshal. It was compared with the copy of the paper granted to your dead father. There was no conflict. The boundary was clearly indicated. That land belongs to me."

Arthur O'Rawn was sitting his handsome black horse with easy grace. His long legs were bent slightly at the knees to accommodate them to the stirrups and he kept both gauntleted hands on the reins. There was a scornful twitch at his nostrils.

"What is in your mind?" he demanded. "It cannot be that you think of resorting to force?"

"Yes, I shall resort to force if necessary. But I beg you, young neighbor, to consider well before you drive me to that step. I would not want any of your fine blooded stock—the best in all Ireland—to suffer from the arrows I would loose among them."

"A clash between us might prove most disastrous for you," suggested the debonair youth, still smiling. "I have numbers on my side. And I have influence."

"I am hearing his grandfather, Prince Geoffrey, and his great-grandfather, old Harry Secund, speak through his mouth," thought Tostig. "How true he runs to form! He is a Plantagenet, and one of the worst of them."

"Why are you staring at me, Sir Herdsman?"

"I was thinking that your father was a great knight in his day who had the surest seat in the saddle in all Christendom. I wonder how much you take after him? Can you splinter a lance and keep your seat, even though your opponent rolls on the sod? You must have something of your father's power." He caught himself on the point of adding, "And of your great-uncle, the lionhearted Richard's," but checked himself in time. "You have thirty years the better of me. Would you care, young sir, to settle this dispute between us in personal combat?"

"It might be an interesting encounter," smiled the youth.

"The suggestion is mine, the choice of weapons would be yours. The lance? The mace? The broadsword? It occurs to me that I have heard you fancy yourself in tests of personal strength. You are adept at wrestling. On the latter point, I give you a word of warning. I could take you between my two arms and crack that proud spine of yours in two."

Richard's son gave his shoulders a shrug. "It has come to me, Sir Herdsman," he said, "that my courage might be questioned if I fought a man of your advanced years. Perhaps after all it would be best to leave this matter to the courts. It would be settled there quickly. And for all time."

Tostig said to himself, "He is very sure of this influence of which he spoke." He allowed no doubt to show in what he said, however. "The costs of going to court are heavy. Think it over well before you act. And in the meantime, be both reasonable and prudent. Take your horses back where they belong."

After a long delay, and with obvious reluctance, the horses were driven back to the O'Rawn side of the boundary. For weeks thereafter Tostig waited for his friend's son to take the next step but nothing happened. It seemed that the incident was ended.

But it was not ended. Not as far as Tostig himself was concerned. A short time before, while hunting for a knife in a pile of discarded matter, he had found his silver spurs, bound together and black with tarnish. He had held them in his hands and studied them for several moments, thinking what little good they had brought him. Then he had tossed them back with the rest.

Now he got them out again. With great care and industry, he polished them until they shone as brightly as when his squire had first strapped them on his heels.

"When I am called to join the loved friends who have gone before me," he thought, "there will be no one to uphold my claims. That gilded hoberdehoy will use his influence to get all of it into his hands. *That* must not be allowed to happen. Not," he said, with the depth of his feeling showing in the tightening of his lips and the knotting of his forehead, "if I have to resort to this step I have been fighting against all these years. I must have a son. A son of my own loins."

He attached the glistening silver spurs to his heels. He brushed the plume in a velvet hat he had not worn since the news had come of Giselle's death. He wrapped his once best cloak about him, glad to see that the excellence of the cloth had kept it in good condition. Thus attired, he rode into town.

6

The ladies who had been interested in him once had all been married long since. The blue-eyed daughter of the man who owned the other side of the Slippers had given her hand to a young Irishman from the far north and had a family of youngsters like steppingstones. But he had been aware for a while back of a widow who lived in the town and had sometimes passed him going into church. Her husband had been a linen weaver with a house on an ascending street above William the Marshal's great stone castle. It was wedged in between two large ones and was so small that it was an easy matter not to notice it at all.

It was to this humble domicile that Tostig directed his steps. His knock on the narrow door brought the widow to open it. She was wearing a starchy blue kirtle which rustled as she moved and a cap of the same color, and she looked very much surprised when she discovered the identity of her visitor.

"Madame, may I have a few words with you?"

She dropped a somewhat hurried curtsy. "Pray come in, Sir Tostig."

The ground floor of the house contained one long room only, at the back of which the weaver had worked at his looms. They were covered with cloths now but their presence left little space at the front for social uses. There were two chairs, a table, and little else.

"You will be seated, please."

Tostig took one of the chairs and looked so hard and long at her that she colored and lowered her eyes. He noticed with approval the length of her lashes and the air of extreme neatness about her.

"I do not believe in using a lot of words, madame," he said. "I like to come direct to the point. Your name is Sheila, is it not? May I ask you other questions?"

"Yes, Sir Tostig."

"Do you find being a widow to your taste?"

She looked up hurriedly and then dropped the long lashes again over her slate-colored eyes. This was coming quickly to the point with a vengeance.

"I know not, sir, the purpose of your question but it's an honest answer you will be wanting. No, I am not pleased. There are drawbacks to being a widow, sir."

"May I ask what they are?"

She began to speak slowly. "Men seem to think you have set your mind on being wed again and they—they bother you, sir. All the widowers and the unweds come to see you, and the"—she hesitated over the right word and then used a colloquialism—"all the silly old kimes of the town, even those with no teeth left and bald heads and bent over with the rheums. They think all they have to do is speak and you'll fall at their feet. I have been very rude and most of them have stopped coming."

"And what about your property, madame?"

Her manner changed. It was clear to be seen that in such matters she knew her own mind. "That is the worst of all, sir. The brothers of my poor husband—there are seven of them and nip-cheeses all of them —come here all the time. They ask questions, they want to know everything. They demand I turn what I have over to them. They are all in a rage because my husband left me this place and such money as he had. They catch me by the arms and shake me. They shove papers in front of me."

"Madame," said Tostig, nodding his head soberly, "all the laws have been drawn to take property rights away from women. When a rich heiress marries, she loses the control of her property. A widow is a target for everyone. Those seven sharp brothers will trap you if you are not careful."

A silence fell between them. Sheila reached nervously for a small workbasket on the table and began to employ her hands with some sewing task. Everything about her added to Tostig's resolution. "I think the good saints directed my steps here," he said to himself.

"Madame," he said, breaking the long pause, "I have never married. There was a reason of which I never speak and which I shall never explain. Save to say this: that what kept me from seeking a wife was not a disinclination to marriage."

An observant eye might have noticed that her hands, busy with the sewing, were none too steady at this point.

"How long have you been a widow?"

"Two years and a little matter of a month or so."

"How long were you married?"

"Six years, sir."

"And you bore your husband no children?"

At this question a flush mounted in her cheeks and even invaded her brow, which was quite wide and surprisingly white. "No, Sir Tostig. But my failure to bear children was not due"—she looked up at him for a moment as though to point the fact that she was borrowing his own words—"was not due to a disinclination to motherhood."

He began then to question her along less personal lines. "I was surprised to hear you use my name. I didn't think you were aware of my existence."

"Oh, sir, I have seen you at mass. Many times. Twice I saw you riding through town. And, of course, sir, there has been much talk of you. It's said you were knighted after a great battle, for your bravery. You might be surprised if you knew all the things that are said about you."

Tostig spread out one leg so the spur showed. "There is this much truth in it. I won my spurs in a battle. It was called the Fair of Lincoln, where the French were so badly beaten that Prince Louis took his army, what was left of it, back to France. I haven't worn them in many years. They had not been cleaned or shined in all that time until today when I decided I was coming to see you."

If her cheeks had shown a tendency to blush before, they really blossomed now in that telltale manifestation of womanly confusion.

"It's a pretty way of speech you have, sir."

He decided now to come as directly to the point as he had promised in the beginning. "Madame, I desire a wife. I don't want my land taken over after I die by neighbors or sharp men of the law. I want a son of my own. Or, better still, sons. I have seen you a few times only and our talk today has been very brief; but I have taken a liking to you. If I should ask you to marry me, and you were kind enough to say yes, do you think I might have my wish for sons fulfilled?"

The widow dropped the sewing in her lap and her hands became idle. She looked at him with grave eyes. She had dropped all feminine artifices, all the conventional hesitations and evasions. She spoke in a low voice.

"I—I think so. And if you do ask me, as I hope you will, I shall say yes, Sir Tostig. Quickly and happily."

Chapter XXVII

1

WHEN Arthur O'Rawn took his pretty heiress wife home he made a boast that was repeated all over the countryside. "I am going to have many sons," he declared. "Enough of them to have my own Round Table."

Within the year his wife was taken to bed and gave birth to a female child who was named Eleanor. The haughty young father was bitterly disappointed, particularly when he heard that Tostig's wife had chosen the same day to present her husband with a large and healthy son who was given the name of Sigurd.

The next year a second daughter arrived at Castle O'Rawn, to be given the name of Maude. In the same week Tostig became the father of a second son, who was christened Harold.

The third year, but with a month separating the events, the lady of Castle O'Rawn produced still another girl. This one was called Blanche. Tostig's wife had a third son, who was given the name of William after the old marshal.

Men began to laugh behind the back of the tall owner of Green Hedges and to say: "If he's going to fill the seats at that Round Table, he'll have to depend on the bastards all over the neighborhood who have that high and mighty nose of his and his yellow hair."

The race continued another year with exactly the same result: a girl named Joan at Castle O'Rawn, a boy named Patrick at the small house of Tostig. Patrick lacked the physical perfection of the first three. His entry into life had been a difficult one and his right leg had suffered. He never did attain the stature of his brothers and, because of the shortness of the one leg, he was to go through life as Paddy-with-the-Limp.

The race seemed to end at this point. Perhaps Tostig's wife felt she had done all that might be expected of her; at any rate, no more children arrived. The strain of childbearing had told on the chatelaine of Castle O'Rawn. Her plumpness and high color had deserted her. She seldom crossed the drawbridge over the dry moat but moped inside the walls, a pallid wraith of her former self. After five years, however, she made one more effort to give her demanding husband his wish. As her time drew close, there was much anxiety over her condition, much shaking of heads and conferring, in which the husband took no part. "One more female to find a husband for," he grunted. He was hunting when the accouchement took place and on his return a white-faced seneschal greeted him at the door of the keep.

"Hurry, my lord!" said the seneschal. "The angel of death hovers over us!"

"What do you mean?"

"Her ladyship!" quavered the officer of the household. "I am feared, my lord, she is very weak."

The quavering wail of a newborn child, that unmistakable whimper of an arriving soul, greeted the father's ears as he climbed the steps to the solar. The midwife and several maidservants stood about the tall Norman bed on which the lady of the house was lying, motionless and waxen of face.

"She has gone, sir!" said the midwife.

"What's the brat?" demanded the husband. "Another girl?"

"No, sir. A boy. And a healthy one he seems to be."

At first Arthur O'Rawn was incredulous of his good luck. He looked in the direction of the cradle from which the whimpering sounds proceeded. "A boy!" he whispered. Then he gave his thigh a resounding slap with a self-congratulatory palm. "A boy at last! I wasn't letting myself build any hopes on it. Anything wrong with him? 'Od's collarbone, I don't want a cripple like the one the weaver's widow presented to my neighbor, Squire So-and-So."

"There's nothing wrong with his legs, my lord. They're straight and strong."

The new-made father looked down at his own legs, which were probably the finest in all Ireland. "Takes after his sire, eh? 'Egad, I don't know of a better model." He rubbed his nose speculatively. "I think I shall name this son of mine Henry. They don't like the name hereabouts and they say they owe all their troubles to old Harry Secund. But, by St. Hubert, I have Norman blood in me from somewhere. Why shouldn't I call my son after the greatest of the Norman kings? Henry it shall be, and let them fume and spit their contempt!" He glanced with a hint of apprehension at the still figure on the bed. "I want more sons, so I suppose I'll have to find another wife."

With three noisy and active sons in the family, not to mention the quiet Paddy-with-the-Limp, Tostig had found it necessary to add a wing to his compact stone house. It jutted out from a side where the ground fell away sharply and so entailed the building of a stone-walled cellar. This was converted into a stable for the horses and cattle.

On the day of the arrival of the son and heir at Castle O'Rawn, Tostig came home early. He grinned affectionately at his wife, who was busying herself at the hearth with some preparations for the evening meal.

"A son," he announced.

Sheila turned about, holding a long metal spoon in one hand. She did not look a day older than she had on the memorable occasion when Tostig had called at her little house in the town.

"A son!" she exclaimed. "I'm happy for that poor woman. Now she won't have to go on endangering her life this way."

"No. She won't be concerned about such things any more. Sheila, she's gone."

"Dead!" His wife's eyes opened wide with the shock she felt and she crossed herself devoutly. "Oh, kind Mother of Jesus, have mercy on her soul! The poor frail thing."

"He'll marry again soon," predicted Tostig, seating himself by the fire. "It's said he's been casting an eye on the daughter of Turlough O'Byrne." He motioned with one hand. "From up north, you know. Connaught way. Turlough's as rich as a sultan and the girl's a good catch. Then it's said, too, that our fine neighbor with the roving eye has been seeing a certain widow in Dublin. The widow has ropes of pearls as long as her tinted hair and coffers filled with the fine yellow coins. It is my guess it will be the widow woman he decides on."

His wife was sprinkling herbs into the contents of an iron pot and filling the room thereby with a most delicious aroma. "Will this widow woman be giving him the sons he hankers after?"

They looked at each other for a moment in silence and then both smiled. "All widow women are not like you, dear wife," said Tostig.

"All four of them were out riding today," said Sheila. "The O'Rawn girls. I suppose they didn't want them to stay inside. Even the small Joan, sitting her pony like she was born to it. Ah, the sadness for them when they got home!"

"Did they stay on their own side of the boundary?" asked Tostig sharply.

"They did not. Man, man, 'tis no use to be getting angry at them, the poor childers. They're so full of good spirits. 'Tis a pleasant thing to hear them laughing and calling one to another. What harm does it do if they come over on our land once in a while?"

"Once in a while, wife? It's every day in the year, rain or shine or blowing hard. Something must be done about it."

"Leave them be, Tostig, leave them be."

"Where are the boys?"

He was watching his wife as they talked and marveling as always at the coolness of her. No matter how brisk the fire she had to tend, her brow remained white and clear. She looked up at him now with a smile which also was cool and pleasant to see.

"Where they always are. The three eldest, such busy rascals that they are, are out on their horses. Our poor little Paddy sits back there on his cot and studies his letters. And him with so few years!"

"It's not pity we should be giving the boy," declared Tostig. "That one will make his mark. He could sit down right now and read any book. Even though he's never seen one."

"He will make a fine priest, our little Paddy."

Tostig nodded proudly. "He has a clear fine head on him. If only the great archbishop were alive still! I would send our Patrick to him and he would make a cardinal of the boy."

2

Tostig had been correct in his guess. The master of Castle O'Rawn married the widow woman in Dublin and brought her home with him. They were followed by a long train of servants and men-at-arms, the bride traveling in a covered litter and occasionally looking out through the curtains to study the country. "How green it is," she said once. And then she shuddered. "And how very, very damp!"

She was a slender woman with red hair and green eyes. Her name was Tsigane.

When they reached the castle she went at once on a tour of inspection and, after the first few steps, she kept her nose muffled in a highly scented handkerchief. Things had been going to rack and ruin and the need for repairs could be noticed on every hand. Worst of all, the seepage from the garderobes had been piped to the outside walls and al-

lowed to drain down them, with no moat water to carry it away. Even
the inner bailey was not free of domestic animals, and a huge sow with
her brood had to be dislodged to make room for the dainty feet of the
newcomer. Inside the keep it was dark and gloomy and there was soon
a desperate look in the eyes of the new wife.

The son of the house toddled to greet her and was received with the
first sign of pleasure she had been able to display. When the four daughters came in from their morning ride, their eyes round with curiosity, it
was a different matter. She looked at them with an almost hostile light
in her jade eyes.

They were slender little creatures; fair and blue-eyed and bearing
the stamp of their grandmother's beauty on them. Their hair inclined
perhaps to the honey tint of blondeness rather than the vibrant Plantagenet yellow, and their eyes were less brilliant and more of a light corn-
flower shade. To some tastes they would seem even more lovely than
the Pearl of Brittany. Their stepmother greeted each one of them, repeating their names and saying how beautiful they were, even patting
their cheeks in a perfunctory way.

Then Tsigane took her husband by the arm and led him to a bench
in what passed as the Great Hall.

"My handsome barbarian!" she said. "Is this where you expect me
to live?"

"This," declared Arthur proudly, "is Castle O'Rawn, your new home."

"In spite of your masterful ways, my sweet spouse, you have never
grown up," declared the new wife. "Did you expect me to settle down
and spend the rest of my life in this hog sty? How could gentle people—
I am granting you gentility, my own—exist in such a place? Arthur,
Arthur, those garderobes! This terrible odor!"

The master of the castle had turned red with mortification and an
anger he dared not express. He felt like a schoolboy caught in some
gross error as he faced the accusing green eyes of his new wife.

"How long is it since these rushes were changed?" she asked, pointing to the floor.

"Not more than a year," he declared defensively.

"A year? They should be changed much oftener. Three or four times
a year. I have known places where they were changed"—she paused to
lend additional emphasis—"every month."

"I am afraid," said Arthur, the picture of dejection, "we have been
getting careless since my first wife died."

"Nonsense, my beloved simpleton! Your wife has been dead less than a year. What I see here is the result of years of neglect. How can these pretty children exist in such a place?"

The father of the pretty children could think of nothing more to say than, "They've always lived here."

"Are they clean? I have a suspicion they are not. And who looks after their clothes?"

"Why look at me? Is it the duty of a father to attend to such things?" He laughed scornfully. "This is the first time I have thought of it. There are servants to look after the children."

"These dirty sluts I've seen around the place?"

There was a moment of silence while the new wife gave careful thought to the situation. Then she nodded her head with decision. "Arthur, listen closely to what I am going to say. I want you to believe that I mean it. We are going to get to horse at once and return to Dublin. I have no intention of remaining here and I shall never return. For two reasons. The first I have already told you; I couldn't live in such a wallow. The second reason is your four daughters."

"What's wrong with them?" cried the head of the family, his mouth open in the slackness of utter bewilderment.

"Nothing at all. They are the most beautiful young creatures I have ever seen. If they are properly looked after, they will become quite ravishing. *That* is the difficulty. Do you think, my great foolish fellow, that I could live with them about me? I don't want you to lose your respect for my own charms but—but do you think I want to look like an aging dowager surrounded by lovely ladies in waiting? At my first glimpse of them, I shuddered. I was thinking of the future. I felt chilled—as though a cold wind was blowing across the grave of my own pretensions."

Arthur O'Rawn did not reply. All this was beyond his understanding. He stood before his new wife and wondered what she meant.

"We are going back to Dublin. Now." The new wife's tone was filled with decision. Her mind was made up and nothing was going to change it. "We'll take the little boy with us. He is a sweet babe and it will be a pleasure to raise him properly. Those four lovely angels straight from heaven will remain here. We will find some female relative to take them in charge. Have you any unmarried cousins or aunts on your family tree?"

Her husband had to confess that he knew nothing of his lineage. "I suspect my father was Norman," he said, "but I could never get him to tell me anything. The four girls resemble my mother, who was the most beautiful woman in the world. I always thought she looked like a Plantagenet princess."

"Well, I am afraid we can't ask King Henry III to spare us some distant relative for the purpose. I shall have to find someone on my side. And I'll send down my own Torfrida first to see that this place is cleaned from top to bottom. Those poor children can't be left a day longer than is necessary in such condition."

The perplexed husband decided that the time had come to assert himself. He swallowed hard and began to speak in explosive tones. "I was born here and I have lived here all my life. There is no sweeter country in the world. The grass is rich and the horses I raise can't be equaled anywhere. It is here I want all my sons to be born and raised."

The new wife rose and took him by the arm. "Calm yourself, my beautiful and beloved barbarian, my tall charmer," she said. "The first thing for you to understand, and to accept, is that there will be no more sons. There will be no more children. Is that understood? We have more children at this moment than we need. Four more, in fact."

Her view of the future proved to be correct. She settled her husband down with her in the house she owned in Dublin. There were no more sons. There were no more children.

The woman Torfrida arrived at Castle O'Rawn and for a matter of weeks there was such a flurry of house cleaning as had never been heard of before in all of Kilkenny. Carpenters were brought in, and masons, and men to do plastering. The inside of the keep was scraped and washed and cleansed. The sheds in the inner bailey were torn down and replaced by new. The domestic animals were moved to pen and byre and sty. Then a formidable relative of the new wife arrived to take charge of the household. She was a stout widow with a stern eye and a will. The servants jumped at her bidding and no one dreamed of disobeying her. She took the four daughters of the house in hand and saw to it that they were well looked after and fed properly and clothed as young ladies of high station should be. A new order had been established at Castle O'Rawn and, it must be acknowledged, a better one.

The master of the domain returned at intervals, generally to see that the feeding and training of the horses proceeded on proper and orderly lines. He was glad, of course, to find that his four daughters were growing up and becoming more lovely all the time. His second wife never accompanied him.

The four girls became more adept in the handling of horses as the years rolled on. Each day they went riding in a body and sometimes they used a level stretch of land close to the boundary for racing. Their high clear voices and their laughter could then be heard as far as the house Tostig had built. The sons of Tostig often walked over to the line to watch, and this always put a certain restraint on the proceedings. The pretty blonde heads of the four girls would be raised high in the air and never under any circumstances would they look in the direction of the four silent watchers. Their noses seemed to stay up in disdain and they giggled among themselves and passed inaudible comments, undoubtedly uncomplimentary. The boys, who were dark and stocky, never said a word, even among themselves. They would watch for a while and then go away in a body, still silent. They knew that the daughters of the house of O'Rawn regarded them as inferior beings and in a silent, dark way they resented it.

Their mother resented it openly. "Them!" she would say to her sons. "Proud and spiteful and as silly as twittering birds! Don't they know your father rides with silver spurs at his heels? Has no one told them he was a great man in his day and that kings and earls and bishops listened to what he had to say?"

Something quite different happened on one occasion. The youngest of the four girls, the little Joan, came out alone and at the time only Patrick was within range. She rode carelessly over the boundary and within speaking distance of him.

"I suppose you are going to tell me I'm trespassing," she remarked, tossing her head in the air.

"You are on our land, demoiselle," said the boy. "But I had no intention of mentioning it."

"You should consider it an honor for me to be on your land."

"I think it a great pleasure, demoiselle, to see you here," answered the boy. "But I don't regard it as an honor."

Little Joan wrinkled up her forehead for a moment as though she did not understand the distinction he was drawing. Then she began to laugh.

"I see what you mean. There is a difference, isn't there?"

Patrick was not holding his head down as the sons of Tostig usually did when the girls of O'Rawn were in sight. He was looking straight up at her and thinking: "She's the prettiest of them all. What a lovely nose and what bright eyes! Her hair is like the sun!"

"Yes, demoiselle," he said. "But I did not want to seem rude."

"Aren't you the one they call Paddy-with-the-Limp?"

"Yes, I am called Paddy-with-the-Limp."

"They say," declared the girl, "that you are the best of the lot."

And then she kicked a heel into the flank of her horse and was off, giving him a smile of farewell over her shoulder.

Things were different after that, for the small Joan as well as for Paddy-with-the-Limp. When the girls rode by she was always the last in line and, if his brothers did not seem to be noticing, she would raise her hand and wave to him.

To Patrick this was the beginning of something as wonderful as a sunrise or the smooth pull of a bow in his hand (he was a skillful archer) or even the free action of a finely brèd horse. But one day he discovered it was not a beginning at all, that it was instead an ending. There were only three girls riding that day and he heard when he returned home that the small Joan was sick.

His mother said to him, "'Tis the pox the small one has." Her tone hinted at solicitude but there was a matter-of-factness about it as well, for illness and death were everyday affairs. That all of the children of the master of O'Rawn Castle had survived so far was nothing short of miraculous in an age when six or seven out of ten died in their earliest infancy.

Patrick had kept his interest in the youngest of the four girls locked up tightly inside himself. He still thought it necessary to affect a casual tone in speaking. "Is the pox very dangerous?" he asked.

"'Tis sure death, Patrick, my son," was the answer. "Only three of them will we be seeing ever again from this day."

Then she sensed that his attitude was not casual. She turned and looked at him sharply. His face was white and he compressed his lips tightly to keep his emotions under control.

"Patrick, did you like the small one?" she asked.

He swallowed hard before venturing to respond. "Yes, Mother mine," he said. Several moments passed before he found it possible to ask a question. "What are they doing for her?"

"'Tis said, my son, that they've removed her to the old house."

"Do you mean," in incredulous tones, "where the horses are kept?"

She was watching him closely now, with an aroused motherly alarm. "You see, when it's the pox, there's nothing can be done for the one struck down. It's in the hands of the Holy Father and the blessed saints. But this black kind of death can't be let to get at others like a snake weaving through the grass. No one is allowed to go near for fear of catching it. Even the chirurgeon has to be very careful. Oh, very careful indeed."

"Do you mean," he asked in an ominously still voice, "that the Lady Joan is alone? That no one goes near her?"

"That's the way it always is, my son." Then she sensed for the first time the depth of his feeling. He reached for his hat, hanging on the wall with those of his three brothers, on the last of the pegs, of course. "Where are you going? You must do nothing foolish, my son."

"I am going there. Surely, Mother, there is something can be done. I must find out. I must!"

"Patrick, my foolish son!" cried his mother. "You mustn't go near. You'll catch it yourself. And you'll be bringing it back to your brothers and your good father. You must think of them."

"There's only one thing I can think of, Mother: that I must go at once."

The house to which Richard of Rawen had taken his princess wife when they first came to Ireland was hard to recognize. Large doors had been opened at each end and the partitions inside had been removed to make way for stalls. The doors were kept wide open and a continuous sound of neighing and of stamping hoofs could be heard. Three men in woolen drawers to the knee and armless shirts worked thereabouts with mattock and spade and the tools of grooming. At this particular season the horses were out at pasture but the three seemed to have no difficulty in keeping busy. Conn Ragen, with his long white beard and head as bald as a tonsured monk's, came by at regular intervals to make sure they did.

An ancient wooden shed leaned crazily against one wall of the main building. Its door was closed and barred and its single window had been covered with an old shutter, nailed tight to the frame. Cracks and crevices everywhere had been stuffed with remnants of cloth. Piles of refuse rotted against the boards and even the valiant hens were being kept at a distance.

A man sat on a three-legged stool sufficiently far from the place to be free of danger but close enough to prevent any attempt at opening the door. Patrick knew this was the chirurgeon from the tools and properties of his trade which were on display about him. He was, above everything else, a drawer of teeth; for teeth were not easy to keep, they dropped out of a night or were jerked loose with strings or, if they were obdurate and refused to be got rid of by such means, the chirurgeon used some curious kind of instrument which brought them out in a great hurry. This particular caterer to the science of bodily comfort had set up two sticks in the ground with a rope between them from which dangled already a dozen trophies of his skill. A basin on the ground at his feet was an invitation to step forward and be shaved, for barbering was also one of his major occupations.

At a still greater distance from the lean-to, the three sisters of the sick child sat silently together in the shade of a clump of trees. They were looking pale and unhappy and for once they said little.

Limping more than usual in the intensity of his mood, Patrick approached the man into whose far from clean hands the fate of the youngest daughter of the house had been entrusted.

"Where is the Lady Joan?" he asked.

The chirurgeon paid no attention to him at first. It became quite apparent that the man of medicine had been doing more than attend his patient and perform a little dentistry and barbering as the chance arose. A nearly empty tankard on the ground beside him, and a vagueness of eye and uncertainty of movement, indicated that he was well advanced in his cups.

"Can a broomstick make a coward of me?" he demanded of Patrick in a belligerent tone. "I am a man of courage, I tell you. Did I not draw a bow in the fighting up Cashel way many years agone? It's true, and I acknowledge it freely, that I did not kick the heels of the bold Bart Turrough, our leader. Can everyone be in front? Do you want it in a quiditty? It is impossible for more than a few to be in the first rank. I yielded the honor with the best of grace. Then," scowling at Patrick, "what is all this talk of broomsticks?"

"I don't know, sir. I came to see the Lady Joan."

"No one can see her," declared the giver of health and comfort, holding out a restraining arm. "Broomsticks!" he went on bitterly. "What if I did hand in the medicines to her on the head of a broom? The tincture of saffron and the salt of wormwood, than which the best doctor in Paris town could do no better. It was not a broom of long handle so I could remain outside in the clean air the while. Had it been so, then perhaps the tongues might have waggled. I tell you this, young fellow, the broomstick I used was no more than four feet in length."

"Did she drink the medicines, sir?"

The beery eyes of the savior of the ill became doubly bellicose. "Questions, is it now? From the mouths of sucklings. She did not drink those inspired potions! Am I to be blamed for that? Was her mind clear so she could tell what I told her? I do not know. Was she strong enough to reach the medicines? That I do not know either. I had done my duty. What more can be asked?"

Patrick saw that he must employ bold methods if he expected to get by the man of medicine. He drew closer, pointing to a broom on the ground and asking, "Is that the one you used?" The chirurgeon glanced down and at that instant Patrick kicked one of the three legs of the stool, sending him sprawling on the ground. In a matter of seconds he had thrown back the bar and opened the door of the temporary pesthouse.

A heavy and sickening odor poured out from the dark interior and he had to clamp a hand over his nose before venturing in. He could make out a small cot against the interior wall but it was difficult to see much of the small figure lying upon it.

He began to weep in the extremity of his grief. "Sweet little lady, what have they done to you?" he asked aloud. "Is it too late? Oh, is it too late!"

The chirurgeon, not daring to venture within the door, was bellowing commands to him to come out. Patrick paid no attention. He could now see that there was a small table beside the bed, on which were two containers filled with the medicines conveyed to the sickroom on the head of the broom. It was apparent that neither had been touched. The red hangings strung around the bed on a cord (there was a belief among the medically learned that red had a curative effect on victims of the pox) had collapsed in a heap. The cover of the same color was wrapped in a crumpled pile about her feet. The intruder did not raise his eyes to the inflamed face of the sufferer.

"My lady!" he said. "My lady Joan! Can you hear me?"

There was no response. The form on the bed did not move.

"Answer me, my lady!" he entreated. "This is Paddy-with-the-Limp. You remember me. You spoke to me once. So nice and friendly. You waved to me many times. Oh, sweet lady, I want to help you!"

The body still did not move. No sound of breathing reached his ears. He waited a few moments longer, hoping for some evidence to disprove what he feared. Finally, convinced, he turned and stumbled to the door, blinded by his tears.

"It's too late," he said to the chirurgeon. "The Lady Joan is dead!"

The man of medicine retreated hastily to avoid contact with him. The three sisters, making mewing sounds of grief and repugnance, turned and ran in the direction of the castle.

For a week after the wasted body of the youngest sister had been laid in the grave, Patrick lived in a grain crib and his mother brought his meals out and deposited them in the Marshal's Seat. This was a stone shaped like a chair, so called because old Earl William had once rested in it while he sampled a flagon of native brew. At the end of the week the youth was as clear of cheek and sound of health as he had ever been; and so, his old clothes having been burned, he dressed himself in new leggings and tunic and took his place again in the life of the household.

During his period of sequestration he had spent much time gazing across the property line at the O'Rawn domain. A hatred of everything he saw grew in him because of the negligence which had condemned the little Joan to a loathsome death. He came to hate the castle on the hill, the three daughters who had occasionally put in an appearance, the servants who went about their tasks, the doddering Conn Ragen, the fields, the hedges, the trees. The horses alone were not included in this bitterness of feeling. He still admired them and watched with wide eyes of admiration the fineness of them, the grace and ease of their pacing.

Chapter XXVIII

1

WHILE the annals of the two families were thus enfolding in Ireland, there was a continuous struggle in England to maintain the Great Charter. Henry III, son of John, was proving himself an oath-breaking, conniving, sly, indecisive, wasteful, boastful, stupid king. His one consistent aim was to be rid of this Charter which imposed restrictions on his divinely given right to rule as he pleased. Every time he broke it, however, his muddleheadedness or his indolence or his treachery would involve him in fresh difficulties and, to get out of them, he would once more swear to be a good king. The promise made, he would send off in great haste to the Pope to secure absolution in advance for breaking his oath still another time; and so very soon again the nation would suffer the unedifying spectacle of the crowned simpleton pounding with an impotent hammer at the bars he hated.

Events were shaping, nevertheless, for the next great advance along the road to freedom. There was in England at this time a nobleman of high lineage named Simon de Montfort, who was married to Henry's beautiful and high-spirited sister Eleanor (so many of the royal Eleanors were beautiful and high-spirited that it is hard to keep their identities separate) and in time would wrest power from Henry's feeble grasp long enough to establish the right of common men to sit in Parliament with barons and bishops.

England's constitutional advances were not being followed in other countries but in all other directions the ice of the Dark Ages was breaking. Men were beginning again to think, to create, to sing, to paint, to build magnificently. The tall spires of the breath-taking cathedrals were rising to the clouds. The Holy Ghost hospitals were being opened in all large cities. The first light of the Renaissance in arts was burning fitfully through the medieval murk. Most important of all, perhaps, was another contribution from England. A Franciscan monk named Roger Bacon was to settle down in Oxford and to produce during the latter half of the century a new conception of research on which the advances in modern times in science and industry would be based. Bacon is given credit for the invention of gunpowder, which perhaps should be put on the other side of the ledger. Certainly, however, this remarkable monk, living and dying in obscurity, predicted a day when men would see great distances through cylinders of glass and sail through the air in flying ships.

2

Tostig was now an old man. Always stocky, his shoulders had become as bulky as a bear's, and he moved with difficulty. He seldom got to horse, preferring to occupy the Marshal's Seat and direct his sons from there, like a rusty old knight with four squires.

With the advance of the years, he had come more and more to depend on Paddy-with-the-Limp. "Well, my son," he would say when some small crisis faced them, "what do you think we should do now?" Patrick would begin to speak but he seldom got very far. The old man would clap him on the back and say: "You have it, my boy. I knew that would be your way of thinking but I wanted to be sure. You and I, we are very much alike."

Meals were eaten in silence, save for the remarks which passed between husband and wife. When the last slice of bread, serving as a plate, had been raised on the tip of a knife and engulfed, when the last gulp of wine or beer had brought the repast to a close, Tostig would get slowly to his feet. "Wait until I am out of earshot, my sons," he would say, "and then you may gabble as much as you like." Their mother would remain with the four and their eager chatter would sometimes reach the ears of the old man as he sat in the comfort of the Marshal's Seat, all but the voice of little Patrick, who spoke in low tones. He would hear Sigurd talking stubbornly, Harold angrily, William in flights of noisy fancy. Sometimes he would shake his head and mutter: "The only complaint I have of that woman of mine is that she didn't bear me Patrick first. Then I could have willed him the land."

One day when all four had come to the years of manhood, he summoned his sons to his presence. They came dutifully and squatted in a row in front of him. Their mother followed them out, thinking she would be wanted at a family council, but Tostig waved an imperious hand at her. "Go away, wife," he said. But the sight of her walking slowly back to the house, her head held low, caused him to change his mind. "Come back!" he called. "You may be of help to me." He even went to the length of ensconcing her in his seat and remaining on foot himself.

His first words made it clear that he had become deeply religious. "There are times, my sons, and you also, wife, when I feel a kinship with Moses. Was it not said that when he was one hundred and twenty years of age, and marked for death, he went up from the plain of Moab unto the mountain of Nebo and looked out over the Promised Land? From there he studied the country which was to be divided among the children of Israel and decided where each tribe was to go." His eyes passed quickly over his three eldest sons and then came to rest on Patrick. "The time has come for me to decide what is to be done with the land deeded to us by the good old earl. How best can the interests of all of you be helped? If I divided it up equally among you, I would be condemning you to lives of want. There is not enough land here for four families to subsist on with any degree of plenty. When your children grew up and had children of their own, these fair acres would become as squalid as the Valley of the Cheesemakers in the Holy City. I have thought it over with the deepest care and have decided it cannot be done that way."

After a moment's pause, he nodded in the direction of his wife. "I have discussed this with you but not with our sons. I know they have thought me grasping because I have expected them to work without wages for their toil, and have kept them from clothing themselves in fine linens so they could go to the fairs and buy presents for young wantons. What they have not known is that every penny I could get my hands on has been saved against the day when I must die. When that happens, the land will go to the first-born, to Sigurd. The money I have saved will be divided among the other three. It is my advice to you, Harold, and to you, William, that you take your share of the money and your share of the livestock, and seek land elsewhere. To the north and the west of us there is much that is not being put to use."

Sigurd was looking triumphant while Harold and William appeared glum and disappointed. Patrick did not seem much concerned, for he had never expected that any of the land would be his.

"My dear sons," said the mother, "your father is thinking of your best interests. We have talked it over many times and have not been able to see any other course."

"You must not think I am being partial to Sigurd," said Tostig. "He will be starting with no more than his own share of the stock. He will face the danger that our covetous neighbor will go to law and perhaps steal some of the land from him. His lot may not be an easy one at all."

"We must remember that he is the first-born," said the mother gently.

Tostig turned to face Patrick. "On you, Paddy, I am laying a heavy burden. I expect you to remain here. To help Sigurd with the flocks, to give him the wise counsel I know you capable of, and to stand beside him in the event of trouble with the O'Rawn family. Are you prepared to do that?"

There was a moment of silence and then Patrick said, "I am ready to do your bidding, Father."

Tostig then turned to his first-born. "And now, Sigurd, I lay this injunction on you. You must agree that Patrick is to have a share of whatever profits you make. I think the fairest plan would be to base the division on the number of children each of you brings into the world. I am certain, Sigurd, that you will marry soon and beget plenty of children."

"That is as it may be," declared the first-born, scowling darkly.

"I have no intention of taking a wife," said Patrick quietly.

"In the event you do not marry, you will receive a quarter of the profits. Under no circumstances are you to have more than a share of three sevenths, Sigurd being the oldest son." The old man looked from one son to the other. "Is all this understood? Are you in agreement with the plan I have made?"

Patrick said at once, "I am content, Father." Sigurd was the next to agree, although his manner lacked cordiality. Harold and William sat for some time in sullen thought before declaring their willingness to abide by the arrangements. Harold said finally: "There is a young woman who fills my eye. Give me my share now and I will marry her and go to find some of this land you speak of." William, as perhaps befitted his Norman name, had a different plan. "I am tired of raising wool. I would rather be concerned with the selling of it. Give me my share now and I will go to Dublin."

When left alone, Tostig sat for a long time, staring at the western sky where the sun was sinking behind a rack of threatening clouds. Then he studied the crest of the Slippers and came finally to the clump of trees in which he had erected his house. A garden of autumn flowers supplied a red oasis in the sea of green. "There's no place more beautiful in the world or more peaceful," he said to himself. Then his thoughts took another course. "How strange things have turned out. We had high hopes when Richard and I planned the escape from Corfe Castle. We were certain the princess would be chosen when John was put out of the way, and Richard asked nothing better than to go on serving her for the rest of his life. He wanted to carry her colors on his lance, and fight for her, and die for her. I was much clearer in my mind about my part in things. I would marry Giselle and become in time chancellor to the queen. Why not? I would have been her brother-in-law, albeit by the left hand. And I knew I was better fitted for the post than anyone else."

He shook his head glumly as his thoughts ran on. "And now the princess is long dead and my poor Richard has followed her into the grave. No one, saving myself, has any idea who they were, that beautiful golden-haired lady and her gallant husband. And here am I, grown heavy of body and slow of mind, a small raiser of sheep in a foreign land. I have only one thing left to do before I lay my old bones down: to make sure that the secret the three of us shared among us does not die with me."

Tostig had felt the end of things drawing on but time dragged slowly. A few years later he roused himself when a message reached him that raiders were riding in from the west. He was needed to command the defense against them. Four times in the past he had been asked to undertake this task, and four times he had been successful.

"I think my bones will stand one more shaking up," he said to himself as he buckled on a breastplate of hardened leather and donned a steel cap. He gave his sword a cut or two before getting into the saddle and it seemed to him that his arm was not lacking in strength. "This is the last time. I won't be here if there are more raids."

The results followed the pattern of previous contests. The raiders were repulsed and driven back into the mists and the autumnal winds from which they had emerged. The parallel was even closer, for Tostig himself returned with an arrow wound, as on a previous occasion. It was not in the arm this time. The shaft had penetrated his right breast.

He was very weak when they brought him home and helped him down from his horse. A mist seemed to be obstructing his vision and he lacked the strength to walk. He sighed with intense relief when his youngest son put an arm around his shoulders.

"God be praised, it is you!" he said in a hoarse whisper. "I have things to—to say to you."

"Where is Sigurd?" asked Patrick apprehensively. The first-born of the family had ridden with his father because neither Harold nor William was available. Harold had married the young woman who filled his eye and had betaken himself into the north. William was in Dublin, where he had a booth of his own with a scrivener and an apprentice; and reports had it that he was doing very well.

"Sigurd is safe," whispered the old man. "He rode on with the pursuit. They are—they are to be taught a lesson this time." After a long pause, while his breathing became heavy and painful, he went on. "Let me lie here, my son. On our own fine green turf. I don't want to die in my bed. Listen, listen well, to what I have to say."

Patrick's eyes opened wide with wonder when he learned that the beautiful mother of their arrogant neighbor had been the Lost Princess of Brittany. "He does not know," went on the old man, referring to Arthur O'Rawn. "When his father died, the duty of telling him fell to me. And now it is too late for that. I leave the secret with you, my son."

"We have heard," said Patrick, "that the master of the O'Rawn lands is taking steps to seize some of ours. Is it your command that I am to tell him the truth about his descent? It will go bitterly against the grain, my father. He considers us as dirt beneath his feet."

These were the last words that Tostig heard spoken before the darkness, which happily would not last long, closed about him.

Here ends the story told by Richard O'Rawn
to John Foraday.

BOOK THREE

Chapter I

1

I T W A S again the hour which had been dedicated, at one time, to cocktails but which now, alas, was no more than the quiet space of time immediately preceding the serving of a very plain dinner. Richard O'Rawn was seated again on the open terrace of his Riviera villa, watching the sun disappear in the western sky and thinking, no doubt, that it was a very inferior sunset to what he would see if he were back at his home in the American West. John Foraday emerged from the house with an air of triumph and a bundle under his arm.

"It's finished!" he announced.

"Well now," said the old man, "that's good news. You've had your nose to the grindstone for a long time, my boy."

"I typed the last sentence at five twenty-three exactly. And here it is, neatly packed and ready to be sent off. Boy, what a relief! Don't you think we could celebrate a little tonight?"

The old man sat up in his chair. "Martinis!" he exclaimed. "And we'll open a bottle of wine with the dinner. This is a great occasion and must be commemorated properly." He threw back his head and bellowed, "Peterkin!"

John almost skipped as he made his way to a chair. He sat down and sighed with explosive relief. "Do you think they'll publish it?"

"Why not?" said the old man. "Haven't you told them I'm ready to take the rap and acknowledge it to be my own true story?"

Peterkin arrived with two cocktails on a tray. Two, no more. No shaker with the ammunition for dividends.

"When I saw Mr. John with the package under his arm," said the servant, "I knew you would be yelping for a drink. I decided to give in graciously, boss. I didn't wait for orders. I just came."

"Graciously perhaps but not generously," grumbled the former senator, with an eye on the contents of the tray.

"You shouldn't be having it, celebration or no celebration," declared Peterkin sharply.

"For God's sake, take that doleful mug of yours out of my sight!" said the old man. "I want to enjoy this one little lonely drink."

While they sipped their martinis, Richard O'Rawn asked many questions, chiefly about John's reactions to the events he had been setting down on paper. Finally he came to an important one.

"Do you think that life behind the Iron Curtain is as bad today as the kind of thing I have been telling you about the days of Magna Charta?"

"I know it's grim. But I have no way of comparing."

The old man settled back into his chair and shifted his gaze to the east, where the clouds were banked up, a menacing black-gray. "The conditions are different, of course. They have doctors in Russia, and dentists, and there are railway trains, and some automobiles and telephones. They have planes. They even have radio. But, my boy, they are no better off than the poor villeins in King John's day. Why? Because they lack personal freedom. They can't do what they want, they can't say what they please. Even what they should think is dictated to them. *And they are bound to the land!* That is what does it, they can't leave the country, they can't even travel without permission. That, and their lack of a say in things. They have no more than a mockery of the right to vote."

He paused. The heaviness of the eastern sky seemed like a symbol of the life lived beneath it. "Instead of one master, they have many; enough of them to fill arenas at convention times when the self-appointed bosses get together—tough fellows, sly, unscrupulous, cruel. There are King Johns in the villages, in city blocks, in the factories, in the regiments. How long do you think men can live under such conditions without the world in which they exist slipping back to the Dark Ages again?"

John indulged in a rather shamefaced grin. "Do you know, Uncle Richard, when you first started to tell me your story, I had a secret impression that I could have enjoyed living in the thirteenth century. I had visions of wandering about the country in a green jerkin—no, not a jerkin, that didn't come into use for quite a while, I looked it up—with a harp over my shoulder, singing in country inns and tossing off bumpers of ale——"

"The ale," interjected the senator, "was never chilled and it was as flat as stale soda pop."

"It seemed to me fine and noble to ride in tournaments and make love to beautiful ladies."

"John, John, that is one of the great myths. Some of the ladies were lovely enough. When they were young and healthy—up to the age of twenty-five, say—they had fresh complexions and they were quite lively. But they couldn't read, they had never been anywhere, they were dumb, by our standards."

John grinned again. "Well, as the story went on, I got over all that. Everything you told me helped to dispel my illusions. For instance that poor groom who couldn't marry the girl he wanted unless they ran away and became outcasts, sleeping under hedges and wandering always like gypsies."

"That was taken care of. Stephen Langton bought the man's freedom."

Peterkin came out on the terrace. "Dinner is ready, boss, and Mr. John," he announced. "There's a steak tonight."

"Peterkin," cried the old man, "you have a heart after all!"

John had been so deeply absorbed in his work that he had paid little attention to his surroundings. He looked about him now, when they entered the dining salon, and saw it practically for the first time: a gracious room, lighted only with an abundance of candles (a luxury imposed on them by the whims of the owner), looking out over the terrace to the almost Stygian darkness of the Mediterranean. The apartment had four french doors, curtained and valanced in blue and gold, a rare tapestry, and an old master which John regarded with awe if not critical admiration.

"I would be sorry to leave this place now that the work is done," he said, "if the prospect of another visit to Ireland didn't seem so—so very much better."

When the senator had finished a second helping of the beefsteak and, because of this indulgence had refused the creamy concoction reluctantly proffered as dessert by Peterkin, he sat back in his chair. "And now, John," he announced, "I come to the important point, my reason for having you looked up in the first place and for bringing you here with me."

"Yes," said John, feeling a certain constriction of the heart in the intensity of his interest. "I—I haven't asked you any questions. But I've been waiting."

"The reason," went on the old man, "why I broke my engagement to your grandmother. I've dreaded coming to the point, my boy. I'm not sure you are going to accept my explanation." He looked about him for the humidor but failed to see it. "Peterkin, no cigars tonight?"

"No cigars," said Peterkin, putting his head in through the door and then withdrawing it.

The senator groaned. "That makes it still harder. I think I could have made out a better case for myself with a good cigar between my teeth. But I'm sure he's right." He paused and then looked at John and smiled. "Well, here goes."

2

"I was twenty-six years old," began the senator. "Doing well in business. Getting a foothold in the political world. I had money saved up. I was engaged to be married to a lovely girl—and I was very happy about it. The world was my oyster. Young Dick O'Rawn was going places. And then I suddenly became very ill. A fever took hold of me and I lost consciousness. The doctors told me all about it later. Of the days when they didn't expect me to pull through. How I tossed about in the grip of a high temperature, and gabbled in delirium. They called it by a name I don't hear at all nowadays. Brain fever.

"I came through it with difficulty. While I was so very ill something most peculiar happened to me. Perhaps there's a part of every brain which is closed off. Perhaps it carries a sign which the rest of your intelligence machine respects. Marked, *Keep Out, This means you.* My thoughts had taken possession of this forbidden territory.

"I found myself sitting on a sunny field which was filled to overflowing with strange men. Some were in what would have seemed like fantastic costumes to anyone else. Most of them wore armor. They talked in an almost foreign tongue and they used queer words. But not for me. I understood what they were saying. I felt completely at home. I knew why I was there and that the name of the great field was Runnymede. I knew my name was Tostig and that I was a special kind of squire to my lord the archbishop. I knew that Richard of Rawen was in Ireland, that he was married to the Princess Eleanor. I had been with them a short time before and I remembered everything we had said and done. I remembered Giselle. As soon as I thought of her, I could think of nothing else. She was in prison and I didn't know how we could get her free.

"You may find it hard to believe, my boy, that I had no sense at all that this was a dream. I was sure that the other was the dream—my nineteenth-century existence. I was sure I had wakened up and come back to real life again. I remember saying to myself: 'How clear it all was! What a long dream it must have been! And what a strange and wonderful world it was that I was seeing!' I sat there in wonderment about this great life; and all the time exciting things were going on about me, there on the field of Runnymede. There was a constant clashing of arms and blaring of trumpets around the pavilion. History was being made but for the moment I didn't care. I kept thinking: 'How grand it would be to live in that world I was dreaming about. It was so clean, so comfortable, so safe, so—so *fine*. And what unbelievable things men were doing with all those strange machines.' And then things became hazy. A great pain filled my head. I cried out. I heard a voice speaking to me. A pleasant womanly voice, telling me to lie still, that everything was going to be all right. This voice spoke to me, not in the words and the musical tones I heard at Runnymede but in a tongue familiar to me. In a matter of minutes, I think, I fell again into blackness and oblivion.

"When I recovered consciousness again, I was back in the modern world. The nurse was there in her starched uniform to wait on me. Doctors came in and felt my pulse and smiled encouragingly at me. I was weak and dizzy and still very ill. But I was happy. I can't tell you how happy I was. This, I knew, was the real life. The other one, the barbaric time when I had been filled with barbaric emotions—great hate and fear and also abounding hope and love—that was the dream.

"But as I recovered, I gradually realized that although it might be all a dream it had been something strangely new and unbelievable in that line. I still remembered everything. My boyhood at Rawen Priory, the years when I was a squire, the wild exultation of riding out into the west with Richard of Rawen on a great quest, the tilting with the Sire Tohu-Bohu, the lovely Eleanor, the sweet and loyal Giselle, Corfe Castle, the escape, Ireland, my land there, my marriage, my sons, my death while Paddy-with-the-Limp sat near me and wept.

"Gradually I became convinced that for some reason, far outside my powers of understanding, I had been sent back into the world. There must be a purpose in it. I was here to accomplish something, not to live an aimless life like the people around me. When would I know what I was supposed to do about it?

"Inevitably I believed that the people in my first existence must be in the world also. Why should I have been the only one to come back? They were somewhere, Richard and the princess and Paddy-with-the-Limp and, above all the rest, Giselle. Giselle! She would no longer be separated from me by prison bars. She would be free and waiting. My heart bounded at the thought. It was foreordained that we would meet again.

"When that thought first took possession of my mind, I let the wonder of it control all my thinking. To see her again, that lovely and loyal woman, to be able to lay my heart at her feet. The seven hundred years would roll up like a scroll and be as nothing! At first I did not recall, so great was my excitement and joy, that there was an equally sweet and lovely lady named Lucy Congdon to whom I was engaged to be married. When it did come back to me—I suspect it was actually a matter of minutes only—I realized that I had a serious problem on my hands. I loved them both. How could I go on with the engagement to marry Lucy? How could I have a modern wife when I met my love from the past at the appointed time and in the preordained way?

"I was too unhappy to do anything else while I wrestled with this problem. I did not write to Lucy, although I was receiving letters from her. What could I have said to her? Finally I received an urgent telegram. Was I ill again? Had I received her letters? What, what, what, was wrong? I knew then that I could delay no longer. I must make my decision. I wired to her that I was taking the next train east."

There was a pause. The old man, looking tired after his long recital, sat still and watched the face of his companion.

"What a situation you were in!" said John. "I should have guessed what your reason was, after I got to know the whole story. I suppose I was too busy with the writing job to go into that."

"Yes," said the senator, "I had those four days on the train to make my decision. I didn't think of anything else the whole time. Finally I made up my mind. I was the victim of destiny. I would be called upon in due course. When, where, or how, I didn't know. But I must be ready and free when the call came."

"Yes," said John. "I can understand how you felt. But—but what a blow it must have been to my poor grandmother!"

"She also understood. John, there was never in this world a braver or more wonderful woman than Lucy Congdon. I have broken it to you gradually. But my poor little Lucy had to bear it without any preparation. She had to listen to my wild story, and my incoherent way of telling it, and try to believe it. She did believe it, John. I don't think she even thought, as almost any other woman would have done, that I wanted to be free and had invented this story. She took me at my word. Yes, my boy, that wonderful grandmother of yours believed what I was telling her. We decided that—well, that we could not go through with the wedding."

"It must have been hard for both of you," said John. "But I can't see that you could have done anything else."

"Thank you, my boy. You've lifted quite a load off my mind."

Richard O'Rawn was now obviously very tired. His face was gray and drawn. His hands had fallen limply into his lap.

"Well," he said after a time, "that is how it came about. It turned out, of course, that the signal, the call, the summons, never came. Knowing what I did, I tried to correct in myself the faults which I remembered in Tostig. That was as far as things went. If any of the—the other members of the cast had come back into the world with me, I never encountered them. I never heard the faintest whisper of their existence. That applied to Giselle, of course." He sighed, deeply. "When your grandmother married that Beal fellow, I knew she was making a mistake. It proved even worse than I had expected. For my part, I never looked at another woman. I suppose you might say that my decision had ruined both of our lives."

3

John Foraday rose early. Over his breakfast on the terrace, with a soft sun overhead and a faint breeze stirring leaves along the edges of the maroon flagging, he studied timetables. "If we fly," he said to himself, with a smile of the deepest satisfaction, "we could be in Kilkenny for lunch tomorrow. And I would see my beautiful, my wonderful Eleanor in the afternoon. I hope Uncle Richard feels up to going right away."

Peterkin came out and stood beside the table, gnawing a toothpick with a worried air. "Mr. John," he said, "the senator ain't very well. He didn't sleep much. I heard him tossing about and I went in to see what was wrong. He was lying there with his eyes open, staring at the window. He waved me to go away when I spoke to him. This morning he gave in. Said he was feeling pretty low down and miserable."

"He was very tired when he went to bed," said John.

"Mr. John, there's just one thing to be done. We must get him back home. He hasn't much time left and he doesn't want to waste any of it in these furrin parts. He wants to watch good American sunsets and taste good American beef again. There's no time to be lost."

John's heart had gone down into his boots. What chance would he have if he did not get back to Ireland for months, for a year, for several years perhaps? The O'Rawn place would be buzzing all the time with competition (his own inward expression), young Irish squires, riding fools all of them, wise in the ways of horse and dog, talking her language. What was that advice the old man had given him? Whenever you hear the bell, always come out fighting. How could he fight if there was an ocean and a continent between them? He couldn't hope to accomplish much with a mail-order campaign.

Still, his benefactor was a very sick man. There was nothing to be done but to get him home quickly. No other course was thinkable.

He got out his timetables again and studied them carefully.

"How long will it take you to pack?" he asked.

"Two hours," answered Peterkin.

"Go ahead," said John. "I'll get on the telephone and make our reservations on the first plane for America."

Chapter II

1

JOHN FORADAY came out of the hotel in Kilkenny and looked down at the gray stone walls of what had once been William the Marshal's castle. A year had passed and many things had happened. The old senator had enjoyed a few months at his place in the Western hills and then one morning he had failed to wake up. He had been buried there; and the number of people who came for the last rites, by plane, by train, by automobile, had broken all records. Soon afterward Patrick O'Rawn had died in Ireland, even before he knew of the provision made for him in his American cousin's will. The book had been accepted and published on the same day in New York and London. Hints had crept into the papers that it was Richard O'Rawn's own story and, although a discreet silence had been maintained by those in a position to know, the public appetite had been sharpened. John had waited just long enough to put his name to papers concerning the little hat factory at home, for which Richard O'Rawn's will had provided funds, and had boarded a plane for Shannon Airport. The will had been most kind to him also and he was in a hopeful mood.

"If it's a clean, steady ride ye'll be wanting," said a voice, "it will be convenient to me to oblige."

It was Jamesey Boy Callaghan, wearing the same disreputable coat, tied in at the waist with the same frayed rope, and it was the same car at the curb; more shaky and ramshackle, if possible, than before.

"This is a sign!" said John to himself. "I rode out to see her the first time in this old tin can and it will bring me luck to do the same now." He said, aloud: "It's you, is it, Callaghan? Do you promise me it will run as far as the O'Rawn property?"

"Glory be!" said the jehu. "It's the handsome and rich young fellah from Ameriky. Come back to see the young leddy; and her so rich and luvelly and with all the swains of old Ireland at her fate. But where may the old gintleman be?"

John answered in a solemn tone, "He died. Six months ago. And it was a great loss to his country, and to everyone."

"Do ye say, now! God and Mary rest his soul. He was a fine gintleman and as generous as the shepherd king as gave a gold piece to every beggar man he met."

"Let's go," said John.

As the car groaned and snorted and spouted steam and belched gas, and threatened to stall on every upward grade, the driver kept half turned in his seat and talked to his passenger.

"It's such a grand place now ye'll not be knowing it. Such state as was never seen! Two cars, belike, and horses and the little tellyphone, and stoves that make a comfort like the seat nearest the fire in a snug bar. It's many the fine lad would like to pack his bag, like, and move in for good."

"She is in good health?"

"And for why shouldn't she be? Diamonds she has, and pearls she has, and rubies. And purses stuffed with the luvelly paper. But niver a husband." Callaghan desisted long enough to give the wheel a sharp tug as they came to a turn in the road. "Perhaps ye've come back to ask her yerself. It's luck I wish ye, for a generous man ye are."

A little later he said: "It's a pity, now, that the young leddy was willed a lack of trust in me by her own uncle, God rest his soul, though a hard man he was and a suspicious. Unfair it is, and not justly earned."

Later again he almost turned full around. "It's been seen again, sor. The Tostigan ghost. And a shivery thing it is."

John was interested at once. "Who saw it?" he asked.

"A gintleman from Ameriky. It was a home he was looking for, having Irish blood in him, and he was sent to look at the Tostigan land. It was at night he wint there, having been told of the ghost and wanting for brags to make back home. It was sitting there in the Seat as big as life. It seems it was a man and it limped."

"Limped!" cried John in such a loud and sudden voice that Callaghan winced as though he had encountered a tack.

"Ay, it limps. Well, not quite a limp, as you might say. It just sort of favors one foot like a dog with a thorn in its paw."

"The ghost that limps," said John to himself. There was much food for thought in the information which had been given him.

He told Jamesey Boy Callaghan to stop when they got their first glimpse of what had once been called Green Hedges, lying so peacefully below them, with the Nore rippling along between. It was, he thought, more beautiful than his most roseate memories of it. The fields about the old stone house were of a lush green but where the sunlight rested on the tips of the hills there was a hint of purple and warm russets and yellow. Birds in a nearby thicket were singing what seemed to him a song of welcome and the neigh of a horse came thinly from a distance.

"There's nothing to equal it," said John aloud.

"You think not, sor? There's plenty other places where you get your enough of beauty. Say the word and someday I'll make it convenient to drive ye there. Have ye seen the Rock?"

"The Rock of Cashel? No, I haven't."

"I'll take ye there first. And a low rate I'll be making ye because of the danger we might never be getting back."

Eleanor heard the thump and rattle of the car on the drive and came to the front door. There was no beauty anywhere in Ireland, thought John, with a tugging in his heart, to equal the play of the sun on her golden hair. He sprang out of the car.

"Eleanor!" he cried.

She had not expected him. When he saw how pleased she was, his small and uncertain hopes took on a substance and boldness they had never had before.

"John of the Fine Hats!" she cried. "My great, kind, sweet friend, Johnny-O!"

She actually ran to greet him, with a sort of skipping step, she kissed him, sending shivers down his spine; in fact she did everything a lover might have hoped for, save fall into his arms and whisper, "At last, my own, you have answered the call of my heart."

"Why didn't you send word?" she asked.

"But I did. I came as soon as I signed the last paper and so it was in a great rush. I cabled from the airport in New York."

"It hasn't been delivered. I suppose the people in town will get around to sending it. No one seems to believe we have a telephone here now." Her eyes hardened. "I see you engaged that incredible creature again."

"For luck. He brought me here the first time and that was the greatest piece of luck I ever had in my life."

She looked at him with surprise. "John! You've changed. You're not the quiet one, with so little to say, who came here the first time. But where are your bags? Were they jolted out on the way in that excuse of a car?"

"I left everything at the hotel in town. I'll hold the car here, if you don't mind, and run back to town this afternoon."

"You are wrong on all counts, John of the Fine Hats. I won't have that false, sniveling fellow here all day—even if you do think he brings you luck. Besides, you're going to stay here. Oh, everything will be quite right and proper. A distant connection by marriage, Miss Martha MacGovern from Cork, is living with me and I have guests as well. A very sweet couple from California. You *will* think you're in luck when you see Gerda. She was born Irish but they used her when they were making a picture here, and now she's in Hollywood and married to a producer. *He* says there's a picture in your book and he'll be talking to you about it." She became aware again of the presence of Jamesey Boy Callaghan. "Pay him off, John, and send him about his business. We'll drive over later and pick your bags up. Your own room is waiting for you. I've been keeping it ready."

The first glimpse inside the house made it clear that Eleanor had shown the best of sense in the changes she had made; in fact she had made no real changes at all. True, there was a telephone (a stemwinder of the most ancient model), and John caught glimpses of two quaint porcelain stoves of continental variety, but the rooms otherwise maintained their old charm. The same family furniture, the same heavy hangings, the same faded rugs, all the family portraits on the walls. He detected one new piece, an Act of Parliament clock in the hall, with a Georgian buck in knee breeches painted on the long wooden panel.

John stood very still and breathed it all in with the delight almost of a homecomer.

The two guests proved to be quite unusual. James Forest was a movie mogul, a youngish man with a neatly trimmed goatee, an alert eye, and an inquisitive nose. His wife, whose stage name was Gerda Delaney, was a redheaded, blue-eyed little creature on whom Ballycannon had relinquished its hold to Hollywood, even in the matter of speech. They issued from somewhere in the house and greeted John with immediate interest.

"So," said the producer, "you're the fellow who's been kicking up all this dust."

When John looked rather blank, Eleanor supplied the explanation. "He means the rumors about the book."

"Yes, this reincarnation stuff," supplemented Forest. "You've got everybody talking."

"I thought all that had been settled," said John.

"Not a bit of it. You see, Mr. Foraday, my company is going to make the picture. At least, the deal seems on the point of going through. The Head phoned me from his home last night—forgetting the difference in time, of course, and disturbing the whole household at three o'clock this morning—and he said they would be at it hammer and tongs this morning. Your unexpected arrival here is a gift from on high, because they're going to hand the job over to me."

"It certainly is a coincidence."

"So naturally I'm interested in getting the lowdown. If it *is* the story of Senator O'Rawn, it will make a difference in the treatment."

John felt quite ill at ease. He was thinking of his final words on the subject with Richard O'Rawn.

It was a week before the old man died and he had rallied sufficiently for a long discussion. John recalled every word that had been spoken. The scene, in the smallest of detail, was stamped clearly on his mind.

It was in the late afternoon. There was a touch of winter in the air and so it had been impossible to take him out. Instead he had been wheeled in front of the fireplace where a fine fire was blazing. At first he seemed a little dazed, having just wakened from a heavy nap, and he began to talk in a reminiscent vein. "We were always cold," he said. "We couldn't get away from it, not even when the summer sun came out, because then there were the rains to drench us and no clothes to change into. Cold and snow and wind, and the Devil behind it all. Why do we always think of hell as a place of fire and brimstone, with the Devil using a pitchfork to prod the flames? Hell should be black as midnight and cold as the grave, with the lost souls clustered together in sleazy cloaks and chilled to the bone. And the Devil about like a north wind with ice on his breath."

It was clear that his thoughts had gone a long way back. "How the wind roared through the trees when I would go out to drive the sheep into shelter behind the priory walls! How often the snow sifted through chinks in the roof and I would waken to find the floor of the solar white with it and several inches covering my blanket! The whole world was cold and there was no such thing as comfort."

He stretched his feet out closer to the fire and drew a deep breath of satisfaction. He looked at John, who had pulled up a chair close to his, and his mind seemed to clear. "Well, my boy," he said, "I don't believe I'll be here when that book comes out. We had better get it settled. What you're to say, I mean. At first, as you'll remember, I wanted to get people damned well convinced that we can't afford to go back by as much as a step. But, after all, they'll have the story as it stands. Will they need anything more?"

He brushed a hand wearily across his eyes. "I have a confession to make. I don't seem sure of anything any more. Did I actually live through all that? Or was it the most extraordinary dream any man ever had? I was sick a long time and I don't know what my mind was busy with. Perhaps I was dreaming the whole time. Could *that* be the explanation? Of course, there's the matter of the coins; but there may be an explanation of that if we could get down to the bottom of things." He sighed deeply. "I'm too tired to make any decisions. I'll just leave it in your hands, John."

After a long pause, he rallied sufficiently to say: "I don't envy you, my boy. Gad, how they'll come at you! Reporters are hard to fend off." He smiled faintly. "Fine fellows, though. I always liked them. I played it straight with them and they did the same with me." His voice grew fainter. "I would have enjoyed fencing with them about this story when I was going strong. But not now. I can't even cope with that damned tyrant in the house." A final word came some moments after but John could not be sure that the old man's mind had not wandered to something else. "You pays your money and you takes your choice. You takes your choice."

John looked at Eleanor but it was apparent that her curiosity equaled that of the producer. "All I can tell you," he said finally, "is what I've already said. The senator was an authority on the period. He had much of the story in his mind and he took me around to see all the places that came into it. It certainly was his story in a very real sense. It got out somehow that he had actually lived in the days of Magna Charta. But—well, I would rather stand on what I've said."

"But see here," protested Forest. "I think you ought to come clean. If I'm to make the picture, I must start off with a full understanding of it. Should I make it straight? Or should I use this other angle?"

"Well," said John, "that's your problem, isn't it? You pays your money and you takes your choice."

The producer denied this vehemently. "You can't brush me off as easily as that. I must have the real story. Didn't he show where the

original O'Rawn Castle stood? Didn't he tell the exact number of coins
they would find in the crypt? Didn't he say that the course of the river
had changed? How did he know all that?"

"Aw, shut up, Jimmy!" said his beautiful little wife. "Must you jump
down his throat the moment he comes through the door? Give him a
chance to catch his breath. He's too nice to be treated this way. If you
keep bothering him, I'll just tuck him in that sweet little roadster of
mine and take him away for a good long drive."

The producer grinned. "Well, babe, there's something in what you
say. Skip it, Foraday. We had better get ourselves acquainted before
I begin batting you around like this. Of course," he added, "I'm on the
ragged edge myself. If the deal goes through, they'll keep the cables hot
with instructions and demands. They'll expect me to get my story line
right away."

"After lunch," said Eleanor firmly. "No more business talk until then."

There was another guest at lunch, a neighbor named Daniel O'Hoolihan. He was an oldish man with wisps of red hair standing up from
various elevations of his head, which gave him something of the appearance of a leprechaun. He seemed in rather poor circumstances, for
he was wearing an old shooting jacket, with pockets so worn that the
edges had been covered with tape, and there was a neat patch on one
of his knees. It was equally clear, however, that he was a gentleman;
his voice, on the rare occasions when he had a chance to use it, was
low and cultured and his diction was in the best tradition.

Eleanor was full of plans. That afternoon, if the fair weather held,
they would all go out and find the places which had been mentioned
in the book. This suited James Forest because it offered an opportunity
to get John talking. His bride (they had been married a few weeks only,
the ceremony having been delayed while she completed her work in
her first starring picture) was even more pleased.

"It will give me a chance to really get the feel of the part, won't it,
Jimmy darling?" she said.

The producer glared at her across the table. "My angel from on
high," he said, "my devastating little beauty, my sheer bundle of kitten-
ishness and Irish charm, must you keep harping on that?" He turned
to John. "This bride of mine—and God how I love her!—has got it into
her damned stubborn head that I can give her the lead—*if* we buy the
story and *if* they confide it into my able hands." He turned again to
glare accusingly at her. "Don't you realize, my sweet simpleton, that

the first picture in which you appear—in a secondary role—isn't out yet? I acknowledge the rushes were fine. But can I go to those highbinders who rule the celluloid universe, can I actually go into the dread presence of the Head, and say, 'I'm going to give my wife the lead'? They would say I was crazy. Remember, babe, it's a double part, the Pearl of Brittany and the half sister. We have three dames with established box-office appeal on the pay roll. The Head will want me to use one of them and he'll probably make the choice himself."

"I can play the role, Jimmy," declared the redheaded starlet. "I want to show them what I can do. All I ask is that you fix it for me to go in and see the Head. I'll talk him into it."

"I wouldn't trust you with him," declared her husband.

While this pleasant little squabble was going on, John was watching Eleanor and thinking how absurd it was to believe any Hollywood star —of the first magnitude, let alone the starlet variety—could play her in a picture; for, of course, Eleanor *was* the Pearl of Brittany, the most perfect cast-back ever accomplished over the centuries. Prosperity had done a great deal for her already. She was well dressed, expensively and exquisitely, in fact, in a gray-fawn tweed with flecks of gold in it, a sweater under the coat the color of unminted gold, and a yellow kerchief tied loosely around her neck. She had so much poise that he knew she would never again depend on a harp and an old Irish song to make an initial impression.

Their eyes met and she smiled delightedly at him as though to say, "Perhaps I could give some pointers as to how the princess should be played?"

When the casting discussion subsided, Eleanor turned to the quiet Mr. O'Hoolihan. "Have you anything of interest to report?" she asked.

It became apparent then that the neighbor was engaged on a most difficult task, the tracing of the O'Rawn family tree, and that, when he had it completed, he intended to write a history around it. He had notes on scraps of paper in every pocket.

"I have indeed, Miss Eleanor," answered the shabby little man. "I have all the facts on a most colorful ancestor of yours." He began an almost feverish search through his pockets and succeeded finally in drawing forth a dog-eared card. He gave this a shortsighted scrutiny. "Ah, yes, this is it. Thomas Aloysius O'Rawn. Born 1765. Married 1788 to Rebecca Moore of Wexford. Ah, my dear child, what a story there is behind these bare statistics! This Ally O'Rawn was a great rider and his like was nowhere to be found. The horses he raised were the proudest and finest still in all Ireland and he rode them himself in all the great races of the day; and, moreover, he brought his colors in ahead most of the time.

"He was one of the first to join up when rebellion flared in Wexford in '98. He carried a musket and picked off the redcoats with the best of them. But he was taken, poor fellow, and kept in chains in a prison. The English intended to hang him at first but his life was spared finally. They kept him in prison for more than six months, which was a long and dreary spell for one as active as he was.

"Thomas Aloysius O'Rawn was released with other political prisoners. May 1799. He reached his home here to find that his beautiful wife had eloped the day before with his best friend, having received word of his coming. They went to the Continent, this precious pair, and never came back. That was a very bad situation indeed. You see, the wife had not presented the head of the O'Rawns—indeed, Thomas Aloysius was the sole surviving representative of the family at that time—with an heir. There could be no question of a divorce and so it began to look certain that the family would come to an end, as all great families seem to do sooner or later."

"My friend," commented Forest, "you're off to a good start. This has some of the elements of a damned good picture."

"It may or may not be the basis for a cinematographic presentation," said Mr. O'Hoolihan, gazing up rather quizzically at the ceiling, "but I think the problem must have been given a great deal of thought up there. It must have been very clear that something ought to be done about it."

He replaced the notes in his pockets and gave an involuntary sigh. "It looked for a long time as though nothing would be done. The runaway pair got along by playing whist skillfully for high stakes. To eke it out, Rebecca had a way of fluttering her eyelashes—she was a handsome jade—at elderly men with property, and this resulted always in generous financial contributions."

"Ha! Another Becky Sharp."

"Exactly, sir. The absconders got along so easily that they lived on and on, in the very best of health. In fact it was not until Thomas Aloysius O'Rawn was seventy-four years old that his wife finally died in Brussels.

"The head of the family was still what used to be called a fine figure of a man. When he heard the news, he slapped a hand against his muscular thigh and cried, 'Saved by the kind and holy Timekeeper of us all!' He changed his stock, brushed his hair, gave the ends of his mustache a devilish twirl, had a horse saddled, and rode into town. It's said he quietly looked over all the widow women, just to be certain in his own mind. They didn't please him. Every mother's son of them—your pardon, please, every mother's daughter—had kind of run to seed. So he went out on the street and looked about him. He saw a girl. She had black hair and blue eyes and a nice swing to her. He took her by the wrist. 'You're the one,' he said. 'What do you mean?' she said. 'Stop wasting my time,' he said, 'standing here and asking all these questions.' They were married right away and in nine months there was a fine male son and heir yowling in the house."

"How very lucky for me," said Eleanor. "I wouldn't have been born, would I, if the flirtatious Becky hadn't died just when she did?"

"I'll add something to that," declared the producer. "Richard O'Rawn wouldn't have been born either and the Plantagenet line would have come to an end. And this book wouldn't have been written."

"And I," said his redheaded wife, "wouldn't have this chance to play a big double role."

The producer scowled at her. "You die hard, my pet, my sweet possessor of all those endearing young charms. But take it from me, my beautiful angel, you can be as damn pigheaded about it as you please but you will *not* get the part."

2

John was the first down for breakfast the next morning. He found himself facing a strip of Irish bacon at least fifteen inches long, thick and crunchy and rich, and a double-yolked egg. The bacon had been reduced to a meager six inches when Eleanor came in. Her short blue skirt swirled and swished about her in the most approved American fashion. She took a chair beside him.

"If Eleanor of Brittany came in to join us," said John, "I'm sure she would look plain by comparison."

Eleanor said severely: "Only husbands are supposed to pay compliments before breakfast. And I've heard that they seldom do. I don't want to seem prying but I believe, Mr. John Foraday, you left the house last night at eleven-thirty and did not get back until two. I know the exact time when you came in because I was worried and stayed awake."

John's mood sobered at once. "I tried to leave without disturbing you. I was paying a call." He hesitated. "On a ghost."

She responded to that with a sudden great interest. "The Tostigan ghost, of course."

"Of course. You see, I had been told something. That he limps."

Eleanor's eyes opened wide with excited speculation. "The ghost limps! Oh, John, do you suppose it's the spirit of poor little Paddy-with-the-Limp?"

"That was the conclusion I reached. It's clear he hadn't obeyed the injunction laid upon him by his father. Perhaps some of the Tostigan land had been taken over and the feeling between the two families ran too high for any communication between them. We can be sure of this: if Arthur O'Rawn had been told his mother was Eleanor of Brittany, he would have done something about it. I asked myself if Paddy had been coming back all these centuries in the hope of conveying the message he should have delivered before he died."

Eleanor nodded eagerly. "Of course. That explains it."

"You believe in ghosts, then?"

"Yes, I believe in ghosts." After a moment she added in a reproachful tone, "Why didn't you tell me before you went? I would have gone with you. I really resent your not giving me the chance."

"Dear Eleanor, this ghost business can be—well, pretty grim and frightening. I didn't want to expose you to it. And besides, there were your guests, who would have clamored to go along too. That wouldn't have done. Ghosts don't like excursion parties. So I slipped out quietly and hoped to get away with it."

There was a pause. Eleanor, it was clear, was still rather resentful. "Well," she said finally, "did you see the spirit, and was it our little Paddy?"

John shook his head. "I saw nothing. Not so much as a gray wisp near the walls. I heard nothing. Not even a ghostly footstep on the empty stairs."

"How *very* disappointing." Eleanor clearly had hoped for something better than this. "But you must have done something about it. Did you say anything?"

"I made one effort. I said aloud: 'If Patrick, son of Tostig, is here, I have a message for him. I have come to tell him that he needn't reproach himself any longer. The message has been given to the last of the O'Rawns.'"

"And what happened then?"

"Nothing. Nothing at all." After a moment John went on with a somewhat shamefaced smile. "There was an owl in the Tostigan tower and it hooted at me. It was the most dreadful sound I ever heard in my life. I turned and came away and I'm afraid the gait I struck wasn't strictly heel-and-toe."

"I've always believed in the Tostigan ghost," said Eleanor reproachfully. "And now I have to give it up."

"The whole thing is completely absurd. And yet——"

"Yes," she agreed. "The whole thing *is* absurd. And yet——"

The honeymooning Forests came in at this point and attacked their long strips of bacon with enthusiastic appetites. The bride's auburn hair was piled up rather carelessly on the top of her head and she would have seemed ravishingly pretty if the competition had been less severe. The white and gold dressing gown she was wearing would have caused raised eyebrows in Ballycannon and a brisk campaign of shocked comment.

"Did you sleep well?" asked Eleanor.

They both asserted they had slept like tops and Eleanor gave John a relieved look from the corner of one eye; it would not be necessary to have a second explanation of his midnight wanderings.

The sharp eye of the producer picked out a large sheet of paper on which John had been working as he attacked his breakfast and which he had relegated to a serving table when Eleanor joined him. It contained a rough sketch of what seemed like a monument with a long and irregular column of printed letters.

"What's that?" asked Forest. "Something to do with the Dead Sea scrolls?"

Eleanor rose from her place and went over to examine it. After a moment or two she turned in John's direction with shining eyes. "What a wonderful idea!" she said.

It was now necessary to make an explanation. John regretted this because he had wanted to discuss it first with Eleanor alone. "Well, it's a plan for a column," he said. "I want to raise it on the land over there which belongs to the Tostigan tract. None of them are left now and it seems to me something should be done to give them a permanent remembrance. They were a remarkable family."

"What do you intend to say about them?"

"Read it, John," said Eleanor, handing him the sheet.

So he read what he had been setting down.

This unadorned shaft
has been erected in memory
of the TOSTIGAN family
who held these lands
for seven centuries
and fought bravely in many
wars for liberty.
It is dedicated particularly
to the memory of
SIGURD and TERENCE
the last survivors of the family,
who fell in 1915 fighting
against the forces
of aggression,
And above all else to
TOSTIG
the founder,
whose great exploits
have long been forgotten.
On a day when men's
hopes were as high
as the warm sun above
he stood under arms
on the field of Runnymede.

Miss Martha MacGovern from Cork, starchily dressed for the day's duties, came in at this point. She looked disapprovingly at the distracting Gerda and then shared in the study of the sketch. She gave her head a toss.

"Why such a pother over the Tostigans?" she asked. "All of my life, may St. Agnes believe me, I heard nothing but bad of them."

Marty Lacey came in to clear the table, looking quite clean and trim and not liking it. He sniffed when he heard what the chaperone had said.

"The murtherin' davils!" he muttered. "The black, fightin' hounds o' Sathan!"

Chapter III

A CABLE arrived with the news that Forest's studio had not bought the book after all, and on the heels of this came a second, summoning him home by the next plane to discuss other plans. John remained on and enjoyed the exclusive company of his hostess; and he counted the picture sale well lost for this privilege. They spent a great many hours going about the grounds together and finding the places which had provided backgrounds for the story. The first, and the easiest, was the hill where Richard of Rawen had built his castle. They traced again the line of the enclosing walls and found some remains of the keep. John was the first to point out the deep scar in the side of the hill which had served as a dry moat and the particular spot where, he was convinced, Tostig had supervised the building of the drawbridge. They located the stretch of flat land where the four little O'Rawn daughters had raced their horses while the dark sons of Tostig watched in silence.

It was Eleanor who found evidences of the first stone house to which Richard had brought his royal bride. "Uncle Patrick went to digging here once," she explained, "and he came to some foundations of rough stone; so this must be it." She looked about her. "If that's right, we're standing where the poor little Lady Joan died all by herself in that dreadful shed."

They found Domligh Crest on the extreme edge of the property and Eleanor remained here in silence for several moments, thinking of her gallant ancestress. "What a bold rider she must have been," she said to John. "I like to take chances also but I—I never come this way. I don't want to be tempted. There must be no more falls on the Domligh Crest."

It began to drizzle a little at this point. They had mackintoshes with them, having come on foot, and these were hurriedly produced. John helped Eleanor into hers, his hands unsteady as they encountered the ends of her crisply curling hair.

"Shall we run for it?" he asked.

Eleanor shook her head. "I like walking in the rain. There's something so pleasant about the feel of the gentle moisture on your face. Of course, if it starts to pour, we'll have to make a dash for home. Or take shelter."

He insisted on buttoning the mackintosh up around her neck and he trembled when his knuckles touched her chin. It was because of this that he decided to speak. Ever since the departure of the other guests, he had been hovering on the brink, watching for the ideal moment, hesitating, and finally remaining silent. "I can't wait any longer," he said to himself now. "I must find out where I stand."

They were trudging along together and keeping step, and Eleanor for once had nothing to say. This must be the ideal moment. He began to make his declaration, realizing that his approach was both stiff and unsatisfactory. "I've been so long back in the past," he began, "that I actually find myself thinking sometimes in terms of what went on then. I even find myself talking their way. I—I've no idea how men really propose nowadays. Except I'm pretty sure they don't go down on their knees and kiss the girl's hand." He swallowed hard. "Well, I'll have to do it my own way. I—I love you so much that I don't know where to begin. I've been this way since the first moment I saw you. Uncle Richard advised me not to be meek about it but to—to take a high hand. I can't do that. No one could be more meek than I feel at this minute. I know all my—my shortcomings. You are beautiful and you have royal blood in your veins. I have nothing to put forward in my own favor except that I've written a book; and that's a pretty thin argument. It's sheer presumption on my part. But I—I love you to distraction. That's the whole of my case."

She looked up at him and she seemed quite cool and collected. "You want me to be your wife, John?"

"That is it. Perhaps I should have chosen a time when I could have gone down on my knees after all. That's the way I feel."

"Uncle Richard was right," she said quietly. "There's no reason why you should feel meek. You were like a knight in shining armor when you first came into my life and proceeded to set things to rights. I owe so much to you! Would you like my answer now?"

He hesitated before replying. "Yes," he said. "I had better know. For better or for worse."

Suddenly Eleanor laughed. "You are going to be very angry, John. My answer has to be yes and no."

It was beginning to pour now and they were forced to take immediate shelter under the branches of an old and thick oak. Eleanor looked up at him and indulged in a smile which seemed somewhat wistful.

"How very unfortunate!" she said. "We're going to get soaked. And you'll look at me and say, 'It's not possible that I'm in love with this bedraggled mouse.' You'll be sorry you spoke and you'll wonder how you can get out of it."

John laughed exuberantly. To know that she was at least halfway persuaded was so wonderful that he felt like doing an Irish jig. They could not be seen where they were but it did not occur to him to kiss her. His newly aroused confidence did not go as far as that.

"I guess I don't understand," he said. "I'm bowled over that you are even partly willing. That's more than I've ever dared hope for. But if you think yes, why is there also a no?"

"It's this way, my dearest and truest friend," said the girl. "I do love you. I know there are several kinds of love that a woman can feel for a man but I think the kind I have for you is the—the right kind—— No, no! No demonstrations yet. There's still so much to be said about it. I have a kind of difficult explanation to make."

"I'm no longer afraid of the 'no' part," declared John. His face was radiant. The words kept galloping through his mind, "She loves me, she loves, she loves me! I heard her say it. The right kind of love, she said. Now that I know *that* much, I can dispose of any objections."

"I don't care how high the jumps may be," he declared. "We can take them together."

Eleanor sighed. "I wish I could be as sure as that. You see, it's not enough for us to say we love each other. We still have to consider what we're going to do with our lives. Where are we to live them? There's nothing I want to do but stay here in Ireland. To live all my life in this beautiful land, with these sweet people around me. To hear their soft voices. To go on thinking about things the Irish way. To love horses and dogs and believe in the Little People." She delayed for a moment. "John, are you going to write more books?"

"I expect to devote my life to writing."

"Then why can't you do it in Ireland? Right—right here. In this lovely spot which you called Green Hedges. There's no place quieter or sweeter in the whole world, I'm sure."

John fell into a long silence. Now he could understand the reasons behind the "no" half of her answer. This was not an easy jump at all. It was, he could see, the hardest and steepest he might ever face in his life.

"Don't you think you would like it in America?" he asked finally.

"The very thought frightens me," she confessed. "The noise, the crowds, the rush! I must be perfectly frank, John. I shudder at the prospect."

He studied her earnest, damp face. "But you've never been there. You've taken too seriously the things you've heard and read. America is full of places as sweet and lovely as this. And the cities are wonderful. They are so alive and stimulating."

"Perhaps we have the wrong impression here," she said. "No attempt is made to set it right; and I've always thought it would be as impossible for me to live in America as in England."

"There are reasons," John explained, "why I must live in my own country. I hope to write other books and, of course, they'll have American themes and backgrounds. I couldn't work here, so far away from the home base and separated from my publishing connections. Then I must keep an eye on the spending of the money Uncle Richard left for the hat factory; that seems to me nothing short of a sacred obligation. And there's this above everything else. I am filled with American traditions. I would always be a stranger here."

The storm passed over and the sun came out. It was almost as though Nature had said, "I'll take a hand in this argument, I'll show this heathen that there's nothing to compare with Old Ireland." At any rate, the sky cleared save for a smatter of fleecy gray clouds, as fine as ostrich plumes in the headdress of a barbaric queen. The trees and the hedges and the fields were so green that they might have retained the freshness of the first creation. It was easy to believe that all the birds in Kilkenny had come to this one spot to join in protesting the unequaled quality of everything Irish.

There was a paddock close to the house. As they strolled by, keeping their eyes raised to enjoy this sudden pouring forth of beauty, there was a brisk neigh and a handsome chestnut crossed the springy turf at an easy lope. He came to the fence and leaned over it so that Eleanor could throw an arm over his neck and lay her cheek against his velvety muzzle.

"My fine fellow," she said. "My very fine fellow."

Cassius MacMurdo, who was in charge of the horses, came out from the stables and joined them to sing the praises of the two-year-old. "I

clocked him for a quarter this marnin'," he said, the wrinkles around
his faded blue eyes deepening in his enthusiasm. "It's not telling I dare
how fast it was, for ye'll be left thinkin' he's another Man o' War. If he
lives to be a hundred, he'll never equal the time he showed me the
marnin'." Then his excitement mounted still higher. "And I'll swear,
miss, it's clipping a bit off it he'll be tomorra."

Eleanor turned away from the fence and looked at John with a
suggestion of rueful delight. "You see?" she said. "This is Ireland, John.
Can I ever leave it? I'm afraid the answer is still: yes, I love you, but
no, I can't go with you."

2

There was a car of ancient vintage on the drive; one of the old models
which stood high up from the ground and could be depended on to
run forever. The maid who helped Marty Lacey with the household
work, a small and very industrious girl with long black eyelashes but
no other pretentions to looks, met them at the door.

"Ma'am," she said. "There's a gintleman."

The card she handed to her mistress contained the name Harold
Willowbie Hemingbroke. "English," commented Eleanor, with no evidence of interest.

"Wait a minute!" said John. "Hemingbroke. I had a letter from him.
Two letters, in fact." He began to smile. "My beautiful scion of the
long-lost Plantagenets, you're in for it. Mr. Hemingbroke is the president
of the Plantagenet Society of the British Empire. Perhaps he has come
to denounce you as an impostor. Or, more likely, he's here to swear
fealty to you."

Eleanor smiled back, with a hint of excitement. "How *very* interesting. Let's go in, John."

John held back. "I shouldn't be in on this. It may be strictly confidential. If an Indian turned up in New York and announced himself
as a direct descendant of Old Chief Stung Plenty, who sold Manhattan
for a quart of brandy, it wouldn't be a matter for everyone to listen in
on. The society may have things to say to you that are not for every
pair of ears."

"I must say that I don't care for the comparison," declared Eleanor,
with the merest toss of her head.

"Perhaps this Mr. Hemingbroke will be wanting to make some claims
for you. Like that fellow Dudley who lost Lady Jane Grey her head.

On second thoughts, I think I ought to go in and hear what he has on his mind."

"What did he write you about?"

"Oh, he was asking for more information about this and that. I wasn't able to help him much."

"Well, you got me into this. So in you come, Mr. John Foraday."

The visitor, who rose with great dignity from a chair and bowed low to Eleanor with a motion of his right arm which suggested the sweep of a plumed hat, was tall and thin and correctly arrayed in morning coat and striped trousers. Rimless glasses were clamped tight on the bridge of his long, thin nose. He was quite serious in mien. There was about him, in fact, a suggestion of complete lack of humor.

"Ma'am," he said, "it is gracious of you to accord me this audience."

John lingered behind watching Eleanor and admiring the way she carried herself: her head high, a hint of warmth in her eyes, a queen to the life.

"How do you do, Mr. Hemingbroke," she said. "You are from London?"

The visitor cleared his throat. "My cards say London, ma'am, because the offices of our society are there. Actually I live a short distance from Basingstoke. May I say that my visit today is the result of a fortnight of earnest discussion with the inner circle of our membership. As soon as the book appeared, we began an intensive investigation. We have satisfied ourselves now that the family of O'Rawn, and the Tostigans also, have been in Ireland many generations. Before we get through, we hope to have proofs that they were first heard of in the reign of King John. If we can prove *that*, the skeptics—who number in the millions now—will be utterly confounded. We are confident, I may tell you, that we shall prove Eleanor O'Rawn to be a direct descendant of Eleanor of Brittany. Ah, Your Highness, what an achievement that will be! A serious purpose will have been given us at last in place of the somewhat nebulous proceedings which have occupied us to date." He bowed again. "I am one of a committee, Your Highness. A committee of eight. The others remained behind while I came on to ask if you would deign to receive us all tomorrow."

"I shall be most happy to meet your other members, Mr. Hemingbroke," said Eleanor. "Perhaps you will be kind enough to come for tea. And may I present my guest and friend, Mr. John Foraday?"

"John Foraday!" The visitor's pale gray eyes opened with surprise. "The writer of the book! I am happy to make your acquaintance, sir."

"You spoke of a more serious purpose for your society," said John. "What are you planning, may I ask? Something in the way of throne-shaking?"

"No, no, no!" cried Mr. Hemingbroke in a dismayed tone. "I must have expressed myself very badly if you think that possible. Very badly indeed."

Eleanor was holding his card in her hand and stealing quick glances at it. "I am rather at a loss," she confessed. "You spoke of your—I think you said, your nebulous proceedings."

"Permit me to explain, ma'am. The Plantagenet Society is made up of people who take a deep interest in the past. Our interest is historical and"—he glanced at John—"in no sense political. We are loyal subjects of our beloved young queen and we have no desire to see present conditions altered in any respect. But we have specialized—shall I say?—in the story of the Plantagenets. It has been our custom to meet once a month and hold discussions. Generally there are papers by our members; all having to do, naturally, with those great English kings. The last was a most excellent dissertation prepared by Dr. Edgar Colson of York on that unfortunate and well-meaning man, King Henry VI. I shall be happy to send you copies, ma'am. Both you and Mr. Foraday will be interested, I am sure."

"We will be happy to have the copies, Mr. Hemingbroke."

"Often," went on the visitor, "we have discussed the possibility that direct descendants would be found. But our interests and our activities are purely academic. It was, may I say, an academic excitement which shook us when it became likely that our hopes were to be fulfilled. . . . My fellow members will be waiting most anxiously for my report. How uplifted they will feel when I tell them you are the personification of all that was best in your ancestors."

The conversation continued for some minutes. There was a little discussion as to Eleanor's plans, in the course of which she asserted that she intended to remain in Ireland, a decision which the president of the society seemed to approve. John took no further part in the talk. He kept an eye on the girl and was afraid he could detect in her the first evidences of a stirring ambition. "She's taking all this seriously," he thought. This made him unhappy; it did not bode well for his own hopes and plans. He felt a hearty dislike growing in him for the Plantagenet Society and everything it represented.

3

Eleanor did not put in an appearance next morning. This was surprising. She generally rose early and had set the domestic wheels to turning before breakfast was served. When she did not come down for the morning meal, John found little pleasure in his crisp rasher of bacon.

"That idiot!" he said to himself, referring to the dignified president of the Plantagenet Society. "He has upset her. I could see the effect his talk was having. She's beginning to visualize herself as a member of royalty and at this moment she isn't in the least interested in a humble house guest. The odds were bad enough before. Now—well, I'm afraid I might as well go home."

He sat in glum consideration of the unfavorable situation which had developed, thinking particularly of the occasion when Richard O'Rawn had said to him: "I'm sure she's marked by destiny for something unusual. God alone knows what. But whatever it is, she'll follow the course marked for her. Even if it means leaving everyone far behind her."

"He was right," thought John. The cigarette he had lighted was tasteless and he tamped it out.

The birds were singing under the eaves, the neighing of horses reached him from the paddock. It was going to be a perfect day; but it seemed to him that the sun had been obscured suddenly by menacing clouds.

He spent a restless morning without getting so much as a glimpse of his young hostess. The maid, when questioned, said that "Mistress be a-writing in her room."

"Letters? I'll be happy to ride to the post office with them."

"No s'r. Not letters. She were writing on whole sheets and sheets o' paper."

Not letters! Then quite clearly Eleanor had become posterity-minded and was committing to paper on this fateful morning all her impressions and reflections. She was beginning to follow the course marked for her. He, John Foraday, was already being left far behind.

Around noon he heard a familiar sound coming from around a bend in the road. Rattle, clump, clash! A car was approaching and only one automobile in the world could make just that sound: the ramshackle vehicle belonging to Jamesey Boy Callaghan. John walked down to the gate beyond the ford.

It was Callaghan, sure enough; and he had a passenger with him, a young man with the imprint of the United States of America upon him. The car stopped.

"Wait for me," said the passenger, getting out. "I may be an hour, two hours, a day, a week. You can't tell. But no matter how long it is, you wait. Is that clear?"

"Yes, sor." Callaghan then called to John. "Good marnin', Mr. Fer'day. And when is it ye'll be going back, sor?"

"Soon, I think. I'll send for you."

The newcomer, who had red hair and a sharp brown eye, walked briskly over to John. "My name," he said, "is Quincy McComber. I'm with the Farley Syndicate in New York. I've come to have a talk with Miss Eleanor O'Rawn."

"This is her place. She'll be putting in an appearance any minute now, I think. My name is John Foraday."

Quincy McComber shook hands with him enthusiastically. "I'm glad to find you here, Mr. Foraday. I don't need to tell you, I'm sure, that it's your book which brings me here. I want to interest her in writing something for us." Noting a surprised look in John's eye, he went on. "The usual thing. Her girlhood in New Zealand. Her life here in Ireland. What it means to discover you have royal blood in your veins after all these centuries. I'm very curious to see her, Mr. Foraday. From what I hear, she's a raving beauty."

"She's all of that. Come along to the house."

Eleanor did not appear until lunchtime. John had taken it on himself to invite the visitor to join them for the meal and Eleanor was surprised to find herself with two guests instead of one. The newcomer plunged at once into the purpose of his visit.

"If you are interested," he said, after outlining what the syndicate had in mind, "I am authorized to make you a proposition. So much a word. We're willing to make it rather handsome, I don't mind saying."

"How handsome?" asked John.

"That would depend, of course, on how much material there is."

Eleanor seemed doubtful of the idea. "I'm not a writer and it doesn't seem to me there's much to tell."

"Perhaps you would need a ghost," suggested the visitor.

Eleanor turned a startled glance, first at John and then at Mr. McComber. "A ghost?" she said. She was thinking, no doubt, of the only ghost she had ever had any acquaintance with, the midnight visitor at the Tostigan tower. "What have ghosts to do with it?"

The visitor laughed. "Forgive me, Miss O'Rawn. That's a term we use in the publishing business in America. Mr. Foraday knows all about it, of course."

"What does it mean, John?"

"Well, sometimes when a person has a story to tell—a movie actress or a heavyweight champion, say—and doesn't have the gift to tell it, a writer is employed to help. The writer is called a ghost."

"I've heard of that being done. But why is the writer called a ghost?"

"Generally it's a matter of vanity. The principal doesn't want to acknowledge that it's necessary to hire a professional writer. So the writer has to hover around in the background and is never mentioned. He's really not supposed to exist."

"I see. It's rather apt, after all," said Eleanor.

"Most American slang is pretty apt, you'll find. Although there's one I've never got the hang of. A ghost writer is sometimes called a trained seal."

McComber shook his head. "No, you're a bit twisted there. The person for whom the ghost works is sometimes called a trained seal. But you don't hear it much any more. It's going out."

Eleanor laughed delightedly. "So you've come all the way to Ireland, Mr. McComber, to turn me into a trained seal!"

McComber shook his head in emphatic haste. "No indeed! Far, far from it, dear lady! You must remain exactly as you are. You must never turn into anything else."

By the time they reached the gooseberry tart, Eleanor had made up her mind and had said a definite no to the proposition, but the syndicate man was not one to give in easily. He followed them around all the early part of the afternoon, arguing his case and raising his price regularly each hour. Once he took John aside and said to him earnestly: "You should be backing me up, Foraday. She'll want you to ghost the job and that will mean a nice slice for you." But John did not see things in that light. He felt it would be a mistake.

4

The argument was still going on at four-thirty when two large prewar limousines deposited the Plantagenet Society committee at the front door. Three men got out, Mr. Hemingbroke, a Colonel Shaftley, and the Honorable Gerald Grenadin, and five ladies. The ladies were of a striking similarity in type: spare, rather tight-lipped, shortsighted, and wearing large bonnets of an ancient vintage.

Quincy McComber took one look at the party and then propounded some questions to John. "What's this invasion? Have they come over for a croquet tournament? Or is it going to be one of those old-time garden parties?"

"They are all members of a society which is much interested in Miss O'Rawn."

The syndicate man looked the new arrivals over more closely. "I'm going to stick around," he announced. "When these five battle-axes get through with the fair Eleanor, her powers of resistance will be at a low ebb."

Eleanor greeted her guests at the front door. She was dressed very simply in a suit of heathery cloth, in which green predominated, with something lacy at the neck; but she could not have looked her part better if she had been wearing a diamond-studded gown with a seven-foot train and a coronet in her hair. This was John's opinion but it must be considered, of course, that he was not an impartial witness.

Some of the committee shared his opinion, however. He heard a lady with a treble voice say to a companion, "Eleanor of Aquitaine on the morning of her coronation!" and the companion answer in a decided bass: "Allowing, dear Daisy, for some differences in dress styles. But I agree with you. She's a Plantagenet to her fingertips!"

It had been understood that John would take a part in the proceedings and assist Eleanor in every way possible but, as it happened, he did not go inside the house. As the deputation trailed through the front door, a dogcart and pony came clopping up the drive with the reins in the cautious hands of Mr. O'Hoolihan. John remained behind to greet him.

The visitor came to a stop and studied the limousines with one eyebrow raised, which gave him the appearance of an elderly fox terrier. "Our fair lady has guests of some distinction," he said. He consulted a fat old-fashioned watch on the end of a slender gold chain and frowned dubiously. "I have only a short time, as it happens. And there are matters I should discuss with Miss Eleanor without any delay."

"Having to do with the family tree?" asked John.

"Well, yes."

"Then why not tell me? In this matter our interests are closely allied."

The shabby little man considered this suggestion with pursed lips. Then he nodded. "I think it might be in order. You will hear of it at once in any event. And I have hardly more than an hour. I shall take the liberty of laying the facts before you, sir, and later you will be good enough to repeat them to Miss Eleanor."

They sought a place some distance down the drive and here they seated themselves on the soft greensward. It was a long conversation which followed because the worthy Mr. O'Hoolihan lacked the gift of swift and spare narrative. He could never resist taking a bypath but must enter upon it and pursue his way to its end. In fact the better part of an hour had been wasted in these excursions before he came to his main point.

"I very much doubt if our fair young lady will like what I must tell you. She is keenly interested in tracing back the history of her family but my quest in her behalf can be no more than halfway successful. I have found there are no records earlier than midway of the sixteenth century. That means, my good sir, that the authentic annals of the O'Rawns may not be traced back further than the days of Edward Emanuel O'Rawn, who was born," drawing out a card and consulting it, "who was born in 1488 and died in 1556. He it was who married Leueen Tostigan and who, moreover, ran away to sea when he was a very young spark and served for two years in the piratical ship of the great Grace O'Malley."

"Were no records kept prior to that date?" asked John.

"Either they were not kept or they were destroyed; wantonly, perhaps, or by fire. How great a tragedy it is!"

John shook his head. "This is very bad news, Mr. O'Hoolihan. I confess I've been hoping it would be possible to find records to prove the authenticity of the story I published."

"Is it any compensation," asked the old man, "that it works the other way as well, that now it won't be possible to produce anything to the contrary?"

"Is there any possibility that the papers might turn up in some other part of the country?"

"I doubt it, my dear fellow. We are looking back into the emptiness and silence of a dark age when men had no conception of the value of such records."

It was too late now to join the party inside. John sought out Quincy McComber, who was loafing impatiently by the side of the road. "In my opinion the final word will be no. Of course, you'll want to have it from the lady herself but I'm certain it would be unwise to bother her now. Get in touch with her in the morning."

"Okay," said the syndicate man. "I'll stick around. I'll talk her into it yet."

"And hold the car a few minutes," said John. "It's more than likely I'll be riding in with you."

Chapter IV

1

JOHN found Eleanor in the sewing room at the head of the stairs. He had hoped she would be there, because they had come to regard it as their room and to use it for anything in the way of a confidential talk. It was in every respect a pleasant apartment. An atmosphere of old-fashioned housewifery pervaded it. There was an ancient model of a sewing machine in one corner, surely one of the first ever made. On one wall was a silken frame with pockets for spools of thread of all colors. In the center, the place of honor, stood a little old grandmother of a worktable, of obviously distinguished pedigree, holding all the instruments for dressmaking. In still another corner stood a tall judy, chastely draped with the satiny beginnings of a new gown for the mistress of the house.

She was sitting on a couch on the order of a love seat, although it was barely capacious enough for even the most devoted pair. She looked very tired.

"I learned a lesson today," she said.

John seated himself, facing her, and waited.

"It must be a difficult life that members of royal families live," she went on. "To be subject to rules about everything! To be watched and questioned and controlled. Oh yes, I'm sure they are actually kept under control. Even today—and, after all, you know, I am no more than an outsider, a myth, with no prospect of ever being more than a myth—even with me those dear, gentle ladies probed into everything! They were like inquisitors. Or should I say inquisitresses?"

John waited for her to go on, realizing that she had much to say.

"It must be hard enough to be a member of a reigning house. Even to be a queen. But when you belong to the outer fringe, where it seems you are subject to all the rules and restrictions and have none of the compensations—the power and grandeur, you know—that must be an uncomfortable life.

"I've been reading about the little court kept up by the Stuarts after they were expelled from England. Do you know anything about it?" John shook his head. "They lived all together, the Pretender and his wife and children, and all the noblemen who had followed him into exile and *their* families. They had a place in northern Italy and they lived on an allowance from the Pope. A lump sum was paid each year to the Pretender and he gave shares to the others. Such pitifully small amounts! It must have been a terrible life: the bickerings over seniority in the household and the division of silly little offices, the gossip, the backbiting, the hatreds! And yet they always had the hope of a return to power to keep their spirits up and to work for." She paused and smiled rather ruefully. "Those gentle old ladies talked as though I would have a court. I have been wondering since if there could be anything less important in the whole world than the court of the last of the Plantagenets!

"They even went into my matrimonial plans. Or rather, their plans for me. It seems I must marry some insignificant scion of royalty. A nephew twice removed from a dethroned king at the least. They mentioned a Karl Anton, who comes from some small German line. From Wolfenbüttel, I think. Is there such a place?"

"Yes, I believe so."

"At a pinch they might be satisfied with a British peer. They mentioned a Freddie Threnoble, the nephew of a duke, and an impoverished Scot whose first name is Dermot. I asked if I couldn't marry anyone I liked, even a commoner, and they said most decidedly no, it would be better to remain single like the Virgin Queen of glorious memory than be a plain Mrs. This or That."

"What a dim view they would take of me," said John.

Eleanor indulged in a tired semblance of a giggle. "I brought that point up. At least, I asked how they would regard an American. You should have seen the horror on their faces. One of them said, 'My lady, how can you even think of such a dreadful idea!' and another said, 'It wouldn't be allowed. There surely is a law against such a thing.' I asked, 'Not even a millionaire?' and they shook their heads. One thought there would be a bare chance for the owner of huge landholdings in the Argentine, because there was something grand and feudal about that."

There was a pause and then John asked, "Do you think you could keep it up?"

She nodded seriously. "Oh yes, I could keep it up. But the question in my mind now is, do I want to?"

For the first time since the conclusion of their talk the day before John felt a stirring of optimism, even of hope.

"Yes?" he said. "That, I think, is the most momentous problem in the whole wide world today. Do you want to, Eleanor?"

She leaned forward, clasping her hands about her knees. "I think it depends," she said. "On one thing."

"Can it be," he cried eagerly, "that this one thing is what I hope it is? Eleanor, will you allow me to—to carry on from here?"

"Yes, John. I am very tired. You do the talking now."

"In the first place," he began, "I know your plans for this place. You want to buy the Tostigan property, don't you?"

"Yes. That above everything else. The lands belong together."

"I'm sure your uncle Richard would have wanted it. In fact he spoke of it several times. I expected to find some provision for it in his will but he must have forgotten about it near the end. I know, too, that you want to build a wing on your house."

"Opening off the drawing room," nodding her head. "To be used as a library. I think it should be reached by several steps leading down, in order to give the ceiling greater height. And we need two new bathrooms. All shiny and artistic like the ones I see advertised in magazines. I've thought about it a great deal."

John leaned forward in turn, so that their heads were very close together.

"All that could be done, you know. Even if you married me and we went to America. We could always spend a great deal of our time over here. We—we might reach a compromise, don't you think?"

"My uncle Patrick always said there had never been a case in the history of law which couldn't be compromised somehow. He went through for the law, you know. Although he never did much at it."

John drew himself still closer and took possession of her hands.

"It's foolish to speak of compromises!" he cried fervently. "What I want to propose isn't one at all. It's an unconditional surrender. I intended to be firm but I—I give in. Write your own ticket, darling. We'll live half of the year in Ireland. Or seven months. Or eight. Or ten. Whatever your heart desires."

There was a long moment of silence. Then she shook her head. "No, no, that wouldn't be fair. You are always so generous, John, and I mustn't take advantage of you. You have your books to write and your hat factory. And I'm so tired that I don't want to talk any more right now or I'll begin to cry. I don't want you to see me being as weak and silly as that. I think I would like to leave it all in your hands. When you have thought it over and decided what seems to you to be best, come and tell me what you have decided."

John rose to his feet. With the exultation which had swept over him at this surrender, which was even more complete than his own, there went a deep sense of compassion. "Those old crows have tired you out!" he said. "I think you had better go right to bed and have some dinner brought up on a tray. And then have a good night's sleep. In the meantime I mustn't take advantage of *your* generosity. I spoke to McComber about driving into town with him. I'll do that, and I'll come back tomorrow morning. Bright and early. You will be rested then and we'll settle down to making our plans."

It was settled that way and John went out to signal the car not to leave without him. Lacey came down with his bags and John was on the point of getting into the back seat when Eleanor appeared at the front entrance.

"John!" she called. "Don't go! I want to talk to you now."

He sprang off the running board with such vigor that this part of the equipment on Jamesey Boy Callaghan's ancient vehicle parted company from the rest of the body. He ran up the drive as fast as his legs would carry him.

It was a different Eleanor who greeted him. She did not seem tired at all. Her eyes were shining.

"I've talked to Cousin Martha," she said eagerly. "We can finish packing tomorrow if we start now. John, my mind is made up. Could you telephone from here and make all the arrangements—for the marriage, and the tickets, and everything? I want to go with you. As for the future—well, let the future take care of itself!"